Jill Mansell worked for many years at the Burden Neuro-logical Hospital, Bristol, and now writes full-time. Her novels include TWO'S COMPANY, NADIA KNOWS BEST, STAYING AT DAISY'S and FALLING FOR YOU, all of which have been *Sunday Times* bestsellers.

Head Over Heels

and

Perfect Timing

Jill Mansell

headline

HEAD OVER HEELS first published in 1998
by HEADLINE BOOK PUBLISHING

PERFECT TIMING first published in 1997
by HEADLINE BOOK PUBLISHING

First published in this omnibus edition in 2005
by HEADLINE BOOK PUBLISHING

A HEADLINE paperback

10 9 8 7 6 5 4 3 2

ISBN 978 0 7553 2669 3

Typeset in Times by Avon DataSet Ltd,
Bidford-on-Avon, Warwickshire

Printed and bound in Great Britain by
Mackays of Chatham plc, Chatham, Kent

Headline's policy is to use papers that are natural, renewable and
recyclable products and made from wood grown in sustainable
forests. The logging and manufacturing processes are expected to
conform to the environmental regulations of the country of origin.

HEADLINE PUBLISHING GROUP
A division of Hodder Headline
338 Euston Road
London NW1 3BH

www.headline.co.uk
www.hodderheadline.com

Head Over Heels

For my mum

Big Top Under Canvas Inverness

Bught Road, Inverness, IV3 5SS

Sun 03rd Jul 2022 6:00 PM Gates Open

LCC Live presents

Texas

No seats allowed to be taken into the venue
Under 16s must be accompanied by an adult over 18

Ticket £42.50 Plus Booking Fee

General Admission Standing

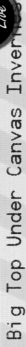

powered by
TICKETLINE.co.uk

081268541189

Terms & Conditions of Sale:

1. Once you have purchased tickets, they can only be exchanged, refunded or returned in the circumstances described below.

   - If we fail to fulfil an order as a result of any negligence, or similar act or omission of our own or on breach of contract The customer on a full refund including any booking fee charged.
   - If the event is cancelled, postponed or material changes are made to the Event, namely a change of the venue or the headline act, the original tickets that you have purchased will remain valid for the event (except for in the case of cancellation) unless otherwise advised. However if you are unable to attend the revised event only the face value of the tickets will be refunded as these are circumstances beyond our control. If the tickets have not been posted out, the processing fee will also be refunded.
   - There will be no refund for lost, stolen or damaged tickets (save that duplicate tickets may be possible (if for resale) or if the venue or Event organiser provides different seats to those specified on the ticket.
   - For any refund of face value you will be required to return the tickets, on receipt of which we will make the refund. The refund will be made using the same method of payment that was used to purchase the tickets.
   - By secure post to Ticketline. PO Box 4081, Manchester M60 1YT
   - Refund requests will be accepted up until 1 week before the date of the revised event or 1 week before notification of the change (whichever is the later) unless otherwise advised.

   We are unable to refund tickets that are received after this time.

2. It is your responsibility to ensure that tickets returned are received by us. We therefore advise/leave to return any tickets by secure post.

3. When events are cancelled, postponed or content is significantly changed, we will do our best to inform all purchasers using the contact details provided when the booking was made. However it is the responsibility of the purchaser to check whether the event is taking place ahead at the scheduled date, time and venue. We cannot guarantee that we will be able to make contact with you.

4. It is the responsibility of our customers to inform Ticketline of any change of address, contact telephone number or email address both before and after receipt of your tickets.

5. Always check your tickets on receipt, as mistakes cannot always be rectified later.

6. Although Ticketline will use their best endeavours to indicate any age or other restrictions that apply to events, it is the customer's responsibility to ensure that they are eligible for entry to the event that they are purchasing tickets for.

7. Promoters and Venues always reserve the right to refuse admission to an Event and tickets are issued subject to the rules and regulations of the venue. We will therefore not offer refunds to any ticket holders who may be refused entry or ejected from a venue through the unauthorised use of photographic and recording equipment at venues is usually prohibited.

8. We will not be liable to you for any loss of enjoyment or profit nor any indirect, consequential, exemplary, incidental, special or punitive damages.

9. We will not be liable for any misrepresentation, negligence, contractual or tortious loss of any kind suffered by you from the products, or services, or actions of any venue, performer, promoter or others.

10. Tickets are only for your personal use and that of your party. We reserve the right to cancel tickets purchased if there is any resale or attempted resale of tickets at a higher price than purchased. This includes tickets being resold to the public at an inflated price including via auction sites such as EBAY. The holder of a resold ticket may be refused entry or rejected from the venue.

11. If you are collecting your tickets, the cardholder must be present on collection. The cardholder's signature will be required on collection and the ticket(s) collected by the cardholder in person, and that the credit/debit card must be presented on collection. The cardholder's signature will be required on collection.

12. There is no refund for tickets as tickets for different events have different dispatch times. However, all tickets should be received at least one week before the event, unless they are being collected from the venue. Tickets booked within 10 days of an event that are being posted, may be received slightly later, but should be received at least 2 days before an event.

13. If a venue changes its time for tickets as tickets for different events have different dispatch times, this is beyond Ticketline's control, we reserve the right to make the tickets available for collection at the venue and will inform you accordingly.

14. For certain events there may be a restriction on the maximum number of tickets that may be purchased. We and use our best endeavours to publish this information on the Site and at the point of ticket selection for the event. In such case, we reserve the right to only offer for sale the maximum number of tickets available and to cancel any orders made that exceed the maximum authorised tickets per customer without notice.

15. If tickets despatched by secure delivery are returned as addressee unknown, we reserve the right to cancel the order.

Terms & Conditions of Sale

1. Once you have purchased tickets, they can only be exchanged, refunded or returned in the circumstances described below:
   - Once you have an order as a result of any change in the circumstances described above.
   - booking fee charged.
   - If the event is cancelled, postponed or material changes are made (namely a change of the venue or the headline act, the original tickets that you have purchased will remain valid for the revised event (except for in the case of cancellation) unless otherwise advised. However if you are unable to attend the revised event only, the face value of the tickets will be refunded as these are circumstances beyond our control. If the tickets have not been posted out, the processing fee will also be refunded
   - There will be no refund for lost, stolen or damaged tickets (save that duplicate tickets may be possible if for seats) or if the venue or Event organiser provides different seats to those specified on the ticket.
   - For any refund of face value you will be required to return the tickets, on receipt of which we will make the refund. The refund will be made using the same method of payment that was used to purchase the tickets unless otherwise advised to:
     - By secure post to Ticketline, PO Box 6051, Manchester, M60 1YT
     - Refund requests will be accepted up until 1 week before the date of the revised event or 1 week within notification of the change (whichever is the later) unless otherwise advised
   - We are unable to refund tickets that are received after this time.

2. It is your responsibility to ensure that tickets returned in time to reach us. It is therefore advisable to return any tickets by secure post.

3. When events are cancelled, postponed or changed in some other way, it is the responsibility of the purchaser to check whether the event is going ahead and at what time. We will do our best to inform all purchasers using the contact details provided when the booking was made. However it is the responsibility of the purchaser to check whether the event is going ahead and at what time and venue. We cannot guarantee that we will be able to make contact with you.

4. It is the responsibility of our customers to inform Ticketline of any change of address, contact telephone number or email address both before and after receipt of your tickets.

5. Always check your tickets on receipt, as mistakes cannot always be rectified later

6. Although Ticketline will use their best endeavours to ensure that duplicate tickets may be possible (if for seats) it is the customer's responsibility to ensure that they are eligible for entry to the event that they have purchased tickets for.

7. Promoters and Venues always reserve the right to refuse admission to an Event and tickets are issued subject to the rules and regulations of the venue. We are therefore not able to offer refunds to any ticket holders who may be refused entry. The unauthorised use of photographic and recording equipment at venues is usually prohibited.

8. We will not be liable to you in respect of any loss of enjoyment or profit nor any indirect, consequential, incidental, special or punitive damages

9. We will not be liable for any misrepresentation, negligence, contractual or tortious loss of any kind suffered by you from the products, or services, or actions of any venue, performer, promoter or others.

10. Tickets are only for your personal use and that of your party. We reserve the right to cancel tickets purchased if there is any resale or attempted resale of tickets at a higher price than purchased. This includes tickets being resold to the public at an inflated price including via auction sites such as EBAY. The holder of a resold ticket may be refused entry or rejected from the venue.

11. If you are collecting your tickets rather than having them posted out, please be advised that the tickets must be collected by the cardholder in person, and that the credit/debit card must be presented upon collection, otherwise tickets cannot be collected.

12. There is no guaranteed dispatch time for tickets as different events have different dispatch times. However, all tickets should be received at least one week before the event, unless they are being collected from the venue. Tickets booked within 10 days of an event that are being posted, may be received slightly later, but should be received at least 2 days before an event.

13. If it becomes impractical to post tickets due to proximity of an event or circumstances beyond Ticketline's control, we reserve the right to make tickets available for collection at the venue and will inform you accordingly.

14. For some events there may be a restriction on the maximum number of tickets that may be purchased. We will use our best endeavours to publish this information on the Site and at the point of sale. Selection of the event. In such case, we reserve the right to only offer for sale the maximum number of tickets available and to cancel any orders made that exceed the maximum authorised tickets per customer without notice.

15. If tickets dispatched by secure delivery are returned as 'addressee unknown', we reserve the right to cancel the order

Inverness Northern Meeting Park

Ardross Street, Inverness, IV3 5NS

Fri 12th Aug 2022 6:00 PM Gates Open

LCC Live present

Amy Macdonald plus Guests

No seats allowed to be taken into the venue
Under 16s must be accompanied by an adult over 18

Ticket £35.00 Plus Booking Fee

General Admission Standing

00886509872 4

Chapter 1

'I can't decide, cider or a glass of Chablis.' Jessie Roscoe leaned her elbows on the bar and chewed one arm of her paint-splattered sunglasses while she gave the matter some thought.

'I don't know if I should serve you. Are you sure you're old enough to drink?' said Oliver.

'Oh,' Lili sighed, 'I wish someone would say that to me.'

Jessie searched energetically in the pockets of her jeans, at last unearthing a fiver. She waved it lovingly under Oliver's nose.

'Cider for your dear old mother. Better make it a shandy, don't want to fall off my ladder. Lili, how about you?'

'Coke. Don't want to fall into a drunken stupor.' Lili looked regretful. A proper drink would be lovely, but that was the drawback with small children: when they were around you had to be so alert.

The lounge bar of the Seven Bells was cool, dark and faintly musty, the ingrained aromas of beer and cigarette smoke mingling with beeswax polish and the smell of sizzling onions and garlic wafting through from the kitchen. When Oliver had finished serving them, they made their way through the empty pub and out into the enclosed back garden.

It was five past twelve and the sun was blazing down. Lili parked the cumbersome double buggy in the shade of a lilac tree while Jessie batted curious wasps away from their drinks and tore open a packet of Twiglets.

'Look at them. Like a couple of pensioners on the beach at Bournemouth.' Jessie nodded at the children, both fast asleep in the buggy, facing away from each other with mouths open, chins lolling on chests and knees apart. Two-year-old William, Lili's youngest, clutched a naked Action Man. One-year-old Freya, whom Lili looked after for another couple in the village, was managing to snore gently and simultaneously suck her thumb.

Lili prayed they'd stay asleep. If they woke up, William would bellow to be pushed on the swing and Freya would scream even louder because she wanted to go on it too. They would then yell for crisps, drinks and more drinks, and since they were both at that stage where they were driven to investigate everything – bits of broken glass, other people's drinks, the contents of ashtrays – Lili knew she may as well give in at once and take them home.

Twenty minutes, that's all I ask, she thought without much hope of getting it. Twenty minutes of blessed peace and adult conversation.

'God, that's better,' Jessie gasped, having gulped down half her ice-cold shandy in one go. Swivelling round on the bench she patted both back pockets, located a tube of Ambre Solaire and passed it over her shoulder to Lili. 'Could you put some on my back?' Her scoop-necked vest was low-cut, front and rear, and although her skin tanned easily there was a definite pink tinge to it. She squirmed as Lili dribbled cream on to a burnt bit, and said, 'Heard from Michael?'

'He phoned last night.' Lili heard the lack of enthusiasm in her own voice and was secretly appalled by it. Her husband had been away for six months, for heaven's sake, working half-way across the world in Dubai, and she couldn't even summon up the energy to miss him. Honestly, what kind of a wife was she? 'He's flying back next Friday – for eight weeks. I'll have to get some marmalade in.'

'And plenty of tranquillisers,' Jessie glanced over one shoulder at her, 'in case you explode with over-excitement.'

Lili pulled a face and screwed the top back on the sun cream. It wasn't just her. Absence didn't appear to make Michael's heart grow fonder either.

'Do you know, when he first took the job out there I

2

thought it would be so romantic.' She scooped a dog-paddling greenfly out of her glass and deposited it carefully on the rose bush behind her. 'I imagined astronomical phone bills, not being able to sleep at night because I missed him so much, driving up to Heathrow at four in the morning to meet him off the plane, the two of us running towards each other in slow motion, him lifting me into the air and twirling me round' – in Lili's fantasy she was a sylphlike seven stone – 'and after that,' she concluded with a shrug, 'well, overwhelming lust and passion, I suppose. And wall-to-wall, non-stop shagging.'

'Do it next Friday.' As she spoke, Jessie pulled the purple scarf out of her falling-down hair, flipped her head over, gathered together the mass of dark ringlets and retied the scarf in a lopsided bow. 'Drive up to Heathrow at four in the morning and throw yourself into his arms. See what happens.'

'One, I'd look a berk because his plane doesn't get in 'til eleven. Two, he'd say, "What the bloody hell are you doing here and if that's lipstick you're wearing don't get it on my shirt." And three,' Lili finished counting off on her fingers, 'I'd squash him.'

Jessie ignored this last remark. To listen to Lili you'd think she was the size of a tank, which she wasn't. Lili was simply well rounded, with big hazel eyes, shiny light-brown hair, terrific dimples and a little mouth like a rosebud. If it weren't for the old jeans and the stripy cotton shirt she could have been a character out of a painting by Renoir. She certainly didn't weigh enough to squash her husband.

Which was a shame, Jessie felt. Because if anyone needed a good squashing, it was Michael Ferguson.

As they sat there idly mulling over Lili's husband's deficiencies, they heard the low rumbling sound of a lorry accelerating away up Water's Lane, interrupting the peaceful silence of Upper Sisley on a hot Wednesday afternoon.

'Removals van,' Lili said brightly, remembering that this was the bit of news she'd meant to tell Jessie. 'Two of them turned up at Sisley House this morning, huge great things. Someone's going to be living there at last.'

3

She sounded so much more animated now. Jessie saw the spark of interest in her eyes. The prospect of new people moving into Sisley House was clearly a far more enticing prospect than that of Michael's return.

'Removals lorry,' Oliver announced, ducking his head to avoid the honeysuckle framing the doorway as he came out to join them in the garden. 'Signs of life up at the house.'

'Old news,' Jessie said airily. 'We already know that.'

Oliver looked disappointed. 'Okay, but you don't know who's bought the place.' Leaning across the table, he helped himself to the Twiglets. An irritating air of mystery had been engendered by Harry Norton, the local estate agent handling the sale of the property, who had remained uncharacteristically tight-lipped about the identity of the new owner. Even Jessie, whom Harry fancied like mad, had been unable to weasel it out of him.

'Soon find out,' she said, slapping Oliver's hand away as it slid back for more Twiglets. 'Don't you have any work to do?'

'You're the only customers.' Oliver grinned at his mother in her paint-splashed sunglasses and pinched another Twiglet anyway. 'I'm clearing the table for you.'

'If Harry's being this secretive it must be someone famous,' said Lili.

'We told old Cecil it was Madonna,' Oliver's grin broadened, 'and he went out and bought one of her CDs.'

'I heard about that.' Jessie gave him a look. 'Poor Cecil. He tried to play it on his wind-up gramophone.'

'Might be royalty,' said Lili, her hazel eyes widening.

'Might be a drugs baron,' said Oliver, 'or an arms dealer. Or a recluse.'

Freya stirred and whimpered in her sleep as Jessie's mobile phone rang.

'J.R. Decorating Services, can I help you?'

'I hope so.' It was a male voice. 'I need some work done and I've been given your number. I understand you're a small firm based in Upper Sisley?'

'That's right.' Jessie pulled an apologetic face at Lili, who was on her knees frantically attempting to lull Freya back to sleep. Disturbed by the girl's fretful cries, William's eyes snapped open and he too began to wail.

'Oh dear, sounds like trouble.' The voice at the other end of the phone seemed amused. 'Look, I'll just give you my number. Maybe you could ask your husband to call me back.'

Jessie watched as Oliver gamely tried to help. He flinched as Freya jabbed a finger in his eye.

'I haven't got a husband.'

'Well, sorry – whoever does the work. If he rings me, we can arrange a time for him to come and look at the job.'

'Actually,' Jessie raised her voice to make herself heard over the bawling, 'it's not a him. It's me.'

'Good grief. What about the children?'

He sounded appalled.

'Aaaargh,' yelled Oliver, clutching the front of his jeans as William made a furious bid for freedom. 'He *kicked* me.'

Jessie grinned and forced herself to concentrate. The line wasn't great. 'Don't worry, hardly any of them are mine.' She stood up and moved away from the noise, angling the phone this way and that in an effort to improve the reception. 'Now, whereabouts are you, and when would you like me to come round?'

She still couldn't hear properly. Where was this guy phoning from, Bucharest? She hopped on to one of the rustic benches, then up again on to the table. Now she had a clear view over the high wall bordering the pub's garden, right across the village green. Another removals van was just arriving, inching around the corner and slowing as it approached the entrance gates to Sisley House.

'Sisley House,' said the voice on the phone, 'and you can call round as soon as you like. We're pretty chaotic here, but the work needs to be done.'

The reception had abruptly improved, the crackling had cleared. Jessie felt her stomach do a slow, swooping somersault. She gazed stupidly at the gabled roof of Sisley House, and at the few upstairs windows not obscured by trees. If she was speaking to who she thought she was speaking to . . .

Oh God, thought Jessie, how could I not have recognised that voice before?

Behind her the screaming had stopped. Oliver was wearing Freya's pink and white sunhat and pulling fearsome faces, reducing William to fits of giggles. Lili, still on her knees, was placating Freya with a bottle of blackcurrant juice.

'You do know where we are?' prompted the voice at the other end of the phone.

I'm in shock, that's what it is, thought Jessie. She pulled herself together. She was standing, suddenly, at the edge of an ice-cold river, and she could either ease herself into the water inch by inch, or close her eyes, take a deep breath, and dive.

'Yes.' She took the necessary deep breath. 'I know where you are. In fact I'm in the pub just across the road from you. Why don't I come over now?'

'Mum's gone a funny colour,' said Oliver, looking up. 'Is she going to faint? Mum, are you all right?'

'Sorry, could I have your name?' said Jessie, just to be sure. No point making a twit of herself if it wasn't him after all.

'Gillespie. Toby Gillespie.'

'Come on Mum, get down from there.' Oliver grasped her hand and helped her off the table. The line promptly went fuzzy again.

Jessie said, 'Okay, I'll be with you in a minute,' and switched off the phone.

Oliver gave her an odd look. 'Who was that?'

'The new owner of Sisley House.'

'Seriously? Who is it?'

'Toby Gillespie.'

'No!' squeaked Lili, lighting up like a Christmas tree. 'You mean Toby Gillespie the actor?'

If you were about to plunge head-first into an ice-cold river, thought Jessie, it was only sensible to take precautions.

She looked at Lili, who never went anywhere without the contents of Boots the Chemist in her massive shoulder-bag.

'That's the one. Um . . . got any waterproof mascara?'

6

Chapter 2

The lorry she had just seen arriving was now parked at the top of the drive. As Jessie approached, two removals men, perspiring freely, carried a dark blue velvet Chesterfield down the ramp, across the gravel and into the house.

The heavy oak-panelled front door was wide open, but by the time Jessie reached it the men had disappeared. Trying the doorbell, she discovered it had been disconnected. She hovered uncertainly in the doorway, feeling a bit of a lemon. It almost came as a relief to hear a tinny crash behind the door ahead of her and to the left, and a bored-sounding male voice drawl, 'Oh shit.'

Time to take that plunge.

Pushing the door open, Jessie found herself in the kitchen. Crates were piled everywhere, and a teenage boy with shoulder-length dark hair was standing by the sink staring down helplessly at an empty green tin and an explosion of sugar on the floor. A pretty blonde girl wearing a white T-shirt and plenty of lilac eyeshadow to match her shorts was sitting cross-legged on one of the unpacked crates reading a magazine.

The boy looked at Jessie, his expression defensive.

'I didn't do it on purpose. It just slipped out of my hand.'

The blonde girl, without bothering to glance up, said, 'I bet you say that to all the girls.'

The boy went red.

'Mum said I had to make the removal men a cup of tea. It's not fair. What am I going to do now?'

As he spoke, the kettle at his elbow came to the boil. Steam billowed out over his arm and he let out a yell,

7

leaping away from the sink and crunching sugar underfoot.

'Scoop it back into the tin,' suggested the girl. She looked up at Jessie, eyebrows raised. 'They won't notice, will they?'

Jessie hesitated. The boy's trainers didn't look that hygienic. Not very hopefully she said, 'Do you have a dustpan and brush?'

'Somewhere. In one of the crates, probably.'

The boy finished pouring boiling water into five unmatched cups and a blue and gold gravy boat. He threw teabags into each of them, wiped a spoon on the leg of his jeans, then knelt down and began painstakingly piling sugar from the floor into the spoon.

'Hang on.' Jessie held up her hands like a traffic cop. 'Leave it. I'll be back in a second, okay?'

'Who are you, anyway?' The blonde girl seemed curious rather than concerned.

'Painter and decorator. I'm here to see your father.'

'Oh, right. He's around here somewhere.' The girl pushed her fingers through her silky, white-blonde hair and smiled at Jessie. Then she resumed reading her magazine.

Next door, at Keeper's Cottage, Drew answered the door dressed in a pair of crumpled black and white striped boxer shorts.

'Can I borrow a dustpan and brush?' said Jessie.

'God, I love it when you talk dirty.'

'And some sugar?'

She followed him through to the kitchen, six times smaller and every bit as chaotic as the Gillespies'. Drew and Jamie, who were both vets, shared the rented cottage with Doug Flynn, an SHO in casualty at Harleston General. When they weren't working they played rugby and cricket, and when they weren't playing rugby and cricket they downed astonishing quantities of lager and watched rugby and cricket on TV.

All three were fast approaching thirty but none showed any sign of settling down yet. As far as Jessie could make out, Drew and Jamie spent a lot of time talking laddishly about girls while Doug just slept with an endless stream of

8

them. She got on well with all three of them, but was especially fond of Drew, with his merry eyes and boyish, self-deprecating smile.

Since domesticity wasn't high on their agenda, she was impressed when he found the dustpan and brush almost straight away. She watched him yawn as he poured sugar into a mug.

'Sorry, I woke you up. You look shattered.'

He turned and grinned at Jessie. 'Not your fault. I was up all night with a cow.'

'Good result?'

'Twins.' He yawned again, checked his watch, and glanced out of the kitchen window at the hopelessly over-grown lawn. 'I'd better get a move on, surgery starts at two. Weird,' he went on, shaking his head, 'I dreamt the back garden was full of army tanks.'

'You must have heard the removals vans reversing up next door's drive.'

'Someone's moving in?' Drew opened the fridge, sniffed a carton of orange juice and gulped down the contents. 'Do we know who it is yet?'

'Some actor chap.' Jessie felt her stomach do that thing again, that nervous loop-the-loop. 'Toby Gillespie and his family.'

Drew's blond eyebrows went up. 'Toby Gillespie? The one with the wife?'

'Lots of people have wives, Drew.' It was hard work, Jessie discovered, sounding normal.

But Drew was really grinning now, his wide mouth stretching practically from ear to ear. 'Ah, but he has The Wife. Deborah – that's her name, isn't it? Now *she's* what I call a serious bit of totty.'

'She's older than I am,' Jessie protested. 'She must be forty, for heaven's sake. How can you call a forty-year-old a bit of totty?'

Drew's shrug was good-natured. 'Whatever. I'll call her anything else she likes. Well well, Deborah Gillespie, our new neighbour.' He winked lasciviously at Jessie. 'Could be fun.'

9

★ ★ ★

By the time she got back it was too late. The removals men, now somewhat unattractively stripped to the waist, had made themselves comfortable on two black suede sofas on the driveway and were stretched out in the sun, smoking and drinking their tea.

'Need any more sugar?' Jessie offered them Drew's chipped mug, but they shook their heads.

'No thanks, love, got plenty,' one of them said happily. 'The lad gave us some. We're fine.'

There was no sign of the lad in the kitchen, just a pile of sopping teabags on the worktop next to the kettle and more footprints in the sugar scattered across the floor.

'Hi,' said the blonde girl, evidently unfazed by Jessie's reappearance. 'If the men keel over and die, we can blame Dizzy. He's just found something putrid stuck to the bottom of his shoe. Looks like a dead mouse.' She shook her head. 'Honestly, he's such a pillock.'

'Um . . . have you seen your father yet? The thing is, he's expecting me.'

'Don't panic, he'll come and find you when he's ready. Why don't you just relax?' Toby's daughter suggested. 'Feel free to make yourself a cup of tea,' she added generously, reaching down from her packing case and offering Jessie the Royal Doulton gravy boat. 'Here, you can use my mug.'

Jessie was on her hands and knees sweeping up sugar under the kitchen table when the door burst open behind her.

'Sav, put that bloody magazine down for a minute. Why didn't you come and tell me the decorator was here? According to Dizzy she turned up ages ago and bloody went away again.'

It was Toby's voice, and he sounded exasperated. Motionless under the table, Jessie swivelled her gaze to the left and saw his feet. Before she could move, the faded navy deck shoes were joined by a pair of flat bronze and white sandals, encasing possibly the most shapely, tanned, *glamorous* feet she had ever clapped eyes on.

'Darling, you'll have to tell those removal men to put

10

some clothes back on. They're sweating like pigs all over the black sofas.'

'She came back.' Savannah Gillespie sounded bewildered. 'I don't know where she's gone now. She was here just a minute ago.'

'I still am,' said Jessie, hugely tempting though it was to stay under the table. Coming face to face again with Toby for the first time in over twenty years wasn't turning out quite as she had expected.

Like my life, Jessie thought as she backed gingerly out of her hiding place. Rule number one: Nothing ever goes according to plan.

Deborah Gillespie, the rest of her every bit as elegant as her feet, burst out laughing.

'Good heavens! What were you doing down there – hiding from us?'

Jessie couldn't look at Toby; all she was dimly able to register was a faded denim shirt and battered jeans. She held up the half-full dustpan. 'Some sugar got spilled. I was just sweeping it up.'

Deborah looked mystified. 'I don't understand. How did you manage to spill sugar in the first place? Don't tell me my useless children stood by and let *you* make the tea for the removal men.'

'No, you see, I—'

'Jess? Jess, is that you?'

Toby was staring at her.

Jessie returned his astonished gaze. Smiling slightly, she nodded.

'Yes, it's me. Hello, Toby.'

'Jess! This is . . . amazing.'

He took a step forwards, hesitated for a second, then moved around the table and reached for her, clutching her forearms. Jessie wished she didn't have a loaded dustpan in one hand and a brush in the other.

She glimpsed the astonished expression in Deborah Gillespie's dark brown eyes as Toby kissed her warmly on both cheeks. Even Savannah had by this time put down her magazine in order to watch.

11

'I take it you two know each other,' Deborah said at last.

'From way back. Years and years ago. My God, I can't believe it.' Still marvelling, Toby squeezed her wrists. Delight mingled with a flicker of guilt as he studied Jessie's flushed face. 'We were . . . well . . .'

'Pretty close?' Deborah guessed.

Jessie nodded. As she moved to balance herself, more sugar crunched underfoot. She'd made a lousy job of sweeping up.

'You look just the same,' said Toby. 'You look great.' He shook his head. 'I'm still in shock.'

'Weird,' Savannah intoned. 'Dad, lost for words.'

Toby turned to Deborah. 'Do you remember when the estate agent first showed us details of this house? You asked him where Upper Sisley was and I said I knew it, I came here once, years ago.' He waited until Deborah had nodded, then went on, 'Well, this is who I came here with. Jess and I were on a cycling holiday—'

'A cycling holiday!' Savannah rolled her eyes; this was clearly hysterical. 'Dad, that is so *sad*.'

'I was a drama student. We didn't have any money. We'd borrowed a tent,' Toby remembered, 'and even that was full of holes.'

'Not to mention insects,' said Jessie. Heavens, what was Deborah making of all this?

Clapping her hands over her mouth, Savannah gurgled, 'I don't believe it, a tent . . .'

'You can mock,' Toby grinned at his daughter, 'but we had a brilliant time. When we came to Upper Sisley there was a cricket match being played on the village green. It was a blisteringly hot summer afternoon. We lay on the grass and watched the cricket. And when the players had finished their tea, we were invited to help ourselves to all the leftover cakes and sandwiches.'

Savannah began playing an imaginary violin. 'So the good people of the village saved you from starving to death in your manky, wasp-infested tent. This is better than Oliver Twist.'

'I think it's romantic,' Deborah protested.

'Actually, it wasn't,' said Jessie. 'The tuna sandwiches had been left in the sun too long. We spent the night rushing in and out of the tent bringing our boots up.'

'But it didn't put us off Upper Sisley,' Toby went on. 'I remember saying to Jess at the time how great it would be to live somewhere like this.' He stopped abruptly and looked at her, and Jessie saw it again in his dark blue eyes: that brief, unspoken flicker of guilt.

'And now you are,' she said. 'Living here, I mean.'

He nodded, clearly desperate to say more but handicapped by the presence of his family. 'And you moved here too.'

'I'm starving,' Savannah announced, uncrossing her brown legs and waggling her toes.

'Run over to the cricket club,' said Toby, 'see if they've got any leftover sandwiches.'

'Ha ha. Mum, what can I eat?'

'Don't ask me.' Deborah looked alarmed. 'I haven't a clue where anything is.'

Savannah clutched her flat stomach and pulled a piteous face. 'This is serious, I'm really *really* hungry.'

'There's the village shop,' said Jessie.

'The pub!' Toby exclaimed. 'When I spoke to you on the phone you told me you were in the pub. Does it do food?'

Jessie was gripped with panic.

13

Chapter 3

'Um . . . um . . . the village shop does great food. All kinds of stuff. Frozen, too.' Wildly Jessie said, 'How about pizzas?'

Deborah was looking unenthusiastic. 'A pub lunch sounds far nicer. Anyway, we could all do with a break. Pub, Savvy?'

'Great! Won't be a sec,' Savannah slid off her crate and out of the kitchen, 'just need to brush my hair.'

'That means back in twenty minutes,' said Toby with an air of long-suffering, 'while she trowels on a faceful of make-up.'

'Men, they just don't understand. Come on,' Deborah grinned at Jessie, 'while we're waiting, you can see what needs to be done.'

The rooms they wanted her to decorate were upstairs. Two sunny south-facing bedrooms and a bathroom. Taking measurements and sketching a brief plan of each room in her notebook, Jessie said, 'I'm busy for the next fortnight, but I could make a start the week after that.'

'That's fine,' said Deborah. 'Isn't it, darling?'

Toby had been miles away, gazing out of the uncurtained bedroom window. He turned to look at them both.

'Sorry?'

'Jess can start on this in a fortnight's time.'

'Oh.' He nodded. 'Great.'

Jessie wondered what he had been so lost in thought about. She felt that strange, swallow-diving sensation again in the pit of her stomach. She wondered if, when she told him what she clearly must tell him, Toby would still think that having her working here in this house was oh, great.

14

★ ★ ★

Jessie did her best to get out of going back to the Seven Bells with them, but Toby wasn't having any of it.

'Don't be silly. Of course you're coming for a drink,' he said as he dragged her along the hall. 'Isn't she, Sav?'

Savannah's baby-pink lipstick glistened in the sunlight.

'Definitely. You can tell us all about Dad and the things he got up to eighty years ago, when he was young.'

Leaving the removals men to it, they made their way across the village green towards the Seven Bells. Dizzy slouched along, kicking the heads off dandelions as he went. Deborah, effortlessly elegant in a black off-the-shoulder jersey top and white Capri pants, walked arm-in-arm with Savannah. Jessie, walking behind them with Toby alongside, realised he was holding back, attempting to slow her down.

At last he murmured, 'Jess, I tried to contact you.'

They were a hundred yards from the pub and less than three yards from his wife and children. Hardly ideal.

'I know. I moved away.'

'Your parents wouldn't tell me where you were. I was frantic—'

'Not now,' said Jessie.

'No, I know. But we do have to talk.'

'Plenty of time.'

Toby glanced over his shoulder at Sisley House. 'We drove down from London the day after the estate agent gave us the details. As soon as I saw this place I knew we had to live here.' He shook his head. 'Is that fate?'

'No, it's a coincidence.'

'How long ago did you move here?'

'Fifteen years.'

'And did you ever—'

'We're here,' Jessie interrupted before they cannoned into Deborah and Savannah in the doorway.

'Come on, Dad, get your wallet out.' Savannah pushed open the door. 'Your shout.'

Lorna Blake, the landlady, was serving behind the bar with Oliver. Lorna had run the pub for the last five years. A

15

forty-something divorcee with a tough, no-nonsense manner, a gin-soaked voice, an endless capacity for cigarettes and a piercing bright-blue gaze, she always reminded Jessie of a female Al Capone. Moll Harper, the other full-time barmaid, was carrying trays of food through from the kitchen, holding them high as she sashayed between the crowded tables. The Seven Bells, with its picturesque setting and glowing reviews in all the pub guides, attracted tourists as well as locals. The pub was far busier now than it had been at midday.

There was a brief, stunned silence as heads turned and brains registered who had just joined them. It was, thought Jessie, like walking into the OK Corrall.

But the Gillespies, presumably, were used to this. If they noticed, they didn't show it. Jessie introduced them to Lorna Blake, who could be guaranteed not to gush and make an idiot of herself. Blunt, down-to-earth, chain-smoking Lorna never got excited about anything.

'Pleased to meet you.' As she shook Toby's hand, she mustered a faint smile. 'Welcome to the village.'

'And this is Oliver,' Jessie went on hurriedly, 'and that's Moll over there . . . Now, everyone's starving, so let's get some food ordered, then why don't we sit outside?'

Oliver was giving her an odd look. Deeply aware of this, Jessie ignored him and grabbed a handful of menus.

Oliver leaned across the bar to attract her attention. 'Lili had to take the kids home, by the way.' Meaningfully, he added, 'She said she'd see you later.'

'Okay. The fish pie's good,' Jessie announced, feeling slightly frantic. 'Or the fettucine Alfredo, that's my favourite . . .'

'Can you believe it?' Deborah was speaking to Lorna, but her husky, actressy voice could be heard by everyone in the bar. 'We move to a new house in the back of beyond and the first person we bump into,' she turned and lightly touched Jessie's arm, 'turns out to be one of my husband's old flames.'

Another silence, of positively Hitchcockian duration.

'If you don't feel like pasta,' Jessie blurted out, 'there's always steak and chips.'

16

Oliver had been pouring a pint of draught Stella. The lager, unchecked, foamed over the rim of the glass. 'You didn't tell me you *knew* him,' he said, his tone accusing.

Savannah, who had hopped up on to a bar stool, sat with her elbows on the bar and her chin resting on one hand. 'Don't panic, it's ancient history.' Amused, she tilted her head at Oliver. 'Why so bothered, anyway? What are you, her boyfriend?'

Outraged, Oliver said, 'Don't be ridiculous. I'm her son.'

'Good heavens! Are you really?' Deborah clapped her hands in delight. 'A strapping great lad like you! What are you, six two? Six three?'

'It's half past one,' said Jessie, by this time close to meltdown. 'Oh God, I really, really have to go . . . I promised the Hartwells I'd have their kitchen finished by five . . .'

Nobody took the slightest bit of notice. Jessie watched in horror as Savannah, now perking up considerably, wriggled her bottom on the bar stool, crossed her arms beneath her pert breasts and focused all her attention on Oliver.

'So you live in the village too? Well, that's something. I was scared it'd be full of miserable old folk.' She leaned closer and lowered her voice, too late to avoid offending all the miserable old folk hunched around a nearby table playing crib. 'What's it like, then? Dead boring around here – or are there places to go?'

Oliver began to unbend. 'Oh, there are places to go. You just need to know the right people. A mate of mine from college has just opened a new club in Harleston—'

'So you're at college.' Savannah's lilac-shadowed eyes were bright with interest. 'Whereabouts?'

'Exeter. Maths.'

'What year?'

'I've just finished my finals.'

Oliver knew the grin was spreading all over his face. He couldn't help it; every time he remembered the exams were over, it happened.

Savannah grinned back.

Deborah lit a cigarette and offered Jessie one. Jessie, who

17

didn't smoke, wondered if this was the moment to take it up.

'The Hartwells will have my guts for garters if I don't get back to work. I'm sorry, I really must go—'

'Maths. Crikey.' Savannah pulled a face. 'I couldn't do that. Still, must come in handy when you're working behind a bar.' She sounded impressed. 'You're older than I thought, then. You must be twenty-one – three years older than me . . .'

'Which makes you eighteen. See?' Oliver said modestly. 'I'm a genius.'

Savannah was giggling. Jessie, feeling horribly hot and sweaty, fumbled for her car keys. They promptly slid out of her hand and clattered to the flagstone floor.

Toby reached down for them at the same time as she did. Their heads met at table level. Jessie couldn't bring herself to meet his eye.

'I must go, I really must.'

'Jess . . .'

Toby's voice sounded strange. As well it might, Jessie had to concede. Trembling, she snatched the keys out of his hand.

But this time he forced her to look at him.

'Oh, Jess, we definitely need to talk.'

Chapter 4

Visiting her mother-in-law wasn't Lili's favourite pastime, but since William had been chanting 'Gra'ma, Gra'ma' like a demented football supporter for the past hour, she decided she may as well bite the bullet. Lili was terrified of Eleanor Ferguson, but William adored her – which just went to show there was no accounting for taste.

Piling an ecstatic William and a fractious Freya back into the double buggy, Lili remembered to drag a comb through her hair and squirt on some scent before leaving the house. If she didn't, Eleanor would only remark acerbically, 'Oh my, look at you. Just because your husband's away, dear, that's no reason to let yourself go . . .'

But Lili's spirits began to lift as she set out with the children. Living in the same village as one's mother-in-law might be construed as another bit of bad luck, but at least they lived at opposite ends of it, and the walk from the Old Vicarage in the High Street to Eleanor's cottage at the far end of Water's Lane was a scenic one.

It's a glorious day, thought Lili, determinedly counting her blessings. I've finished a mountain of ironing; Jessie's bound to call round later to give me all the gossip on the new people at Sisley House – could it *really* be Toby Gillespie, or had that been a joke, like the Madonna one? And, best of all, Michael's not here, so I can watch *Sleepless in Seattle* tonight in peace.

This was yet another blip on their compatibility chart. If he bothered to watch anything, Michael was a *Panorama*-type man who disapproved mightily of Lili's frivolous taste in TV. *Sleepless in Seattle* wasn't his thing at all.

19

'Gra'ma! Gra'ma!' William yodelled, feverish with anticipation and drumming his heels on the pushchair's foot-rest.

Lili had to smile. 'That's right, going to see Grandma.'

William let out a scream of delight and pointed across the road.

'Raddit. *Raddit*!'

'So it is.' Lili manoeuvred the buggy so Freya could see it too. 'Look, darling, a rabbit.'

'Raddit raddit raddit!' William screeched joyfully, his flailing arm almost knocking Freya horizontal. 'Mum, radd—'

The car, an old blood-red Granada belching exhaust fumes, came tearing around the corner of Compass Lane doing at least sixty. Instinctively, almost wrenching her arms out of their sockets, Lili jerked the buggy up on to the verge.

There were two men in the car, she saw them grinning as they swerved across the road. The rabbit didn't stand a chance. A bone-crunching thud was followed by a jubilant double thumbs-up from the driver of the car.

Lili screamed. William screamed louder. Freya stuck her thumb in her mouth and gazed wide-eyed at the dust cloud kicked up by the Granada's filthy wheels.

'You bastards!' Lili bellowed as the car disappeared up Water's Lane. She ran over to the animal, praying it was dead.

'Raddit,' said William, behind her.

Oh God, oh God, it was still alive. The rabbit's eyes were open. It lay, frozen with shock, on the verge. Blood seeped through the brownish-grey fur and its ribcage rose and fell in rapid, panicky breaths.

'Bastards,' Lili whispered, crouching over the terrified, quivering body and wondering what on earth to do. She couldn't, she *couldn't* just leave it there to die.

'Bas-tid,' William said helpfully when she ran back across the road to the pushchair.

Hands trembling, Lili unzipped the haversack packed with baby-changing paraphernalia. Dry-mouthed, she said croakily, 'I know.'

★ ★ ★

Further along Compass Lane, in Keeper's Cottage, Drew finished brushing his teeth, spat into the wash-basin – bullseye – and surveyed his reflection in the bathroom mirror without enthusiasm.

If his surname were Smith it wouldn't be so bad. Or Saunders or Webb or even Witherspoon. But it wasn't. His name was Andrew Darcy, and after thirty years it still had the ability to depress him. People about to meet Mr Darcy for the first time had certain expectations. Women, particularly. And Drew, with his untamed muddy-blond hair, big broken nose, wide, friendly mouth and generally unchiselled features, knew what a disappointment he must be in the flesh. He was a let-down. Okay, maybe not downright ugly. But average, certainly. Average enough to need to get by on personality where the opposite sex was concerned.

That was the trouble with girls. When they knew his name in advance, they anticipated so much more. He was supposed to look like Colin wet-shirt Firth, for Christ's sake.

It was bloody unfair – and it had happened again yesterday, when a stunning blonde in a scarlet sundress had brought her Siamese kitten into the surgery for its inoculations.

'Oh.' Her pretty face had fallen when she'd seen Drew. 'Are *you* Mr Darcy?'

Her hopes had been cruelly dashed, and so had his. Drew had found himself wishing for the millionth time that his name could be something ordinary, like Lewis, or even something ugly like Snark . . . At least then he could come as a nice surprise instead of a let-down.

He would have changed it by deed poll if it wasn't such a nancyish thing to do. Besides, that would really give the game away. Then everyone would know how much it bothered him.

Drew, who had his pride, turned his back on his less than satisfactory reflection and raced downstairs, taking them three at a time. It was twenty to two; he'd better get a move on if he wasn't going to be late.

He was by the front door when someone began frantically

21

hammering on it. Pulling it open, he found Lili Ferguson leaning against the porch in a frightful state.

'Oh, Drew, thank goodness you're in—'

'What is it?' His forehead puckered. She had a pushchair full of children with her and was clutching a Tesco bag in her arms. Her hair, wet with perspiration, was plastered against her temples and her shirt clung damply to her breasts.

Her eyes filled with tears as she opened the bag and showed him the rabbit. It lay there, quite still and bleeding profusely, wrapped in one of William's spare nappies.

'It's his leg.'

'Poor old thing,' said Drew. 'Been run over by the look of it.'

'We saw it happen. They didn't stop . . .' Lili bit her lip. 'They did it on purpose. It was deliberate.'

'Bas-tid,' William announced, waving cheerfully at Drew.

'You can save it, can't you?' Lili knew she was overreacting – this was the countryside, wild animals died all the time – but she couldn't help it, she didn't care.

'Well . . .'

'It costs money, I know that. I'll pay.'

'Bas-tid, bas-tid,' sang William. Reaching sideways, he grabbed a fistful of dandelions and wrenched them out of the untended stone tub next to the porch. Rubbing them happily in Freya's face, he yelled, 'Bas-tid Gra'ma.'

Oh heavens, thought Lili, this is all I need.

Drew glanced at his watch. Quarter to. 'Look, I'm on my way into the surgery now. I'll take him with me and see what I can do.'

'Money's no object,' said Lili recklessly, gladder than ever that Michael was thousands of miles away in Dubai. He was about as fond of rabbits as he was of *Sleepless in Seattle*.

Lili was in the kitchen slicing up tomatoes and mushrooms for a Bolognese sauce when Jessie tapped on the back door and let herself in.

'You've had your phone turned off all afternoon.' Lili wagged an accusing vegetable knife. 'And you haven't been

22

home yet either. I spoke to Oliver.'

Jessie went straight to the fridge, poured two enormous glasses of white wine and plonked them on the kitchen table. It was six o'clock. Feeling guilty about the phone, she switched it back on.

'I had to finish the Hartwells' kitchen. And I needed time to think.'

'I'm not surprised.' Lili's eyebrows went up. 'Oliver told me everything.'

Jessie swallowed. 'Everything?'

'About you and Toby Gillespie, and the fact that the two of you were childhood sweethearts,' Lili said, 'which for some reason you've never seen fit to mention to either your son or your best friend.'

'Ah.' Phew.

'Well, quite.' Lili abandoned the mushrooms and folded her arms across her pneumatic chest. 'If I were in your shoes I expect I'd want time to think about it too.'

Jessie dived into her drink.

Frowning, Lili went on, 'And why did you pour me one when Freya's still here? You know what Hugh and Felicity are like.'

Jessie drained her glass. 'I didn't pour you one, they're both for me.'

'Crikey.'

'Where are the kids?'

Lili poked her head around the kitchen door. In the living room Harriet, Lottie, William and Freya – like a row of Russian dolls – sat motionless on the sofa.

'Glued to the TV.'

Jessie pulled out a chair, fell onto it, dragged the purple scarf out of her hair and began winding it round and round her knuckles like worry beads. Which was apt. 'Toby Gillespie is Oliver's father.'

'Oh!' Lili's hands flew to her mouth. She stared wide-eyed at Jessie, unable to speak.

'Well, quite,' Jessie mimicked.

'Jess, are you *serious*?'

Jessie examined the ends of her hair, which were

23

encrusted with sunflower yellow emulsion. 'Of course I'm serious. It's hardly the kind of thing you'd make up.'

'Good grief.' The Bolognese sauce was well and truly forgotten now. Lili checked again through the living room door, making sure they hadn't been overheard, then plonked herself down at the table opposite Jessie.

'Does he know?'

'Who?'

'Toby Gillespie.'

'Up until today? No.' Jessie tried biting one of her fingernails but they were all spotted with paint. 'Although I think he was putting two and two together as I left the pub.'

'Does Oliver know?'

'Of course he doesn't.'

'Are you going to tell him?'

The taste of paint was disgusting. Jessie wound the purple scarf tightly round her left wrist instead and watched her hand change colour.

'Jess?'

Now her fingers were as purple as the scarf.

'I don't know, I don't know. It's up to Toby, I suppose. Blimey, today's been a big enough shock for me. God knows what it'll be like for him.'

Lili was still open-mouthed with shock. This was riveting stuff. Reaching behind her, she flicked the fridge open with one expert finger, tilted her chair on to its hind legs and grabbed the bottle of wine.

'So why didn't you ever tell me the truth?'

'The first rule of deception,' Jessie said with an apologetic shrug, 'is keep it simple. And stick to your story. I told you the same as I told Oliver.'

Lili ran through in her mind what she had been told, which was basically that, upon finding herself pregnant, Jessie and her boyfriend of the time, Tony something-or-other, had tried to make a go of things and failed dismally. They had split up before Oliver was born, and Tony had emigrated to Australia without ever seeing his son or showing the least amount of concern for either him or Jess.

It was a boring story, a story deliberately designed – Lili

24

now realised – not to arouse interest. If anyone ever tried to question Jessie on the subject of Oliver's father she even used a dull voice to describe him. Tony had fair hair, he was quite tall, in looks and intelligence he was average. This was about as much as she had ever been prepared to admit. No, they'd never really loved each other, and living together, let alone marriage, would have been a disaster. Tony just wasn't the settling-down type.

And no, she hadn't missed him particularly when he'd disappeared from her life. He was no loss.

As Lili put her elbows on the table, ready to listen to the real – and far more enthralling – story, Jessie's phone rang.

'Switched it back on then,' Toby Gillespie remarked in laconic fashion when she answered.

'Sorry, I was . . . busy.'

'I think cowardly's the word you're looking for.'

'Toby, I know we have to—'

'Talk, yes. Nine o'clock at your house?'

'Um, nine—'

'I checked with Oliver. He's working tonight, so we won't be interrupted.'

Jessie's hands had gone all sweaty again. 'Does he . . . er, has he . . .?'

'Nine o'clock, Jess. I'll see you then.'

She opened her mouth to dither some more but it was too late. Toby had hung up.

'Right,' announced Lili, quite forcibly for her. 'I think you'd better tell me the truth, the whole truth and nothing but the— *bugger.*'

Even Jessie had to smile. As Lili went to answer the door she called after her, 'It's a conspiracy.'

'Worse than that,' Lili hissed back, 'it's Hugh and Felicity.'

Easygoing Lili, who liked most people, tried hard to like Hugh and Felicity Seymour, but it was hard to warm to a couple so perfect that they made you feel like something stuck to the bottom of a dustbin by comparison.

Felicity was superwoman in a power suit, with her geometric ash-blonde bob, flawless make-up and Vuitton briefcase. Hugh, who had sleek conker-brown hair and a year-round tan, was the belted trenchcoat type. They were both tall, both thin, both successful in business. They were wealthy, intelligent, charming and utterly devoted to their only daughter, Freya.

Every now and again Lili was seized with an overwhelming urge to tie them up, lead them along to Paddy Birley's dairy farm and roll them around in a yardful of cow pats.

'Hello, how are you? How's she been today?' cried Felicity as she always did, while Hugh swung Freya up into his arms and covered her face with kisses.

'She's been great,' said Lili, wondering how quickly she could get rid of them. Hugh and Felicity loved to hear every detail of Freya's day, down to the last soggy rusk. 'Ate well, slept well, hasn't been sick, she and William played with the Duplo—'

'Blood,' William announced, perking up at the sound of his name. 'Raddit leg off.' He rolled his eyes dramatically. 'All blood.'

'Good heavens!' Felicity looked petrified. 'What's this all about?'

'Bas-tid,' William said with pride.

'Sounds like I'm not the only one who's had an eventful day,' Jessie observed when the Seymours had at last been despatched.

Lili looked worried. 'I meant to phone Drew to find out how the rabbit is.'

'Ring him now.'

Lili recognised a last feeble stab at procrastination when she heard one.

'I can't,' she told Jessie, sitting back down and emptying the bottle of wine into their glasses. 'I'm too busy listening to you telling me absolutely everything there is to know about you and Toby Gillespie.'

Chapter 5

'We met at a party in London. Toby was at RADA, I was still at school in Cheltenham. We were so happy together. It was brilliant, real first-love stuff.'

'Oh my God.' Lili was so excited she was biting her knuckles. 'I *knew* this was going to be good.'

'It couldn't have been better.' Jessie dabbed her finger in a spilt drop of wine and doodled a wet spiral on the kitchen table. 'We saw each other every weekend. Neither of us had a bean, of course, but that didn't matter. We did all those poor-but-happy things students do, and we made a million plans for the future. But one of the things we did backfired on us,' she added with a faint smile, 'and a baby didn't fit in with any of those plans. I was seventeen, half-way through my A-levels. Toby was twenty and a drama student. The same thing had happened to one of the boys in his year. He married his girlfriend, dropped out of RADA and got a job in an abattoir.'

There was an odd look in Jessie's eyes. Lili guessed what was coming next and couldn't bear it.

'You didn't tell him,' she gasped. 'You didn't even tell him you were pregnant!'

'Oh I did. I told him. He said he'd marry me. But I knew it wasn't what he wanted.' Fidgeting uncontrollably now, Jessie swirled the wine round in her glass, creating a mini whirlpool. 'Acting was Toby's life. He was going to be the next Al Pacino. I couldn't see him working in an abattoir.'

'So . . .?'

'Everyone seemed to think the best thing all round was an

abortion. Not least my parents,' Jessie said drily. 'A penniless drama student wasn't their idea of ideal son-in-law material. So we agreed that's what would happen. It was all arranged.' She took a deep breath. 'Except, at the last minute I couldn't go through with it.'

'Good grief. And Toby finished with you? The bastard.' Lili bristled with indignation.

'Will you stop jumping to conclusions?' Jessie demanded. 'He didn't know I hadn't had it done. I decided it wasn't fair on him. He'd sold practically all his possessions to raise the money for the operation – after doing all that, how could I tell him I'd changed my mind?'

'But it was his baby!'

'I know, but he didn't really want it.'

'What did your parents say?'

Jessie pulled a face. 'Went mental. I was this major embarrassment to them – they could hardly bear to look at me. So I shot up to Scotland and stayed with my Auntie Morag in Glasgow. I wrote to Toby and told him it was all over between us. I said I'd had the abortion and that was it – I didn't want to see him any more. When he turned up on my parents' doorstep they told him the same.' She shrugged. 'He kept on phoning them, but they weren't going to tell him where I was. Then, six months later, they moved to Oxford and that really *was* it. Toby couldn't contact them any more. They'd disappeared.'

'Oh, Jess. And now he's found you.' Lili could hardly breathe. 'What's he going to *say*?'

Jessie stood up, stuffed the purple scarf into the back pocket of her jeans and reached across the table for her keys. 'Haven't the foggiest. But I'd like to have a bath before I find out.'

Lili jumped a mile when the doorbell rang at ten to eight. Desperately on edge on Jessie's behalf, she hadn't been able to concentrate on anything else. 'Mum, you're missing out pages,' an aggrieved Lottie had complained during *Postman Pat and the Mystery Thief*. 'This is hopeless! You'll just have to start again from the beginning.'

Having at last managed to get William and five-year-old Lottie up to bed, Lili had followed Jessie's example and wallowed in a hot bath, wriggling her toes in time with the music belting out of Harriet's room (because according to Harriet you couldn't truly appreciate the Spice Girls unless they were causing bits of plaster to vibrate off the walls).

The doorbell ringing coincided with Lili taking her first cautious sip of just-made hot chocolate. She groaned as it slopped down the front of her white towelling dressing gown, then let out a squeak as the scalding liquid seeped through to her skin.

'Ooh . . . ow . . . Oh, hi! . . . Ooh . . .'

Drew Darcy, on the doorstep, broke into a grin. 'This is exciting. You sound like one of those sex lines – just dial 0898 something-or-other and speak to Luscious Lucy. Not,' he added hastily, 'that I've ever phoned one.'

'It's hot chocolate,' Lili gasped. 'I've gone and burnt my . . . chest.' She risked a quick peek between the lapels and saw angry blotches spring up. 'Ow, it still hurts.'

Drew marched her through to the kitchen, held a tea towel under the cold tap, expertly wrung it out and handed it to Lili.

'Hold this against your . . . er, affected area. Go on, right inside your dressing gown. I won't look.'

Heavens, what a peculiar sensation, thought Lili. Ice-cold water was dripping down her breasts, sliding over her stomach and puddling on the floor, while the rest of her was warm and dry.

'Any blisters forming?' Drew asked.

Lili peeped again, shook her head and peeled the top edge of the tea towel away to reassure him. Drew was a vet after all, the next best thing to a doctor. Anyway, what was she showing him? Just a bit of cleavage.

'You'll live.' His grin broadened, revealing lots of creamy white teeth, many of them capped as a result of tussles on the rugby pitch. 'Sorry, it obviously wasn't a great time to call round.'

'How's the rabbit?' Lili was still dripping. She wondered if she looked as incontinent as she felt.

Drew stopped smiling.

'I'm sorry. He died.'

'Oh no. Did you operate on him?'

'He died in the car, on the way to the surgery,' Drew said gently. 'Just closed his eyes and went. He must have had internal bleeding. I really am sorry, Lili.'

Lili wiped her eyes with her sleeve, feeling a bit stupid. You were allowed to cry when a pet died, but this had been just a wild rabbit, a complete stranger . . .

'Here.' Drew passed her a handkerchief and patted her hand.

She hoped he didn't think she was barmy, a hopelessly soft case.

'This is embarrassing.'

'Of course it isn't. You're upset because some idiot ran that rabbit over for fun.'

So I am, thought Lili, snuffling into his hanky and marvelling at how clean and fresh-smelling it was. Drew must keep a special supply for weepy pet owners. Gosh, he was kind.

'I just don't understand how anyone can do something like that. I mean, when I'm driving I swerve to avoid animals.' Lili shook her head, shuddering as she remembered a heartstopping moment last year when she'd only just managed to steer out of the way of a bolting fox cub. 'What kind of a person sees something in the road and actually aims *for* it?'

Drew nodded. 'They aren't people, they're monsters. I tell you, some of the cases I see make me want to batter whoever did it to a pulp. Animals starved, beaten, neglected . . .' His eyes hardened as he spoke. 'Like this morning we had a puppy brought in. The owners had done a moonlight flit. When the landlord went to the house the place was a tip and they'd left the dog behind, locked up in one room with no food. Another couple of days and he'd have died. Sorry,' Drew said, glancing up and seeing the tears rolling freely down Lili's cheeks. 'I'm not doing much of a job here, am I? I'm supposed to be cheering you up.'

'What will happen to him?'

'Dogs' home. He's only four or five months old, just a puppy. Not what you'd call Mr Good Looking,' Drew added with a brief smile. 'Not exactly the Brad Pitt of the doggy world, but he has a lovely nature. I'm sure somebody will take him.'

'And if they don't, he'll be put down,' said Lili, feeling sick. 'What make is he?"

'What make *isn't* he?' Drew replied. 'They don't come much more mongrel than this. Terrier, greyhound, collie, maybe a dash of spaniel in there somewhere—'

'I'll have him,' Lili blurted out.

'You haven't seen him.'

'Doesn't matter. I want him.' She marvelled at the certainty in her voice.

Drew, who was being more cautious, said, 'Lili, this isn't dial-a-pizza. You're upset because the rabbit died. I've just made you cry – twice. You're in what we professional medical types call a bit of a state.' He smiled again, to show he understood. 'By all means come into the surgery tomorrow and meet him, but don't make any rash promises tonight.'

Lili, who had by this time stopped crying, knew she wouldn't change her mind. She wanted this dog more than anything, and as soon as he recovered she was going to bring him home.

And I'm not even going to think about what Michael will say, Lili told herself with great firmness.

This was chiefly because she already knew what he would say. Michael had about as much time for dogs as he did for wild rabbits.

Chapter 6

Having bathed and washed her hair, Jessie was finding the process of deciding what to wear a complicated business. Too much effort and Toby might think she was trying to impress him. Too little, on the other, and he might think she was trying to make a point of deliberately not impressing him.

Or something like that.

In the end she settled for a black cotton sundress, sleeveless and ankle-length and a bit on the tenty side, but easy to wear. On the one hand it was a dress, so she didn't look as if she was making too little effort; on the other hand it wasn't what you'd call smart.

She stayed barefoot, but tied up her hair with a yellow bow. She put on mascara but not lipstick, deodorant but no perfume, knickers but no bra, and Bruce Springsteen but not Bryan Ferry.

Oh God, definitely not Bryan Ferry.

What a lot of fuss, thought Jessie – and talk about pointless! Why am I so bothered about what I look like when he's seen me already, covered in paint and wearing boots and my least flattering jeans?

'It's not very fair, is it?' Jessie said when she opened the front door twenty minutes later. 'I mean, here I am looking twenty years older than when you last saw me, but you're always in the papers or on TV so there's no shock value, no twenty-year gap to get over—'

'Twenty-one,' Toby corrected, his dark blue eyes steady. 'Twenty-one and a half years, actually.'

'Okay, fine. I'm just saying it must be more of a—'

'Jess, stop wittering.' Toby stepped into the hall and closed the door behind him. 'Don't you think we have more important things to talk about?'

Jessie's plan to be cool and calm and laid-back about it all didn't seem to be going terribly well. Things had been a lot easier, she realised, when Toby's family had been around him, serving as unwitting bodyguards. With an apologetic shake of her head, she backed her way into the living room.

'Sorry. Right. Well, fire away . . .'

'Fire being the operative word, seeing as I've spent the whole day torn between wanting to shoot you and kiss you senseless. Dammit, Jess.' Toby pushed his dark-blond hair out of his eyes just as she remembered him doing all those years ago. 'I knew moving house was supposed to be a stressful experience, but I wasn't expecting this.'

'Well,' said Jessie, stung, 'neither was I.'

It *had* all been a bit sudden.

'Oliver's my son,' Toby said.

'Of course he's your son.'

'I came face to face with him today. No warning, nothing.'

'I didn't have time to tell you, did I?' Jessie protested.

Now Toby really looked as if he could throttle her. She watched his knuckles gleam as he gripped the back of the sofa.

Finally he said in a low voice, 'Jess, you've had twenty-one years to tell me.'

There was a framed photograph on the mantelpiece of Oliver as a laughing, gap-toothed five-year-old. It embarrassed him hugely, but Jess adored it. She looked at it now. 'You didn't want him,' she told Toby. 'You didn't want to be tied down. A baby wasn't part of the plan, was it?'

'But *Jess*—'

'You had no money and another year to go at drama school. You said an abortion was the best thing, and gave me the money to do it. When the time came . . .' Jessie said slowly, 'I couldn't.'

'You should have told me,' said Toby. 'You shouldn't have just disappeared.'

'Except that would have been like emotional blackmail,

wouldn't it?' There was pain and pride in Jessie's dark brown eyes. 'You'd have stuck by me and secretly resented me, and sooner or later you'd have ended up hating me for forcing you into a situation you needn't have been in.' She shrugged and looked again at the photograph. 'I just thought it was better to go away and have the baby on my own.'

'Jesus, your parents must have really hated me. They wouldn't tell me a thing,' said Toby. He stuffed his hands into the pockets of his jeans. 'So, where did you go?'

'Scotland. To stay with my Auntie Morag. And after Oliver was born I managed to get a council flat. It wasn't much of a place, but we managed.' Jessie didn't elaborate. The flat, on the seventeenth floor of a high-rise in Glasgow, had been mouldy and dilapidated, with walls so thin you could hear the click of the needles as syringefuls of heroin were injected into the veins of the addicts next door.

'Did it never occur to you to contact me?' Toby said carefully.

'Of course it did. I thought about it hundreds of times. But when Oliver was tiny, you were just another struggling actor. Then you landed the part in *Fast and Loose* and became a star practically overnight.' Jessie lifted her eyebrows at him. 'And how would it have looked if I'd contacted you then? I'd have looked like a groupie, crawling out of the woodwork, only interested in you because you'd become a success.'

Toby was still gripping the back of the sofa for dear life. 'I was desperate to find you again,' he told Jessie. 'You have no idea. If you'd contacted me, I'd have been so . . . happy . . .'

'Yes, well.' She shrugged flippantly. 'I was tempted, I can tell you. When you're eighteen and a single mother, you have your low points.'

'I wish you had contacted me.'

Jessie smiled to herself, deciding he might as well know everything.

'Actually, I did write to you once. I addressed it to the TV company that made *Fast and Loose*. I couldn't tell you about Oliver, of course, not in a letter that was going to be opened and read by a complete stranger, but I asked you to get in touch with me and gave you my Glasgow address.'

Toby was staring at her, his expression appalled, already shaking his head.

'But I didn't—'

'I know you didn't see it. The letter was in my bag waiting to be posted,' Jessie's voice caught as she remembered the long-ago moment, 'when it was announced on the radio that you'd just got married.'

'Oh my God,' sighed Toby.

'And there it was, the next day, in all the papers – your fairytale secret wedding to stunning actress Deborah Lane.' Jessie realised she could probably still recite the articles word for word. 'I saw the photographs and read all that stuff about how you'd spotted her on TV, fallen in love at first sight and tracked her down . . . You were quoted as saying you were the luckiest man in the world with the most beautiful wife in the world and you couldn't wait to start a family together.'

She stopped. Toby was staring at her with the oddest expression on his face.

'Well, that was pretty much that,' Jessie went on when he didn't speak. To compensate, she felt herself beginning to babble again. 'I felt a bit of an idiot, I can tell you. And of course I didn't post the letter. I tore it into a million pieces, actually, and flung it out of my kitchen window like confetti . . .'

Toby was moving towards her.

'. . . very melodramatic of me, I know—'

'Jess, shut up.'

'Oh Toby, please don't, you really mustn't.' Unsteadily she backed away.

'Oh Jess,' he mimicked softly. 'I must, I really must.'

He bent his head and kissed her, gently at first, then harder, and the extraordinary thing, Jessie realised as she clung to him, was that his kiss hadn't changed at all. It was just as she remembered it, as unique as any fingerprint. And every bit as miraculous.

'Hang on,' she muttered shakily, managing to pull away at last. 'This is wrong, wrong, wrong.'

'How can it be?' Toby's warm hands were on either side of her face. 'We should have stayed together.'

Maybe. And with hindsight, Jessie thought sadly, they could have done. The drawback at the time, of course, had been that they had been too practical, too realistic. It hadn't occurred to either of them that just months after graduating from RADA, Toby would land the lead role in what was to become one of the most popular and hugely successful TV series of all time.

The odds against that happening . . . Well, Jessie mused, you'd have more luck at Ladbroke's betting on the Loch Ness monster bursting out the water dangling a Yeti in one flipper and a winning Lottery ticket in the other.

Trying hard to look as if the kiss hadn't knocked her for six, Jessie perched on the arm of the sofa. 'You've got Deborah now,' she told Toby. 'And one of the happiest marriages in show business.'

It was true. Everyone knew that. When any magazine ran a feature on enduring celebrity marriages, the Gillespies were always mentioned up there along with the Newmans, the Connerys and the Caines.

'What about you?' Toby's fingers, disconcertingly, were still stroking her face. 'Who have you got?'

'Oliver,' Jessie replied simply, 'my son.'

'You've never married?'

'Don't look at me like that!' Horrified, she thought she glimpsed pity in his eyes. 'I haven't spent the last twenty years celibate! I've had my moments, I can assure you.'

'But you didn't find Mr Right.'

'Sometimes,' Jessie replied with spirit, 'you can have more fun with Mr Wrong.'

This was her excuse anyway, and she was sticking to it.

To her relief Toby let the matter drop. 'We've got so much catching up to do. I still don't know how you got from Glasgow to here.'

'My parents died fifteen years ago,' Jessie said matter-of-factly. 'When they moved from Cheltenham they bought a bungalow in Oxford.'

'I hitch-hiked down from London one weekend,' Toby

interrupted, 'and they'd just gone . . .' His expression changed. 'How did they die?'

Jessie remained calm. In truth, her parents' what-will-the-neighbours-say attitude and total lack of interest in their grandson had reduced her relationship with them to Christmas-card level. She had no regrets. They had been ashamed of her for being an unmarried mother, and she had been ashamed of them for taking it out on Oliver.

'There was a massive gas explosion. The bungalow was destroyed. They were killed outright.'

'Oh Jess, I'm sorry.'

'But they were insured to the hilt,' she went on, 'and with the money I was able to buy this place. I remembered Upper Sisley, and drove down here to have a look at the village. After a high-rise in Glasgow, Duck Cottage was like a palace. As soon as I saw it, I knew I wanted to live here.'

Toby nodded. He had felt it too.

'And I've been happy here ever since.' Jessie looked up at him. 'So there you go. That's me up to date and I haven't even offered you a drink yet. Red wine or tea?'

They sat out in the back garden and watched the sun slide behind the trees as they drank their wine.

'Your turn now,' said Jessie. She tucked her feet up on the bench and smoothed the black cotton folds of her dress over her ankles until only her red painted toenails peeped out. 'You've met Oliver. So what did you think of him?'

'Bearing in mind that I was in shock at the time, it seems to me you've done a pretty good job.' Toby shook his head. 'I can't believe how much I've missed. As for Oliver . . . I mean, has it been hard for him, growing up without a father?'

'Probably.' Jessie's voice was steady. It was an awful lot easier to breathe now that Toby was sitting opposite her with a wooden table between them. 'But he's never accused me of wrecking his life.'

'No, of course you—'

'The thing is, what happens next?' Jessie twirled the stem of her glass between her fingers. 'Do we keep this to ourselves, or do we tell him?'

Toby frowned. It hadn't occurred to him that they had a choice. 'What do you think? Which would be best for you?'

'It's going to affect you more than it'll affect me,' Jessie said. 'There's Deborah to consider. And your children. It might not be good news for your career—'

'Sod my career!' Toby retorted, sounding almost angry. Jessie wondered if he thought she was having a go at him.

'Okay, but how's Deborah going to react?'

'No idea.'

Deeply curious, Jessie couldn't resist asking, 'Did you tell her you were coming over to see me tonight?'

Toby nodded and helped himself to more wine.

'She didn't mind?'

He shook his head.

'Oh.'

This was good in one way, Jessie told herself. Jealousy was boring and seriously overrated as an occupation, and what did it ever achieve? She was glad Deborah – who seemed so nice – didn't go in for that kind of thing.

On the other hand, it wasn't terribly flattering to be shrugged off with quite this much lack of concern. Toby did fancy me once, after all, Jessie thought with mild indignation. It would be nice to be regarded as just a *bit* of a threat.

'I want Oliver to know I'm his father.' Toby nodded, to show he'd made his decision.

'Right. You break it to your family first,' said Jessie, 'then I'll tell Oliver.'

'Do you hate me?' said Toby.

'No.'

'Do you wish I hadn't bought Sisley House?'

'I don't know yet.' Jessie smiled slightly. 'We'll have to wait and see how all this turns out.'

There were so many things to say, it was hard to know where to start. She tucked her feet right under the hem of her dress, suddenly aware of how chipped the red polish was on her toes. Toby might only be wearing a yellow polo shirt and Levi's, but the discreetly slim watch on his wrist was a Cartier and his shoes were hand-made. By comparison she couldn't help feeling a bit . . . well, a bit Oxfam.

38

'I never stopped thinking about you.' His voice was low. 'You broke my heart when you disappeared.'

'For at least a week,' Jessie riposted, alarm mingling with desire as she saw the expression in his eyes.

'Longer than that.' Toby shook his head and stood up, dangling the empty wine bottle between his fingers. 'Any more where this came from?'

'No,' Jessie lied. 'Look, why don't you go home now and tell them?'

'Are you kicking me out?' Toby laughed. 'What happened, did I miss last orders?'

Her heart was hammering away now, under the black cotton. 'I'd just rather you went. I'm tired,' she said, 'it's been a hell of a day.'

But Toby, still smiling that heart-breaking, oh-so-familiar smile, was moving towards her again.

'You aren't tired.' Briefly he touched her shoulder. 'You're trembling.'

'No.' Jessie tried to back hastily along the wooden bench, a surefire way to get splinters. 'Please, Toby, stop it. I don't want you to kiss me again. Ever,' she added as firmly as she could manage.

'That's not true either.'

This, of course, *was* true.

'Okay, okay! You *mustn't* kiss me again. It isn't fair on Deborah, for a start.'

Nor on me, Jessie thought.

'A lot of things aren't fair. All these years,' said Toby, 'I've blamed myself for what happened. I'd forced you to have an abortion, and as a result you couldn't bear to see me again. So you disappeared, and I lost you.' He put the empty bottle on the table and reached for Jessie's hands, pulling her to her feet. 'Now I've found you again – *both* of you – and I can't even begin to describe how that feels.'

'Don't kiss me,' Jessie squeaked.

'Okay, relax.' He was grinning. 'You can show me out instead. We'll shake hands politely over the garden gate . . . will that keep the neighbours happy?'

He did too, in solemn, bank-managerish fashion.

'I can't see anybody watching.'

'Well you wouldn't.' Jessie glanced briefly across the green. 'They aren't amateurs, you know. We're talking SAS tactics here.'

'I'll see you tomorrow.'

'Right. Good luck.'

Before she could stop him, Toby had lifted a stray ringlet away from her damp cheek and smoothed it behind her ear. 'As beautiful as ever.' He sounded almost sad. 'Oh, Jess.'

Oh God! I want you to kiss me, kiss me, *kiss me*! Jessie almost shouted aloud. But it was only a temporary lapse. She managed to control herself.

This was Upper Sisley, after all.

Beyond those motionless net curtains a crack surveillance team lurked. The binoculars would be out in force.

Chapter 7

Lili didn't have long to wait to discover why Felicity Seymour stayed in the car the next morning.

Hugh, carrying Freya into the house, said, 'Felicity was a bit concerned. She asked me to mention the bottle of wine yesterday.'

'Oh, that was Jessie, not me,' Lili told him cheerfully. 'She'd had a bit of a shock.'

'There were two glasses.' Hugh smiled his charming, apologetic smile to show he wasn't about to dispense with her services on the spot. 'I'm sure you think we're making a fuss about nothing—'

'They were both Jessie's!' Lili began to feel a bit sick – even to her own ears that sounded lame. She tried again. 'Really, I never drink when I'm working.'

She wondered whether Hugh and Felicity were planning to report her to the social services, with whom she was registered, and her cheeks flamed. Here she was, innocent, and practically being accused of being drunk in charge of a baby.

Then her cheeks went even redder as she recalled grabbing one of the glasses and taking a hefty gulp of wine. Oh God, she *had* had a drink – and she hadn't even remembered doing it, a sure sign of alcoholism if ever there was one . . .

'Well, I just said I'd mention it.' Hugh glanced at his expensive watch. 'I'm sure it won't happen again. We both know how happy Freya is coming here to you.'

Plus there are no other registered childminders in the village, Lili thought. She watched the way Hugh's glossy, conker-brown hair flopped forwards as he bent to kiss his daughter goodbye, then fell effortlessly back into place when he straightened up again. She wondered jealously what it must be like to have hair that did what you wanted it to do. To be perfect *and* to have perfect hair.

Lili was on her knees unloading the washing machine when she heard horribly familiar footsteps on the path leading up to the front door.

Oh God, unfair, she thought frantically. Why can't she ring first?

But there was nowhere to run, no place to hide – not even inside the washing machine. There was a clink of glass, a sharp rap on the door, and Eleanor Ferguson's face – alarmingly distorted – appeared pressed against the bubbled glass.

When Lili opened the door she found her mother-in-law brandishing four slightly cloudy milk bottles.

'Morning, Lili, I'll just give these a rinse, shall I? We don't want people walking past the house thinking you don't know how to wash a milk bottle.'

Lili had had sixteen years of this. She was fairly used to it by now. Instead of feeling as if a time bomb were about to go off in her chest, and bursting into tears of frustration, she treasured Eleanor's crashingly insensitive remarks, collecting them like Green Shield stamps, saving them up and relaying them to Jessie afterwards, when they would scream with laughter and award each new insult points out of ten.

'Help yourself,' Lili said with a bright smile, because this was probably a seven and a half. She picked up the top-heavy washing basket. 'I've just got to shove these in the tumble dryer.'

'The tumble dryer!' Eleanor looked as horrified as if Lili had suggested the shredder. 'Don't be ridiculous, Lili. It's a beautiful sunny day – those clothes will dry in no time.'

'I know they will,' Lili replied patiently, 'but they'll be creased and need ironing. This way, they don't.'

'Oh, Lili.' Eleanor's tone spoke volumes. She shook her head. 'Those machines cost a fortune to run.'

'Yes, but it saves electricity not having to iron—'

'Here, give that to me.' Eleanor seized the washing basket from her. 'I'll take it home, peg everything out on the line, iron it all when it's dry and bring it back this evening.'

And happen to mention it to everyone you pass in the street until the whole village knows, Lili thought. Still, they were as used to Eleanor as she was. And properly ironed clothes would make a nice change.

'Fine then – if you're sure.' She rummaged in the freezer as she spoke, hunting for a packet of fish fingers for William and Freya's lunch.

'I could bring a casserole as well, if you like. Something nutritious for the children's tea,' said Eleanor. 'It can't do them any good, growing up on all this junk food.'

Lili looked at the packet of pure cod fillet fish fingers in her hand. They didn't seem to have done Captain Birdseye any harm. 'Eleanor, if you'd like to make a casserole, that would be great,' she said, because Eleanor was clearly dying to. It would give her the opportunity to boast – yet again – about the time she almost auditioned for *Masterchef*. 'Actually, I wanted to ask another favour – but you do so much for us already.'

'Some of us are just more organised than others,' Eleanor preened. 'What is it you need help with?'

'Could you look after the children this evening, around sixish? Just for an hour?'

'That's no problem. Why – where are you going?' Eleanor said briskly. 'The doctor's? What's the matter this time?' She did that Kenneth Williams thing with her nostrils. 'Not more thrush?'

Lili took a deep breath. Some months back, Eleanor had gone upstairs to the loo and returned twenty minutes later with a handful of rusty razors.

'I've sorted out your bathroom cabinet, given it a good scrub and a tidy up,' she had announced, dropping the razors into the bin. 'I presume the tub of Canesten cream belongs to you, Lili.'

Lili, stunned, had only been able to nod.

'So you've got thrush, have you? That's not very nice, is

43

it? Maybe if you washed your underwear properly by hand instead of throwing it all into that washing machine of yours, this kind of thing wouldn't happen.'

That had been one of Jessie's favourites – she'd given it a nine.

'No, I don't have thrush,' Lili said patiently now, as Freya stirred in her sleep, 'and I'm not going to see the doctor, I'm going to see the vet.'

'What on earth for?' Eleanor looked indignant. 'You don't have any animals.'

'Drew Darcy was telling me yesterday about a puppy they've taken in. It's in need of a home,' Lili braced herself, 'and I said we might have it.'

'But Michael doesn't like dogs!' Indignation turned to outrage. 'He won't want a puppy in his house.'

'It's my house too,' said Lili bravely, 'and I do.'

On the rare occasions when Lili did stand up for herself, Eleanor never knew how to react. Consequently – as now – several seconds of stunned silence were followed by an abrupt change of subject.

'I'll put the kettle on,' Eleanor announced, filling it under the tap to the two-cup level, because anything more would be wasteful. Before plugging it in, she ran a J-Cloth over the base. 'Anyway, I wonder what my next door neighbour's been up to. There was a journalist knocking on her door this morning.'

Lili had to bite her lip. So this was the reason for today's unscheduled visit. When Eleanor assumed her only-mildly-interested voice it meant she was about to explode with curiosity.

There was a triumphant light in Eleanor's pale grey eyes. Bernadette Thomas kept herself frustratingly to herself. 'Not that I knew it was a journalist at first, of course. I just saw the chap knocking at the door and getting no reply, so I went and told him Mrs Thomas had gone out earlier. Then I said if he'd like to leave a message I'd be happy to pass it on, and he gave me a card.' Swelling with pride, Eleanor produced it from her cardigan pocket and waved it at Lili. 'See? With his name and number printed on it. He's a freelance journalist, very interested in doing a piece on my next door neighbour for *The Times*, no less. Now what do you suppose that could be about?'

Freya had woken up. As she lifted the baby up, Lili smelled the deliciously clean baby smell of her head and hid another smile. 'Why don't you ask her?'

Eleanor was now unloading the dishwasher, peering with deep suspicion at the inside of every mug because you could only really trust something to be clean if it was scoured by hand. 'Bernadette Thomas moved into this village six months ago, and I've tried to strike up numerous conversations . . .'

Interrogations, thought Lili.

'I've done my best to be friendly . . .'

Nosy, thought Lili.

'But she never tells me anything,' Eleanor concluded irritably. 'She's just one of those antisocial women, determined to keep herself to herself.'

'Hang on, something's wrong here,' said Jessie. 'It's your day off, it's only one o'clock in the afternoon, and you're *up*. Dressed, even. Quick, give me a Valium—'

'Ha ha,' Oliver said as she squeezed past him in the narrow kitchen, pinching a slice of toast from his plate en route. 'It's the lowest form of wit.'

Having slung two more slices of bread into the toaster, Jessie began spreading the stolen slice thickly with peanut butter. Oliver was wearing dark green jeans and a T-shirt that actually looked as if it might have been ironed.

'So where are you off to?'

He shrugged. 'Driving into Harleston.'

'On your own?' said Jessie.

'I'm going with Savannah Gillespie.'

The toast popped up.

Looking at it, Jessie said, 'Oh.'

'I saw her from my bedroom window this morning. She was sitting on the wall by the pond feeding the ducks,' Oliver explained. 'We got chatting again, and I said if she wasn't doing anything this afternoon I could show her round the town.'

Jessie could only assume that Savannah hadn't Been Told yet. 'Er . . . were her parents happy with that?'

Oliver looked amused. 'I have passed my driving test, you know. And Savannah's eighteen. She doesn't have to ask their permission.'

'Yes, well, drive carefully.' Jessie concentrated on scraping the last of the peanut butter out of the jar. 'And be . . . be polite.'

'Mum, are you on drugs or something?'

Jessie checked for the fiftieth time that the battery on her phone hadn't gone flat. Oh, Toby, what's going on? Why haven't you rung yet?

Turning to Oliver she said, 'And don't be late home.'

'Yoo hoo!'

Bernadette Thomas's heart sank when she saw Eleanor Ferguson's permed grey head bobbing over the fence that divided their cottages. She wouldn't make the same mistake next time she bought a house, that was for sure. She'd hire a private detective to check out the neighbours in advance.

'Yoo hoo-oo, Bernadette!'

The silly woman was waving at her. Bernadette, who had been peacefully clipping the edges of her lawn, stood up and made her way over to the fence.

'You had a visitor earlier, while you were out. A journalist,' Eleanor announced with pride and extremely thinly disguised curiosity. 'Here, he left his card, and he'd like you to contact him at your earliest convenience. I said to him, What's going on here? Is Bernadette a celebrity and we don't even know it?' She laughed a bit too heartily. 'Or a bank robber, or a Russian spy?'

'I'm not a Russian spy,' said Bernadette, her palms sweating. She took the card and stepped backwards, landing awkwardly on one of the stones bordering the flowerbed and almost stumbling in her hurry to get away. 'I don't rob banks either.'

'But you are very secretive.' Eleanor's tone was arch; she'd had enough of this prevarication. 'The thing is, people are beginning to wonder, Bernadette. You know how some folk

46

are about a bit of a mystery. Before long they'll be imagining all sorts.'

Bernadette's scalp began to prickle beneath her gardening
hat. She knew Eleanor was right. And now a journalist was
sniffing around . . . Oh God, it didn't bear thinking about.
'Excuse me,' she said hurriedly, needing time to think, to
prepare. 'I'm sure I can hear my phone.'

Bernadette's phone might not have been ringing, but Jessie's
was. Balanced on the top of a step-ladder with a tray of
pistachio-green matt emulsion in one hand a roller in the
other, she had to grip the roller's handle between her teeth
and squeeze the phone out of a narrow pocket single-
handed.

'It's me.' Toby sounded relaxed. 'I've spoken to Deborah
and she's fine about it. So why don't you tell Oliver this
evening, and I'll tell my two, then you can both come over
here for a drink and a chat . . .'

'Is it really that simple?' said Jessie. Heavens, how civi-
lised. Somehow she'd imagined it would be a bit more
dramatic than this.

But then, Jessie realised as she set to with the roller once
more, I've clearly been moving in hopelessly unsophisti-
cated circles. Maybe when you were a member of London's
glitterati, long-lost sons popping up out of the woodwork
were par for the course.

The journalist, when Bernadette spoke to him, was thankfully not the pushy type. He was disappointed when she
explained apologetically that she was unable to help him,
but assured her that he understood.

Bernadette breathed a sigh of relief as she replaced the
receiver. That was one crisis averted – or postponed, at
least.

Now she just had Eleanor Ferguson to deal with.

An hour later, Bernadette parked on a meter in the centre of
Harleston. She checked her reflection in the rear-view
mirror before getting out of the car. An anonymous woman

in her mid-forties stared back at her, neatly made up and unobtrusively dressed in a navy blouse and grey linen skirt. She ran a comb briefly through the straight brown hair she wore in a simple centre-parted bob. She touched her plain gold earrings – an habitual gesture of reassurance – then, satisfied that all was well, took her purse out of her bag. She needed a pound coin for the meter.

Waterstone's was moderately busy but nobody bothered Bernadette, who blended in with the browsers. She spent twenty minutes searching along the fiction shelves before finding what she was looking for.

Antonia Kay was the author of four Aga-saga type novels. Bernadette had never heard of her, and since the company that brought out her books wasn't one of the more successful ones, it stood to reason that Antonia, as a novelist, wasn't one of the publishing industry's great successes either.

Best of all, there was no author biography included in any of the four novels, nor were there any photographs to show the readers what Antonia Kay looked like. But from the style of novel, you would imagine her to be a quiet, nondescript, middle-aged woman who maybe lived, alone, in a village . . .

'You'll do,' Bernadette murmured, piling all four paperbacks into the crook of her arm and carrying them over to the pay desk.

Chapter 8

Harriet Ferguson, home from school, made her traditional Thursday-afternoon trip to the village shop to pick up her copy of *Boyz!!* Magazine.

'Muck. That's all it is, nothing but muck,' declared Myrtle Armitage, who had run the shop for the last thirty years. 'I don't know how your mother lets you read all that smutty stuff. Things aren't like they were in my day, I can tell you.'

'I know,' said Harriet patiently, 'you tell me every week. But Myrtle, magazines hadn't been invented in your day.' God, sex probably hadn't been invented.

'Cheeky madam.' Myrtle totted up the cost of the magazine and the fruit gums. 'Lads – that's all you young girls think about. You'll end up in trouble.'

'I won't,' Harriet flicked back her thick brown hair, 'because I'm choosy.'

'Oh aye, there's plenty've said that in their time,' Myrtle chuckled, 'and ended up in pudding club just the same.'

Harriet knew Myrtle didn't believe her, but it was true, she was choosy. She didn't mean to be, she didn't even *want* to be, it was just an unfortunate side-effect of reading magazines like *Boyz!!*. After drooling over endless photographs of all the dishiest, coolest, wickedest pop and soap stars in the country, Harriet had discovered, the real boys – the ones she went to school with – were a massive let-down.

The bell above the shop door went ding but Harriet, her nose stuck in the magazine, was too engrossed in How To Become The Snogger Of The Century to notice.

Myrtle Armitage said, 'Yes, love?'

'Uh . . . Blutack. Got any Blutack?' Dizzy asked hopefully.

Myrtle shot him a suspicious look, clearly wondering if Blutack was a contraceptive. 'What is it?'

Dizzy began to look worried. 'You use it to stick posters on your wall.'

'We've got Sellotape,' said Myrtle. 'That'll do the trick.'

'It's for my bedroom. My parents'd go mad.' Dizzy sounded resigned; he'd been down that road before. 'It'll wreck the wallpaper or something. They said definitely no Sellotape.'

'Oh.'

Harriet looked up from her article. ('Don't go at it like a vacuum-cleaner! Give the poor guy a chance to breathe!!!') 'Are you the one who's just moved into Sisley House?'

Dizzy went pink around the ears. 'Yeah.'

'What's your name?'

'Dizzy.'

Harriet's forehead creased. 'That's a bit weird, isn't it?'

He went pinker. 'It's Thaddeus really. Gross. Dizzy was my dad's idea of a joke when I was a baby. Because of Dizzy Gillespie, y'know?'

Harriet didn't know, but surely anything was better than Thaddeus. And she'd thought her name was bad.

'Anyway . . .' Dizzy shoved his hands into his pockets and scuffed his trainers against the counter. 'It kind of stuck. Everyone calls me Dizzy now.'

'Oh well, could be worse.' Harriet decided to be kind. 'I was sick in assembly once, and for years afterwards my nickname was Puke.'

Myrtle Armitage – whose nickname at school, somewhat predictably, had been Myrtle the Turtle – straightened a pile of *Country Life*s and registered her disapproval with a sniff.

'My sister's name is Savannah,' said Dizzy, 'and everyone calls her Savlon.' He looked pleased with himself. 'I thought that one up.'

'Anyway,' said Harriet, 'the thing is, I've got some Blutack at home. You can have a bit of mine if you like.'

'Hey, nice one!' Dizzy's face lit up. 'That'd be neat. Thanks . . . er . . . Puke.'

'Nobody calls me Puke any more,' Harriet said, walking with him to the door. 'My name's Harriet.'

Harriet enjoyed talking to Dizzy for all of two minutes. The other trouble with real boys, as she had already begun to discover, was that it never took them long to show themselves up.

And Dizzy, it soon became apparent, was no exception.

As they dawdled their way along the High Street towards The Old Vicarage they approached the Seven Bells. The pub was closed but Moll Harper, the full-time barmaid who lived above it, was stretched out on the village green making the most of the sun before they opened again at five thirty. She was lying on a red towel. She wore a dark green bikini, and her tortoiseshell curls were spread out Medusa-style around her head. Even when she lay flat on her back, Harriet couldn't help noticing, her astonishing boobs still pointed skywards.

Men were besotted with Moll Harper, and it mystified Harriet, who couldn't for the life of her imagine why. Moll wore peasanty, serving-wench clothes, never anything fashionable. When the magazines told you frosted pale eyeshadows and metallic lipsticks were in, Moll wore sooty, smudgy eyeliner and left her broad red mouth bare. She had a huge bosom, curves everywhere, big hips, and had to be at least two stone overweight. Anyone else sunbathing in public in a bikini, Harriet thought, would hold their stomach in. But not Moll. She had a spare tyre and she wasn't afraid to show it. She simply didn't give a fig.

You couldn't imagine anyone less like a supermodel, yet the men clearly weren't bothered about that. They fell like ninepins under Moll's spell. She was famous for it; all she had to do was look at them and smile her lazy, insolent smile, and they were lost.

It'll be a test, Harriet thought as they drew closer. If Dizzy doesn't say anything, we'll be friends for ever. If he does say something . . . well, that'll be it. He'll just be another dork.

Thankfully, Moll was asleep.

'Phwoar,' said Dizzy, veering across the road like a heat-seeking missile in order to get a better look. He ogled for a few seconds then swerved excitedly back. 'I saw her yesterday lunchtime, working in the pub. What a body, what a bird! She's top.'

Huh. Top-heavy, certainly. 'I'm surprised you didn't wolf whistle,' Harriet sneered.

'Well, she's asleep. Don't want to wake her up, do I?'

Harriet contemplated telling him that Moll Harper was a slut – practically a prostitute, in fact, she slept with so many men – but guessed it would only fuel Dizzy's interest. Instead she glanced down at her blue school shirt and vile pleated skirt and wondered if she was ever going to grow a bust.

'Is she married or anything?' Dizzy asked eagerly, still peering over his shoulder at Moll.

I'll tell him to wait in the garden and chuck the Blutack out of the window, Harriet decided. He's not coming into my house.

Men, boys – they're all the same, she thought with scornful resignation. Dizzy Gillespie was just another sex-crazed dork.

Lili was being subversive, and it was a thrilling experience. She felt naughty and rebellious and quite unlike herself. She also felt as if she should be striding along in a leather jacket with the collar turned up, and dark glasses, and maybe a pair of radically ripped 501s.

It came as something of a let-down when she glimpsed her reflection in the plate glass double doors of the veterinary surgery and remembered that she was actually wearing a pink and white flowered T-shirt and radically ironed jeans from M&S.

Furthermore, since they had been ironed by Eleanor Ferguson, they sported creases down the front of each leg sharp enough to slice bread.

Lili consoled herself with the knowledge that though she might not look subversive she was certainly going to *be* it. The more objections Eleanor had dredged up, the more determined she had become to bring the puppy home.

'Gosh, you look different,' she told Drew when the receptionist showed her into his surgery.

He grinned. 'It's the white coat. Makes me look intelligent. Have a seat and I'll go and get him.'

When he returned less than a minute later, Lili was almost knocked off her chair by a brown blur with a frantically wagging tail. He flung himself at her, whimpering with pleasure, scrambled clumsily onto her lap and joyously licked her face.

'See? Why can't I do that when I meet a woman I like?' marvelled Drew.

'Oh, he's divine!' Lili's eyes filled with tears of happiness. She held the dog's face between her hands and gazed with adoration into his chocolate-brown eyes. 'Can I really take him home?'

'Looks like love at first sight.' Drew was leaning back against the examination table with his arms folded across his chest, watching the pair of them. 'Who am I to come between a match made in heaven?'

'Oh, Drew—'

'We don't know his name, I'm afraid.'

The dog was still licking Lili's wet cheeks. He was lanky and gawky, like a self-conscious teenager, and when he realised Lili was studying him again he cocked his head to one side like a Page 3 girl posing coyly for the camera.

'I've left the kids at home with my mother-in-law,' said Lili.

At once, Drew looked sympathetic: Eleanor disapproved of Drew, Jamie and Doug almost as much as she disapproved of Lili. 'I called into the shop on my way here this afternoon,' he told her, 'and she was in there telling Myrtle Armitage she'd just spent the last three hours doing your ironing.'

'She brought it back this evening.' Lili pulled a face. 'She stood in the middle of the kitchen and looked around and said, "Do you know what this place needs, Lili? This place needs a jolly good blitz." So I think that's what we're going to have to call him,' she concluded happily, rubbing the dog's lop-sided ears. 'Blitz.'

Blitz peed in the car three times on the way to his new home. When they reached The Old Vicarage he launched himself first at Harriet, then at Eleanor, his paws in all directions like Bambi's as he shot from one end of the kitchen to the other.

He peed twice more on the quarry-tiled floor, leapt up on to the window seats to admire the view, let out a series of ecstatic howls and hurdled the kitchen table in one go, sending Eleanor's basket of faultlessly ironed clothes flying.

'He's not even house-trained!' shouted Eleanor, purple in the face with outrage.

'He is,' Lili assured her, keeping her fingers crossed behind her back. 'He's just pleased to see us.'

'I don't know what Michael's going to say about this, I really don't.'

Feeling amazingly brave, Lili said, 'Oh, I thought you did.' She looked innocent. 'You said he'd be furious.'

'Well, he'll certainly be that.' Eleanor's lips were welded together. She knew Lili had visited the shop earlier this afternoon. Six cans of Pedigree Chum and a bag of dog biscuits, that's what she'd bought. She'd had no intention of coming back from Harleston without that blasted dog.

'Mum, he's *cool*,' Harriet exclaimed, her eyes shining. 'What's he called? Can we wake up Lottie and show her?'

'No you cannot.' Eleanor was horrified by the suggestion. 'Children need their routine. I put her to bed twenty minutes ago—'

'But it is a special occasion,' said Lili. Golly, *more* subversion. 'And Lottie would so love to meet him. Go on, run upstairs and get her,' she told Harriet. 'And he's called Blitz.'

'I might have known,' said Eleanor disparagingly. Her nostrils flared like tents. 'It's a ridiculous name for a dog.'

Chapter 9

Blitz wasn't the only one being introduced to his new family that evening.

'Are you sure you're okay?' said Jessie for the twentieth time as she and Oliver made their way along Compass Lane towards Sisley House.

'Mum, don't fuss. Why wouldn't I be okay?'

She had sat Oliver down and told him everything, just as yesterday she had told Lili. Except it had been altogether easier telling Lili.

'I don't know.' Jessie hated not knowing the answers to questions; she was just trying to help. 'I suppose I'm saying don't worry if you feel a bit funny about it. I know how much of a shock it must be—'

'But some shocks are nicer than others. I mean, if you'd told me my father was a mass-murderer, that would be one of the nastier ones,' Oliver pointed out reasonably. 'This is Toby Gillespie we're talking about. I've met him, I've met his family . . . They're all great. Okay, it's a shock,' he went on, 'but when you think about it, it's a pretty nice shock. It could be a hell of a lot worse.'

'Oh darling . . .' Jessie longed to throw her arms around him but she wasn't allowed to, not in public. Oliver had put a stop to that at the age of eight.

'The weird thing is,' Oliver sounded thoughtful, 'when I was little I used to fantasise that my Dad was rich and famous.' He smiled briefly. 'And it was true, he was.'

They were approaching the gates of Sisley House. Jessie slowed down. 'Should I have told you before now?' She looked worried. 'Did I do the wrong thing?' She felt terrible.

Oliver had never mentioned this before. It broke her heart to imagine him fantasising about his absent father.

Oliver guessed at once what was on her mind. 'Look, nearly everyone does it. We talked about it at college; it's just something kids like to do. Even the ones who knew their parents were their biological parents. They still day-dreamed about discovering they were adopted. Then they could fantasise that their real father was Steve McQueen or Rod Stewart or someone, and that their real mother was . . . God, I don't know . . . Cher.'

Toby answered the front door. To Jessie's relief he didn't try anything embarrassing, like putting his arms around Oliver. He just winked and smiled and ushered Jessie past him into the hall.

'Let me have a quiet word with Oliver. Jess, go on through to the sitting room, would you? Oliver can come into the kitchen and help me with the drinks.'

The sitting room, with its yellow-gold walls and impracti-cal pale yellow carpet, was flooded with early evening sunlight. Jessie felt her heart begin to break into a canter. She felt as if she were on a stage, in a play, and nobody had let her see a copy of the script.

Deborah was standing by the French windows, her black hair gleaming, her flawless body wrapped in a plain grey silk vest and narrow grey trousers. The only splashes of colour were the red lipstick and red strappy leather sandals.

She was smoking a menthol cigarette and her eyes nar-rowed as she caught sight of Jessie in the doorway.

If this was a play, Jessie hardly needed a script to know that here was the prize bitch, the ultimate baddie.

Except it wasn't a play.

'Bloody cigarettes.' Deborah stubbed it out in a nearby ashtray, blinking and dabbing a forefinger under each eye in turn to check her mascara hadn't run. 'God, I'm useless at smoking. It always gets in my eyes.' And then, in a rush, 'Oh Jess, can you believe it? We're practically related to one another! Living here is going to be so much *fun*.'

'You don't mind?' said Jessie, hugely relieved. 'About Oliver?'

Deborah looked amazed. 'Why would I? That all happened before Toby and I even met. Heavens, it's not as if he's suddenly produced a bawling baby out of nowhere.' She raised her dark eyebrows and said, straight-faced, 'if he tried that I might be a bit miffed.'

'I'm glad you're okay about it.' Jessie perched on the arm of one of the sofas and gazed admiringly around the sitting room. 'You've settled in fast. You must have put in some hours to get this much done.'

'The men did most of it. I just supervised the unpacking and told them where to put everything.' Deborah broke into a grin. 'Bossed them about, made them cry, threatened to make them drink another cup of Dizzy's tea, that kind of thing.'

I like you, thought Jessie. You're brilliant, I really like you. I wish I didn't, but I do. Her stomach lurched with shock as the implications of this last thought struck home. This last *rogue* thought—

'Drinks,' Toby announced, pushing the door open and coming through with Oliver.

'. . . Most people take their gap year before college, but I couldn't wait to get there,' Oliver was saying, 'so I'm taking mine now. That's why I'm working in the Seven Bells, to get some money together. As soon as I've saved enough I'm going to travel around Europe.'

'Jess tells me you got a two-one,' Toby said. 'I'm impressed.'

'Come on, let's have a proper look at the two of you,' Deborah urged. She studied them in silence for several seconds, then turned to Jessie. 'It's definitely there, isn't it? I mean, you wouldn't catch sight of Oliver and say straight away, God, that boy's the spitting image of Toby Gillespie. But when they're side by side you can see the likeness in the eyes, the cheekbones are there . . . they even stand in the same way.'

'Same blond hair,' said Jessie, nodding.

'Like Savannah.' Toby looked amused. 'Except she has more of it.'

'Speaking of Savannah,' said Oliver, 'where is she?'

The door creaked and opened wider.

'I'm here.'

Savannah seemed to be clutching the door handle for support as she surveyed the assembled company. She had changed into a midriff-baring black top and an orange denim skirt, and Jessie wondered if she had been crying.

Turning to her, holding his breath, Oliver mouthed, 'Okay?' and for a long, terrifying moment Savannah didn't react.

Then, breaking into a huge grin, she rushed over and threw her arms around him. 'Of *course* I'm okay. You're my new big brother. And you know what that means?'

Oliver shook his head. 'What?'

'Somebody else buying me fantastic presents at Christmas.'

Phew. Jessie relaxed, thankful to have been wrong. For several appalling seconds she'd thought Savannah was genuinely upset. She watched her kiss Oliver noisily on both cheeks.

'We were just looking at the similarities between us,' said Toby.

'Do we look like brother and sister?' Savannah sounded delighted. 'There's the hair, of course. Are we really alike? What else is the same?'

She was gaily standing next to Oliver, ready for inspection, when Dizzy slouched in almost unnoticed.

'Bet you Oliver doesn't have a tattoo on his bum,' he remarked, almost to himself. 'At least not one that says I love Jez.'

'You little *sneak*!' Savannah squealed, going bright red. She seized Oliver's arm. 'Here, this is a job for big brother. Just beat him to a pulp, will you? No – better make it a purée.'

Toby, sounding appalled, said, 'Savannah, for God's sake, tell me you don't have a tattoo.'

Jessie and Deborah, exchanging glances, tried not to laugh.

'Darling, I can't keep track of all these boys.' Deborah frowned as she struggled to remember. 'Which one was Jez?'

'Look at the state of you two.'

Home from the hospital, Doug Flynn good-naturedly surveyed the living room of Keeper's Cottage. Cricket from Australia was on the TV. Drew and Jamie, in shorts and T-shirts bearing the respective slogans 'I'm a Baywatch Babe' and 'Look Out – Here Come the Rugger Buggers', were sprawled in armchairs clutching cans of lager. More cans littered the coffee table. Empty cheese and onion crisp packets, crumpled up and hurled at the TV set whenever the Aussies hit a six, dotted the carpet. Drew wore a hat with corks bobbing around the brim. Jamie was wearing a pair of red and white striped Y-fronts on his head.

'Join us.' Drew waved his half-full can enticingly under Doug's nose. 'Plenty more in the fridge. Australia are two hundred and eight for six. Actually, it's a bloody good match.'

'Can't, I'm going out.' Doug was already pulling off his shirt and heading upstairs for a shower.

'Alison?' Jamie's eyes were fixed on the screen, but he was interested enough to ask. He liked Alison; she had colossal boobs.

'Melissa.'

Ten minutes later Doug clattered down the stairs again, showered, changed and clearly ready for anything. For someone who had just finished a twenty-four-hour shift in casualty he looked unfairly good. Drew never knew how he did it. Even his shirt was ironed.

'Busy today?'

Doug grinned. 'A chap came in complaining of lower abdominal pain. Real bank manager type. We X-rayed him and he had a Marmite jar up his bum.'

Drew snorted into his lager. 'Full of Marmite?'

'No, peanuts.'

This was par for the course in casualty. You could think of the weirdest things and put them in the most unlikely orifices and somebody somewhere would have thought of it before you.

'Did he say why?' Jamie marvelled.

59

'No. Just cried and begged us not to tell his wife.'

'When did you iron that shirt anyway?' Drew was mystified.

'I didn't. Alison volunteered. She did a whole stack of stuff.'

'Didn't do any of mine,' Jamie said gloomily.

Doug laughed. 'Ah, but you have to earn it.'

First Drew wondered how Alison would feel if she knew Doug was wearing one of the shirts she had so lovingly ironed out on a date with someone else. Then he wondered how it would feel to go out with one girl actually wearing a shirt that had been lovingly ironed for you by another. Finally he wondered what it must be like to be Doug Flynn, to be *so* good-looking and apparently irresistible that wherever you went there were girls – gorgeous girls at that – falling over themselves to go out with you. And to iron your shirts.

'Look at that, look at that!' howled Jamie, leaping out of his seat. 'Catch it, you idiot! Catch it, catch it – YES! OUT!'

'Me too.' Doug glanced out of the window as a car pulled up on the verge outside the cottage.

'You're kidding,' Drew exclaimed. 'You mean she's actually come to pick *you* up?'

How did the jammy sod do it?

'She offered. What could I say?' Shrugging, Doug slung a cream linen jacket over his shoulder and headed for the door.

'Don't go straight out. Bring her in and introduce her,' Jamie begged. 'I haven't seen Melissa yet.'

He was on his knees in front of the TV, his Y-fronts falling over one eye.

'The thing is,' said Doug, 'would she want to see you?'

By ten o'clock the Australians were two hundred and seventy for eight and Drew was beginning to wish he hadn't eaten five packets of cheese and onion crisps. The taste in his mouth was diabolical. He took another swig of lager and tried swilling it, mouthwash-style, around his teeth. No good. He balanced the half-empty can on his knee and that was no good either; it promptly toppled over, tipping its contents over his shorts.

Still, it was a hot night. At least the lager was cool. And, Drew thought contentedly, there was plenty left in the fridge.

'You get it,' he told Jamie when the doorbell rang.

'No, you.'

Drew indicated the sodden front of his shorts. 'What, in this state?'

'Look,' said Jamie, who was lying on the floor, 'I'd love to answer the door, but I think I'm too pissed to stand.'

'Good grief,' said Drew when he saw who was on the doorstep. 'I mean . . . hello.'

When he swallowed there was an audible gulping sound, just like in a cartoon.

Embarrassing or what?

Chapter 10

Deborah Gillespie – understandably – looked entertained.

'Hi. I'm your new neighbour.' She held up the dustpan and brush Jessie Roscoe had borrowed the day before. 'Just returning these.'

Numb with shock, Drew took them. He knew, of course, that the Gillespies had moved into Sisley House, but it was still something of a first, opening the front door and coming unexpectedly face to face with someone you'd only ever seen before on TV or in the papers.

'Oh, right, great . . . thanks.' Instinctively he held the dustpan in front of his groin, attempting to cover the stain. Oh God, that looked even worse. He saw Deborah Gillespie's gaze drop to his shorts.

'I spilled some lager. It isn't . . . I mean, I haven't—'

'Wet yourself?' said Deborah, straight-faced. 'Well, good.'

Hell, he felt like a fourteen-year-old. What on earth was he supposed to say next?

Mercifully, Deborah did it for him. 'So, are you the doctor or one of the vets? You see,' she smiled a disarming smile, 'I've been hearing all about you.'

What? What have you heard? Was it *all* bad? wondered Drew, mesmerised by her dark eyes and dazzling beauty. Hell, she'd asked him a question . . . he was supposed to be coming up with a sensible answer.

'Um, vet.'

'On your own tonight?'

Drew cringed as Deborah peered past him. If she'd been any normal visitor he would have invited her in without a second thought.

'Who is it?' yelled Jamie from the living room.

Oh God, oh God . . .

'Doctor?' Deborah enquired brightly.

'Another vet.'

'Oh, right.' She nodded. 'Actually, I dropped by to ask if I could borrow some milk. And if you can spare a bit of washing-up liquid, even better.'

This was ridiculous, Drew realised. How long could he reasonably stand here like this – like a prison warder, for heaven's sake – barring her way?

'Look,' he blurted out in desperation, 'you can come in but the place is a tip. And I mean a *real* tip.'

'Are you worried I might be shocked?' Deborah sounded cheerful.

'Well, it's not a pretty sight.'

'You're three single males sharing a house,' she consoled him. 'If it were immaculate, I'd just assume you were gay.'

'Who's gay?' Jamie demanded indignantly from the floor as Drew led her through to the living room. 'Not me, that's for bloody sure . . .' Having started on the lager earlier than Drew, he peered up from beneath the drooping Y-fronts at Deborah. 'Drew, are you sure this is the pizza delivery boy? He doesn't have nearly enough spots.'

Drew flushed, embarrassed already, and gave Jamie's bare foot a hefty warning kick. 'It's our new neighbour, you moron – Deborah Gillespie. I'm really sorry about Jamie,' he added, glancing at Deborah, 'he's pissed.'

'At least I haven't pissed myself,' cackled Jamie, pointing to the front of Drew's shorts.

'Right. What was it you wanted – milk and washing-up liquid?' Drew made for the kitchen; the quicker he got her out of here the better.

'Only if you can spare them.'

'Milk and washing-up liquid?' Jamie sounded bemused. 'What is that, some kind of cocktail? Okay, I'll try one,' he called through the open doorway, 'but stick a vodka in mine.'

'Coming from London, we're used to shops that stay open all night,' Deborah explained. 'It's going to take some getting used to, remembering not to run out of things after six o'clock in the evening.'

'Well, you can always borrow from us.' Drew's hands trembled slightly as he poured most of their own remaining milk into a chipped Independence Day cup. When he had squeezed a decent amount of Fairy Liquid into the only other clean container – it had to be, didn't it, the mug featuring the over-endowed girl whose bikini disappeared when it heated up – he handed them to Deborah. 'There you go.'

'You're an angel.' Smiling, she put them down on the crowded worktop. 'The thing is, I don't have to dash straight back. You wouldn't by any chance have a lager going begging?'

'Our lagers don't beg,' Jamie yelled. 'We're the ones who beg – for lager!'

'I'm sorry, he's *so* bloody rude.' Drew grabbed another can from the fridge and gazed around frantically, wondering what to pour it into.

'Come on, calm down.' Taking the icy can, Deborah patted his arm. 'Don't panic, and stop trying to treat me like the Queen Mother. I have seen a man a little the worse for drink before,' she added with an innocent smile. 'I've mixed with actors for the last twenty years.'

'Okay. Right.' Drew tried to smile back but he still felt like rolling Jamie up in the un-Hoovered carpet and chucking him, stupid Y-fronts and all, into the village pond.

He was still hunting without success for a glass that wasn't a pint mug. Deborah grinned and tackled the ring pull. 'Don't bother, I'm fine like this.'

As they headed back to the living room she clinked her can, first against Drew's, then – leaning down – Jamie's. 'New neighbours and happy times ahead. Cheers.'

Drew found he'd gone weak at the knees – an alarmingly cissy thing to happen to a grown man. He wondered if Deborah Gillespie was the most hypnotically beautiful, charming and totally amazing woman he'd ever met in his life, decided almost at once that of course she was, and murmured, 'Cheers.'

What was he getting so het up about anyway? That was the thing about hypnotically beautiful, charming and amazing women: they were way, way, *way* out of his league.

'Where have you been?' Toby protested when Deborah finally reappeared. 'You said you were going to make coffee.' He looked at his watch. 'That was almost an hour ago.'

'We'd run out of milk.' Deborah balanced the tray on the table. 'I borrowed some from the boys next door. Stayed to chat. You were right,' she told Jessie cheerfully, 'they're sweet.'

Sweet? Jessie hid a smile. She hadn't gone quite that far. She'd said they were good fun.

'Was Doug there?' she asked. She especially couldn't imagine anyone calling Doug Flynn 'sweet'.

'The doctor? Oh, he was out. I just met the vets. Jamie, and the big freckly one . . . what's his name? Drew, is it?'

Oliver was on the sofa comparing GCSE results with Savannah. He looked up.

'Drew Darcy.'

Deborah started to laugh.

'Really, that's his surname? Was that who I met – the dashing Mr Darcy? Oh dear, poor lamb. How dreadful to be a big, freckly rugby player and saddled with a name like that.'

Jamie was snoring on the carpet, but Drew couldn't sleep. He was still thinking about the events of the evening when Doug came in with his arm around Melissa. He glanced at the hideous state of the living room and at Jamie's inert form, and led Melissa promptly towards the stairs.

'What happened?' he said over his shoulder to Drew, meaning the Test match.

'Oh, nothing much. Deborah Gillespie dropped by . . . that's all.' Drew yawned and stretched as if this was the kind of thing that went on in his life all the time. 'We chatted, sank a few lagers – quite a few lagers, actually. Got on pretty well together . . .'

'Yeah, yeah.' Grinning, Doug patted Melissa's perky

bottom. 'Hear that, sweetheart? The sad fantasies of the lonely sex-starved single bloke. Promise you'll never let that happen to me.'

'Just one thing before you go,' Toby said as they all made their way into the hall. It was past midnight and Jessie had to make an early start in the morning. 'Any odd-bods in the village that you know of?'

'Why?' Jessie winked at Deborah. 'Are you dying to meet some?'

But Toby wasn't smiling. He pulled a folded envelope from his back pocket and handed it to her with a shrug. 'It's probably nothing, a one-off. I just wondered if anyone sprung to mind.'

Jessie unfolded the envelope, which had been hand delivered, and drew out a single sheet of paper. On it were the words: 'Mr Gillespie, You are not wanted here.'

That was all, written in shaky capitals in the centre of the page.

'Someone right-handed, writing with their left hand,' said Jessie. She looked up, feeling like Miss Marple.

Toby raised an eyebrow. 'Any ideas?'

'I can't imagine who'd do something like this.'

'It's probably kids,' said Deborah, unconcerned.

'When did you get it?'

'Shoved through the letter box sometime last night. When we came downstairs this morning it was on the mat.'

'Are you going to show it to the police?'

Toby shook his head. 'It's hardly a threatening letter. I only asked because you might have said straight away, "Oh, that'll be old so-and-so, he's always doing stuff like that."'

'Well . . . no, there's no one obvious.' Jessie looked doubtful. Toby and Deborah didn't seem alarmed, but weren't anonymous letters the tiniest bit worrying?

Deborah, reading her thoughts, said, 'This kind of thing happens when you're in the public eye. Toby's had his share of weird letters and obsessed fans over the years. One woman even thought she was married to him.' She shrugged. 'It's boring but harmless. You get used to it after a while.'

'The only difference being, they usually wish you *would* move into their village.' With a faint smile, Toby pushed the letter back into its envelope and shoved it into one of the drawers in the dresser. 'Whereas this one seems to want me out.'

Chapter 11

Another sizzling hot day. By eleven o'clock the sky was a cloudless peacock blue. Since the earth was cracked and dry, and her poor parched plants were screaming out for water, Bernadette Thomas began filling her watering can at the kitchen sink. It would take at least an hour and a great deal of toing and froing, but the hosepipe ban had been put into force – and with a neighbour like Eleanor Ferguson you didn't flout bans lightly. She'd have the hosepipe police on to you in a flash.

As it was, Eleanor's head soon popped up over the fence dividing their gardens. Bernadette made a private bet with herself that the word 'journalist' would feature in the third sentence Eleanor uttered.

'Morning,' sang Eleanor. 'Goodness, that looks like hard work!'

Bernadette smiled and nodded.

One.

'Well, seems a shame to waste a nice sunny drying day like this: I think I'll wash my curtains.'

'Good idea,' said Bernadette, carefully watering her petunias.

Two – just.

'Oh, by the way' – Eleanor's tone was elaborately casual – 'did you manage to get hold of that journalist chappie?'

Three. Bingo.

Without being aware of it – for they had only exchanged smiles and brief pleasantries in passing – Bernadette and Lili Ferguson had hit on precisely the same method of staying sane. Turning Eleanor's incurable nosiness into a form of entertainment made all the difference in the world – it really did the trick.

Bernadette shook her almost empty watering can at the sweet peas and straightened up. 'Yes, thank you, I did.'

'Oh.'

If Eleanor had had whiskers, they would have been aquiver. (Actually she *was* prone to whiskers, but she religiously plucked them out, using the excellent tweezers in her Swiss Army knife.)

'And . . . um, was it about something to do with the . . . the village?'

Bernadette took a deep breath. 'As a matter of fact, he wanted to interview me about my work. But, as you know, I'm a private person. I really do prefer to keep myself to myself.'

'Your work . . .?'

Never mind aquiver; aquiver was old hat. Eleanor was by this time agog.

'I don't give interviews. I told him that and he understood,' Bernadette concluded innocently, turning back towards the house with the empty watering can in her hand. 'So thank you for taking an interest but I'm afraid speaking to journalists isn't my idea of fun.'

'But . . .' Eleanor's mouth was gaping, guppy-fashion. 'But . . . I don't . . . You've never told me what kind of work you do!'

Bernadette paused on her doorstep, as if giving the matter some thought. She exhaled slowly. 'I'm sorry. Some people welcome publicity and some don't. I write books, that's all. Novels.'

'You're a writer? But how *exciting*!' Eleanor's expression was avid. 'I had no idea! What kind of novels do you write?'

Another pause, then Bernadette inclined her head towards her house.

'Come over if you like, and I'll show you.'

Inside, the cottage was sparingly furnished but – Eleanor noted with approval – scrupulously clean.

As Bernadette reached up to the shelf above one of the

recessed alcoves, her white lace petticoat showed beneath the hem of her pale green shirtwaister dress. Eleanor approved of this too. In her opinion, far too many women these days went without petticoats.

'Here we are.' Bernadette passed over a small handful of books. She looked embarrassed. 'They don't exactly sell in their millions, but I scrape a living.'

Eleanor was enthralled. Her next-door neighbour was a published author! Fancy that!

'Antonia Kay . . . That's your pen name, then? Your . . . what-d'you-call-it?'

'Pseudonym.' Bernadette nodded. 'Again, I prefer the privacy.'

'Well, to think you actually wrote these yourself,' Eleanor marvelled. 'I've always meant to write a book, but where would I find the time? Three and a half hours I was, yesterday, doing my daughter-in-law's ironing for her. Always busy, that's me. No time to *read* a book, let alone write one . . .'

'Well, yes. Of course. I understand—'

'But I'll read yours,' Eleanor exclaimed as Bernadette made a move to take the books back. 'If you'd lend me one.'

Bernadette retrieved the books anyway. She shuffled through them in search of the one she had stayed up reading until three o'clock this morning – not because it was unputdownable, but because if she was going to be lending it to Eleanor Ferguson she needed at least some idea of what it was about.

'Here we are. This is the first one I wrote. And don't worry, I won't be offended if you hate it.'

Greedily Eleanor clasped the book in both hands. Weren't first novels always autobiographical? This was the perfect way to get to know her odd, reclusive neighbour. 'I'm sure it's wonderful,' she declared with an air of grandeur. 'I can't wait.'

'And I'd be grateful if you'd keep this to yourself . . .' Bernadette's tone was delicate. 'I know I don't even need to ask; I can rely on your discretion. It's just that . . . well, the rest of the village . . .'

'Say no more, my lips are sealed.' Regally, Eleanor leaned closer. 'And I was thinking earlier, humping that heavy watering can up and down the garden can't be doing your back any good. You could always use your hosepipe, you know. I think under the circumstances I can turn a blind eye.'

On her way out, still clutching the book triumphantly to her chest, she spotted a smallish framed photograph on a highly polished occasional table. Intrigued, since there were no other photos in sight, Eleanor stopped and picked it up.

'She looks pleasant.'

The photograph was of a thin, shyly smiling woman in her early thirties. 'Who's this then?' Eleanor waggled the frame at Bernadette. 'Younger sister?'

'Er . . . just a friend.'

Oh dear. When she saw the brief flush of colour in Bernadette's cheeks, Eleanor understood at once. Her mouth instantly narrowed with disgust and disapproval. She regretted being so friendly now.

No wonder husbandless, childless Bernadette Thomas kept herself to herself.

Eleanor knew perfectly well what 'Er . . . just a friend' meant.

Home from school, Harriet changed out of her uniform and into a T-shirt and shorts. When she looked at herself in the wardrobe mirror, her heart sank. Plain brown hair, plain grey eyes, and a totally useless straight-up-and-down figure like a frankfurter . . . Hell's bells, when was she going to start going in and out?

At this rate I'll end up in an old folk's home, eighty years old, pushing a Zimmer frame and still wearing a trainer bra, she thought, glancing out of her bedroom window and recognising Dizzy Gillespie's lazy, loping walk as he made his way along Compass Lane, no doubt heading for the village shop.

Huh, he's a pillock anyway. Just like all the rest of them – obsessed with boobs.

And why? *Why?* Harriet wondered frustratedly. What is the point?

She dragged her trainers out from under the bed, yanked open her sock drawer and pulled out a pair of last winter's thick grey hockey socks. Then, carefully rolling up each one in turn, she pulled up her T-shirt, tucking it under her chin, and stuffed them into her astonished – but luckily quite stretchy – bra.

'Oh, hi!' Dizzy was careful to look elaborately surprised when he saw Harriet. He would rather have died than admit he'd been hanging around hoping to bump into her ever since he'd seen her jump off the school coach.

'Hi.' Harriet clung on to Blitz's lead as the dog hurled himself, yapping joyfully, at Dizzy. With great pride she said, 'His name's Blitz. He's our new dog, we got him yesterday.'

'That's nothing,' said Dizzy. 'We got a new brother.'

'What? You mean your mother actually gave birth?' Harriet's jaw dropped. 'Crikey!'

'Nah – it's Oliver Roscoe.'

'Oliver? *Crikey.*'

'Seems his old lady had a thing with our old man, yonks ago.' Bending down, Dizzy nonchalantly ruffled Blitz's ears.

'Is that weird?' Harriet looked doubtful. She thought it must feel extremely weird to have a full-grown half-brother suddenly pop out of nowhere.

Dizzy shrugged. 'Dunno. I don't know him properly yet. You can't get a word in edgeways with Savlon around. Still, he seems okay.'

'Down, Blitz!' Harriet yanked the straining lead as the dog tried to scramble into the litter bin outside the shop. 'He's after that Cornetto wrapper. I was about to take him for a walk in Compass Hill wood, give him a bit of a guided tour seeing as he's new to the area.'

When she glanced up, Harriet saw Dizzy staring at her chest. For a split second she panicked – but no, it was okay. It wasn't a you've-got-socks-stuffed-in-your-bra kind of stare. It was an admiring one. For the first time in my life I'm being eyed-up, she thought delightedly. Now I know how Moll Harper feels. Blimey, no wonder she always looks so pleased with herself.

Yesterday's disgust with Dizzy, when he had – *yuk* – so grossly ogled Moll, had evaporated like morning mist. Now he was ogling *her*, and Harriet experienced a heady rush of power.

She no longer felt plain, she felt like . . . oh, like an enchantress . . .

'I'm new to the area,' said Dizzy. 'Can I come on your guided tour too?'

Harriet, flushed with triumph, was too busy being an enchantress to notice that Blitz was inching closer to the tantalising Cornetto wrapper. Nor did she know that already occupying the wrapper was a contented wasp. Blitz launched himself, seizing the paper in his jaws. The wasp, outraged, buzzed furiously and stung the dog on the nose. Howling, Blitz leapt out of the bin and tried to hide behind Harriet. As his lead wrapped itself around her knees, he did another frantic circuit and Harriet, effectively lassooed, toppled to the ground.

'It's okay!' Dizzy shouted, grabbing Blitz by the collar and unravelling the lead from Harriet's bound legs. 'I've got him! Poor old boy, what did that wasp do to you, eh? That'll teach you to stick your nose in rubbish bins.' He crouched down and soothed the dog's wounded pride. When Harriet didn't move he glanced at her. 'You can get up now. What's the matter? Are you hurt?'

Harriet kept her arms clamped across her chest. It may not have been a violent toppling-over, but it had been enough to jolt one of the hockey socks out of her over-stuffed bra.

Dizzy's concern turned to alarm when he saw which part of herself she was clutching. 'Is it your heart?'

Oh yes, brilliant, thought Harriet, flinching as Blitz lunged forward with enthusiasm to lick her forehead. Dial 999 and call an ambulance, why don't you? Tell them I need sock-massage. Humiliate me completely . . .

But since Dizzy looked as if he really might, she said stoically. 'I'm fine, it's not my heart.'

Just my sock.

Dizzy frowned. 'You don't look fine to me.'

'I feel a bit sick.' Harriet pulled a nauseated face and massaged her chest a bit, wondering if she could somehow manage to slide the sock unobtrusively back into place. But it was hopeless. She had more chance of getting a jellyfish into a Coke bottle.

'Maybe if we start walking you'll feel better.' Dizzy was unable to tear his eyes away. He'd give anything for the chance to massage her chest like that.

Harriet levered herself cautiously to her knees. 'I don't think so. Actually, I think I'll just go home.'

'Oh.'

The sock began to slip. Harriet caught it just before it fell out from under her T-shirt. 'I'll take Blitz.' She grabbed the dog's lead with her free hand. Bloody stupid animal. Her cheeks burned as she turned hurriedly away, heading for the Old Vicarage. 'Bye.'

Something was definitely up. She wasn't ill. *Now* what had he said to upset her?

Feeling totally rejected, Dizzy stuffed his hands into the pockets of his baggy, holey jeans and said in a casual, I'm-not-bothered voice, 'Okay, see ya.'

Chapter 12

Jessie called in on Lili when she finished work at six. Harriet was entertaining Lottie and William in the sandpit at the far end of the garden, so they had the sun-baked patio to themselves. Better still, since Freya had already been picked up (by a beady-eyed Felicity), Lili could actually relax and pour herself a glass of wine.

Or even two.

'So what did Oliver call him? Dad?'

'Just Toby.'

'God, imagine . . .' Lili, who couldn't begin to, stretched out her pale legs and wished she could get them as brown as Jessie's. 'Was it awkward?'

Jessie was feeding crisps under the table to Blitz, who had come to cool off in the shade and dribble affectionate ribbons of saliva over her bare feet. 'Not at all. I thought it might be, but it wasn't. Mainly thanks to Deborah, because she could have made it awkward. She didn't though, she was great.'

'And you said she disappeared for an hour – so she isn't bothered about leaving you and Toby alone together. It doesn't worry her,' Lili probed. 'The fact that you two used to be . . . well, you know . . .'

Jessie was busy polishing her sunglasses on the sleeve of her white shirt. 'No, she's not jealous.'

'Oh.' Lili felt miffed on her friend's behalf. 'Well, I suppose that's good in one way . . .'

'And not terribly flattering in the other,' Jessie finished drily.

'Well, she could at least be a bit concerned.' Lili was

indignant. 'How does she know you and Toby won't fall in love with each other all over again? You could be a huge threat to her marriage!'

'You mean, how dare she be so friendly?' Jessie teased, loving the way Lili's eyes grew bright as she sprang to her defence: 'How dare she trust me not to snatch her husband from under her nose?'

'Oh, now you're making fun of me. But how does she know you wouldn't?'

'Come on. Deborah Gillespie is stunning. No best-dressed list is complete without her name on it. She's glamorous and charming and about as nice as it's possible to get without actually making people physically sick. What's more,' Jessie went on, counting the reasons on paint-stained fingers, 'you only have to read the gossip columns to know they're the happiest married couple on the planet. And I should know,' she added with a brief, rueful smile, 'because I've been reading them for the last twenty years. Nobody, I promise you, has paid more attention to those articles than me.'

Lili opened her mouth, then abruptly shut it again. This was an admission and a half, coming from proud, fiercely independent Jess.

A diversion was created by William, at the bottom of the garden, emptying a bucket of sand over Lottie's head. Lottie screamed and gave him a resounding slap. William, grabbing handfuls of sand, flung them furiously in Lottie's face. Lili went to help Harriet separate them, thankful only that Hugh and Felicity weren't here to witness the fracas.

Order was eventually restored.

'So how do you feel about him? I mean, all that old stuff between you?' Lili ventured on her return. 'Is the attraction still there?'

Jessie, prevaricating, said, 'Things are a bit different now.'

'And that's no answer. What I'm saying is, if Toby wasn't married and he came round to your place tonight . . .' Lili's hazel eyes widened, 'and he swept you into his arms and said, "Oh Jess, I've never been able to forget you." . . . *What would you do?*'

'Oh, he's already done all that.'

'You are kidding!'

'Yes, I'm kidding.'

Jessie was bursting to tell Lili everything. She knew she mustn't.

'God, I hate you,' Lili groaned. Her heart had begun to gallop. She flopped back in her chair, patting her ample chest. 'Don't *do* this to me.'

Jessie, smiling faintly and twiddling the stem of her glass between her fingers, thought, I wish Toby hadn't done it to me.

Except that wasn't quite true. She was glad he had. Dammit, she had loved every blissful second.

She just wished he wasn't married.

'What's this?' To change the subject Jessie reached for the book lying face-down on the table. 'Didn't know you were keen on Aga sagas.'

'Eleanor brought it round this afternoon. You know that woman living next door to her? She wrote it.'

'Really? Bernadette Thomas?'

Lili nodded and grinned. 'It's been driving Eleanor mad for months, not being able to find out anything about her new neighbour. But she twisted those thumbscrews a few extra notches and finally wore Bernadette down. She cracked and admitted she was a novelist.'

Interested, Jessie looked at the cover, which featured a rocking chair, a sleeping cat and a grandfather clock. A John Grisham thriller it clearly wasn't. 'So Eleanor's read this, has she? Did she enjoy it?'

'Ah well, this is where it becomes interesting,' said Lili. 'She insisted I read it first. She put on her prune face and told me she had no intention of reading a book with marauding lesbians in it.'

'*Marauding* lesbians? Good grief!' Jessie glanced again at the cover. 'Not terribly likely, is it? Gentle, cake-baking lesbians maybe.'

'Whatever. I'm the official censor, anyway. And Eleanor's torn between being thrilled to be living next door to a writer – even an unfamous one – and horrified by the discovery that she's gay.'

'Poor woman,' sighed Jessie, feeling deeply sorry for Bernadette. She'd feel sorry for anyone who had to live next door to Eleanor Ferguson.

'No wonder she keeps herself to herself.' Lili was thinking along much the same lines. 'I used to wonder if she was a bit odd – you know, one of those weird reclusive types – but I bet that's *why* she's like it. She's probably afraid the rest of the village is as narrow-minded as Eleanor, and that once her secret gets out we'll drown her in the duck pond.'

Odd. Weird. Remembering Toby's words of the night before, Jessie tried to imagine Bernadette Thomas slipping an anonymous note through the letter box of Sisley House. Bernadette: the quiet lady novelist with the lovingly tended garden, the old-fashioned dresses and the neatly bobbed brown-with-a-hint-of-auburn hair.

'Oh my God!' Lili gasped when Jessie told her about the anonymous note. 'But how horrible! How could anyone do it? Nothing like that's ever happened here before.'

It hadn't. And Bernadette Thomas had only moved to Upper Sisley a few months ago . . .

'Maybe it was someone's idea of a joke.' Jessie bent down and rubbed Blitz's big, comforting, silky ears. The fact that Bernadette was a relative newcomer to the village was hardly rock-solid evidence. 'Perhaps it won't happen again.'

'It's who? Oh hi, Melissa! Hang on, he's in the shower. DOUG!'

'What?'

'MELISSA ON THE PHONE!'

'Tell her I'm out.'

'I CAN'T TELL HER YOU'RE OUT, YOU BERK, I JUST SAID YOU WERE IN THE SHOWER!'

Upstairs, Doug laughed to himself and carried on soaping his chest.

Downstairs, Jamie lowered his voice from a bellow to normal volume. 'Melissa, hi. Listen, I *thought* he was in the shower, but— What?'

Even Drew, who was in the kitchen making himself an oven-chip sandwich, could hear the furious squawking at the other end of the phone. The next minute Jamie was staring at a silent receiver.

'She hung up. She called *me* a bastard,' he said, aggrieved, 'and just hung up. I don't get it. Doug's the one who's dumped her, how come I'm the bastard?'

Doug, coming down the stairs with a dark green towel slung around his waist, said, 'Anything to eat?'

'Why did you dump her anyway?' Jamie was fretful. He'd never dump someone like Melissa.

'She snored.'

Hmm. Jamie wondered if – when she'd had a chance to cool down a bit – Melissa might be interested in going out with a vet instead. Snoring wouldn't bother him, he could always wear earplugs.

Drew watched Jamie resume his ironing. It was fascinating to see a man, a qualified vet capable of operating on a canary, make such a pig's ear of a shirt.

But Jamie was intent on his task. It was Friday night, he hadn't pulled in ages, and he was going to the Rattles Club in Harleston. What's more, he wasn't going to come home again until he *had* pulled.

'Sure you don't want to come along?' he said to Drew when he'd finished the shirt – after a fashion. A cab shared, after all, is a cab fare halved. 'Come on, it's Friday night,' he added persuasively, 'the place'll be crawling with crumpet.'

'Most of it underage,' said Drew. God, he was twenty-nine, almost thirty. He was too old to trawl the nightclubs in search of girls who would only bore him rigid within minutes. 'What do you find to *talk* to them about, once you've asked them which school they go to?'

Astonished, Jamie said, 'Who wants to talk?'

'Anyway, you can't call them crumpet. That's at least ten years out of date. It's almost as bad as wearing a toupée and flares and calling girls chicks.'

Jamie looked superior. 'Flares are back in, so there.'

'Wrong,' said Drew. 'Flares are back in for teenage girls. If you tried wearing them, I promise you, you'd be laughed out of the club.'

'So you're not coming tonight?'

The phone rang again. Doug answered it.

'No.' Finishing his chip sandwich, Drew licked his fingers. 'You can keep your jailbait, your pounding music and your overpriced drinks. I'm going to the Bells with Doug.'

'God, you sound ancient,' Jamie scoffed. 'And I'm telling you now, you'll never meet any decent talent in the Bells.'

Doug, still on the phone, said, 'Okay, great. Meet you in the Bells at eight thirty.'

'Not Melissa,' Jamie and Drew chorused when he had hung up.

'Not Melissa.' Doug grinned as he re-emerged from the kitchen, swigging from a can of Coke. 'Patsy.'

'Patsy.' Jamie tried to remember. 'Is she new?'

'Met her this morning. She brought her mother into casualty with a fractured femur.'

Drew's heart sank. He didn't want to spend the evening watching Doug work his all-too-familiar magic while the besotted Patsy fell helplessly under his spell. He sighed.

'What?' said Doug.

Drew looked doubtful. 'Am I going to be the gooseberry?'

'Oh come on,' Doug protested, combing his wet hair into place and raising his eyebrows at Drew in the mirror. 'Of course not.'

Chapter 13

By eight thirty the Seven Bells was filling up nicely. Drew's spirits lifted no end when Moll – looking luscious in a dark red velvet bodice-type thing and a calf-length swirly black skirt – winked at him and ignored Doug completely.

'You two boys out on your own tonight?' asked Lorna Blake as she served them their drinks. Lorna always spoke her mind, wasn't afraid of anyone, looked as if she'd know how to handle a gun and laughed uproariously at all the dirtiest jokes. Yet beneath the armour-plating she was as vulnerable as anyone. Devoted to her beloved cats, she freely admitted they were her surrogate children. When one of them had developed a malignant growth in the oesophagus last year, she had been as distraught as any mother. Yet even this grief she had kept almost entirely to herself. Drew, who had finally been forced to put the cat down, was the only person in Upper Sisley ever to have seen her cry.

'Out on our own and looking for the women of our dreams.' Doug rested his elbows on the bar, doing an unconvincing imitation of forlorn. 'What I'm really after is someone with straight, shoulder-length hair, green eyes, a dazzling smile and a white sleeveless dress with yellow buttons all the way down the front—'

'Oh, *you*!' Patsy cried delightedly over his shoulder. 'I *crept* up behind you! How on earth did you know I was here?'

Drew and Lorna exchanged glances. That was it, done. Patsy was smitten already.

Is that really all it takes? Drew silently marvelled. The

ability to out-blarney the Blarney Stone and a mirror behind the optics?

'So tell me how it happened,' he said to Patsy when Doug had performed the introductions and bought her a vodka and slimline tonic. 'Your mother broke her leg, you went along with her to the hospital, and the next thing you know you're being asked out by this smooth-talking doctor.'

Patsy smiled and glanced up at Doug from beneath her lashes. She carried on lovingly stroking his denim sleeve.

'Not quite,' Doug said. 'Actually, she asked me out.'

Oliver flushed with pleasure twenty minutes later when the door swung open and Savannah, wearing a Manics On Tour T-shirt and frayed khaki shorts, sauntered up to the bar.

'Hi. You're late.'

'Mum and Dad decided to come too.' As she wriggled on to a bar stool Savannah surveyed the drinks. 'They'll be here in a sec. I think I'll have a glass of red.'

'How about white? We've got a terrific new Chardonnay.' Oliver rummaged in the ice bucket, found the bottle he was looking for and showed her the label.

Savannah giggled as droplets of icy water splashed on to her bare legs. 'Okay, big brother, if that's what you recommend.'

'Here they come,' said Oliver as Toby and Deborah appeared.

'Blimey,' Lorna Blake murmured as another brief hush descended on the bar, 'it's like being visited by bloody royalty.' She looked amused. 'Why do people have to gawp? They'll be curtseying next.'

'It'll be okay when the novelty wears off.' Oliver, instinctively defending his new family, nodded towards Toby and Deborah. 'Anyway, it's not their fault.'

A ladybird had landed on Savannah's foot. Seeing that she was temporarily distracted, Lorna gave Oliver a nudge and said archly, 'You're getting on well with the daughter, aren't you? Very cosy. Pretty girl, too. Although I'm not sure the big brother image is quite what you're after, it's hardly—'

'But he is.' Savannah, having flicked the ladybird off her ankle, was paying attention again. 'He is my brother.'

Oliver stared at her.

Stunned, Lorna stared at Oliver.

Savannah looked from one to the other and said, 'Wasn't I supposed to say that? Is it meant to be a secret?' Her eyes widened in self-defence. 'Nobody said anything about having to keep it a secret.'

This was true, nobody had. But only because the subject hadn't come up yet. Feeling uneasy, Oliver poured the chilled wine and wondered how Toby was likely to react.

He didn't have long to wait.

'Are you serious?' Lorna said to Savannah.

'Serious about what?' Reaching the bar, Toby prodded his daughter in the ribs. 'What's she done – asked for a gin and Baileys? Sav, I've told you before, you can't order a drink that looks like something the cat sicked up.'

'Oliver?' said Lorna.

'Don't look at me,' Oliver replied hurriedly. 'I didn't say anything.'

Deborah said, 'What's going on?'

Lorna, never afraid to speak out, turned her attention to Toby Gillespie. 'Is Oliver your son?'

'Yes, he is.' Toby, in turn, smiled at Oliver.

'So . . . so you and Jess . . .'

'Yes, we did.'

'There,' said Savannah, hugely relieved. 'I told you it wasn't a secret.'

Lorna Blake looked stunned. 'But . . . we never knew that. You never told us.' She turned to Oliver.

Oliver said simply, 'I never knew.'

Recognising Drew at one of the tables at the far end of the bar, Deborah made her way over.

'Hello! I haven't forgotten I owe you a cup of milk.'

Drew said, 'And some washing-up liquid.'

'Not to mention several cans of lager.' Clutching her forehead, Deborah mimed a hangover. 'Maybe I should buy you a drink.'

Flushed with pride and pleasure, Drew introduced her to Doug and Patsy.

'So you're the doctor,' said Deborah. 'I missed you last night.'

'I knew I should have stayed in.'

'And you work in casualty, Drew tells me. Is it as exciting as it looks in *ER*?'

'Oh well,' Doug grinned, '*ER*'s pretty slow and dreary compared with Harleston General.'

'So what's it like?' Deborah turned to Patsy. 'Being a doctor's girlfriend?'

Patsy was overwhelmed – she was having quite a day. First her mother's leg, then Doug . . . and now here she was having an actual conversation with Deborah Gillespie. 'I don't know yet, I only met him this morning.' She giggled and squeezed Doug's arm. 'But I don't care if he has to work long hours,' she went on joyfully. 'I'm sure it's going to be great.'

Drew saw the look exchanged between Doug and Deborah.

'Lucky you,' said Deborah. 'There's something about a man in a white coat,' she added with a complicit smile, 'don't you think?'

'I could always introduce you to Ernie Alpass,' Drew offered. 'He's the baker in the next village.'

'Okay, a white coat and a stethoscope. But I'm right, aren't I?' Deborah went on. 'Millions of women just go weak at the knees at the sight of a doctor. Why *is* that?'

If anyone knows the answer it's Doug, Drew thought drily. Over the years he's certainly carried out enough research.

'The thing is, you can be the most respectable woman in the world,' said Doug, 'happily married and utterly faithful. But if a male doctor asks you to take your clothes off and lie down on the couch because he needs to examine you . . . well, you do it. Doctors are the only men in the world apart from your husband who get to see you naked.'

'Unless you pose for *Playboy*,' Drew pointed out.

'So it's a power thing,' Deborah mused, nodding. Leaning closer to Doug, she added, 'Ah, but what about all you young male doctors? Is it ever a turn-on, or does it just get boring in the end – seeing women's naked bodies day in, day out?'

'Are you kidding?' Doug's mouth twitched. 'Why do you suppose we wear those long white coats?'

After that it started to get embarrassing. Drew saw what was happening and wished to God he'd stayed at home. He wished he could bring himself to get up and leave but he couldn't, because then Patsy really wouldn't have anyone to talk to.

Most of all, though, he wished Doug would leave Deborah Gillespie alone.

It wasn't Deborah's fault, he thought with growing irritation; she was treating Doug just as she treated everyone, with natural friendliness and effortless charm. Drew, having experienced this himself for the first time last night, had – okay, he admitted it – been utterly bowled over. Maybe even a bit smitten. But with a woman as stunning as Deborah Gillespie, that was only natural. Being smitten was par for the course. Anyone not smitten had to be pretty weird.

But the difference between us, Drew thought, is I don't automatically assume Deborah Gillespie fancies me in return. And Doug clearly does.

Doug couldn't take his eyes off her. He couldn't stop talking to her and he couldn't talk to her without touching her. He was firing on all cylinders, flirting as Drew had never seen him flirt before.

Poor Patsy wasn't getting a look in. Admittedly she hadn't helped her cause, butting in excitedly at first with such gems as 'I've seen all your husband's films' and 'Fancy famous people like you coming out to a pub', but it was still cruel.

Drew spent an unhappy hour trying to make polite conversation – so that maybe Patsy wouldn't notice the way Doug was ignoring her – and buying hundreds of rounds of drinks. By ten o'clock Patsy had had enough. Tears glittered on her eyelashes as she scraped her chair back and stood up. Drew wondered if she was about to tip Doug's untouched pint over his head – which would have been good – but it didn't happen. All Patsy flung at him was a look of anger, which was wasted, frankly, since Doug was too busy flirting with Deborah to notice.

Chapter 14

Drew caught up with Patsy in the corridor leading to the loos. She slumped against the whitewashed wall, clutching her white leather handbag like a security blanket, her mouth wobbling and her face blotchy with the effort it was taking not to cry.

'What a bastard. Is he always like this?'

'Well, yes.'

'It's so humiliating. I thought he really liked me.'

'I'm sorry,' said Drew. God, talk about pathetic. Doug does this to her and I'm the one saying sorry.

'I was so excited when he asked me out.' Patsy's voice began to break. 'I told all my flatmates how dishy he was and they were really j-j-jealous.'

'Here.' The mascara was beginning to slide. As Drew passed her a handkerchief he realised he was doing it again. The world, it seemed, was divided into two kinds of men: the good-looking ones who make girls cry, and the rest, who supply the mopping-up equipment.

'What am I going to do?' Patsy trumpeted into the hanky, blowing her nose in front of Drew as she would never have dreamt of blowing her nose in front of Doug. 'I told them not to expect me home tonight. I can't drive back now, they'll laugh at me.'

Drew made the supreme sacrifice.

'Look, I'll phone for a cab. We'll go into Harleston.' He didn't want to, but she was so desperate. 'I'll take you to Rattles, how about that?'

'Not likely, that's where my flatmates'll be. I've told them I'm going out with a drop-dead-gorgeous doctor.' Patsy was distraught, beyond caring. 'They're hardly going to be impressed, are they,' she sobbed, 'when I turn up with you instead?'

'Where's . . .?' said Doug when Drew reappeared.

'Patsy. She's gone.'

'What, to buy a drink?'

'She's left. Gone home.' Drew spoke evenly. 'I'm amazed you noticed she was missing. Even if you couldn't remember her name.'

Deborah looked horrified. 'You're not serious! Oh Lord, this is all my fault, I just know it is. I only popped over to say hello and I've been here for' – she peered at her watch – 'good grief, an *hour*. That poor girl! No wonder she got fed up – once I start yakking no one else can get a word in edgeways.'

'Please,' said Doug, 'relax. She wasn't important.'

Drew's fingers closed over the slip of paper in the palm of his hand. Even with the tears rolling down her cheeks as she'd climbed into the taxi, Patsy hadn't been able to stop herself burrowing frantically in her bag and scribbling her phone number on the back of an old Sainsbury's receipt. 'Just in case he wants to ring me,' she had said, embarrassment mingling with desperation as she pressed it into Drew's hand. 'I know, don't say it. But he might change his mind.'

Drew crumpled up the receipt and dropped it on the floor.

'Litter lout,' said Moll, clearing glasses at the next table.

'But you were important to her,' Deborah exclaimed, shaking her head. 'This is awful, I feel *terrible*.'

Moll was humming to herself as she gave the empty table an energetic wipe-down. Glad of the distraction, Drew watched the way her amazing breasts danced a little dance together in absolutely perfect time. They were, he decided, the Torvill and Dean of breasts.

When Moll glanced across and gave him one of her smiles Drew said in a low voice, 'Can I take you out to dinner one night?'

He had drunk enough to enable the words to slip out with ease.

'Sounds great,' said Moll. 'I'm not sure yet which evenings I'm working, but I can always ask Lorna—'

'How about coming back to the cottage with me tonight?' Drew realised he didn't want to sleep with Moll sometime next week, he wanted to sleep with her now.

The great thing about Moll was, she was never offended. The bad thing about her was she sometimes said no.

Moll, who was fond of Drew, smiled again and shook her head. 'I don't think so, not tonight. I'm pretty shattered.'

He didn't even have a chance to try and change her mind. With a last swish of her cloth and a clink of glass, Moll was gone.

Drew sank his pint and ruminated on the fact that tonight clearly wasn't going to be his night for getting laid.

At least neither Doug nor Deborah had heard him being turned down.

'It's been great seeing you again,' Deborah told him, standing up. She turned from Drew to Doug. 'Lovely meeting you, as well. I'd better head back to my lot, they're going to wonder where I've got to.' She winked at Drew. 'Again.'

Drew watched Doug smile at her, and squeeze her hand. 'See you again soon.'

They both watched Deborah make her way back to the far end of the bar, slip her arm around Toby Gillespie's waist and say something that made Lorna Blake throw back her head and laugh.

'She is stunning,' Doug breathed out slowly.

Drew said, 'Her husband thinks so too.'

Amused, Doug changed the subject. 'Shame about Patsy going off in a strop. That's the trouble with girls like her. They're like policemen, never around when you need them.'

'She was crying.'

'She'll live.'

'You are such a shit.' Drew pushed his chair back and drained his glass.

'It's my round,' Doug protested as he rose to his feet. 'I'll get these.'

'Not for me.' Drew couldn't be bothered to stay. He couldn't be bothered to drink any more, even if Doug was buying. 'I'm going home.'

Drew woke up with a start, mid-way through a dream about Lili Ferguson. For a split second he was able to recall the dream with utter clarity: Lili was running across the village green stark naked, being chased by her mother-in-law clutching a pile of white doctors' coats. Eleanor Ferguson was shouting, 'It took me three hours to iron these, for pity's sake put one on, girl! Cover yourself up before anyone sees you, you're a disgrace!'

And I was standing outside the pub watching them, thought Drew, and I yelled out to Lili . . .

Dammit, I yelled something out to Lili. What did I yell?

But it was useless. The dream had gone, slithering away like mercury. Drew gave up trying to remember and rolled on to his back. It was a hot night and he had developed a raging thirst. Peering at the luminous hands on his watch, he discovered he hadn't been asleep for hours after all. It was still only twenty past midnight.

Then he heard a creaking door downstairs, followed by the sound of footsteps, and he realised that this was what had woken him up.

God, he was thirsty! That was what fifteen lagers did for you. Rolling on to his side again, he felt around on the floor next to the bed until he found an empty pint glass. Okay, he'd called Doug a shit earlier, but he wouldn't have taken offence, would he? If he asked him now to fill up the glass from the bathroom tap, Doug would do it. Save having to get out of bed.

About to call out, Drew heard whispering. He closed his mouth again and listened harder.

There were two sets of footsteps on the stairs.

Doug murmured, 'It's okay, he's asleep.'

This was followed moments later by a burst of laughter and a muffled shriek.

'Doug, get off! Not on the staircase!'

Drew closed his eyes. It was Moll's voice.

As his thirst raged on, he clutched the dusty glass to his chest, not even noticing as a hugely grateful hairy-legged spider scuttled out.

Chapter 15

The journalist from the *Daily Mail* arrived the following Tuesday, promptly at eleven thirty.

'Is this going to be awful?' said Jessie, watching the car pull up the drive. She was apprehensive, never having had to deal with the press before.

'Don't worry, it'll be fine.' Toby put down the script he'd been reading and came to stand behind her at the window. 'This woman's one of the best. Anyway, far better to do it like this, all over in one go.' He gave Jessie's shoulder a reassuring squeeze. 'As soon as they've got what they want, they leave you alone. Start slamming doors in their faces and yelling "No comment" and you'll have them pestering you for months, digging for dirt and making up all kinds of rubbish.'

The journalist was climbing out of her car, lowering her dark glasses in order to study the front of the house. Jessie, damp with sweat, wished she could be back upstairs in her dungarees, getting on with the marbling she'd started yesterday in the master bathroom. The walls had already been primed, undercoated and fine-filled. She had given them two coats of eggshell. This morning she had begun applying the glaze, made up from equal parts of raw linseed oil, white spirit and white undercoat. Now, with a fine hog's hair brush, a dust brush with tapered bristles, a goose feather and a soft cloth, she was ready to create the marbling effect.

Except I'm not, thought Jessie as the doorbell rang. I'm down here instead, about to be interviewed by one of the shrewdest journalists in the business.

And if that on its own wasn't scary enough, Jessie had

another worry. The journalist wasn't only going to go over all that old stuff, was she? She was bound to ask how Jessie and Toby felt about each other now.

Fibbing to Lili was one thing, but lying convincingly to an eagle-eyed journalist was quite another.

Jessie just prayed she'd be able to pull it off without going puce.

She didn't blush, thank God. When the subject came up, Toby laughed and said easily, 'Wouldn't it have been great? Like a Hollywood film. Except I wouldn't have married and had a family. I'd have to have been a lonely old bachelor, bitter and miserable for twenty years before finally rediscovering my lost love.'

The journalist laughed too, and Deborah knocked on the door, poking her head round.

'Lunch is ready. We're eating out on the terrace. Jess, are you really allergic to lobster or is Oliver having me on?'

'How about you, Jessie?' the journalist asked as they made their way through the house. 'After all, you never did marry, did you?'

'I haven't spent the last twenty years being bitter and miserable either.' Jessie concentrated on a white wall, which was supposed to help. Oh please don't let me blush, mustn't blush . . .

'Look at him, though. Toby Gillespie, hugely successful, stunningly attractive.' The older woman lowered her voice. 'You must still have some feelings for him.'

'It's water under the bridge now.' Jessie could feel the perspiration prickling along her spine. 'We've both grown up. We get on well together.' She shrugged damply. 'That's as far as it goes.'

'But you *loved* each other . . .'

'Look, did you ever eat a reheated baked potato?'

'Well—'

'It still looks like a baked potato. It even tastes like a baked potato,' Jessie improvised wildly as they stepped out on to the terrace, 'but it's been reheated, so it just isn't the same.'

Oliver, Savannah and Dizzy were already sitting around

the table. The journalist was charmed by Oliver, and he in turn answered her questions with cheerful enthusiasm.

'God no, I've never wanted to be an actor. I was press-ganged into being a donkey once in the school nativity play and that put me off for life.'

'He told me about that,' Savannah giggled. 'He said one of the shepherds spent the entire performance trying to shove a raw carrot up his nose.'

'I did that once,' Dizzy joined in eagerly. 'Well it was a broad bean, but I got it stuck up my nose, didn't I, Mum? Remember – you had to take me to casualty?'

'Speaking of casualty . . .' Deborah was mopping up salad dressing from her plate with a piece of olive bread. 'I forgot to tell you, Jess. We met Doug Flynn on Friday night. He was in the pub with Drew.'

The lobster was heavenly; Jessie was having to force herself not to lick the plate. She confined herself to licking her fingers instead, and glanced across the table at Deborah. 'So, what's the verdict?'

Deborah rolled her dark eyes. 'Well, *doesn't* he think he's gorgeous?'

'Absolutely. The bee's knees.' Jessie was grinning. 'Trouble is, he's not the only one.'

'Um, so I gathered.'

'That chap you were talking to for ages?' Savannah looked indignant. 'Why are you both laughing like that? He *was* gorgeous. I thought he was completely—'

'Don't even think it,' Jessie protested. 'Yogurts have a longer shelf-life than Doug Flynn's girlfriends.'

Deborah gave her daughter's arm a consoling pat. 'There you are, darling. You wouldn't want a use-by date stamped on your bottom.'

'He disappeared with Moll on Friday,' put in Oliver.

'Ah well, that's allowed,' Jessie said easily. 'He won't break her heart, will he? He knows he's safe with Moll; they're two of a kind.'

'God, sorry,' Dizzy exclaimed, accidentally knocking over the journalist's glass of red at the thought of Moll's breasts.

The photographer arrived as they were finishing lunch.

For the next hour and a half he took endless assorted group photos.

Jessie and Deborah were sitting together on the lawn watching him use up another reel of film on Oliver, Savannah and Dizzy when the journalist rejoined them.

'Oliver, move closer to Dizzy,' the photographer instructed. 'And Savannah, pull your skirt down, darling – we don't want to see your knickers.'

'*He* doesn't, certainly,' Deborah murmured to Jessie. 'He's gay.'

The journalist smiled. 'You really do get along together well, don't you? I'm going to enjoy writing this piece. Our readers love a story with a happy ending.'

'Come back and see us in a year,' said Deborah, 'it could all be different then. Just think,' she went on playfully, 'Toby could leave me for Lorna-the-pub-landlady.'

'Dizzy could have a torrid affair with Moll-the-man-eating-trollop,' said Jessie, joining in.

'Oliver can be his rival in love. They can fight a duel on the village green.' Deborah's eyes were alight with laughter. 'And Savvy could get hopelessly entangled with devilish doctor Doug. He'd dump her, of course.'

'I was going to have an affair with him,' Jessie protested.

'Go on then,' Deborah said generously, 'you can tame him. He can fall in love with you and that'll make Savvy madly jealous.'

Jessie, who had been trying to make a daisy chain, pulled a face. 'I'm going off this idea already. You can have Doug if you want.'

'Thanks, but no thanks.' Deborah looked cheerful. 'I've rather got my eye on dashing Mr Darcy.'

The journalist, who had always hankered after a cottage in the country but had worried that village life might be boring, looked enthralled. 'Heavens, is he as handsome and arrogant as he sounds?'

Deborah burst out laughing. 'Drew Darcy, bless his heart, is about as arrogant and handsome as a battered old sofa. Savvy, push your hair away from your face. And stop swinging your legs!'

Shielding her eyes from the mid-afternoon sun, the journalist watched her photographer attempt to organise a shot of Oliver and Savannah sitting together on the wall. 'Look at them, both so blonde and tanned. They certainly make a striking pair.' She smiled at Jessie and Deborah. 'You must be proud of them.'

'I'd be a lot prouder,' said Deborah, 'if my daughter wasn't still flashing her pants. SAVVY!' She raised her voice again. 'Knees together, skirt *down*!'

'She's a stunning girl, though.'

'Oh, she's the one with the looks,' Deborah agreed, rolling on to her front and propping herself up on her elbows. 'Poor old Dizz . . . well, fingers crossed, he'll improve as he gets older.'

Dizzy, lying unnoticed in a hammock some fifteen feet behind them, already knew why the photographer was taking so many more shots of Savannah than he had of him. She was the photogenic one and he was the lank-haired adolescent. He was used to the lack of attention and he didn't need to overhear his mother's tactless remarks to know he was no Brad Pitt.

It still hurt, though.

'Wonderful, great, terrific,' chirruped the photographer, snapping away ecstatically across the lawn. 'Ollie, move your head closer to your sister's. That's it, that's it, you're a *star*.'

The photographer probably fancied Oliver too, Dizzy decided, closing his eyes and making the hammock sway from side to side. He pulled his baseball cap lower over his face and gave himself up to the far more pleasurable fantasy he had overheard earlier, the thrilling one suggested by Jess.

The one about me, Dizzy thought happily, having a torrid affair with man-eating Moll.

When the journalist and the photographer had left for London, Jessie went back upstairs to her marbling. After visiting her briefly, Toby came back down and found Oliver eating left-over salad in the kitchen. Dizzy was still in his hammock, Savannah was chattering on the phone to a schoolfriend and Deborah was in the sitting room catching up with the tennis on television.

'I've had a word with Jess and she's agreed.' Toby plunged straight in. 'Look, this Europe trip of yours. When were you planning to go?'

Oliver was taken aback. What was this about? Surely they weren't suggesting he called it off?

'As soon as I've got enough money,' he said defensively. 'I'm saving as hard as I can. The idea is to work here for three months, go off for three months, come back and work in the pub for another three months then take off again. That's the theory anyway,' he concluded worriedly. 'Cashflow permitting.'

'Well I can help you there.' Toby held out a folded cheque.

Oliver took it and stared at the figures. 'I don't believe it. Five thousand pounds!'

'I've got some catching up to do,' said Toby. 'Please, just take it.'

Oliver was still gazing at the cheque in wonder. 'This is amazing. I could go to Europe straight away. I could go *tomorrow*.'

'You don't have to rush off quite that fast. And don't think I'm trying to get rid of you,' Toby went on hurriedly, 'because that's the last thing I want. I just know it's what you want to do. And I'd like to help out.'

Overwhelmed, Oliver shoved the cheque into his jeans pocket.

'Thanks. I don't know what else to say.' Paris, Tuscany, Rome, Vienna . . . I can do it *all* . . .

'Nothing. You don't need to thank me.'

'Is it okay to tell the others? I mean, can I tell Sav?'

As he said it, the sound of Savannah screeching with laughter drifted through the hall. Toby, who was waiting for a call to come through from his agent, lifted his eyebrows in resignation.

'Of course. That is, if you ever manage to get her off the damn phone.'

Chapter 16

Oliver and Savannah were banished to Savannah's bed-room.

'It's Dad's idea of hell, having to watch himself on TV.' Savannah slotted the video into the machine then threw herself on to the bed and rummaged under the crumpled duvet for the remote control. 'If we ever want to watch anything of his we have to do it well out of earshot. This film's one of my favourites actually. I can't believe you've never seen it.' Pressing fast-forward, whizzing through the opening titles, Savannah jabbered on. 'Four Bafta nominations, an Oscar for best supporting actress, and the theme song went to number one in seven countries *including* Belgium, so if you visit Belgium on your grand tour—'

'Sshh,' said Oliver, taking the remote control from her and pressing play instead. He slid down into a sitting position on the floor and turned the volume up, wondering why Savannah was so rattled. Something was up. He really hoped it wasn't what he thought it was. 'Let's just watch the film.'

He tried, but it was hard to get into a psychological thriller when the person noisily filing their nails behind you kept telling you what was about to happen next.

'As soon as he's fallen asleep she sneaks out to meet the lawyer. She thinks he's on her side but he isn't.'

'Thanks.'

They watched Toby kissing the actress.

'Weird, isn't it? Seeing your own father kiss another woman. Everyone thinks she's so perfect,' Savannah went on, 'but Dad says she had diabolical bad breath, it was like snogging King Kong.'

'I can't hear this.' Oliver turned up the volume again.

'They go to Venice next, to see the lawyer's cousin. I expect you'll visit Venice, won't you? Do all those naff touristy things—'

'Right,' said Oliver, switching off the video and swivelling round to face her. 'That's it. You win. Now why don't you tell me what this is all about?' His jaw was tense. 'Or can I guess?'

Savannah avoided his eyes. She carried on filing her nails, faster and faster. 'I don't know what you mean.'

'Don't you? I think I do.'

'Go on then.' File, file. 'You tell me.'

'It's the money, isn't it?' Oliver reached over and took the emery board away from her; it was a miracle she had any nails left. 'The cheque for five thousand pounds. You don't think he should have given it to me.'

This time Savannah looked straight at him. 'I *wish* he bloody hadn't given it to you, that's for sure.'

'Because you think it's unfair.' Oliver was lacerated with guilt. 'He's given me all that money and he hasn't given you the same amount—'

'Oh come on, don't be such a berk!' Savannah howled suddenly. 'I'm not jealous! I'm . . . I'm . . .'

Bemused, Oliver said, 'You're what?'

'I'm *miserable*.' She promptly burst into tears. 'I don't want you to go.'

What was going on? Helplessly, Oliver said, 'You've lost me.'

'I know, that's just it,' Savannah sobbed, wiping her eyes with a handful of duvet. 'I don't *want* to lose you. We've only just found you and the last week's been so brilliant . . . and now you're going away for months and months . . . and I'm going to h-hate it so m-m-much.'

Touched beyond belief, Oliver ruffled her curtain of blonde hair. There was even a lump in his own throat.

'Please, please don't cry. I'll miss you too, but it won't be for ever. I'll send postcards,' he said soothingly.

'Oh brilliant.' Savannah sniffed. 'That'll make all the difference.'

'We can talk to each other on the phone.'

'It won't be the same!' she wailed.

'I know.' Oliver looked unhappy. Hell, now she was making him feel terrible. 'But if you knew how long I've dreamed of going to Europe. We've never had any money . . . I've never even been abroad, you see. The most Mum could manage was a caravan holiday in Totnes.'

Savannah reached for her nightie – actually an extra-large Oasis T-shirt – and blew her nose on it. Liam's face came off worst. 'And we've been everywhere. God, I'm a selfish cow! It's just such rotten timing, that's all.' She dredged up a watery smile. 'It's your fault. Why couldn't you take your gap year at the same time as everyone else?'

'You really want to know?' Oliver grinned, hugely relieved she'd stopped crying at last. 'I was seeing this girl. We were mad about each other. When she said she was applying for a place at Exeter, I couldn't bear the thought of her meeting someone else. So that was it, I applied too. And we both got in.'

'What was her name?'

'Claire.'

'Pretty?'

He looked offended. 'Of course she was pretty. I don't go out with dogs.'

'So what happened?' Savannah said.

'It lasted about three months.' Oliver's shrug was philosophical; this had all happened three long years ago. 'Then the novelty wore off.'

'But who finished with who?'

'We just gradually drifted apart. I was into sport, she liked singing madrigals.'

Savannah nodded, envisaging a pretty girl warbling churchy-type songs. Was she tall or short, thin or fat, blonde or dark?

Oh my God, thought Savannah, I'm jealous of Claire . . .

'When will you go?' she asked Oliver bravely. 'Did you mean it about setting off next week?'

Quite suddenly next week seemed awfully soon. Oliver thought of the brand new passport he had acquired in April, sitting in his sock drawer at home. It would be short notice, anyway, for Lorna to replace him in the pub. He couldn't leave her in the lurch, could he?

'No hurry,' he told Savannah, his tone reassuring. 'These trips take time to plan properly. Maybe in a couple of months.'

Savannah was relieved. Two months, that was eight weeks. Eight weeks was ages away.

She nodded. 'Okay.'

'Now,' said Oliver, waving the remote control, 'maybe we could watch the rest of this film.'

The doorbell rang at eight o'clock that evening just as Toby was coming down the stairs. When he saw the outline of a motorcyclist's helmet through the stained glass he assumed his agent had arranged for the script he'd been waiting for to be delivered by courier.

Instead, when he opened the door, he was knocked sideways by a great waft of garlic.

'Pizza delivery,' announced a muffled voice, thrusting a pile of eight boxes at Toby. Pulling a bill from his pocket he added, 'That'll be seventy-three pounds eighty.'

'Sorry, wrong address.'

'Gillespie, Sisley House, Upper Sisley,' recited the delivery boy. Now that his own hands were free he flipped up his visor. 'Hey, you're that film star. Can I have your autograph?'

'We haven't ordered any pizzas.'

'Come on,' the boy protested. 'I've come all the way from Harleston. We don't even come this far out normally, but you promised to pay an extra twenty quid for delivery. See?' he pointed to the bill.

'I didn't promise anything,' said Toby, 'because I didn't phone you.'

'What is it?' Dizzy, appearing behind Toby, peered over his shoulders and sniffed. 'Pizzas? Hey Dad, great! I'm starving.'

'But I haven't—'

'Mr Gillespie, I've come all this way. It's my first week in the job.' The boy began to look scared. 'Do you have any idea what my boss'll do to me if I go back with eight cold pizzas and no money?'

Toby heaved a sigh and reached for his wallet. Dizzy joyfully seized the pizzas and disappeared into the kitchen.

'You might want to stick them in the oven,' said the delivery boy as he shoved the bundle of notes into his pocket. 'I had a puncture on the way over.'

'Right.' Wearily Toby began to close the door. The boy put his foot over the step to stop him.

'Aren't you forgetting something, Mr Gillespie? Autograph?'

'Ugh!' Savannah surveyed the pizzas in disgust. 'They've all got extra anchovies. What did you do that for, Dad? You know none of us can stand anchovies.'

'I didn't order the bloody pizzas,' said Toby, exasperated, 'let alone the anchovies.'

'Don't be so fussy.' Dizzy gave his sister a look of scorn. 'You can peel them off.'

Savannah looked mystified. 'So who did order them?'

'I don't know.' The same person, Toby presumed, who had delivered the anonymous note. 'Just someone's idea of a joke.'

'Well, we can't eat all eight,' said Deborah. 'Why don't I take a few next door? Maybe Drew or Doug would be glad of them.'

She took three of the pizzas around to Keeper's Cottage, but both Doug and Drew were out at work.

Jamie, unable to believe his luck, thanked Deborah and offered her a can of Guinness which, regretfully, she declined.

Then he sat down to watch yet more cricket, showered the pizzas with chilli sauce, and happily ate all three.

Chapter 17

Lili was on her hands and knees in the kitchen performing a mass nappy change when Michael arrived home on Friday afternoon.

William, as agile as an eel, squirmed off the changing mat and out of reach the moment Lili had cleaned him up. Rather than hare around trying to catch him, she armed herself with more baby wipes and decided to tackle Freya's nappy. The stench was horrendous. William, screeching with delight, yelled, 'Pooh, yuk!' and raced around the kitchen table weeing at intervals on the floor.

'I'm back,' Michael announced, opening the door. 'God, what a smell! William, Daddy's home, come and give me a hug—'

'Nooo!' howled William, alarmed by the sudden appearance of the father he hadn't seen for three months, and going briskly into reverse. He cannoned into the dog basket, tipped over backwards and landed on Blitz. Yelping, Blitz shot out of the basket, skidded in a puddle of wee and ricocheted off Michael's legs.

'Hello, darling.' Lili scrambled to her feet before Michael – standing behind her – could tell her she'd put on weight. 'You're early. William, stop hiding – it's Daddy. Hang on, I need to get rid of these and wash my hands.'

Michael flinched as she headed past him with the offending nappies. William peered at him over the rim of the dog basket.

'You're a pushover, that's your trouble,' Michael told Lili. He looked without enthusiasm at Blitz, who was tentatively wagging his tail. 'Let me guess. The owners are away on holiday and they asked you to look after it for a couple of weeks, save them forking out on kennel fees—'

'Actually he's ours.' Lili, scrubbing her hands at the sink, gave him a bright, over-the-shoulder smile.

'This is a joke,' said Michael slowly.

'He's adorable. Brilliant with the children – they love him to bits.'

'I don't like dogs.'

'And company for me.' Having dried her hands, Lili crossed the kitchen and dutifully gave her travel-weary husband a peck on the cheek. His suit was crumpled and he smelled of all the different aftershaves he'd tried out in Duty Free. 'He's got a lovely temperament, wouldn't hurt a fly. Anyway, it makes sense to have a guard dog—'

'Oh, perfect sense. Especially one that wouldn't hurt a fly.'

Eagerly, Lili said, 'But he can bark, he's terrific at barking! That'll be enough to scare any burglars away.'

'In other words it's a *fait accompli*.' Michael's jaw tightened. 'You know I can't stand dogs, but you went ahead and got one anyway.' He slung his jacket over his shoulder and headed for the kitchen door. 'I mean, why should I have a say in anything? I'm only the one who slogs his guts out to pay the bills and support you all.'

'Where are you going?' Lili said, feeling a bit sick. This wasn't the best of starts.

'Upstairs, to take a shower. After all,' Michael added, 'I want to be smart for the occasion.'

Freya poked William in the eye. William let out a roar and gave her a thump back.

'What occasion?' Lili had to raise her voice to be heard over the cacophony of wails.

'The massive surprise party you've organised to celebrate my happy homecoming.'

Sarcasm. Oh help.

'Your mother's coming over at seven.'

'That's all I need.'

'It's steak and chips for dinner,' Lili said hopefully. 'I got some really nice sirloin yesterday. Your favourite.' She was patting Blitz, stroking his silky ears as she spoke.

'Well, it's easy to see who's the most popular around here,' Michael said. 'You may as well just open a can of Pedigree Chum for me and give the steak to the dog.'

As he stood under the shower Michael acknowledged that he had overreacted downstairs. The dog was only partly to blame for his short temper; for the first time since leaving school he had suffered the indignity this morning of actually being dumped.

His fling with Sandra had begun three months earlier. When you both worked for the same company in Dubai and socialised with the same crowd, it seemed a natural progression – sooner or later – to end up in the same bed. And Michael had been more than happy with the situation. As with most of his extra-curricular relationships, Sandra was the opposite of Lili. Thin, with short dark hair, she wore business suits and worked as hard as she played. He needed a mistress who knew her own mind, one who didn't faff about, and Sandra fitted the bill.

Annoyingly, she hadn't faffed about this morning either, when Michael had dropped in to say goodbye. 'It's been fun, Mike, but now it's over,' she had told him breezily, quite out of the blue.

His stomach still lurched at the recent memory. Okay, theirs wasn't the romance of the century, but why on earth would she want to end it?

'But . . . but . . .' he had spluttered, standing in the middle of her apartment while she sat back and efficiently lit a cigarette.

'I've been seeing quite a bit of Ned Armstrong,' Sandra announced. 'Oh come on, cheer up. You're going home to little wifey and the kids, aren't you? You'll be gone for eight weeks. What did you expect me to do, put myself on ice until you get back?'

And that had been that. Done and dusted. Sandra had given him a brisk kiss goodbye and he had driven in a daze to the airport, maybe not heartbroken but definitely put out.

105

Hence the filthy mood.

Michael sighed and switched off the shower. It wasn't Lili's fault; he mustn't take it out on her.

Lili was chopping mushrooms to go with the steak when he returned downstairs. Moving up behind her, he slid his arms around her waist and nuzzled her soft neck.

'Rough journey. I'm sorry.'

'Me too.' His chin was bristly. Lili resisted the urge to duck away. Once upon a time, she thought guiltily, I loved having my neck nuzzled by Michael.

He peered out of the window. The dog was in the garden, joyously digging up Lili's prized herbaceous border. Pushing open the door to the sitting room, Michael saw William and Freya fast asleep together on the sofa.

'Where's Lottie?'

'Birthday party.' Lili was deeply envious of Lottie's social life, which was as hectic as any debutante's.

'And Harriet?'

'Swimming.' Oh dear, thought Lili, no wonder he's miffed. He must feel horribly left out. She said apologetically, 'We weren't expecting you back 'til six.'

Michael wasn't the least bit miffed; this was fine by him. When you hadn't seen your wife for three months, the sex was always more fun; it was like riding a new bike.

'Aaargh!' Lili screeched as a warm hand snaked beneath the elasticised waistband of her track-suit bottoms. The chopping knife slipped from her grasp as Michael's other hand deftly unfastened her bra. This was his party trick and he was immensely proud of it but Lili could have done with some warning. Mushrooms went flying and the knife pirouetted to the floor, bouncing off her ankle en route.

'Mike . . . not now!'

'*Yes*, now.'

'But the children—'

'Are asleep.' He began enthusiastically to drag her track-suit trousers down over her hips.

Lili, trying hard to tug them back up again, gasped, 'They might wake up!'

'Any more excuses,' Michael murmured, manoeuvring

106

her towards the kitchen table, 'and I just might take offence.'

'Oh my God!' Lili yelped as a movement at the kitchen window caught her eye. 'Get off me. Felicity's here!'

It was close, but as she stumbled to the door Lili consoled herself with the knowledge that it could have been a hundred times worse. If Felicity had turned up just five minutes later . . .

Except then, she thought, it would have been over and done with and I'd have been back chopping mushrooms.

'You're early,' she exclaimed brightly, smoothing her T-shirt over her hips and thanking her lucky stars Michael hadn't managed to tug her track-suit bottoms right off.

Felicity's jaw was rigid. 'Where's Freya?'

'She's fine – fast asleep in the other room,' Lili babbled. 'Oh, she's been as good as gold—'

'Can I see her?'

'And here's Michael, home again after three months!'

'So I see,' Felicity said, pink-cheeked with disapproval. 'By the way, there's a knife on the floor behind you.'

Lili was consumed with guilt. She pushed open the sitting-room door and watched Felicity scoop the sleeping Freya into her arms, murmuring, 'It's all right, darling, Mummy's here now.'

'I'm so sorry. Michael's just glad to be back.' As she spoke, Lili wondered if this was it, whether this time she really was about to get the sack. She couldn't for the life of her imagine Hugh and Felicity being overcome with lust and Doing It on the kitchen table. She couldn't even imagine them doing it on less-than-perfectly ironed sheets.

To Lili's amazement, it was Michael who came to her rescue.

'I'm entirely to blame,' he announced, appearing in the doorway and smiling broadly at Felicity. 'Please don't be cross with Lili. I ambushed her. The reason I wasn't getting anywhere,' he explained ruefully, 'was because she kept yelling that she couldn't leave the children.'

'I understand.' Felicity's expression softened. She stroked Freya's rosebud mouth adoringly as a ribbon of dribble draped itself across her lime green Jasper Conran jacket. 'Anyway, we'll be off.' With a flicker of a smile she said to Michael, 'Have a nice evening.'

'You *charmed* her,' Lili exclaimed when Felicity and Freya had left. 'I don't believe it, how did you *do* that? You actually made the Ice Queen smile!'

Michael wondered for a brief moment if a fling with Felicity Seymour would be playing it a bit too close to home. Reluctantly he decided it would. That was the trouble with small villages, you couldn't get away with a damn thing.

Happily, William was still sprawled across the sofa, fast asleep and lovingly clutching a naked Barbie to his chest.

Moving towards Lili with a familiar sparkle in his eyes, Michael said, 'Like father, like son. I think he has the right idea, don't you?'

'Did Lili tell you about that new next-door neighbour of mine?' asked Eleanor that evening, over coffee and slices of the fruit cake she had brought round in a tin because 'I guessed you wouldn't have had time to make him one, dear.'

Lili had fought back the urge to reply innocently, 'No, we were too busy having sex.'

Michael looked bemused. 'No.'

'Writes books,' Eleanor began triumphantly.

'Ahem,' said Lili. 'Didn't she want to keep it quiet?'

'Ha! That's not all she wants kept quiet! Being a writer wasn't the only thing I found out about her,' Eleanor declared with satisfaction.

Michael tried to sound interested. 'Oh yes?'

Eleanor mouthed the word *lesbian* across the table at him.

Michael had never mastered lip reading. 'What?'

'You know. One of them.'

'One of what?'

Harriet, who had been doing her best to pick out all the sultanas and leave the cake, watched her grandmother mouth the terrible word again. 'You can say it out loud,' she told Eleanor, 'I do know what lesbian means.'

'Well, really.' Eleanor looked shocked.

Harriet shrugged and ate another sultana. What was the big deal? 'Everyone knows.'

'Well you shouldn't.' Eleanor turned to Lili, who had already guessed this would be her fault. 'This is what happens when you let children read those dreadful magazines. Myrtle Armitage showed me one the other day in the shop. Disgusting,' she pronounced heatedly. 'What do fourteen-year-olds need to know about those matters?'

'One of our teachers at school is a lesbian,' said Harriet, unperturbed. 'Miss Hegarty. She lives with her girlfriend.'

'Then she should be reported,' Eleanor snapped.

'But she's our favourite teacher,' Harriet protested. 'She's great.'

Eleanor's eyes narrowed. 'The next thing you know, she'll be making improper advances.'

'Huh, if you want improper advances try Mr Florian, our chemistry teacher,' Harriet declared. 'Or Fingers Florian as we call him. Disgusting old letch.'

'Can we change the subject?' Lili pleaded, before Eleanor's blood pressure reached eruption level.

'How are the Gillespies settling into the village?' said Michael, to be helpful.

'That Jessie Roscoe.' Eleanor tutted and shot a disapproving glance – yet another one – in Lili's direction. 'That friend of yours. I always said she was a shameless trollop. Sleeping around with film stars . . .'

Patiently Lili said, 'He wasn't a film star when she slept with him.'

'Hmm.' Eleanor sniffed and raised her eyebrows meaningfully at Michael. Trust Lili to defend her friend.

'The children seem nice, anyway,' said Lili.

The urge to boast was too much for Eleanor Ferguson to resist.

'I was chatting to the boy yesterday outside the shop. Thaddeus, his name is, though everyone calls him Dizzy. We had a most pleasant conversation about the weather.'

In reality Eleanor had been the one carrying on the pleasant conversation while Thaddeus had examined his trainers and mumbled the odd reply – but he'd seemed a nice enough lad.

Eleanor prepared to make amends with Harriet, who was now kneading her picked-to-pieces cake into pellets. 'I saw you talking to him the other afternoon, didn't I, dear? What with school and exams coming up, the two of you must have lots in common.'

'You must be joking,' said Harriet disparagingly. 'The only thing Dizzy Gillespie's interested in is massive breasts.'

Chapter 18

The phone in Bernadette's tiny cottage was out in the hallway. Every time she answered it, she glanced at the framed photograph of April on the hall table as she spoke. Once a week, usually on a Saturday morning, the caller would be April. They would chat for several minutes, talk about their respective careers, catch up on any news, tell each other how they were getting on, and generally pass the time of day.

Which was what they were doing now.

'My nosy neighbour asked me yesterday when my next book was coming out.' As she spoke, Bernadette gazed at the photograph. With her big Bambi eyes and the familiar shy tilt of her head, April looked far younger than thirty-six. Then again, the photograph had been taken last year when her hair was short. It could have grown; she might look different now.

They hadn't seen each other since Christmas. Realising how upsetting April found their meetings, Bernadette had suggested they should leave it for a while. But the regular phone calls, which they both looked forward to, had continued. They could still speak to each other; they could still be friends.

Bernadette was truly grateful for that.

'The dreaded Eleanor, you mean?' April hadn't met Eleanor, but she'd heard plenty about her. 'What did you say?'

'I told her I wasn't sure because my editor was juggling publishing schedules. Afterwards, I rang up the publishers and asked them when the new Antonia Kay novel would be out. Keeping my fingers crossed,' she went on drily, 'that they wouldn't say, "Oh I'm sorry, Antonia Kay's dead." '

April giggled. 'And is she?'

'No, thank God. Her next novel hits the bookshelves on August the tenth and it's called *A Frond of Honeysuckle*. Poor old Antonia,' Bernadette mused. 'I can't help thinking she might sell a few more copies if she could come up with snappier titles.'

'At least you can tell Eleanor. Just pray she doesn't ask to see an advance copy. Damn, is that the time?' April sounded distracted, 'I'm going to be late. I'm meeting someone for lunch at one.'

Meeting someone.

Her tone deceptively casual, Bernadette said, 'A man?'

'No, not a man. Just one of the girls from work. We're having lunch at Webster's, then going for a bit of a shop. There's this gorgeous dress in Principles I've had my eye on for weeks . . . you'd love it . . .'

'Off you go, then.' Bernadette stepped firmly into the breach, filling the awkward silence. 'Have a great afternoon and make sure you buy that dress. I'll speak to you next week.'

For a moment April sounded almost tearful. 'I will, Bernie. You look after yourself. Bye.'

Bernadette knew she was being weak, but she couldn't help herself. Anyway, where was the harm? She wanted to see April, that was all. And if April wasn't to be upset, she had to do it this way – without April seeing her.

Bernadette hovered inside the entrance to Habitat, across the road from Webster's. It was ten to one, which meant that April – who was far too courteous to keep a friend waiting – would be arriving any minute now.

'Can I help you, madam?' asked a friendly salesgirl.

'No thanks.' Bernadette shook her head. 'I'm just waiting for someone.'

And there, moments later, was April. Safely tucked out of sight, Bernadette watched her make her way along the street. Her shiny light-brown hair was still short, she was wearing a pale blue shirt and a white skirt, and her beautiful eyes were revealed as she approached the entrance to Webster's and took off her dark glasses.

In less than ten seconds it was all over. April had disappeared from sight. This was what I drove into Harleston for, thought Bernadette, and it was worth it.

She pulled a lace-edged handkerchief from her handbag and dabbed carefully at her brimming eyes.

The kind salesgirl, watching from the other side of the shop, came back over and said, 'Are you sure you're okay?'

'Yes, thank you.' Bernadette took a deep breath before putting the mascara-stained handkerchief away again. She mustered a faint smile. 'I'm fine.'

Dizzy was bored. There was nothing to do in this dump, and since it was still only the end of June he had weeks and weeks more of nothingness to endure before going back to school in September.

He wondered gloomily why villages had to be so dull. God, no amusement arcades, nothing. You couldn't even drink because everyone in the pub knew you were underage.

When the telephone rang for the seventh time that morning he answered it without getting his hopes up. This was just as well, since not one of his mates in London had bothered to get in touch, despite breezily assuring him they would. Dizzy hadn't rung them either, but that wasn't the point.

He picked up the receiver. 'No, she's out,' he said with a sigh. Even the receiver reeked of his sister's revolting perfume. 'Okay, yeah, I'll tell her.'

He hung up, feeling more depressed than ever. Yet another call for Savannah. How come, Dizzy thought resentfully, her friends hadn't forgotten *her*?

Jessie was upstairs putting the finishing touches to the spare bedroom when the door was nudged open and Dizzy appeared carrying two mugs.

'Brought you some tea,' he announced, slopping a fair amount on to the floorboards as he approached.

'Great.'

'Only because I'm bored.'

'Oh, right.' Jessie, who had been ragging bronze glaze over a matt bottle-green basecoat, flexed her fingers and stepped back to survey the results.

Dizzy handed her the mug and she flinched as droplets of hot tea spattered her bare feet. She flinched again when she drank the tea, which was too sweet, too milky and tasted of tomato ketchup.

Dizzy slumped down in the window seat and looked at the green and gold walls. 'It's not bad,' he said, sounding surprised. This was huge praise coming from him. 'Looks like crushed velvet. How'd you do that?'

Jessie held up the linen rag she'd been using. 'You just scrunch this up and press it into the wet glaze. Pretty, isn't it?'

'Yeah. Can I have a go?'

'Um . . .' Jessie hesitated. Ragging was like handwriting, it was personal. If Dizzy did a bit, the difference would show.

'Doesn't matter.' Dizzy lost interest as soon as he saw the look on Jessie's face. He was used to that look – it was the same one his chemistry teacher used when he offered to light the bunsen burners in the lab.

'I'm almost finished.' Jessie wiped her bronze-glazed fingers on her dungarees. 'This is the last room. I'm starting at Lorna's next week.' She looked regretful. Lorna wasn't interested in marbling and scumble glazes. 'Magnolia emulsion everywhere. Nothing like the stuff I've been doing here.'

'You're decorating the pub?'

'Not downstairs, just the living quarters.'

Dizzy perked right up. Moll lived over the pub. That meant Jessie would be decorating Moll's room, the one she actually slept in. 'I could give you a hand if you like,' he blurted out. Upstairs would mean the bathroom too, wouldn't it? Imagine decorating the room where Moll took her baths. Better still, imagine decorating the room while she was in it . . .

Taken aback by this astonishing show of enthusiasm, Jessie said, 'Well, I would speak to your dad. I had no idea you were interested in decorating, Dizzy.'

Dizzy, who wasn't, shrugged and said, 'It's okay.' He paused, then realised he should pretend to be. 'I mean, it's great.' He put on his interested face, like the one his dad used when he was being introduced to royalty. 'Uh . . . what made you go into this line of work?'

Jessie took another slurp of ketchupy tea and shuddered. 'It was an accident. I'd done all sorts of jobs, anything that fitted in with bringing up Oliver. Then I moved to Upper Sisley. Our cottage was a tip; it hadn't been decorated for fifty years, so to save money I did everything myself. One of the neighbours saw what I'd done and asked if I'd paint a couple of rooms in her house. After that, word got around. Not that I was particularly brilliant,' Jessie admitted, 'not then, anyway. It was just that the nearest painter and decorator lived miles away and people trusted me not to rip them off.'

'Right,' murmured Dizzy, his thoughts elsewhere. Maybe Moll preferred showers to baths.

'Well, I'd better get on.' This evidently wasn't interesting enough for Dizzy; she'd lost him. Jessie picked up her crumpled rag. 'Thanks for the tea.'

Still slumped in the window seat, Dizzy nodded vaguely. The next second a flash of scarlet in the distance caught his eye and his head whipped round so fast he almost knocked himself out on the glass.

It was Moll, in an amazing red dress, sauntering along the High Street with a bag slung over one shoulder and her hair tumbling down her back. Dizzy watched, hypnotised, as she approached the bus shelter and slowed down. He saw her take a pair of sunglasses and a red and white scarf out of her bag. She put on the glasses first, then dabbed at her perspiring breasts and began fanning herself with the scarf.

Only two buses a day passed through Upper Sisley; Dizzy knew that. This one, heading into town, and the one that brought you back again several hours later.

'Think I'll go into Harleston,' he muttered, scrambling

115

down from the window seat and sending Jessie's cans of paint flying. Luckily the lids were on.

'Catching the bus?' Jessie glanced at her watch. 'It takes ages. I'm driving in myself later – I could give you a lift if you like.'

Dizzy didn't care if the journey by bus took ages. He *wanted* it to take ages. Sounding oddly breathless he said, 'It's okay, I'd rather go now,' and raced out of the room.

Chapter 19

Standing less than six feet away from Moll, actually being able to see at close range the sheen of perspiration on her awesome chest, was a mind-blowing experience. Dizzy tried to look as if he wasn't looking, but it wasn't easy.

When he managed to smile at Moll, she smiled back. When he cleared his throat and said, 'Are you waiting for the bus too?' she smiled again.

Dizzy could have kicked himself. Not only a totally dumb question, but his voice had come out all weird and squeaky. God, what must Moll think of him now?

He looked away, embarrassed, and tried to comb his hair with his fingers, but basically it needed more than that.

Like him, it was badly in need of help.

'Know any good hairdressers?' Dizzy blurted out, inspired. 'That's why I'm going into Harleston, to get it cut.'

'There's a place in Church Street,' she said at last. 'Rococo. They're good.'

'Oh, right . . .'

'You could get it cheered up a bit while you're there. Have some highlights.'

She was still smiling at him. There were dimples in her cheeks. Dizzy wondered if she was serious, or if it was a wind-up. He cleared his throat again and said, 'You reckon?' The squeak had gone, thank God. 'Uh . . . what colour?'

Moll studied him, her head still tilted sideways, one hand idly rubbing her throat. Dizzy Gillespie had a teenage crush on her, that much was obvious, but would he really change his hair that drastically on her say-so?

Oh well, thought Moll, only one way to find out.

117

Her mouth twitched. Finally she said, 'I think blonds have more fun, don't you?'

That wasn't cruel, Moll reassured herself. Blond was okay. She could have said purple.

Dizzy still didn't know if she was having him on, but that was okay – he had plenty of time yet. They could sit together on the bus and talk about hair all the way to Harleston.

Oh, what wouldn't he give to stroke her throat like that . . .

'Here it comes,' said Moll as the bus rounded the corner of Waters Lane and trundled towards them.

Dizzy said, 'It's tiny. Not like the double-deckers we have in London.'

'Ah well, size isn't always everything.' Moll waved at the driver as the bus approached. Grinning back at her, he began to brake. Moments later a dark blue MG with its roof down screeched to a halt behind the bus and Doug Flynn, in the driver's seat, shouted, 'Hey, Moll! I'm on my way into work – I'll give you a lift.'

Dizzy almost yelled, 'Don't you DARE,' at Doug Flynn. Mercifully the words died in his throat. He watched, dry-mouthed, as Moll lifted up her full skirts and leapt joyfully into the passenger seat of the MG.

Why does stuff like this always happen to me? Dizzy thought miserably.

'Getting on?' sighed the bus driver, who was disappointed too.

'I don't know.'

'Son, do I look like a personal chauffeur? This is a bus, not an executive limo.'

In desperation Dizzy glanced at Moll.

'Sorry, it's only a two-seater,' Doug said, not sounding sorry at all.

'Can't wait to see the new hairdo,' Moll shouted, waving her fingers at him as Doug reversed rapidly then accelerated away in a cloud of dust.

'Look, are you catching this bus or what?' the bus driver demanded.

With Moll's last words echoing in his brain, Dizzy climbed aboard.

He was half-way to Harleston before he discovered he only had two pounds fifty in his pocket. Not even enough for a trim.

Toby, who had spent the last two hours sitting with his feet up in the conservatory reading scripts, watched unnoticed from the bedroom doorway as Jess, the tip of her pink tongue just visible between her teeth, eased the scrunched-up linen rag into the corner where the wall met the fireplace. He waited until she had finished before pushing the door shut behind him, the squeaking hinge letting her know he was there.

Jessie sat back on her heels, arched her shoulders and stretched. 'I'm getting old. Backache.'

Toby helped her up. 'It's looking great.'

'Thanks. And you look harassed.' Jessie gestured with amusement towards his ruffled blond hair.

Toby, who habitually ran his fingers through his hair when he had a decision to make, heaved a sigh. 'I've just read through two scripts. Which one do I go with – the low-budget British comedy drama or the big bucks American thriller?'

'Which one did you like most?'

'The thriller.'

'Which one pays best?'

'Are you serious?' Toby grinned. 'Moneywise, we're talking about the difference between a mile-long buffet on the QE2 and a chip butty at an all-night caff.'

'So why can't you decide?' said Jessie, who was rather fond of chip butties.

'The American film will be shot on location in LA and Acapulco. Six weeks minimum.'

'Oh you poor thing. It's a hard life.'

Toby held up his hands. 'Okay, I know. But six weeks is a long time to be away.'

'And you'll miss Deborah and the kids.' Jessie stopped teasing him. She nodded, realising what he was getting at.

'But couldn't they come out and visit you, stay for a couple of weeks? Or Deborah could fly out on her own . . . I could easily keep an eye on Dizzy and Savannah, it wouldn't be any trouble.'

Was it her imagination, or was this suggestion followed by a bit of a pregnant pause?

And why was Toby looking at her in that funny way?

He spoke at last. 'The trouble is, Deborah wouldn't be the one I'd miss.' Toby chose his words with care. 'The one I'd miss would be you.'

There, he'd said it.

Oh shit, thought Jessie. Her stomach lurched. He said it.

'Don't be stupid.'

'I'm not being stupid.'

'Look, you managed perfectly well for twenty-one years. Another six weeks is hardly going to make a difference.'

'I might have *managed* without you for twenty-one years,' Toby shook his head at her wilful stupidity, 'but I missed you too. All the time. And now we've—'

'Don't say it,' Jessie pleaded. 'Don't say any more.'

'It isn't easy, you know, feeling like this. I want to kiss you,' Toby said slowly, 'all the time. Every time I see you. It's driving me mad, Jess. This whole just-good-friends bit is doing my head in. And what I really can't figure out is if you feel the same way about me.'

Oh God, oh God. Jessie closed her eyes for a second and went to lean against the still-wet wall. With a yelp of horror she jerked herself away just in time.

Toby's gaze was still on her, unwavering.

'I'm doing my best not to,' Jessie told him, her voice unsteady.

'So you *do*—'

'Toby, it doesn't matter how we feel about each other. It just can't happen. You've got Deborah and the children. You have a fantastically happy marr— *mmmfph*!'

Toby's mouth came down on hers. His hands held each side of her face and as his tongue slid into her mouth she felt the frantic hammering of his heart against her chest.

It was blissful, totally blissful.

And utterly, utterly wrong.

'Now you've got paint all over you,' Jessie mumbled when she finally pulled away, clutching his arms for support. She gazed at the smudges of green and gold on the front of his white shirt, perfectly mirroring the ones on her T-shirt. Talk about a dead giveaway.

'Don't change the subject.'

'Oh Toby, for God's sake, we *have* to change the subject.'

'Okay. I love you.'

'That isn't changing—'

'Look, either you listen to me, hear what I have to say, or I kiss you again.' Toby's mouth twitched. 'So it's up to you. I'm easy.'

'You're married. And don't you dare try and make me laugh,' said Jessie. 'Because this isn't a laughing matter.'

'It's still there, though, isn't it? You do feel the same way about me.'

'Toby! You have to listen to me.' Jessie was beginning to feel like a student teacher struggling to keep an unruly class in check. 'Deborah is one of the nicest women I've ever met. I really like her. Even if I did want to—'

'Ah, but you *do* want to.'

He was grinning now. Jessie could have thumped him.

'But don't you *see*?' It came out as a wail. 'It only makes it *more* impossible.'

Toby held her hands and stroked her balled-up fists. He shook his head. 'What if I were to tell you my fantastically happy marriage isn't quite as fantastically happy as it looks?'

The moment the words were out he regretted them. The look on Jessie's face said it all. He felt her withdraw. He could have kicked himself. The timing was all wrong. If he'd told her some other day, told her when everything that had just happened hadn't just happened . . . well, it would have sounded more valid. She might even have believed him. Saying it now just made it sound like some desperate excuse, along the well-worn lines of My Wife Doesn't Understand Me, Since The Baby She's Not Interested In Me Any More, And We Haven't Had Sex For Years. The kind of persuasive patter used by casually unfaithful husbands the world over, when the women they pick up protest feebly that they don't sleep with married men.

'Well, yes . . .' Jessie drawled. 'I had noticed, of course. You two can't stand the sight of each other. It's blindingly obvious.'

This time the mockery was humourless. Toby knew he had blown it. Anything he said now would only make the situation worse.

Even if it was true.

Jessie stared hard out of the window. She felt sickened and horribly cheap. Until now she'd believed Toby when he'd told her he had never been unfaithful to Deborah. Now she realised how naive she had been.

That famous line of Mandy Rice-Davies's came to mind: 'Well, he would say that, wouldn't he?'

And Toby's an actor too. He can say anything – from 'The aliens have landed!' to 'And now I'm going to shoot you' – and make it sound totally believable. That's what he's good at. It's his job.

He probably sleeps with all his co-stars, Jessie thought. He could have notched up dozens of affairs behind Deborah's back. God, how could I have been so *stupid*?

'Jess, I'm sorry, I can't—'

'Time I got back to work.' Without looking at him, she reached for the linen cloth and carefully re-crumpled it into the palm of her hand. 'I want to be finished by tomorrow.'

What a complete and utter balls-up.

Since there was nothing more he could say, Toby quietly left the room.

Chapter 20

The next morning Toby – thank God – had driven up to London to meet with a producer friend of his. Deborah and Savannah had gone into Harleston. When Jessie heard a blood-curdling howl coming from the bathroom, her paint-brush flew out of her hand and clattered against the window-sill. For the last hour the house had been silent; she hadn't realised Dizzy was still here.

The bathroom door was shut.

'Dizzy? Are you all right?'

No reply.

Jessie knocked. 'Dizzy, it's me, Jessie. Say something.'

Nothing.

'Look, I know you're in there. If you don't answer me, I'm opening the door.'

'Don't.' Dizzy sounded anguished. 'Just don't, okay?'

Jessie leaned against the wall, relieved that at least Dizzy wasn't lying unconscious in the bath. But something was definitely still up.

'What's the matter?' she called out. 'Are you ill?'

'No.'

'What then?'

She heard a sigh, followed by a clunk as something fell over.

'Dizzy, have you fainted?'

'God you're nosy!' Dizzy sounded exasperated and dangerously close to tears. 'Can't you just leave me alone?'

'Not until you tell me what's wrong.'

Moments later, the door abruptly swung open.

'I thought you were dead,' said Jessie. 'You frightened the

life out of me. When I heard that yell, I thought you'd electrocuted yourself in the bath.'

'I wish I had,' Dizzy groaned, his voice muffled by the dark blue towel draped over his head.

Glancing behind him, Jessie saw what had made the hefty clunk just now. A bottle of Domestos with its top off had toppled into the bath. The contents were quietly dissolving the bath mat. The plughole was clogged with what looked like yellow teddy bear fur.

'Oh Dizzy, come here.' Gently she pulled the towel away to reveal the matted, orangey-yellow tufts of hair sticking out all over his head.

'I wish I was dead.' Furiously, Dizzy blinked back tears of shame.

'No you don't.' Jessie touched the still-damp hair, which had the texture of coconut matting. She wanted to hug him. 'We'll sort it out.'

'Nothing's going to sort this out.' His shoulders slumped. 'Christ, what a mess! I just . . . All I wanted was to be a bit blond.'

Jessie screwed the top back on the Domestos and ran the taps into the bath. The rubber mat was like chewing gum where the bleach had eaten into it.

'You're lucky it didn't burn your scalp. Neat bleach can take your skin off.'

'I didn't use neat bleach. I diluted it.' Dizzy was defensive. 'I'm not stupid, you know.'

'No, of course not.'

Jessie's tone was soothing, but he didn't even hear her. The mirror had claimed his attention once more.

'Oh hell. Oh bloody *bloody* hell!'

'I'll drive you into Harleston,' Jessie offered for the second time in two days. 'We'll find a brilliant hairdresser—'

'They'll laugh at me,' Dizzy wailed, on the verge of hysteria. 'I can't bear it, I won't go!' Knowing his luck he'd be bound to bump into his mother and sister. Or worse still, Moll.

'Okay. Hang on.' Jessie ran downstairs. When she reappeared two minutes later Dizzy was hunched, looking more suicidal than ever, on the side of the bath.

'All arranged.' She grabbed his arm and yanked him towards the door. 'Lili's doing it.'

'Lili who?'

'My friend Lili, Harriet's mother. Don't panic – Harriet won't be there,' Jessie pointed out before Dizzy could open his mouth to protest. 'She's at school.'

'Is her mother a proper hairdresser?' He looked terrified.

'Well, she's a qualified hedge-trimmer, but it's all pretty much the same thing, isn't it?' said Jessie. She broke into a grin and pushed Dizzy in the direction of the stairs. 'Joke.'

'This is great,' Jessie announced, driving out through the gates of Sisley House, turning right along Compass Lane and waving cheerily as she passed old Cecil Barker walking his dogs. 'I feel like the SAS. Keep your head down and don't move a muscle until I tell you.'

'This blanket stinks of turps,' Dizzy grumbled.

'Stay under it. Here's Lili's nightmare of a mother-in-law coming out of the shop. Morning, Eleanor!' Jessie shouted, beaming through the open window as she rounded the left-hand bend and headed up the High Street.

'Are we there?' said Dizzy moments later when the car stopped.

'Just opening the gate so I can park on the drive,' Jessie explained. 'Then you'll be able to sneak in the back door. Oh look, there's Moll. Hi, Moll! Gorgeous day!'

'Right, Jess said it was an emergency,' said Lili, 'so take off your hood and let's have a look. Will, leave those dog biscuits alone.'

'I'll look after Will and Freya, keep them occupied.' Jessie scooped both children into her arms and whisked them outside before they could laugh.

Miserably, without much hope that anything could be done, Dizzy removed his hood.

Lili examined the evidence. 'The hair's breaking off. We'll have to cut it short.'

'I know. I don't care about that.' He did, but even he

could see he didn't have much choice. 'It's just the colour.'

'What I can do,' said Lili, thoughtfully investigating the tangled mess, 'is restore the natural pigments. Get it back, more or less, to your own colour. It isn't easy, and it'll take a while—'

'When will Harriet be back?'

'Not for ages. She's gone to a tennis tournament.'

For the first time, the muscles in Dizzy's shoulders unclenched. He even managed a brief smile. 'Okay. Thanks.'

'Any danger of anything to eat?' said Michael, coming into the kitchen two hours later.

'Sorry, darling, I've been a bit tied up. There's some cold chicken in the fridge.' Lili gestured vaguely with plastic-gloved hands stained red like a surgeon's. 'This is Dizzy, by the way. Dizzy, this is my husband Michael.'

'He won't tell anyone will he?' Dizzy turned to her in anguish when Michael had gone.

Lili, patting his skinny shoulder, said, 'Don't worry, I'll make sure he doesn't.'

When Hugh and Felicity arrived at five o'clock on the dot they found the back door open and Lili carefully cutting the hair of a nervous-looking teenage boy.

'Goodness, aren't you busy?' Felicity announced. 'Doing two jobs at once.' Her perfectly made-up eyes darted around the kitchen. 'Although I can't actually see Freya anywhere . . .'

'Sorry, I usually keep the hairdressing to the evenings.' Lili felt herself going red. 'But this was such an emergency—'

'Thanks a lot,' Dizzy muttered, going even redder.

'—And Freya's fine, really she is. She's playing outside with Will and Jess—'

'Of course. There she is,' Felicity cut in as the three of them burst out of the Wendy house. 'I didn't realise your friend Jessie was a qualified child-minder too.'

★ ★ ★

126

'She disapproves of me so much,' Lili fretted over dinner later that evening. 'She picks up on every tiny thing. Honestly, she's worse than your mother.'

Michael's mouth tightened. He didn't mind criticising his own mother but he wasn't amused when someone else tried it, particularly when that person was Lili. 'My mother does a great deal for you,' he announced coolly. He knew this because Eleanor had told him so only yesterday. 'You should be grateful for her help.'

'Dad, I need new trainers,' said Harriet. 'My old ones are too small.'

'Now who did I see wearing a pair of trainers with lights in the soles?' Michael looked thoughtful. 'Every time he tapped his foot, the lights flashed. Oh right, got it now – the lad who was here this afternoon.'

Lili stared at him and slowly shook her head.

Harriet frowned. There was only one person in the village with that kind of trainers. 'Dizzy Gillespie? Is that who you mean, Dad?' Her eyes widened in astonishment. 'What was *he* doing here?'

Lili was still giving him one of her iciest looks – which, being Lili, wasn't actually that icy. Michael, who hadn't forgiven her yet for the anti-Eleanor remark, decided he didn't much care for the silent threat, however feeble.

'Dizzy. That's it, that was his name. Your mother was doing something drastic to his hair.'

Harriet swivelled round to Lili. 'Mum?'

'Michael,' Lili warned, 'I told you not to—'

'Tipped a bottle of Domestos over his head, apparently.' Michael smiled, taking great pleasure in watching the dismay on Lili's face. That, he thought with satisfaction, would teach her to have a dig at Mother.

'Domestos!' Harriet squealed, almost falling off her chair. 'What colour did his hair go?'

'According to your mother, something pretty similar to Colman's Mustard. The bits that were left, that is. Most of it,' Michael concluded with malicious relish, 'shrivelled up and dropped off.'

★ ★ ★

Dizzy had to dawdle casually past the Seven Bells half a dozen times before Moll emerged to clear up the accumulation of empty glasses littering the tables outside the pub.

She was wearing an almost transparent emerald green shirt over a red boob tube. A lacy black bra strap was sliding off one shoulder. Dizzy watched longingly as she leaned across one of the tables, her heavenly breasts – one slightly lower than the other – almost brushing the weather-beaten surface. Oh lucky, lucky table . . .

'Hi,' he said, when Moll had straightened up again.

She turned, her arms full of stacked-up glasses clutched to her chest.

'Well well, look at you.' Moll smiled her slow, appraising, come-to-bed smile. 'Decided to give the highlights a miss then? Went for the snip instead.'

'The snip' was what Dizzy's mother called vasectomies. Thinking of vasectomies made Dizzy think of sex even more than he was thinking of it already. His ears, long hidden from public view but now hopelessly exposed, grew hot. He prayed they weren't glowing as neon-red as he thought they were.

'Thought it was time for a change.' Bravely he ignored his flaming ears.

'Very smart. Can't beat a nice short-back-and-sides.' Still smiling to herself, Moll began to move towards the pub.

Desperate to keep the conversational ball rolling, Dizzy blurted out, 'That's a nice top. Is it new? Did you buy it this afternoon in Harleston?'

Moll glanced down at the gauzy green shirt, frayed at the neckline and damp where the dregs from one of the beer mugs had spilled over. 'This old thing? God no, it's ancient.' She hauled the lacy black bra strap back on to her shoulder and proudly gave it a twang. 'New bra, though.'

Dizzy couldn't speak. His tongue had glued itself to the roof of his mouth.

'Well, I'd better get back inside,' said Moll, 'or Lorna'll think I've done a bunk with one of her precious customers.'

'Is that doctor bloke . . . the one who gave you the lift into town . . . is he your boyfriend?' Dizzy rushed the words out before his courage failed.

'What, Doug?' Dimpling, Moll shook her head. 'He's a good friend, that's all. The kind who'll stop and give you a lift when you need one. That's what having friends is all about, isn't it, sweetpea?'

What was she implying? Was there some hidden agenda here? Assuming his man-of-the-world stance, pretending he knew exactly what she meant, Dizzy peeled his tongue unstuck again and stammered, 'I s-suppose so.'

'No suppose about it.' Moll's cat-like eyes glittered with amusement. 'I make sure I look after my friends.' As she disappeared through the doorway she added lightly over her shoulder, 'That way, everybody's happy. I do favours for them, they do favours for me.'

Chapter 21

Accident and Emergency at Harleston General had been frantically busy all day. Doug Flynn, who was due off at six, had dealt with a constant stream of casualties ranging from a severed leg to a lost-behind-the-eye contact lens. Fifteen cases of heat-stroke, two dog bites and a functional hemiparesis later – not to mention a paralytic fourteen-year-old who had thrown up in truly spectacular fashion in the waiting room – he was ready for a drink of his own. Unlike the teenager, however, he wouldn't be downing eighteen pints of lager and black.

At four o'clock Doug stuck his head around the door of the coffee room. 'Who's for a session at the Antelope later? Susie? James? Esther, you'll definitely come.'

'Promises, promises.' Esther, one of the SRNs, giggled.

James, who was a senior charge nurse, looked regretful. 'I've got to pick the kids up.'

'April,' said Doug, clasping the receptionist's arm as she tried to slip past him. 'How about you?'

April blushed. Doug Flynn had never invited her along before; in fact he seldom paid her much attention at all. She knew he was only asking her now to make up the numbers. 'Well, thanks . . . but I don't think I—'

'No excuses.' Dimly aware that she was divorced and not having much of a time of it, Doug flashed her a reassuring grin. April was totally not his type but even he was capable of the occasional altruistic gesture. 'Do you good to get out for a bit. And don't worry about transport,' he added casually, 'I'll give you a lift.'

By six o'clock Doug had managed to rustle up several

more willing contenders. In the event there were eight of them, in three cars, travelling in convoy to the Antelope, a pretty riverside pub on the outskirts of Harleston.

The top was down on Doug's dark-blue MG. April, touched that he hadn't forgotten her, was nevertheless thankful the journey was a short one. She'd always wanted to be driven in an open-topped sports car with the wind blowing through her hair. The trouble was, now it was actually happening, she was terrified to open her mouth in case she swallowed a wasp.

The Antelope heaved with after-work drinkers. As they made their way up to the bar, April's courage began to falter. She knew she should be making an effort to get out more, but staying at home was so much easier, so much less hassle. Going out, on the other hand, forcing herself to socialise, attempting to rebuild her life . . . Heavens, just the thought of it was enough to bring on a panic attack.

'What would you like?' said Doug, effortlessly attracting the attention of the prettiest barmaid.

'Oh, um, an orange juice? Hang on, let me—'

'Boring,' said Doug. 'Have a glass of wine. Don't worry,' he added, gently pushing April's purse away, 'I'm getting these.'

April was under no illusions, she knew he was just being kind. With his dauntingly glamorous good looks, Doug Flynn could have any woman he wanted and, from what she could gather, frequently did. The last person he would be interested in was someone as mousy as her.

Still, he had bought her a drink, and horribly out of practice though she might be, even April knew this meant she now had to engage in a spot of polite conversation in return.

'Did Esther tell you, the chap who fell off his ladder yesterday sent us a basket of fruit this afternoon?' Oh *well done*, April. Riveting stuff. Battling on in desperation, she said, 'He owns a chain of greengrocers, apparently. I don't know how he'll manage to run them with both arms in plaster.'

'Let's not talk about work,' said Doug.

'Oh, right.'

'Why don't you tell me about you?'

'N-nothing to tell,' April stammered, hopelessly unprepared for all this attention.

'Did I hear Susie mention you were divorced?'

'Well . . . yes.'

'Kids?'

'No.'

'Met anyone else yet?'

'No.'

'Sorry, I know this sounds like an interrogation.' Doug's smile was the one he used when he was putting a nervous patient at ease. 'It really isn't meant to. I'm just curious. You don't have to answer if you don't want to.'

'That's okay.' April took a reassuring gulp of icy white wine. If she was ever going to rejoin the rest of the world she'd have to get used to questions like these. 'I don't mind. My husband and I separated three years ago. Now we're divorced. I live in a one-bedroomed flat on the other side of Harleston. I'm afraid I've become a bit of a hermit.'

Doug's dark eyes, trained on hers, were mesmerising. 'Why did you split up?'

Not that mesmerising.

'Just didn't work out,' said April, her fingers tightening around the stem of the glass.

Doug nodded and wisely didn't press her for details. 'These things happen,' he observed lightly. 'Sitting at home on your own isn't going to help much, though.'

'I know, I know. It's just hard to make the—'

'Hello there,' said a male voice inches from April's right ear, and she jerked round in astonishment only to feel a complete idiot when she realised the owner of the voice hadn't been saying hello to her.

'Hi,' Doug replied easily, recognising Michael Ferguson, husband of pretty, overweight Lili from the village. Michael wasn't around much – he worked abroad for months on end, something to do with computers – but they saw each other from time to time, chiefly in the bar of the Seven Bells.

'Busy here,' Michael commented, taking his change from

the barmaid and easing his pint of lager through the crush of bodies. He smiled briefly at April as he began to move away. 'Sorry, didn't mean to make you jump just now.'

April went pink, only thankful she hadn't made an even greater fool of herself and said hello back.

'Who's he – a friend of yours?' she asked Doug when the man was out of earshot, but Doug was busy peering over heads searching for the rest of their party.

'Not a friend, just someone I vaguely know to say hello to.' Without bothering to elaborate he added with some relief, 'There are the others, outside on the terrace. Let's join them.'

April left the Antelope at eight thirty, having assured Doug – who clearly didn't want to leave yet – that she was fine, she could catch the bus home, there was one that ran past the Antelope practically all the way to her front door.

Exhilarated by the success of her first proper social outing in over a year, she half-smiled at the man who had earlier spoken to Doug as she made her way towards the exit. Then, because three glasses of wine and a rattling bus journey could be uncomfortable, she veered left and nipped into the ladies' loo.

Above the mirror in the cloakroom someone had stuck a poster advertising 'Singles Nite at the Antelope'. It was held each Wednesday, April read, admission was free and everyone who arrived before nine o'clock received a complimentary drink.

A plump girl emerged from one of the cubicles tucking her shirt into her jeans. She saw April looking at the poster. 'You should come along,' she announced. 'Everyone's dead friendly and there's always loads of blokes.'

Taken aback by the girl's up-front approach, April said, 'Oh, I don't know . . .'

'Go on, live a little!' The girl washed her hands, dried them on her jeans and began re-doing her lipstick. 'No need to feel awkward, we're all in the same boat.' She shrugged cheerfully at April's reflection in the mirror. 'What have you got to lose anyway? It's just a laugh.'

Chapter 22

The following afternoon, as soon as Hugh and Felicity had picked up Freya, Lili spruced up Will and Lottie and took them to stay with Eleanor for a couple of hours.

Bernadette Thomas was tending the hollyhocks in her front garden. She waved at Will, who had been bawling 'HELLO! HELLO!' at her all the way along Waters Lane and clearly had no intention of stopping until he got a reply.

'Hello.' Bernadette turned to Lottie. 'That's a pretty dress. Have you come to visit Grandma?'

'Mum, that's the lady who smells.'

'*Nice*, Lottie. That's the lady who smells *nice*.' Lili pulled an apologetic face at Bernadette, who wore Arpège and always smelled wonderful.

'Anyway,' Lottie told Bernadette with an air of lofty disdain, 'she isn't your Grandma, she's *our* Grandma.'

'Kids,' Lili sighed, shaking her head. 'Couldn't you just chuck them in a sound-proof cupboard and leave them there for a fortnight?'

'Don't worry about it.' Bernadette smiled reassuringly and pushed a loose strand of hair behind one ear. In the sunlight, a pretty opal and sapphire ring glinted on her right hand.

'I'm dropping them off for a couple of hours,' Lili explained. 'Our dog's got a sore paw so I'm taking him into Harleston. Drew Darcy's going to have a look at him. Lottie, don't take your shoes off, your feet will get filthy.'

Lottie looked mutinous. 'Don't want to wear shoes.'

'Yes, well, Grandma likes you to wear them.' Lili exchanged a glance with Bernadette. 'She says only tinkers' children run around barefoot.'

'Better keep them on.' Bernadette nodded kindly at Lottie. 'Don't want to upset your Grandma.'

As their eyes met again, Lili and Bernadette silently sympathised with each other, acknowledging the respective difficulties of being Eleanor Ferguson's daughter-in-law and next-door neighbour.

'Do you do Postman Pat?' Lottie demanded suddenly.

Confused, Bernadette said, 'Excuse me?'

'Grandma said you write books. Do you write Postman Pat stories?'

'Er . . . no. Sorry.'

'That's all right, I just wondered. Anyway,' Lottie announced, 'you only have to say excuse me if you do a burp or a—'

'I read the novel you lent Eleanor.' Lili dived in hastily before she could finish; bodily functions were currently Lottie's big interest. 'I know you don't want the whole village knowing about your work, but she just happened to mention to us that you wrote novels.'

Bernadette sounded faintly amused. 'You mean the whole village doesn't know?'

'Oh I'm sure she wouldn't tell anyone else.' Mentally Lili crossed her fingers. 'But I really enjoyed your book.' Damn – she couldn't remember the title. 'I thought it was brilliant.'

This was another fib; she'd found the book soporific, genteel, and extremely average, but at least it hadn't had any lesbians in it. Anyway, Lili reasoned, when you were telling an author you'd read one of their books you could hardly say you'd found it average, could you?

Unless of course you were Eleanor.

Bernadette smiled, but rather embarrassingly looked as if she didn't believe her. 'Thank you.'

'When's the next one out?' Lili was floundering, but she knew it was a good question to ask.

'September. The fourth. It's called . . . um, *A Frond of Honeysuckle*.'

Good grief.

'Well, I'll definitely buy it.'

135

'There's Grandma!' Lottie yelled as the front door opened. Running up the path, she hurled herself into Eleanor's outstretched arms.

Lili scooped Will up on to her hip and smiled at Bernadette as she followed Lottie into the house.

'Bye. See you again.'

'I've been watching from the bedroom window.' Eleanor's tone was frosty. 'You were very friendly, chatting away like that, laughing together . . .'

Puzzled by her evident disapproval, Lili said, 'She seems nice.'

'I daresay she does. But you should be careful, Lili. Too much fraternising . . . well, it could be construed as encouragement.'

'Encouragement?' A couple of seconds later Lili figured out what Eleanor was getting at. 'Oh! You mean she might think I'm a—'

'You know perfectly well what I mean, no need to spell it out.' Eleanor's mouth looked like a purse with the drawstring pulled tight. She shepherded Lottie through to the kitchen. 'And how you can let this child run around without shoes on is beyond me, Lili. She looks like a tinker's child. The next thing you know she'll step on a piece of glass and get blood poisoning.' She shook her head in sorrowful, told-you-so fashion. 'Mark my words, they'll end up having to amputate her leg.'

'Lili, come on in. How nice to see you.'

Drew was touched that Lili had made an appointment and taken the trouble to drive over to the surgery. Just as Doug was plagued by people accosting him at parties with, 'You're a doctor, aren't you? What d'you think could be wrong with my shoulder?' so he and Jamie were used to people in the village bringing their pets along to Keeper's Cottage and explaining that they were sure it wasn't serious, but could Drew or Jamie just take a quick look . . .?

Ironically, Lili Ferguson was one of the very few people he wouldn't have minded seeing on his doorstep. Entertained by her efforts to persuade Blitz to sit on the examination table,

Drew was so pleased to see her he forgot he was supposed to be keeping his feet out of sight.

'I heard him give a yelp in the garden this morning, as if he'd hurt himself,' Lili explained. 'And now he's limping. Something's wrong but I can't see what. Did you know you're wearing odd shoes?'

She flipped her shaggy light-brown hair away from her face and held Blitz still while Drew examined the sore paw.

'I was in a hurry, had to take my car to the garage. I only found out at lunchtime why everyone was smirking at me.' He sounded resigned. 'Our receptionist ran a sweepstake all morning, taking bets on when I'd cotton on.'

'Poor you.' Lili giggled. 'Is the car all right, at least?'

Drew searched in a drawer for a magnifying glass. 'The mechanical equivalent of going to the doctor with a dizzy spell and finding out you've got a brain tumour the size of a turnip. I only took the damn thing in for a service.' He looked rueful. 'From what I could make out when I rang the garage just now, they're about to give it the last rites.'

'Oh dear, poor you *and* poor car,' said Lili. She watched him study Blitz's paw through the magnifying glass. 'How will you manage?'

Drew had located the problem, a deeply embedded thorn. He reached for the fine tweezers.

'They're lending me a replacement car, but not until tomorrow. I told our receptionist she can have the pleasure of driving me home, to make up for taking the piss out of me all morning.'

'Does she live near us?'

'Nope, it's miles out of her way,' Drew announced with relish.

'Well that's silly. I can give you a lift home,' said Lili.

With a deft movement Drew tweezered the thorn out of Blitz's paw. 'There, done.'

'Drew, tell her she doesn't have to do it.'

'Now where's the fun in that?' His grin was unrepentant. 'Anyway, I won't finish before seven.'

'It's okay, darling, all over now.' Lili gave Blitz a reassuring hug. 'I mean it, Drew. Look, it's six fifteen already. I'll take Blitz for a run in Canford Park. By the time I get back you'll be ready to go.'

Blitz, evidently having forgiven Drew for attacking him with a pair of tweezers, was now vigorously licking his hand.

'Go on then, I always was a sucker for a wet tongue. Oh God,' Drew groaned, clapping his hand to his forehead and going hot and cold all over, 'I can't believe I just said that.'

'I'm glad you did.' Lili smiled her dimpliest smile at poor, perspiring Drew. 'It's so lovely to know that accidentally coming out with something daft happens to other people too.'

'It must be great having your husband home.' Drew held Blitz on his lap in the passenger seat as Lili tried hard not to crunch gears. She never did as a rule, but the minute any man climbed into her car she became hopelessly self-conscious. Probably because Michael had spent the last twenty years moaning in long-suffering fashion, 'And for God's sake don't crunch the gears.'

'I don't know about great. It takes a bit of getting used to,' she admitted. 'You get yourself into a routine, then all of a sudden there's this huge disruption. Of course it isn't easy for Michael either,' Lili went on hastily, in case she sounded disloyal. 'After a week or two the novelty of being home wears off. He gets bored, he feels in the way, we both start getting irritable . . . Ah well, thank goodness for snooker.' Lili sounded rueful. 'That's where he is this evening, at the Take A Cue club in Harleston.' She accelerated violently through an orange light because Michael always bawled 'GO GO GO!' at her like a demented cox. 'At least it keeps him out of mischief.'

'Oh dear. And there was me thinking you were one of the blissfully-married brigade.'

Lili couldn't imagine what was happening to her. She didn't normally go around blurting out details of her private life to strange men.

Except Drew wasn't strange. Well, not if you didn't count the odd shoes. And he'd been in a rush, Lili thought with a surge of protectiveness. They weren't really his fault.

138

'I wouldn't call us blissful.' She thought back to this afternoon's argument, triggered off by Blitz shredding her entire stock of Pampers. This had prompted a furious 'that bloody dog' reaction from Michael, swiftly compounded when Lili had asked him to pick up a couple more packs of nappies before disappearing off to the snooker club. 'Oh, we muddle along, but we're no Hugo and Felicity.' She glanced sideways at Drew. 'If it's blissful you're after, they're your couple.'

Drew laughed. 'We call them the Thunderbirds. Perfect cars, perfect clothes, perfect hair. I wonder if they have perfect sex?'

'Oh, definitely. Orgasms on tap, multiple *and* simultaneous.'

They reached Upper Sisley. As she approached the brow of Compass Hill, Lili braked and nodded towards Treetops, the Seymours' splendid house, ahead of them on the right. Their garden was immaculate, the gravel freshly raked, and even their cars were parked with geometric precision on the driveway.

'I'm only saying it because I'm jealous,' she admitted. 'Hugh and Felicity are devoted to each other. It must be wonderful to feel like that. I mean, how many couples are truly happy these days? One in a hundred? One in a thousand?'

'Now I'm depressed,' said Drew. 'If things are that bad, I may as well give up now.' He gave Blitz's arched neck an affectionate rub. 'Settle for a dog instead.'

Lili pulled up outside Keeper's Cottage, whose garden was in no danger whatsoever of being described as immaculate. Through the wide-open sitting-room window came the sound of Jamie bawling tunelessly along to Blur.

Blitz, recognising the song from Harriet's CD, pricked up his ears and began to whimper with excitement.

'Just so long as it's a faithful dog,' said Lili.

'Come in for a drink?' Drew offered casually.

'Better not.' She checked her watch with regret. 'Eleanor's expecting me.'

'Maybe some other time then.' Something about the way

Lili's cheeks dimpled when she smiled was getting to Drew. Without stopping to think he leaned across and landed a brief kiss on the nearest dimple. 'Thanks for the lift.'

'I could drive you in tomorrow morning,' said Lili. Good grief, what's going on here? Is this how it feels to be possessed – when you open your mouth and words you never meant to say come tumbling out?

'That's really kind, but I couldn't let you. It's too far . . .' Drew felt himself go hot again. There was definitely something happening and he wasn't sure he liked it. Or rather he liked the feelings but he wasn't at all sure Lili Ferguson was the right person to be causing them.

'It's no trouble, honestly.' Lili's eyes were wide, her expression earnest. 'I need to go to the supermarket anyway for nappies.'

Nappies.

The dreaded N-word. As if I needed reminding, thought Drew, exasperated because this wasn't supposed to be happening to him. Let's face it, he was youngish, free and single, and – in his own way – a reasonably eligible bloke. What was more, he had a picture fixed in his mind of his ideal woman – the one he would one day meet and fall in love with – and she was young, blonde and busty, the kind of girl who wouldn't look out of place on Page 3 of the *Sun*.

'What time do you have to be at the surgery?'

'Eight thirty.'

'That's fine. I don't have Freya tomorrow anyway.' Lili smiled across at him. 'Michael can look after the kids and I'll pick you up at eight.'

'Well, if you're sure.' Drew felt his insides beginning to churn. God, how ridiculous! He was getting butterflies already. Twenty-nine years old and acting like a teenager on a first date.

This was wrong, all wrong. It didn't fit in with his plans at all.

The woman of his dreams definitely wasn't supposed to be seven years older than him with floppy light-brown hair, a rounded figure, three noisy children and an irritable husband to boot.

Chapter 23

'For you,' said Oliver, handing Jessie the phone. He spent the next five minutes listening to her chattering happily to Jonathan, a divorced sculptor from Cheltenham, of whom she had seen a fair bit last year. But chatting, it seemed, was as far as it went nowadays. Before long, Oliver heard Jessie making her usual feeble excuses.

Sometimes he despaired of his mother; at this rate she was never going to settle down with a man.

'He was asking you out, wasn't he?' he said when she had hung up. 'You like him, you get on well together . . . so why don't you go?'

Jessie ruffled his blond hair as she wandered through to the kitchen in search of food. 'Can't be bothered.' She shrugged; it was the truth. 'Fancied a night in, just me and a video and a condensed milk sandwich.' Taking the tin out of the fridge she waved it enticingly at Oliver. 'Want one?'

'You are gross.'

This was a term he had picked up from Savannah. Having got by without it for so many years, it had recently begun to feature heavily in Oliver's conversation. Everything from advocaat to zebra print wallpaper was gross.

Smiling to herself, Jessie grabbed a knife and began energetically slicing bread. 'Anyway, you turn girls down. I've heard you do it a million times.'

'That's different. I'm not a middle-aged spinster,' said Oliver.

Jessie was only briefly tempted to pour condensed milk over his head; that would be a waste.

'What about the girl from Bath, the pretty redhead?' she

persisted. 'I thought you were keen on her. Now you won't even return her calls.'

It was Oliver's turn to shrug and gaze out of the window. Across the village green, Drew Darcy was climbing out of Lili Ferguson's filthy red Volvo. 'I got bored.'

As she was putting the tin back in the fridge, Jessie spotted a bottle of already opened wine, rough but just about drinkable. She sloshed some into a glass and carried her sandwich back through to the living room.

'What are you looking at?'

'Your friend Lili, trying to pull away in third gear. Ha, now she's stalled.' He shook his head in amusement. 'She's a terrible driver.'

'Don't you have to be at work by seven thirty?' said Jessie.

'Yes.'

'It's seven thirty.'

'Hell, my watch must've stopped—' Oliver raced upstairs to shower and change.

Jessie was licking her fingers, watching *EastEnders* and making the discovery that cheap white wine and condensed milk sandwiches didn't go, when the doorbell went.

Toby stood on the doorstep, looking dauntingly handsome in a dark blue shirt and white jeans. His blond hair lifted in the breeze as he took off his dark glasses, fixing Jessie with those famous – and even more daunting – navy blue eyes.

'I've brought the rest of your money. I thought you'd prefer cash.'

He was holding a manila envelope, but not offering it to her.

'Cash or cheque, either's fine. I do pay tax on my earnings.' Meaningfully Jessie added, 'I'm not a cheat.'

'Look, are you going to invite me in?' Toby lowered his voice. 'Jess, we need to talk.'

At that moment Oliver clattered down the stairs, combing his wet hair with one hand and carrying his shoes in the other. He panted, 'Oh, hi – I'm late for work.'

'I'm in a hurry too,' Jessie told Toby. 'I'm going out.'

Oliver was in the middle of pulling his shoes on. He

142

stopped and stared up at her. 'Who with?'

'Jonathan.'

'You turned him down!'

'He rang back while you were in the shower,' Jessie lied. 'He's picking me up at eight o'clock.' She whisked the envelope from Toby's grasp, tore it open and flipped briefly through the wad of twenty-pound notes. 'That's fine. Thanks very much. Now if you'll excuse me, I have to change.'

From upstairs, she heard Toby and Oliver leaving together. Oliver was saying, 'Don't take any notice of Mum, she's been in a funny mood for the last couple of days.'

Huh, thought Jessie, I wonder why.

'Who's this chap then?' said Toby. 'This Jonathan?'

'Oh, he's okay. Mad about Mum.' Oliver sounded amused. 'Just goes to show there's no accounting for taste. Coming over for a drink later?'

'Could do,' said Toby.

Jessie had forgotten Jonathan's number. She had to look it up. Absence makes the heart forgetful . . .

'It's me. I'm sorry, can I change my mind?'

'About what?'

'I'd really like to see you tonight.'

'Call that a grovel?' said Jonathan.

'I'd really really *really* like to see you tonight.'

'What a shame, you're too late,' Jonathan sighed. 'I've made other plans.'

'You haven't!'

'Okay, I haven't. What time do you want me to pick you up?'

This wasn't as wholly unselfish as it sounded. Jonathan, a classic car enthusiast, couldn't bear to be driven anywhere in anything remotely ordinary. If he wasn't behind the wheel of his beloved yellow Lagonda he didn't see the point in going out.

'Eight o'clock?' said Jessie.

'It's ten to eight now,' Jonathan protested. 'Give me a break.'

'Okay, half past.'

This was definitely what she needed, Jessie realised later that evening in The Seven Bells. A partner. An Other Half. Someone whose name people could link with hers so that whenever they were thinking of having a party they could happily invite not just Jessie-on-her-own, but Jessie-and-Thing.

And the next time some philandering married man made a pass at her he wouldn't be able to insinuate that she should be grateful for the attention, what with her being so . . . well, so embarrassingly *single*.

It was just a shame there wasn't some magic switch she could flick that would make her suddenly fancy Jonathan.

'Why does Oliver think I phoned you twice this evening and *begged* you to come out with me?'

'Probably because I told him you had.'

Jonathan was nothing if not easygoing. He merely raised a quizzical eyebrow. 'Am I allowed to ask why?'

'It's complicated,' Jessie said with a sigh.

'Could it have anything to do with that piece in the *Daily Mail* last week?'

Jessie, her eyes bright, rattled the ice cubes around her empty glass like dice. 'Why should it be anything to do with that?'

'Oh, no reason. I just wondered why we were sitting over *here* and Toby Gillespie was standing at the bar over *there*,' Jonathan remarked mildly. 'I also can't help noticing the way he keeps looking at me. As if he'd quite like to hit me over the head with a shovel.'

Jessie trusted Jonathan, but she wasn't sure she trusted him one hundred per cent. 'Don't be daft. He's happily married.'

Jonathan shrugged. 'I'm just telling you what I see.'

'Shall we go?' said Jessie. It was nine o'clock, she was starving and she had made her point.

Jonathan smiled slightly. So he was right. Poor Jess, what kind of a mess had she got herself into now?

'Would you like me to put my arm around you as we leave?' he offered, since she had clearly dragged him along for a reason.

Jessie shot him a look of gratitude. 'Yes, please.'

'So Jess and Jonathan are back together,' Lorna Blake observed, wiping the bar with such vigour she almost sent Toby's tumbler of Glenfiddich flying.

'Looks like it.' Oliver listened to the throaty roar of Jonathan's Lagonda as it pulled out of the car park. 'That could be the sound of my future stepfather.' He grinned at Savannah. 'Except he'd never let me borrow his precious car.'

'I'll have another Scotch,' said Toby.

Lorna gave him a pointed look. 'Please.'

'Sorry.' He exaggerated the word. '*Please.*'

'You've had loads, Dad,' Savannah said with a frown.

A middle-aged couple who had been murmuring encouragement to each other now approached the bar.

'Toby Gillespie? We're great fans of yours,' gushed the woman, thrusting a beer mat under his nose. 'Could we have your autograph?'

'Please,' prompted Toby.

The woman blushed all the way to her frizzy grey roots.

Toby shook his head. 'No.'

'Dad!' exclaimed Savannah.

'I don't want to.'

'I'm really sorry.' Savannah turned to the couple. 'He's had a bit of a bad day.'

'One of his friends has died,' Oliver joined in. 'A dear old actor friend—'

'Oh you poor thing.' The woman touched Toby's arm. 'How horrid for you. Who was it? Anyone we'd know?'

'He wasn't famous.' Oliver's tone was sombre. 'They were just very close.' Glimpsing the look of astonishment in the woman's eye, he hastily added, 'Not that kind of close.'

Toby still wasn't saying anything.

'We're sorry to have disturbed you.' Crestfallen, the woman and her husband backed away. The next minute, their drinks still unfinished, they had left the pub.

'Well that was bloody rude,' snapped Lorna.

'Look, people have been coming up to me asking for my autograph for the last twenty years.' Toby wasn't in the mood to defend himself. 'This is the first time I've ever said no.'

'It is, it is,' said Savannah loyally.

'Once in twenty years. That's not a bad record, is it?'

'I don't know,' said Lorna Blake, nodding in the direction of the door. 'Ask the couple who just left.'

Guilt began to kick in. Defensively Toby said, 'They'll survive.'

'Of course they will. Don't you worry about them,' Lorna said coldly. 'They're not important, are they? You're the one that matters.' As she turned away to serve another customer she added, 'So long as you feel good about yourself, that's what counts.'

'Oh shit,' sighed Toby, finishing his drink and sliding off his stool. 'Goodnight.'

'Did you see Dad go home?' Savannah asked when Moll came back in weighed down with empties.

'He's still outside. Breathe in.' As Moll squeezed past Oliver, she wiggled her hips teasingly against his jean-clad bottom. She winked at Savannah. 'I can't resist this boy's body. Couldn't you just see him getting his kit off in one of those Levi's ads?'

'What's he doing outside?' Oliver looked worried.

'Sitting at one of the tables talking to some middle-aged couple.'

'Saying what to them?'

'What is this – twenty questions?' Wondering why Oliver should be so concerned, Moll gave him a playful dig in the ribs. 'The usual stuff, that's all. I had to lend him my pen so he could give them an autograph. Now are you going to stack these glasses in the dishwasher?' She aimed another teasing prod at Oliver's flat stomach. 'Or am I going to have to tickle you until you beg for mer—'

'I'll do it!' gasped Oliver, who was hopelessly ticklish. He tried to back away. 'Moll! I'll do it, just stop!'

'Has anything ever happened between you two?' said Savannah when Moll had disappeared for a five-minute fag break.

'What, me and Moll?' Oliver looked amused. 'No.'

'Why not?'

'What do you mean?'

Savannah shrugged and fiddled with the thin straps of her stripy cotton top. 'Just that she seems to have slept with pretty much everyone else around here. And it's obvious she's keen on you.'

'She's just friendly,' Oliver protested, laughing.

But Savannah had been watching Moll Harper; she'd figured out her method. Any man Moll wasn't interested in got the saucy, flirty, you-should-be-so-lucky smile. The ones who did interest her, meanwhile, were treated to the slow, sultry, think-of-the-fun-*we*-could-have variety.

And while the banter she exchanged with Oliver might be saucy, the smile certainly wasn't.

Savannah, not fooled for a second, gave him a long look. 'Bullshit. She fancies you rotten.'

He shrugged. 'Okay, maybe she's not my type.'

'Well, good.' Savannah was torn between relief and confusion that it should have mattered so much to her in the first place. The compulsion to protect Oliver from the attentions of other girls was as strong as ever.

She just wished she knew why.

Chapter 24

Now this is what I call stupid, Lili thought at seven thirty the next morning as she stood in her bra and pants in front of the wardrobe wondering what to wear.

Pink shirt or orange top?

White skirt held together at the waist with a safety pin, or black trousers?

Green sandals or purple flip-flops?

Hair up in a ponytail or—

'Decisions, decisions.' Harriet, wearing the Spice Girls T-shirt she used as a nightie and clutching a bowl of Cheerios, appeared in the bedroom doorway. 'You must be going somewhere brilliant.'

'Sainsbury's, actually.' It was too hot for black trousers and the orange top had gone weird around the neckline. Lili seized the pale pink shirt and safety-pinned skirt and tried to look as if she always gave such careful thought to what clothes she put on each morning, rather than rummaging in the heap on the chair for yesterday's T-shirt and leggings.

'Oh, wow, Mum! You've got lipstick on!'

Um, um . . .

'It's a very smart Sainsbury's.'

'But you never—'

'Lili, QUICK! Get down here and sort out this son of yours,' Michael bawled up the stairs.

'He's done something hideous in his nappy,' Lottie screeched, determined to sound as outraged as her father, 'and it's all shot up his back.'

As she made her way downstairs, grateful for the diversion,

it occurred to Lili that Michael had never actually changed a nappy in his life.

Doug Flynn was rushing out of Keeper's Cottage as she arrived.

'I'm giving Drew a lift into work,' Lili explained.

'Are you?' Doug looked surprised but held the front door open for her. 'He isn't up yet.'

When Doug's car had roared away up Compass Hill, Lili realised how utterly silent it was in the cottage.

The place was messy – certainly messy enough to send a shiver down Eleanor's fastidious, germ-free spine – but it wasn't as awful as it could have been. There was just the kind of general clutter you'd expect in a cottage shared by three single blokes. It actually had quite a relaxed atmosphere, Lili decided, feeling like Goldilocks as she wandered about.

Except one of the three bears, presumably, was still in the house.

'Uh . . . hello?' Lili aimed the words tentatively up the stairs.

No reply.

'Drew, are you there?'

Still nothing. This was getting silly. What if Drew had gone out last night, with his girlfriend for example, and stayed over at her place? What if he's simply forgotten about her offer of a lift?

But Lili was fairly sure Drew didn't have a girlfriend. And although the sensible thing would be to go home and see if he phoned her, she couldn't do it without just checking first . . .

'Hello? Drew?' Ridiculously, she realised she was creeping up the stairs, trying not to make the floorboards creak. Lili cleared her throat as she reached the landing and called out again. 'Drew? It's me – Lili.'

The bathroom door was wide open, as was the door to Doug's bedroom. Lili could tell it was his by the reek in the air of recently applied Eau Savage and the upturned copy of Gray's Anatomy lying on the unmade bed.

149

She knocked on the first of the two closed doors, peered inside and saw a heap of Jamie's sweatshirts kicked into a corner. Lili wrinkled her nose; no sign of any aftershave in here, more's the pity.

The last door had to be Drew's. Lili tapped and pushed it open, convinced by now that he wouldn't be here.

The room was in almost total darkness, the curtains drawn. She let out a squeak of alarm when the bedclothes shifted and Drew's head poked out from under the duvet.

'Lili?'

'Oh good grief, I'm sorry!' She scuttled backwards, clinging to the door handle for support. 'I thought you were . . . I mean, I didn't think you'd be—'

'What time is it?' Drew groaned, cutting across her babble.

'Five past eight. Um, shall I open the curtains?'

'Five past eight! Hell.'

He sounded terrible. Lili wondered if he was horribly hung-over.

She switched the light on, then cautiously approached the bed. 'Don't you have to be at the surgery by half past—'

'Mind the bucket,' Drew mumbled, not quite fast enough.

There was a resounding clunk as Lili stumbled against the aluminium bucket. At least it was empty.

'God, how much did you have to drink last night? Are you going to be sick?'

Now that the gloom had dissipated she could see Drew's face. He was the colour of dish-water and looked every bit as terrible as he sounded.

'I didn't have anything to drink,' he croaked. 'It's that bloody bug . . . I've been throwing up all night.'

'Oh, Drew, you poor thing!' The stomach bug had been doing the rounds of the village, knocking its sufferers for six in dramatic fashion. Lottie and Will had both gone down with it the week before. Happily they hadn't been ill for long; it was only a twenty-four-hour virus.

Lili pressed a cool hand to Drew's forehead and felt how hot he was.

'You might catch it,' he protested feebly.

'I won't, I'm never ill.'

'Neither am I.'

'I'll get you a drink. Mineral water's good,' said Lili. 'And that sheet's all twisted. Let me sort your bed out for you, then you'll be more comfortable.'

'You shouldn't be here. What if I'm sick again?' Drew miserably shook his head from side to side on the pillow. He'd never felt this terrible before.

'I'm a mother. I'm terrific at clearing up sick. Now, what about work?'

'I'll need to ring Jamie on his mobile. He was called out to help with a difficult foaling last night. He'll have to cover my shift . . . Where are you going?'

'I'll get that water for you and bring up the phone.'

He gave her a soulful look. 'I could be dead by the time you get back.'

Lili smiled. 'Try and keep breathing for the next couple of minutes.'

By half past eight Drew was sitting up in a freshly made bed, sipping mineral water and actually feeling a bit better.

'You're an angel. You know that, don't you? I'm pathetically grateful,' he told Lili. 'Not to mention ravenous. I think I could manage some toast.'

She shook her head. 'It's too soon.'

'No, really, I'll be okay.'

Lili made him some toast.

At nine o'clock Drew threw up again into his bucket.

'Why don't you try and get some more sleep?' Lili sponged his burning forehead with a blissfully cold flannel.

'You haven't even said I told you so,' Drew marvelled, closing his eyes.

She sounded amused. 'I hate it when anyone says it to me.'

'Is your car outside?'

'Yes.'

He raised an eyebrow. 'People will talk.'

Glad that his eyes were still closed, Lili said lightly, 'Shows how thick they are, then. If we were having a mad passionate affair I'd hardly park my car right outside your front door, would I?'

Slowly, Drew opened his eyes. 'Unless it was a double bluff.'

'Anyway, I'm sure people are talking already. When I pulled your curtains earlier, Myrtle Armitage was walking past. She looked pretty scandalised,' said Lili.

Drew mustered a faint smile. 'She'll tell everyone. If you switch on the TV, it's probably on Ceefax.'

'Or she's working her way through every newspaper in the shop,' Lili giggled, 'sticking Post-it notes onto the bottom of all the gossip column pages. News just in from Upper Sisley. Frumpy mother-of-three flaunts fling with dashing Darcy.'

'You aren't frumpy and I'm not dashing. Well, only to the loo,' said Drew.

His eyelids were closing again. He sounded as if he was having to struggle to stay awake.

'I'll leave you in peace.' Lili put the phone on the bedside table next to his glass of water. 'Give me a ring if you need anything. I'll pop back later anyway, shall I? Make sure you're all right.'

She half expected Drew to protest that there was no need, he'd be fine. But he didn't.

'Thanks. There's a spare front door key on the mantel-piece.' Sounding resigned, he went on, 'If I'm not breathing when you get here, just give me mouth-to-mouth resuscitation.'

'Don't worry. Jamie said on the phone he'd be home by three,' Lili consoled him. 'If you're not breathing I'll ask him to do it.'

Chapter 25

Lili was on her hands and knees in the garden digging up Beachcomber Barbie when a shadow fell over the flower bed.

'What's going on?' said Jessie.

'Oh, Lottie buried her yesterday. Ken's down here some-where too – under that rose bush, I think. She said they were just too old.' Lili imitated her younger daughter's dramatic manner. 'It was time for them to die.'

'I'm not talking about Barbie and Ken, I'm more inter-ested in you and Drew Darcy,' said Jessie. 'I came home for lunch and Oliver told me.'

'Oliver?'

'He heard it from Lorna.'

'Who told Lorna?'

'Who d'you think? Myrtle.'

'Ah.' Lili nodded and smiled and shook a lump of earth out of Barbie's hair.

'Shameless, that's what you are. Pulling open Drew's bedroom curtains and not caring who sees you.' Jessie mimicked the shopkeeper's outraged tone. She might only have heard the gossip third-hand, but it wasn't hard to imagine how Myrtle would have put it. 'Bold as brass, pleased as Punch, happy as Larry,' she began to improvise freely, 'whoever Larry might be . . .'

'Did she really say that?'

'Well, maybe not. But apparently there was some mention of a mid-life crisis.'

'Cheek!' exclaimed Lili. 'I'm only thirty-six.'

Jessie grinned. 'So what was he like in bed?'

'Sick.'

'What – like perverted?'

'Like in a bucket.' Lili jacked Barbie into a bent-over position and mimed her throwing up into the flower bed. 'Poor thing, he's got that bug.'

'And you were just doing your Florence Nightingale bit?' Jessie looked disappointed. 'Mopping up puke? This is such a let-down.'

Lili sat back on her heels and dusted the earth off her hands. She knew when she was being teased. She was the least likely person in the village to carry on an affair. Well – one of the least likely, she corrected herself as a mental picture of her mother-in-law in a negligée flitted through her mind.

She wondered what Jessie would say if she told her how long she'd spent in front of the mirror this morning, dithering over what to wear. 'Anyway,' she said to divert attention from herself, 'why aren't you working?'

'I wanted to talk to you.'

Lili could guess what this was about. The village grapevine travelled in both directions. Last night, while Harriet had been walking Blitz around the green, she had reported seeing Jess being driven away from the pub in a bright yellow sports car.

'You're seeing Jonathan again.'

Jessie sank down on the grass next to her and nodded. 'Kind of.'

'Why? I mean, he's really nice,' Lili amended hastily, 'but . . . well, I thought you'd got bored with all that tinkering-under-the-bonnet business. You told me if he spent as much time on foreplay as he spent polishing his spark plugs he'd be able to give Warren Beatty a run for his money.'

'I'm not sleeping with him this time. Just seeing him. It isn't a romantic thing.' Jessie was fiddling with the orange scarf in her hair. Since it didn't need fiddling with, this was a sure sign that she was plucking up the courage to say something else.

'Come on,' pressed Lili. 'What?'

'Oh God. I just want people to *think* we're a couple.'

'Why?'

Here goes, thought Jessie. She stopped twiddling the ends of the orange scarf, took a deep breath and told her what had been going on with Toby.

'What a toad,' Lili gasped when she had finished. Then, 'Oh poor *you*,' as Jessie's eyes filled up with tears. Jessie never cried, not even at *Little House on the Prairie*.

'Isn't it stupid?' Jessie found a use for the scarf at last, furiously wiping her eyes with one end. 'I can't believe I actually fell for it, all that stuff about how he'd never stopped loving me, never felt like this about anyone else . . . and all the time it was just a stinking *line* . . .'

Wondering if she'd missed something, Lili said cautiously, 'You didn't go to bed with him, though?'

Jessie shook her head. 'But I wanted to.'

'Oh Jess . . .'

'I wouldn't, because of Deborah.' Jessie struggled to make herself understood. 'But if he weren't married I would have.' Sadly she added, 'Like a shot.'

Lili was still trying to think of something consoling to say when Michael appeared outside.

'Haven't you been to Sainsbury's yet?' he grumbled. 'We've run out of coffee.'

'I've been busy.' Lili pushed her shaggy fringe out of her eyes and gazed up at him, determined not to apologise.

'Looks like it. Gossiping with your friends on the lawn.' He smiled slightly at Jess to soften the accusation. 'Nice work if you can get it.'

'If you're desperate for coffee, walk up to Myrtle's,' said Lili.

'She doesn't sell the kind I like.'

This was what drove Lili mad. After a week or two of being back at home, the novelty wore off. Michael grew as bored and fractious as any teenager, and – quite unfairly – she felt obliged to keep him occupied. She found herself saying things like, 'Well, the lawn needs mowing,' or, 'Why don't you have a nice game of golf?'

'You could go to Sainsbury's if you like,' she suggested

now, keen to get him out of the house so she and Jess could carry on uninterrupted. 'The list's on the kitchen table.'

Michael looked underwhelmed. He'd seen the list; it was a mile long and full of riveting stuff like toilet bleach, potatoes and J-Cloths.

'Or you could fix those shelves in the bathroom,' Lili went on brightly.

Shelves. Steady on there, too much excitement couldn't be good for a man.

He hated fixing bloody shelves anyway.

'I'll get the shopping.'

'Oh, and while I think of it, can you look after the kids on Wednesday evening? Myrtle wants me to perm her hair and it's easier if I do it at her house.'

Irritation welled up. Trawl around Sainsbury's, babysit the kids . . . What was he, the sodding hired help?

'I'll get the shopping,' Michael repeated tightly, 'but you'll have to manage without me on Wednesday. I'm playing snooker. There's a competition on at the club.'

He had no intention of going to the snooker club. He was sick to death of snooker. He would pay another visit to the Antelope, he decided, and check out Singles Nite instead.

Oliver and Savannah were going swimming as soon as Oliver finished his lunchtime shift at the pub.

'We're rushed off our feet,' he told her when she wandered into the bar at two thirty with a rolled-up towel under her arm.

Savannah, who was wearing a pale grey cropped top and frayed white shorts, wasn't concerned. 'I'll have a drink and wait outside.' She patted her brown midriff and grinned. 'Work on my tan.'

Plenty of people had chosen to eat their lunch in the back garden. When Oliver emerged into the blazing sunshine twenty minutes later carrying two plates of vegetarian cannelloni, all the tables were occupied and he couldn't immediately pick out Savannah.

Then he saw her at the far end of the garden, squashed on to a bench between two men he didn't know. Three more sat opposite her and they were all howling with laughter. When Oliver moved to one side to get a better view, he saw why. One of the men was wearing Savannah's pink and black striped bikini top over his shirt.

'Um . . . excuse me, are those our cannellonis?'

Savannah was laughing so much she choked on her orange juice. The chap next to her began patting her on the back. The man in the bikini top pretended to choke as well, and got the strap across his back vigorously twanged.

Feeling increasingly uneasy, Oliver watched Savannah murmur something to the one who'd been patting her on the back. The man leaned across, lifted the curtain of blonde hair away from her ear and whispered something that made her burst out laughing again.

Moments later she looked up and spotted Oliver. Still giggling, she beckoned him over, clearly eager to introduce him to her new friends.

Oliver had no intention of going over to be introduced. Why would he want to meet that bunch of idiots?

'Are they for us?' said the same slightly irritated voice behind Oliver as he stood there with the cannellonis going cold.

'Sorry? Oh, right.' He put the plates down on the table, bits of glistening lollo rosso and tomato spilling to the ground.

The man on the other side of Savannah had progressed to rubbing his thigh against her bare leg. Now he was checking out the amount of fray on her shorts. Oliver quashed a terrifying urge to rush across and deck him.

'Hang on, this is vegetarian. We aren't vegetarians,' complained the customer, who was overweight and perspiring freely in the heat. 'We ordered ordinary.'

The pink and black striped bikini top was coming off now, striptease style. Its wearer swung it around his head and gyrated his hips suggestively. The next minute it sailed through the air, landing in one of the apple trees and catching on a low branch.

'Are you listening to me? I *said*, we don't want this vegetarian rubbish.'

'It might do you some good,' Oliver couldn't stop himself snapping back. 'Just stop moaning and eat it.'

It was her job to unpack and put away, Lili realised when she opened the door to the kitchen and saw the dozen or so carriers groaning with groceries. Michael had already disappeared upstairs to have a shower. Oh well, he deserves a rest, she thought drily, discovering three tubs of rapidly melting Crunchy Nut Toffee Explosion ice cream in the first bag she peered into. He's only a man, after all. He can't be expected to do everything.

'Can you keep an eye on the children for ten minutes?' She asked an hour later. Michael, evidently still suffering from shop-lag, was stretched out on one of the sun-loungers listening to cricket on the radio. This, to Lili's mind, was about as riveting as listening to knitting on the radio.

He deigned to raise his dark glasses. 'What?'

'Just for ten minutes. I promised Drew I'd pop back and make sure he's okay.'

Michael squinted up at her. 'Are you wearing lipstick?'

'No!' Lili felt the back of her neck prickle with belated guilt; after this morning she hadn't had the nerve to risk it again. Instead, purely to combat lip-dryness, she had grabbed one of the million tubes of lip salve Harriet was addicted to and had applied a quick layer as she was running downstairs.

Michael shrugged. 'Okay. Don't be long, I'm starving.'

As she made her way across the sun-bleached village green, Lili felt like Gary Cooper in *High Noon*. Myrtle Armitage was bound to be watching avidly, informing anyone else who happened to be in the shop that there she was, as bold as brass and old enough to know better, off again to visit her fancy man.

Lili wondered if the fact that Jamie's car was now parked on the verge outside Keeper's Cottage would defeat the gossips or add to the intrigue. Myrtle might start spreading even wilder rumours about threesomes.

'Hi!' Jamie said cheerfully, opening the front door. 'He must be ill – I offered him a beer and he turned it down.'

Jamie wasn't helping much by wearing only a pair of beige shorts. If Myrtle had her Hubble-strength binoculars trained on Keeper's Cottage, she might just think he was naked.

'I brought him another bottle of mineral water,' said Lili.

Jamie looked appalled. 'He'll never get drunk on that. Still, come on in. At least he's stopped throwing up.'

Drew was lying in bed, watching cricket – God, what *was* it with men and that stupid game? – on a grainy black and white portable TV. He was still looking white and drawn, but smiled and sat up when Lili came into the room.

'Am I glad to see you.'

'Why?'

'I need sympathy.' He rumpled his hair and looked sorry for himself. 'No danger of that Philistine downstairs being sympathetic.'

'You poor wounded soldier.' Lili grinned.

'He came home with an Indian takeaway,' Drew protested. 'Asked me if I fancied some of his chicken vindaloo.'

'Ah well, men are beasts.'

'I'm not a beast. I'm just thirsty.'

She held up the family-size bottle of mineral water. 'Ta-raa!'

'Brilliant.'

Drew heaved a sigh of relief and watched her unscrew the top. Sadly, Lili's hurried progress across the green had given the bottle a thorough shaking-up. The next moment icy carbonated water fountained everywhere, drenching them both.

'Are you trying to tell me I need a shower?' said Drew.

There was a box of man-size tissues half hidden under the bed. Hooking it out with her foot, Lili went pink as she realised she had dragged out a packet of condoms along with the Kleenex. Hurriedly, before Drew saw what she'd done, she tried to kick them back.

'Owww!'

'What's happened?' Drew leaned over the side of the bed.

Lili, who had missed the condoms completely, collapsed to the floor clutching her big toe.

'Ow ow ow . . .' she moaned, rocking to and fro and feeling quite sick. The pain was excruciating.

'Here, let me have a look.' Drew threw back the covers, hopped out and lifted her on to the bed.

'I'm so clumsy,' Lili wailed. Last time it had been her scalded chest. 'I'm such an idiot. Oh yuk, and this pillow's soaking wet.'

Having pulled off her dusty sandal, Drew sat on the edge of the mattress and examined her foot. Lili prayed it wasn't dirty, then she prayed even harder that it didn't smell.

'Not broken. You'll have a bit of a bruise.'

The pain was beginning to wear off. Lili, wondering why her mouth felt so weird, licked her lips. 'You're the one who's supposed to be in bed, not me.'

Drew grinned at her. He was wearing nothing but a pair of red boxer shorts, and his face and chest were still damp. The boxer shorts were covered with mini *Baywatch* babes, Lili couldn't help noticing. She wondered if he was holding his stomach in.

'Jamie's idea of a witty Christmas present,' Drew said, holding his stomach in so hard he was in danger of getting cramp. 'Sophisticated or what?'

Lili's mouth still felt really odd. She licked her lips again, then wondered if Drew would think she was doing it for his benefit, trying to be provocative.

'Anyone fancy a coffee? Lili, how about you?'

Jamie, appearing in the doorway, stopped dead as he took in the scene: Lili on the bed licking her lips; Drew – looking decidedly damp – sitting next to her in his *Baywatch* boxers. On the floor, the condoms had shot out of their packet.

'Blimey.' Jamie gazed at Drew and let out a low whistle of admiration. 'That's what I call fast work.'

'What's the matter with your mouth?' said Michael when Lili arrived back at the house.

'I don't know.'

Mystified, she rummaged in the drawer of the Welsh dresser where she had thrown Harriet's lip salve after using it.

'And why are you limping?'

'I stubbed my toe.'

'You're all wet, too. What have you been doing, giving the poor sod a blanket bath?'

'Oh for pity's sake!' Lili exclaimed, half-laughing as she found the black and white tube and read the words printed on the side. 'It isn't lip salve at all, it's Pritt-stick.'

Chapter 26

Doug Flynn hadn't spoken much to April since their outing last week to the Antelope, but she was flattered on Wednesday morning when he noticed her hair.

'Had it cut,' he said with a nod of approval as he leaned against the desk in reception and flipped idly through a set of notes. 'I like it.'

'Thanks.' April touched the new, feathery tendrils around the nape of her neck, her confidence boosted. She wondered how Doug would react if he knew she was going back to the Antelope tonight. Find it hugely amusing, no doubt. When you were as outrageously good-looking as Doug Flynn, wondering how you were ever going to meet a potential partner simply wasn't an issue. Women swarmed out of the woodwork wherever you went.

'Hmm, can't wait,' Doug murmured, turning a page. The set of case notes, as thick as a telephone directory, belonged to one of their regulars, a homeless alcoholic in his twenties with a reputation for peeing in the waste bin next to the coffee machine and roaring that all doctors in this dump were murderers. He smelled outrageous and, to amuse himself, liked to scrawl four letter words across the tattered copies of *People's Friend* and *Reader's Digest* peppering the waiting room.

He had deigned to visit them today because his latest tattoo had gone violently septic.

'He's just visiting the loo,' said April when Doug heaved the notes under one arm without much enthusiasm and turned to scan the rows of seats.

'Lucky loo.' Glancing at his watch, Doug dumped the

notes back on the desk. 'In that case he can wait another five minutes. I don't know if I can face this on an empty stomach – I'm going to grab a sandwich.'

April was busily tapping details into the computer when the bell on the desk went *ding* to attract her attention. Hoping it wasn't Doug's patient come back to tell her she was a whore and a bloody murderer just like the rest of them, she glanced cautiously over her shoulder and said, 'Won't be a sec.'

It took her a couple of seconds to recognise the woman standing there, simply because her presence was so out of context. Just as you didn't expect to find Margaret Thatcher queuing behind you in the post office, you didn't expect to look up and see Deborah Gillespie smiling at you across the desk in the casualty department of Harleston General.

It was weird, coming face to face with someone you'd only ever seen before in the papers or on television.

'Sorry.' Realising how moronic she must look, April stopped staring and pulled herself together. 'Can I help you?'

'I'm such an idiot,' said Deborah Gillespie, gripping her stomach and wincing. 'We just moved down here and I haven't got around yet to registering with the local GP. The thing is, I think I've got appendicitis.'

Although clearly in pain, she managed a rueful smile. April was dazzled. She couldn't imagine how anyone could look so effortlessly chic in just a pale grey cardigan and faded jeans.

Neither could Doug's next patient, back from the loo and eyeing Deborah's rear view with interest.

'If you give me your details I'll make up a file,' April told her. 'Don't worry, we'll get someone to take a look at you.'

'I'll take a look at you,' Doug's patient leered, breathing hideous alcohol fumes over Deborah's shoulder, patently under the impression that he was in with a chance here. 'C'mon, c'mon . . .' clumsily he tried to grab her wrist. 'Let's go and find an empty cubicle. You're my kind of woman, y'know that?'

The security guard was on his break. Mortified, April

looked around for Doug. The sooner he cleaned up this awful man's septic tattoo and sent him back out into the real world the better. Heavens, what must poor Deborah Gillespie be making of this?

Deborah leaned across the desk and said in a low voice, 'It's okay, I'm married to an actor. I'm used to drunks.'

'Yeah? This is your lucky day, sweetheart,' Doug's patient crooned happily. 'Just be careful with my back, all right? No getting carried away and digging your nails in.' He twisted round, showing her which shoulder blade to avoid. 'This tattoo's giving me gyp.'

'Hang on a sec,' April said to Deborah. 'I'll just go and find this gentleman's doctor, then—'

'Before you go, is Doug Flynn on duty?' Deborah interrupted. 'Sorry, it's an awful cheek – but I know him, you see. If he isn't here it doesn't matter,' she went on, skilfully ignoring the alcoholic's grubby fingers pawing her arm, 'but if he is, I'd prefer to be dealt with by Doug.'

Septic Tattoo was swiftly delegated to Rosie, the junior house officer. 'Oh great,' she grumbled. 'You get Deborah Gillespie, I get *him*. Just how fair is that?'

Doug gave her shoulder a reassuring squeeze. 'When Tom Cruise walks in, he's all yours. Promise.'

Walking carefully, holding her stomach, Deborah followed him along the corridor to the examination cubicle.

'Lie down on the couch,' said Doug, 'and I'll have a look at you. Why don't you tell me how this started?'

'I think it's appendicitis.' She half-unzipped her jeans and lifted the pale grey angora cardigan out of the way. 'It started this morning.'

Gently Doug began to palpate her abdomen.

'Tell me if it hurts.'

'Ouch,' said Deborah as his cool fingers pressed beneath her ribs. 'Ouch,' as they moved down to the left. 'Ouch, ouch,' she murmured when he slid them to the right.

'That was McBurney's point,' Doug told her, having elicited an 'ouch' much the same as all the others upon investigating the area on the right side, two thirds of the way from navel to jutting hip bone. 'You don't have appendicitis.'

'I don't?'

'If you had, you'd hit the ceiling when I did this.' He pressed again.

Deborah, trying to keep a straight face, said, 'Ouch.'

'Pulse normal,' Doug remarked, dropping her wrist and scribbling a figure in the notes. 'How did you get here? Did your husband bring you?'

'He's in London. I drove.'

'Is that sensible, when you're in this much pain?'

'I knew you were on duty today. I heard your car going up the road at half past nine.'

'Respiration's normal. Blood pressure normal.' Carefully, playing for time, Doug wrote down the results. Something was going on here. Deborah was smiling up at him now, not paying the least bit of attention to the findings of his examination.

'Appetite okay?' As he spoke, Doug heard one of the nurses talking to another patient as she pushed him along in a wheelchair. The flimsy curtain separating the cubicle from the corridor fluttered as they moved past.

'Fine,' said Deborah.

Doug couldn't look at her. He didn't want to say this, but it was a question that had to be asked: 'How are your bowels?'

'Very well, thank you. How are yours?' Still smiling up at him, Deborah watched the curtain billow again as an ECG trolley was wheeled past. She put a finger to her lips and beckoned Doug closer.

Doug wondered if the fact that they could be overheard so easily was embarrassing her. Maybe she wanted to tell him something incredibly intimate about her bowels. He leaned down, breathing in her soapy scent, trying to keep his eyes averted from her cleavage.

Deborah lifted her head and kissed him, slowly and very thoroughly, full on the mouth.

Jesus, thought Doug, stunned by the unexpectedness of the kiss, and both appalled and hopelessly aroused by the fear of being caught.

Jesus . . .

'Guess what, doctor?' Deborah breathed in his ear. 'My stomach ache's all gone. Almost as if it were never there in the first place. It's a miracle.'

Unable to speak – not daring to utter a word – Doug nodded his head. His heart was kicking against his chest like a demented donkey. This was unbelievable. How could it be happening? What did it *mean*?

Deborah smiled and kissed him again, sliding her tongue into his mouth and arching her back as she pulled him closer still.

'Have any of your patients ever done this to you before?' she murmured.

Thankfully the words were barely audible. Doug shook his head. If someone came into the cubicle now he would face instant dismissal. He'd be struck off. All those gruelling years of training would have been for nothing.

'No.'

'Good.' Deborah winked. 'I'd hate to be unoriginal.'

With some difficulty, Doug pulled himself upright. He reached for the notes on the trolley.

'I have to write something down; I can't just leave it—'

'Anything you like,' Deborah murmured back, handing him the pen which had rolled under her leg. She surveyed Doug with evident pleasure. 'So long as it isn't the truth. What time do you finish work?'

More voices outside. Doug, so used to being in control of every situation, knew he wasn't the one in control now.

He mouthed, 'Six o'clock,' and Deborah nodded.

'That's fine. Come to my house.' Glimpsing the expression on Doug's face, she added, 'Toby won't be back before midnight.'

'And the rest of your family?'

Deborah looked amused. 'All under control, Doctor. I'm not a complete novice, you know.'

Dear God . . .

'So how was the glorious Mrs Gillespie?' said Rosie an hour later, launching herself into the coffee room for what was laughingly known as a lunch break. This meant ten minutes on a good day. More often than not it meant no break at all.

Doug frowned, pretending to be engrossed in an article on Marfan's Syndrome in this month's *BMJ*. Without even glancing up, he said, 'Who? Oh, she was okay.'

'Wow, such enthusiasm.' Rosie threw herself into a chair and tore the wrapper off a half-melted Mars bar. 'What was the problem in the end? I noticed you didn't admit her.'

'Didn't need admitting. All she had was trapped wind,' Doug said shortly. 'I prescribed charcoal tablets, sent her home and told her to get herself registered with a GP.'

Rosie pulled a face. 'What a let-down. That's not very glamorous, is it? You don't expect women like her to suffer from wind.'

Doug let her babble on between mouthfuls of Mars bar. If she dragged the *BMJ* out of his hands and announced that she was going to test him on it, he would fail abysmally. The game would be well and truly up.

She didn't, thank goodness.

As he turned a page for appearance's sake, he checked his watch. Four and a half hours to go before six o'clock.

'Still . . .' Rosie swallowed the last bit of Mars, licked her fingers and wiped her hands happily on the inside of her white coat. 'Look on the bright side. At least your patient didn't pee in the sink like mine did.'

Chapter 27

The back garden of Keeper's Cottage was a dandelion-infested no-go area. Hardly able to believe he was doing this, Doug made his way through the chest-high cow parsley to the stone wall separating their untamed jungle from the landscaped grounds of Sisley House.

As he hopped over the wall he saw Deborah waiting for him on the terrace.

'Handy, having adjoining gardens,' she announced cheerfully when he reached her. 'This way nobody can start asking awkward questions.'

Doug's mouth was dry. Deborah was leading him over to the French windows.

'Asking awkward questions about what?'

'About why, every time the rest of the family are away, you turn up at my house.'

Every time? My God, Doug thought, this is Deborah Gillespie speaking. This is unreal. 'The rest of your family . . .' he croaked as she unfastened his shirt with deft fingers and pushed him gently backwards on to a crimson velvet-upholstered sofa.

'. . . are all in London.' Deborah undid the last button with a flourish. 'Toby's doing a chat show and the other guests are the Spice Girls.' She shrugged. 'That was it. Sav and Dizzy were out of here. I didn't see them for dust.'

Doug had a million questions but he didn't get a chance to ask them. Deborah slid the straps of her black dress off her shoulders and stood naked before him, lithe and golden, every red-blooded male's fantasy come true.

Her dark eyes sparkled as she unbuckled the belt on his

jeans and said, 'Well, Doctor, my turn to examine you now. I think this is going to be fun.'

Afterwards Doug had to put his jeans and shirt back on straight away. It felt too weird, lying there on the sofa naked. Imagine if Toby came back early.

'Ready for the quick getaway?' Teasing, Deborah reached over for the remote control and flipped the television on. 'Relax, you're quite safe. It's a live show.'

Doug turned and there was Toby on the screen, making an appearance in order to plug the release on video of last year's film.

'So . . . you and Deborah, still happily married after all these years . . .' marvelled the interviewer, who was divorced four times himself. 'How *do* you do it?'

It was a run-of-the-mill question, one that Toby had been asked a thousand times before.

'We're great friends, I suppose.' His smile was self-deprecating. 'We talk, we trust each other, we don't—'

The screen abruptly went blank.

Doug, who had grabbed the remote control from Deborah's hand, said, 'Aren't you taking a bit of a risk here? How do you know I won't go to the papers? I could sell a story like this for thousands.'

'You could.' Deborah nodded, unperturbed. 'But you'd be struck off. I was your patient.'

'This afternoon, when you said you weren't a complete novice . . .' Doug hesitated, searching for the right words. 'Do you . . . I mean, is it a regular thing?'

Laughing, Deborah pulled him back down next to her. 'Look, you aren't the first. But you aren't the hundredth either. I'm very fussy, extremely discreet, and I only get involved with men who have as much to lose as I do.' She stroked Doug's tanned chest. 'I have a nice life and I don't want to put my marriage at risk. But some opportunities are just too good to pass up.' With a grin, Deborah went on, 'We moved into this house and there you were, our new next-door neighbour. Not only dishy but something of an expert when it comes to covering your tracks with women.'

She waved a teasing index finger at him and added, 'Plus, you have a career you wouldn't want to put at risk.'

'Does Toby do this as well?' Doug was stunned by her matter-of-factness.

'God, no!'

'Never?'

'Never.'

'Does he know *you* do it?'

Patiently Deborah shook her head. 'I told you, I'm very discreet.'

'What would happen if he found out?'

'About you and me?' Sweeping back her dark hair, Deborah wriggled down on the sofa, her words becoming muffled as she trailed kisses across his flat stomach. 'He won't find out about us. I trust you,' she added, glancing up briefly and breaking into a bewitching smile. 'You're a doctor.'

'Don't you even love him?' said Doug when he could speak again.

'Of course I do.' Deborah sounded amused.

'So why do this?'

She shrugged carelessly. 'Adventure, I suppose. Fun. Why not, if no one gets hurt?'

'I still can't believe this is happening.' Doug shook his head. 'You're Deborah Gillespie. You're married to Toby Gil—'

'And you have no idea how bloody *boring* it is, being constantly described as Mr and Mrs Happy-Showbusiness-Couple,' Deborah blurted out. 'You have no idea how humiliating it is when the only reason people know you is because you're Toby Gillespie's wife.'

The phone rang and Deborah answered it, still naked. Doug, watching her, recalled that she had once been a bit-part actress, the highlight of her career an appearance in a TV commercial for shampoo. That was when Toby had, famously, spotted her and tracked her down. Soon afterwards they had married, the children had come along in smart succession, and as far as Deborah's fledgling career was concerned, that had been that.

'How do you spell Spielberg?' Deborah sighed, hanging up the phone and frowning at what she'd written. Doug reached across and corrected it. The message was for Toby to ring Steven Spielberg's office first thing tomorrow.

He tried to imagine how that made Deborah feel. Was she envious of Toby's success? Did she wonder if it could have been her, being rung up by Steven Spielberg, desperate for her to star in his next movie?

Doug followed Deborah through to the kitchen and watched her bottom wiggle as she pinned the note up on the message board behind the door.

'What are those? Fan mail?' He pointed to a cluster of envelopes bulldog-clipped together and addressed to Toby in oddly childish writing.

'Hate mail.' Deborah unpinned them and held them out to him. 'Someone in the village isn't overjoyed to have us here.'

'Have you told the police?' Doug skimmed through the contents. 'They could check for fingerprints.'

'The letters aren't threatening. The police have more important things to worry about. What are they going to do – fingerprint the whole village?'

'But—'

'Don't let it bother you,' Deborah said lightly. Drawing him against her, she wound her arms around his neck. 'We've got far more interesting things to think about,' she murmured in his ear, 'like when and where we're going to meet next.'

April knew she looked hopelessly out of place. She'd been so determined not to appear tarty, she'd ended up resembling an off-duty nun instead. The white high-necked blouse felt as if it would choke her; the navy skirt was too long and too dark; sixty denier tights had been a huge mistake. If the temperature outside was Mediterranean, the heat inside the Antelope Inn was positively tropical. I might not look tarty but I definitely look stupid, she thought, leaning against a wall and feeling the sweat crawling down the backs of her legs.

Singles Nite was more popular than she had imagined – but nobody else had come dressed as a nun.

She checked her watch. Her new way of coping was to set herself small challenges and see them through. Coming along here tonight had been the first challenge. Sticking it out for an hour, no matter how awful it turned out to be, was another. According to the magazine someone had left behind in the waiting room, this was a surefire method of getting your life back on track. Before you knew it, you'd find yourself brimming over with bucketloads of confidence and fabulous men would be falling over themselves to whisk you off on a paragliding adventure in Peru.

'Test your Mettle!' the article had urged. 'Take Risks! Seize the Moment *and* the Man of your Dreams!'

April wasn't sure about the paragliding in Peru bit, but she wouldn't say no to a cottage in Cornwall. The man of her dreams wouldn't even need to be fabulous, she had decided wistfully. Just caring and decent and . . . well, nice.

But she couldn't help wondering if maybe she'd been meant to read this advice. If Doug Flynn's patient – the one with the septic tattoo – hadn't scrawled 'FUCK' and 'BOLLOCKS' all over the front cover of the glossy magazine, she wouldn't have had to take it out of the waiting room, the article would have passed her by, and she might well have given in to the temptation to stay in tonight and sob her way through *Ghost* on television.

Oh well, so much for fate. It was eight forty-five. Fifteen more minutes, then she could go home. Nobody had spoken to her yet and it was looking increasingly unlikely that anyone would.

Serves me right for getting my hopes up, thought April, sipping her lukewarm grapefruit juice to make it last.

The bad news was that being whisked away by Mr Fabulous clearly wasn't going to happen. The good news, though, was that at least she'd set herself a goal and stuck to it. The even better news was, she'd taped *Ghost*.

At two minutes to nine, someone did actually speak to her.

'Oh, hi, it's you!'

It was the girl April had met in the loo last week, the friendly one who had urged her to come along to Singles Nite.

'Hello.' Clutching her empty glass, April attempted to shrink away from a noisy group of women swarming past. She managed to smile at the girl, who was wearing a fluorescent pink blouse tied under her breasts and a microscopic pair of orange shorts. But the clothes didn't matter; she was just glad to be having a conversation.

'Told you it was a laugh here, didn't I?' The girl in turn beamed at April and accidentally sloshed red wine down the leg of a tall man's cream trousers. 'Oops, sorry!' She gave his arm an apologetic pat. 'Let me buy you a drink, love. See you around,' she added over her shoulder to April, winking as she led the man towards the bar. 'Don't do anything I wouldn't do, eh?'

'No,' said April, chastened. 'Bye.'

Chapter 28

'Must be nice for the kiddies,' said Myrtle, 'having their Dad back.'

'Mmm.' Lili gave Myrtle's freshly permed, just washed, grey-with-a-hint-of-lilac curls a brisk rub with the towel.

'Nice for you too.'

'Well, yes.' Lili ran a comb through Myrtle's hair and picked up her scissors. 'Just a trim, is that what you want? A general tidy-up?'

'Your Michael doesn't mind you visiting other men then?' Myrtle enquired archly. 'I mean, he's not bothered about you spending time over at Keeper's Cottage?'

The scissors, nice and sharp, could snip out Myrtle's tongue with no trouble at all. Resisting the urge, Lili smiled into the mirror and began cutting her hair instead. 'Drew was ill. He caught that rotten bug. I was making sure he was okay, Myrtle, that's all.'

'Hmm.'

'It's called being neighbourly. What did you imagine?' Lili went on brightly. 'That Drew and I are having a torrid affair?'

'Of course not.' Myrtle pursed her lips as the scissors snip-snipped around the nape of her bulbous neck. 'But you know what some folk around here are like for gossip.'

'Anyway, Drew's years younger than me. He's a young man and I'm almost forty. Heavens,' Lili said cheerfully. 'I've even got cellulite!'

'I'm just saying some women go a bit funny when they reach that age.' Myrtle was partial to a bit of doom and gloom. 'I'm talking about the change, dear. Their hormones

174

start going up the creek and that's it, they're off, having hot flushes all over the place and chasing after anything in trousers.'

Was this what had happened when Myrtle had hit the menopause? Stifling a grin, Lili said, 'I didn't know that.'

Myrtle, who spent much of her free time in the shop, propped against the counter idly leafing through magazines, regarded herself as something of an expert. She frequently got her facts wrong, but always pronounced them with authority. 'Mark my words, there's a lot of it about these days,' she told Lili sternly. 'These women have to have tablets to keep them under control. Maybe that's what you need.'

Amazed, Lili said, 'What kind of tablets?'

'You go along to your GP, dear, and tell him you're nearing the change.' Myrtle turned to make sure Lili was paying attention, and almost got her ear sliced off. 'He'll put you on some of that UHT.'

The car park at the Antelope was full. Michael, forced to leave the car on the opposite side of the road, only realised who the girl in the high-necked white shirt and unflattering blue skirt was when he walked past her at the bus stop.

'Hello there.' His eyes crinkled in friendly recognition. 'We met briefly last week, didn't we? You're Doug's friend.'

'Well, kind of. We just work together.' Flustered, April realised how foolish she must sound. As if anyone would assume she was one of Doug Flynn's girlfriends. 'I mean . . . only vaguely, in the same department,' she stumbled on. 'He's a doctor . . . of course you know that. And I'm just one of the receptionists.'

'No "just" about it. Where would a hospital be without receptionists to keep everything running smoothly?'

The road was clear now but Michael didn't attempt to cross it. Instead he nodded in the direction of the pub. 'I saw you coming out while I was trying to find somewhere to park. Is Doug inside?' The prospect didn't alarm him. Doug Flynn wasn't the type to whisper a word of friendly warning to Lili along the lines of 'Guess where I bumped into your husband the other night . . . ?'

But April shook her head. 'No, he's not there.'

'And you've given up already, at . . .' Michael consulted his watch, '. . . ten past nine. That's a bad sign. What's it like inside?'

'Hot,' said April. 'The air conditioning's broken down.'

'And busy, by the look of the car park.'

'I . . . I was meant to be meeting a friend there, but she didn't turn up,' April fibbed. This was the excuse she had prepared in case she bumped into anyone she knew.

'Some friend.' Not believing her for a minute, Michael was touched by her air of vulnerability. 'Well, I'm here now. Why don't we go in and have a drink together?'

He was really quite good looking. And he seemed kind. If only she hadn't worn these stupid clothes. 'Actually, I thought I'd just go home.' April gestured apologetically at her skirt and tights. 'I feel a bit overdressed.'

He looked sympathetic. 'Is that your receptionist's uniform?'

'No, I just wore the wrong thing.' In a burst of honesty she admitted, 'I didn't want to look like a tart.'

She wasn't Michael's usual type at all, but there was something about her that attracted him – definitely. He glanced across once more at the Antelope. 'Well you've put me off the idea of that place.'

'I'm sorry,' April said humbly.

'Don't be sorry, you've done me a favour. No air conditioning and a heaving bar isn't my idea of fun. Look,' he went on, as if on impulse, 'I don't even know your name.'

'April.'

'And I'm Michael.' He grinned at her. 'Why don't we both give this a miss and find somewhere quieter? Do you live far from here?'

'Um . . . a couple of miles.'

'I could drive you to your house, you could dash in and change into something more . . . summery, then we can go wherever we like.'

April was lost for words. She wanted to, more than

anything – but how could she? Hopping into a car with a virtual stranger was dangerous. Testing Your Mettle and Seizing The Moment was all very well, but what about those dreadful stories you saw in the papers . . .?

'I know, I know,' Michael said when she hesitated, 'I could be a murderer, a raving psychopath. I'm not,' he told her with a smile, 'but you don't know that. So look, how about this for a plan? You catch the bus home. Change your clothes. Name a nice pub or restaurant, and I'll see you there in an hour. That way I won't even know where you live.'

April shifted from foot to foot, hotter than ever with embarrassment and racked with indecision. She imagined Bernadette's reaction if she told her she'd climbed into the car of a strange man she'd met at a bus stop.

'Okay,' she said finally.

'Okay.' Michael's smile broadened. He took his car keys from his pocket. 'Where shall we meet?'

He had nice eyes. They crinkled at the corners.

And there was still no sign of the bus.

April was beginning to wonder if she had missed it.

Oh what the hell, who said she needed to tell Bernadette anyway?

Blinking rapidly, she looked at Michael and took the plunge. 'It's okay, I'll come with you.'

Chapter 29

'That's us in Sardinia. We spent a month there after Dad finished filming *The Weekenders*.' Savannah pointed to a photo of Dizzy and herself on a beach, wearing shorts and floppy sun hats and waving frisbees.

'How old were you then?' said Oliver.

'Eight. And Dizzy was six.' She shook her head. 'God, he was a real pain when he was six.'

'I was not,' Dizzy retorted from the depths of the hammock.

'You were. You still are.' Savannah lobbed a peach stone at him. 'Go back to sleep.'

Oliver flipped over to the next page of the album. Savannah had found the photographs in an old suitcase and stuck them in willy-nilly, paying no attention to chronological order. The next picture, far more recent, was of Toby, Deborah, Savannah and a good-looking boy he didn't recognise. They were all sitting around a restaurant table studded with bottles. Savannah, wearing a sequinned white dress, was deeply tanned and showing miles of leg.

'That was in Cannes,' she told Oliver, 'at the film festival. After that meal we went on to Bruce Willis's party. I drank three tequila slammers and fell into the pool.'

'Who's he?' Oliver pointed to the good-looking boy.

'Henri. Wasn't he gorgeous? He had a part in one of the French films nominated for the Palme d'Or.' Savannah sighed happily. 'He was brilliant; we were mad about each other. That was one of the best holidays of my life.'

Oliver looked at her, lying on her front on the lawn, a

dreamy expression on her face. 'How long were you seeing each other?'

'Oh, it was hopeless. He had to fly off to do a film in Toronto, then he went on location with Dad to Switzerland . . . We wrote to each other for a few weeks, but it was never the same.'

She was still gazing at the photograph. Oliver felt a knot tighten in the pit of his stomach. 'Do you still like him?'

'Of course she still likes him,' Dizzy's scornful voice drifted across from the hammock. 'She keeps a photo of him in her diary.'

'You little sneak!' Savannah said furiously. 'How *dare* you read my diary.'

'And saying you wrote to each other's a bit of an exaggeration.' Dizzy, slotting a Blur tape into his Walkman, sounded triumphant. 'You wrote him about fifty letters and he sent you one postcard of a Canadian Mountie. It's hardly the same, is it? Ouch, get off!'

Savannah, on her feet and across the lawn in a flash, tipped Dizzy out of the hammock. She wrenched the Walkman off him, unravelled his precious *Parklife* tape and threw it in his face. 'You're a beastly little shit and I hate you!'

'You smell of garlic,' Dizzy retaliated. 'It's probably the only reason Henri liked you in the first place. He always stank of garlic too.'

Oliver, who was getting used to their fights by now, turned to the next page in the album. At least this one was Henri-free.

He studied a photograph of Savannah and Deborah in Rome, throwing coins into the Trevi fountain. The Gillespies had been everywhere. He'd been nowhere. And the money Toby had given him was just sitting gathering dust in his building society account.

'That's where I'm going,' he said when Savannah had finished beating up Dizzy and thrown herself back down on the grass next to him.

'Not yet though.'

Oliver didn't look at her. He couldn't carry on like this,

feeling jealous whenever he thought of Savannah with past boyfriends. He had to get away.

'You promised you wouldn't go yet,' said Savannah when he didn't reply.

'I know, but I've changed my mind.'

'What did I tell you?' Dizzy jeered from a safe distance. 'It's your garlic breath.'

Savannah sat up, her heart racing. As she moved, her long blonde hair brushed against Oliver's bare arm and she saw him flinch away.

Actually *flinch*.

'Why?' she demanded, beginning to panic.

Oliver shrugged, feeling sick and unable to meet her wounded gaze. 'I'm bored here. I just want to go.'

Dizzy had disappeared on one of his aimless meanderings around the village, Toby was on the phone to his agent and Deborah was in the bath when the doorbell went.

Up in her bedroom, Savannah stuck her fingers in her ears but the ringing didn't stop. She was in no mood to answer the door. Her life was a disaster, she didn't know what the hell to do about it, and worst of all, there was no one she could tell.

'Would somebody *please* answer that bloody door?' Toby yelled from his study, and Savannah heaved herself off the bed. Only the faint hope that it could be Oliver, come back to forgive her for screaming at him, propelled her down the stairs.

But it wasn't Oliver, it was a taxi driver.

'Cab for Mr Gillespie,' he announced, stubbing his cigarette out on the doorstep.

Savannah frowned. Her father wasn't due to go anywhere. 'I don't think we ordered one.'

'Toby Gillespie, Sisley House. A cab was ordered to take him to London.'

'Dad?' Savannah poked her head around the door of the study. 'There's a taxi here to take you to London.'

'Oh for God's sake.' Toby sighed into the phone. 'Hal, can I ring you back in five minutes?'

Savannah, chewing one of her thumbnails in the hall, listened to her father explain to the taxi driver that the call had been a hoax.

'It's the third time it's happened this week,' he said wearily. 'I'm sorry, it's a pain for you and it's a pain for me.'

'So there's no fare to London?'

London, Savannah thought, wincing as she chewed her nail down to the quick. Maybe that was what she needed to do – escape for a while and sort herself out.

But how?

And who could she stay with?

For the third time in a week, Toby gave twenty quid to a taxi driver to console him for missing out on a lucrative fare. The driver left and Toby, unamused, disappeared back into his study.

And Savannah, taken with the idea of disappearing for a few days, suddenly had a brainwave.

Of course! There was someone she could stay with *and* confide in. How silly not to have thought of it before!

Savannah raced after Toby, snatched the receiver out of his hand before he could begin dialling and said breathlessly, 'Dad, before you ring Hal, could I just call Aunt Phoebe, pleeease?'

'You mean you're off to London *now*?' said Dizzy the next morning, watching Savannah lug a suitcase down the stairs. He'd give anything to get out of this boring crappy village for a few days, see a bit of action, visit a few amusement arcades.

'I am. And here – this is for you.' Savannah, who was feeling unusually magnanimous, slid a ten pound note out of the back pocket of her jeans. 'Buy yourself another tape.'

Dizzy beamed. He had two more copies of *Parklife* anyway.

'And you're staying with Aunt Phoebe?'

'Yup.' Bending down, Savannah tightened the strap on the case. She didn't want all her knickers bursting out on the train.

'Can I come too?' said Dizzy hopefully. Seeing as they were friends again.

Straightening up, Savannah wondered if ringing a local taxi company would work. They'd probably think it was another hoax and tell her to bugger off. She looked at Dizzy, who was still standing there with an eager expression on his face.

'No you bloody well can't.'

Bernadette knew at once what had happened – she could tell by the sound of April's voice – and her heart began to race. Clutching her chest, glancing instinctively at the photograph on the table next to the phone, she experienced a peculiar mix of emotions. She would do anything, anything in the world for April. All she wanted was for her to be happy again. But at the same time it was odd, hearing her breathless words as she spoke about the wonderful new man in her life.

'Of course it's early days yet, I know that,' April couldn't conceal her joy, 'but he really seems to like me. I haven't felt this way since . . . well . . .'

'I'm so glad,' Bernadette said gently. 'Now, tell me all about him. What does he do?'

His name was Michael, she learned. He was something in computers. They'd met on Wednesday night and gone to an Italian restaurant and . . . oh, just talked and talked for hours, about *everything* . . .

'Everything?' Bernadette asked.

'Well, no – not that of course. I just told him I was divorced. But I couldn't believe how quickly the time went,' April babbled on. 'One minute the restaurant was full, the next minute we looked around and all the chairs were up on the tables. This sweet old Italian woman was hoovering the carpet and winking at us . . . Oh, it was *so* romantic,' she sighed, 'like something out of a film.'

Since Bernadette could hardly ask how the evening had ended, she said instead, 'How old is he?'

'Early forties.'

'Single? Divorced?'

'Almost divorced. Separated.'

Bernadette frowned. 'How long?'

'I don't know, quite a long time I think, he isn't—'

'Why did they split up?'

'He didn't go into detail.' April sounded edgy, almost irritated. 'Just something to do with him locking her in the cellar for a week with nothing to eat or drink. Bernie, what are you trying to do – spoil everything for me?'

Bernadette watched a bluebottle launch itself dementedly around the narrow hallway, buzzing and bouncing off walls. She opened the front door and let it out. 'Of course not. I just don't want you to get hurt, that's all. You know what I'm talking about. There are some men out there who—'

'My God, you have a nerve,' April whispered, and hung up.

Chapter 30

Freya had been asleep when Hugh and Felicity had picked her up from The Old Vicarage. Lili, tidying the sitting room an hour later, found Colin the Crocodile stuffed behind the cushions on the sofa and realised that Freya couldn't have woken up yet. If she had, she'd be yelling blue murder by now.

'I'll be five minutes,' she told Michael, waggling Colin's chewed tail at him in silent explanation. Will was asleep, and Lottie was in the garden teaching Blitz how to dance on his hind legs. ('No, no, not like that – try and be like a Spice Girl.')

'Fine.' Michael glanced up at Lili as she made her way past him. 'I could make a start on dinner if you like. What shall I do, peel some potatoes?'

Startled, Lili saw that he was actually smiling at her. Actually smiling and offering to peel potatoes.

Spooky.

'Potatoes . . . that'll be great.' She said it casually, as if this were the kind of offer he made every week.

Michael, who had been sprawled across the sofa reading the *Radio Times*, yawned and stood up.

'Nothing much on television tonight. I was going to stay in, but Harry rang earlier to see if I fancied a game of snooker.'

'Oh well, if there isn't anything on the telly . . .' Lili was relieved; too busy with Myrtle Armitage's hair on Wednesday night to watch *Ghost*, she'd taped it instead. If Michael went out, she and Harriet would be able to sit down and enjoy it in peace. 'If I were you I'd go down to the club.'

Freya had woken up. Lili heard her indignant wails the moment she stepped out of the car. Indeed, Freya was yelling so loudly she drowned out the doorbell.

'Oh thank heavens,' Felicity sighed when Lili, having made her way around to the side of the house, tapped on the kitchen window. 'Come in. Brilliant. I tried ringing just now but you were engaged. There there, darling, it's all right. Look, Colin's here . . .'

Freya stopped wailing in an instant. She clasped the battered velvet reptile to her chest, gave Lili a dazzling smile and wriggled to be put down. The transformation was so sudden it was comical.

'If only all our problems could be solved so easily,' said Lili with a grin. She gazed around the showroom of a kitchen and admired a white ceramic bowl overflowing with pink and yellow streaked roses.

'Are those from your garden? They're amazing.'

Felicity was watching Freya's wriggling, nappy-clad bottom disappear under the kitchen table. She nodded absently.

'Has Hugh gone out?' Lili had noticed his car wasn't there. When Felicity nodded again she added cheerfully, 'Got rid of him for the evening, have you? Me too. Michael's playing snooker in Harleston.'

Felicity was wearing only one earring, Lili realised – a smooth, beaten-gold oval the size of a sparrow's egg. Opening her mouth to tell her, Lili promptly shut it again, remembering that Felicity had just tried to ring her. Unclipping an earring before speaking on the phone was one of those things high-flying female executives did.

But Felicity still seemed distracted. Lili took a step towards the door.

'Well, Freya's happy now. I'll be going.'

'Yes. Right. Well, thanks.'

'Bye, sweetheart.' Bending down, Lili waved at Freya as she tottered out from beneath the table. 'Goodness, what's happened to you?'

Freya was walking but her eyes were half-closed. She looked odd.

'Freya? You can't still be sleepy,' Felicity exclaimed. 'You've only just woken up.'

Lili saw the blue-grey tinge around the child's lips and picked her up. 'She's swallowed something. She's choking.'

'No she isn't.' Felicity's eyes widened in astonishment. 'How can she be choking? She hasn't made a sound!'

Lili sat down, opened Freya's mouth, gently felt inside and flipped her over on to her stomach. A gurgling noise began to escape from Freya's throat.

'Omigod!' Felicity shrieked, losing it in an instant and trying to snatch her daughter off Lili's lap. 'She's going to die, she's going to die! What do we do? Shall I phone 999?'

'Not yet.' Lili held Freya face-down on her lap, keeping her head tilted below her trunk. She banged the heel of her hand sharply between the child's shoulder blades. If this didn't work she would have to perform chest thrusts. If that failed, it was on to the Heimlich manoeuvre.

The fourth bang between the shoulder blades did the trick. The smooth gold earring shot out of Freya's throat and bounced off Lili's dusty sandal. Freya took a great gulp of air and Lili gave her a quick hug before handing her over to her mother.

'There you go, she's fine.'

Felicity burst into noisy tears. 'She could have died! You saved her life. Oh, to think what might have happened—'

'Babies swallow anything that looks interesting. Lottie choked on a pickled onion once. When Harriet was tiny she had a thing about pebbles,' said Lili. 'Nightmare on the beach.'

The shuddering sobs finally subsided. Felicity, still clutching an indignant Freya, shook her head. 'You were so calm.'

'I've got three children.' Lili shrugged and smiled. 'Like I said, I'm used to it.'

'Well, thank you.' Wiping her eyes, Felicity handed Freya back to her. She crossed the kitchen, opened a cupboard and took out an old newspaper. 'The least I can do,' she told Lili as she lifted the glorious mass of yellow and pink roses from the bowl and laid them, dripping, on to the newspaper, 'is give you these.'

When Lili got home Michael was watching the news. Next to a saucepan of cold water on top of the cooker lay a polythene bag of potatoes and a potato peeler.

'It says on the bag you don't have to peel them.'

Ah well, it's the thought that counts, Lili decided.

Carefully she laid the roses on the table and began to unwrap the wet stems, peeling back layers of sodden newspaper and wincing when a thorn speared the base of her thumb.

Blood dripped as she carried on unwrapping. Lili used the dry outer pages to blot up the blood. When she unfolded another sheet of the paper and saw more red, she wondered if a thorn had got the better of Felicity too, but this was a less muddy, altogether more vibrant shade.

Although Lili wouldn't put it past Felicity to have more attractive blood than her.

Except it wasn't blood, it was felt pen. As she smoothed out the damp page and inspected the three circled adverts more closely, Lili's heart sank.

Helping Hands Nannies. Our quality of service is second to none.

Au Pairs A La Carte.

and

The Happy Mother Agency. Qualified and experienced staff available.

Well that puts me in my place, thought Lili, crumpling up the soggy papers and biting her lip as she squashed them into the bin.

It hadn't taken Jessie long to freshen up the living quarters of the Seven Bells. True to form, all Lorna had wanted was a couple of coats of white-with-a-hint-of-apricot splashed on throughout.

'It's dry,' she told Moll, who was peering into her room. It was seven o'clock on Friday evening but Jessie was determined to get the job finished. As she carried on rollering matt emulsion on to the landing wall she added, 'You can take the dust sheets off if you like.'

187

Moll pulled off the sheets, straightened her bedspread and pushed the small amount of furniture in the room back into place. From a wooden chest in the living room she lifted all the framed paintings and photographs that had been placed there for safekeeping.

'That's better,' she said with satisfaction when she'd finished, and Jessie climbed off her stepladder to admire the transformation.

It was bizarre. Moll's fringed and tasselled silks and velvets clashed violently with the sterile walls.

'Hmm,' said Jessie.

'I know.' Moll grinned, unconcerned. 'Gypsy Rose Lee meets Barratt Homes.'

'Wouldn't Lorna have let you choose your own colour scheme?'

'I'm not bothered.' Picking up a purple satin scarf, Moll tied it around the waist of her black cotton dress. 'It's only a bedroom. Anyway, who knows when I might move on?'

The pictures on the walls were an eclectic assortment of prints, but Jessie's attention was drawn to a photograph in a plain wooden frame, propped up on the bedside table. Whoever would have thought that Moll, of all people, would sleep with a photo of a good-looking young man next to her bed? Jessie couldn't resist taking a closer look. She glanced over her shoulder at Moll.

'I know.' Moll's eyes sparkled. 'Bit gorgeous.'

'Who is he, an ex?'

'His name's Stevie,' Moll said with pride. 'He's my little brother.'

Moll made them both a cup of tea. In the living room, repainted and already returned to normality, Jessie's gaze fell on another photograph left on the mantelpiece.

'That's one of Lorna's,' Moll explained. 'It's her twin sister.'

Jessie knew about this already; Lorna had mentioned it once or twice in passing. But in response to the question everyone automatically asked, all she ever said was, 'No, we weren't identical.'

'How long ago did she die?' Jessie asked now, studying

the photograph of the young woman in a wheelchair.

'Ten years ago, something like that.' Moll blew on her hot tea. 'Before Lorna took over the pub here. They were close though. She still gets upset when she talks about her.'

Jessie put the photograph carefully back on the mantelpiece and wondered why Lorna Blake had never mentioned the fact that her twin sister was disabled.

'So, what's up with Oliver?' Moll asked easily, changing the subject. 'Girlfriend trouble or what?'

'I don't think so.' Jessie shrugged. Oliver definitely hadn't been himself for the last couple of days. 'I tried asking, but I'm only his mother,' she added with a brief smile. 'He won't tell me.'

Chapter 31

Coming to stay with Aunt Phoebe had been a brilliant idea, Savannah thought happily. The moment she had rung the bell and Phoebe had flung open the front door she had known she'd done exactly the right thing.

'Oh, Aunt Phoebe, I'm soooo glad to see you!'

Phoebe gave her a mock clip around the ear. 'Don't call me aunt! We're going out to lunch and I want everyone to think we're sisters.'

Savannah gave her a bear hug. Phoebe wasn't a real aunt anyway, she was one of her mother's oldest and dearest friends, christened 'aunt' by Toby and Deborah because it irritated her so much.

But even if she wasn't family, she had made a terrific pretend aunt over the years, buying Savannah all manner of wildly unsuitable gifts, treating her to memorable days out and carting her along to glamorous parties.

Savannah loved to hear Phoebe's tales of the old days, when she and Deborah had shared a flat off the Kings Road. This had been in the late seventies while they were still single and doing their actressy-modelly stuff, and by all accounts their social life had been a riot.

'Then Deborah went and spoiled it all, of course,' Phoebe would drawl, exhaling a plume of Marlboro Light, 'and fell in love with this incredibly ugly failed actor.'

'You mean Daddy.' Savannah grinned. She never tired of hearing these stories. 'And you got married too, don't forget. To Baz.'

This was where Phoebe shuddered theatrically. Baz, the lead singer with Whinegum, had been the first of four useless husbands. The marriage had been over within seven months. The alimony, thankfully, had lasted a lot longer . . .

'Right,' Phoebe announced now, taking Savannah's heavy case from her and dumping it in the hall. 'No time to lose. I've booked us a table at Babania for one o'clock. After that, we shop. Okay with you, sweetheart?' She took Savannah's chin between tanned fingers, turning her face up to the light. 'You look peaky. And you sounded desperate on the phone. Am I going to hear about this, hmm? Is that why you're here?'

'Yeah.' Savannah nodded and pressed her lips together, desperate not to cry. If you looked a mess you'd never get into Babania.

Phoebe seemed dubious. 'I could cancel the table . . .'

'God, no!' Savannah shook her head. 'I want to go. I won't show you up, I promise. Let's just have some fun first,' she begged, 'then I'll tell you all the horrid stuff later.'

'Come on then.' As Phoebe led the way down the steps of the ultra-smart Islington townhouse, she tucked her arm through Savannah's and gave it a reassuring squeeze. 'Fun's what I do best.'

Fun, it transpired, also involved a fair amount to drink. Between them they put away three bottles of wine over lunch, and Phoebe soon had Savannah in fits of giggles, regaling her with wicked details of her latest affair with a high-profile cartoonist. By unspoken common consent they talked only about Phoebe, and when lunch was over they launched into a frenzy of shopping.

Cushioned by the wine, they tried on a dozen different outfits in Harvey Nicks. Phoebe would flash her platinum American Express card and glossy carrier bags would appear as if by magic. Hazily Savannah realised she was having an absolute fortune spent on her and she couldn't even remember if she liked any of the stuff she'd tried on.

'You can't buy me all these,' she protested, waving the carriers in feeble fashion as Phoebe steered her towards Donna Karan.

'I already have.' Phoebe looked pleased with herself.

'Anyway, I can do anything I like. You're the daughter I never had.' She waved an index finger at Savannah's chest. 'I'm your doting aunt and it's my job to spoil you rotten.' She studied the girl's face intently. 'Is it working? Are you cheering up?'

'Oh yes,' Savannah nodded because – let's face it – what else could you say when someone had just spent eight hundred pounds on you? 'Definitely, much better now.'

It didn't last. By six o'clock they were back home and the post-lunch hangover had begun to kick in. Phoebe sent Savannah upstairs for a bath, poured herself a reviving gin and tonic and switched on the television. If they were going to have that heart-to-heart she preferred the murmur of voices on television as background noise, rather than music.

'. . . after the news, tonight's feature film,' purred the continuity announcer, '*The Battle of The Sandersons*.' And even after all these years, something in Phoebe's chest – behind the silicone bosoms – went *zinnggg*.

It was so silly. Simon Colman wasn't the star of the film – he'd never starred in any film – but she knew she'd have to watch it again anyway, just to see him in his feeble supporting role.

A friend of a friend, bumping into Simon last summer, had reported joyfully back to Phoebe that he was overweight and losing his hair. The looks that had made her heart skip more than its fair share of beats over the years had faded as spectacularly as his career. According to the informant he was out of the business now, working as a driving instructor and living with his frump of a wife and four children in Hounslow.

Phoebe stirred the ice in her glass with her finger and pondered the vagaries of fate. She had been married four times and had notched up no children. Each of her husbands had been a millionaire – heavens, Asil had practically been a trillionaire – yet she had loved none of them as much as she had loved Simon.

It was impossible not to wonder how her life might have turned out if they'd never split up. Would she be happier now, living in Middlesex, the wife of a balding, flabby driving instructor, surrounded by kids?

The sitting room door opened and Savannah trailed in. She was wearing a pink and white *Love Is . . .* nightshirt, and her blonde hair hung damply over her shoulders. She looked about fourteen and heartbreakingly in need of comfort.

It was time to talk.

Phoebe adored her surrogate daughter. She patted the sofa cushion next to her and let Savannah snuggle up.

'I like your slippers.'

'They're my Oasis slippers.' Savannah wiggled each furry monster in turn. 'That one's Liam and this is Noel.'

Shifting herself for maximum comfort, Phoebe kissed the top of Savannah's head. This was what mothering was all about. I should have had children, I really should, she thought emotionally, I'd have made a great mother.

Phoebe wondered if Simon ever thought back to the old days and regretted giving her the heave-ho.

They could have had such beautiful children together. Even in a semi-detached in Hounslow . . .

But that wasn't why they were here now.

'So, what's up?'

Savannah leaned across, took a sip of Phoebe's drink and said, 'Can I have one as well?'

'It's gin. It'll make you depressed.'

'I'm there already.'

'In that case it'll make you suicidal. And nothing's that bad,' Phoebe said. She uncurled herself and headed for the kitchen.

'I haven't told you yet.' Savannah's bottom lip began to tremble.

'Wait there. I've got a bottle of Moët in the fridge.'

Chapter 32

Too late, Phoebe remembered that champagne only cheered you up if you were cheerful in the first place. Savannah, gulping it down at a rate of knots, was in flood of tears in no time flat.

Phoebe listened, appalled, as the whole story came tumbling out.

'. . . I just don't know how I'm going to cope with it,' Savannah sobbed, reaching for another tissue. 'That's why I had to get away . . . and then he's going away . . . but the problem's still there, isn't it? In six months, or a year, whenever Oliver gets back, he's still going to be my brother and I'll still feel the same about him, I *know* I will . . . and I'm s-s-soooo ashamed!'

Her fragile body shook and Phoebe rocked her in her arms, lost for words. Over Savannah's heaving shoulder she saw that the film was about to start. In less than five minutes she would catch her first glimpse of Simon. It hadn't been a large part – he was the dishy young neighbour of the battling Sanderson family – but he reappeared several times as the story unfolded.

Simon was my love, thought Phoebe, the Moët going to her head. My one and only true love, and I lost him. And to this day I don't even know why.

'It's so unfair,' Savannah stormed, letting it all out now. 'If we'd met on holiday, if I'd been lying on a beach somewhere and he'd come up and started chatting to me . . . we wouldn't even have known we were related. I mean, when you meet someone gorgeous and you fancy each other rotten, you don't say, "Hang on a sec, we'd

194

better not kiss each other, just in case your mum once had a fling with my dad . . ." '

'Oh, Savvy.'

Savannah lifted her head from Phoebe's shoulder. Her eyes were red-rimmed, her expression desolate. 'You see? There's nothing you can do to help. There's nothing anyone can do to make me feel better. There are some problems,' she concluded mournfully, 'you just can't solve.'

Phoebe emptied the bottle into their glasses, a lump the size of a golf ball in her throat. 'You'll get over this.'

'I won't.' Savannah closed her eyes and shook her head, hot tears trickling down her cheeks. 'I know I won't. I love him, Aunt Phoebe. Like I've never loved anyone before.'

'Does . . . does Oliver feel the same way?'

'He hasn't said he does. But I'm pretty sure – yes. And it explains why he's been acting weird.'

Phoebe was desperate for another drink but she knew she mustn't have one. Any more and she risked blurting out things she absolutely mustn't blurt out. Exerting heroic self-control, she said brightly, 'Strong coffee, that's what we need. I'll put the machine on.'

When emotions and alcohol levels were running high, it was so easy to let your tongue run away with you. And I can't let that happen, Phoebe thought, carefully levering herself up from the sofa, I just can't.

The next moment her heart did its familiar skip-and-a-jolt as Simon, behind her, said, 'Morning Mr Sanderson. How's Mrs Sanderson feeling today? Hey, that was some party last night!'

Oh, that corny seventies dialogue.

And that *voice* . . .

Phoebe turned and looked at Simon: young and beautiful then, plump and balding now.

But so what?

Savannah was right. There were some men you just never stopped loving.

Only by the time I realised it, thought Phoebe, it was too late.

'Coffee?'

'Please.' Savannah gave her nose a last honking blow, collected up the scattered tissues and dumped them in the nearby waste-paper basket. 'End of round one,' she said with a watery smile, and glanced at the television screen. 'What's this film?'

'*The Battle of The Sandersons*.'

Savannah nodded. 'That's it.'

Phoebe watched her unfold her legs, slowly, like an invalid. 'Where are you going?'

'Just to the loo.'

Phoebe was engrossed in the film when Savannah came back. She kicked off her hairy monster slippers and curled her feet beneath her on the sofa, her eyes dry now but her face still pinched and pale.

'I've seen this before.'

Nobly Phoebe said, 'Would you rather watch something else?'

Well, she could always tape it.

But Savannah shook her head. 'It's okay, I like it. I love the bit at the barbecue when he throws his wife and all the food in next door's swimming pool.'

Simon's swimming pool. With Simon diving in to fish his neighbour out, emerging from the water with his dark hair slicked back and his white shirt clinging to his body . . .

Phoebe smiled and said, 'That's my favourite bit too.'

They didn't have long to wait. Savannah actually laughed when the wife was launched, screaming, into the pool.

'Mum had a bit of a fling once with that chap there.'

She was pointing at the screen. Phoebe frowned. What chap where?

'Him,' Savannah said as the camera zoomed in on Simon lifting the woman, kicking and yelling, over his shoulder.

Phoebe opened her mouth to say no, she'd got it wrong, *she* was the one who'd had a bit of a fling with Simon. But Savannah was chattering on.

'Before she met Dad, of course. She told me about it once when we were watching this film together. His name's Simon something, isn't it?'

Numbly Phoebe nodded.

'He was supposed to be seeing one of Mum's friends but he kept pestering her to go out with him. In the end he whisked her off to Paris. The next thing Mum knew he was going down on one knee at the top of the Eiffel Tower.' Savannah giggled. 'He produced this whacking great emerald ring and asked Mum to marry him, but she wasn't interested. She said she went off him when she found out he wore purple Y-fronts in bed.'

Until this moment Phoebe had been praying that this was all a silly mistake, that Savannah had muddled Simon with someone else.

But Simon had always worn Y-fronts in bed.

And his favourite pair had been purple.

'So . . . so what happened?'

'Mum said thanks but no thanks and dumped him, smartish.' Savannah shrugged. 'Told him to go back to his girlfriend. But he took it badly, apparently. Said if he couldn't have Mum he didn't want second best. He dumped the girlfriend and went off to make his name in Hollywood. Except he didn't,' she concluded, 'because I've never seen him in anything else since.' Savannah turned her head and grinned. 'Just as well Mum turned him down and married Dad instead.'

Second best . . .

There was a pain in Phoebe's chest, like a serrated knife being twisted beneath her ribs. She could hardly breathe. Fury and grief rose up like bile. Simon and Deborah, her lover and her best friend, had both cheated on her.

It was the ultimate double betrayal.

So much for her long-cherished fantasies. Simon – the bastard – had never loved her. She'd been second best.

Phoebe felt the blade of the knife jab a little deeper.

And as for Deborah . . . Well, what did she owe her oldest friend now?

Nothing at all.

'Listen to me,' said Phoebe. All of a sudden she felt eerily calm. She had kept Deborah's secret for eighteen years and had vowed to take it with her to the grave.

But that had been then, when she had been blissfully unaware of the secret Deborah had in turn been keeping from her. She had no compunction about breaking that vow of silence now. Especially when it could make all the difference in the world to Savannah.

'What?' Savannah looked bemused as Phoebe reached out with a trembling hand and switched off the television.

The room abruptly fell silent. All Phoebe could hear was the sound of her own blood thrumming in her ears. 'This problem of yours,' she said slowly, taking Savannah's thin fingers between her own, 'this thing with Oliver . . .'

Tears sprang instantly to Savannah's eyes once more. She managed a hopeless little nod. 'Yes?'

'How would you feel,' said Phoebe, 'if I told you that Toby Gillespie might not be your father?'

Chapter 33

'It's me,' said Savannah. 'Are you working today?'

Oliver hesitated, twiddling the phone cord around his index finger. 'Not until five.'

'Will you meet me? I'm catching the eleven thirty train from—'

'Look, I'm pretty busy,' Oliver cut in. 'I have to see my travel agent, he's helping me work out an itinerary.' He paused. Savannah had sounded excited. 'Where are you going?'

'I'm not going anywhere, I'm coming home,' she explained impatiently. 'I'm at Paddington now. The train gets into Harleston at twelve fifty-five. Please, Oliver. Say you'll meet me.'

'Well . . .'

'It's important,' said Savannah, and hung up.

'More flowers?' Lili gasped. 'Oh, really, you shouldn't have. This is far too—'

'You saved Freya's life,' Felicity insisted, thrusting the glossy, cellophane-wrapped bouquet into Lili's arms and holding out an even glossier box of chocolates. Charbonnel et Walker, no less. 'It's the least, the *very* least we can do to thank you. If you hadn't been there when it happened . . . Well, it gives me nightmares to think about it.' She shook her head, looking as if she were about to cry. 'I wouldn't have had a clue what to do.'

Overcome, Lili tried to bury her nose in the roses to admire their scent. She felt a twit when she remembered, too late, that they were sealed in cellophane.

'Well, thanks.'

'And I have to apologise,' Felicity went pink, 'for something else.'

'Oh?'

'The newspaper I wrapped those roses in yesterday. Heavens, this is embarrassing. Um . . . the thing is, I don't even know if you . . . if you saw . . .'

'The adverts,' Lili said, to put her out of her misery. 'Yes, I did see them. But it's okay, I understand.'

'No – that's what I needed to tell you. We *want* you to keep on looking after Freya. The nanny thing . . . well, it was just a silly idea.' Felicity was getting redder by the second, but she stumbled on towards the finishing line. 'Anyway, just to let you know – we won't be pursuing it. We're more than happy for her to stay with you.'

Hanging out of the train's open window, Savannah saw Oliver waiting for her on the dusty station platform. He was wearing a red shirt and his oldest Levi's, and – typically impatient – he was jangling his car keys with one hand and twiddling his sunglasses in the other.

Her heart did a little leap of joy. Oliver had never looked more gorgeous. She wished she could race along the platform and just throw herself into his arms.

Except if I did that, she thought, someone would be bound to nick my suitcase.

Anyway, she couldn't.

Yet.

'Here, give that to me.' Wasting no time, Oliver seized her case and began to head for the exit.

Savannah hurried after him. She had been playing this scene in her mind all the way from Paddington.

'Can we have a coffee?' She jerked her head in the direction of the station buffet. It didn't bear much relation to the one in *Brief Encounter*, but the film had made a lasting impression on Savannah. In her mind, station buffets seethed with dramatic possibilities. Besides, she wanted the comfort of other people around her.

Oliver wasn't slowing down. 'I've parked on double yellows.'

'Please. Just five minutes.'

'I thought you had something important to sort out.'

'I do.' Savannah stopped at the entrance to the buffet and gave him a long look. Even her expression, she felt, seethed with dramatic possibilities. 'We both do.'

'If I get clamped, you can pay the fine,' warned Oliver.

She grinned back at him, so happy she could burst. 'Okay.'

Biting her lip with excitement, Savannah waited until they had sat down with their coffees at a red Formica-topped table. She tore open a sachet of sugar and spilled most of it over her orange Lycra skirt.

'So what's this about?' asked Oliver.

'I know why you've been avoiding me. I know why you're going away,' said Savannah.

He looked uncomfortable. 'I haven't been avoiding you.'

'Oh yes you have.' She couldn't stop the smile spreading across her face. 'But I may have the answer.'

Oliver tore the edge off a sachet and poured salt into his coffee. His hand shook as he stirred it in.

'The answer to what?'

Savannah couldn't contain herself a minute longer. 'I might not be Dad's daughter.'

'What?'

'Mum had an affair with someone else. Dad might not be my real dad. Which would mean,' Savannah said simply, 'you and I aren't related.'

'Don't be ridiculous!' Oliver was scandalised. 'Your mum? Someone's been winding you up. Deborah would never have an affair.'

'Oliver, trust me. This is on the level.'

'But this is your mother we're talking about.'

'I know, I know. She's so wonderful, everyone loves her, she's the perfect wife.' Laughing at the expression on his face, Savannah said, 'Think about it, it's the perfect cover. She's the last person in the world people would suspect of ever having an affair. Her very niceness is her alibi . . .'

'You don't seem too stunned,' said Oliver.

Savannah shrugged. 'I never knew for sure, but I've had my suspicions.'

'You mean about Toby not being—'

'Oh no! The Dad thing came as a surprise. But over the years I have wondered if she sees other men.'

The Dad thing. Oliver was too dumbstruck to absorb all the implications. He couldn't get over how calmly Savannah appeared to be taking the news.

He looked across the Formica table, deep into her eyes. Blue eyes, a lighter shade of blue than Toby's. And silky white-blonde hair. 'Are you upset?'

'What, about Dad? Nooo, he's still my dad. Just not biologically,' Savannah added with remarkable sang-froid. 'Which, basically, is the answer to all our prayers.'

'But you don't know for certain.' Still dazed, Oliver took a mouthful of tea. As he spat it back into the cup an elderly woman at a nearby table shook her head in disgust and ostentatiously buried herself behind the *Daily Telegraph*.

'I know, but I'm pretty sure.'

'How did you find all this out anyway?'

'My Aunt Phoebe. She told me everything – about Dad working abroad for weeks on end and Mum meeting this chap. He was married too, so they had to be really careful. That's how Phoebe got involved,' Savannah explained patiently. 'She used to let them meet at her place.'

'What makes you so sure this other man's your father?'

Another shrug. 'As soon as Phoebe told me who he was, I just thought, *of course*.'

Oliver took a deep breath. This was getting weirder by the minute. 'You mean he's someone you already *know*?'

'Only by sight,' said Savannah. 'Not to say hello to.'

'Who is it?' Oliver knocked his cup with his elbow, sending it clattering across the table. The elderly woman behind Savannah glared and rattled her paper.

Following Oliver's gaze, Savannah looked over her shoulder.

'Well, that's handy.' She started to laugh. 'See that

photograph on the front page?'

Oliver frowned and nodded. 'So what?'

Her blue eyes sparkled. 'So – that's him.'

'Oh Jesus!' exclaimed Oliver. 'Not a politician.'

Savannah, on dazzling form, managed to persuade the traffic warden to put his pen and ticket pad away.

As they drove towards Harleston she filled Oliver in with the rest of the details. 'He wasn't a member of the cabinet then, of course. He'd only just been elected as an MP. But he was in London all week and his wife and kids were hundreds of miles away in his constituency. You can see how these things happen.'

Oliver was in deep shock. This was too much to take in. David Mansfield's entire political career had been built up around a staunch commitment to honesty, loyalty and family values. If it got out that he was an adulterer, he would be finished, forced to resign, out on his ear—

Hell's bells, this was *serious*.

'Sav, what are you going to do?'

'Hmm?' On their way out of the station she had stopped at the newspaper stand and bought a copy of the *Telegraph*. Now, her blonde head bent over the front-page photograph, she was scrutinising David Mansfield's facial features. Short blond hair, cobalt blue eyes, the trademark lopsided smile that had won the hearts and votes of women all over the country.

The implications could be catastrophic.

'What are you going to do?' Oliver repeated.

Savannah looked surprised. 'Find out if he's my father, of course.'

Shit.

'How?'

She shrugged. 'Blood tests. DNA, that kind of thing.'

'And then what?'

'Come on, Oliver! What planet are you on? What do you *think* I'm going to do?'

Wreck a few lives? Create wholesale political turmoil? With Savannah, who knew?

He heaved a sigh. 'I don't know. Tell me.'

'If I'm his daughter,' Savannah jabbed happily at the photograph on her lap, 'it means we aren't related.' Her grin was jaunty, no-holds-barred. 'It means we can be together!'

Chapter 34

Deborah and Doug were in bed when they heard the crunch of tyres on gravel outside.

'Christ, who's that?' Doug was out of bed in a flash. He peered around the edge of the curtain. 'It's Oliver's car . . . Bloody hell, he's got Savannah with him!'

'He can't have. She's in London.'

'She isn't. She's getting her suitcase out of the boot.'

Doug, thankfully, had had plenty of practice at getting dressed at the speed of light. Deborah stayed where she was.

'Down the back staircase and out through the French windows.' Amused, she lifted her face for a fleeting kiss. 'Never mind, maybe we can catch up later. When the coast's clear I'll give you a ring.'

'Mum?' The bedroom door swung open. 'What are you doing in bed?'

'Oh darling, I've got the most stinking headache. A real killer.' Deborah rolled on to her side and held her hand an inch above her forehead. 'I've taken heaps of pain-killers but it won't go away.'

'Have you seen a doctor?'

'Oh, I don't want to be a nuisance. Anyway, what are you doing back?'

Savannah plonked herself down on the bed. 'Mum, Aunt Phoebe told me something and I have to find out if it's true.'

'Heavens,' said Deborah, 'what kind of something? That Rotterdam is the capital of Belgium? That horizontal stripes make your hips look bigger? That you can't get pregnant standing up?'

'Actually she told me that this chap might be my father.'
Savannah produced the folded-up front page of the newspaper from her shirt pocket. 'Is he?'

Deborah sat bolt upright. 'No.'

'Don't say "no", just like that. And mind your head –
here, let me put a pillow behind you – that's better. Now
come on, Mum. Is he?'

'Sweetheart, what an extraordinary thing to—'

'Mum, Phoebe told me all about it. The whole thing. You
had an affair with David Mansfield, you used her house,
you met him at a charity fund-raising dinner and he phoned
you the next day to ask if you'd like to—'

'Oh good grief, that's enough,' said Deborah faintly,
closing her eyes. The fictitious headache threatened to
become real. 'Yes, yes – that's all true.'

'And when you found out you were pregnant you didn't
know if I was his or Daddy's,' Savannah persisted.

'Darling, I'm *sure* you're Daddy's.'

'Well, we need a blood test.'

This was too much. This was a nightmare.

Deborah clutched at Savannah's hand. 'We *don't* need a
blood test. You're Toby's daughter. I don't know why
Phoebe told you all this, but it really is best forgotten. Think
of the trouble it would cause. Sweetheart, Toby *loves* you.
He's your father—'

'I know he's my father, but he might not be my *biological*
father.' Savannah was implacable, her blue eyes bright. 'And
I don't want him to be, either, because he's Oliver's father
too. And I love Oliver,' she said.

'Why?' Deborah demanded when Phoebe picked up the
phone. 'Why did you tell her?'

It was still only three o'clock in the afternoon. Phoebe
had to hand it to Savannah, she didn't hang around. When
she had a job to do, she got on and did it.

'I thought she had a right to know. She's in love with that
boy.'

'She is *not* in love with him!' Deborah was ready to
explode with frustration. 'She's got a stupid crush on him.

206

She's had them before and she'll have them again. She's eighteen, for God's sake! Getting crushes on boys is what eighteen-year-olds *do*.'

'Didn't sound like a crush me.' In London, Phoebe poured herself a hefty vodka and tonic.

'You promised, Phoebe. You're my oldest friend and you promised *never* to tell anyone.'

'So?'

'*So?*' Deborah almost screamed. 'I can't believe you've done this to me!'

'Well, snap.' Phoebe spat out the words with grim satisfaction.

'What?' Deborah closed her eyes. 'What are you talking about now?'

'I think you mean *who* am I talking about now. Let me put this simply.' Phoebe's tumbler clinked against the receiver as she took an icy gulp. 'Simon Colman – that's who.'

'Where are you going?' Oliver asked when Jessie came downstairs carrying a small overnight case.

'Cornwall. With Jonathan. He'll be here by five.'

'It's going to rain.' Oliver nodded at the TV, where a manically cheerful weathergirl was gleefully pointing at thunder and lightning symbols on a map.

'Never mind.' Jessie checked her watch; she wasn't planning to lie on a beach. 'Are you okay?'

Oliver nodded again. He wasn't okay, he was sick with worry. Savannah was on a mission, she was unstoppable, and there was nothing he could do to dissuade her.

God knows what was going on over at Sisley House right now.

Oliver was just glad Toby was in New York. Maybe Deborah would be able to make her wilful daughter see sense.

'I'll be back tomorrow evening.' In the distance came the roar of Jonathan's car approaching the crest of Compass Hill. Jessie picked up her case, sunglasses and emergency supply of Rolos. She looked at Oliver, who seemed distracted. 'Sure you're all right?'

'I'm fine. You and Jonathan have a good time.' He smiled up at Jessie to reassure her. They got on well; they had always been close. But this time Oliver couldn't bring himself to tell her what was going on.

It was just easier if she didn't know.

'Are you sure you want to do this?' Jonathan had to raise his voice to be heard above the noise of the car.

'What, eat four packets of Rolos all at once?'

'No thanks.' He shook his head as Jessie offered him one. 'I'm talking about Cornwall. I don't want you to do something you might regret afterwards.'

'This is what I want,' Jessie said. 'Of course I won't regret it afterwards.' She unwrapped another Rolo. 'I never regret anything I do.'

'Would that be a double room?' asked the receptionist at the hotel overlooking St Austell Bay.

Jonathan cast a hopeful sidelong glance in Jessie's direction.

'No thanks. Two singles.' Jessie wasn't looking, but she knew his face had fallen. Jonathan lived in hope of resuming their old relationship.

The receptionist handed them their keys. 'Well, enjoy your stay.'

'I'll do my best,' Jonathan told her mournfully.

'Come on.' Jessie tapped his arm. 'Before the restaurant closes. I'll buy you dinner to make up for the lack of sex.'

They ate on the terrace, admiring the view of the bay and sifting through the dozens of estate agents' details Jessie had had sent to her during the last couple of days. There were eight properties she particularly wanted to inspect.

'Couldn't you just rent one for the summer?' Jonathan frowned, shaking his head at the shortlist. 'Selling Duck Cottage, buying something down here . . . It's pretty final. You might hate it.'

The terrace was bordered by palm trees. Far below them,

an inky sea glittered in the moonlight. The lights from the cottages dotted along the curve of the bay illuminated the waves lapping the shoreline.

'How could I hate living here?' Jessie waved an airy hand at the view. 'It's beautiful.'

Besides, the whole point of selling her home and buying another was to *make* it final.

'No friends,' Jonathan pointed out. 'You could be lonely.'

'I'll make new ones.'

'Oliver won't approve.'

'Oliver's twenty-one, he doesn't need to approve. He can live where he likes.'

'You'll have to build up your business again from scratch.'

'Jonathan, if I wanted to be depressed I'd read Anita Brookner novels. It was your idea to come down here with me,' Jessie reminded him. 'The least you can do is be on my side.'

'You're running away.' His tone was blunt.

'I'm not running away.' Jessie sighed and watched him signal the waiter for more wine. 'I just can't stay there any more. I thought I could cope with Toby being there, but I can't.'

Jonathan was incredibly fond of Jessie, but he was glad he no longer loved her. If he'd been sitting here now, pining for her to come to her senses and love him back . . . Well, thank goodness he wasn't, that was all he could say. Otherwise, the look on her face when she talked about Toby Gillespie would be breaking his heart.

'I don't want you making a huge mistake.' He reached across the table, covering her hand with his long thin fingers.

'I won't be,' said Jessie, inwardly touched by his concern. She plastered on a bright smile. 'I told you before, I never regret anything I do.'

But her flippant manner was no longer fooling Jonathan. And it wasn't the first time Jessie had run away.

'Really?' He gave her a shrewd look. 'Not even jumping on a train to Scotland all those years ago and not letting Toby Gillespie know he was about to become a father?'

Chapter 35

Deborah had done her best but she was getting nowhere. It was like trying to persuade a spoilt six-year-old that she didn't want an ice cream with a flake in it, she'd be much happier with a plate of steamed vegetables instead.

'It's no good, Mum. This is the most important thing in the world to me and I'm not going to let you fob me off.' It was midnight, and Savannah, frustratingly, was showing no signs of caving in. 'One way or another we're going to find out the truth. Either Dad has the blood test—'

'Not your father. No, *no*!' Deborah had always taken such care not to be found out. If there was a way around this, any way at all that meant Toby needn't know about her infidelity, she would take it.

After all, Savannah could still be his.

'Okay.' Savannah flicked the newspaper photograph of David Mansfield with her finger. 'So we get it from him.'

'For goodness sake, have you any idea—?'

'Mum, chill out, it's not that big a deal. We can be discreet.'

Discreet. Deborah buried her face in her hands and shook her head. 'I don't know how you think—'

'Right, that's enough,' Savannah announced briskly. 'We're going round in circles here. All you have to do is phone him up and explain the situation. He seems a decent enough chap, I'm sure he'll understand.'

Deborah wished she could press Rewind, just go back a couple of days and start from scratch.

'But darling . . .'

'I mean it, Mum.' Pushing back her blonde hair, Savannah spoke with an air of horrible finality. 'If you don't do it, I will.'

Leaving the message was ridiculously simple. Directory Enquiries gave Deborah the number of the House of Commons. Dialling, she expected an answering machine, but a cheerful man replied, explaining that the switchboard was manned twenty-four hours a day.

Feeling sick, Deborah gave him a brief message to pass on to David Mansfield. Just her name and number and that it was urgent. She had to add this last bit because Savannah was sitting directly opposite her, cross-legged on the sofa, saying, 'Tell him it's urgent. Make sure he knows he has to call you back. Say it's a matter of life and death.'

'He'll be given the message tomorrow.' Deborah hung up and massaged her aching temples. 'Now, can we please go to bed?'

Not that she'd be able to sleep a wink. So this was how it felt to be emotionally drained.

Savannah flung her arms around her.

'Isn't this just *fantastic*? Sorry, Mum. I know it's a bit awkward for you, but if it means Oliver and I can be together . . .'

There were tears of elation in her eyes. As she kissed her, Deborah wiped them away.

'If you are his daughter, have you thought what else it could mean? He might want to meet you, get to know you. God, even introduce you to his family . . .'

'No thanks,' Savannah said firmly. 'I'm not interested in any of that stuff. Just so long as his blood matches mine, that'll do me.'

Savannah was still in bed and Deborah was downstairs in the kitchen when the phone rang at ten the next morning.

The voice on the other end of the line was unmistakable. 'Deborah? It's me. I got your message.'

'Oh, right. Hang on a sec.' Jerkily she reached for her purse on the dresser. 'Dizzy, we need bread and . . . um, teabags. Get some from the shop, would you?'

Dizzy frowned. What was going on? Yesterday his mother had slipped him twenty quid and told him to spend the day in Harleston. And now here she was, getting rid of him again.

'*Now*, darling, please.'

When he had ambled out, glancing suspiciously over his shoulder, Deborah returned her attention to the phone. The blood was pounding through her body like a herd of marathon runners; she hadn't expected him to get back to her so soon.

'David, hello. Um . . . is this phone safe?'

It was weird, speaking to him again.

'Absolutely. Now, what's all this about?'

David Mansfield sat in his office and thought back to the last time he had slept with Deborah, all those years ago. His parliamentary career had begun to take off shortly afterwards and he had never risked another affair since then. There was far too much at stake.

Deborah told him everything.

David listened in silence.

'I'm so sorry, David. I've done my best to talk her out of it but she won't listen. You know how strong-willed teenage girls can be.'

'I can't believe I'm hearing this.' In his oak-panelled office David Mansfield experienced a vivid mental image of his career flashing before his eyes before disappearing down the nearest toilet. 'Deborah, Deborah. This cannot happen.'

'Oh David, it's happening. I'm not thrilled about it either.' Fumbling in the kitchen drawer, Deborah found an old packet of Rothmans and lit one up. 'If Toby finds out, he's not going to forgive me. He'll want a divorce.'

David thought about his own marriage. He loved his wife. He loved her almost as much as he loved being a government minister.

Jesus Christ, what had he ever done to deserve this?

'We need to stop her.'

'We can't,' Deborah sighed. 'You'll have to go along with it. It's the only way.'

'Oh yes, right. Terrific.'

'Look, Savannah doesn't want publicity, just proof that you're her father. Nobody else needs to know.'

'Deborah, my whole life is at stake here!' David Mansfield closed his eyes – those famous blue eyes – and willed himself to come up with some kind of solution.

'Okay, let me put it this way.' The time had come, Deborah decided, to be blunt. 'If you provide the blood sample, you can cross your fingers and pray the story doesn't leak out. If you don't . . .' She paused, making sure he understood. '. . . Savannah will go to the press and the Pickfords vans will be pulling up outside your office faster than you can say "This is Trevor McDonald with The News at Ten".'

The film Toby was promoting in the States wasn't great, but until its target audience saw it for themselves they wouldn't know that. The advance publicity had been expertly orchestrated, the advertising had had millions of dollars poured into it, and the stars were doing the rounds of the talk shows, hyping it like mad and making it sound like the best thing to hit the cinema screens since *The Godfather*.

Toby had just done Letterman – *big* honour – and thirteen magazine interviews. From tomorrow, he had another nine TV appearances lined up and twenty radio shows to do. You had to try not to repeat yourself, though this was all but impossible. You had to be endlessly enthusiastic. You had to remember the names of the people interviewing you and use them. You had to shuttle from one radio or TV station to the next and look as if you were actually enjoying yourself.

You even had to stay awake.

Jessie was dreaming she'd bought a house in St Austell Bay. Literally *in* the bay, so it could be reached only by boat. In her dream she was gazing out of her bedroom window at Toby, standing on the beach with a megaphone. He was yelling across the water at her: 'You won't get rid of me that easily, you know! I CAN SWIM!'

When the phone began to ring beside the bed, Jessie answered it without waking up properly first.

'Jess?'

'Toby?'

'It's a terrible line. Jess, is that you?'

'Use your megaphone,' said Jessie. 'No, never mind, just swim across.'

A stunned silence greeted this suggestion. Jessie opened her eyes and got her bearings.

It was one o'clock in the morning and she'd forgotten to close her curtains. Through the window, an almost full moon hung above Compass Hill Wood, silhouetting the trees against the grey-black sky. In the distance a fox cried out. She was in her own bed, surrounded by estate agents' leaflets that crackled when she moved. She didn't live in a cottage in the middle of St Austell Bay and Toby Gillespie wasn't standing barefoot on the beach, bawling at her through a megaphone.

That had been a dream.

Frowning, she looked at the receiver in her hand.

The only puzzle now was, who was this on the other end of the phone?

'Jess?'

Toby. It was still him.

'I was asleep. It's okay, I'm awake now.'

'I'm sorry.'

'I was dreaming about you.'

Jessie knew it was a stupid thing to say but she hadn't had time to gather her wits.

Toby was absurdly pleased. He couldn't bear it that they'd parted on chilly terms. The reason he'd rung now was because he missed her so much.

'What was the dream about?' He pictured Jessie lying in bed. Maybe in the dream he'd been lying in it with her.

'You were chasing after me. I was trying to get away but you kept chasing me.'

So much for romance.

'Oh.' Despite the disappointment, Toby managed a brief smile. 'I do apologise.'

'Where are you anyway?' Jessie sat up, sending her map of Cornwall and a few sheets of house details slithering to the floor.

'New York. The St Regis Hotel. Shall I describe my room to you? The carpet is light blue, the curtains are dark blue, the wallpaper is a kind of stripy blue and—'

'Toby, why are you ringing?'

A pause. 'I just wanted to talk.'

'Couldn't you have phoned Deborah?'

'You know what I mean.'

'Toby—'

'I know, I know.' His tone was rueful. 'But I can't help how I feel, Jess.'

Jessie picked up one of the leaflets on the bed. There was a photograph fixed to the front of a pink-washed cottage with an overgrown front garden. What it didn't show was the fish and chip shop next door and the tattoo parlour opposite.

'This isn't fair.'

'I know that too. But some things—'

'I'm selling the cottage,' said Jessie. 'Moving away.'

Toby clenched the receiver in alarm. The hairs stood up on the back of his neck. 'Shit, no! Jess, you mustn't do that. You *can't*.'

'I'm not sure I have a choice.' Oh hell, Jessie thought, now I sound totally pathetic. But he'd caught her at a vulnerable time and she had to make him understand. 'It isn't easy for me either, you know.'

'I'm sorry. God, I'm so sorry,' said Toby. 'But you don't have to move away. Jess, I love you, you already know that. But I don't want there to be any awkwardness between us. I know I screwed things up the other week, but I swear that won't happen again. You have my word on it. No more hassle,' he went on urgently, 'I promise. From now on we'll be just friends.'

'Hello,' Savannah said cheerfully, 'is Doug in? I wondered if I could have a word with him.'

Jamie, who had answered the door, gazed in wonder at

215

Savannah's cropped white vest and handkerchief-sized skirt. Bloody hell, Doug was a lucky sod.

'He's here, but he's . . . uh . . . upstairs. Asleep.'

'Actually, it's quite urgent.' Savannah beamed at Jamie. 'Could you wake him up?'

Drew wandered out of the kitchen clutching a bowl of cornflakes and a fork. 'Maybe it's something we could help you with,' he offered. Doug had only finished his night shift two hours earlier.

'I don't think so. You see, I've got this massive splinter in my bottom.'

'I'm great with splinters,' Jamie volunteered enthusiastically.

Savannah gave him an apologetic look. 'Well, I think I'd prefer a doctor to take it out.'

Chapter 36

'I don't really have a splinter,' Savannah explained as they made their way back to Sisley House. 'I need to ask you a favour.'

'I see.'

Doug gave her a guarded look. Something was up. Surely she hadn't seen him legging it across her back garden yesterday morning.

'A big favour. Huge, actually.'

'What?'

'The thing is,' Savannah said, 'you know how to keep secrets, don't you? I mean, you're a doctor and you take that oath-thingy, so I can definitely trust you one hundred per cent. Whatever it is, you won't breathe a word to another living soul.'

Doug frowned. 'Well no, of course I wouldn't. But if it's something serious, you really should be seeing—'

'It isn't that kind of serious,' Savannah assured him gaily. 'More . . . well, sensitive. Not open heart surgery on the kitchen table if that's what's worrying you.'

'Maybe you'd better tell me what this is about,' Doug said, although he could hazard a guess. Either Savannah thought she might be pregnant or she was afraid she'd caught some form of sexually transmitted disease.

But as they rounded the corner he was taken aback to see Deborah's car parked at the top of the drive.

'Um . . . does this involve your mother?'

'Oh yes.'

Shit. He hoped Deborah didn't have some form of sexually transmitted disease. 'Look,' he said warily, 'if someone's ill—'

'Nobody's ill. We're expecting a visitor.' There was an air of excitement about Savannah; her eyes were almost feverishly bright. 'And I want you to take a couple of blood samples, that's all.'

Doug looked at her.

'*Blood* samples?'

'You mustn't let them out of your sight until you send them off to the lab.' Savannah had read enough Jeffrey Archer novels to know you couldn't trust politicians. 'Then when the results come back,' she concluded triumphantly, 'you give them to me.'

This was surreal.

Doug slid the hypodermic needle into the bulging vein and slowly drew back the plunger. Right first time, thank God; the blood flowed smoothly into the syringe.

David Mansfield watched him withdraw the needle and decant the sample into a thin plastic phial. He had driven down, alone, to Upper Sisley. Now he watched Doug Flynn write a fictitious name on the phial's label.

He rolled down his sleeve and looked across at Deborah Gillespie's daughter, perched on the edge of the kitchen table in a barely-there skirt and a vest that stopped short of her navel. If she were his daughter, he thought with an irrational flash of annoyance, he'd tell her to put some proper clothes on and stop dressing like a tart.

'Well, that's done,' said Deborah with some relief. 'Now, can I get anyone a drink?'

David Mansfield stood up. 'I should be going.'

Deborah poured herself a massive vodka and tonic anyway. She needed it, even if nobody else did.

'I'll show you out,' Savannah said, jumping down from the table. 'It's all right,' she added kindly as she saw David Mansfield to the front door. 'I'm doing this for love, not money. You don't have to worry, I won't blab.'

'Where's Dizzy?' Doug asked while he and Deborah were alone in the kitchen.

'Up in his room.'

'Christ, isn't that a bit risky?'

'I drove into Harleston this morning and bought him a new game for his computer.' Deborah managed a faint smile. 'Thank goodness for *Command & Conquer.* He won't come downstairs for a week.'

Doug shook his head. 'I can't believe I just did that. I can't believe you had an affair with David Mansfield.'

'I know, weird isn't it? I never even voted for him.' Deborah rattled the ice in her tumbler. 'Are you sure you wouldn't like a drink?'

'No thanks.' A drink was the last thing he wanted.

'Anyway, we don't have to worry,' said Deborah. 'All you need to do now is swap his blood for some of your own. Then it'll come back negative.'

Doug had just finished a gruelling twenty-four-hour shift. He had been asleep for less than an hour when Savannah had got him out of bed. He wasn't normally so slow on the uptake.

'You mean switch the samples?'

'Of course switch the samples! Savannah's won't match yours, will it? And she'll never know—'

'I can't do that,' said Doug. He began to sweat. This was too much; he was already far more involved than he wanted to be. But at least so far he hadn't done anything unethical. 'I'm sorry, there's no way I'm doing that,' he told Deborah abruptly. 'Tampering with blood samples is fraudulent. We're talking gross professional misconduct.'

'Phuh, some father he is!' Savannah remarked cheerfully, coming back into the kitchen and helping herself to a can of Coke from the fridge. 'What a grumpy-drawers. He didn't even wave goodbye.'

'Well?' Jamie was avid for details. He'd been fantasising about Savannah Gillespie's wondrous bottom for the last twenty minutes. Now Doug was back he could hear about it from the horse's mouth . . . so to speak.

'Well what?'

'What was it *like*!'

Doug put his medical bag into the cupboard under the stairs. The medical bag containing a phial of David

219

Mansfield's blood. He stood looking at it, deep in thought.

'He's in shock,' Drew said with a grin. 'It's all been too much for him.'

Ever hopeful, Jamie said, 'Was it like a little peach?'

'What?' Doug was still hovering by the cupboard, wondering if he should take the samples straight to the lab.

'Savannah's bottom, you idiot! Did she squeal when you took the splinter out?' Jamie's eyes lit up. 'Did you keep it as a souvenir?'

'Oh, right . . . no.'

It was useless. Doug simply wasn't going to tell him what he wanted to hear. He was selfishly keeping the details to himself. 'Life is so unfair,' Jamie grumbled. 'If you'd been at work she would've asked me to help. I'd've have done it, I'd been over there like a shot.'

Damn, I wish you had, thought Doug.

When the phone rang on Wednesday afternoon Deborah picked it up and held her breath.

'Well?'

'The results just came back. It's a match,' said Doug.

'Oh shit.' Fumbling for her lighter, Deborah lit a cigarette.

'I'm sorry.'

'You know what this means, don't you? The end of my marriage. And it's going to kill Toby—'

'Look, I'm pretty busy. I have to get back to work.'

'It still isn't too late,' Deborah glanced sideways over her shoulder to make sure she wasn't being overheard. But Dizzy was still upstairs, closeted in his room with *Command & Conquer*, and she hadn't seen Savannah all day. 'You can alter the report, Doug. Just Tippex out the crucial bits, write negative instead of positive, then photocopy it! Savannah will never know.'

'Er . . . actually,' said Doug, 'she already does.'

'But how—'

'Hi, Mum!' Savannah's voice, in the background, sang down the phone before Doug could speak again.

'She's been sitting here in reception since nine o'clock this morning,' he said drily, 'waiting for the results to come back.'

Jessie was sitting in the back garden painting her toenails, drinking Tizer and half-listening to a problems phone-in on the radio. She was making short work of a packet of liquorice allsorts and thinking about Toby's phone call the other night, when the familiar sound of Oliver's car pulling up outside reminded her that it was high time she told him about Cornwall.

Poor Oliver, at this rate he was going to come back one day from a lunchtime shift at the Bells and find somebody else living in his house.

'There you are,' Jessie said when he appeared clutching two chilled cans of Fosters. Heavens, this was quite nerve-wracking; she wasn't sure where to start. 'Sit down, Olly, I've got something to tell you.' There, she'd done it, she'd started. 'The thing is, I saw this brilliant cottage when Jonathan and I were down in Cornwall and I'd really like to buy it. I want to sell this place and move to St Austell. Now, how do you feel about that, is it okay with you?' As she ran out of breath, Jessie wondered why Oliver wasn't reacting. He seemed to be paying more attention to the kleptomaniac on the radio than to her own big news.

'Uh . . . fine.'

'I mean, I know it must come as a bit of a shock, but this won't really affect you that much, will it? You're twenty-one, off to Europe . . . and when you get back you'll be going wherever your career takes you, sharing flats, living your own life—'

'Mum, it's okay, I don't *mind*,' said Oliver, wondering when he might get a word in edgeways.

'The thing is, you'd be able to come and stay whenever you liked,' Jessie rattled on frantically, 'and if you wanted to come here, I'm sure Toby would be glad to have you at his house. So really it means you'll have more choice than before, which is *great*—'

'Mum, I've got something to tell you too.'

'Oh.' Jessie ground to a halt, surprised by the abruptness of Oliver's tone. Still, at least that was that out of the way now. She'd done it, told him she was going, and he hadn't asked her why.

No awkward questions about Toby – phew.

Rummaging in the liquorice allsorts bag, Jessie found one left – only a boring pink coconut one, but better than nothing. Then she took a swig of Fosters.

Ugh, it didn't go.

Oliver closed his eyes for a second. He had to say it, he had to. No backing out now.

'It's about Savannah. She isn't my sister.'

'Oliver, of course she is! What a thing to say!' Jessie protested. 'Why else would I have told you about Toby and me? It's hardly the kind of thing I'd make up.'

'We aren't talking about me. I know Toby's my father,' said Oliver. 'The thing is, he isn't Savannah's.'

'Oh, now this is too—'

'Mum, it's true. Deborah had an affair.'

Briefly, without naming names, he ran through the facts. Jessie was horrified.

'Poor Toby. Poor Savannah! She must be devastated. This Phoebe person has to be mad. Whatever possessed her to suddenly blurt everything out like that?'

'I don't know, she just did.' Oliver had finished his lager. He could do with another one. Considering that none of this was his fault, he was feeling strangely racked with guilt.

On the radio, a worried-sounding woman from Gwent was saying, 'You see, Anna, I don't know how to break it to him. He worked so hard for that money and I spent it all on scratchcards. He's going to be so upset when he finds out.'

Jessie found herself listening without meaning to.

Anna, who had a firm authoritative voice laced with compassion, heaved a sigh and said, 'Oh dear, oh dear, you've got yourself into a right pickle, haven't you?'

'I have, Anna, I know I have.'

'Well, my advice to you is, *don't* tell him.' Anna paused for dramatic effect, then went on, 'Take a part-time job, earn back all the money you lost, pay it into that joint bank account of yours, and' – in a voice like a kindly rumble of thunder – 'DO NOT SPEND IT ON SCRATCH CARDS.'

What this country needs, Jessie thought, is someone like Anna running it. She'd soon have us all sorted.

'Hang on.' She sat up abruptly as the significance of Anna's wise words sank in. 'There's no need for Toby to know about this! Savannah doesn't have to tell him.'

'She does.'

Oliver was fiddling with his empty lager can, denting and undenting it.

'But *why*?'

As he hesitated, Jessie saw his neck begin to redden. This had to be the first flush she had seen on her handsome twenty-one-year-old son since he was about fourteen.

Oliver simply wasn't the going-red type.

'Because me and . . . and Savannah . . .'

Jessie continued to watch, mystified. Heavens, even his grammar was going to pot.

'Yes?' she prompted helpfully. 'You and Savannah *what*?'

'Um . . . er . . . well, we're in love.'

Chapter 37

Deborah had three cigarettes on the trot before ringing the private number David Mansfield had given her. Remembering how violently opposed he was to smoking, she pinched one of Dizzy's Juicy Fruits before picking up the phone. Just in time – since he'd never been mad about the sound of gum being chewed either – she took it out of her mouth.

'Oh, hello.' David didn't sound enchanted to hear from her. 'Well?'

Deborah tried to drop the bit of gum into the ashtray but it was stuck to her finger. She shook her hand and the chewed wodge flew across the kitchen.

'It was a positive match.'

'Shit.'

'Sorry.'

'Bit late for sorry.'

Deborah wished she'd hung on to the chewing gum now. Wasn't this just typical of bloody men?

'Well,' she bristled, 'what else do you want me to say?'

'Not a lot you can say.' David sounded resigned rather than angry. 'Apart from, "Wake up, David, you've been having a bad dream." '

'Don't tell me you never suspected,' Deborah sighed. 'You aren't stupid. One minute we were fine, the next I was telling you I couldn't see you again. And eight months later – hey presto – Savannah was born. David, it must have occurred to you that she could be . . . well, yours.'

She had been about to say government issue, but sensed that David wasn't in the mood for humour.

'You didn't say anything. I took that to mean she wasn't.

Shit. *Shit!*' he raged down the phone. 'This is my *career*!'

God, he was so selfish.

'Savannah won't go to the papers,' Deborah said consolingly.

David Mansfield's laughter was hollow. 'Come on, she's eighteen years old. She dresses like a trollop and all she cares about is getting her own way. Of course she'll go to the papers.'

When Deborah had hung up she rang Doug's mobile.

'Where are you?'

'At home.'

'I need cheering up,' said Deborah. 'Can I come over?'

'Drew's here.'

Next door at Keeper's Cottage, Drew was putting on his jacket.

'I'm just off,' he said, in case Doug hadn't noticed.

But Doug shook his head. 'No, he'll be in all evening. And I'm on duty tomorrow. No, no, that would be difficult . . . Yes, I'll ring you.'

Drew was grinning by the time Doug switched off the phone.

'Who was that?'

'New physio at the hospital.'

'New married physio, if the only place she can meet you is here.' Drew, who had been called out to a heifer in labour, said briskly, 'Could be trouble.'

Tell me about it, thought Doug. He couldn't cope with Deborah Gillespie right now; he needed breathing space.

'I know.' He yawned, feigning boredom. 'That's why I turned her down.'

The Sindy Silverman Show went out live at nine in the evening. Afterwards in hospitality Sindy chatted briefly with her two other guests – a blind snake-charmer and a raddled rock star fresh out of rehab – before homing in on Toby.

'Hey, you were good tonight.'

'Not really.' Toby thought he'd been okay, but good was pushing it.

'At least you were on this planet.' She nodded briefly in

the direction of the leather-clad rock star. 'That guy is coked to the eyeballs. He kept calling me Barbie. One more trip to the bathroom and he won't even know his own name.'

Never mind drugs, Toby was beginning to know how he felt. This publicity tour felt as if it had been going on for months. Stifling a yawn, he put down his empty glass.

'We could go out to dinner.' Sindy lowered her voice and moved nearer. Up close, her heavy make-up was showing signs of wear. It made her look like a drag queen.

Without it, thought Toby, she'd be fine. Beneath all that glistening foundation and trowelled-on orange lipstick she had a sweet smile and a pretty face.

'Thanks, but I had something earlier. And I'm pretty tired.'

'Maybe you're just tired of being alone.' Sindy gave his arm a sympathetic pat. 'Look, we don't have to eat. I could show you my apartment,' she offered with a playful lift of her eyebrows. 'It's only five blocks from here.'

Toby looked at her. How old was she? Thirty-five? Her nose had been fixed, so had the cheekbones, and the lips were collagen-enhanced. Was she on her second face-lift or third?

'Thank you,' he said again, 'but I'm married.'

'Well I know that.' The collagen mouth twitched with amusement. 'I do read my researchers' notes, you know. But she's in England, right? And you're over here . . .'

'It's not that kind of marriage,' said Toby.

The plucked eyebrows shot up even higher. 'You're not serious! You mean you're actually *faithful*?'

'The dreaded f-word.' Toby smiled briefly and nodded. 'I'm afraid so.'

'Amazing. Nice for her, shame for me.' Sindy Silverman gave a good-natured shrug. 'She's a lucky lady.'

'Thanks.'

For the first time all evening she seemed genuinely curious. 'Is it . . . you know, *easy*?'

Toby watched the rock star reel towards the door, almost crashing into the snake-charmer's basket of cobras en route.

He thought of all the times in the last few days when he had looked at a telephone and longed – Christ, *ached* – to ring Jessie. 'Not always easy,' he admitted.

Sometimes it wasn't easy at all.

Oliver could smell Savannah's perfume as they made their way across the village green together by moonlight. An old Simon and Garfunkel song was playing over and over again in his head. It wasn't until Savannah slipped her fingers into his that he figured out why.

God, it was the music from *The Graduate*, and he was as twitchy as Dustin Hoffman, faced with the terrifying, predatory advances of Mrs Robinson . . .

'Olly, come on. Don't do that.'

'Don't do what?'

'Take your hand away.' Savannah reached for it again and held it more firmly this time. 'It's okay now, it's allowed.'

Oh Christ.

'Someone could see us,' said Oliver.

'So?'

'So, *they* don't know it's allowed. Please, just let go.'

'I don't care what other people think. It's none of their business.' She stopped walking and turned to face him. 'Olly, I love you. We aren't related. That means we can do anything we like!' In the darkness, the whites of her eyes gleamed like opals. 'It's been three whole days now and you still won't even *kiss* me.'

Oliver carried on walking. 'It doesn't feel right.'

'But it *is* right. It's what you wanted.' Savannah sounded as if she were about to explode with frustration. 'It's what we *both* wanted.'

Oliver couldn't speak. He just wanted to go home. Okay, he had fancied Savannah, he'd fancied her quite a lot. And seeing her being chatted up by other blokes had been awful. But on a scale of one to ten his lust for her had rated . . . what, a seven?

Maybe an eight.

The trouble was, Savannah had gone overboard. Her feelings for him rated two hundred and ninety.

'Your Dad doesn't even know yet.' This was Oliver's excuse, but he could only use it for another forty-eight hours. And what would happen when Toby found out was anybody's guess. He couldn't bring himself even to think that far ahead.

'We don't have to go home yet,' Savannah urged. 'We could go for a walk in the woods. Nobody would see us there.'

Oliver, who had no intention of taking her anywhere, said, 'Compass Hill Wood is full of bats.'

It was almost midnight when Savannah let herself into the house, but Dizzy was downstairs in the kitchen foraging for food.

'That looks so gross.' She prised the lid off the biscuit tin, took out a handful of chocolate digestives and pushed past him on the way to the fridge.

Dizzy was painstakingly – and messily – putting together a doorstep sandwich of ham, peanut butter, Marmite and mayonnaise. He watched Savannah crumble the biscuits into a bowl and pour double cream on top.

The words pot, kettle and black sprang to mind.

'What d'you want to be when you grow up?' he countered, 'Roseanne Barr?'

A thump on the arm would have been par for the course but Savannah couldn't be bothered. She found a teaspoon and began to eat, ignoring Dizzy and brooding fretfully over Oliver.

It isn't going well, she thought, suffused with misery. Everything should be great and it isn't. Oh shit, I love him, I love him, I love him *so much*—

'Look, am I missing something here?' Dizzy was frowning. Now he came to think about it, his mother had been pretty quiet for the past few days as well. Okay, he hadn't spent much time downstairs, but was it his imagination or was there a bit of a strained atmosphere in this house?

And why hadn't Savannah thumped him just now? She always gave him a thump when he called her fat.

Savannah, leaning against the fridge, ignored him and carried on eating.

228

'Is something going on that I don't know about?' Dizzy persisted.

'No.'

'There is.' He shot her an accusing look. 'You're acting weird. Mum's acting weird too. And when I saw Jessie coming out of the shop this afternoon she asked me if I was okay.'

Toby had to be told before Dizzy. Her mother had been adamant on that score.

Savannah mashed the last dregs of the chocolate digestives into the cream and piled it on to her spoon. She flicked Dizzy a you-don't-need-to-know look and a dismissive shrug. 'Nobody's acting weird.'

'Don't give me that.' He hated it when she acted all condescending and superior, deliberately treating him like a kid. 'Something *is* going on,' he whined. 'Tell me what it is.'

'Oh shut up, Dizzy! Don't pester me, okay? Give it a rest.' Losing patience, Savannah clattered her bowl into the sink and stalked towards the door. 'Just get back to your precious computer,' she snapped over her shoulder. 'Zap a few aliens and leave me alone.'

Chapter 38

Jessie got home from work at six o'clock. Toby was due back at around eight. Unable to relax, she had a shower, sorted out her knicker drawer and finally – heavens, she must be desperate – lugged a great armful of ironing downstairs.

Twenty minutes later she saw Deborah coming up the front path.

'Hi. I've got the jitters.' Deborah held out a bottle of wine, her smile rueful. 'Can I come in?'

'I've got the jitters too,' said Jessie. She fetched two glasses and followed Deborah into the laundry-strewn living room. 'Ironing's supposed to be soothing.'

'And is it?'

'Can't say it's doing much for me.' Gloomily Jessie held up a white silk shirt complete with shrivelled scorch mark down the front, the shape of South America. 'I didn't feel very soothed when I did this.'

'That's your favourite shirt,' Deborah protested.

'Well, it was.'

'I've got one I don't wear any more. It's a Jasper Conran. You can have it.' Deftly Deborah uncorked the wine and filled the glasses.

'Why?'

'Because I've got four white silk shirts and you've just wrecked your only one.' She shrugged and rolled her dark eyes. 'If only all our problems could be so easily solved. Oh well, cheers!'

They made short work of the first two glasses. When Jessie went to unplug the iron, Deborah stopped her.

'No, leave it on. If it's soothing I'll give it a go.' She

picked up one of Oliver's Nike sweatshirts and began ironing the sleeves.

'Are you hungry?' Jessie asked. 'I could stick a pizza in the oven.'

Deborah shook her head. 'I couldn't eat a thing. My stomach feels like a washing machine stuck on spin. Anyway, reeking of garlic may not be such a great move. Toby might regard it as the ultimate insult.'

Jessie privately felt that the ultimate insult as far as Toby was concerned was the fact that his wife had had an affair – and a child – with a super-smooth, if not downright slimy, politician.

Still, this was Deborah's problem, not hers.

'Are you scared?'

'Witless. Oh God, everyone makes mistakes, don't they? I made mine eighteen years ago,' Deborah heaved a mammoth sigh, 'and now I'm about to get my come-uppance.'

She couldn't stop looking at her watch, and every few seconds she put the iron down and took another swig of Frascati. Jessie didn't hold out much hope for Oliver's beloved pink sweatshirt; any minute now the lettering on the front was going to end up melted like toffee and super-glued to the iron.

'Have you tried reasoning with Savannah? I mean, does she understand just how much chaos she's going to cause?'

Deborah gave her a wry look. 'I've reasoned with her until I'm navy blue in the face. I'd have more joy persuading Dizzy to listen to Radio Four. You know what teenagers are like, endlessly self-centred.' She flipped back her dark hair with a weary gesture and the lettering on the sweatshirt, trapped beneath the iron, went *sssssss*. 'The trouble is, I can't even be angry with her. It's all my own fault. Oh *shit*.' She gazed in dismay at the frazzled letters on the bottom of the iron. 'I'm sorry. Now Oliver's going to want to kill me too, and he'll be so pissed off when he finds out he can't because Toby's done it alr—'

'Here, sit down.' Jessie took the iron and guided her over to the sofa. 'Maybe it won't be as bad as you think.' Hmm, long shot. 'Toby might be okay about it, once he gets over the . . . um, shock . . .'

'Oh, please!' Deborah intercepted, half-laughing. 'We both know that won't happen. I don't want us to split up – God knows, my marriage is more important to me than anything – but I'm really going to have my work cut out, persuading Toby not to divorce me.'

Jessie watched her twirl the broad silver bracelet on her wrist. Sitting there, so elegant in a topaz yellow vest, narrow white trousers and yellow and silver strappy sandals, it was hard to imagine anyone wanting to divorce her.

'Do you know what I think he'll do?' Deborah said suddenly. 'I think he'll throw me out of the house like the cheap shameless hussy I am, and get back together with you.'

What?

Jessie took another hasty slurp of wine, praying that the glass at least partly shielded her face from Deborah's disconcertingly piercing gaze. 'Me! Heavens, why me? What on earth makes you say that?'

'Come on, I'm not daft.' Deborah's dark brown eyes lit up with genuine amusement. Affectionately she reached over and patted Jessie's wrist. 'And you aren't, either. You know Toby still likes you.'

Oh good grief.

'Er . . . well, we get on okay, I suppose.'

'Trust me, Jess, it's more than that. If Toby and I were to split up, I'm telling you, he'd be round here like a shot. It's the old hurt pride thing, that male need to retaliate. And he wouldn't have to go out and *find* someone else,' she explained brightly, '. . . well, because you're already here!'

'I don't think so,' Jessie lied. She picked up the Frascati bottle but it was empty.

'I'm sorry, I'm really not trying to embarrass you,' said Deborah, 'I just know I'm right. It's what men are like. Why go to all the trouble of introducing yourself to somebody new when you can just leap into bed with an old flame?' She shrugged. 'They always do that, given the choice. They're so predictable.'

This had a certain ring of truth to it. The dear old better-the-devil-you-know syndrome was something Jessie had, in the past, been on nodding acquaintance with herself. It wasn't very flattering, that was the trouble. Being rung up out of the blue by some ex-bloke who's just broken up with his girlfriend always felt, somehow, like being awarded fourth prize in a talent competition when only four people have bothered to turn up.

'So what are you saying?' Jessie peered into the depths of her glass. Empty as well. At this rate she'd soon be making arrangements with Lorna Blake for fresh bottles of wine to be delivered from the pub to her doorstep each day, like milk.

'Oh Lord, I'm not trying to warn you off!' Deborah cried, appalled. 'That isn't what I mean at all. If you want to sleep with Toby, feel free,' she urged, 'please, just go ahead! It's what I deserve and I wouldn't dream of asking you not to.'

'I might not want to,' said Jessie, by this time thoroughly confused.

'Well, as I say, it's up to you.' Deborah checked her watch again and rose with reluctance to her feet. 'All I'm asking is for you to put in a good word for me.'

Jessie's mind was a blank. Her brain felt as if it had been Etch-A-Sketched and wiped clean.

'A good word?'

'We're friends, aren't we?' Deborah gave her a pleading look. 'Oh God, I really have to go now . . . it's just scary, this is my whole life at stake here. Well, wish me tons of luck, Jess.' Deborah's dark eyes swam with tears for a second, then she smiled a bracing smile and brushed them away. 'And stick up for me every now and again.' She gave Jessie a quick Chanel-scented hug. 'I know I did a bad thing, but it all happened so long ago, and I love Toby so much. If anyone can save my marriage, you can.'

'But,' Jessie felt sick, 'but—'

'Oh please, Jess, he'll listen to you . . . *Please* say you'll be on my side.'

★ ★ ★

Falling asleep clearly wasn't going to happen, it wasn't on the night's agenda. At half past two, after three hours of frenzied tossing, turning and pillow-punching, Jessie gave up and climbed out of bed.

Opening the back door, she stepped outside. The garden was in darkness but that didn't matter, she could find her way around it with her eyes shut.

The smooth Cotswold stone paving slabs beneath her bare feet were still warm from the day's sun. Jessie reached the wooden seat at the far end of the garden and sat down, hugging her knees and wrapping her long white nightie around her ankles.

A moth whirred past her head and in the distance an owl hooted, but Jessie was oblivious to these distractions. Less than three hundred yards separated her cottage from Sisley House, and she couldn't stop her mind running feverishly through all the likely scenarios of what might be going on there.

And quite a few unlikely ones too.

It was horrible, not knowing and not being able to do anything. Jessie hated feeling so helpless. She didn't know how Oliver could just sleep, as if nothing had happened . . .

Suddenly it occurred to her that Toby, fresh off the plane from New York, could well be sleeping too. Deborah had told him what she had to tell him and he had been shocked, appalled, furious etc. etc., but in the end jet-lag had knocked him for six.

Outraged, Jessie sat bolt upright on the wooden bench. She didn't want to be the only person awake and worrying herself sick at three o'clock in the morning. Bloody hell, that simply wasn't *fair*.

She ran up the path, in through the back door, out through the front door and across Compass Lane. The village was silent – no sounds of anguished screaming or plate smashing, at least.

Jessie was on the green now. She slowed to a walk and felt the dry grass tickle her ankles and the soles of her feet. As she approached the duck pond, the first rushes brushed against her knees. From this angle she couldn't quite see

Sisley House, but if she moved a little to the left she would just be able to glimpse it through the trees—

'Oh shit,' she squeaked as one foot hit an unexpected slope and the other – cartoon style – stepped into fresh air.

Chapter 39

Not very gracefully, Jessie half-slithered, half-tumbled into the water. Luckily she didn't make much noise, landing with a muted plop rather than a splash.

'Quaa-aack,' murmured a mallard duck, registering his irritation at being woken up.

'Bugger, bugger,' Jessie muttered, hauling herself upright and wading towards the bank. Bits of weed clung to her arms and legs; the bottom of the pond was squishy and she was going to have her work cut out scrambling back up on to dry land.

At least the water was warm.

'Here, grab hold of me,' said a familiar voice, and a hand appeared through the rushes.

Jessie, astonished but grateful, gripped the strong hand and was efficiently hauled out.

'Phew. Thanks.'

'No problem.' Moll Harper was grinning at her. 'Do I ask what you were doing in the pond or shall we gloss over that one?'

'Um . . . I just couldn't sleep . . .'

Feeble, feeble.

'Don't worry, I'm discreet.' Moll's teeth gleamed white in the darkness.

'Why are you here, anyway?' Jess countered, genuinely puzzled.

Moll jerked her head in the direction of Keeper's Cottage, next to Sisley House.

'Went back with Doug after the pub closed this evening. But Jamie's snoring like a train in the next bedroom,' she pulled a face, 'and Doug has to be up at six. I decided I'd rather spend the rest of the night in my own bed.'

'Lucky for me you did,' said Jessie, wringing out her sopping wet nightie. 'Well, I'd better get inside and dry off. Thanks for winching me out.'

'No problem.' Moll shook back her hair and gazed around her, listening to the rhythmic rasp of a nearby grasshopper. 'Quiet, isn't it? Peaceful. Feels like we're the only ones awake.'

'It's three o'clock in the morning,' said Jessie. 'I should think we are.'

'Hmm. There are lights on over at the Gillespies' place.' Moll smiled slightly, watching Jessie's face. 'Bye.'

Jessie watched her make her way across the village green. When she had disappeared, Jessie turned and headed slowly back towards the cottage. Only when she reached the front gate was she able to make out the dark silhouette of a figure, half-obscured by the branches of an overhanging ash tree, further up Compass Lane.

Jessie stopped in her tracks and the figure moved towards her. When he stepped out of the shadows she saw that it was Toby.

It was dark, but she recognised the outline of his body. When he drew closer she saw how pale he was, with shock and grief.

'I knew you'd be awake.' His voice was low. 'I had to see you.'

Jessie reached for his hand.

'Come in.'

'What happened?' Toby said when they were in the living room. 'And who was that with you by the pond?'

'Moll. I fell in. She appeared from nowhere and pulled me out.'

Although it wasn't cold, Jessie began to shiver. Puddles of pondwater were dripping on to the carpet and there were bits of weed stuck to her feet. But changing out of a sodden nightie didn't seem important right now.

'How did you fall into the pond?'

'Not looking where I was going. Trying to see if there

were any lights on in your house.' He looked exhausted; there were charcoal-grey shadows under his eyes and the muscles around his jaw were clenched. Jessie wished she had more to offer him than tea, but she'd finished the wine. 'I'll put the kettle on. I'm sorry, there's nothing stronger, I should have—'

'I don't want anything to drink.' Shaking his head, Toby moved one step closer and took both her hands in his. 'I came to see *you*, Jess. To say I told you so.'

She blinked. 'Told me so what?'

'You didn't believe me when I tried to tell you my marriage wasn't that perfect. You thought it was a line and you despised me for it. Well,' he said evenly, 'maybe now you'll believe me.'

'I'm sorry.'

'I've never lied to you in my life, Jess.' He shook his head. 'And I never will.'

'I'm so sorry about everything.' Jessie's knees were trembling. She sank down on to the sofa. 'You must be feeling . . . Oh, I can't imagine how horrible it must have been, finding out about . . . well, you know.'

'You mean finding out that my daughter is in love with my son – except it doesn't matter, it's not illegal or anything, because my daughter isn't actually my daughter anyway,' Toby said grimly. 'But my unfaithful wife never told me about this because she was never absolutely sure herself . . . that's the great thing about having an affair with a man whose colouring roughly matches that of your husband . . . and besides, she wasn't terribly keen on me finding out she had been unfaithful, what with us being such a *happily* married couple.'

He had to talk; he had to get it out of his system. Bottling it up, Jessie knew, would be the worst thing he could do.

She said gently, 'Did you never suspect anything?'

Another shake of the head. 'Not then.' Toby sounded bitter. 'Last year, maybe. And two years ago, almost definitely. Deborah's good, but she's not that good at covering her tracks.' He closed his eyes for a second. 'But eighteen years ago? No, I had no idea she was screwing someone behind my back. Jesus!' he exclaimed furiously. 'We'd only been married a year or so ourselves. Why would she even *want* to?'

There was no answer to this, Jessie thought miserably. Some people just did.

'So that's it,' Toby declared. 'Marriage over.'

'But—'

'Not because my wife slept with someone else. Not just because of that,' he amended, rubbing his hand hard against his forehead. 'It's the deceit I can't handle. How dare she pass off some other bloke's child as mine?'

He was shaking with fury. Jessie felt the clammy wetness of her nightie around her bottom. She stood up again before it seeped into the sofa and made her look incontinent.

'So what are you saying – that you don't love Savannah any more?' Under the circumstances, maybe blunt was best. 'She isn't genetically yours, so from now on she's on her own? You no longer *have* a daughter?'

'Of course I'm not saying that. Don't be ridiculous,' Toby almost shouted back. 'I'm not angry with Savannah. This isn't her fault, is it? It's Deborah's fault. She's the one I don't love any more.'

'The main thing is not to rush into anything. You don't have to make any decisions straight away.' Jessie knew this was good honest agony-aunt advice. It might not be the kind of thing she'd ever do herself, but it sounded excellent.

'Oh shut up,' Toby drawled, not taken in for a minute. 'I know exactly what I'm going to do.'

Jessie tried shaking her head at him. 'You might regret it.'

'I'll get a divorce.'

'Toby, you've had a terrible shock. You *think* you want a divorce—'

'Then I'll marry you.'

'Oh good grief!'

'But first things first.' Toby moved towards her. 'Can I stay here tonight?'

He didn't want to go home. It was perfectly understandable. It was, Jessie told herself, a reasonable enough request.

'Well, yes, of course . . .' She patted the back of the sofa in a vague this-is-*really*-comfortable manner, but Toby was shaking his head.

'I meant with you, Jess. I want to sleep with you.'

It felt almost as if Deborah were in the room with them, Jessie could hear her words so clearly: 'Trust me, Jess, if Toby and I were to split up, he'd be round here like a shot . . . It's the old hurt pride thing, that male need to retaliate . . . he wouldn't have to go out and find someone else because you're already here.'

Worst of all, Deborah hadn't even said it bitchily. It wasn't meant as a put-down, Jessie realised, it was just . . . well, true.

'You want to sleep with me as a way of getting back at Deborah,' she said, to make him understand.

'I don't.'

'You do. It's a revenge thing. You want to hurt her as much as she's hurt you.'

'I wanted to sleep with you before,' Toby reminded her. 'And she hadn't hurt me then.'

'Look, this wouldn't be the right thing to do.'

It was hard, saying no when you didn't want to. Bloody hard.

'Anyway.' Toby ignored Jessie's feeble protest and slid the strap of her nightie off her shoulder. 'It's not as if we're talking about a quick screw here, a meaningless one-off. I meant it about the divorce, you know. And I want to marry you, Jess. Christ, I should have married you twenty *years* ago.'

Jessie watched the other strap go. The clammy wet nightie slid off her and plopped – not very romantically – to the ground.

Chapter 40

Glad to be out of it at least, Jessie reached into the laundry basket of things that hadn't earlier got around to being ironed, pulled out a crumpled blue shirt and put that on instead.

'Toby, you can have the sofa. I'm going up to bed. I'll throw down a couple of blankets, but I'm sure you won't be—'

'Jess, I want to sleep with you.'

'Toby, you can't.'

'Why not?' His eyes darkened. 'If this has something to do with that chap with the sports car . . .'

'Actually, it's more to do with contraception,' Jessie sighed. Oh well, sometimes honesty was the best policy. Especially when you'd run out of plausible lies. When in doubt, be blunt.

Who said romance was dead?

'I don't care about that.'

Hmm, certainly not Toby.

'Oh, thanks,' Jessie exclaimed

'I want to make you pregnant. I want us to have another baby.'

'Well, I don't!'

'Jess, I love you.' He held her shoulders and gazed down at her, his eyes serious but his mouth beginning to twitch. 'Even if you are as bloody stubborn as you ever were.'

She kissed his cheek and moved towards the stairs. 'I just don't fancy climbing ladders and painting ceilings with a baby slung over my shoulder, that's all.'

Condoms, condoms, thought Jessie . . . How about

Keeper's Cottage? Three healthy rugby-playing lager-swilling lads like that must have whole cupboards full of the things. For heaven's sake, there was probably a vending machine by the front door.

She tried to imagine knocking on their front door at half past three in the morning and asking if they had any to spare.

'You wouldn't have to paint ceilings,' said Toby. 'Not if you were my wife.'

He had just seen her stark naked, but Jessie still found herself clutching the crumpled shirt-tails around her thighs as she climbed the stairs. It wasn't even a gorgeous shirt, just one of Oliver's ancient cast-offs that she used when she was painting. Lord, thought Jessie, talk about glamorous.

And then another thought occurred to her – *ding* – like a light bulb going on in her head.

'All right, I give in,' Toby said. 'You can relax. I'll sleep down here.'

'Right.'

'I can tell when you aren't going to change your mind.'

'Good,' said Jessie.

'You're a cruel, heartless woman. You know that, don't you?'

'Oh yes.'

'I shouldn't think I'll be able to sleep at all.' He looked mournful.

Jessie smiled. 'Toby, you'll sleep like a log.'

Oliver had only half-drawn his bedroom curtains. Pale moonlight filtered through the gap, enabling Jessie to find her way across the room without breaking her toes on bits of furniture.

She eased the top right-hand drawer of the old chest of drawers open, terrified it might squeak. Next to her, sprawled diagonally across his bed, Oliver breathed in and out, undisturbed.

There were car magazines, old keyrings, Oliver's passport, a battered copy of *The Traveller's Guide to Europe*, a broken watch and a penknife.

She found what she was looking for in the left-hand drawer.

Twenty minutes later, Jessie heard the creak of footsteps on the stairs.

Her bedroom door swung open.

Toby, his voice low, said, 'Are you still awake?'

'Yes.'

'You didn't throw a blanket down.'

'You're cold?'

He nodded. 'And there's a bloody damp patch on the sofa from your nightdress.'

Jessie bit her lip, trying not to smile. 'I'm sorry.'

'What are those?'

'Well if you don't know . . .'

'Okay. Where did you get them?'

Jessie watched him pick up the unopened packet of condoms from the bedside table. Now why hadn't she hidden them? Why hadn't she stuffed them under her pillow when she heard him coming up the stairs?

Silly question.

'I found them in Oliver's room.'

Even sillier answer.

'And?' Toby sat down on the bed next to her. 'What was the plan?'

'I don't know.'

'Were you going to blow them up and twist them into animal shapes, maybe? Here's a giraffe, here's a rabbit . . .'

Jessie trembled. He was so close to her. Half of her wanted desperately to undress him and pull him into bed, but the other half – the one bearing an alarming resemblance to Lili's mother-in-law – was tapping a disapproving foot and reminding her tartly that these kinds of shenanigans weren't going to solve anything at all.

The worst bit, the most humiliating part of all this, was having practically been given permission to sleep with Toby by his wife.

I want to, Jessie thought helplessly, and Toby wants to. The trouble is, the really off-putting thing is, Deborah wants us to as well.

'Okay, I get the message.' Toby stood up again. 'It's cold

down there, but never mind. I'll ignore the damp patch and the fact that you have the most uncomfortable sofa in England. If not sleeping with me means that much to you, then fine, I understand. I may even still respect you in the mor— What are you doing?'

'What does it look like?'

Toby watched, dry-mouthed, as Jessie peeled the cellophane off the pack of condoms. The muted gold glow from the bedside lamp lit up her tumbling ringlets. She was frowning with concentration, her mouth slightly open. The crumpled shirt was sliding off one brown shoulder.

She looked so, so beautiful . . .

'Come on.' She reached for his hand. Her expression might be casual but she didn't fool Toby. 'Wouldn't want you to get cold.'

As she pulled him into bed he felt the manic hammering of her heart against his chest.

'Jess, are you sure?' Christ, thought Toby, I must be mad. What am I trying to do now – put her off?

But it wasn't that. He just didn't want her to hate herself in the morning. Not that he could see why she should, but Jess had never been one for doing things by the book. She was wilful and stubborn and fiercely proud.

A real one-off.

Jessie smiled up at him, one warm arm curling around his neck. 'I changed my mind. And I'm really, really sure. Well, on one condition.'

Anything, anything. Dress up in a rubber diving suit? Do it in the village pond, singing 'Yellow Submarine' through a snorkel? No problem at all.

'What?' Toby murmured, kissing her neck and sliding one hand beneath the crumpled, fresh-from-the-laundry-basket shirt.

Jessie tapped him on the nose with the condom packet. 'First thing in the morning, you get out of here without being seen. *By anyone*. Then you have to drive into Harleston and buy another packet exactly like this one.'

'Good grief, what are you?' said Toby with a grin. 'Sex mad?'

She tapped him again. 'Look, I stole these from Oliver's drawer. Do you have any idea how embarrassing that is? They *have* to be replaced before he wakes up.'

Oh Jessie Roscoe, I love you . . .

'You mean whatever happens, Oliver mustn't find out his mother's had sex with his father?' Toby's smile broadened.

'It's not that,' Jessie fibbed, because it *was* partly that. 'It's the sneaking into his bedroom in the middle of the night and stealing them.' She went pink at the awful thought of Oliver finding out. 'It sounds so teenagey, so . . . so desperate.'

'I've waited twenty-one years for this.' Toby helped her out of the faded blue shirt. 'I *am* desperate.'

'You still have to promise.'

The shirt slid to the floor. Jessie might not go around flaunting it, he thought, but she had a terrific figure.

'All right, I promise. But I don't need to drive all the way into Harleston.' Innocently Toby said, 'I'll just pop across and pick some up from Myrtle Armitage's shop.'

Chapter 41

'Impotent! What d'you mean, impotent? You can't be!'

'I can,' said Oliver sadly. 'I am.' He hung his head. 'I'm sorry.'

It was Thursday morning. By the time he had staggered downstairs at ten o'clock, the cottage was empty. Jessie, who had left for work earlier, had been in a bit of a daze herself, by the look of things. In the kitchen Oliver had discovered six slices of charcoaled toast, an untouched cup of coffee and the milk left out of the fridge. In the living room, on the floor by the sofa, there was a dripping wet nightdress.

Frowning, Oliver had struggled to figure it out. Jessie must have jumped under the shower, forgetting to take off her nightie first. In a fit of tidiness he'd bent down and picked it up. Mysteriously, a long strand of something resembling pondweed had been stuck to the hem.

Oliver had given up. Anyway, he had other things to think about. Savannah would be here soon – she had said tennish, which meant eleven – and he hadn't even figured out yet what he was going to say.

Crikey, that was more important than a bit of slimy old pondweed!

'You're early,' he had told Savannah when she arrived.

She'd looked taken aback.

'I'm not. It's ten to eleven.'

'Well, earlier than I expected.' Oliver had been nervous. He'd pushed his hands through his blond hair and wondered – not for the first time – how he had managed to get himself into this mess. 'So, how did it go last night?'

He hadn't been in her way, but Savannah had squeezed

past him and made sure her hips brushed suggestively against his as she made her way through to the kitchen.

'Pretty much as expected. Dad got back from Heathrow. Mum told Dad. Dad went berserk. Mum cried a bit. I came downstairs and cried a bit too. I hugged Dad, he hugged me, I told him I loved him and how happy I was with you. Then Dizzy wandered in like a pillock and said "What's going on?", so Mum had to explain everything all over again and Dizzy kept whining "Why didn't anybody tell me about this before?" As if *that* was all that mattered.' Savannah had rolled her eyes as she dumped a carrier bag on the fridge and pulled out a box of frozen banana doughnuts. 'Here, stick these in the microwave. We can have three each.'

'What's going to happen now?' Oliver had asked. He didn't know if he could face one banana doughnut, let alone three.

'Nothing much.' Savannah had shrugged. 'It'll blow over.'

Oliver was feeling horribly responsible for all this. He had to check. 'They're not going to split up, then?'

'Nooo! Oh, Dad ranted on a bit about getting a divorce, but he'd never do it. That's just what people say when they're upset. Anyway, Mum'll get round him, she's great at that kind of stuff.'

'But—'

'*Bee-eep,*' went the microwave. Greedily Savannah had swung the door open and tried to pick up a steaming doughnut.

'Honestly, aren't microwaves brilliant? One minute everything's frozen, and the next – OUCH!'

She'd fanned her mouth violently, hopping from one foot to the other.

'. . . Everything's hot?' Oliver had suggested.

Savannah had come up to him, looking plaintive and pointing to her lower lip.

'Well, it's a bit red.' Personally, Oliver thought anyone daft enough to eat doughnuts straight from the microwave deserved to be scalded with molten banana purée.

'You could kiss it better,' Savannah had whispered.

Oh God, thought Oliver, flinching away. Here we go again.

'Ollie, what's the matter?'

'Nothing, nothing . . .' There was something else in the carrier bag on top of the fridge. Desperate to change the subject, he had begun to investigate. 'God, what's this?' Delving further, he'd pulled out a small paintbrush. He'd stared at it in utter bewilderment. 'Sav?'

Savannah's eyes were bright. She'd pointed to the jar in his left hand. 'It's chocolate body-paint. You paint it on,' she had touched the brush in his other hand, 'with this.' Her voice had dropped to a whisper. 'Then you lick it off . . .'

Oliver had dropped the brush. 'Jesus! *Why?*'

'It's fun. And it's sexy.' Savannah had stood her ground; there was a feverish glitter in her eye. Those things hadn't just accidentally toppled into the carrier bag, Oliver realised. They'd been put there for a purpose.

'Sounds messy to me,' he'd prevaricated, wondering desperately how to change the subject.

God, this was crazy. Two weeks ago he'd have given both arms for this to be happening . . . and now that it was, he was backing away like a startled sheep.

'It's *meant* to be messy. That's part of the fun,' Savannah had insisted. She'd smiled and run her pink tongue around her lips. To Oliver it was all horribly reminiscent of a cat about to pounce.

I'm not even a sheep any more, he thought. I'm a mouse.

Just tell her, just tell her you don't fancy her any more, a voice in his head had howled, but Oliver knew he couldn't bring himself to do it.

Too much had happened and it was all his fault. He had been attracted to Savannah and he hadn't been able to hide it. Now, thanks to him, a perfectly good marriage lay in tatters, Savannah's father was no longer her father . . . and, doubtless, somewhere in Westminster a philandering Cabinet Minister was knocking back blood-pressure pills by the bucketful and rehearsing his resignation speech.

Oliver's mouth had gone dry at the thought of all the havoc his hormones had unwittingly caused.

There was no way, no way on earth, he could back out now.

'I know what it is,' Savannah had announced. 'I've figured it out. You're shy.'

Shy was okay, shy was good. Shy would definitely buy him time.

Numbly Oliver had nodded.

Savannah had looked triumphant.

'See? I *knew* there had to be a reason for the way you've been acting lately. But you don't have to worry, because this is why I'm here today. To get you over it!'

'Um . . . I don't think you—'

'Of *course* I can!' Gaily Savannah had waved the brush and jar at him. 'That's the brilliant thing about body paint. Once you're covered in this stuff, it's impossible to be shy. You just relax, go with the flow, and before you know it all your inhibitions have—'

'I'm not shy, I'm impotent,' Oliver had blurted out in desperation.

Stunned silence. At least he'd managed to shut her up.

Finally she'd said, 'What?'

'I'm impotent, that's why I've been a bit . . . well, offish. I just didn't know how to tell you.'

'Impotent! What d'you mean, impotent?' Savannah wailed. 'You can't be!'

'I can,' said Oliver sadly. 'I am.' He hung his head. 'I'm sorry.'

'But I could cure that too, I know I could. There are all sorts of things you can do to—'

'Tried them,' he cut in firmly.

'Not with me!'

'It's no good, Sav. Nothing works.'

Horrified, Savannah clutched his arm. 'But you can't just suffer in silence! You have to see a doctor, get it sorted out.' Beseechingly she added, 'I could ask Doug Flynn to take a look at you.'

Oh yes, terrific, thought Oliver, that's all I need.

'No.' He shook his head, quite pleased with himself, and wondering why he hadn't thought of this before. 'I've

249

already been seen by the specialists. It all started in the spring when I got kneed during a college rugby match. There's nothing they can do, but at least it isn't permanent. I just have to be patient,' he explained with regret, 'and wait for the . . . um . . . feeling to come back. But it's going to be out of action for at least a year.'

Upstairs in his room, Dizzy was doing his best to destroy the enemy and conquer the universe but things weren't going too well. It was hard to conquer the universe when you couldn't see the screen properly and everything was blurred.

Dizzy gave up and rubbed his eyes with the sleeve of his Guns 'n' Roses sweatshirt. He wasn't crying. Only cissies cried. His eyes were just watering a bit because he'd been staring at the screen for too long.

But it isn't fair, it bloody *isn't*, he thought, biting his lip. Nobody tells me anything in this house, they don't care about me . . . I don't know why they bothered to bring me down here with them; they might as well have left me in London, chucked me into that skip along with the rest of the unwanted rubbish that would only clutter up their smart new house.

What really got to him was how it hadn't seemed to occur to any of them that he might have wanted to be told what was going on.

Bloody hell, he thought miserably, was that so unreasonable? It was pretty major stuff, after all. But no – all Savannah had snapped when he'd protested that nobody had said anything to him was, 'Oh stop whingeing, Dizzy. Why would anyone in their right mind *want* to?'

Bitch. At that moment he had hated her so much he could have pulled all her stupid blonde hair out.

Dizzy sighed and switched off his computer. He would go over to the shop, buy a load of chocolate and eat it all in one go. Maybe he'd bump into Moll and she'd sense how pissed off he was and say in that slow sexy voice of hers, 'Hey, Dizzy, you look down in the dumps, why don't we go somewhere quiet, just the two of us, and you can tell me all about it? Maybe I could help to cheer you up . . .'

'Two Crunchies.' Dizzy dug into the pocket of his baggy jeans and pulled out a fiver. 'A Kit-Kat, a Lion bar and one of those big packets of Maltesers. Oh, and ten Marlboro Lights,' he added. 'For my mother.'

Myrtle Armitage gave him a who-are-you-trying-to-kid look. 'I don't sell cigarettes to minors. Tell your mother she'll have to buy her own.'

'She's ill,' said Dizzy, 'in bed. That's why she asked me to get them for her.'

'If she's ill,' Myrtle replied with an air of triumph, 'she won't be needing cigarettes, will she?'

Look, I'm under a lot of *stress*, Dizzy wanted to yell – but it was no good. He knew he couldn't win. The whole world was against him, treating him like some stupid little kid.

Outside the shop he collided with Harriet Ferguson and Blitz. Harriet was trying, without much success, to tie the dog's lead to the litter bin.

'Oh, hi.' She looked relieved to see Dizzy. 'Dogs aren't allowed in the shop. Could you just hold him for a minute while I run inside?'

'Why should I?' said Dizzy. Too right. Nobody ever did him any sodding favours.

Taken aback, Harriet said, 'I'd only be a second. I wanted to pick up my magazine.'

'Wanted' was the understatement of the year. There was a full-sized poster of Brad Pitt free with this week's issue. She'd spent the last hour clearing a space for it on her bedroom wall.

'I can't hold him, right?' Dizzy's tone was dismissive. 'My hands are full.'

Harriet looked at the half dozen or so bars of chocolate he was clutching. 'Put them in your pockets.'

He shot her a look of disgust. 'Oh great, then they'd melt.'

'Well, why don't you—'

'Woof!'

Recognising the smell of chocolate, Blitz leapt up ecstatically on his back legs. Startled, Dizzy took a step backwards and the Lion bar slipped from his grasp. Blitz caught it before it hit the ground and wolfed it down in three seconds flat, wrapper and all.

He eyed Dizzy eagerly, hopeful of an action reply.

'That was my Lion bar!' Dizzy howled. 'You stupid bloody dog! How dare you eat my Lion bar! It was *MINE*!'

'Sor-ry.' Harriet privately felt he was making a big fuss over nothing. How many bars of chocolate could anyone eat in one go anyway? But to humour Dizzy she wagged a finger at Blitz and said, 'Naughty boy.'

Blitz wagged his tail back at her, happily.

'Isn't he gorgeous?' Harriet grinned, forgetting all about Dizzy's strop.

Dizzy hadn't. 'No he isn't,' he sneered, 'he's bloody ugly. And I don't know what you're looking so smug about, because you're buying me another Lion bar.'

'I am not!' Harriet was outraged. 'You shouldn't have dropped it in the first place. Anyway, I haven't got enough money.' Her voice rose. 'And our dog isn't ugly! How *dare* you call him that!'

Dizzy hated the world. He scowled mightily, kicked his trainer against the litter bin – *clanggg* – and muttered, 'He is. He's as ugly as you are.'

Blitz began to gag as a bit of chewed wrapper worked its way back into his throat. Harriet was delighted when he brought up the Lion bar over Dizzy's other trainer.

She fixed Dizzy with the disdainful glare she'd been practising for ages in front of her bedroom mirror. It was a Scary-Spice-meets-Arnold-Schwarzenegger kind of glare, and rather effective if she did say so herself. Whenever she used it on her little brother it reduced him to tears.

Dizzy didn't cry. He said mockingly, 'Oh, I'm *sooo* frightened.'

Harriet bent down and gave Blitz a consoling ear-rub. 'Come on, darling, I'm taking you home. We might be ugly,' she smiled sweetly up at Dizzy, 'but at least we don't dye our hair with Harpic.'

Chapter 42

Dizzy had to do something about his vomit-stained trainer. He sat on the bank, dangled both feet in the village pond and ate his way morosely through the family bag of Maltesers and one of the Crunchie bars.

He couldn't decide whom he hated most. Harriet, for taunting him about the toilet bleach, her mother for telling her about it, or Jessie Roscoe, for dragging him over there in the first place and *promising* him that no one else would ever find out.

Ha, Dizzy thought bitterly. And now the whole village knew. Bloody women, they were all the same.

Well, nearly.

He didn't look up when he heard a front door slam shut. It wasn't until he heard footsteps rustling across the dry grass that he bothered to raise his head.

And there she was, sauntering towards him. Like the way you always wish it would happen, thought Dizzy – but it never does in real life.

But wasn't that weird – when he'd just that moment been thinking about her?

It had to be fate.

Without thinking what he was doing, he put his hand up and waved.

Moll was wearing a tight-fitting black vest, a long, flowing yellow and black skirt, and her usual armfuls of bangles. Her tawny hair was loose today, streaming down her back, and she was carrying an orange cardigan.

Dizzy watched her veer towards him. In his earlier fantasy she had said, 'You look down in the dumps, Dizzy,' and offered to cheer him up. The trouble was, she could hardly say that now. Not when he had a daft grin plastered all over his face.

'Hi,' she said, glancing at Dizzy's thin legs with his jeans rolled up and his big trainers bobbing like torpedoes beneath the surface of the water. 'Bet that feels nice.'

'Join me.' Dizzy felt like a character in a film. Recklessly he patted the grass next to him. 'Got a fag?'

Moll grinned and stuck her hand into the side pocket of her skirt. She pulled out a packet of Superkings and a heavy gold lighter.

'Help yourself.' She sat down next to him on the grass.

Dizzy, who had seen it done in the films, lit two cigarettes and handed one to Moll.

'Ta.'

'What were you doing over there?' He nodded casually in the direction of Keeper's Cottage, where Doug's dark-blue MG was parked outside.

'Popped back for a beer with the boys after closing last night. Left this behind.' Moll patted the orange cardigan, then blew a lazy smoke ring. 'Just called round to pick it up.'

Dizzy couldn't help noticing the black lacy bra-strap poking out from between the folds of orange wool. The cardigan clearly wasn't the only thing she'd taken off and left behind last night.

He wondered if Moll had slept with Doug or Drew or Jamie.

Or all three.

Perspiration prickled behind his ears and down his neck.

'Watch that lighter,' Moll said. 'Don't drop it in the pond.'

Dizzy stopped fiddling with the heavy lighter. 'It's nice,' he said lamely, holding it up and turning it this way and that. 'Did someone give it to you?'

Moll winked. 'Call it a present from a grateful customer.'

What does that wink mean? Dizzy wondered in a frenzy of indecision. Why's she winking at me – and what *kind* of grateful customer?

'Enjoying the school holidays?'

'Boring,' muttered Dizzy.

'And your family, how are they?'

'Huh, don't ask.'

Sex, Dizzy thought. That's what I need. I'm sixteen and I haven't done it yet. That's why I'm so miserable.

He was sex-starved, it was bound to be having an effect. It couldn't be natural to have this many hormones and be celibate.

'Hello.' Moll passed her hand in front of his face. 'What's up? You're miles away.'

Dizzy looked at her. He was having trouble breathing.

'I've got seventy-three pounds in my Post Office savings account. If I gave it to you, would you have sex with me?'

Moll chucked her cigarette end into the pond, an act of vandalism guaranteed to send Eleanor Ferguson – if she were watching – into paroxysms of rage.

'Dizzy, I don't sleep with men for money.'

Oh dear, she thought wryly, is that the kind of reputation I have around here? Is that really what everyone thinks?

'No?' In desperation he said, 'Well, how about for free?'

Moll almost smiled. She shook her head. 'Sorry. I only sleep with men because I want to.'

Dizzy could have cried. He wanted to sleep with Moll Harper more than anything in the world. It was *so unfair*.

'Who gave you this, then?' he said sulkily, nudging the gold lighter with his elbow.

'Ah, I get it.' Moll looked entertained. 'You thought I meant *that* kind of grateful customer.'

Dizzy could feel his lower lip beginning to jut. He'd taken the risk and been rejected. Moll could have taken his Godawful hideous life and made it better, but she hadn't, she'd chosen not to.

It was just another let-down to add to all the rest.

'I don't see why any bloke would give you a gold lighter just because you served him a drink at the bar.' It came out as a challenge.

'Actually, I did more than that. Some guy came into the pub and when I went outside this lad was breaking into his Rolls-Royce.' Moll smiled to herself, remembering the events of that afternoon. 'I dragged him out by his earrings and sat on him until the police arrived.' She shrugged. 'The guy was grateful. He gave me his lighter, that's all.'

Honestly, some blokes had all the luck. Dizzy wished he could be sat on by Moll.

'Anyway,' Moll stretched and yawned, 'I'd better be off.'

Dizzy watched her stand up and brush the grass from her skirt. It was only a cheap one, nothing like the kind of thing his mother would wear.

Seventy-three pounds and she still won't have sex with me, he thought morosely. God, I'm a loser.

'I hate this place.' Dizzy chucked a stone into the pond.

'What you need is to get yourself a girlfriend. That'd buck you up.' Poor lad, she felt quite sorry for him.

Oh yeah, thought Dizzy, and there are so many thousands of girls to choose from.

'Here, have another fag,' Moll said kindly.

'Thanks. Uh . . . you won't tell anyone about what I . . . um . . .'

'Your business proposal, you mean?' She looked amused. 'Don't worry, I'm discreet.'

Dizzy watched her go. Outside the pub Lorna Blake was putting out ashtrays. He saw her speak to Moll, and Moll say something in return. Then half-turning, Moll gestured towards the pond with the hand clutching the orange cardigan and said something else. Lorna burst out laughing and swivelled round to follow the direction of Moll's arm.

Dizzy wanted to die. So much for discretion. It was obvious what they were laughing about.

Him.

When he got home the house was empty. Not even a note on the kitchen table to let him know where everyone else had gone or when they might be back.

That's how much they care about me, Dizzy thought, squelching upstairs in his waterlogged trainers.

It didn't take him long to chuck a few T-shirts and a couple of pairs of jeans into a sportsbag. He added his Post Office savings book, his Walkman, half a dozen favourite tapes and a baseball cap. Half-way down the stairs he remembered bathroom stuff and went back for his toothbrush, shampoo, Clearasil and a bottle of Savannah's expensive conditioner because his hair still went like coconut matting after he washed it.

In the kitchen he made himself a sandwich and emptied the milk money out of the teapot on the top shelf of the dresser. This netted him an extra twenty-three pounds, which would come in handy until he mastered the art of sitting outside a tube station on a grubby blanket looking suitably hungry and homeless.

A grubby blanket . . .

But they didn't have one. Dizzy had to make do with his mother's rather smart tartan picnic rug instead.

'Hop in, if you want a lift,' Jessie said, pulling up at the bus stop. 'Blimey, what's in there?'

Dizzy thudded his Slazenger bag into the back of the van and climbed into the passenger seat. 'Just stuff.'

'Quite a lot of stuff.' When Jessie had seen him with his sportsbag she had assumed he was going swimming. 'What's up? Running away from home?'

'Nah. Staying with a mate in London for a few days. He phoned up this morning.' Dizzy wound the window down so he could rest his arm out of it. 'Mum said it was a great idea.'

Jessie could believe that. The goings-on in Sisley House must have unsettled Dizzy; it would do him good to be away from all the hassle for a few days.

Wary of saying the wrong thing, she waited for Dizzy to raise the subject. When he didn't, she turned on the radio and let him hum happily along to the music instead.

'Enjoy yourself.' Jessie dropped Dizzy and his overloaded bag outside the coach station. 'Have fun.'

'Oh, I will.' Dizzy looked and sounded more cheerful than she'd ever seen him look before. 'I'll have a great time, don't worry about me.'

Chapter 43

Jamie Lyall was a pig.

Drew, who could think of a hundred things he'd rather be doing than tackling the mountain of washing-up left by Jamie, ploughed on with the grim business of scraping two-day-old Cheerios off bowls, dried-up curry off plates, and mould off the inside of half a dozen mugs. The kitchen bin bulged with empty lager cans. He had already discovered an ancient pizza welded to the wire rack in the oven. And wherever he walked, Sugar Puffs crunched under his feet.

It took an hour, but Drew finally got the kitchen looking tidy and moderately hygienic once more. What irritated him most was knowing that when Jamie came home he wouldn't stop and admire his efforts because he simply wouldn't notice. He'd just make himself a coffee, a mountain of toast and another bowl of cereal, wander through to the sitting room and make yet more mess.

Because that, basically, was what he always did.

The coffee might taste a bit better than usual because it wasn't flavoured with mould, but that was all. It wouldn't occur to Jamie that the mug had actually been washed.

I must be getting old, Drew mused. Living in squalor never used to bother me like this.

It wasn't as if he loved housework; it had just gradually crept up on him that doing some every now and again made day-to-day living that much more bearable. It was actually a reasonable thing to do.

Jesus, I'll be taking up tapestry next, Drew thought in alarm. Buying cushions and dried flowers and becoming really interested in discovering what all those mysterious attachments on the Hoover actually *do*.

Still, that was enough domesticity for one day. Now he deserved a reward. Idly glancing out of the sitting-room window, Drew saw Blitz hurtling around the village green like a one-dog relay team, only instead of a baton he had his lead between his teeth.

Lili and Harriet were trying to catch him, without much luck. Blitz, his tail going like a propeller, was enjoying himself far too much.

Grinning broadly, Drew watched as Harriet crept to the left and Lili to the right, attempting to corner him sheepdog-style. Except the green had no corners and Blitz was quicker than both of them. Stopping dead, he crouched on the grass and let them get within a few feet of him. Then he leapt up again, zig-zagging around Lili and haring past Harriet faster than a whippet.

Drew left the cottage, crossed the lane to the green, stuck his fingers in his mouth and let out a piercing whistle. Blitz, recognising him, spun round in delight and bounded over.

'You dimwit,' Drew said affectionately, grabbing the dog by the collar and removing the end of the lead from his drooling mouth.

'My hero,' puffed Lili, staggering up to them. 'Thanks, Drew. From the bottom of my lungs.'

'Good exercise,' he remarked while she got her breath back. 'Maybe Blitz should release a work-out video. He could give Jane Fonda a run for her money.'

Harriet took the lead from him. 'Poor Blitz, he thought you were on his side. Now he'll never trust you again.'

'No more Mr Nice Guy.' Drew winked at her. 'Story of my life.'

'I'm supposed to be taking him up to Compass Hill Wood.' Lili was still panting. 'And I'm shattered already.'

On the spur of the moment – and encouraged by the fact that she had said 'I' rather than 'we' – Drew said, 'I could do with some exercise myself. Would you mind if I came too?'

He directed the question at Harriet, who shrugged.

'I'm not going, I only came out to help Mum catch Blitz. There's something I want to watch on TV.'

'Oh well,' said Drew. He looked at Lili. 'Fancy some company then? Say no if you'd rather be—'

'Why not?' Just slightly pink, Lili smiled up at him. 'I could do with some professional know-how. You can teach this useless animal to do as he's told.'

They walked companionably together up Compass Hill with Blitz straining on his lead between them. By the time they reached the path leading into the woods they had talked about Jamie's allergy to housework, Doug's complicated sex life – though neither of them knew quite *how* complicated – and how to crush garlic without getting the smell of it on your hands.

'We haven't talked about you yet.' Lili bent to unclip Blitz's lead so he could run on ahead and chase squirrels. 'What have you been up to lately?'

'Washing up, mainly.' Looking soulful, Drew splayed his fingers in front of him. 'What can I say? Dishpan hands.'

'Very soft.' Teasingly, Lili touched them. 'Much nicer for the cows when you have to stick your arm up their bottoms.'

He looked at her, bright-eyed from their uphill walk and with wisps of hair escaping from her pony-tail. She was wearing a pale-green shirt over slightly crumpled white trousers and her face was free of make-up. She looked comfortable rather than smart, which he liked. If Lili had been done-up he would have felt scruffy by comparison in his faded Guinness T-shirt and jogging pants.

'I've been working. Nothing much else.' Drew was more interested in finding out more about Lili. 'How's it going at home? Got used to having Michael back yet?'

'I suppose.' Lili sighed without meaning to. Ahead of them Blitz spotted his first squirrel and let out a yelp of delight. 'He goes out a lot. Sometimes I have a moan about it, other times I'm secretly relieved. He's out again this evening,' she went on. 'That's why he's looking after Will and Lottie now. I told him he could jolly well spend a bit of quality time with them while I took Blitz for a walk.'

'Couldn't you all have come out together?'

Lili half-smiled. 'You mean like a story-book family? If I suggested that he'd just look horrified and say, "What's the point?" '

More yelps of frustration echoed through the woods as Blitz attempted to scramble up a vertical tree trunk. Forty feet above his head, a squirrel leapt from branch to branch with elaborate ease, taunting him.

'Is he faithful?'

'Who?' Lili thought for a moment he meant Blitz.

'Your husband.'

'Oh. Well . . . maybe not all the time.'

Drew saw the telltale flush creep up her neck.

'Not *all* the time?' Incredulous, he stopped walking.

'I mean, he might have the odd fling when he's working abroad, but that's kind of . . . well, understandable, isn't it? When you're away from your wife and family for months on end, you're bound to get a bit fed up, a bit bored . . .'

'Lili, you don't have to make excuses for him!'

'I'm not. It's called being realistic. I'm not naive; I know these things go on.' Lili stuffed her hands into the front pockets of her trousers, avoiding Drew's gaze. 'But it's only when he's away, when I'm not around. He wouldn't do it here.' She shrugged. 'Why would he need to?'

Because he's a prize shit, probably, thought Drew. He was furious.

'If he loved you, he wouldn't do it at all,' he said coldly.

'Oh shut up, I wish I'd never told you now.'

Lili felt her throat begin to tighten. She didn't even know why she *had* told Drew. Bleating on about her husband's suspected infidelities – okay, okay, *probable* infidelities – wasn't something she made a habit of.

'Wo-oof!' Blitz howled, losing his grip and sliding in an undignified fashion down the tree trunk. He landed in a heap at the bottom and glanced over his shoulder, embarrassed, to see if anyone had noticed.

'You're criticising me. You think I'm stupid.' Lili tried to swallow the lump in her throat. Dammit, now she *felt* stupid. She really, really wished she'd kept her mouth shut.

261

'I don't, it's not that. I just think you deserve so much better.' Drew was struggling to explain. Michael Ferguson was a philanderer, and Drew wanted to punch his lights out. He wanted Lili to understand that she didn't have to settle for being cheated on, that she was worth more than that.

But mainly, he wanted to put his arms around her and kiss her and kiss her and kiss her . . .

'It isn't as simple as that.' Lili was shaking her head, kicking her way through a pile of dead leaves. 'When you have children, they come first. And they need their Dad.'

From the sound of it, Michael Ferguson wasn't likely to be shortlisted for Father of the Year. But Drew was more interested in hearing more from Lili than arguing with her.

He forced himself to say, 'Of course they do.'

'Then there's that other thing, the old devil-you-know business,' Lili went on. She was doing it again, saying more than she meant to say; how did Drew *do* that?

'You mean, at least he's not a raving psychopath.'

'Look, a lot of women leave their husbands and regret it later. They think it'll be fun, being single again, but it doesn't turn out like that. They end up lonely and depressed instead. They search and search but they never find Mr Right. And in the end they realise the chap they were once married to was actually Mr Almost-Right, which is about as good as it gets.'

Drew stared at Lili in amazement. 'Finished?'

She nodded, embarrassed. 'Finished.'

'Well, that is the most depressing reason I've ever heard for staying married to a jerk.'

'Trust me, it happens. I read the personal columns,' said Lili. 'The world is full of stunning divorcées who can't find a half-decent man. And if *they* can't manage it . . .' she added with a dismissive shake of her head. 'Well, let's be honest, how much hope is there for someone like me?'

Enough was enough.

'Come here.' Drew grabbed her hand and kissed her, very firmly indeed, until Lili began to make running-out-of-air noises.

'That's for being stupid,' Drew told her, trembling with emotion but determined to sound cross. 'And I don't ever want to hear you say anything so ridiculous again. Got it?'

'Got it,' whispered Lili.

'What was all that gurgle-gurgle business, anyway?'

She hung her head, ashamed. The last time she'd been kissed with anything approaching passion must have been twenty years ago. 'Sorry. Forgot to breathe.'

'Well, just don't forget next time.'

'Oh, Drew . . .'

'You know what your trouble is?' he said gruffly.

'What?'

'It doesn't seem to have occurred to you that splitting up doesn't have to mean being miserable for the rest of your life. You don't hear about all the thousands of happily remarried divorcées because they don't advertise in the personal columns.'

'It's easy for you to say that. You've never been married, and you don't have . . . um, children . . .'

Lili was having trouble concentrating. Drew's hands were on her shoulders, his thumbs gently massaging her collarbones. He looked as if he was about to kiss her again. She could smell his warm skin and her knees were buckling. Up ahead, sunlight filtered through the canopy of trees, dappling the ground. Blitz crashed like a hooligan through a maze of young bracken. High above them – and sounding badly in need of Strepsils – a rook cawed.

'I know I haven't, but I'll tell you something.' Drew's mouth was moving closer. 'If I had a wife and family, we'd all walk the dog together. And we'd have fun doing it.'

Lili closed her eyes. Heavens, what a voice. It was like lying in a bath of warm, melted chocolate and not giving a damn about the calories . . .

'I'm going to kiss you again now.' Drew sounded serious. 'Don't forget, okay?'

'Forget what?'

'To keep breathing this time.'

Maybe I'm having an out-of-body experience, Lili thought. Her fingers had somehow managed to creep upwards and start stroking his cheek completely of their own accord.

'Things like this just don't happen to me,' she murmured.

'They do now.'

'We really shouldn't be doing . . .' she gestured idiotically around her. '. . . all this stuff.'

Drew punctuated his reply with kisses. 'Oh yes' – kiss – 'we definitely' – kiss – 'definitely' – kiss – 'should.'

'I'm still breathing,' Lili murmured as his arms slid around her. Drew was such a fantastic kisser. And as for the sensations her poor, tired old body was experiencing . . .

Oops, nearly forgot to breathe again.

In, out.

In, out.

In, out.

'Oh Drew . . .' She pressed herself quite shamelessly against him.

'Oh shit,' Drew groaned. The kiss stopped abruptly. Looking stricken, he half-pulled away.

Oh no. Poor Drew, Lili thought, her heart going out to him. How awful to suffer from premature ejaculation.

And heavens, that *had* been premature!

'I'm so sorry about this,' Drew muttered into her hair.

'It doesn't matter, really it doesn't.' Rushing to reassure him, Lili buried her head against his broad chest and hugged him tighter still. 'Golly, it happens to loads of men. If anything I'm flattered—'

'Perhaps you should look behind you,' Drew said, gently turning her around.

Chapter 44

Felicity stood in a sun-dappled clearing less than fifty yards away from Lili and Drew. Blitz was close by, snuffling in the undergrowth, undeterred by her arrival. Used to seeing Felicity every day when she dropped Freya off at the house, it clearly hadn't occurred to him to bark.

Lili couldn't move. All the old clichés seemed to be clamouring to get out of her brain. She wished a big hole would open up and swallow her; she wished it could be a terrible dream. She wished she could do what two-year-old Will did when he didn't want anyone to see him, and cover her own eyes.

It took a second or two before Lili realised that Felicity was standing there, in her immaculate black and white shirt dress and black patent leather court shoes, *crying*.

'Felicity . . .?'

Lili's whole body was drenched in panicky sweat. She didn't have a clue what to say next, but she knew she had to try and say something. This was awful, her worse night-mare; she needed to come up with some kind of plausible excuse, fast.

But Felicity was shaking her head, signalling her not to speak. The tears were still pouring down her cheeks and she was clearly without a handkerchief. She stood there, staring at them through red-rimmed eyes, sniffing and gulping like a child.

'Felicity, I'm sorry. I know what you must be th-thinking,' Lili faltered, 'but I swear to you, we—'

'Don't,' Felicity sobbed, making no attempt to wipe her eyes. The expression in them was utterly desolate. 'Just don't try and explain, okay? Because right now I can't bear to hear it.'

She turned and ran back through the woods the way she had come, her thin legs gawky and stumbling on the uneven path in her rush to get away.

Blitz, his tail wagging and a politely bemused expression on his face, watched her go.

'Oh my God oh my God,' groaned Lili, 'this is *awful* . . .'

Drew longed to put a comforting arm around her but he didn't quite dare. All the blissful intimacy between them had vanished in a moment, evaporated into thin air.

'She won't say anything,' he tried to reassure Lili, who was now trembling for a different reason. She was in deep shock.

'You don't know Felicity. She disapproves of me so much already.'

'Okay, but it was only a kiss.'

Drew wished he was better at spur-of-the-moment excuses. Unlike Doug, he simply hadn't had the practice.

'Drew.' Despite her panic-stricken state, Lili gave him a pitying look. 'There are kisses and there are kisses. What Felicity saw just now was pretty much of a giveaway, I'd say. It hardly fell into the category of quick social peck on the cheek.'

'I didn't mean it like that,' said Drew. 'Look, you're fairly convinced Michael's played away himself, in the past. How much of a fuss can he kick up if he does get to hear about this?'

'I've no idea.' Lili didn't hold out much hope for instant understanding and total forgiveness. 'I'll give you a ring, shall I, and let you know when I find out?'

Drew hated feeling so useless. What a balls-up! How many blokes, he thought with a surge of self-disgust, could wreck a meaningful relationship before it was even two minutes old?

Lili had been thinking, too.

'Was Felicity crying already? Was she walking through the woods having a good old cry when she happened to bump into us?'

She looked hopeful until Drew shook his head.

'Sorry, other way round. She saw us, *then* burst into tears.'

Eleanor Ferguson, who had been on one of her periodic knitting benders, arrived at The Old Vicarage just as Michael was reversing the Volvo out of the drive.

'Snooker,' he told his mother, dutifully admiring the three Aran cardigans she whisked out of a carrier bag to show him. 'The kids'll love them. Mum, I've got a match at seven, mustn't keep the others waiting—'

'You go and enjoy yourself,' Eleanor told him fondly. 'You deserve an evening off.'

Lili wished she had film in her camera, to capture the expressions on the faces of Will, Lottie and Harriet as their grandmother lined them up, von Trapp fashion, in their matching porridge-toned cardigans.

'You all look very smart.' Eleanor moved briskly from one to the next, tweaking leather buttons and turned-up sleeves into place. 'And don't worry, there's plenty of room for growth.'

Lili knew her children would have to be chloroformed before they would ever wear these cardigans of their own free will. She said, 'Eleanor, they're wonderful. I don't know how you do it. You could win competitions with knitting as brilliant as that.'

Unused to such fulsome flattery from her daughter-in-law, Eleanor was more than happy to babysit for an hour while Lili popped over to Duck Cottage.

As she raced across the green, Lili couldn't help wondering how Eleanor would react if she knew the real reason she was so eager to see Jess.

'We have to talk,' Lili announced breathlessly, barging in without knocking and almost tripping over a suitcase in the hall. 'Jess, I'm desperate. I've done something terrible and now Michael's going to find out.' She hopped from foot to foot in anguish. 'I need you to tell me what to do.'

Jessie looked up from her packing. 'You've been putting rat poison in his bacon sandwiches?'

'No.' Lili cringed. 'Worse.'

'What, then?'

'Oh help, I'm going to blush. I kissed Drew Darcy.'

Jessie watched her blush.

'And who saw you?'

'Felicity.'

'What did she do?'

'Burst into tears.'

'Was it nice?'

Lili gazed at her in astonishment. Was Jessie trying not to smile?

'What, watching Felicity burst into tears?'

'Don't be daft. Kissing Drew.'

'It was heaven,' Lili said miserably. 'Oh God, I know it's hopeless but I really like him. And I think he really likes me. Except now everything's ruined. Felicity's going to take Freya away because I'm a bad moral influence, and she's bound to tell Michael, who'll go ballistic—'

'Right, let's get this sorted out.' Jessie stood up and stepped over the open suitcase. 'First we go and see Felicity. Find out if she *is* going to tell Michael.'

Horrified, Lili gasped, 'Oh, we can't do that!'

'You need to know, don't you?' Jessie grabbed her by the arm, pulling her over the suitcase and through the front door. 'Look, you can grovel if you want to. Shed a few tears yourself, tell Felicity it was a one-off, a momentary lapse . . . God, you're only human, after all—'

'Except Felicity *isn't* human, is she?' said Lili, petrified. 'She's perfect.'

Hugh's car, thankfully, wasn't in the driveway.

Jessie rang the doorbell three times before Felicity came to the door.

'Hi,' said Jessie, 'Lili would like to talk to you and I'm here as moral support.'

More like immoral support, thought Lili.

'So,' Jessie went on cheerfully, 'can we come in?'

Felicity was pale, wet-haired and wrapped in an eau-de-nil satin dressing gown. The make-up was gone and her eyelids were swollen. She looked as if she'd been crying for hours.

As she nodded and led the way through to the sitting room, Lili wondered suddenly if Felicity was this distraught because she too had a crush on Drew Darcy. Mortified, blushing furiously and hating every second, she gazed down at the flawless pistachio-green carpet and stumbled through her excuses and apologies. It was shameful and not terribly likely to work, but she begged anyway.

'. . . so there it is. It's up to you. I know I shouldn't have done what I did, but I promise you I'm not having an affair with Drew Darcy.' Dry-mouthed and still unable to drag her eyes above skirting-board level – incredibly *clean* boards they were too – Lili reached the end of her grovel. 'It's just one more mistake to add to all my other hundreds of mistakes,' she concluded hopelessly. 'I wish I could be perfect, like you and Hugh, but I'm not.'

Felicity stood up, clutching her robe tightly around her narrow waist. 'Wait there. I've got something to show you.'

She was back less than a minute later with an ivory leather photograph album.

'Your wedding album?' Lili's heart sank at the sight of gold-edged pages. Oh crikey, what now? Was she really in for a stern lecture on the sanctity of marriage?

269

Chapter 45

Felicity placed the heavy album on the floor in front of them and knelt down next to it.

'This is what I was doing when you rang the doorbell.'

She flipped over the first page and Lili's hand flew to her mouth.

The photograph of Felicity arriving at the church had been neatly cut into quarters.

In silence, Felicity leafed steadily through the pages, showing them that she hadn't stopped until she'd reached the end. Every single photograph had been snipped to pieces.

'That's how perfect my marriage is.' Felicity spoke at last, her voice wobbling with emotion. 'See that wedding dress? Sonia Rykiel. See the limos and the bridesmaids' outfits and the hotel where we had the reception?' With her index finger she prodded chopped-up sections of different photographs, pointing them out. 'Everything cost a fortune. All our guests kept telling us it was the most fabulous wedding they'd ever been to. And all the time they were saying it I was thinking, *you have no idea.*' She stopped and glanced up, her eyes brimming with fresh tears. 'Because do you know how much Hugh loved me? Well, he didn't. Not at all.'

This was awful. Lili couldn't bear it. Impulsively she reached over and squeezed Felicity's arm. Heavens, it was thinner than one of Bambi's ankles. 'You don't know that. Even if you've had a fight and he said it, I bet you anything he didn't mean it. Sometimes people yell terrible things when they don't—'

'It wasn't a fight. And Hugh didn't tell me.' Felicity took

a deep, shuddery breath. 'I've just always known it.'

'Where is he now?' Jessie, asked. Felicity had used a sharp pair of scissors on those photos. She hoped they weren't dealing with a body-in-the-bedroom situation here.

'He's left me.' Felicity propped her knees under her chin and wrapped her arms around her legs. 'He promised he never would, but he has.'

'How awful! You poor, poor thing,' Lili said. 'I'm so sorry.'

'And I know what you're both thinking,' Felicity blurted out. 'But no, he didn't leave me for another woman. Hugh's gay, you see. He's left me for another man.'

Lili gasped. 'Oh good grief!'

'You don't have to tell us this,' said Jessie, but Felicity was shaking her blonde head.

'If I don't tell someone, I'll explode.'

'Maybe he'll change his mind and come back,' Lili suggested. 'He might just be . . . well, confused.'

Felicity examined a fingernail with a jagged edge. Without even bothering to phone her manicurist for an emergency consultation, she bit off the end. 'Hugh isn't bisexual. He's *gay*. One hundred per cent.'

Lili frowned. 'He can't be. What about Freya?'

'We bought a plastic syringe at the chemist.'

'So you've never had sex?' Lili was finding this hard to fathom; her perfect couple was disintegrating around her ears.

'Never had sex,' Felicity agreed simply. 'Not with Hugh.' A pause. 'Not with anyone else either.'

'What, *no one*?'

Before Lili's astonishment went into orbit, Jessie intervened. 'If you knew he was gay, why did you marry him?'

Felicity heaved a sigh. 'I was naive, and lonely, and he swept me off my feet. By the time he told me it was too late. I was so in love with him I said it didn't matter. After all,' she said sadly, 'what you've never had, you can't miss. And people are always saying sex isn't as important as friendship.'

'I'm sorry if this is a rude question,' said Jessie, 'but could we open a bottle of wine?'

271

The wine was fetched from the fridge and poured into Waterford crystal glasses.

'Hugh had to marry. His boss was a complete bigot, obsessed with the image of the company,' Felicity explained. 'If you weren't a family man, basically, you didn't get promoted.'

'He's brilliant with Freya,' said Lili.

'Of course he is, he adores her. We both do.'

'If this comes out, will he get the sack?' Jessie asked.

'I don't know. Maybe. But he doesn't care.' Felicity shrugged. 'It isn't a fling this time, you see. For the first time in his life Hugh's fallen in love. And I can't begin to compete.'

She paused and took a great swig of Chablis, shuddering as the iciness of it caught in her throat.

'Heavens,' said Lili, feeling humble. 'I don't know what to say. No wonder you were upset when we saw you this afternoon in the woods.'

'Well, yes.' For the first time a faint, wry smile lit up Felicity's pale features. 'But the reason I burst into tears at the sight of the two of you was because I was so . . . so *jealous*.'

Lili's eyebrows shot up. 'Jealous?'

'No, not jealous. Envious. In the same way that you envied me my marriage, I suppose.' Another smile, a bit broader this time. 'You see, I envy *you*, Lili. As far as I'm concerned, you're the one with the perfect life.'

'Another drink,' Lili gasped, holding out her empty glass. 'My God, you think *my* life is perfect!'

'I'm not a relaxed person. I love the way you treat Freya. And nothing ever fazes you, and you have three happy children and a husband who adores you . . .'

'I say, steady on there.' Lili was half-laughing, half-embarrassed.

'Okay, but you have a husband who comes home and makes mad passionate love to you on the kitchen table. Or would have done if we hadn't turned up at the wrong moment. Thanks,' Felicity said as Jess refilled her glass to the brim. 'If that's empty there's another one in the fridge. You see, nobody's ever done that to me,' she went on sadly. 'And when I realised what we'd interrupted, I was so *envious*.'

'You must have thought I was a right trollop,' said Lili, 'when you caught me today, cheating on Michael.'

Felicity shook her head. 'But I didn't, not at all. I just thought how lucky you were, to have a husband *and* a lover. You see, I was envious of that too.'

Jessie fetched the second bottle from the fridge. Through the baby alarm they heard Freya upstairs, stirring then settling again in her cot.

'I feel better now I've said all that.' Felicity combed her pale fingers through her hair. 'It's such a relief to talk about it. Even if you do think I'm stupid.'

'You aren't stupid,' Lili protested.

'Gullible, then. A bit of a sad case.' Felicity bit her lip. 'God, wait until this gets out. I'll be the laughing stock of the village.'

'You won't be. It won't get out. Nobody in the village needs to know,' said Jessie. 'We won't tell anyone.'

Lili was shaking her head vigorously, but Felicity seemed unconvinced.

'Look,' said Lili, 'I'm not going to breathe a word, am I? Because I know if I did, you could run round the village blabbing about me and Drew.'

Felicity nodded.

The silence in the room lengthened.

Felicity glanced up from under her eyelashes at Jessie.

'Okay, okay,' Jessie caved in, 'if it makes you happier, I'll throw my secret into the pot too.'

'What secret?' Lili demanded.

'I slept with Toby last night.'

'You did WHAT?' Lili shrieked, almost bouncing off the sofa. 'You didn't tell me about this!'

'There hasn't been time,' Jessie protested mildly.

'Gosh.' Enthralled, Felicity refilled their glasses.

Lili dismissed the thought of her mother-in-law sitting at home minding her children and casting disapproving glances at the clock 'Go on then,' she declared, 'tell us everything. We've got time now.'

'You've had your nose pressed against that window for the last two hours,' said Jamie, chucking a pizza crust at Drew's head. 'What's going on out there – Melinda Messenger getting her kit off?'

Drew ignored him. Jamie was sprawled in his favourite armchair in front of the television, laughing himself sick at an ancient Benny Hill re-run. He clearly had big tits on the brain.

Anyway, nothing was going on outside now. Earlier, he had watched Lili scurrying over to Jessie's cottage. Within minutes they had set off together up Compass Hill – making for Hugh and Felicity Seymour's house, presumably.

But that had been ages ago. There had been no sign of them since.

Not knowing what was going on was hideous; it was doing Drew's head in. He longed to rush after them and hammer on the Seymours' front door, yelling, 'Don't blame Lili! It was all my fault . . . I *love* her!' Except he wouldn't, of course. Because though it might be true it would also make him look a prize berk.

And it was hardly likely to help Lili.

'This is bloody funny,' Jamie cackled as Benny Hill fell out of a plane and landed in a haystack with a parachute made of suspender belts and bras. He tossed a handful of peanuts into the air, tried to catch them in his mouth and missed. 'You should be watching this, it's brilliant.'

Not half as brilliant as the way I feel about Lili Ferguson, thought Drew, wishing he could phone her.

Blimey, he must have it bad. Right now the thought of Lili with all her clothes on was far more of a thrill than Melinda Messenger getting her kit off.

Chapter 46

Oliver was working in the pub but his mind wasn't on the job. He had overcharged one customer tonight, under-charged several others and given one chap fifteen pounds' change from a fiver.

Lorna, keeping a close eye on him, watched him fill a pint glass to the brim with Fosters. 'The customer asked for shandy,' she reminded him.

He shook his head apologetically, tipped half the lager away and began filling the glass with draught tonic water instead.

'Olly, let me do that. One of the barrels needs changing in the cellar.'

Lorna watched him thread his way through the pub. Savannah, she realised, was keeping an eye on him too, swivelling round on her bar stool so her pink skirt rode all the way up her thighs. It hadn't escaped Lorna's notice that the atmosphere between them this evening had been strained.

'Haven't seen your mum and dad in here for a while.' Lighting a cigarette, she offered one to Savannah.

'That's because they haven't been in for a while.' Realising this sounded ruder than she'd meant it to, Savannah took a cigarette even though she didn't want one. To make amends she said, 'They've been pretty busy . . . working, that kind of thing.'

Lorna, who didn't believe in shilly-shallying around, propped her elbows on the bar and said bluntly, 'Oliver's not himself tonight.'

Savannah didn't reply to this; she simply shrugged and took a drag of her cigarette.

'Look, he's a good boy. I'm very fond of him,' Lorna said,

'and something's troubling him. Before he comes back, why don't you tell me what's up?'

Up. How apt.

Savannah wanted to cry. She was wearing her shortest skirt, and not once this evening had Oliver glanced at her legs. She'd even squashed herself into a too-tight Wonder-bra – unbelievably uncomfortable, but the results were dramatic – and for all the attention he'd paid her cleavage she might as well be wearing a sack.

Oliver wasn't just impotent, it seemed. He'd turned into a full-blown eunuch.

'Nothing's up,' Savannah said bitterly, avoiding Lorna's gaze. 'Nothing at all.'

'It's ten o'clock,' came the frosty accusation when Lili slipped into the sitting room, as if by doing so stealthily Eleanor somehow wouldn't notice the time.

'I know, I'm sorry.'

Lili, breathless from running, tried to breathe through her nose so Eleanor wouldn't smell the alcohol fumes. Oh Lord, she sounded like a steam train.

'You're late.'

Lili wondered rebelliously why she always had to get the ticking-off. Michael was late too, later than she was, but Eleanor would never dream of implying that he was a thoughtless, neglectful father. Oh no, Michael was her precious son, Lili thought, swaying a bit. That made him perfect . . .

But she forced herself to look suitably penitent. 'I really am sorry. It won't happen again. Did . . . um . . . anybody ring?'

'Like who?'

Like Drew, you nosy old witch. 'I don't know.' Lili shrugged. 'Anyone.'

But Eleanor shook her head. 'Only some chap selling double glazing. I told him you weren't interested.'

Lili's heart did a back flip. Had it been Drew?

When she had grovelled some more and Eleanor had left, she rang 1471.

Number withheld.
Oh bum.

Begging wasn't all it was cracked up to be. Dizzy had made seventy-two pence in five hours and been given a soggy corned-beef sandwich by some old dear who'd ranted on at him to confess his sins to the Good Lord and pray for entrance to the Kingdom of Heaven.

'She's barking, mate. Barking Beryl we call her,' announced a skinny lad with dyed yellow hair, squatting down in the doorway next to him. 'Don't touch that sandwich whatever you do. It ain't corned beef, it's Pedigree Chum. Hey, neat blanket.'

'Nicked it,' Dizzy mumbled. Privately he blamed the picnic rug for his low earnings. He'd muddied it up a bit, but it still didn't look authentic.

'Who'd you nick it from, the Queen?' The boy grinned. 'I'm Skunk, by the way. Got anything on you?' He winked and patted the filthy pocket of his denim shirt.

'Um . . . no.'

'Well if you want any, I'm your man. See y'around.' The boy gave Dizzy a friendly nudge in the ribs and hauled himself to his feet.

'Yeah, great.' Dizzy nodded and stifled a yawn. It had been an eventful day. 'Anyway, I'm going to have a kip.'

He woke up shivering an hour later, minus his mother's picnic rug. The sports bag was gone too.

This is more like it, thought Dizzy, relieved to feel his wallet still stuffed down the front of his jeans. This is more authentic.

He lay back down in the newsagent's doorway and imagined the chaos at home. His family would be frantic with worry, they'd have called out the police by now. The news that he was missing would have spread around the village and Moll would be feeling terrible, blaming herself.

Happily, Dizzy closed his eyes, imagining his mother and sister in floods of tears and his father, distraught, telling the police he'd do anything, pay any amount of money, so long as his son was returned safe and sound.

Bugger, he thought as he drifted back to sleep, should have left a ransom note.

April didn't need to study the evidence in her bathroom mirror to see if she looked different these days; she *knew* she looked different. She felt different too, as if her whole personality had been locked up for years in a box too small for it, and had now burst free.

Everyone at work had noticed the transformation – the nurses, the cleaners, some of the doctors . . . even Doug Flynn had winked at her across the reception desk the other day and said, 'Whatever you're on, sweetheart, I wouldn't mind some of it.'

She had blushed, of course – that hadn't gone away – and Rosie the junior house officer had joined in with a grin, 'I think April's won the lottery and isn't telling us.'

April had wanted to say, 'Better than that,' because winning a squillion pounds was nothing compared with falling in love with the most wonderful man in the world . . . particularly when you'd given up hope of ever finding happiness again.

There was a tap on the bathroom door before Michael pushed it open. 'What are you doing in here? You've been ages.' He came up behind her and slid his arms around her waist, growling, 'Come back to bed this minute.'

They smiled at each other in the mirror and Michael pretended to bite her neck.

'I was just thinking how lucky I am.' April leaned back against him. Oh, how she loved that solid feeling, that sense of utter security.

'I was just thinking how lonely I was, all on my own in that big old bed.'

Laughing, she let him carry her back into the bedroom and make love to her again. It was so easy to let herself go with Michael; his enthusiasm was infectious. To April, it felt as if she'd been on the strictest possible diet all her life, and now she was being introduced to the joys of real food by a gourmet.

'Next time we'll have to try out your bed,' she told him afterwards, her head nestling against his shoulder. 'I haven't even seen your house yet.'

'I told you, I've got the decorators in.' Over the top of her head, Michael glanced at his watch: ten thirty already. 'Pots of paint and dust sheets everywhere.'

'I wouldn't mind. I'd still like to see where you live.'

'It's a mess, and I'd mind.' He gave her a hug. 'God, I'm hot. Okay if I take a quick shower before I go?'

Go?

'Have a shower if you want. But don't go,' April begged, stroking his collarbone. 'Please.'

'I must.'

'Why? Will the pots of paint miss you?'

Michael sighed. It was no good, this was getting too complicated. He had to tell her.

'April, listen to me.'

'Hmm?'

She was busy trailing kisses across his chest.

'I told you I was separated from my wife . . .'

April's head jerked up in alarm.

'. . . and I am,' Michael said hastily. 'I mean, the marriage is over, I swear it is . . .'

'But . . .' April's eyes were as big as Bambi's. She looked terrified. 'But what?'

'But – the property market being as it is, I haven't been able to move out yet.'

April felt her heart crashing painfully against her ribs. She whispered, 'You still live with your wife?'

Michael nodded. 'We live separate lives. I sleep in the spare room, of course. But you have to understand I can't exactly take you home and introduce you to the family. That would be . . . well, cruel.'

April was too shocked to cry. All she could hear was Bernadette's voice on the phone the other night, gently warning her not to get too carried away because Things Could Go Wrong.

'Why do you have to *do* this?' she had demanded at the time, irritated by Bernadette's prophecies of doom and gloom. 'I'm happy. Nothing's going to go wrong. Stop trying to depress me.'

Bernadette had tried to placate her. 'I'm not, I just don't want you to get hurt.'

'Oh, change the record,' she had snapped back, 'that one's stuck.'

'April, nothing's changed.' Michael climbed out of bed. 'I still love you. But if you don't want to see me any more, I'll understand.'

He looked sad as he headed for the bathroom. April lay in bed listening to the muffled roar of the shower.

Oh God, I can't lose him, not now.

And he was right, she thought, chewing a thumbnail, nothing *had* changed. They still shared the same feelings for each other, didn't they?

Okay, it was inconvenient, but that wasn't Michael's fault.

It wasn't the end of the world either.

Just a housing problem, really.

When Michael emerged from the shower with one of her pink towels slung around his hips, April held her arms out to him.

'I'm sorry. It was the shock, that's all.' She clung to him. 'I love you too.'

Chapter 47

Toby had been ringing and ringing Jessie's number but there was still no answer.

'That's weird,' said Deborah, coming into his study. 'I thought Dizzy was in his room. But I've just been up there and it's empty.'

It was a sign of the current dismal state of their marriage, Toby thought, that these were the first words she had spoken to him all day. They were like two strangers, he realised, in a hospital waiting room. Deliberately avoiding eye contact, each lost in their own thoughts. The easygoing rapport between them had well and truly vanished.

What was more, he no longer even cared.

Still no reply. Wearily Toby hung up the phone. 'Where is he, then? I haven't seen him.'

Deborah shrugged. 'No idea.'

When Toby came back downstairs, she was in the kitchen spreading Brie on Bath Olivers.

'His Walkman's gone. And his GameBoy. And some stuff's missing from the bathroom,' he announced grimly.

Deborah looked up. 'What, you mean he's taken them with him? He's run away? What about clothes?'

'I can't tell. The wardrobe isn't bare, if that's what you mean,' Toby pushed his fingers through his blond hair, 'but some things may have gone.'

'Toby! What do we do?'

'I'll try the pub. Ask Savannah. Maybe he said something to her.'

Deborah licked gooey Brie from her fingers. 'Will you go and see Jess, too?'

'I might.'

Was Jessie out, or had she simply not been answering the phone?'

'You slept with her last night.'

Toby's eyes didn't flicker. 'Yes.'

'It's okay,' Deborah said with a faint smile. 'I told her you would.'

'Dizzy?' Jessie stood in the doorway of the cottage, frowning. 'Yes, I saw him. I gave him a lift to the coach station this afternoon.'

Toby exhaled slowly. 'The coach station. Did he say where he was going?'

'Well of course he did – to stay with a friend in London.' She looked puzzled. 'Didn't Deborah tell you?'

'Deborah's just been up to his room and discovered he's missing.'

'But he said she thought it was a great idea . . . Oh well, he was obviously lying. Sorry,' said Jessie, shaking her head. 'I just saw him waiting at the bus stop with his bag, thought I was doing him a favour.'

'Did he seem upset?'

'No. Quite cheerful actually.'

Toby said, 'Can I come in?'

'What will you do, phone the police?'

He hesitated. 'No, not yet anyway. I've got a few of his friends' parents' numbers somewhere. I'll ring around tomorrow, see if I can track him down.' He gazed steadily at Jessie. 'But I'd still like to come in. I've spent the last two hours trying to ring you.'

'Look, last night was a huge mistake.' Jessie followed him into the dimly lit living room but didn't sit down. She fiddled with the sleeves of her grey sweatshirt, pulling them over her knuckles and folding her arms across her chest.

'It wasn't a mistake.' Toby's voice was gentle. 'You know how much I love you.'

'Deborah was unfaithful to you, so you were unfaithful to her. It was a revenge thing.' Jessie blinked and turned away. 'And two wrongs don't make a right.'

Toby thought they did. 'Jess, you aren't—'

'I shouldn't have slept with you last night and I'm definitely not going to sleep with you again.'

First Dizzy, now this. It was too much to cope with in one evening.

With a sense of impending doom, Toby said, 'Why not?'

'Because it's humiliating. Next time you want to get your own back on Deborah, you'll just have to find someone else to have sex with.' Meaning it, Jessie said, 'Let them find out how it feels to be the consolation prize.'

Despite the gallons of wine she had swallowed, Lili woke up at once when the bedroom door creaked open. She watched through her eyelashes as Michael moved quietly around the room, taking off his clothes and dropping them on the floor for her to pick up in the morning. Everything except his trousers, anyway, which for some reason were exempt from this routine. The trousers were always meticulously folded and hung up.

In the dim and distant past, Lili remembered, she had found this foible quaint.

'I'm awake,' she murmured when he climbed into bed next to her.

'Sshh, go to sleep.'

'Did you win?'

'Win what?'

'The snooker match.'

'Knocked out in the semi-finals. Missed the pink.'

'Bad luck. Okay, g'night.'

Michael patted her thigh and leaned over to give her a brief kiss on the ear. For a worrying second Lili wondered if this meant he wanted to have sex with her, but he turned back over and hauled the duvet up over his shoulders, sign language for Goodnight, Irene.

As she drifted back to sleep, Lili caught the faint whiff of magnolias. In the dim, subconscious recess of her mind, it occurred to her that, for a man who had just spent six hours in the smoky confines of a snooker club, Michael smelled astonishingly clean.

'Oi, you! Out the way.'

Dizzy blinked, screwed up his face and winced as a none-too-gentle boot prodded him in the back.

'Ouch. What time is it?'

'Four thirty.'

'*What?*'

The man above him cackled with unsympathetic laughter. 'And you must be new to this lark, else you wouldn't sleep in my doorway. This is a newsagent's, sunbeam. If it's a lie-in you're after, try the shoe shop next door. They don't open 'til nine.'

But Dizzy was out of luck. The doorway of the shoe shop was already taken, as were most of the other doorways in the street. Now he knew why the other occupants had been smirking at him and nudging each other last night.

He'd even managed to get sleeping rough wrong.

By lunchtime, the novelty of being on the streets was beginning to wear off. Dizzy had been cornered by Barking Beryl again and forced to endure a Bible reading. Two teenage boys whizzing past on skateboards had spat at him with hideous accuracy. A middle-aged businessman had called him scum. And when a pretty girl had dropped something into his upturned baseball cap, Dizzy had called 'Thank you' after her before realising it wasn't a coin but a wodge of used chewing gum.

Being minus his Walkman was no fun either. Time dragged horribly without U2 and Oasis blasting holes in your eardrums.

Worst of all, with no feeling left in his bottom from sitting on the pavement, Dizzy had ventured into a small park and sunk thankfully on to the softer grass. It wasn't until an hour later when he was searching for more daisies for his daisy chain that he swivelled round and discovered a used syringe – complete with bloodstained needle – lying under a dandelion leaf just inches from his previously numb bum. Shaking, he imagined the consequences if he'd sat on it. His mind conjured up terrifying images of himself riddled with Aids.

Dizzy ran out of the park, across the main road and into the warm, welcoming, blissfully familiar arms of Burger King. But even the perky little redhead serving behind the counter didn't seem to smile at him as brightly as she did the other customers. Sitting down at a table by the window, Dizzy surreptitiously sniffed his armpits. Without deodorant and a change of clothes he was definitely beginning to pong.

Oh dear, there was such a thing as *too* authentic.

He found himself gazing longingly at the telephone box across the street. Could he phone Baz, his best friend from school, and ask him to put him up for a couple of days? Then he could have a bath, wash his hair and sleep in a real bed.

Maybe even borrow a Walkman.

No, that was no good. Dispiritedly, Dizzy picked a shred of lettuce out of his BK Flamer. Baz's mother would be suspicious; she'd only phone up his mother and give the game away. Tempting though the thought of a hot bath was – and Dizzy had never imagined he'd hear himself thinking *that* – it simply wasn't on. He wanted his parents – okay, and Moll, and even stupid Harriet Ferguson – to worry themselves sick about him. And how could they be worried sick if they knew he was swanning around Baz's mother's bloody great five-storey house – Christ, it was practically a *palace* – in Kensington?

Dizzy was gripped suddenly by a great wave of homesickness. He shredded his bun, rolled the bits of bread into pellets and watched a girl in a baseball cap roller-blade into the phone box. She was wearing pink shorts and one of those tiny stretchy top things, and when she took off her cap he saw that she had long, silver-blonde hair.

The effect was both attention-getting and familiar. She looked, Dizzy realised, a lot like Sav.

Blimey, things had to be tough when you were reduced to missing your own stroppy pain-in-the-neck sister.

Savannah was painting her toenails white when the phone began to ring. Cursing with annoyance she waddled like a goose across the room to answer it.

'Hello?'

Nothing.

'Hello?'

Still nothing.

'Look, is anybody there?' she said briskly, 'because this is getting boring.'

No reply.

'Right.' She hung up.

In London, deeply disappointed, Dizzy hung up too.

Well, so much for everyone being out of their minds with worry.

As he pushed his way out of the phone box, which reeked of the roller-blading girl's cheap perfume, Dizzy was struck by a terrible thought.

What if nobody had even noticed yet that he'd gone?

Chapter 48

'I'm amazed I managed to make it through the door, my nose feels so long,' said Lili. 'I've never told so many lies before in my life.'

'I'm glad you came.'

Drew hadn't been able to stop thinking about her; he had hardly slept last night. He wanted to kiss Lili now; but there were three vet nurses in the next room and the door could be flung open at any moment.

Instead, he lifted Blitz up on to the examination table and gave his ears an affectionate rub.

Blitz wagged his tail.

'He's fine, I take it?'

Lili blushed and nodded.

'I told Michael he'd swallowed a tennis ball.'

Blitz looked astonished.

'And then I thought if I tell your receptionist that, you'll have to do loads of X-rays, so I said he'd been sick a few times instead.'

Blitz panted happily and licked Drew's hand.

'We'll just say he ate something that disagreed with him. And you can tell Michael that the tennis ball passed through . . . er . . . naturally.'

A pained expression appeared in the dog's soulful dark eyes.

'Ouch,' said Lili.

Drew glanced across at her. 'Anyway, I pity the next poor sod who tries to sell double glazing to your mother-in-law.'

'So it was you.' She grinned. 'I wondered, but the number was withheld.'

'Ah well, you don't share a house with Doug Flynn without picking up a few pointers.' Then he grew serious. 'I saw you and Jess setting out last night. How did it go?'

'Felicity's fine about it. She won't tell anyone. She and Hugh have broken up,' Lili added briefly, without going into details. 'She was crying because she envied me having a husband and a hunky lover too.'

'Hunky!' It made him sound like Jean-Claud van Damme. 'I'm not hunky.'

Lili, who thought he was, said, 'You're not my lover either.'

No, but I want to be, thought Drew.

The charged silence was broken by Fiona, one of the nurses, popping her head around the door.

'Drew, Mrs Childerley's outside with her boa constrictor. Any chance of seeing them before it swallows Richie Bigelow's kitten?'

Relieved not to be playing gooseberry any more, Blitz leapt off the table and licked Fiona's hand.

'Right, well, we're just about finished here. I'll be out in a sec,' said Drew, a bit too heartily.

'You're busy,' said Lili when the door had closed behind them. 'I shouldn't have come. I could've just phoned to let you know all this.'

But she hadn't been able to stay away. A phone call wouldn't have been enough. Just the thought of seeing Drew again had made her go fizzy all over, like a sherbet dip.

It was a full-blown addiction, and Lili couldn't say no.

'This is better than a phone call.' Drew recognised the craving; he had it too. Quickly, taking her by surprise, he kissed Lili's half-open mouth. She tasted of Opal Fruits.

Out in the waiting room, someone screamed. A woman's voice scolded, 'Bad boy, Percy! The lady doesn't want you on her lap.'

'See if you can get away this afternoon. I'm off at three,' Drew murmured, lovingly stroking Lili's hair. 'Ring me.'

I'm practically an adulteress, Lili marvelled, nodding happily. I should be ashamed of myself.

Oh, but how could something so wicked feel so *right*?

Savannah was sunbathing on the terrace when she heard Toby and Deborah return home. They had driven into Harleston to report Dizzy's disappearance to the police. Shielding her eyes from the one o'clock sun, Savannah thought how desperately worried her father looked.

'Any news?' he said. 'Any phone calls?'

'Nope. Well, one call,' she amended, to be accurate, 'but there was nobody there.'

Toby frowned. 'You mean it was a silent call?'

Savannah shrugged. 'I guess.'

'It could have been Dizzy.'

Oh God, could it? She experienced a spasm of guilt. 'But that's stupid. Why would he phone up and not say anything?'

Toby sighed. 'Look, I have to take some photos of Dizzy over to the police station. If the phone rings again, let your mother answer it.'

'Are they out looking for him?' Savannah said brightly. 'Is it like that film with Harrison Ford . . . you know, *The Fugitive*?' She imagined helicopters circling noisily overhead, convoys of police cars closing in on Dizzy, officers with loud-hailers ordering him to give himself up—

'They took down his details,' said Toby, 'that's all.'

Savannah looked disappointed. 'What's the point of that?'

Toby shook his head. The point of it was that a body plucked out of the Thames could be compared with the descriptions of all reported missing persons.

But he couldn't tell Savannah that.

'It's just the best they can do.' As he ran his fingers through his hair, it occurred to him that he could dial 1471 and ring the number back. Maybe Dizzy – if it had been Dizzy – was still there.

But as he was heading back to the house, the phone shrilled again.

'Who was that?' he said as Deborah replaced the receiver.

'Baz's mother. She hasn't seen Dizzy, she just wondered if we'd heard anything yet.'

'Great.' Now it was pointless dialling 1471.

Toby flipped through the photograph album Deborah had brought into the kitchen and took out three of the most recent pictures of Dizzy.

'I'm off then. I'll be back in an hour.'

Dizzy would be fine, Deborah reassured herself. He was a teenager going through a tricky phase, but he'd be back in no time at all. Toby might be in a complete state about his disappearance, but he was overreacting as usual. Typical actor, Deborah thought. Having to make a drama out of the situation, automatically imagining the worst.

As the front door slammed behind Toby, Savannah wandered into the kitchen pulling a lime-green T-shirt over her bikini. 'May as well go to the pub,' she said. 'Oliver's working over there.'

'Good idea, sweetheart.'

Fondly, Deborah watched her go. Then she dialled the number of Keeper's Cottage.

When Doug answered, she murmured, 'I'm free.'

Telling yourself you weren't going to get involved with someone as potentially risky as Deborah Gillespie was all very well, but when you picked up the phone and heard that silky voice breathing those words down your ear, saying 'Well, actually, it's very kind of you to offer but I'm busy right now' wasn't the response that sprang most immediately to mind.

And Doug hadn't been busy.

And it was certainly a more entertaining way of spending forty minutes than reading up on the latest pharmaceutical treatment for syphilis.

'Where the hell have you been?' demanded Jamie, who was in the kitchen making himself a fried egg sandwich. He stared at Doug, standing at the open back door. 'I came home half an hour ago. Your car was here and the house was empty.' He looked confused. 'What were you doing out *there*?'

This was a fair question. The garden of Keeper's Cottage

was a waist-high jungle of grass and weeds. Nobody ventured out into it of their own free will.

Apart from Doug, of course, when he was hopping discreetly over the back wall.

'I saw something on TV about crop circles. Wondered how they were made, that's all.'

Jamie's eggs were burning. He frowned and gave them a prod. 'Crop circles? You mean you've been out there making a *weed* circle?'

Doug stretched his arms and yawned. 'Thought about it, sat down to think about it, must have crashed out. Next thing I knew it was an hour later and I heard you banging around in here.'

'You fell asleep in the garden?' Jamie still didn't sound convinced. 'But there isn't anywhere to lie down, you must—'

Doug was saved by Melinda clattering to the floor.

Jamie's Melinda Messenger calendar, signed by Melinda herself, was his most treasured possession. He rushed over to rescue her. It was the third time in a week she'd done this.

'You need a nail in that wall,' Doug observed. 'Blutack isn't strong enough.'

The implausibility of him having fallen asleep in the garden was forgotten. All Jamie cared about was Melinda's well-being.

Still, she seemed unharmed. Lovingly he stroked her astonishing cleavage.

'Poor darling, must be the weight of her boobs.'

Dizzy took a deep breath, fed the coins into the slot and tried again.

This time, to his relief, his father answered.

'Hello?'

Dizzy said nothing.

'Dizzy, is that you?'

Yes, yes, it's me!

'Dizzy, if that's you, say something. We need to know you're safe.'

So you've noticed I've gone, then.

'Listen, Dizzy, we want you to come home. We love you. We miss you. Please.' Toby's voice, so urgent, began to crack with emotion, 'Nothing else matters. I know things have been difficult lately, but we can sort that out. We just need you back with us.'

Silence.

'And nobody's going to yell at you for running away, or for taking that money.'

Ah, so the milkman had called round.

'Dizzy, speak to me. Your mother's frantic with worry. We all are.'

What, even Savannah?

'Dizzy, *please* . . .'

The pips went.

Dizzy put the phone down and backed out of the phone box, smiling to himself.

Yeah, result!

But he wouldn't go home just yet.

Chapter 49

Lili watched from the kitchen window as Michael, with Will hoisted on to his shoulders, chased Lottie around the garden. She heard their screams of delight as Lottie raced across a flowerbed and Michael, roaring like a dinosaur, charged after her. Giggling helplessly, Will yelled, 'Again, Daddy, again!'

Michael couldn't be bothered, as a rule, to play rough-and-tumble with them, so they appreciated it all the more when he did.

Even more unexpectedly, upon returning from Harleston she had found him in the kitchen doing the washing-up.

Lili wished he hadn't chosen today of all days to be Mr Wonderful-husband-and-father.

'Can't catch me, can't catch me!' Lottie screamed, flashing her Pocahontas knickers as she dived into the Wendy house.

Will shouted, 'Huff and puff, Daddy, and blow the house down!'

As Michael began to huff and puff, Lili thought: What am I *doing*? How can I even contemplate having an affair with Drew Darcy?

It had seem so much easier yesterday. When Drew had gently questioned her about the state of her marriage she had almost managed to convince herself that sleeping with him wouldn't be that terrible a thing to do, because Michael had probably, in the past, been unfaithful to her.

And if he had, then it was only fair that she should have her turn.

But I don't have any proof, Lili thought guiltily. Maybe I

just want him to have slept around, to make it all right.

And what if he never had? What if he'd been tempted but had always said no, because he was married . . . happily married . . .?

Oh God.

'Lunch ready?' Michael said, coming into the kitchen with a child under each arm. 'We're starving.'

'As starving as dinosaurs,' giggled Lottie.

'Poo,' Will announced with pride. 'Big poo.'

'Ah well, that's your department.' Deftly Michael handed his son over to Lili. 'I'll go and get my kit together while you deal with him. Where are my cricket trousers, in the airing cupboard?'

'Your cricket trousers?'

'I got chatting to one of the guys at the snooker club last night. Told him I hadn't played for ages, but he offered me a place on his team. We're playing a match this afternoon.'

'Who for?' said Lili, bemused.

'Just some pub thing. I didn't think you'd mind.' Michael sounded peeved. 'I've spent enough time entertaining the kids, haven't I? And clearing all that washing-up.'

'I don't mind,' Lili assured him, her smile bright. If he could be nice, so could she. Maybe this was all their marriage needed, a bit of extra effort. 'It's a gorgeous afternoon, we could come and watch. Bring a picnic, cheer you on, give your team some support—'

'Trouble is, they're playing away. No idea where. I just know we're being picked up in a coach – er, mini-bus, at four.'

'Oh. So you won't be back until . . .?'

'Your guess is as good as mine.' Michael shrugged and tickled the back of Will's neck, making him squeal with delight. 'Late-ish.'

Lili nodded. It meant she wouldn't be able to see Drew.

Hmm, maybe this was just as well.

It wasn't the most comfortable of situations, walking into the village shop and bumping unexpectedly into the wife of someone you'd recently slept with.

It was even more awkward when you looked a wreck and she was exuding more glamour than Sophia Loren and Diana Ross put together.

Jessie, who had called in on her way home from work to pick up a pint of milk and a packet of toilet rolls – *très chic* – was acutely aware of her shiny, unmade-face, messy hair and scruffy dungarees. There were circles of sweat under the arms of her mauve T-shirt and splashes of bottle-green emulsion on her face and chest.

Oh, and she smelled of turps.

'Jess, hi!' Deborah finished paying for her copy of *Vogue* and waited while Jessie bought her milk.

The toilet rolls would just have to wait. Jessie couldn't face buying them in front of Deborah.

'You look as if you've got green measles,' Deborah cheerfully informed her when they were outside.

'I know. I've been rollering a ceiling.' For something to do, Jessie rubbed at her speckled forearms. 'So. How is, um, everything?'

Deborah shrugged and leaned against the dusty bonnet of Jessie's van. 'No news yet about Dizzy. Toby's raced up to London to pound the streets looking for him, although I told him it was a waste of time. Still, fingers crossed.' She fiddled with the arms of her sunglasses and glanced at Jessie. 'As for me and Toby – you know as much as I do. We're just getting through it, taking things day by day.'

'Well . . . good.'

Jessie didn't know if she meant it. She couldn't think of anything else to say. All she could really think of was how much she wanted a bath.

'I'd better be getting back. Dizzy might ring.' Deborah smiled and pulled herself upright, adding easily, 'Pop over later for a drink if you'd like to.'

'Maybe.' This was definitely a lie.

'Oh Jess, I forget to ask.' Turning back, Deborah gazed at her with concern. 'What happened last night? Toby came home looking completely fed up. I wasn't even expecting him back,' she added. 'I thought he'd stay with you.'

★ ★ ★

295

Parking the car as she returned from her monthly visit to the hairdresser in Harleston, Bernadette Thomas saw her next-door neighbour eagerly poking her head out of her open sitting-room window.

'Yoo hoo,' Eleanor Ferguson trilled, emerging from her front door clutching a parcel before Bernadette even had her key out of the ignition. 'This arrived while you were out. From your publishers, by the look of it.'

'Thank you.' As she held out her hands, Bernadette was grateful her neighbour was basically uninterested in books, otherwise she might have noticed that this parcel hadn't been sent by the firm that published Antonia Kay's dreary efforts.

'How exciting! Copies of the new novel, hot off the press?'

Eleanor might not be interested in books, but she still enjoyed telling all her friends she lived next door to a real author.

'Afraid not. Just proofs,' Bernadette replied firmly, before the older woman could grab the parcel back from her and tear the wrapper off.

'Oh.'

Eleanor didn't know what proofs were.

'For copy-editing.'

'Ah, I see.' Eleanor was still gazing at it longingly.

'Very dull job,' Bernadette assured her.

'Still, not long now before the next book comes out.' Eleanor brightened. 'You said August, didn't you?'

'That's right. August the tenth.'

'What's it called again?'

Damn, what was it called?

'*A Strand of Honeysuckle*. No, a *Frond*,' Bernadette corrected herself rapidly. '*A Frond of Honeysuckle*.' She patted her newly done hair. 'My editor was keen on strand, but I managed to convince her frond was better.'

'Well, it sounds marvellous.' Eleanor wondered if this one had any lesbians in it. She sincerely hoped not, although she probably wouldn't read it anyway. The last one had been about as much fun as darning a string vest.

'You shall have a signed copy,' Bernadette told her gravely.

'Lovely!' trilled Eleanor. 'Can't wait!'

While she was waiting for Michael to arrive, April phoned Bernadette. Instead of defending herself against Bernadette's thinly veiled warnings, she had decided, from now on she would take the initiative and tell her how wonderful Michael was.

First she had to listen to the story of Bernadette's most recent encounter with Eleanor, her terrifyingly bossy next-door neighbour.

'Why aren't you at the hospital?' Bernadette said at last. 'You told me you were working days this week.'

'I swapped shifts with one of the other girls. Michael's coming over at four.' April curled up on the sofa and hugged her knees to her chest. 'He's taking me to this fantastic restaurant he knows in Cheltenham.'

'At four o'clock in the afternoon?'

Ah, here we go.

'He said he couldn't wait to see me. The table's booked for eight.' Defiantly April added, 'Don't worry, I'm sure we'll find something to occupy us until then.'

A brief silence. 'Has he told his wife about you?'

Be calm, be calm.

'He doesn't have to report back to his wife. They're almost divorced.' Instead of snapping, April kept her tone pleasant and flexed her toes, admiring the neat, freshly painted nails. 'The decree nisi's due any day now.' As she said the words she could almost believe them to be true. The more she thought about Michael's unknown but clearly neurotic wife, the easier it became to imagine the divorce going through.

Not right away, perhaps, but *soon*.

'You haven't told me where he lives,' Bernadette said.

April smiled to herself. 'Oh, he's letting his wife keep the house. He's just bought a gorgeous new one on the outskirts of Harleston. Detached, of course. Four bedrooms, huge garden. At the moment we're knee-deep in paint charts and wallpaper samples, trying to decide how it should look.'

Another pause, lengthier this time. 'Well, there's someone here in the village who's an excellent painter and decorator. I've heard very good reports of her work. If you'd like her number I could get it for you,' Bernadette offered. 'Her name's Jessie something-or-other.'

'Perhaps.' April checked her watch: twenty to four. She wondered how Jessie something-or-other would feel about being hired to hang imaginary wallpaper on walls in a house that didn't exist.

'So, will you be moving in with this, um . . .?'

'Michael,' April prompted. She loved saying his name aloud.

'Yes. Michael.'

'Oh, I'm sure I will. He's asked me to marry him, of course.' April shivered with pleasure. 'But there's no need to rush into things, is there? We'll probably just live together first.'

In our invisible four-bedroomed house . . .

'Well,' Bernadette hesitated, still not sounding convinced, 'you seem happy enough. But don't forget what I said the other—'

Rrrrring!

Phew, saved by the bell and not a moment too soon.

Relieved to be spared the lecture, April jumped up and ran her fingers through her short, newly highlighted hair. 'Bernie, he's here! I have to go. I'll speak to you soon, okay?'

'Remember, any problems at all and you know where I am—' Bernadette began, but April had already hung up.

When she flung open the front door, Michael was frowning.

'I haven't asked you to marry me.'

'What? Oh!' Whoosh, April felt herself go bright red. 'How long have you been here?'

He smiled slightly. 'Couple of minutes.'

'On the – um, on the doorstep.'

'Less than six feet away from where you were sitting.' Michael nodded in the direction of the living-room window, flung open to coax some air into the stuffy flat. 'A word of advice, sweetheart. If you'd prefer not to be overheard, keep your windows shut. I don't know . . .' He tutted. 'At this rate, you're never going to get that job with MI5.'

April was awash with embarrassment. She hung her head. 'No – sorry. I know you didn't ask me to marry you.'

'Haven't bought a house, either.' Michael raised a quizzical eyebrow. 'So who were you talking to? What's going on?'

'It was just a friend being all disapproving about you,' April admitted. 'I don't think she wants me to be happy, basically. She's all on her own and probably jealous.'

'Sure she's a friend?' Michael observed drily.

'Well, we were close once. S-sometimes it's hard,' she stammered, 'to break away.'

'Maybe you should try it. After all,' his arms slipped around her waist, 'you've got me now. I'm your new friend.'

Relieved, April clung to him. 'I didn't mean to say all those things, I just wanted her to know how happy I am.'

'So you thought you'd gee her up, make her a bit more jealous?' Michael idly stroked her clean hair. 'Who is she? D'you see much of her?'

April shook her head. 'Not for ages. We just talk on the phone every now and again. She's no one special.'

Grinning, Michael lifted her into his arms, kicked the front door shut and carried her through the flat to the bedroom. 'Glad to hear it. Now, we've got a few hours to kill before dinner.' Skilfully, through the thin cotton of her shirt, he unfastened April's bra. 'Don't want to waste them, do we?'

It didn't take Toby long to concede that Deborah had been right. Coming up to London was something he'd felt compelled to do, simply because the alternative – sitting at home, *waiting* – was unbearable.

But six hours traipsing around the West End, searching frantically for Dizzy, had only served to emphasise the hopelessness of the situation. Thousands upon thousands of people were milling around. And this was just Piccadilly Circus, Toby thought, close to despair as he scanned the sea of bobbing heads around him.

Worse still, he didn't even know if Dizzy was in London. Dialling 1471 after this morning's call had been no help. The number had been withheld. Dizzy could be anywhere in the country.

Toby's shoulders sagged. He was, as Deborah had pointed out so dismissively, never going to get anywhere. Time to go home, he thought, feeling useless.

Oh well, at least he'd tried.

Chapter 50

When Dizzy had booked into an hotel just off Piccadilly Circus, the plan had been to have a bath and spend the rest of the evening quietly in the bar. This meant he would have just enough money left for a train ticket back to Harleston the next morning. He much preferred travelling by rail than in a stupid coach.

In the event, however, the hotel bar had been deserted and the bartender had, humiliatingly, demanded to see some ID before he'd serve Dizzy with anything stronger than a Coke.

Determined by this stage at least to have a proper drink while he was in London, Dizzy had wandered out on to the streets, finally managing to buy four bottles of Hooch in an off-licence. When he had guzzled them down one after the other, he made his way unsteadily towards Soho, where a friendly bloke invited him into a club where the girls – he assured Dizzy – had to be seen to be believed.

So had the prices of the drinks they served, but by this time Dizzy no longer cared. One of the girls, who looked a bit like Moll if you half-closed your eyes and squinted, invited him in a friendly fashion to press a ten pound note down the front of her G-string. Half-closing his eyes and squinting for all he was worth, Dizzy happily did as he was told and almost fell backwards off his chair when she gyrated her pelvis just inches from his face. Her fake tan was blotchy and she was on the flabby side, but Dizzy didn't mind. What was a bit of cellulite between friends?

Waking up in his hotel room the next morning, he was irritated to find himself on the floor next to his bed, which seemed an awful waste of forty-six pounds.

Struggling to his feet – ouch, his head hurt – Dizzy then made the even more annoying discovery that his wallet was empty.

This was seriously bad news. Now he didn't even have enough money for a coach, let alone a train ticket.

Downstairs in the dining room, determined to get his money's worth – breakfast was inclusive – he drank four cups of coffee and ate seven hot croissants with butter and black cherry jam.

He only just made it to the loo before throwing up.

There were four black cabs lined up outside the hotel with their For Hire signs up. After two 'On-yer-bike's and a 'You must be bleedin' jokin', mate', Dizzy realised he was going to have to pull out all the stops.

He was the son of an actor, wasn't he?

Right, he'd see if he could act.

''Ere comes Mr Popular,' the fourth cab driver declared as Dizzy approached his window. He watched him over the top of yesterday's *Evening Standard*. 'If that lot sent you packing, what makes you think I'm gonna do any different?'

Dizzy summoned up his worst-ever, most humiliating fantasy, where a beautiful woman – okay, let's call her Moll – announced in a loud voice in front of a huge crowd of people: 'My God, Dizzy Gillespie, that is the smallest willy I have ever seen in my life!'

'Well?' the cab driver demanded with an impatient flick of the sports section, 'are ya gonna say somethin' or aren't ya?'

Everyone in the crowd was turning to look and laugh at Dizzy. He wanted to run away and hide but there was no escape. And now people were beginning to tug enthusiastically at his jeans, all wanting to see the world's smallest willy for themselves . . .

Dizzy promptly burst into tears. 'You'll think I'm lying, but I'm not,' he told the startled cabbie between sobs. 'I ran away from home and now I want to go back, but someone stole my wallet. If you take me, my parents'll pay the fare, honest they will. They'll probably give you a reward too.'

The driver hesitated. 'Where d'you live?'

'Um, Harleston.'

'What, in Gloucestershire? Christ, you must be joking!'

Crying was a doddle. For the first time, Dizzy experienced the thrill of real acting. He might not be on a stage but this was a challenge he couldn't resist. He was going to make this bloke take him to Upper Sisley if it killed him.

'Please, please . . .' he wept. 'I just want to go home. I want my m-m-mum!'

The tears streaming down his face would have done Kenneth Branagh proud. They were Oscar-winning tears.

'Look, why don't I take you to the nearest police station and—'

'Nooo!' wailed Dizzy, clutching the side of the cab. Wow, talk about street theatre. Thrillingly, people were stopping to watch him. This was like starring in *Hamlet*.

'Or you could phone them?' the cab driver suggested helplessly.

'Nooo! I want my mum!'

'Will they definitely pay the fare?'

'Yeees!'

The boy was clearly distraught. But he was also wellspoken.

The story rang true.

The cab driver, who had read enough newspaper articles in his time about runaway teenagers and the anguish they caused their parents, heaved a sigh and put aside his crumpled *Evening Standard*. 'Okay, hop in. Too soft-hearted for my own good, that's what I am.' He shook his head, touched by the woebegone look on the lad's tear-streaked face. 'They'd just bleedin' better pay up, that's all.'

It was one of the best moments of Dizzy's life.

When the cab pulled up on the gravelled drive, nothing happened for a second. Then a bedroom window was flung open and Savannah's blonde head poked out. All the anxiety she had worked so hard to conceal from her parents crumbled in an instant.

'It's Dizzy! Mum, it's Dizzy, he's *here*!' she yelled, and the next minute his mother was racing down the front steps crying, 'Oh Dizzy, I can't believe you're back!'

Dizzy found himself crying real tears this time, which was a bit embarrassing, but most of them got soaked into his mother's white shirt so it probably didn't notice too much. And when his dad came out and hugged him too, saying, 'Was that you on the phone, Dizzy? Was it?' his joy was complete.

He was the centre of attention, the prodigal son come home at last.

It felt great.

The cab driver, dazed to discover who Dizzy's parents were, longed to be invited into the house so he could tell them the heroic part he had played in their son's return.

'You didn't tell me your old man was Toby Gillespie,' he said to Dizzy, thinking a cup of tea wouldn't go amiss either.

Course not, Dizzy thought, then it wouldn't have been a challenge, would it?

'All the others turned 'im away,' the cabbie told Toby modestly. 'But I couldn't do it, could I? Got an 'eart of gold, me. If someone needs an 'elping 'and, I can't turn 'em away, it just ain't in my nature, see—'

'How much do I owe you?' Toby said, picturing the story on the front of next week's *News of the World*.

'Call it an 'undred and forty, guv. Course, I've met some stars in my time. I've 'ad Su Pollard in this cab; almost 'ad Paul Merton once—'

'Here's two hundred.' Toby counted the notes into the man's hand. 'We're very grateful, but I'm sure you understand that this is a private matter. Any publicity is the last thing my son needs.'

'I get your drift, guv. Don't worry about it. Soul of discretion, me. 'Ad Mick Jagger in the back of me cab once – shoulda seen the fings 'e was gettin' up to wiv this blonde bird—'

'Right,' said Toby, 'well, thanks again. Have a safe journey home.'

Embellishing wildly, Dizzy regaled his family with stories of drug dealers, rent boys and muggers with knives.

'But I really liked that picnic rug,' said Deborah, dismayed. 'It was cashmere.'

'Didn't have much choice,' Dizzy told her sorrowfully. 'This bloke was desperate. It was a case of my picnic rug or my life.'

'Never mind, we'll get another one.' His mother hugged him. 'You're back, that's all that matters.'

'Why did you do it, Dizzy?' Toby was frowning. 'What made you run away?'

'I didn't think you cared about me. I was miserable.' Dizzy revelled unashamedly in their attention; this would make a great film, especially if he starred in it. 'Ever since we moved here, it's been all Sav-this and Sav-that.' His chin began to wobble. 'I felt like she was the only one you cared about.'

'Oh great.' Savannah rolled her eyes. 'I might have known I'd get the blame.'

'You called me a nerd.'

'You *are* a nerd.'

'Sav, Dizzy, stop it!' Deborah protested. 'We love *both* of you—'

'And then there was the Oliver thing.' Suppressing a qualm of guilt, because he really liked Oliver, Dizzy looked miserable. 'He's cleverer than I am, and better looking, and everyone thinks he's great. I just thought you liked him better than me.'

Savannah made sick noises. 'That's it, blame Oliver as well.'

'Savannah, that's enough!' Toby said sharply.

'Now listen to me, Dizzy.' Deborah's arm tightened around his shoulders. 'We love you and don't you ever forget it. I know the last couple of months haven't been easy, but that's all in the past. From now on things will be better. We just want you to be happy, because that's all that matters.' She kissed him on the forehead. 'Promise.'

'Thanks, Mum.'

Blimey, thought Dizzy, it was like waking up and finding yourself in *The Waltons*. Maybe he should change his name to Jim-Bob.

'Are you hungry?' Toby asked.

305

Dizzy nodded. He was, actually.

'Of course he's hungry!' Deborah jumped up from the sofa. 'Tell me what you'd like, Dizzy. Your favourite meal – anything at all. I'll make it!'

Savannah stared at her mother in astonishment.

This is more like it, Dizzy thought happily. I could get used to this.

'Uh . . . how about a takeaway pizza?'

A letter addressed to Toby in familiar writing arrived in the post the next morning.

Wondering why he even bothered to open it, Toby tore apart the envelope.

'A second-class stamp for a second-rate actor,' the note informed him. 'What did Upper Sisley ever do to deserve you? When are you going to leave?'

Charming, thought Toby.

The note was the usual, wobbly-lettered affair, and as a bonus the sender had included an old newspaper review of a West End play Toby had appeared in months earlier. The famously acerbic theatre critic had lain into all aspects of the production, and had called Toby's performance 'singularly underwhelming'.

Everyone suffered the occasional bad review but nobody enjoyed getting them. Toby was as hurt reading this one again as he had been the first time he'd seen it.

He wished he had the address of whoever had posted it to him. Then he could send copies of some of his brilliant reviews back.

He phoned Jessie. 'Dizzy's home.'

'I know. Savannah told Oliver. I'm so glad.'

'Jess, we need to talk.'

'Why?'

'I want to see you.'

'Well you can't,' said Jessie, and hung up.

Toby knew why.

Dizzy had run away from home because he was unhappy. Seeing his parents split up wasn't going to make him happier.

Jessie was letting him know he owed it to his children to sort out his troubled marriage.

When Toby made his way back to the kitchen he found Dizzy ploughing through a bowl of cereal. Rice Krispies littered the table and the milk jug was sitting in a puddle of milk.

'Hi, Dad.' Dizzy spoke through a mouthful of Rice Krispies.

'You're up early.'

'Going into Harleston, aren't I? Dad, can I have some money?'

Toby poured himself a ferociously strong black coffee. 'What d'you want money for?'

When he looked up, Dizzy was rolling his eyes in amazement. It was clearly a dumb question. 'I got mugged, didn't I? I need a new Walkman, new tapes, new Gameboy . . . new *everything*.'

Loving your children, Toby discovered, didn't mean you weren't tempted, sometimes, to shake them until their teeth rattled.

'It's not long to your birthday. We could buy you a Walkman then.' He spoke evenly. 'And you could have the Gameboy at Christmas.'

'Da-ad!'

'What?'

'I can't wait 'til then,' said Dizzy, outraged. 'I need them *now*.'

Toby lost his temper. 'You spoilt brat! If you want the money, you'll bloody well earn it.'

'I can't.' Horrified, Dizzy stopped eating. 'Where can I get a job? There isn't anything around here that—'

'As soon as you've finished your breakfast, you can clean the cars. When they're done, you can mow the lawn. And when that's finished,' said Toby, his expression ominously grim, 'I'll give you ten pounds.'

Mow the lawn? What, *all* of it?

'Is this a joke?'

'No joke.'

'But we've got that gardening bloke,' Dizzy protested. 'He mows the lawn. It's *his* job.'

'Dizzy, I'm am not doling out money like a crazed lottery winner.'

Take it from me, Dizzy thought sulkily, you're nothing like any kind of lottery winner.

'If mowing lawns isn't your thing, Paddy Birley's looking for a lad to work on his farm.' Untrue, but a pretty safe fib, Toby felt. 'If you'd rather clean out cowsheds for three pounds an hour, that's fine by me.'

Chapter 51

Harriet was sitting on the garden wall drumming her heels against the stonework when she saw Dizzy meandering across the green towards her. His hands were in his pockets and he was kicking a stone along, pretending not to have noticed her.

'You're back then,' said Harriet.

Wow, original.

'No, this is just a hologram.' Dizzy smirked and poked himself in the chest. 'Looks real though, doesn't it?'

Harriet immediately hated him for making her feel stupid. 'You weren't gone for long. Chicken out, did you?'

'Living rough doesn't scare me,' Dizzy sneered. 'I just knew everyone was worried about me, so I came home.'

'I wasn't worried about you. Didn't bother me.'

This wasn't going to plan at all. Dizzy had wanted to be welcomed home like a hero. He'd wanted Harriet Ferguson to be pleased to see him, and apologetic for the toilet bleach slur; then he could have forgiven her and told her all about his adventures on the streets of London – the exciting version, of course. Not the real one.

But Harriet didn't appear to be interested. All she was doing was swinging her skinny legs and smirking down at him in a really stupid and immature way.

Now he definitely couldn't ask her if she had a spare Walkman he could borrow.

So much for the honeymoon period, thought Dizzy, filled with resentment. Less than twenty-four hours and it was over. Everything was back to boring normality. And his arms ached like nobody's business from all that bloody car washing.

God, life was *so* unfair.

'Out of interest,' Harriet said eagerly, 'why *did* you run away? Was it anything to do with my joke about the Harpic?'

There was an avid gleam in her eye. Dizzy itched to shove her off the wall. So much for thinking Harriet might have been sobbing into her pillow, blaming herself. Huh, all she wanted to do was take the credit.

'Funny,' he mused, 'I always thought your dog was the one with the bad breath. Now that Blitz isn't here I realise it was you all along.'

Mowing the lawn was even worse than washing the cars, but Dizzy grimly carried on until the job was done. Since his father had warned his mother not to give in and slip him a cheque, he didn't have a lot of choice.

Slave labour, that's what it was. At this rate, by the time he had enough money to buy one, Walkmans would be obsolete.

Two hours later and ten measly quid better off, Dizzy was bored again. He was stuck here in this crappy village with nothing to do, no friends, nothing to look forward to and no money.

Mooching around, trailing grass cuttings into the hall, he pulled open the drawer where bills were generally slung, in case by some miracle any post had arrived for him while he was away.

None had. All that was in there was a bunch of fan mail, a red electricity bill, last week's *Stage* and a couple of requests for Toby to donate something to charity or show up at some function in aid of Save The Earwig.

To amuse himself, Dizzy skimmed through a few of the fan letters. It was a pretty weird experience, reading stuff from women drooling over your own father, but they kept on writing and sending photos, and sometimes they were good for a laugh, especially the really gross ones who sent in pictures of themselves all dressed up in basques with stockings and suspenders.

There weren't any of those today, just half a dozen pretty normal letters. Toby made an effort to sit down each week and reply to them, otherwise they mounted up.

Dizzy turned over the last letter and realised it wasn't from a fan.

As Toby had done earlier, he read the anonymous note. Brief and to the point, as usual. And this time a newspaper cutting too.

Nice touch.

Dizzy thought idly that whoever was sending this stuff must get a real kick out of it, otherwise why would they bother?

It must be quite exciting, going as far as you dared and making sure you didn't get caught. Thinking up new things to do, hugging the secret to yourself, experiencing that buzz . . .

This is right up my street, thought Dizzy, his mind working overtime. This is my chance to get my own back on all of them.

This could be a real laugh.

'Dizzy, are you okay?'

Deborah knocked and waited before popping her head around the door. Dizzy was in bed with only his head visible. He nodded and raised a feeble smile.

'Yeah. Just tired. And I ache all over.' He moved a bit and winced. 'Still, never mind. Thought I'd have an early night. Dad says I can clean the windows tomorrow.'

It was only eight thirty.

'Darling, don't worry about the money,' Deborah whispered. 'Your father's in a bad mood, that's all. We'll sort something out.'

As soon as his mother had gone, Dizzy sat up, snapped the bedroom light back on, gleefully flexed his rubber-gloved fingers and pulled the box of work in progress out from under the bed.

By eleven o'clock he was almost finished. The adverts in the paper had been great; within days, that bossy old cow Eleanor Ferguson would be receiving a free brochure telling her what to do about Embarrassing Facial Hair. Doug Flynn was getting Transform Your Sex Life With A Penile

311

Extension. He had answered a lonely hearts ad in Harriet Ferguson's name – to a seventy-three-year-old pig farmer, ha! And Paddy Birley, who lived in a bungalow, could look forward to a visit from someone keen to sell him a stairlift.

Dizzy sniggered to himself and shuffled through the rest of the letters, which looked just like the ones downstairs. He had written them with his left hand and kept the style much the same, only this time Toby Gillespie wouldn't be the only recipient.

Dear Moll,
Silicone is *bad* for you. Get those implants taken out at once!

Dear Myrtle Armitage
You couldn't run an egg and spoon race, let alone a shop.

Dear Mr Gillespie,
You are a useless actor. Why don't you and your family move back to London?

This was what Dizzy wanted more than anything.

He put the letters back into the box, carefully peeled off his rubber globes – ugh, his hands were really sweaty – and settled happily down to sleep.

A week later the villagers were in high dudgeon.

Dizzy loved every minute.

'A bloody stairlift, I ask you!' spluttered Paddy Birley when he called into the shop. 'Couldn't get rid of the bloke! I said to him, I said, look at this place, it ain't *got* no bleeding stairs, but did that put him off? Did it heck as like; he spent two hours trying to persuade me to put in an upstairs extension.'

'Everybody's got something,' Myrtle Armitage chuntered.

'Old Cecil got one of them brochure things about hair transplants,' Paddy Birley told her as the door clanged open and Dizzy came in. 'And yesterday they phoned him up. He

312

told them he'd managed all right without hair for the last fifty years and he wasn't about to start buying shampoo now.'

'That Lorna from the pub got sent a load of bumph on how to get your teeth white.' Myrtle narrowed her eyes in Dizzy's direction. 'What d'you want? And before you ask, I'm not selling you no cigarettes.'

'Just a packet of chewing gum,' said Dizzy politely. 'Please.' He looked at the envelope in Myrtle's heavily veined hand. 'You got one as well, did you? What did yours say?'

Myrtle bristled. 'Told me I didn't know how to run a shop.'

Dizzy kept a straight face. This was brilliant.

'Dad's been getting them for ages, ever since we moved in. Saying he's a crap actor and why doesn't he go back to London. Poor old Dad, it really upsets him.' He frowned. 'Who do you think's sending all this stuff?'

The devil makes work for idle hands, and Dizzy was certainly idle. It was, Myrtle had decided, just the sort of trick a bored schoolboy would play.

Now, though, her private suspicion that Dizzy could have been behind the campaign began to crumble. If his own father was receiving letters, it couldn't be him. Surely.

Promptly reverting to second choice, she said, 'One of them lads from Keeper's Cottage, I reckon. Not Doug, he's a doctor. But I wouldn't put it past that Jamie,' she went on, her tone brisk. 'He's always up to mischief. It's the kind of prank he'd think was funny.'

Dizzy paid for his chewing gum. 'Well I don't think it's funny. It's cruel. I mean, you're hurting people's feelings, aren't you? I think you run a brilliant shop.'

Myrtle, whose feelings had definitely been hurt, softened towards the boy at once. Of course it wasn't Dizzy. He was a kind lad, nicely brought up. And he'd been to a posh school. 'My money's on that young vet,' she pronounced. 'And he won't get away with it, I'm telling you now. Next time I see him, I'll give him a piece of my mind.'

★ ★ ★

Harriet was mystified to receive a letter from someone called Frank Huntingdon. Written on musty-smelling Basildon Bond in an old-fashioned hand, it went:

Dear Harriet,
Many thanks for your nice letter and yes, I would very much like to meet you. I was also extremely pleased to learn that you share my passion for pigs. Maybe in due course I could show you over my farm.

As requested, I am enclosing a snapshot of myself, which I hope won't scare you off. Country dancing and hard work has kept me in pretty good health over the years. Not bad for seventy-three, all in all, and I still have my own teeth.

Please do ring me, so we can arrange a meeting. As you say, loneliness is a terrible thing, and so unnecessary. Who knows, maybe we can find happiness together?

Yours most respectfully,
Frank Huntingdon

Harriet turned over the snap, which had been taken in one of those passport photo booths. Frank had white hair, a ruddy, outdoorsy complexion, a big grin and an even bigger hole in his ancient hand-knitted sweater.

Poor old bugger, all alone and desperate for company. Glancing at the address at the top of the letter, she saw that he lived less than twelve miles away. He had advertised for a partner in the local paper and somebody – one of her daft friends from school, no doubt – had written back pretending to be Harriet.

I should ring and tell him it was a prank, thought Harriet, but the prospect was too toe-curling. Frank was seventy-three and she was fourteen. He would be embarrassed and so would she.

Anyway, he was bound to have had dozens of other women writing to him, she decided with some relief, real women who were every bit as ancient as they said they were.

Frank, bless his lonely heart, would be rushed off his feet.

He wouldn't even notice her name missing from the list.

Glad that she was on her own in the kitchen, Harriet tore up the letter and the photo and shoved the pieces deep into the bin.

Chapter 52

'It's okay, I know he isn't there,' said Drew. 'I just saw him leave.'

Oh, how she loved the sound of his voice: low-pitched, intimate and sexy.

'Where are you?'

'Living room.'

Lili felt her insides do a lightning squirm, like a shoal of tiny fish darting around within her stomach. She stretched the phone lead as far as it would go and walked across to the bedroom window.

There he was, on the other side of the green.

'I can see you, just.' It was so heavenly to hear from him. 'What are you doing?'

'Grinning like an idiot. What's that white thing you're wearing, a strapless dress?'

'Strapless bath towel.' Lili giggled. 'I've just had a shower.'

'You mean . . .' Drew let out a low whistle. 'So what's under the bath towel?'

'Stretch marks, mainly. I wouldn't bother getting out your binoculars. Some things are better viewed from a distance.'

'I'd rather see you close up.' Drew marvelled at her lack of self-esteem; if Lili would only let him, he'd happily kiss each and every stretch mark. 'Go on, I dare you. Accidentally drop the towel.'

'Unfair.' Lili blushed with pleasure. 'Would you take your clothes off in full view of the village?'

'Love to. Except if I did it, I'd be arrested. Whereas you'd get a round of applause.'

'I'm still not going to,' said Lili.

'Chicken.'

'But not exactly a spring one.'

She was always running herself down. Drew wished he could restore some of that shattered self-confidence.

'Lili, you're gorgeous. If you were twenty-two with a figure like a wire coat-hanger I wouldn't be on this phone to you now.' Before she could come up with some new derogatory remark about herself he went on, 'I've got to see you again. It's killing me, only being able to talk on the phone.'

It was killing her too, but she didn't know what else they could do. Before, she had been able to visit Keeper's Cottage without a qualm. Waving to Myrtle Armitage from Drew's bedroom window had been funny. But that was when they'd had nothing to hide. Now that they did, waltzing over to the cottage was out of the question. The idea that anyone might suspect them of being up to no good wasn't funny at all.

'How about tonight?' Drew persisted. 'Say you've taken up evening classes in Harleston. Tell Michael he's babysitting because you'll be weaving baskets between seven and ten.'

As he spoke, Jessie's clapped-out van roared into view down Compass Hill and along the High Street.

'Michael's got another cricket match on.' Lili peered out of the window as the van drew to a halt outside the front of the house. 'Anyway, here's Jess. I must go.'

'I don't want you to go,' Drew said. He watched Jessie jump out of the driver's seat, pause to re-tie the yellow scarf in her hair and wave up at Lili.

'Back door's open,' Lili bellowed out of the window. To Drew she added, 'I have to hang up now.'

Where there's a will there's a way, thought Drew.

'No you don't.' He spoke quickly. 'Let me talk to Jess.'

Lili was so nervous she missed the turning and drove straight past the entrance to the hotel. Two miles down the road, doing a clumsy, sweaty-palmed U-turn, she almost ended up in a ditch. By the time she pulled up at the top of the drive it was twenty past eight and the butterflies in her stomach had reached fever pitch.

Drew was standing on the hotel steps waiting for her. He looked smarter than she'd ever seen him look before, in a dark suit, freshly ironed white shirt and an actual, honest-to-goodness tie.

'Wow!' Lili kissed him, touched that he should have made such an effort. Even the wayward hair had been combed into submission.

Up close, she saw that the tie was patterned with golden retrievers.

Drew gave her a stern look. 'You're late.'

'Sorry, got lost.'

In the stone doorway, he stroked her flushed cheek. 'I thought you weren't coming.'

'I'm here,' Lili whispered, 'but I have to be home by eleven.'

Two and a half hours. Not ideal, but better than nothing at all.

'Right,' said Drew, 'this place has three bars, two restaurants and eighty-four rooms.' He gazed steadily into Lili's wide hazel eyes. 'Up to you.'

'Oh Drew, we can't book a room.'

We can, we *can*.

'Okay, fine.'

Over drinks in a secluded corner of the first bar they came to, Lili struggled to explain.

'It's not that I don't want to . . .'

Me neither, thought Drew, filled with longing.

'. . . But I'm married.'

Lili shook her head. She had spent the last few days wrestling with her conscience.

'What if Michael's been unfaithful to you hundreds of times?'

'What if he hasn't?'

She looked so miserable. Drew couldn't bear it. For the first time in his life, he now realised, he was in love.

And as if the fact that she was married wasn't bad

318

enough, he'd had to go and fall for someone with – oh God, could you credit it? – *scruples*.

'Well?' Jessie demanded, twisting round on the sofa when the sitting-room door opened and closed behind her. Blitz, curled up on her lap, opened an equally enquiring eye and – like a conductor calling his orchestra to attention – thumped his tail three times against the arm of the sofa.

'We had a great time.' Lili threw herself into the scruffy but comfortable chair opposite.

Jess raised an eyebrow. 'Doesn't look as if you did.'

Lili's eyes filled with tears. 'It was the best two hours of my life. I didn't want to leave.'

'Oh!' Agog, Jessie bounced into a sitting position. 'And did you . . . you know?'

Lili fumbled up her sleeve for a tissue. She blew her nose and shook her head, praying that Michael wouldn't choose this moment to come home.

'I couldn't, I just couldn't. I'm in deep enough water as it is. I told him we had to stop it while we still could. Oh Jess, it's all over. I said I wasn't going to see him again. What we're doing is *wrong* . . .'

Silently Jessie reached for the half-empty bottle of rough-and-ready Spanish wine she had brought with her on babysitting duty. She poured, handed the glass to Lili and made her drink.

'What did Drew say?'

'That he loved me.' More hot tears trickled down Lili's cheeks. 'But if it was what I wanted, he wouldn't try and change my mind.'

Jessie put her arms around her.

'God, I hope Michael knows how lucky he is,' she told Lili. 'Not only an angel for a wife, but a considerate rival for her affections, too.'

'You look a mess,' said Michael the next morning. 'What happened to your eyes?'

Lili flinched. She had pretended to be asleep when he had crept in shortly after midnight, but when Michael's snores had begun to shake the bed, she had given up trying to hold back the tears. They had slid into her ears, down her neck and into the pillow. Knowing that she had done the honourable thing didn't make it any easier to bear.

She had managed an hour's sleep at the very most, and now her brain felt full of grit.

'Lili?' When she didn't say anything, Michael stopped spreading marmalade on his toast and looked up. What was going on? Had she somehow found out about April? Christ, had someone seen them together last night?

He put down the knife. Deny everything, deny, deny . . .

'Sweetheart, what's wrong?'

Oh, how could I ever have thought of cheating on him? thought Lili, awash with shame. Look, he's worried about me! He can see I'm upset and he *cares*—

'Mum, when can Aunt Jess look after us again?' Lottie raced into the kitchen grabbing two bananas from the fruit bowl. 'She told us a story about monsters with knickers on their heads and hats on their bottoms, it was loads better than Postman-boring-Pat.'

'I'd forgotten about Jess babysitting last night,' said Michael when Lottie had left them to it. Outside in the garden she was shooting Will with both bananas. 'Doing someone's hair, weren't you? Where was that?' He floundered, wondering if Lili had followed him, had actually watched him disappear inside April's flat. 'In Harleston?'

Guilt was gnawing away at Lili's stomach like battery acid. She'd always been a useless liar.

She nodded.

'But you've been crying.' Michael couldn't give up now; he had to know. 'Lili, tell me what's wrong.'

'It's nothing. One of Felicity's friends wanted a perm, that's all. And when I'd finished she didn't like it. Said I'd made her l-look like a sheep.' Haltingly Lili stammered out the excuse Jess had had the foresight to concoct. 'She called me a useless amateur. That's why I was upset.'

It was a toss-up who was more relieved; Lili because he believed her story or Michael because he hadn't, after all, been found out.

320

He gave her an awkward hug. 'There there, you're a terrific hairdresser. Come on, sit down and I'll make you a cup of tea.'

I'm sorry. I'm so sorry I was almost unfaithful to you, Lili thought, biting her lip and trying desperately hard not to compare the hug with one of Drew's.

'Can I make a catapult out of a pair of knickers like Aunt Jess taught me last night?' Lottie, hurtling back into the kitchen, skidded to a halt. 'Then I can shoot grapes at Will's head – Oh yuk, don't hug each other, that's how babies get born. And you don't want any more children,' she informed them scornfully. 'Three's *quite* enough.'

Chapter 53

Dizzy was keen to branch out. The letters had been great, but now it was time to diversify. Come nightfall, he decided, he would sneak out of the house and see what he could do. He'd already set his heart on scrawling something obscene, with weedkiller, across the middle of the village green.

Now, as he dawdled along with his hands stuffed into his pockets, he saw Bernadette Thomas heading towards him in her car.

Dizzy nodded and waved as she drove past, and Bernadette acknowledged him with a brief smile in return. Odd woman, never said much, kept herself to herself. Dizzy, turning to watch her go, realised that Bernadette Thomas was heading for Harleston.

Which meant her cottage was empty.

When a frog landed with a plop on the front of his left trainer less than a minute later, Dizzy decided it must be fate.

Yeah!

All women were scared stupid of frogs.

Bending down, he swiftly scooped up the creature and dropped it into his jeans pocket. Then he sauntered casually back past the pond, across the road and along Waters Lane.

Eleanor Ferguson's was the first house he came to, but a quick glance up at the windows revealed no sign of her.

Quick as a flash, while no one else was in sight, Dizzy raced up the path to Bernadette Thomas's front door, held open the letterbox and posted the frog into the hall.

Then, unable to resist the temptation, he crouched and peered through the slit to follow its progress.

Brilliant!

Boingg, boingg, the frog sprang through the hallway into the sitting room. That would make Bernadette scream, thought Dizzy, trampling a flowerbed and pressing his nose against the sitting-room window, just in time to see the frog leap up on to the mantelpiece and send a china candlestick flying.

'What on earth do you think you're doing?' barked a terrifying voice behind him.

Dizzy, leaning precariously sideways, lost his footing and fell into a rose bush.

Shit, bugger, *ouch*.

'Well?' demanded Eleanor Ferguson, who had been in the back garden tending her tomato plants.

'I-I was just p-passing,' Dizzy stammered. 'I thought I heard s-somebody shout for help.'

He was an actor, wasn't he? He could act his way out of this.

But Eleanor Ferguson was giving him a forbidding look. 'There's no one in there. And when you were peering through the window just now you were laughing to yourself.'

'I wasn't,' Dizzy protested, wide-eyed, but it was no good. Eleanor marched round to join him. When she glanced through her neighbour's window it didn't take her long to spot the frog, by this time leaping happily on and off the sofa like Gene Kelly in *Singin' in the Rain*.

'It was only meant to be a joke,' Dizzy mumbled.

'A joke? What, like the anonymous letters everyone's been getting in the post?' Eleanor's sidelong glance was shrewd. 'That was you as well, I imagine.'

Dizzy's acting abilities promptly deserted him. He shook his head and muttered, 'No.'

Hopeless, *hopeless*.

'Oh, I think it was.'

Eleanor watched him trying to avoid her gaze. She wondered why she wasn't shouting at him. Then it came to her. With that truculent expression and those drooping, defeated shoulders, Dizzy reminded her of her own son at fifteen. She had caught Michael letting down the tyres on the bikes of a group of lads who hadn't wanted him to join their gang.

'Dizzy.' Her voice softened. 'Why are you doing it?'

And this time, when he desperately didn't want to cry, Dizzy found himself with tears dripping down his cheeks.

'Everyone ignores me.' He hiccuped and wiped his eyes on his sleeve. 'It was so great when I came back from London, being made a fuss of and stuff, but it didn't last two minutes. Now it's just as awful as it was before.'

Eleanor remembered Michael, all those years ago, wailing, 'Why haven't I got any *friends*?'

A lump came to her throat. 'Look, I won't tell Bernadette this was your doing.' She indicated the frog through the window. 'And I won't say anything about the letters either. But you must stop now, Dizzy. Don't send any more. There's talk of the police being called in, and if you're caught you'll only be in more trouble.'

Dizzy could hardly believe what he was hearing. Eleanor Ferguson was an old witch, everyone knew that. He sniffed loudly. Why would a bossy interfering old witch be on his side?

'I know what you're thinking,' Eleanor said without rancour. She rummaged up her sleeve and passed him a clean tissue, 'but this shall be our secret, you have my word. As long as it stops.' Firmly she added, 'No more letters, no more frogs. And nobody but you and me will be any the wiser, all right?'

Back at the house, Savannah was forty minutes into a phone call to her best friend from school and seriously beginning to regret ever picking up the phone in the first place. There was nothing more sick-making than being forced to listen to someone else spout on and on about the fantastic new love of their life. But having to hear every last tedious detail of what they were getting up to when you yourself weren't getting up to *anything at all* – well, that was deeply depressing stuff.

'. . . and the next night we did it in the sea,' Mandy

giggled. 'Sav, you *have* to try it, I can't describe how it feels . . .!'

But you'll give it a damn good try, thought Savannah, gloomily picking at a hole in the knee of her jeans. What was she going to do about Oliver? What was she going to *do*?

'God, listen to me rabbiting away and not letting you get a word in edgeways,' Mandy trilled twenty minutes later. 'Tell me how things are going with you and your chap!'

'Oh, you know, same as you.' Savannah twiddled the telephone cord around her finger and forced herself to sound jaunty. 'Brilliant sex, every position you can think of—'

'I know, I know, aren't men just insatiable? Honestly, I don't know where Harry gets his energy from, we're just doing it morning noon and night!'

'Yeah, we are too.'

Savannah wanted to cry. How could she ever confide in anyone, admit to them that Oliver was impotent?

Oh, the shame, the terrible humiliation.

She would never live it down.

Lili was on the phone to Felicity two days later when she saw Lottie, in the front garden, struggling to climb one of the walnut trees.

'Lottie, get down!' she shouted through the window.

Puffing and struggling to get a better foothold, Lottie yelled back, 'I can *do* it!'

'I won't keep you,' Felicity said. 'I just rang to let you know I'm taking a few more days off work, so I won't need you to look after Freya this week.' Apologetically she added, 'If that's okay with you.'

'No problem.' Lili, who would get paid anyway, was grateful for the reprieve. As the long summer holiday wore on, she had enough on her plate coping with her own boisterous brood. 'Felicity, thanks for ringing but I'm going to have to go. Lottie's half-way up a tree . . .'

As she was running out of the front door Lottie lost her precarious grip on a branch. With an ear-splitting scream she tumbled out of the tree, ricocheted off the stone wall beneath it and landed on the narrow pavement with a thud.

'Oh my God, Lottie!'

'MUMMEEEE!'

Lili, her heart pounding, knelt beside her grey-faced daughter. Lottie's eyes rolled and flickered momentarily with the shock, then she opened her mouth and let out a howl like a wild animal.

'Ow . . . ow . . . it hurts. Don't touch me! Don't touch my arm, it HURTS!'

'All right, darling, you're all right, don't try to move. Michael!' Lili shouted, but she knew he was in the shower – he wouldn't be able to hear her.

'I'm not all right!' Lottie roared between screams. 'Ow, Mummy, ow, make it *go away*!'

Lili heard the sound of running footsteps. When she looked up and saw Drew she almost wept with relief.

'I was just leaving the pub.' He crouched down and took Lottie's pulse. 'Heard the screams. It's okay, sweetheart, I'm not going to hurt you. Looks like you've broken that arm.'

'Is Doug at home?' Lili asked, but Drew shook his head.

'On duty.'

'Oh God, shall I phone for an ambulance?'

'It'll be twenty minutes before it gets here. Was she knocked out?'

'No. Did you bang your head, sweetheart?'

'No!' Lottie howled, struggling to sit up. 'Not my head, my ARM!'

'Quicker if we take her ourselves,' Drew said, rolling up his sleeves. 'There don't seem to be any other injuries but she needs to be checked over.' He glanced at the open front door. 'Where's Michael?'

'In the shower. And Will's asleep upstairs – and Harriet's taken Blitz for a walk—'

'Okay, I'll bring my car over and we'll put Lottie across the back seat. Michael can bring Will and Harriet along to the hospital in his own time.'

He knew just what to do. Speechless with gratitude, Lili nodded.

'Pull my dress down!' Lottie bellowed, tugging frantically

at the hem with her good arm. 'I don't want everyone to see my knickers!'

Doug came through to see Lottie as soon as they arrived in Casualty. Lili guiltily avoided the glares of outrage from the other patients who had been sitting there for hours without so much as a sniff of a doctor. The female patients in particular, when they saw how good-looking Doug was, were clearly wondering what Lili had that they didn't.

'This is like nepotism,' she whispered to Drew.

'I know, good isn't it?' he replied cheerfully. 'Unless of course you'd rather sit here for the rest of the afternoon listening to Lottie yelling her head off.'

Doug finished his brief preliminary examination and straightened up. 'Right, we'll take her through to a cubicle. When I've had a proper look at her we'll get the X-rays organised. Lili, you'll need to give the receptionist some details.'

Lili stroked her daughter's clammy forehead. 'Shouldn't I stay with Lottie?'

But Lottie's good arm tightened possessively around Drew's neck.

'Drew can come with me. I like Drew.'

Doug's mouth twitched. 'Come on then, he can carry you to the cubicle. Your Mum'll be through in a minute. Over there,' he told Lili, nodding in the direction of the reception desk.

'Why?' Lottie demanded.

Doug was surprisingly good with children. Keeping a straight face, he leaned closer to her. 'Because that's April, our receptionist behind the desk.' His whisper was conspiratorial. 'And she needs to know everything there is to know about you.'

Lottie looked outraged. 'What, even the colour of my knickers?'

Chapter 54

Biting her lip, Lili watched Drew lift her daughter effort-lessly into his arms and carry her off down the corridor. Then she made her way over to the desk.

The receptionist's neat hair and freshly applied lipstick made Lili acutely conscious of how dishevelled she must look by comparison. She had been polishing windows before Felicity had rung, and her old yellow shirt was smudged with Windolene. Worse still, she couldn't remember brushing her hair this morning – a look that only the Goldie Hawns of this world could carry off – and yester-day's mascara had welded her eyelashes into clumps.

There are two kinds of women in this world, Lili thought: the ones like me and the receptionist types who always take their mascara off at night.

She wondered with a pang what Drew must have thought when he saw her like this.

No, no – mustn't even think about Drew. Definitely not allowed.

'Sorry.' Hastily Lili tried to comb Windolene-impregnated fingers through her embarrassing hair. 'I just realised what a fright I must look.'

'Not at all.' The receptionist's smile was reassuring. 'You're a friend of Doug's, I take it?'

'Well, kind of. We live in the same village.'

Manicured fingernails hovered above the computer key-board.

'Could you tell me your daughter's name?'

'Lottie Ferguson. Charlotte Ferguson,' Lili corrected her-self. 'Date of birth, twentieth of May 1993.'

The receptionist keyed in the details. 'Address?'

'The Old Vicarage, Upper Sisley.'

The tap-tapping faltered for a second. April gazed at the screen, saw that she had typed Siz instead of Sis, and hurriedly deleted the z. How extraordinary – she hadn't realised that Doug Flynn lived in the same village as Bernadette . . .

It didn't matter, of course it didn't. Just a coincidence, that was all.

She composed herself and glanced up at the woman in front of her. The woman must also know Bernadette.

'Any previous admissions?'

Lili shook her head. 'No.'

'Name and address of GP?'

'Dr Mather. Um . . . Oh Lord, I can't remember her address.'

'Would your husband know?' The receptionist glanced briefly behind her, in the direction of the corridor, and Lili realised what she meant.

'Oh no. Gosh, that isn't my husband. Drew shares a house with Doug; he just gave us a lift here.' Flushing at the implication, Lili hurried to explain. 'My husband's at home with the baby. He'll come in as soon as our elder daughter gets home. In fact I need to ring him, tell him what to bring in case Lottie has to stay here overnight.' She scrabbled in the pocket of her jeans for the emergency fiver she had grabbed on the way out of the house. 'You wouldn't have change for the phone, would you? I want to catch him before he leaves.'

It was against the rules, but April didn't have any change on her. She pushed her phone across the desk and lowered her voice. 'Here, use this one.'

'Thanks. I'll be quick, I promise.' Grinning with relief, Lili punched out the number. It was answered on the second ring.

'Darling? Yes, it's me. Doug's seeing to Lottie now.' Pause. 'No, they're doing X-rays but he doesn't think there's anything to worry about, just the arm. Yes, definitely broken.' Long pause. 'No, Michael, it can't wait. If his nappy's dirty you have to change it *now*.' Lili rolled her eyes in disbelief. 'Why? Because if you leave it, he'll get raging nappy rash. Now listen, I have to get off this phone. Throw a few things together before you leave, in case they keep Lottie in. A couple of clean nighties, toothbrush, that kind of thing. No, I washed and dried them this morning – they're in a big pile on our bed . . .'

April dropped the file she had been putting together and slid off her stool to retrieve it from under her desk. Her hands were shaking, her heart was pounding and she didn't know if she was going to be able to get up again.

Ferguson.

Michael Ferguson.

Surely not. Oh please, it couldn't be . . .

Her mind raced. All the separate details were battering around inside her head.

Not *her* Michael.

He and Doug knew each other, but Michael had only described him as a passing acquaintance; he hadn't said they lived in the same village.

But Michael had never told her exactly where he *did* live. Not in a deliberate I-don't-want-you-to-know way, of course; he had simply veered away from the question, describing it vaguely as a quiet little place and turning the conversation to something else.

And she, not wanting to irritate him, had let it pass. He had his family to consider, after all. April understood that. He might be living separately from his wife but there were still her feelings to consider. If she'd pressed for details, he might start to panic that he had a Fatal Attraction-type scenario on his hands.

Except . . .

Still crouched on the floor, April experienced a tidal wave of nausea.

Except . . . if they were talking about the same Michael Ferguson here, he wasn't sounding too separated from his wife.

'Darling', this woman had just called him. And not in that polite, teeth-gritted-together way some couples do when they clearly can't stand each other.

She'd said 'Our bed', too.

Our bed, meaning the one *they* slept in.

Together.

April was feeling sicker by the minute. She might actually have to throw up in her waste-paper basket.

'. . . okay darling, come as soon as Harriet gets back. See you soon.'

Above her, Lili hung up. Seconds later she was peering over the edge of the desk.

'Hello. Are you okay down there?'

April forced herself to nod. 'Just dropped the file.'

'Oh. Well, thanks for letting me use your phone. Have you got all the details you need?'

Another nod.

'I'll go through then, see how Lottie is. Will you be able to let me know when the troops arrive?'

'Troops?'

'Husband, teenage daughter, small noisy son, even noisier dog.' Lili grinned down at her. 'Well, maybe not the dog.'

April's hands were still trembling uncontrollably as she gathered together the sheets from the file. She forced herself to take a deep breath. 'Right, yes, I'll tell you.'

'Brilliant.' With a cheery wave Lili disappeared from view. 'Thanks!'

The next thirty minutes were the longest of April's life, as she waited for Lottie Ferguson's father to appear through the sliding doors. When he did, she knew at once that the desperate excuses she had spent the last half-hour manufacturing on his behalf had been a waste of time.

The expression on Michael's face when he saw her behind the desk said it all. A combination of shifty-eyed guilt and bravado – because as far as he was concerned there was still a chance he could get away with this.

He does, he really does, April thought incredulously as he and the children approached the desk. He thinks he can pull this off.

'Hello, my name's Michael Ferguson.' He winked at her

with the eye furthest from his teenage daughter. 'I'm Lottie Ferguson's father; she's here with my . . . er, wife.'

The '. . . er' bit, April realised, was significant too. He was implying that Lili might be his wife but it was a marriage in name only.

Feeling numb, she nodded. 'If you take a seat, I'll tell her you're here.'

April heard herself saying the words but only just. There was a rushing noise, like an approaching typhoon, in her ears. She wanted to scream at Michael but she couldn't, not with the children at his side. Wondering how she was going to make it along the corridor, she turned. But luck was on her side and Doug's friend was coming towards her.

'Um . . . Mr Ferguson's arrived.'

Drew glanced across at Harriet and Michael, and smiled briefly at Will, who was sitting on the floor playing with his beloved headless Barbie. That was it, he wasn't needed any more. Michael was here now. 'I'll tell Lili,' he offered, 'then it's time I was gone.'

'Oh help,' April murmured, realising she could no longer see properly. Everything was spinning, going grey, and the typhoon noise in her ears was getting louder.

'Oh help what? Is something wrong?' Drew frowned, then saw the colour drain from her face.

He managed to catch her just as she crumpled to the floor.

Eleanor Ferguson loved to boast that she was far too busy to watch TV . . . It was such rubbish, and there always seemed to be so many more worthwhile things to do.

But every now and again in the privacy of your own sitting room, it was nice to be able to make yourself a cup of tea, throw a couple of homemade biscuits on to a plate, put your feet up and let a bit of mindless afternoon television wash over you.

As long as nobody else knew you were doing it.

Eleanor almost choked on her flapjack when she heard the continuity announcer talking about *The Jack Astley Show*, due to be broadcast at five thirty.

'. . . and Jack's guest today is little-known novelist Antonia Kay, whose latest book is about to be turned into a Hollywood blockbuster.'

This time there was no 'almost' about it. Eleanor did choke on her flapjack. Spluttering and banging her bony chest, she sat bolt upright and stared at the screen. Her very own next-door neighbour . . . Good grief, this was unbelievable! A film company in Hollywood was actually making a film of Bernadette's novel . . .

And she hadn't told anyone, Eleanor realised with a jolt of betrayal. Not even *me*.

She leapt up, tea and flapjack forgotten, and ran to the window. Bernadette's car wasn't parked in its usual place and the windows next door were all shut. There was no one at home.

Of course, she would be at the television studios, Eleanor reminded herself. *The Jack Astley Show* went out live.

It would be a huge ordeal for someone as private and publicity-shy as Bernadette. Eleanor wondered why she had agreed to appear, then dismissed the question from her mind. That was irrelevant now. The show was set to start in an hour and it was up to her – it was her *duty*, no less – to spread the word to as many of the villagers as possible.

After all, if Bernadette was going to flaunt herself on national television, her identity was hardly going to be a secret any more.

Fifty minutes later and still bristling with importance, Eleanor swept into the shop.

'Well well,' marvelled Myrtle Armitage when she heard the news. 'Who'd've thought it? Quiet as a mouse, looks like she wouldn't say boo to a bowl of custard . . . and all this time she's been doing deals with them Hollywood types.' She cast a regretful glance at her watch. 'Looks like I'm going to have to miss it. I can't close the shop yet.'

Eleanor couldn't bear anyone to miss this. Bernadette was her next-door neighbour and she felt as if she'd discovered her single-handedly.

'Set your TV up out here. It's a portable, isn't it?' She

pushed the carefully arranged rows of magazines to one side, clearing a space on the counter. 'You wait there, I'll bring it through myself.'

As Eleanor disappeared through the door leading into Myrtle's living room, Myrtle called after her, 'But it's half past five now. You won't be home in time.'

Eleanor returned, holding the portable television aloft. Dust free, she was pleased to note.

'No problem. I'll watch it here with you.'

Chapter 55

As she had been recovering from her faint, April had heard Lili greeting Michael over by the coffee machine.

'Hello, sweetheart! I was wondering when you'd get here!'

If April had looked up at that moment she would have seen that Lili was kissing Harriet, not Michael. But all she heard was the sound of the kiss, then Lili's voice again, pitched lower this time.

'What's going on over there?'

'One of the receptionists fainted.' Michael had sounded vague, uninterested.

'Oh, that poor girl! She didn't seem well when I was talking to her earlier. I wondered then if she felt a bit—'

'Anyway,' Michael had interrupted brusquely, 'how's Lottie?'

'Oh, fine. Come and see her, she's dying to show off her plaster cast.'

That had been over an hour ago. Shortly afterwards, one of the nurses who was going off duty had given April a lift home.

'Take it easy,' she had advised. 'You still look dreadful. I'd go to bed if I were you.'

April had managed a nod and a brief frozen smile of thanks, but bed was out of the question. She was seized with rage and grief and helplessness. Michael Ferguson had lied to her, made an utter fool of her, destroyed her chance of happiness.

April couldn't believe it was happening to her all over again.

★ ★ ★

'We're here, love.' The taxi driver pulled up outside the cottage and twisted around, checking that his fare hadn't thrown up all over the back seat. 'That'll be eight quid.'

At least Bernie's car was outside. When April had called for a cab it hadn't occurred to her to phone and check first. But then it hadn't occurred to her either to wonder if what she was doing was right. Coming here had been instinctive, simply the only thing *to* do.

Because, despite everything that had happened in the past, she knew Bernie loved her.

And what April needed now, more than ever before, was someone who would understand and sympathise.

Someone who would be on her side.

Bernadette, just back from a trip to the garden centre, heard the sound of an unfamiliar car outside. When she went to the window and saw who was climbing out of the idling taxi she had to step back and catch her breath.

April.

What in heaven's name was she doing here?

Bernadette didn't have to wait long to find out. When she opened the door April was stumbling up the front path, tears streaming from her eyes. Instinctively Bernadette held out her arms. The last time she had seen April was less than two months ago, when she had hidden in a shop doorway in Harleston in order to glimpse her across the street.

But it had been over two years since April had set eyes on her.

'Oh Bernie, I had to come. Please don't be angry with me.' She buried her head against Bernadette's shoulder, the stiff lace-edged frill of Bernadette's blouse scratching her wet cheek. 'I'm so sorry, I just didn't know what else to do.'

'Shhh, it's okay. I'm glad you came,' Bernadette murmured in soothing tones. 'Now, tell me what's wrong.' As she led her into the sitting room, Bernadette stroked April's soft blonde hair. She had never stopped loving her. If there was anything, *anything* she could do to make the pain go away, she would do it.

Over at the village shop, Eleanor Ferguson was quivering

like a rat's whiskers. Outrage vied with bitter humiliation, and she could scarcely bear to meet Myrtle Armitage's beady gaze.

Because Antonia Kay was on the television exchanging flirtatious banter with Jack Astley. What was more, Jack Astley was visibly enjoying himself, because Antonia Kay was blonde and pretty and wore a mini-skirt that showed off her long, shapely legs.

There had been no mistake, because they were talking about *A Frond of Honeysuckle*, and Jack was holding a copy of the book up to the camera.

Eleanor flushed an ever-deepening shade of red. This was more than outrageous, it was intolerable. Bernadette Thomas had lied to her, not just once but over and over again.

She's made me look a complete fool, Eleanor thought, jowls aquiver as she remembered how she had raced around the village boasting about Bernadette's appearance on TV and exhorting everyone to watch.

She's the one pretending – God alone knows why – to be someone she isn't, Eleanor fumed, and *I'm* the one left with egg on my face.

Myrtle Armitage, secretly delighted to be witnessing bossy Eleanor Ferguson's long-awaited come-uppance, spoke with feigned innocence.

'Maybe you misunderstood her. She could've said she *knew* a novelist and you thought she said she *was* one—'

'It wasn't a misunderstanding.' Grimly Eleanor stood up. She'd had enough. 'That woman deliberately lied to me, and I'm going to give her a piece of my mind!'

'What are you doing?' April stammered, clutching fearfully at Bernadette's sleeve.

But Bernadette had already wrenched open the front door. Michael Ferguson had done this to April and – one way or another – he would pay for it.

So angry she could barely see straight, Bernadette marched slap into Eleanor Ferguson storming through the front gate.

'You,' Eleanor pointed a rigid, accusing finger at Bernadette, 'have some explaining to do, madam.'

'If anyone has any explaining to do, it's your son. Where is he?'

Open-mouthed, Eleanor took a step backwards. Who was supposed to be the accuser here?

The next second she recognised the slender, distraught-looking blonde clinging to Bernadette's arm. This was the girl whose photograph stood in a silver frame on the table in Bernadette's hall. Eleanor's nostrils twitched with disgust. Ugh! Filthy lesbians the pair of them—

'Bernie, no, leave it,' the girl pleaded. 'He's probably still at the hospital anyway.'

'Hospital? *Hospital?*' Eleanor barked. 'My son Michael – is that who you're talking about? How ridiculous! I saw him myself less than two minutes ago, walking across to the pub.' To her eternal shame she remembered how she had poked her head around the door of the Seven Bells and said archly to Lorna Blake: 'Tune in to *The Jack Astley Show* at five thirty and you could be in for a big surprise.'

With grim satisfaction, Bernadette said, 'Right, the pub it is!'

'Bernie, you mustn't!' April begged, but her protesting hand was shaken off. And April, who knew she didn't mean it anyway, experienced a furtive thrill deep down in the pit of her stomach.

Was this why I came here? she wondered as they set off at speed down the lane. Was this why I had to see Bernie again – for comfort *and* some kind of revenge?

'I don't know what you think you're playing at,' Eleanor spoke through gritted teeth, racing to keep up as they approached the village green, 'but I've just been watching the *real* Antonia Kay on television. Now you'd better tell me what this is all about.'

'You'll find out soon enough.'

'Heaven knows, I tried to be a good neighbour to you, and this is how you repay me. You're nothing but a liar and a cheat!'

Bernadette strode on ahead without speaking, leading the

mini-convoy of three. She didn't even glance at Eleanor as she reached the far side of the green, marched across the road to the Seven Bells and pushed open the heavy oak door.

Despite never having actually set foot in the pub before, Bernadette recognised quite a few of the people in there. For six o'clock in the evening it was busier than she had expected too – another bonus. Maybe forty or fifty customers in all, among them Toby and Savannah Gillespie, and the two young vets from Keeper's Cottage.

As people turned their attention from the TV set up on the wall, Bernadette's level gaze swung the length of the pub. Tall, good-looking Oliver Roscoe was working behind the bar, one hand on a beer pump as he filled a pint mug to the brim. Next to him, unloading a tray of glasses, Moll-the-trollop, whose reputation even Bernadette was aware of. And further along, smoking a cigarette and chatting to a customer perched on one of the leather-topped bar stools, gravel-voiced Lorna Blake.

Bernadette heard April behind her, still gasping for breath.

She looked directly at Michael Ferguson, the customer perched on the stool engaged in desultory conversation with Lorna.

Bernadette coughed and announced in a clear voice, 'Mr Ferguson.'

Michael turned, a questioning tilt to his eyebrows. 'Yes?'

Then he saw April, standing two feet behind Bernadette, her eyes desolate and swollen with tears.

'What's this about?' The sudden pallor of Michael's face matched the frothy just-poured beer.

'Oh, I think you know,' said Bernadette.

Michael's jaw stuck out at a belligerent angle. 'Should I?'

'You recognise this lady, I take it?'

He hesitated, then shrugged. 'I saw her at the hospital earlier, if that's what you mean.'

In the doorway, Eleanor protested furiously, 'This is ridiculous! You can't—'

But Bernadette was off. In less than a second she had

crossed the stone-flagged floor, pulled back her arm and delivered a right hook like a hammer-blow to Michael Ferguson's jutting chin.

He fell off his stool, crashed heavily to the ground and lay there, dazed, as Bernadette picked up his pint glass and poured the frothy contents over his head.

'And you think *I'm* a liar and a cheat,' she told Eleanor, her tone almost conversational as she flicked the last dregs of Courage Best dismissively in his face.

The rest of the pub stared, agog, at the surreal sight of Bernadette standing over Michael Ferguson. It had been a punch like no other they had ever witnessed, a punch that would have done credit to Prince Naseem.

'Wh-what's going on?' Michael was spluttering and wiping the beer from his stinging eyes. 'What's this got to do with you, for Christ's sake?'

'Let's just say I care about what happens to April,' Bernadette told him icily. It might have been twenty years ago now, but once a boxer always a boxer. 'You see, she's my ex-wife.'

Chapter 56

'I still can't believe it,' Lili exclaimed the next morning, shaking her head as she tipped a packet of chocolate digestives into the biscuit tin. 'Bernadette Thomas used to be a *man*.'

'I wish I could have been there.' Jessie winced and shot her a semi-apologetic glance across the kitchen table. 'Sorry, I know Michael's your husband and all that, but Oliver did say it was the most amazing sight.'

Lili was busy cramming a biscuit into her mouth. 'Don't look so guilty. I wish I'd been there too. I just thought you could always tell when men had had a sex change. You know, five-o'clock shadow breaking through their foundation.'

'Gruff voices.'

'Thick black hairs poking out through their tights.'

'And leather-studded mini-skirts.' Jessie helped herself to another digestive.

If it hadn't been such a hot day the kitchen door wouldn't have been left wide open and Bernadette Thomas, about to tap on it, would not have overheard this conversation.

But since it was, and she had, she cleared her throat instead and said from the doorway, 'Electrolysis works wonders these days. And the hormone replacements, they help too. As for the clothes . . . well, we don't all want to wear leather-studded mini-skirts.'

Across the table, Lili gasped and went pink. Jessie coughed, struggling to swallow her mouthful of biscuit.

'Hi! Come in. God, sorry, what must you think of us? We were just—'

341

'Saying what everyone else in the village has been saying since word got out?' Bernadette suggested drily. 'Don't worry, I understand. Transsexuals are an object of fascination. It's only natural to be curious.'

'Which is why you kept quiet about it for so long.' Jessie could sympathise, she knew how it felt to be gossiped about. 'But now everybody knows. So what made you decide to blow your cover?'

A brief smile from Bernadette, who was as carefully made-up as ever. She brushed a stray thread from the front of her high-necked cream blouse. 'Well yes, of course I could have rushed in there and scratched his eyes out,' she admitted, 'or tried stabbing him with a crochet hook, that would have been more ladylike. But I wasn't thinking that clearly. Or maybe I didn't care any more. When you work yourself up into that much of a state the old instincts take over. You see, I was in the army for many years, did a lot of boxing . . . All I wanted to do was hurt him as much as he'd hurt April.' Bernadette paused, gazing down at her clenched knuckles. 'And possibly to assuage my own guilt, because of course I'd hurt April too. I should never have married her, I know that, but at the time I thought it might make the other feelings go away. And I loved her,' Bernadette concluded sadly, 'very much indeed. I still do.'

There were so many questions. Jessie pushed the sugar bowl across the table as Lili poured Bernadette a mug of tea.

'Why did you tell Eleanor you were Antonia Kay?'

'A journalist came round. Somebody from the support group I used to attend gave him my name and address. When Eleanor started asking questions I had to come up with a plausible answer.'

'But a writer!'

'Ah, but I *am* a writer.' Bernadette looked amused as she sipped her tea. 'I'm just not Antonia Kay.'

Bewildered, Lili said, 'Who are you then?'

'Bernard Thomas.'

'You write spy thrillers!' Jessie recognised the name at once. 'Oliver's got all your books. He tried to make me read one once but it was so tough, so hard-hitting . . . Gosh, sorry, that sounds rude—'

'They're men's books.' Bernadette waved aside the apology. 'It's okay, I'm not offended. Men love them, women hate them.'

Lili was fascinated. 'Do your publishers know about . . .?'

'Oh yes, I told them. They almost fainted,' Bernadette said good-naturedly. 'Made me promise not to let the cat out of the bag. If word got out, they knew sales would plummet. It's a question of image, you see. As my editor pointed out, it would be rather like asking the public to accept James Bond in stockings and a basque.'

'Have some more tea.' Lili picked up the teapot. 'I have to say, I'm not sure my mother-in-law will ever speak to you again. But then again, that could be a blessing.'

Bernadette took the teapot from Lili's trembling hands and set it back down on the table. 'Look, we've talked enough about me. That's not why I came here. I wanted to apologise to you.'

'Oh Lord, no need for that,' said Lili, embarrassed.

'Of course there is. Your husband was carrying on with April and now, thanks to me, the whole village knows. You must be devastated.' Bernadette frowned. 'Unless . . . you already knew?'

Lili's hands had stopped trembling. Really, she didn't feel too bad at all.

'No, I didn't know.' She shook her fringe out of her eyes. 'But – well, put it this way, it was a relief to find out.'

Having made himself scarce for most of the day, Michael felt he had given Lili time to get over the shock.

'Look, okay, I accept that I shouldn't have done it,' he said generously, facing Lili across their double bed while she threw shirt after crumpled shirt into an open case. 'But don't you think you're overreacting here? It was a fling, that's all. She didn't *mean* anything. It's no reason to break up a perfectly good marriage.'

As he finished speaking, something registered that hadn't registered before. *Unironed* shirts.

What a slut, Michael thought, outraged. His mother had always told him he deserved better, and she'd been right.

'This isn't a perfectly good marriage,' Lili said with unnerving calm, 'it's a completely crappy one.'

'But we've got three children!'

'Which is why I stuck it out for so long. Otherwise, believe me, I'd have been out of here years ago.' She pulled open Michael's underwear drawer and began hurling socks and pants higgledy-piggledy on top of the mountain of shirts. 'Still, never mind. This time you can be the one to go.'

Michael glared at her. Lili never ironed underwear either. Unlike his mother, who had always lovingly pressed and folded them in serried ranks in his drawer.

'You're being ridiculous!' he snapped. 'Thousands of women accept their husbands' harmless little affairs . . . Why can't you? Why do *you* have to be the one who kicks up an almighty fuss?'

'Maybe because this is the last straw.' Lili knew the way she was flinging stuff into the suitcase was irritating him, which only made doing it more enjoyable. 'Maybe they figured out the pros and cons and decided their marriages were worth saving.' She held up an orange and pink Argyle sock and raised an eyebrow. 'Whereas I've just had enough.'

'But—'

'No, let me say it. I've put up with all sorts of stuff from you, because I always told myself that at least you were faithful. Then, when I began to think that maybe you were playing away in Dubai, I told myself that at least you weren't doing it here, right under my nose.' Lili chucked a can of shaving foam on top of the underwear and watched the lid roll on to the floor. 'So you see, we've pretty much hit rock bottom now, haven't we? I can't think of a single reason why I should stay married to you any more.'

Michael began to sweat; he felt himself go hot and cold all over. He'd never seen Lili like this before. God, what with child-support payments and alimony, she could totally wipe him out.

'The children . . . *our* children,' he blustered, 'need a father.'

Lili had had enough. This was hypocrisy on a grand scale. 'I know they do,' she said flatly. 'Still, they've managed without one for this long—'

'Lili, I love you!'

But even begging, it seemed, wasn't going to work. She snapped the case shut and pushed it across the bed.

'Don't lie, Michael. And don't try to make me feel guilty, because I just won't. All this is your fault, not mine.'

'You can't do this to me!' he retaliated furiously. 'Where the hell am I supposed to go?'

Lili shrugged. 'I don't know and I don't care. Ask Bernadette's ex-wife – what's her name? April. Maybe she'll put you up.'

Chapter 57

Two hours later Michael dragged his cases – properly packed this time – down the stairs. A hurried phone call to Head Office followed by another to Heathrow had completed the arrangements to return to Dubai sooner than planned. If Lili needed a while to cool off, he would give it to her. By the time of his next leave, Michael had confidently decided, she would be more than happy to welcome him back.

'Dad, look at my arm,' Lottie waved the plaster cast under his nose, her expression gleeful. 'I wrote my name on it, and then I wrote bum!' Spotting the cases in the hall, she said, 'Where are you going?'

Lili was in the kitchen. Making sure she could overhear, Michael crouched down and gave Lottie an emotional hug.

'Away, sweetheart. Back to Dubai, I'm afraid. I'll be gone for a long time.'

But Lottie, disappointingly, planted only a dutiful peck on his cheek before wriggling out of his grasp. 'Okay. And see what Harriet drew? A picture of Blitz. It's meant to look like a tattoo.'

'I'll bring back lots of presents,' Michael promised in desperation.

'You always tell us that but you never do. You always say you forgot.'

Harriet seemed equally unimpressed when, wandering out into the hall, she found herself on the receiving end of a suffocating embrace and the promise of regular postcards.

She frowned. 'But you always said you were too busy to buy them.'

'Not this time,' Michael told her humbly. How had this happened? When had his own children turned against him?

It was galling to realise that the most enthusiastic goodbye came from Blitz. He didn't even like the wretched dog, but at least he got his hand licked. All Will could manage, when roused from his afternoon nap, was an indignant wail and a raspberry yoghurt-flavoured burp.

Rubbing his chin, still sore from yesterday and sorer now from finding itself on the receiving end of one of Will's flailing rabbit punches, Michael made his way through to the kitchen.

'Right, I'm off.'

Lili was at the sink, draining pasta. She turned, half enveloped in clouds of steam. 'Okay.'

He gave her one last chance.

'It was a one-off, you have to believe that. It's never happened before, *ever*.'

Lili looked at him for several seconds. 'Yes it has.'

He shook his head. 'You're wrong.'

'Michael, she rang me. From Dubai.'

Jesus Christ, that bitch!

'When?' Reddening, Michael silently cursed Sandra; whatever had possessed her to do something so stupid? 'She had no right to do that! When did she ring? And what did she tell you?'

Lili exhaled slowly. 'Nothing. Nobody rang. I just said it to see how you'd react.'

She wondered if she should be bursting into tears – surely she should be more upset than this? – but all she felt was an overwhelming sense of release.

'You mean you were *bluffing*?' Michael was incredulous.

'I just wanted to make sure I was right.' Lili gave the colander one last shake, then carefully began tipping pasta on to plates. 'And now I know I am.'

Toby tore open the familiarly addressed envelope, wondering why he was even bothering to do so. He should be throwing these letters, unopened, straight into the bin.

Or handing them over to the police, he thought wearily.

Maybe the time had come to take that step.

'Toby Gillespie, useless actor. Isn't it time you moved on?'

That was all it said. Hardly a death threat.

He glanced up as Dizzy ambled into the sitting room.

'What's that?'

'Another of those letters, if you can call it that.'

Frowning, Dizzy took it and read the wobbly words. He hadn't written this one, but if Eleanor Ferguson got to hear about it she would think he had. And let's face it, he thought morosely, everyone in this bloody village gets to hear about everything.

Still, he couldn't help experiencing a brief pang of envy. Somebody else was still getting a kick out of doing what he was no longer allowed to do.

It was so unfair.

He handed the letter back to his father. 'What are you going to do?'

'I don't know.' Toby sighed. 'Pass it on to the police.'

Startled, Dizzy said, 'They might get fed up and stop doing it. Then you wouldn't need to.'

'I've been thinking that for months, but it hasn't happened yet. And now other people are getting them as well.'

'I was in the shop this morning. Nobody's had anything for the last three days.'

Grimly Toby held up the letter. 'I have.'

'I'd still leave it for a week or so.' Dizzy was beginning to sweat. 'You never know, this could be the last one.'

Twenty minutes later Toby heard footsteps on the stairs. When he glanced up he saw Deborah rubbing scent into her neck and wrists. She had changed her clothes and put on fresh make-up, he noticed.

Am I meant to ask where she's going?

Appalled, Toby realised he simply didn't care. The atmosphere in the house remained at sub-zero, and he had no urge to remedy it.

For all her surface charm, Deborah had always done exactly what she wanted.

Well, she could carry on doing it now, Toby thought, unmoved. It no longer bothered him.

Living separate lives suited him just fine.

Doug Flynn didn't look thrilled when he answered the door and found Deborah on the front step. He glanced across the green, wondering who else had spotted her there.

'This isn't a good idea.'

'I didn't have much choice.' Deborah was as elegant as ever in a black silk sweater, black trousers and a cloud of Rive Gauche. 'You've been avoiding me, Doug. And you aren't returning my calls.'

These days, when Doug's mobile began to ring, he habitually checked the caller's number as it flashed up. If he recognised it as Deborah's he let the answering service take a message.

It had taken quite a few lately.

'I told you, it's all too much of a risk. I don't want to be involved any more.'

'And I told you, I don't care about that.' Deborah's dark eyes were bright with impatience. She wasn't the type to stamp her foot but she looked as if she wanted to. Pushing the door further open, she moved towards him. 'Doug, let me in. I have to talk to you. I'm going mad next door . . . Toby's being a *pig*—'

'Jamie's upstairs.'

'So? We'll talk quietly.'

He sighed and let Deborah into the cottage. A scene on the doorstep was the last thing either of them needed. 'Five minutes then. I'm on duty at six.'

'But you aren't working this weekend, are you?'

Taken aback, Doug said, 'How do you know?'

'Well, I hardly needed to hire a private investigator.' Deborah gently mocked his astonishment. 'I rang the Casualty Department, asked if you'd be there on Saturday afternoon. They said you had the whole weekend off.'

'So?'

'So I thought we could go away together. I'll tell Toby I'm going up to London to stay with friends. You can—'

'I'm already going away.'

'Great, I'll come with you.'

'I've made other arrangements.'

'Unmake them.' Smiling, Deborah trailed her fingers down his cheek. 'I mean, be honest. She wouldn't have been a patch on me anyway, would she?'

Upstairs, they heard Jamie crashing around in his bedroom, hunting in his wardrobe for something clean to wear.

'At least she isn't married,' said Doug. He wasn't taking anyone with him – he had an interview for a job in Manchester – but he was buggered if he was going to let Deborah know that.

'I may not be married for much longer,' she said calmly. 'I did my best, but Toby's never going to forgive me. I'm telling you, it's hell in that house. But you and I . . . we'd be brilliant together.' Deborah's tone grew more urgent. 'I've been thinking about it – you could jack in that lousy NHS job and go into private practice. Imagine, your own consulting rooms in Harley Street! With your looks and my connections, how could it fail? You'd make a fortune as doctor to the stars . . . We could get you a stint on TV—'

'I don't want to be on television,' Doug said coldly. 'And I certainly don't want to spend my days doling out diet pills and telling neurotic thirty-year-old actresses they need a face-lift. Now, I have to get to work.'

'Phone in, tell them you're sick,' Deborah pleaded, pressing herself against him. 'You can't do this to me. Toby's such a bastard he won't even sleep with me. I haven't had sex for weeks!'

Her desperation repulsed him. Doug managed to push her away moments before Jamie clattered downstairs in jeans and one of Drew's best shirts.

'It's just a minor eye infection,' he told Deborah. 'Keep using the drops and it'll clear up in a couple of days.'

When he had shown her out and closed the front door, Jamie gave him an odd look.

'What was she doing here?'

'Nothing.' Doug picked up his jacket and car keys. 'Getting hysterical over a bit of conjunctivitis.'

'But I thought I heard her say . . .' Jamie's courage failed him. '. . . Um, I couldn't see any sign of conjunctivitis.'

'Exactly.' Doug's tone was curt as he made his way out. 'She was just making a big fuss.'

Drew and Jamie were the last to leave the Seven Bells that night. As they made their way across the green, Jamie was still harping on about Deborah Gillespie.

'I do, I reckon there's something going on between those two. It's that perfume she wears. I smelled it once before, that time Doug said he'd fallen asleep in the back garden. It was on his shirt, I swear it was.'

'You've already told me this. About fifty times this evening.' Drew was less enthralled. All he could think about was Lili, whom he hadn't dared to phone.

'I'm allowed to repeat myself, I'm pissed. And I swear I heard her say she hadn't had sex for weeks.'

Drew muttered, 'I know the feeling.'

'Lucky bastard, what's he got that we haven't?'

'Good looks,' said Drew.

'Huh.'

'Sports car.'

'Oh well.'

'The letters MD after his name.'

'Pssh.'

'And he treats women like dirt.'

'I tried treating a bird like dirt once,' Jamie said gloomily, 'I really fancied her.'

'What happened?'

'Bloody bitch dumped me.'

'Who's that over there?'

'Eh?'

Drew squinted across the green. Ahead of them, fifty yards to the right of Keeper's Cottage where Compass Lane joined Waters Lane, something was glinting in the darkness.

'Someone's trying to hide behind those bushes.'

Jamie sounded hopeful. 'Could be Deborah Gillespie and Doug having a shag.'

Drew didn't think this was likely, but whoever it was, they

351

were acting in a pretty furtive manner.

'Come on, let's see what they're up to.'

When they reached the bushes, it didn't take a genius to work it out. The glinting had come from a can of spray paint. The sign saying WATERS LANE – the road in which Bernadette Thomas and Eleanor Ferguson lived – had been altered to read SEX-CHANGE LANE.

And the person crouching in the undergrowth clutching the spray can was Toby Gillespie's son, Dizzy.

Afterwards, Drew realised that if the boy had looked a bit sheepish, given them an apologetic grin and maybe made a bit of a joke of it, they would more than likely have let him go. Compared with the drunken pranks they had played at college, defacing a road sign was pretty tame. But Dizzy hadn't tried to laugh it off. He had gazed at them, wide-eyed with horror, and made a frantic bid for freedom.

This had been his big mistake; years of rugby training had induced an almost Pavlovian reaction in Jamie.

If it moves, tackle it.

Jamie promptly hurled himself after Dizzy, grabbing him by the knees and bringing him to the ground with a thud.

Two white envelopes flew out of the back pocket of Dizzy's jeans and the can of paint skidded across the grass.

'Let go of me! Just leave me alone!' Dizzy begged.

'Yes, let go of him,' said Drew, embarrassed by Jamie's overreaction. Before the wind could catch Dizzy's envelopes and carry them off, he bent down and picked them up himself.

'What?' Deeply disappointed, Jamie said, 'Can't I make a citizen's arrest?'

This was what nine pints of Guinness did to you. Made you all of a sudden astonishingly law-abiding.

'No you can't.'

Idly Drew turned the envelopes over. The next second his pulse began to quicken. Even in almost total blackness he could make out the writing on the front of them.

They were both stamped, and one was addressed to Toby Gillespie.

The other was for Moll.

'Hang on to him,' Drew instructed Jamie as he began to tear open the second envelope.

'Don't,' Dizzy bleated, white-faced with terror. 'You can't read that,' he added in desperation, 'it's private – it's not addressed to you!'

Chapter 58

'What's going on?' Toby Gillespie looked concerned when he opened the front door at midnight and found Drew Darcy on his front doorstep.

'Sorry about this,' said Drew, 'but it's about your son.'

'Dizzy? He's in bed.'

Jamie dragged Dizzy across the gravel and into view.

'Here.' Drew handed the two letters over to Toby. 'I'll leave these with you. They fell out of Dizzy's pocket earlier.'

Toby skimmed the contents in less than five seconds:

> Moll,
> It's no fun sleeping with you any more. All that silicone sloshing about sounds like two hot-water bottles strapped to your chest.

The second one, addressed to him, said:

> You're a lousy actor. Nobody wants you here. Sell your house and move back to London.

Oh Christ, thought Toby, I do not believe this.

'Thanks,' he told Drew evenly, wondering if life could possibly get more disastrous. 'I'll take over now.'

'It's not fair!' Dizzy wailed. 'I get the blame for everything! I didn't *start* it!'

Toby rubbed his hands over his face. 'You mean there are two people in this village sending anonymous letters?'

'Yes, yes!'

'Oh, Dizzy.' He shook his head. Discovering that the person who had been sending you hate mail was your own son . . . now that *was* a kick in the teeth.

'Honest!' Dizzy was desperate; not being believed was awful. 'Somebody else started it and I just kind of . . . joined in. I made them look the same, that's all.'

Still sceptical, Toby said, 'Why?'

'Dunno. For a laugh.'

'A *laugh*?'

Dizzy shifted uncomfortably on the sofa and pulled the frayed sleeves of his jumper up over his knuckles. 'I hate it here. I wanted you to sell the house, move back to London.'

'And how long did you think you'd be able to get away with this?'

Dizzy nodded miserably at the two letters lying on the coffee table between them. 'These were the last ones. Then I was going to stop.' He tried to be as honest as he could. 'I stopped three days ago, then this morning you got one of the other ones. I didn't send that one.' He glanced up to see if his father believed him. 'But you were talking about going to the police, so I thought I'd just have one last go.'

'Go at what?'

'Making you sell the house.'

Toby sighed. Then he tapped the other letter. 'And this one? Have you really slept with Moll?'

Dizzy looked as if he might cry. His bottom lip wobbled.

'No, but everybody else has.'

Felicity Seymour, never having been much of a pub person, was astounded to find herself enjoying her visits to the Seven Bells more and more.

At first, when Hugh had made his twice-weekly visits to the house to see Freya, she had shut herself upstairs in her room and sobbed. After a couple of weeks, however, when the sobbing had subsided, she'd taken to going for a drive, or calling in on Lili for coffee and a chat.

One evening when she had dropped by with three long hours to kill, Lili had been strapping Will into his pushchair and attempting to drag a brush through Lottie's tangled curls.

'It's such a gorgeous evening, I thought we'd go to the pub,' Lili had explained. 'The kids love playing in the garden, and Lorna doesn't mind as long as they stay outside.'

Hesitating, not wanting to play gooseberry, Felicity had asked, 'Will Drew be there?'

Lili had finished brushing Playdough out of Lottie's hair and straightened up. 'I don't know.'

'Have you spoken to him yet?'

Vigorously Lili shook her head. 'God no! Poor chap, he's probably scared witless. One minute he's having a bit of a harmless flirt with an old married woman, then ... *whooomph!* The next thing he knows, she's kicked out her husband.'

'Maybe it's what he wanted to happen.'

'I don't think so.' Lili had spent hours perfecting her careless smile. 'I mean, let's be honest. If you were Drew, would you want to be saddled with someone else's three kids?'

'I still think you should phone him,' said Felicity.

'Better if I don't.' Lili, who had her pride, had spoken as if it couldn't matter less. But inside her brain the same words kept churning round and round like a washing machine: If he wanted to, he could always phone me.

From that first sunny evening at the Seven Bells, Felicity had been struck by the friendliness of the bar staff. When Lili had prepared to leave with her children, Lorna Blake had cornered Felicity and said in her husky, do-as-I-tell-you-voice, 'You can stay for one more, can't you? Go on, I could do with the company.' And whisking her empty glass from her, not even giving her a chance to refuse, she had filled it to the brim with Frascati.

The pair of them had clicked immediately. Felicity had no idea why – they could hardly be more different, after all – but somehow their differences were irrelevant. Lorna was simply easy to talk to. Beneath the brusque exterior, the cynical smile and the trowelled-on make-up, Felicity suspected, lay an altogether gentler character than Lorna liked to make out.

Tonight she had come to the pub on her own and found it practically deserted.

'The darts team are playing an away match,' Lorna drawled, 'and they're such useless buggers they needed the rest of my regulars to cheer them on.'

The lack of customers meant they could talk uninterrupted.

'How's it going with Hugh?' Lorna asked, lighting up her umpteenth cigarette and leaning her elbows companionably on the bar.

Felicity shrugged. 'It's easier being out of the house while he's there.'

'Seeing anyone else, is he?'

Only Lorna could ask such a blunt question and make her laugh. I'm getting better, Felicity thought with gratitude. Only a couple of weeks ago I'd have burst into floods of tears.

Instead she said mischievously, 'Why? Interested?'

Lorna almost choked on her Scotch. 'Not my type!'

'No, well, you aren't his type either.' Felicity took a deep breath; until now she hadn't told anyone other than Lili and Jess. 'Hugh's gay.'

'Is he?' Raising one painted eyebrow, Lorna looked amused. 'So am I.'

'Oh, good Lord!' It simply hadn't occurred to Felicity before. She had vaguely assumed Lorna Blake to be a divorcee, childless by choice. 'Am I the only person in the village who didn't know?'

The corner of Lorna's mouth twitched. 'No, you're the only one who does.'

An hour later, while they were discussing the hopelessness of the darts team with Moll, one of Lorna's cats appeared behind the bar, snaking itself around Moll's shapely legs. Moll looked as if she'd quite like to give it a kick.

Lorna, cooing like a mother hen, scooped the purring creature up into her arms. 'Who's my beautiful boy, then? You shouldn't be down here, oh no you shouldn't.'

Moll made sick noises and rolled her eyes.

'Just ignore her,' Lorna whispered consolingly in the cat's ear. 'She's horrible.'

Felicity put out a hand and stroked the soft fur. 'I love cats. I'm thinking of getting one when I move into the new house.'

Beneath the heftily applied layers of mascara, Lorna's eyes lit up. 'I haven't introduced you to the rest of the family yet! Why don't you come up and meet them properly?'

'Um . . .' Felicity hesitated and checked her watch.

'Of course,' Lorna went on hurriedly, 'if you'd rather not—'

'I'd love to,' said Felicity before Lorna could think she was afraid to venture upstairs alone with her. She slid off her bar stool.

'Think you can manage down here?' Lorna winked at Moll.

At that moment the door swung open and Drew Darcy came in, closely followed by Doug Flynn. Moll, glad she'd worn the emerald-green bra and low-cut red velvet top, felt Doug's dark gaze flicker over her and registered his approval.

Running her tongue briefly over her lips to make them glisten, she breathed in to let Lorna past. 'Don't worry about me.' Moll's grin was confident. 'You know I always give the customers what they want.'

Chapter 59

Upstairs, Felicity was formally introduced to the other two cats. Then Lorna pulled a photograph album out of a drawer and lovingly went through every page, pointing out each of them as kittens.

'We'd only cramp Moll's style if we went back down,' she told Felicity. 'Shall I put the kettle on? I fancy a cup of tea.'

This made Felicity smile. 'You don't seem the tea type. I thought you drank gin for breakfast, gin for lunch and gin for tea.'

'People aren't always the way they seem.' Back from the tiny kitchen, Lorna leaned against the door frame. 'As you've discovered tonight.' She pulled a face. 'As we all discovered the other week when Bernadette Thomas came hurtling in here and punched Michael Ferguson off his stool.'

'I don't know . . .' Felicity sighed, fondling the youngest cat's ears. 'One way or another, husbands always manage to be embarrassing.' *Embarrassing* – that was an understatement. Hers had wrecked her life.

'Do you want to talk about Hugh?'

Felicity glanced nervously again at her watch. 'I said I'd be home by ten. He's meant to be meeting up with . . . um, someone, later.'

'You mean his new chap?' Calmly Lorna picked up the phone and passed it across. 'Give him a ring, say you'll be late.'

Feeling terribly daring, Felicity did as she was told. It gave her a thrill to hear the note of irritation in his voice.

Now Hugh would have to cancel his night out, and he so hated letting people down. Other people, that was. Wives didn't count.

'But who are you with?' he demanded.

Lorna, eavesdropping next to her, shook her head.

'Just a friend,' said Felicity.

'Are you at Lili's house?'

'No.'

Irritation was replaced by curiosity. 'So where then? Is this a male friend?'

Vigorously Lorna nodded.

'Hugh, you aren't the only one allowed to have male friends, okay? I'll be back by midnight.'

Pleased with herself, Felicity put the phone down. 'I don't know why that makes me feel better, but it does.'

Lorna grinned and lit yet another cigarette. 'Make yourself comfortable. I'll go and make that tea.'

Felicity had told her everything, and Lorna listened without interrupting her once. Downstairs as the clock struck eleven, they heard Moll call time at the bar.

Twenty minutes later she poked her head around the door. 'All cleared up. See you in the morning.'

When the door had closed behind her, Lorna glanced with amusement at Felicity, who was clearly confused.

'Must be Doug's lucky night.'

The next moment amusement turned to dismay as Felicity burst into tears.

Feeling helpless, Lorna watched her sob. She so wanted to put a comforting arm around her but didn't quite dare in case Felicity thought it was a come-on.

Instead she made another pot of tea, opened a fresh box of tissues because Felicity had got through the last lot, and waited for the torrent of tears to end.

It did, finally.

'Sorry . . . sorry. It was just saying it was Doug's lucky night.' Miserably Felicity blinked her red-rimmed eyes. 'I mean, it's not that I want to be Moll—'

'I should think not,' Lorna interjected brusquely. 'Girl's a slut. She's slept with more men than I've had double Scotches.'

'But I've never slept with any.' A fresh tear the size of a pea rolled down the side of Felicity's nose. 'It's never been any man's lucky night with me. I'm so useless and stupid and . . . and a-a-shamed of myself . . . Oh God!' She buried her face in her hands. 'I wish I'd never told you now. You must think I'm a pathetic case.'

'I don't, I don't. We've all done things we're ashamed of.' As Lorna said it, the hairs at the back of her neck began to prickle and she knew the time had come. She couldn't bottle it up any longer; she needed to confide in someone as badly as Felicity had needed to confide in her.

Without even thinking, she reached out and touched Felicity's thin hand. 'You've told me your embarrassing thing. Now I'll tell you mine. Hang on, I need a drink before I do this . . .'

When she had splashed an inch of gin into a tumbler, Lorna crossed to the mantelpiece and took down a photograph in a frame.

'I saw it earlier when you were in the kitchen,' Felicity said. She looked again at the picture of a younger Lorna, sitting on a wall with her arm around the shoulder of another girl in a wheelchair. 'Who is she?'

'My twin sister, Paula. She was mentally handicapped.' One of the cats jumped on to Lorna's lap and lay there purring, lazily kneading its paws. Lorna closed her eyes. 'She died ten years ago. I loved her so much.'

Felicity didn't say anything. Lorna gulped down her gin and went on. 'Paula was besotted with Toby Gillespie. Her room was plastered with pictures of him; she watched videos of his films endlessly. She even called her cat Toby.'

'I called my goldfish Adam,' said Felicity, 'after Adam Ant.'

Lorna smiled briefly. 'Anyway, Paula wrote to him asking for a signed photo. After six weeks, when nothing had arrived, I sent her a letter myself, pretending it was from him.' The smile had gone now, her expression was grim.

'Paula didn't know the difference, of course. She was thrilled.'

'Oh no,' said Felicity, 'don't tell me. She found out.'

'No. She developed pneumonia. And I, stupidly giving Toby Gillespie the benefit of the doubt, wrote to him myself.' Lorna took another slug of gin. Her hands shook as she lit a cigarette. 'I told him all about Paula, and how ill she was, and begged him to come and see her.' A longer pause. 'I even offered to pay.'

Felicity's eyes were wide. 'And did he get in touch?'

Lorna shook her head. 'No. He ignored my letter too. We lived in Devon then, and a week later there were pictures in all the papers of the Gillespies on holiday in Devon. They were staying less than five miles away,' she went on bitterly, 'and he couldn't even be bothered to spare an hour to visit my sister.' She took a shuddering breath. 'Three days later, Paula died.'

'But that wasn't your fault!' Felicity exclaimed. 'You didn't do anything to be ashamed of!'

Lorna shook her head. 'Haven't you figured it out yet? It was me, sending the anonymous letters.'

'You! But how could it have been you? It was Dizzy Gillespie,' said Felicity, bewildered. 'They caught him red-handed.'

A crooked smile, wreathed in cigarette smoke. 'Dizzy got the idea from me. He wanted Toby to sell the house almost as much as I did. I couldn't help it,' said Lorna in a low voice. 'Toby Gillespie had let my sister down. I hated him with a vengeance. I couldn't bear the thought of him living here . . . and everyone thinking he was so great. I just wanted to hurt him as much as he'd hurt our family.'

Felicity sat back, struggling to take it all in. She shook her head. 'Well, I can understand that. It seems odd, though,' she said diffidently, 'I mean, I don't know Toby Gillespie, but I do know he does a lot of work for charity. From what I've heard, he doesn't seem the kind of person who'd ignore a cry for help.'

'That's what I thought.' Lorna pressed her lips together. 'But he'd ignored mine, so I carried on sending the letters.'

And the pizzas, and the endless taxis, she thought with a pang of guilt. 'Then last week I overheard Savannah in the bar, complaining that her father was too busy to play tennis with her. She said, "Ten hours he's been sitting there, working through a drawerful of fan mail. He even had the nerve to tell me if I was bored I could stamp the envelopes." And when Oliver asked her why Toby didn't employ a secretary to deal with them, Savannah said, "He doesn't trust anyone else to do it. He had a useless PA years ago." Apparently,' Lorna said drily, 'it wasn't until after he'd sacked her that he discovered she'd been chucking all the fan letters in the bin unopened because she couldn't be bothered to read them.'

Chapter 60

Honestly, Savannah thought, lifting her sunglasses to get a better view. She liked Moll, but there was no getting away from it – the girl was a complete tart.

As she approached the pub and took a closer look at the person Moll was flinging her arms around, Savannah changed that to a tart with taste. This guy, whoever he might be, was gorgeous.

Savannah wondered idly what it was about lean, rangy men on motorbikes, with leather trousers and dark hair curling over their collars, that made them so irresistible.

Moll was still hugging him when she reached them. Turning at the sound of footsteps, she grinned at Savannah.

'What d'you think then? Not bad?'

God, how embarrassing! Aware that the boy on the motorbike was lazily surveying her, Savannah shrugged and went pink.

'Aren't you jealous?' teased Moll.

Aarghh, this was awful. Never mind pink, now she was aubergine. Worse still, she had the most terrifying urge to yell 'YES YES YES!'

'Ignore her,' said the boy on the bike, addressing Savannah and pinching Moll's ample waist, 'she's far too fat for me. I go for girls who can ride pillion without bursting my tyres.'

Savannah gazed at him, lost for words.

'God, you're rude!' In retaliation, Moll gave him a good-natured punch on the arm. But she'd forgiven him already. Never mind bursting tyres, she wanted to burst with pride. Not that he deserved it, of course, thought Moll, she just couldn't help it. She loved him so much. 'Sav, meet Stevie,' she announced joyfully, 'my completely vile little brother.'

I love Oliver, I love Oliver, Savannah repeated over and over in her mind. Perched on her stool next to the bar, she tapped her fingers on her thighs in time with the words in an effort to keep the mantra going.

Oh but it was hard, when your gaze kept sliding – practically of its own accord – to the other end of the bar.

Especially when every time you glimpsed those strong suntanned arms, that dark curly hair and that heavenly smile, something low down in the very pit of your stomach went *pingggg* . . .

Not that Oliver didn't have a heavenly smile too, of course. And a gorgeous body. But there was no getting away from the fact that the *pingggg* factor had been sadly lacking in recent weeks.

Savannah, forgetting to tap and picking at the edges of a beer mat instead, couldn't help reflecting that things in that department weren't what they used to be. Maintaining eternal optimism in the face of impotence wasn't easy. She'd done her level best to be patient and understanding, but where was it getting her?

Not laid, that was for sure.

Oliver, who was wiping down the bar, had noticed the way Savannah kept glancing down the bar and quickly back again. He lowered his voice. 'Do you like him?'

Startled, Savannah said, 'What?'

'Moll's brother. I mean, he's good-looking, isn't he?'

'So?'

She was definitely on the defensive. This could be it, thought Oliver with a surge of hope, this could be the answer to everything.

'Look,' he murmured, 'I'd understand. I know it hasn't been easy for you, what with . . . well, the way things are. I wouldn't mind if you . . . well, you know . . .'

Savannah stared at him. Was he *serious*? What did he expect her to say – 'Oh, okay then, we'll carry on being secretly in love with each other but on Tuesday and Friday evenings I'll slope off with some tall dark total stranger and have mindless sex'?

God, it was like a husband whose idea of hell was trailing round the shops saying, 'You know I don't care much for that kind of thing, dear. Why don't you go with one of your friends instead?'

'Are you *mad*?' Savannah declared furiously. 'What do you think I am, a complete sex maniac?'

'No, no. I just—'

'Shut up then,' she hissed, 'because I don't even fancy him, okay?' She shot a look of disdain in Stevie Harper's direction, to prove her point. 'He couldn't be less my type.'

Ten minutes later, on her way back from the loo, Savannah bumped into Stevie in the corridor.

'You gave me a terrible look just now. I saw you,' he admonished. 'What did I do to deserve that?'

There was no getting away from it – he was outrageously attractive. Her stomach pinging for all it was worth, Savannah flicked back her hair and said, 'Nothing.'

Talk about original.

But Stevie didn't seem to mind.

'I asked Moll about you. I thought the blond guy behind the bar might be your boyfriend, but she tells me he's your brother.'

'That's right.'

'So how about you and me going for a drink tomorrow night?'

He was smiling at her. She could smell soap and leather and that sexy, oily, motorbike smell. He also had the longest eyelashes she'd ever seen.

She squirmed with desire. 'I thought that's what we were doing now.'

'Come on, you know what I mean – without your big brother and my big sister looking on.'

'I don't know anything about you.'

It was a feeble protest.

'Ah well, now's your chance to find out. I'll pick you up at eight. We'll go into Harleston.'

Savannah thought, I haven't even said yes.

But then, was it ever likely that she'd say no?

She nodded quickly. 'Okay, but don't pick me up.' She was buggered if Oliver was going to find out about this. 'I'll meet you at the Iguana Bar in Brunswick Square.'

'Haven't seen you here for a while,' said Lorna.

Toby's smile was brief. 'I've been trying to spend more time with Dizzy. Not that he's too impressed.'

'Scotch?'

Lorna wished her hands would stop shaking. Felicity had said, 'You should tell him, explain everything. Just admit it was you and let him know how sorry you are.' Calmly she'd added, 'I'm sure he'd understand.'

Maybe he would, but Lorna cringed at the thought of admitting the letters had come from her. She wasn't the apologising type.

'A large one,' said Toby as she held the tumbler under the Johnny Walker optic. 'I need it.'

He looked tired. There were dark shadows beneath his eyes and his jaw was set. Hardly surprising, Lorna thought with a rush of guilt. He's been the victim of a hate campaign and he hasn't even done anything to deserve it.

'On the house,' she said brusquely as Toby held out a tenner.

'Oh, thanks.' He looked taken aback, as well he might. She had never offered to buy him a drink before.

Say it, say it.

Don't go on, Lorna begged her nagging conscience, I just can't.

But Oliver, back from the cellar, had spotted Toby. He'd be over in a minute to say hello and the opportunity would be lost.

'Actually, I'm glad you came in. There's something I need to tell you.'

Aargh, what am I *doing*?

'Oh?' Toby looked wary. 'About Savannah? What's she been up to now?'

'Nothing. Well, not that I know of,' Lorna amended. It seemed unlikely that a pretty blonde teenager wouldn't be up to something, somewhere along the line. 'The thing is, being a pub landlady is a bit like being a priest. People have a few drinks and confide in you. And they trust you not to blab their secrets around the village.'

'I see.' Toby wondered just how bad this was going to be. His stomach lurched; was it something to do with Jess?

'Dizzy didn't write all those anonymous letters. Some of them were sent by someone else in the village.' Lorna lit a cigarette, forgetting the one already smouldering in the ashtray.

Toby looked at her. 'Who?'

She shook her head. 'I can't tell you that. I promised I wouldn't. But they're very sorry. It was never meant to be malicious, it was just a – well, a prank that got out of hand.' She swallowed, forcing herself to meet Toby Gillespie's steady gaze. 'And they want you to know it's over now. They'll never do it again.'

Oliver was desperate for sex. It was seriously starting to get him down. What with fending off Savannah – who was so anxious to cure him she had recently started dropping dark hints about counselling and therapists – and not seeing anyone else because there simply wasn't the opportunity, he was beginning to feel like a heroin addict in need of a fix.

'You're working tonight, aren't you?' Savannah asked when she called into Duck Cottage at lunchtime.

'Mm.'

Oliver was eating his way through a packet of Jammy Dodgers and reading an article in the paper about touring Scandinavia by coach. Plenty of beautiful blondes with liberated attitudes in Scandinavia.

'It's just that I won't be coming to the pub. One of my friends is down from London, staying with her stepfather in Cheltenham. She rang and invited me over for the evening.'

Oliver didn't dare look up. Reaching across the kitchen table, he helped himself to another biscuit. 'Fine.'

'You don't mind, do you? It won't be that great, but she

begged me to go. We'll just have a couple of drinks and a girlie gossip—'

'Of course I don't mind.'

Go. Go!

As soon as Savannah had left, Oliver leapt to his feet and dialled the pub.

'Moll, is that you? Moll, you know I love you.'

'What do you want?' said Moll.

'It's your evening off tonight, right?'

'You can't whisk me away to Paris, Oliver. You're working.'

He grinned; she knew exactly what he wanted.

'Swap?'

She kept him dangling for a second. 'What's in it for me?'

'My share of next week's tips.'

'Ha! That just gives you an excuse to spend the next seven days being vile to everybody.'

'Please?'

'Okay.'

'Moll, you're brilliant.'

Exultantly, Oliver reached for the phone book.

'Yeah, I know.'

He picked Mel up from her flat at seven o'clock on the dot.

'So, what's brought this on?' Mel's Lycra skirt slithered up her thighs as she climbed into the passenger seat. 'Three months of deafening silence, then a phone call out of the blue. I thought you'd emigrated or died or something.'

It was good to see Mel again. Oliver leaned over and kissed her. 'No, still alive. There's just been a lot going on recently. Working and family stuff . . . you know.'

'I read about it in the papers. Imagine, Toby Gillespie turning out to be your Dad. What's he like?'

'Great.'

'And the rest of them?' Mel was incurably nosy. 'Are they okay?'

Oliver nodded, still smiling. If it was good to see Mel again, it was even better knowing that four Hooper's

Hooches and she was anybody's.

'I saw the photos of you and the daughter. Savannah, that's her name isn't it? She's really pretty.'

Oliver didn't want to talk about Savannah. He'd come out tonight to get away from all that.

He said, 'So are you.'

The engine was still idling; they hadn't pulled away from the kerb yet.

Mel looked at him. 'I wouldn't want you to think I was cheap . . .'

'I'd never do that,' Oliver assured her. 'Have you seen the price of Alcopops lately?'

Mel burst out laughing. They'd always got on so well together. And the sex had never been less than brilliant. 'I was just going to say, the flat's empty. We don't have to go out yet.'

'You might think I'm cheap,' Oliver protested.

'I won't, I promise.'

'You're a terrible influence on an innocent young country boy,' Oliver sighed, flicking off the ignition. 'Go on then, you've twisted my arm.'

Chapter 61

Less than a mile away, in the Iguana Bar, Savannah was having a weak-at-the-knees experience. Watching heads swivel in admiration as Stevie Harper made his way towards her, she wondered why Oliver no longer had this kind of effect on her.

Except, deep down, she knew the answer. It was because Oliver might give the impression of being sexy, but it was all a façade. It was like trying to have a meaningful relationship with a poster of your favourite pop star.

'Hi.' Stevie looked as if he was about to kiss her, then stopped at the last second. Talk about being in control. God, he was so gorgeous, so *cool* . . .

And that was the difference between him and Oliver, Savannah thought with a shudder of pleasure as she watched him stride easily up to the bar. When you looked at Stevie Harper you knew – you just knew for sure – that he delivered what he promised.

He simply wasn't the impotent type.

Oliver was happy. This was more like it; terrific sex and no complications.

Thank heavens for Mel.

Beneath the duvet, warm fingers began to dance their way up the inside of his thigh.

'We don't have to get up. We could just stay here,' she suggested.

Oliver was tempted, but that wouldn't be fair on her.

'No, we'll go out. You said you wanted to see that friend of yours before she leaves for the States.'

'She'll be in the Iguana Bar,' Mel said happily.

'What's going on?' Oliver breathed out slowly as the warm hand travelled further up his thigh.

Mel, her eyes bright and her hair tousled, murmured, 'We don't have to be there before nine.'

Savannah hoped she didn't look as idiotically besotted as she felt. She was trying so hard to play it cool, but it wasn't easy when your body all of a sudden appeared to be swarming with too much electricity.

Stevie Harper might be only twenty-three, but he had been everywhere and done everything.

Toured the United States on his motorbike.

Worked out there briefly as a stunt double.

Tried – even more briefly – a spot of modelling.

'It was a nightmare. They kept nagging at me to wear moisturiser,' Stevie told her with disgust, 'and panicking that I'd fly off my bike and wreck my face.'

Savannah was mesmerised. 'What did you do next?'

'Worked as a croupier in Las Vegas, washed dishes in a few hotels, had a bash at male prostitution. Anything really,' he shrugged, 'to earn a bit of cash.'

Savannah's mouth dropped open.

'Joke,' said Stevie. 'Just wanted to make sure you were paying attention.'

He's teasing me, Savannah thought joyfully, I love it, love it, *love* it.

'So how long have you been back in this country?'

'Three months. I headed down to the south coast, took a job with a travelling fair.'

'A fair! Which ride?'

She knew at once it had to be one of the rides. Stevie wasn't the three-darts-for-a-pound, win-a-goldfish type.

'Waltzers.' His dark eyes glittered with remembered amusement. 'Spinning the chairs, making all the girls scream for more.'

'This is making me feel *so* much better about failing my A levels,' Savannah sighed.

'Why?'

'Well, look at you!' Crikey, she couldn't *stop* looking at him; he was the long-haired leather-trousered rebellious bad boy of her dreams. 'You didn't need them, did you? You just went out there and did stuff,' she flung her arms wide, '*exciting stuff*—'

'I've got a GCSE in music,' Stevie offered.

'Exactly!'

'And eleven in academic subjects. And four A levels. Oh,' he added, 'and a degree in physics.'

'Wow!' Savannah was dumbfounded.

But impressed.

'I'm sorry.' Stevie raised an enquiring eyebrow. 'Have I blown it? Do you prefer your men thick?'

'No, *no*!'

Heavens, he was perfect. Now even her parents would love him too.

Except . . . oh God—

'What?' said Stevie.

'How long are you going to be here?' The words tumbled out in a panic. If he was only visiting Moll for a few days before disappearing again, how could she bear it?

Stevie looked at her. 'No plans. If there's a good reason to stay, I'll stay.'

'Oh.'

'So which would you prefer?'

'What?'

'Shall I stick around?' He put his drink down and rose to his feet. 'Or go?'

'Don't!' Savannah shrieked without thinking.

People at nearby tables turned and stared. She bit her lip, trying to ignore them.

'Oh dear,' Stevie started to laugh, 'now everyone thinks I put my hand up your skirt.'

'Sit down,' Savannah pleaded, but instead of sitting he was pulling her upright.

'In a minute. I'm afraid I have to kiss you first.'

By this time they were the centre of attention but Savannah no longer cared. Stevie Harper was a heavenly kisser and the way his hands were sliding over her bare shoulders made all the little hairs on her arms stand on end.

Keeping her eyes closed, Savannah willed the kiss to go on for ever and let her own trembling fingers begin to roam over the back pockets of his leather jeans.

She didn't know how she was going to break the news to Oliver; he'd be devastated when he found out.

Still, never mind about that now.

This was meant to happen, Savannah thought ecstatically, this is fate.

When the kiss finally ended, she opened her eyes and gazed up at Stevie. God, he was divine . . .

'Somebody's watching us,' he told her.

'Blimey, I should think everyone is.'

'I'm talking about your brother.'

It was like someone saying, 'Don't look now, but there's a spider the size of a *dinner* plate behind you.' You still had to look.

Cringing, because this was worse than any spider, Savannah peeled herself away from Stevie and turned slowly around.

There was Oliver with a strange expression on his face.

And a pretty, dark-haired girl clinging lovingly to his arm.

'Well,' Oliver said when everyone had been introduced. Mel had dashed to the loo and Stevie was over at the bar ordering more drinks. 'This is . . . interesting.'

Since they only had a couple of minutes, Savannah thought she may as well come right out and say it.

'I really like him.'

Oliver nodded. 'So I noticed.'

'Do you really like her?' She jerked her head in the direction of the loos.

'Mel's an ex of mine. She's good fun.'

Baffled, recalling the way Mel had acted while Oliver was introducing her, Savannah said, 'Does she know she's an ex? Have you *told* her you're impotent?'

Oliver's dark eyes flickered.

'Oh, oh I *see*.' All of a sudden Savannah understood; it

was like finally figuring out a magic trick. 'You aren't, are you? You're not impotent.'

'Sorry.'

Savannah knew she should be outraged. Instead, she felt like a caged bird unexpectedly set free. All these weeks she had done her best to convince herself she still loved Oliver.

But she hadn't, not really. He had been a crush, that was all, a fixation that had escalated because it was forbidden. And by the time that hurdle had been overcome, the crush had run its course.

As teenage crushes do.

'Well, I'm glad,' said Savannah with a faint smile. 'For your sake, I mean.'

'It wouldn't have felt right,' Oliver sounded relieved too. 'I think we get on better as brother and sister.'

Back from the loo, Mel bounced up to them.

'What's this about getting on better? God, that's abnormal – me and my brother fight like cat and dog!'

Savannah and Oliver grinned at each other.

'We're pretty new to it,' said Oliver, as Stevie returned with the drinks. 'Give us time, we will too.'

'What have you got that the rest of us haven't?' Jamie protested. 'Lorna never says "On the house" when I'm buying a drink.'

'It's Felicity's last night in the village,' said Lorna. 'She's moving to Cheltenham tomorrow.'

'I'll buy you a drink,' Felicity told him.

'Will you?' Jamie looked surprised and ridiculously pleased.

'There.' Lorna filled his pint glass with best bitter and slid it in front of him. 'Now perhaps you'll cheer up.'

'I can't cheer up.' Jamie sounded mournful. 'I'm depressed.'

Lorna snorted with laughter and winked at Felicity. 'You! A strapping young lad with a good job . . . What have you got to be depressed about?'

'I'm a strapping young lad with a good job and no

girlfriend,' Jamie announced gloomily. 'And no bloody sex life.'

This was his seventh pint.

'Oh well, that's tragic.' Lorna lifted his elbow out of a puddle of beer and briskly wiped the bar dry.

'It is, it's *bloody* tragic. Especially when you're sharing a house with Dr Kil-bloody-dare. It's sickening, I tell you.' Jamie shook his head. 'And it's not *fair*. He gets sex sex sex all the time, and I don't get any of it.'

Well, thought Felicity, I know how that feels.

Lorna was doing her best to be philosophical. 'Ah, but is he happy?'

Jamie gazed at her in incredulous, slightly cross-eyed fashion. 'Wouldn't you be?'

'Look,' said Felicity, feeling unaccountably brave, 'sex isn't the be-all and end-all. There are other things in life, you know.'

'Huh,' said Jamie. 'Name five.'

'Rugby, cricket, lager.' Lorna was still trying to help. 'Um, getting legless . . .'

'That doesn't count.' Jamie was scornful. 'It's the same as lager.'

Lorna's patience ran out. 'Oh well, maybe Mother Nature's trying to tell you something. You could just be useless in bed.'

Felicity winced. The expression on Jamie's face was so despondent she wanted to give him a big hug.

'But the thing is, I'm not. I'm pretty good,' he said sorrowfully, 'when I get the chance.'

An hour later Lorna called time, and the few remaining regulars made their way out. Felicity, by now sitting at a corner table with Jamie, watched Lorna busy herself with the clearing up.

'I should be getting home,' she told Jamie.

Five gin and tonics were more than she was used to, but Felicity didn't feel fuzzy-headed. And why shouldn't she have a few drinks, anyway? The house had been sold. It was her last night in the village and Hugh had taken Freya over to his place to allow her to get the packing finished without interruption. That was all done now. Everything was in boxes ready to go into the removals van. By this time tomorrow, she'd be back with her parents. Just temporarily, of course, until she found a place of her own – but she knew only too well what the next few weeks would be like.

Back in my old bedroom, thought Felicity, not much looking forward to the prospect, with my mother fussing over me, telling me I'm too thin and forcing me to eat steak and kidney pudding.

She knew, too, exactly what her mother would be like with Freya. Trying so hard not to take over but unable to resist saying, 'Darling, why don't we try doing it *this* way?'

I've been married, I've given birth and I'm an intelligent, successful businesswoman . . . and it isn't going to make a blind bit of difference to my mother, Felicity thought with rising frustration. As far as she's concerned I'm still her shy, gawky, virginal teenager.

Well, the virginal bit was still true.

'One more drink,' said Jamie, his hand brushing against hers as he reached for her empty glass.

'The pub's closed.'

'Ah, Lorna won't mind.' He gave her a conspiratorial wink before raising his voice. 'Lorna? One for the road?'

'No. Go home.'

Jamie looked crestfallen. 'You're no fun.'

Lorna was behind the bar, cashing up the till. She looked at the two of them, sitting so close together their knees were practically touching. 'If you want to carry on yakking, why don't you ask Felicity back to your place for a drink?'

Jamie brightened, then his shoulders sagged again. 'Doug's there with some nurse.'

Lorna shrugged and raised an eyebrow fractionally in Felicity's direction.

'What are you doing?' said Felicity, when Jamie had ambled off to the loo.

'Oh come on, I've been watching the pair of you for the last hour. Don't tell me it hasn't occurred to you.'

'Are you serious? You think I should take him home, throw him on to my bed and *ravish* him?'

Lorna shrugged. 'It's your last night. You have a virginity you want to be rid of. And you do *like* him.'

'I hardly know him!' wailed Felicity.

'You knew Hugh, and look where that got you.'

'Lorna, I couldn't possibly. It would be too . . . too . . . sordid for words.'

'Okay, just a suggestion. Forget I mentioned it.'

Felicity hesitated, biting her lip.

'Anyway, he's drunk.'

'Not that drunk,' said Lorna, who had been quietly serving Jamie alcohol-free beer for the last hour and a half. 'I'm sure he'd manage.' She smiled slightly before adding, 'And he did say he was good in bed.'

Chapter 62

Lili was doing a bit of frenzied dusting in the living room when she heard footsteps on the gravel outside.

Quickly hiding the can of spray polish in case it was Eleanor (Oh Lili, you should use Mansion Wax; how can you expect something out of an aerosol to nourish the wood?), she raced through to the kitchen and swept all the cornflake-encrusted cereal bowls off the table and into the sink.

Opening the door, Lili heaved a sigh of relief.

'Thank goodness it's you! I thought you were my mother-in-law carrying out one of her dawn raids. Oh my word, are those for me?'

It wasn't dawn, it was nine thirty in the morning, but Felicity looked as if she'd been up for hours. In a crisp pink shirt and extremely clean jeans, she looked as glossy and bright-eyed as a squirrel.

'Just to say thank you for looking after Freya. Well, and for everything else.' She beamed at Lili, thrust the massive bunch of white lilies into her arms and plonked two bottles of champagne on the kitchen table.

'Heavens, moving house must really suit you.' Lili was full of admiration. 'Most people look totally frazzled, but you're . . . well, you're *glowing*.'

She was. It was extraordinary. Eleanor would certainly approve, Lili decided. Felicity looked as if she'd been given a thorough going over with a tin of Mansion Wax.

'It's a new start. I'm going to make the most of it,' Felicity agreed happily.

Impulsively Lili ripped the foil off one of the bottles and

unfastened the wire. 'Then we definitely have to celebrate. Just one glass each,' she said as the cork flew out, 'to toast your brilliant new life. There, if my mother-in-law turns up now, she'll really know I've gone to the dogs.'

The removals men were arriving at ten o'clock. Lottie, Will and Blitz sat in the other room glued to a Teletubbies video, and Lili wondered why Felicity looked as if she were bursting to tell her a secret but was unable to find the words.

Instead they talked about Freya and the smart nursery she would be attending in Cheltenham while Felicity was at work, then about Will and the decidedly un-smart new habit he had of weeing in his potty then trying to wash his hands in it.

'I was fast asleep this morning,' said Lili, 'when Lottie came into the bedroom, tapped me on the shoulder and said, "Mummy, can you and me sing 'If you're happy and you know it clap your hands'?" '

Felicity grinned. She was happy and she certainly knew it. She was also dying to tell Lili about last night . . . Oh, but what if Lili thought she was a slut?

Instead she said, 'Any news of Drew?'

Lili shook her head. She hadn't seen him for weeks now. Impossible though it seemed in a village this size, Drew had managed to turn himself into the invisible man.

He clearly wasn't interested. There again, why should he be? She was no Pamela Anderson.

Dammit, she wasn't even a Clive Anderson . . .

Oh well, she thought with the resigned sigh of one who has been over it a thousand times, I suppose I'll live.

Two minutes later they both jumped a mile as the front doorbell rang out.

'Shit, it's my mother-in-law! Hide the bottles, give me the glasses, run a tea towel under the cold tap—'

'Why?' Felicity looked startled.

'If Eleanor smells alcohol on my breath she's going to snort fire out of her nostrils.'

But Blitz was barking and Lottie, in the front room, had climbed on to a chair in order to peer out of the bay window. With a shriek of delight she yelled, 'Mum, open the door! It's Drew!'

Even if he hadn't been in love with her already, Drew's heart would have melted at the sight of Lili's tentative, struggling-to-be-normal smile. It was hopeless; keeping his distance for the past few weeks had half-killed him, and what good had it done?

None at all.

Not one bloody iota.

'What's in there?' Lili pointed at the cardboard box he was holding.

'Oh God, I feel like a vacuum cleaner salesman. Look, I've got something to show you, but there's no need to be polite. If you aren't interested, just say so.'

'We don't really need another vacuum cleaner, we've got Blitz.' Oh help, Lili thought, talk about feeble, I'm definitely no Clive Anderson. 'Sorry. Do come in.'

Felicity, looking more cheerful than Drew had ever seen her look before, greeted him with a broad smile. 'Hi! We're celebrating my moving day. That's your glass there.' She gestured to a full one. 'I've got to go in a minute. Lottie, mind that bottle.'

'Open the box!' barked Lottie, and Lili almost said 'Take the money!' Realising that she was probably the only person in the room ancient enough to remember the TV catch-phrase, she stopped herself just in time.

'Oh wow!' Lottie squealed as Drew peeled back the lid and showed her the kittens.

'Paddy Birley dumped them on me an hour ago,' he explained. 'Asked me to get rid of them. Old bugger must be going soft in his old age,' he added in an undertone to Lili. 'He usually drowns them in a bucket. Sorry, this isn't meant to be emotional blackmail. I just wondered if you'd want one.'

This wasn't true. He had been desperate for an excuse to call in on Lili, and Paddy Birley, the world's most unlikely Fairy Godmother, had provided it.

'Oh, Mum, can we have a kitten? Can we can we can we?'

There were five in the box. Lili picked up a mewling black and white bundle of warm fur and wondered if Blitz would eat it. Until five minutes ago she hadn't wanted a cat, but if Drew was offering her one . . . well, that was different.

'I'll have two,' Felicity cried, eagerly scooping them out of the box. 'Hugh would never let me have a cat. And Lorna was saying the other day that she'd love a couple more.'

Blitz, nosing his way between Lili and Drew, sniffed the kitten on Lili's lap. Cautiously he wagged his tail.

Relieved that he wasn't actually salivating, Lili said, 'We'll take this one.'

'Done.' Drew began to relax. He grinned at her. 'Sold to the lady in the pink slippers with the champagne glass in her hand. Maybe I should become a door-to-door vacuum cleaner salesman after all.'

Lili wished she weren't wearing her pink slippers; they were hardly chic.

'I can't take them now.' Felicity checked her watch. 'Damn, and it's ten o'clock—'

'Don't worry, I'll take them into the surgery and give them the once over. Ring me this afternoon,' Drew said easily, 'and we'll sort something out.'

'Cup of tea?' Lili said when they were alone in the kitchen.

'No thanks. How have you been?'

Polite, polite.

'Oh, well, okay.' Lili busied herself with the kettle.

'Is it really all over between you and Michael?'

She nodded and dropped two teabags into the milk jug.

'I wanted to phone you,' said Drew.

'Doesn't matter. I understand.'

'Understand what?'

'Well, that you didn't want to be involved.'

The kettle clicked off. Lili, trembling violently, poured boiling water into the milk jug.

'Not quite right. I *do* want to be involved.' Drew, who wanted it more than anything, chose his words with care. 'But not until you know for certain that it's what you want too.'

She turned to look at him. 'Truly?'

He nodded. 'You'd be on the rebound. And rebound relationships never work out.'

Despite herself, Lili started to laugh.

'What?'

'Look, all the nurses at our practice are female. So is the cleaner, so are the receptionists. You don't work with eight gossiping women,' Drew said gravely, 'without learning all there is to know about relationships doomed to disaster. I don't think you want to drink that,' he added, fishing the teabags out of the milk jug and tipping the murky liquid down the sink.

Lili wondered if it still counted as 'on the rebound' when the marriage you'd just escaped from was as lousy as hers had been. She'd actually experienced a few twinges of guilt, thinking that she should be feeling a lot more miserable than this.

But she knew what Drew meant.

'So what do we do?'

Drew shrugged. He knew exactly what he'd like to do.

'Take it slowly, I suppose. Give you time to get over . . . well, all the stuff you need to get over.'

Right. Lili nodded. That was sensible.

Boring, but definitely sensible.

'Okay. How long d'you think that'll take?'

Drew reached for the glass of champagne he hadn't yet had a chance to drink.

'Five or six years.'

'Five or six *years*?' Lili wailed. 'Oh my God, we could be dead by then! That is *so* unfair—'

'Five or six months then?'

Lili stared at him. It was certainly better, but five or six months still felt like an awfully long way away.

She proceeded with caution. 'Before what?'

'Before we get involved,' said Drew.

'Oh. And what happens in the mean time?'

His mouth twitched. Lili really was adorable. 'Well, I could get to know your children properly. We could see each other, maybe a couple of times a week.'

'Or more,' Lili suggested. Hastily she added, 'So long as we made sure we weren't getting involved.'

Drew looked thoughtful. He nodded his head. 'I could go along with that.'

'Only if you want to.'

'Oh no, I think that'd be fine.'

He was teasing her, Lili realised. Everything was going to be all right. She felt as if she could explode with joy.

'What about kissing and stuff?' she ventured bravely.

'Stuff?'

'Bed-type stuff.'

'Oh well, I'm all in favour of that,' said Drew. 'All that . . . bed-type stuff.'

'And kissing,' Lili reminded him.

'Kissing too.'

'So you think it would be all right to do that,' she double-checked, light-headed with anticipation.

'Oh, definitely.' Unable to help himself, Drew took her in his arms. As his mouth brushed hers he murmured, 'Just so long as we don't get involved.'

Chapter 63

Felicity, balancing Freya on her hip in order to open the front door, was astonished to find Jamie on the doorstep.

'Oh! When I rang Drew he said one of the practice nurses would drop them off on her way home.'

'I was passing,' Jamie fibbed. 'I offered to bring them instead.' Gauche but desperate, he went on, 'I haven't been able to stop thinking about you all day.'

Felicity was lost for words. Last night had been amazing and she hadn't been able to stop thinking about it either. But her thoughts had all been of the sex, not of Jamie.

Since he was so obviously not her type, she hadn't imagined their encounter ever being more than a miraculous one-night stand.

'I did them myself.' Jamie held up the cat basket. 'They've had their worming tablets and inoculations.' Hopefully he said, 'Shall I bring them in?'

'My mother's here.' Felicity glanced nervously over her shoulder. 'I don't really think . . .'

'Okay, I understand, but can I see you again? How about tomorrow night?'

Caught off guard, Felicity found herself prevaricating helplessly. 'Look, how much do I owe you for this?' She was edging towards the hall table, actually reaching for her handbag as she spoke.

'Nothing!'

'But the injections—'

'Let me take you out tomorrow night,' Jamie was close to despair, 'and we'll call it quits.'

Bloody hell, this never happened to Doug.

'Please,' he begged.

'I wasn't expecting this.'

'So? All you have to do is say yes.'

He willed her to say it, but Felicity was shaking her head, unable to speak.

'You don't want to see me.' Jamie was filled with dismay. God, this was so humiliating! 'You used me, and now you don't want to see me ever again.'

Felicity, who had used him precisely *because* she'd thought she wouldn't see him again, said in a low voice, 'I thought you just wanted sex with someone, you didn't care who.'

'Okay, okay, maybe I did, but that was last night,' Jamie blurted out in an anguished whisper. 'And now I *do* care—'

'Who is it, dear? The girl with the kittens?' The voice of Felicity's mother drifted down the hall towards them.

'Please,' Jamie tried again frantically. 'Take a few days to think about it, if you like. But just let me ring you.'

'Look, I've got the number of the surgery.' Flustered, Felicity grabbed the cat basket from him as her mother's footsteps echoed along the parquet floor. 'If I decide to see you again, I'll ring you.'

'What are you doing?' said Toby.

Jess, on her knees in front of a lichen-covered tombstone, was trimming the grass around the grave with a pair of nail scissors.

'I broke my garden shears.'

'Whose grave is this?'

Jessie leaned back on her heels and pushed her hair out of her eyes. She waited for Toby to scan the simple wording on the stone: In Loving Memory of Susan Wilder, Died aged Fifty-Eight. Devoted Wife and Mother.

'She was old Cecil's wife.'

Old Cecil, with his smelly dog and smellier pipe, was a more-or-less permanent fixture in the corner of the Seven Bells, where he spent his days playing either dominoes or cribbage.

'Died twenty-five years ago.' Toby raised an eyebrow.

'He adored her. Look how beautifully he's kept the grave.'

Jessie ran her fingers over the velvety, weed-free grass. 'His rheumatism's bad this week; that's why he asked me to come and give it a tidy-up.'

Toby watched her unwrap the flowers she had brought with her from old Cecil's garden and arrange them in the weighted-down vase.

'I didn't realise old Cecil had been married.'

'Forty-two years. He was seventeen, she was sixteen.' Jessie tweaked a nodding foxglove into place. 'He still misses her dreadfully.'

'What happened to the children?'

'Two boys. Moved away, lost contact.' Jessie shrugged. 'It could happen to any of us. Just because they're our kids, we can't force them to keep in touch.' She glanced up at Toby. 'How's Dizzy?'

'Stroppy, belligerent, sulky, rude. All the normal teenage stuff.'

'And what are you doing here?'

Shielding her eyes from the afternoon sun, Jessie glanced around the churchyard, with its unregimented hotch-potch of tombs and headstones, some centuries old and tilting at jaunty angles, others gleaming and new.

'Learning lines.' Toby took a folded script from his inside jacket pocket. 'Graveyards are great places to learn lines.' With a wry smile he added, 'Unless you bump into someone you know.'

'Don't let me stop you.'

Toby watched her rearrange the flowers. Was this how it was always going to be? Talking about trivia and taking care to avoid anything remotely important?

'You haven't mentioned it,' he said, 'but you must know about Oliver and Savannah.'

Jessie nodded. 'It was bound to happen, sooner or later. Not very nice for you, though.'

'Why not?'

'Well, all that trouble for nothing. You needn't have found out about Deborah's affair, or you not being Savannah's father. Dizzy wouldn't have run away.'

'Jess, I told you months ago that my marriage wasn't all it

was cracked up to be. You were the one who made me realise just—'

'Oh no, don't start that again,' Jessie warned, 'that's not fair. Anyway, you and Deborah have to stay together now. For Dizzy's sake.'

'Even if he doesn't appreciate it?'

'Yes!'

'But—'

'Look, if you two split up and Dizzy runs away again and begs on the streets and becomes a crack addict and *dies*, it'll be on your conscience for the rest of your life.' Jessie took a deep breath before adding slowly, 'And if I were in any way involved with you, it would be on my conscience too.'

Savannah and Stevie were in the garden talking so intently to each other that they wouldn't have noticed if the SAS had swung out of the trees and smoke-bombed the gazebo.

Deborah, watching them together, experienced a pang of envy. No danger of anything like that happening to me just now, she thought with simmering frustration. Toby was being *so* unreasonable. And Doug, damn him, was still refusing to take her calls.

She sighed, drumming her fingers against the window frame, on edge because she wasn't used to being treated like this.

Oh, what the hell.

She picked up the phone, rang Doug's mobile and waited for the electronic voice to inform her – as it always did nowadays – that the person she was calling wasn't available right now, but if she wished to leave a—

'Yes?'

'Doug! Don't hang up.'

'I'm with a patient.'

'Can I see you later?'

'Sorry, busy.'

'If you don't say yes, I'm telling Toby everything.'

God, *listen* to me, Deborah thought, appalled. I sound completely *desperate*. And I'm not, I'm not. I'm Deborah Gillespie; I can have any man I want . . .

'You do that.' Doug sounded bored. 'Although what good you think it'll do, I can't imagine.'

'Please . . .'

Deborah felt the hot tears welling up. Outside, Stevie Harper was kissing her daughter. Toby had disappeared, heaven only knows where. This wasn't how her life was supposed to turn out.

'Have to go now,' Doug said briskly. 'Bye.'

'Nobody in the world has ever been as happy as me-ee-ee,' sang Savannah, reeling into the sitting room twenty minutes later. 'Mum, we're going over to Bath. Are my Levi's clean?'

'Don't know. Try the airing cupboard.'

But Savannah was frowning at the television.

'Have you lost the remote again? *Countdown*'s on Channel 4.'

'It's quite interesting, actually. All about . . . um . . . tax and stuff.'

Deborah had turned on the television intending to watch *Countdown* – she had a soft spot for Richard Whiteley – but had got waylaid by BBC2 instead. *Parliament Today* was on and there was David, addressing a packed House of Commons, effortlessly commanding their attention.

And hers too . . .

'God, there he is. Look at him!' Savannah jeered and made sick noises. 'Mr Smooth. Whatever did you see in him, Mum?'

'He's very good looking.' Deborah was filled with indignation. 'Anyway, that's no way to speak about your father.'

'Don't call him that. Dad's my proper father. And I've already looked in the airing cupboard.'

Savannah might be more concerned with locating her jeans, but Deborah was finding it increasingly hard to tear her eyes away from the figure currently occupying centre stage on the television screen. They had both been so on edge when he had driven down to Sisley House, it had hardly been an ideal reunion.

But that had been two months ago.

And now . . . well, things were quite different.

389

'Mum, you're not listening to me. Where are my *jeans*?'

There was no getting away from it, David Mansfield was an awfully attractive man.

Having stomped out, Savannah stomped back in again.

'I looked in the tumble dryer. It's empty.'

There again, involvement with politics was known to have a remarkable effect on the ugliest of men. It was the power thing, it gave them a kind of glittery aura.

Deborah smiled to herself, relishing the challenge of getting intimate with David's own extra-glittery aura.

Imagine, not just an MP but a member of the Cabinet!

Handsome!

Married!

Terrified by the prospect of scandal but at the same time irresistibly drawn to the idea – because, after all, the greater the risk, the bigger the adrenalin rush. And they didn't come much bigger than this . . .

Gazing at the screen, Deborah wondered what it would be like, actually making love to David on the floor of the House of Commons, with MPs on both sides cheering them on and the Speaker barking, 'Order, order' in an attempt to—

'Mum, WHERE ARE MY JEANS?'

Some fantasies were too enthralling to abandon. Impatiently Deborah waved her away. 'You can borrow mine.'

Savannah shot her a look of undiluted disgust.

'Yours have got creases ironed down the front.'

Chapter 64

Doug pulled open the front door of Keeper's Cottage, hauled his cases out to the car and loaded them into the boot.

It was six thirty in the morning and the sky was a clear duck-egg blue tinged with pink. The village green was silvered with dew.

Doug paused to take one last look around. This was where he had spent the last year. Now it was time to move on. His contract with Harleston General was up and, although the Manchester interview hadn't come to anything, he had struck lucky with his second, at a children's hospital in Kent. Goodbye A & E, hello paediatrics, he thought, watching a pair of undulating squirrels race along the garden wall.

Goodbye Harleston, hello Maidstone.

Goodbye girls, hello more girls.

He left his front-door key on the kitchen table, along with a cheque for the rent owing. He hadn't expected Drew and Jamie to get up at this hour and see him off; this wasn't *Friends*, after all. Just three blokes sharing a house.

Apart from the two squirrels now romping across the green, the village was still and silent. Doug started up the MG's engine and revved it once, wondering if Deborah would hear the noise.

He drove past the entrance to Sisley House. The bedroom curtains were drawn; no signs of life.

Doug shook his head and headed slowly along Compass Lane. That was a lesson he had learned the hard way: some women simply weren't worth getting involved with.

Then again, some were.

Moll was sitting on the front step of the Seven Bells, playing with one of Lorna's new kittens. She looked up and grinned as Doug turned left into the High Street and pulled up alongside the pub.

'Ready?'

'Ready.'

Moll disentangled the kitten's needle-sharp claws from her long red skirt, hauled herself upright and threw her hold-all into the space behind the driver's seat.

'Is that all?'

'I travel light.'

'Are you sure about this?'

Moll looked amused. 'Time to move on.'

Doug leaned across and opened the passenger door for her. He had only told her last night that he was off, but Moll had taken the news in her usual easy stride. When he had half-jokingly said, 'Come with me,' she hadn't hesitated for a moment before replying, 'Okay.'

Now, as she climbed into the MG and shook back her tortoiseshell hair, Doug felt his spirits lift.

They understood each other, he and Moll. They were two of a kind.

'Lorna isn't going to be pleased, losing her star barmaid.'

'She'll be fine. Stevie needs a job to tide him over.'

'I thought your brother was only here for a few days, visiting you.'

'Ah well, that was before he clapped eyes on Savannah Gillespie.'

Doug slid the car into gear. 'That won't last.'

'So? They're enjoying themselves,' Moll said comfortably. 'That's what counts.'

'There's enjoying yourself and there's enjoying yourself,' Doug murmured. 'And if you want to get there in one piece, you'd better take your hand out of my trousers.'

Moll burst out laughing.

'Spoilsport! Myrtle Armitage is watching us from her bedroom window. I wanted to give the old bag one last shock.'

★ ★ ★

It was the last week of the summer holidays, and Harriet was looking forward to getting back to school. She had a new bra to show off in the changing rooms, a new graffiti-free satchel – soon remedy that – and more gossip than usual to relate.

She sat on the front garden wall, kicking her heels against the stonework and dangling a yo-yo inches above the pavement. Every time the kitten launched itself at the yo-yo, she twitched it out of reach.

So:

New bra, which was great, with yellow daisies on it, and padded bits that slotted in and out depending on how pneumatic you wanted to look – which was basically very pneumatic indeed.

New kitten.

New-ish dog.

Parents separated.

Father had affair with the ex-wife of a man-who-became-a-woman. Hmm, maybe she wouldn't mention that bit.

Mother *possibly* having affair with hunky younger vet. Ah, big improvement. Far less shameful too. Since a vet was currently a seriously cool thing to be, this was something you could definitely boast about.

Particularly when his name was Mr Darcy.

Then there's me, thought Harriet, dipping and twitching the yo-yo like a metronome. What have I done with myself these holidays?

Nothing.

Nothing at all.

She closed her eyes for a second, imagining just how left out she was going to feel when all the other girls in her class wittered on and on about their boyfriends. During the course of the last couple of terms it had turned into something of an epidemic.

And I still haven't got one, thought Harriet.

New bra, new cat, new dog . . . no boyfriend.

Talk about a failure.

Realistically, though, how much choice was there when

393

you lived in a stupid village, ten miles from the nearest town?

The only teenage boy in Upper Sisley was Dizzy Gillespie.

And famous parents or no famous parents, Harriet thought with grim satisfaction, she wasn't that desperate.

She knew why she was thinking about boys. Fifty yards away, sitting on the green with his pushbike lying on its side next to him, was one she hadn't seen before. And every time she glanced casually in his direction – hell's bells, it was happening *again* – he seemed to be casually glancing back.

Harriet hadn't been paying attention. With a high-pitched miaow of triumph, the kitten launched itself at the dangling yo-yo and promptly cannoned into the wall.

'You daft animal.' Jumping down, Harriet cradled the kitten in her hands. 'You'll give yourself brain damage.'

The kitten, predictably, weed all over her jeans.

When she looked across, Harriet could have sworn the boy with the bicycle was laughing to himself.

She longed to see his face more clearly. A pair of binoculars would come in useful. You'd have to be discreet about it, of course.

Harriet wished she could stay outside but there was no arguing with the smell of cat pee. She went into the house, changed her jeans, slapped on a bit of blue mascara, checked through the sitting-room window that the boy was still there – yes! – added a dash of lip gloss – oops, not all over her chin – pinched twenty pence from Lottie's piggy bank, and dashed back outside.

She felt the boy's eyes on her as she sauntered casually but sexily past him on her way to the village shop. It really was astonishing the difference a new bra could make, even if it was only a 34AA. Okay, so maybe the results weren't as eye-popping as a pair of hockey socks, but this way was a lot more secure.

Having bought her packet of chewing gum, Harriet headed – casually and sexily – back to the house. But by this time her curiosity was well and truly aroused.

Who was this boy and what was he doing here?

Most weird of all, when she was walking down the road, why on earth did he still keep glancing over at her house?

'Excuse me,' said Harriet, pausing at the edge of the green, 'but you are waiting for someone?'

Now that she was standing less than twenty feet away from him, she could see his face properly.

Hmm, not bad.

No spots, at least.

'Great timing.' The boy grinned up at her. 'I was just about to ask you for help. Although you have to understand, this is an undercover mission.'

There was a conspiratorial twinkle in his eye. Harriet decided she liked him already.

No spots and a sense of humour. Almost too good to be true.

'What, you mean you're a secret agent?'

'Got it in one.'

Harriet giggled. 'Like James Bond?'

'What d'you mean, *like* James Bond?' The boy raised one eyebrow. 'I *am* James Bond. Press the hidden lever,' he went on, patting his bicycle, 'and this turns into an Aston Martin.'

Beaming with delight, Harriet flopped down on to the grass next to him.

'Who are you looking for?'

'Soviet agent.' He lowered his voice to a passable Sean Connery-type growl. 'Known as the Russian Widow, eats men for breakfast. Very beautiful. Extremely dangerous.'

Entranced, Harriet whispered back, 'What's her real name?'

'Harriet Ferguson.'

Hang on a second . . .

'That's my name.'

'Is it? Well, not you, obviously. The other one.'

'Why not me, *obviously*?' Harriet sat up, nettled. 'And *what* other one?'

The boy frowned. 'You're supposed to tell me. Grand-mother was my guess. The Harriet Ferguson I'm looking for is in her late sixties.'

'Well I'm the only one there is.'

He looked across at the house.

'The Old Vicarage, right?'

'Right.'

'Are you sure you aren't in your late sixties?' Eyes narrowing, he peered more closely at her face. 'You could be a master of disguise.'

'You aren't James Bond. James Bond doesn't make mistakes like this,' said Harriet. 'Come on, what's your real name?'

'Alfie Huntingdon.'

'*Alfie?*'

'I know.' He pulled a face. 'Bad news, isn't it? Alfie and Harriet. We sound like a right pair of geriatrics.'

'Huntingdon!' Harriet exclaimed suddenly.

'Oh great, you're going to criticise that too. Actually, I'm quite fond of—'

'The letter. You must be related to Frank.'

'He's my grandfather. So you *did* write to him.' Alfie's eyebrows went up at angles. 'Now I'm definitely confused.'

'I didn't write to him, somebody else did. It was their idea of a joke.' Briefly, Harriet explained. 'When I got your grandfather's letter I meant to write back and tell him. But I thought he'd have hundreds of other replies,' she said apologetically, 'so in the end I didn't bother.'

'He had two, but the other woman wasn't keen on pigs. He liked the sound of you best,' Alfie explained, 'but you didn't write back. He was disappointed, but he didn't want to pester you.'

Harriet loved the way Alfie's eyebrows moved when he talked, as if they had a life of their own.

'So what are you doing here?'

'I volunteered to come over and check the situation out. See what Harriet Ferguson looked like, find out if she was Grandad's type. If I thought she was, I'd have persuaded him to write again, give her another chance.'

'God, I'm sorry.' Harriet felt mortified, as if it were all her fault. 'I wish I was seventy, I really do.'

Alfie leaned back on his elbows and surveyed her without

a trace of embarrassment. 'You aren't to blame. Anyway, every cloud . . .' He broke into a grin. 'I'm glad you're not seventy.'

Harriet was glad too.

'Is your grandad really nice?'

'Yeah, he's great. Just lonely.' Alfie looked unperturbed. 'Don't panic, we'll find someone else for him.'

Harriet wondered how Frank had worded his original ad.

'Maybe it was the pig thing that put them off,' she said helpfully. 'Some women are funny about pigs.'

'Good thinking, Moneypenny.' Alfie wiggled his eyebrows at her. 'Either that or we put the next ad in *Farmer's Weekly*.'

Chapter 65

'I'm telling you, the atmosphere in that house is terrible,' said Oliver. 'You should go up there, then you'd know what I mean.' He was putting together a spaghetti bolognese, practically the only thing he could make. Every work surface in the kitchen was awash with piles of chopped-up mushrooms, tomatoes, onions and garlic.

'That's like saying this milk is off, go on, try it,' Jessie pointed out. 'Why do people always say that?'

But Oliver wasn't going to be side-tracked. 'It's awful. You can't imagine how bad. Have you talked to Toby lately?'

Jessie pinched a mushroom while he wasn't looking. 'What good would that do?'

Oliver shrugged. 'I don't know. It might help.'

Hardly likely, thought Jessie, if just the mention of his name makes my stomach do a double somersault. Toby's remarks in the graveyard last week hadn't been encouraging either. As far as she was concerned, the most helpful thing she could do was keep out of his way.

Well out of his way.

Her hand sidled across to the half-empty bottle of red wine on the kitchen table.

'Don't,' Oliver warned without turning round. 'I need that for the bolognese.'

Oh well, Jessie thought, just have to do it cold turkey.

'I'm putting the cottage on the market,' she said.

He stopped chopping and swung round to look at her, frowning.

'I thought you'd given up on that idea.'

'No.'

'But why?'

'I want to move.'

Oh Olly, don't you see? I *have* to move, she pleaded silently.

'Move where?' He shot her a look of disbelief. 'Not still Cornwall.'

'Yes.'

'But that's miles away!'

That, thought Jessie, is the general idea.

'Look, you're going to Europe.' She tapped the pile of brochures Oliver had brought home from the travel agents that afternoon. 'You'll be gone for the best part of a year. When you get back, you'll find a job and move away . . . Well, you *will*,' she insisted. 'Don't tell me you were planning on living with your old mother for the rest of your life.'

'Is this something to do with Jonathan?' Oliver sounded suspicious. 'Are you two moving in together?'

'No!'

Poor Jonathan, he had given up on her weeks ago. Going out platonically with someone you so badly wanted to sleep with, he had explained with rueful candour to Jess, was hell on wheels. Like gazing for hours at a classic car and not being allowed to lay a finger on it.

Apologising profusely, Jessie had thanked him for being such a good friend, wished him well and kissed him goodbye.

Within a fortnight, Jonathan had found himself another woman, one with a chassis he *could* touch.

'I just don't understand why,' Oliver protested. For something to do, he was chopping the mushrooms into smaller and smaller pieces.

She couldn't bring herself to tell him the real reason.

'I like Cornwall.'

'I thought you liked living here.'

Jessie gazed with longing at the bottle of Valpolicella. When she'd wanted to move before, Toby had persuaded her not to. He had managed to convince her that staying put was the best thing she could do, that running away wasn't the answer. According to Toby, there was no reason why the two of them couldn't co-exist happily together in the same village.

Well, that was where he was wrong.

I gave it my best shot, Jessie reminded herself, *and it didn't work out*. A great wave of sadness swept over her.

'I do like living here,' she told Oliver, semi-truthfully. 'I just think I'll like Cornwall more.'

I'm looking old and tired, thought Eleanor Ferguson as she checked her appearance in the hall mirror before leaving the house. There were deep frown lines between her grey eyebrows and her mouth was turned down at the corners as if gripped with disapproval.

This was hardly surprising, as Eleanor currently had a lot to disapprove of.

What Lili thought she was doing, she had no idea, but these days Eleanor could barely bring herself to speak to her shameless daughter-in-law. Quite clearly, the affair with Drew Darcy had been going on for months – oh, she could see that now – and this had been the reason for the break-up of her son's marriage; it hadn't been Michael's fault at all.

And those poor, innocent children – what they must be going through didn't bear thinking about.

Eleanor opened the front door a couple of inches and peered outside, checking the coast was clear. She was taking immense pains to avoid Bernadette Thomas. How the rest of the village could allow such a creature to carry on living in their midst was beyond Eleanor, but nobody else seemed to care. Eleanor shuddered with revulsion every time she remembered she was living next door to a freak, a man who had undergone a sex change.

Furthermore she would never forgive him for that night-marish scene with Michael in the pub.

Eleanor double-locked the front door and headed for her car. What with Myrtle Armitage's barbed remarks and never knowing who you might bump into without warning, it was easier to avoid the village shop nowadays and drive to Tesco's in Harleston instead.

The car key was slotted into the driver's door when she heard the crackle of wheels on fallen leaves. Looking up, Eleanor saw two teenage boys on mountain bikes swerving along Waters Lane towards her. She didn't recognise them; they certainly weren't from Upper Sisley.

Spotting Eleanor, they glanced at each other and began to giggle.

'It's her. It *is* her,' she heard one of them say to the other. 'You can tell just by looking – that's the bloke who had the sex-change.'

Eleanor froze. She stared at them as they whizzed past, sniggering openly.

When they were safely out of reach, the second boy swivelled round in his saddle and yelled, 'Oi, mate, what's it feel like to have your John Thomas chopped off?'

Tears of humiliation burned the back of Eleanor's eyes like acid. She couldn't go shopping now.

Heading back up the garden path, she saw to her further horror that Bernadette was standing in her front room, gazing out through the open window. Clearly she had heard everything.

She addressed Eleanor with sympathy. 'I'm so sorry about that. They're just boys. I try to ignore them.'

Blinking back tears, Eleanor shot her a look of disdain. Without uttering a word she stalked into the house.

Dizzy was consumed with a jealousy he hadn't known he possessed. Well, not where Harriet Ferguson was concerned at least. Mysteriously, all of a sudden he fancied her like mad.

It was, he acknowledged with reluctance, more than likely something to do with the fact that Moll wasn't around to lust after any more.

He made sure he happened to be sauntering past the village shop when Harriet emerged from it clutching one of her precious magazines. This one, he observed, sported a glossy fluorescent pink cover. It was called *Boyz!!* and had a photo on the front of the hottest new teenage soap star, currently being swooned over by every young girl in the country.

'Met him at a party up in London the other week,' Dizzy lied, casually nodding at the picture. Well, it wasn't a complete lie; he'd met someone who'd stood next to him in a queue at McDonald's. 'I could get you his autograph if you wanted.'

'I'm not bothered.' Harriet shrugged, unimpressed. 'I don't like him much.'

'How's your new kitten? What's its name?'

'Banana.'

Struggling slightly, Dizzy said, 'Banana – that's a good name.'

Harriet shot him a suspicious look. Dizzy? Being complimentary? Surely not.

'It was Lottie's idea. I didn't choose it. Lottie's mad about bananas.'

'I'm not doing anything right now,' Dizzy offered. 'If I came over, you could show me your kitten, I haven't seen it yet.'

Harriet frowned. This was definitely weird. 'It looks like a kitten, that's all. Anyway, I've got a friend coming over,' she checked her watch, 'any minute now.'

Dizzy took a deep breath. He had been practising this bit all morning. 'Look, I was wondering if you'd like to go to the cinema with me. They're showing the new James Bond in Harleston. We could catch the bus into town, get a burger – I'd pay, don't worry about that – then—'

'Seen it.'

Instant deflation. 'Oh. Oh, right.'

Harriet's expression cleared. So that was why Dizzy was being nice!

How completely *amazing*.

'Dizzy, were you asking me out on a date then?'

His ears went beetroot. 'Well, you know, um . . . not exactly a date . . .'

But Harriet was victorious. After all the jibes and putdowns of the past few months, she was going to really enjoy this.

In fact the next couple of minutes could rank among the best of her life.

'You were. You were asking me out on a date,' she announced triumphantly. 'And do you know why I'm turning you down? Two reasons, actually. Because (a) you're a slimeball and I don't fancy you anyway. And (b) I've already got a boyfriend.'

Stung, Dizzy hit back. 'You have not!'

'Oh yes I have.'

'In your dreams.'

'No, he's real. Thanks to you.'

He glared at her, not understanding. 'What are you talking about?'

'You and all those pathetic letters you wrote.' She smirked. 'Surely you remember. You answered an ad in the *Harleston Echo*, pretending to be me.'

Outraged, Dizzy said, 'That was to some old guy! He was *ancient*.'

'But his grandson isn't – he's fifteen.' Harriet's joy was complete as, over Dizzy's shoulder, she spotted Alfie on his bike, pedalling down the High Street towards her. 'So there you go – it all turned out rather well. You should try it, Dizzy. It might even work for you.'

'Hi!' puffed Alfie, screeching to a halt in a cloud of dust and grinning at Harriet.

Wondering if it was possible to actually explode with pride, she grinned back. He was better looking than Dizzy Gillespie. Taller, too. And he thought nothing of cycling twelve miles to see her.

Harriet took immense delight in not introducing him to Dizzy. Tucking her arm through Alfie's, she said joyfully, 'Come on, let's go back to my place.'

'Moneypenny, you always know exactly the right thing to say.'

'Oh, that reminds me.' As they began to move away, Harriet glanced over her shoulder at Dizzy. 'Do go and see the Bond film. We thought it was great.'

Chapter 66

It was mid-September, the leaves were turning and the woody scent of autumn hung in the air. Deborah Gillespie, walking slowly around her garden, saw glossy brown conkers nestling in the long grass beneath the chestnut trees.

Nature's way of telling you your children are growing up, she thought drily. The days of avid collecting and hoarding were over. If she rushed inside now and told Dizzy there were conkers outside, he would roll his eyes and mutter 'Sa-ad'.

Deborah bent and picked up a couple herself, holding them in the palm of her hand and rubbing her fingers over their waxy smoothness. Then she slid them into her jacket pocket alongside her mobile phone.

The one that never rang nowadays.

She had called David Mansfield five days ago. He sounded horrified to hear from her.

'Nothing to panic about,' she had announced cheerfully.

'Is this about Savannah?'

'Why would it be? Don't be so paranoid!'

Evidently thinking about the party conference and the potential scope for scandal, David had let out a groan of relief. She heard him relax. 'So, how can I help?'

'I'm not asking for a favour, David.' Oh, that voice! 'You've been on my mind a lot lately, that's all. I wondered if you'd like to meet up.'

'Ah . . .'

'I'll leave it with you,' Deborah had said lightly. No pressure, no pressure. He knew what she was talking about and he knew he could trust her.

And philandering MPs don't easily change their spots.

'Look, Deborah—'

'You've got my number.' Effortlessly she deflected the protest. 'Have a think about it. Ring me if you're interested.'

Which all sounded great, in theory.

Except he hadn't.

First Toby, then Doug Flynn, Deborah thought. Now David too.

Was this how the fat girls at school felt when they were last to be picked for the hockey team?

Was it how the really ugly ones felt at the end-of-term disco when nobody asked them to dance?

Bloody men!

Conkers in one pocket, terminally non-ringing phone in the other, she made her way back up the garden.

Toby came out on to the terrace as she approached the house.

'We need to talk.'

'Toby, when are you going to stop looking so *grim*?' The last few weeks had been appalling; it was like being in endless detention. 'I've said I'm sorry a hundred times. Why can't we just put it behind us and get back to how we were?'

He shook his head. 'It's not going to work. I want a divorce.'

Deborah felt a dull ache in her stomach.

'You mean you want Jessie. Okay, fine.' She shrugged. 'I owe you that much. Carry on seeing her. I won't say a word.'

Toby only wished he could.

'She won't have anything to do with me,' he said evenly. 'She thinks you and I should stay together for the sake of the children.'

He felt this was particularly bizarre advice, coming as it did from someone who had raised her own child single-handedly.

Deborah began to feel slightly desperate. 'I think she's right.'

But Toby's dark-blue eyes were fixed on the swaying poplars behind her. 'I don't care what either of you think. I just know I can't carry on with this sham of a marriage. Either you move out,' he said slowly, 'or I do.'

It was on the tip of Deborah's tongue to retort, 'Fine – you go,' when it occurred to her that the alternative might not be as dire as she imagined. Okay, this was a big house, but would staying in it be a case of cutting off her nose to spite her face?

There's money in the bank, she thought, and Toby's just signed the deal for the Spielberg film. I could find myself a nice little semi in Putney or Hampstead. Okay, it might not compare pricewise, but at least I'd be back in London.

Because Upper Sisley might be a picturesque village in the Cotswolds, but there was no denying the choice of men was limited.

And in all fairness, how many were really that attractive?

Basically, Deborah decided, the only ones worth having, she'd already had.

'You're splitting up?' Dizzy stared at his parents. 'When?'

It tore at Toby's heart to think that this was what they had to do to gain their son's undivided attention.

'Your father's staying here,' Deborah told him gently, 'and I'm moving back to London.'

'Oh wow, fan-*tas*-tic! Can I come with you?' Dizzy begged. 'Pleeease?'

Deborah was taken aback. 'Darling, that would be lovely – but you've just settled into your new school.'

'I hate it. I'll go back to my old one,' Dizzy promptly announced.

'You've spent the last five years hating that place.'

'Huh, better than that bloody dump in Harleston.'

The fees for the bloody dump amounted to several thousand pounds a year. 'Dizzy, you don't—'

'But what I *really* want to do is go to stage school,' he blurted out.

Savannah snorted with laughter.

'You!'

Dizzy punched her on the shoulder. 'I'm good at acting.'

'Prove it!'

'Oh, Savannah, you're so beautiful, I'm so *lucky* to have a sister as wonderful as you . . .' He smirked and aimed another punch at her arm. 'There, see? If I can say that with a straight face, I can say anything.'

'Dizzy, are you serious about this?' Toby was frowning. This wasn't the reaction he'd expected.

'What, about Savannah being wonderful? Dad, pay attention, I was being an ac-tor!'

But Toby didn't smile. Dizzy realised he had to press his case.

'Deadly serious,' he pleaded.

God, more so than ever since yesterday's humiliating run-in with Harriet Ferguson. As she and that oh-so-witty boyfriend of hers had been making their way back to The Old Vicarage, Dizzy had heard him say: 'Is that the one who sent all the letters?' And Harriet, not even bothering to lower her voice, had replied dismissively, 'Yeah, he's just a nerd.'

Startled, Toby looked across at his daughter. 'How about you?'

Savannah didn't hesitate. 'Oh, I'll stay here, thanks. With you.'

'Can't bear to be away from sexy Stevie, you mean,' Dizzy mocked. 'Ouch, that *hurt*!'

'Unlike you, I care about my education.'

Savannah was so blinded by love that she actually believed this lofty pronouncement. In fact Stevie had persuaded her that retaking her dismally failed A levels was a must. She was also thoroughly enjoying herself at Harleston Tech.

Deborah was lying in the bath when her phone rang. She was so comfortable she almost left it until the answering service picked up.

Almost.

'It's me.'

She closed her eyes in triumph. 'Who's me?'

'You know.'

'Oh, hi.'

Deborah wondered if the news that she and Toby were separating would scare him off. Married women were a far safer bet than the unattached kind.

Maybe she wouldn't tell him just yet.

'Ahem. Well. About this meeting you . . . er . . . suggested.'

Deborah shivered pleasurably. This – *this* was what she most loved. The excitement, the subterfuge, the wicked, intoxicating thrill of it all. Imagine – someone, somewhere right now could be tapping into this very conversation, taping it, ready to do a Camillagate on them . . .

'Thank you for returning my call, I know how busy you must be.' Deborah sank back into the water, still clutching the phone. 'Now,' she said happily, aware that David could hear the sound of splashing, would know she was in the bath, 'you tell me when's good for you, and I'll see if I can fit you in.'

Thanks to a mammoth blackberry picking session, Lottie was stained purple from head to foot. By the time Lili had finished scrubbing her clean in the bath, the smell of cheese on toast was drifting up the stairs.

When she pushed open the sitting-room door, she had to swallow a great lump in her throat.

The fire had been lit. Harriet was sprawled in front of it, reading aloud something incomprehensible from a physics textbook. Drew, in the armchair, had Will balanced on one knee and Blitz draped adoringly over the other. He was listening to Harriet, answering her questions, and playing This Little Piggy with Will's toes. On the rug next to Harriet, Banana lay watching *Tom and Jerry* on the turned-down TV, her skinny tail swishing from side to side.

It was like one of those Victorian Christmas card scenes, thought Lili, feeling ridiculously emotional.

Well – apart from the television.

And Disco Barbie, legs splayed, poking out from behind one of the sofa cushions.

And Harriet's mud-encrusted Nike trainers.

Drew looked up and winked at Lili.

He mouthed 'Marry me' at her.

Lottie, shoving past Lili in her Pocahontas pyjamas and fighting for a place on Drew's knee, howled, 'Get off, Will, it's my turn.'

'Leave Drew alone,' Harriet said. 'He's helping me with my homework.' She glanced up through her fringe. 'So, what's the size of the contingent negative variation, ten microvolts?'

Lili smiled. Her children adored him. He adored them. It was so perfect it was scary – and even scarier because it was all happening so soon.

Drew, it seemed, could do no wrong.

Next moment, Blitz began to bark.

Then the smoke alarm went off in the hall, almost sending Banana into orbit.

Lili reflected that if love was blind, it must also have an effect on your sense of smell, because she'd been the one standing in the doorway and she hadn't even noticed the clouds of smoke billowing from the kitchen.

Drew, having tipped assorted children and animals off his lap, raced past her, silenced the alarm and switched off the grill.

Four slices of cheese on toast, charred beyond recognition, went into the bin.

'Did I ever tell you I was a lousy cook?' said Drew.

Lili pinched his bottom; she felt a lot happier now.

'Just when I was beginning to think you were perfect.'

Much later that evening, with the children in bed, Drew pulled Lili down on the sofa next to him. 'I meant what I said earlier.'

'Sorry about burning the cheese on toast? I should hope so. That was the last of the cheese.'

'The marrying bit.'

Lili looked at him, unable to speak.

'Oh bugger! *Bugger* it! I know I'm not supposed to be saying this.' Drew heaved a sigh. 'It's too soon, we're meant to wait until we're in our nineties at least, but I don't bloody *want* to wait until I'm ninety,' he protested. 'All this stuff about being just-good-friends and not getting emotionally involved . . . it isn't working. I want us to be a proper couple, a proper *family*.'

Lili ran her hand over the bobbly, much-washed wool of his sweater, knitted for him by the grateful elderly owner of a Pekingese with asthma. 'You know what we agreed, that rebound relationships are doomed to failure.'

Gosh, it was hard to be sensible when every atom in your body was willing you to wave your knickers in the air and bellow 'Yes, yes!'

'I'm bored with that rebound stuff.' The beginnings of a smile appeared around Drew's mouth. He slid his fingers beneath Lili's pink sweatshirt and began to tickle her waist. 'I think somebody made it up. They got dumped and used it as an excuse.'

Lili squirmed as he affectionately explored what he called her love-handles.

She called them her fat bits.

'You could meet someone else,' she protested. 'Someone young and firm, with no kids, no stretchmarks . . .'

'Blonde, with huge boobs,' Drew agreed, 'out to here.'

Lili smacked his hand. 'All right, no need to get carried away. I'm just saying, you might go off me.'

'Not going to happen,' Drew said simply. Bending over, no longer teasing, he kissed her on the mouth. 'You see, you're everything I never knew I wanted. I can't imagine life without you, or your children.'

The sitting-room door burst open. Drew just had time to whisk his hand out from under Lili's sweatshirt.

'Mum, I had a dream I was swimming.' Lottie's Pocahontas pyjamas were sodden, and a puddle was forming on the parquet floor. 'And when I woke up, I'd wet the bed.'

Chapter 67

Carla, one of the vet nurses, was reading out the horoscopes in her new *Take-A-Break*.

'What are you, Jamie?'

'Depressed.'

'I mean what *sign*.'

'Dunno. Taurus.'

'Right, let's see.' Carla scanned the lines optimistically, her head going from side to side.

'Don't tell me: I'm useless, my life is miserable and I need to sort myself out.'

'Um . . . basically, yes.'

'Didn't need a stupid horoscope to tell me that.'

Brenda, the receptionist, popped her head around the door. 'Jamie? Mrs Samson's here with Bailey.'

Jamie raised a despairing eyebrow. 'You mean Mrs Bailey's here with Samson.'

'Sorry, yes.' When she giggled, Brenda sounded like Tickle-me-Elmo. 'For neutering.'

But Jamie was unamused. 'Pay attention, Brenda. Imagine if I neutered Mrs Bailey by mistake.'

Brenda's smile faltered.

'Ignore him,' Carla declared breezily, 'he's in a pissy mood, that's all.'

Brenda, who had been away for a few days, gave Jamie a look of sympathy. 'You weren't very cheerful last week either.'

'It's the same pissy mood. It just goes on and on,' Carla rolled her eyes, 'like chewing gum without any taste left.'

Jamie wondered how anyone so kind to animals could be

so heartless when it came to humans. 'Carla, are you sure you want to be a Samaritan when you grow up?'

'Come on, don't be so gloomy. Look on the bright side!' She gave Jamie a reassuring punch on the arm. 'At least *you* aren't the one being neutered.'

Jamie took a mouthful of the coffee she had made him. They'd worked together for almost a year and Carla still couldn't remember that he took sugar.

All in all, he felt, it summed up his situation pretty neatly.

I don't *matter* to anyone, thought Jamie. Nobody cares about me.

Not bossy Carla.

Not Brenda with her Dr Scholl sandals and her stupid giggle.

Not Moll Harper, who had upped and left without so much as a goodbye, in Doug's dark-blue MG.

And not Felicity.

Oh not, certainly not Felicity.

Jamie knew he had to be realistic about this; he had to face facts. It was over a fortnight since he'd seen her. Pretty obviously, she wasn't going to contact him now.

If you liked someone and wanted to see them again, you might leave it a day or two, just to be cool.

But you didn't leave it for fourteen.

Jamie spooned three sugars into his lukewarm coffee and, for the sake of appearances, flicked through Samson's notes. When were things going to get better? He'd lost all interest in his work. The only reason he bothered to come in was because being at home was worse.

In fact home was *worse* than worse – it was bordering on unbearable, what with Drew hardly able to scrape that smug grin off his face and every sentence uttered beginning with 'Lili thinks' this and 'Lili says' that.

If Drew wasn't talking about Lili he was over at The Old Vicarage with her. These days he couldn't stop laughing, whistling and making jokes.

Most irritating of all, as far as Jamie was concerned, he refused point-blank to discuss what was clearly a stupendous sex-life.

Keeper's Cottage wasn't the same any more with Drew in his current state and Doug gone. Doug's replacement hadn't improved matters either.

When Stevie Harper had offered to move in, Jamie had been all for it. Stevie was Moll's brother, he was a good bloke and he was single; they'd have a great laugh.

Except it hadn't worked out like that, because what he hadn't known at the time was that Stevie was seeing Savannah Gillespie. And he liked to have sex with her even more often than Drew had sex with Lili. But at least Drew had the decency to do it over at Lili's house, so Jamie didn't have to listen to every sigh, every shriek of ecstasy, every creak of the bed.

Three blokes sharing a house, Jamie thought sadly. Two of them getting more sex than they knew what to do with.

And me, Norris No-life, sitting up in bed with my copy of *Wisden's Almanack* and cotton wool stuffed in my ears . . .

Jamie gulped down his tepid coffee. He could hear agitated barking coming from the waiting room. Then again, he'd be agitated if he were in Samson's situation.

Time to get gowned and scrubbed up before Samson, poor sod, got cold feet.

Twenty minutes later, Brenda buzzed through to the operating room.

'Jamie, call for you.'

Jamie's heart did its usual jerky flip-flop. He knew it was too late, Felicity would never phone now, but it still happened every time.

Jesus, what am I, some kind of *girl*?

He frowned, concentrating on tying off vessels. It wouldn't be her, it just wouldn't. He wasn't even going to ask.

'Who is it?'

'Walter Clutterbuck. He's worried about his tortoise. Her name's Lady Penelope—'

'What is she, a slow eater? For crying out loud!' Jamie exploded, glaring at the intercom. 'We aren't playing strip pontoon in here, I'm in the middle of surgery. If Walter

413

Clutterbuck wants an appointment he can fucking make one. You do your job and I'll do mine, okay?'

Brenda sounded crushed. 'Sorry, Jamie.'

'And make sure you don't bother me again!'

'You should push that bed of yours up against the wall.' Eyeing him above her mask, Carla slapped the scalpel into Jamie's hand with unnecessary force. 'Then you wouldn't keep getting out the wrong side.'

Morning surgery stretched on through lunch, thanks to an extra hysterectomy mistakenly booked in by last week's useless relief receptionist. By the time Jamie finished the last procedure it was gone two o'clock. His stomach was rumbling with hunger, his hair was plastered to his head and there was an unflattering mark across the bridge of his nose where the plastic clip from his mask had pinched into the skin.

Food. Got to have food.

'Brenda.' Poking his head around the waiting-room door, he forced a smile by way of apology for yelling at her earlier. 'I'm desperate for a shower. Any chance of you popping out and grabbing me a couple of cheese and pickle rolls?'

Brenda leapt to her feet, as wide-eyed and nervous as a rabbit. 'Of course I will! Um—'

'And a Mars bar.' Jamie felt guilty; she tried so hard to please. He dug in his pocket for change.

'Er, sorry, there's someone here to see you,' Brenda blurted out. 'I know it's your lunch-break, but . . .'

Looking up, Jamie saw Felicity sitting on one of the orange plastic chairs at the far end of the waiting room.

'She hasn't got an appointment.' Brenda was clearly petrified.

Flip-flop, went Jamie's heart.

Felicity stood up and came over to the desk. 'Hello Jamie. I know you're busy . . .'

'It's his lunch-break,' said Brenda possessively.

'I phoned three times this morning.'

'I told her you were busy.'

'That's okay, Brenda. Thanks.'

414

'I didn't know if it was just me you didn't want to speak to,' Felicity's smile was uncertain, 'or people in general. Especially when you didn't return my calls last week.'

'Last week?'

Flip-flop, flip-flop.

'I left a couple of messages. Not with you,' Felicity turned to Brenda. 'A woman with a Scottish accent.'

The useless relief receptionist.

Relieved that this was something she couldn't be blamed for, Brenda shook her head. 'That definitely wasn't me.'

'Fine, Brenda.' Jamie pressed a fiver into her palm. 'Two ham and tomato rolls and a Lion bar. Please.'

'But I thought you wanted cheese and—'

'Anything, anything.' The coffee room would be empty. Jamie ran his fingers through his flattened hair and looked at Felicity. 'Please, come on through.'

In the messy, magazine-strewn coffee room, he set about filling the kettle and searching through cupboards for Carla's hidden tin of Earl Grey tea bags.

'I could be making a prize idiot of myself.' Felicity sounded nervous. 'You might have changed your mind about wanting to see me.'

Jamie wasn't like Doug; he couldn't impress girls by knowing the name of their perfume. All he knew was that Felicity smelled gorgeous, and if perfume was supposed to make you want to get closer to someone, it was certainly doing its job.

'Why would I change my mind?'

Blast, where *had* Carla hidden those tea bags? How was he meant to impress someone like Felicity with Co-op's own brand?

'You might have done. You could have met someone else, or decided you just weren't interested any more.'

Jamie couldn't play games like Doug either. 'Well I haven't, okay?'

'Oh. I have.'

'You have what?'

'Changed my mind. About you,' Felicity explained with a shy smile. 'I'd like us to go out – if that's okay with you. I

415

mean, when you have a free evening . . . we could just try it, see how it goes . . . sorry, this isn't coming out very well, I'm horribly out of p-practice,' her voice began to wobble, 'well, more than out of practice really, seeing as I've never asked anyone out before.'

'This evening.' It came out as a croak. Hastily Jamie cleared his throat and tried again. 'This evening. I'm free.' He wasn't, he was on call, but he had done enough favours for Drew in the last few weeks, 'And I think you made a damn good job of it.'

'Of course, we might not get on. We might decide we don't—'

'One step at a time,' Jamie said, unable to resist giving her a quick kiss on the cheek.

Then, when Felicity didn't flinch away, another one an inch closer to her mouth.

She closed her eyes. He took aim for the third time.

Through the closed door a female voice bellowed, 'Where is he? Jamie Lyall, you're a lying bastard and you don't deserve to have people being nice to you!'

Felicity looked stunned.

'There you are!' Carla flung open the door to the coffee room, brandishing a glossy hardback edition of Jeremy Guscott's autobiography. 'I felt sorry for you because your horoscope was so lousy. I thought maybe if I bought you a present, you'd cheer up.'

Jamie, who was a huge fan of Jeremy Guscott, said, 'Carla, that's really kind of—'

'Shut up!' Carla yelled, looking as if she'd like to hurl the book at his head. 'And don't worry, I've learned my lesson. I'm never going to feel sorry for *you* again.'

Jamie could feel Felicity shrinking away from him.

'Why?' Worried, she looked across at Carla. 'What's he done wrong?'

'I've just looked at the calendar. His birthday's in December,' Carla told an uncomprehending Felicity. 'The lying toad isn't even a Taurus!'

Chapter 68

'Dad's not taking it well.'

Savannah was sitting cross-legged on Jessie's sofa, drinking mineral water and absently picking at a hole in the sleeve of her black sweater. It was actually one of Stevie's sweaters, and she was drinking mineral water because Stevie had told her it was better for her than endless cans of Coke.

'No?'

Jessie thought she probably didn't want to hear this. She carried on buttering crumpets.

'I think he's missing Mum terribly.'

Jessie definitely didn't want to hear this. 'Crumpet?'

'Please. I mean, he says he isn't, but that's Dad. Men always bottle up their feelings, don't they? It's stupid.'

'How is your Mum?'

'Oh, having a whale of a time. Guess who she's having a fling with now?'

God, who?

Jessie shook her head, unable to guess. 'Who?'

Savannah, busy cramming half a crumpet into her mouth, wiped melted butter from her chin with the sleeve of Stevie's sweater. 'Yum, these are fab . . . The sperm donor.'

'What?'

'My biological father. That pompous prat! She told me when I was up there last weekend. Top secret, of course.' Savannah rolled her eyes. 'Yuk, can you imagine?'

'I don't think I want to. MI5 might be listening.' Phew, Jessie thought as she crammed another crumpet on to the toasting fork. 'How long's this been going on?'

'Few weeks. Seeing Mum again when he came down here to give the blood sample sparked it off again, apparently.' Marvelling at the sequence of events, Savannah said, 'And now they're mad about each other.'

'Risky.'

'Too right. If they get caught, according to Mum, it could practically bring down the government. And all because I had a bit of a crush on my brother,' Savannah marvelled, polishing off her second crumpet. Innocently she added, 'If that happened, would it be all my fault?'

It seemed safer to steer the conversation away from Deborah. 'Is Dizzy okay?'

'Happier than a pig in a trough. He's starting at the Serena Fox stage school next week. Amazingly, he did a brilliant audition and they snapped him up on the spot. When they found out afterwards he was Toby Gillespie's son they practically wet themselves with joy. Have you two had some kind of argument?' Savannah said suddenly.

Jessie looked astonished. 'Who, me and Dizzy?'

'Come on . . . you and Dad.'

'No.' Fumbling slightly, Jessie stuck yet another crumpet on to the prongs of the fork. She shuffled on her knees closer to the fire.

'Sure?'

'Sure I'm sure.' The heat from the flames – it was definitely the heat from the flames – had brought a rush of colour to Jessie's cheeks. 'What would we argue about?'

Savannah shrugged. 'I don't know. You haven't been over to the house for ages, that's all.'

'I've been busy.' Jessie floundered for an excuse. 'Selling the cottage, helping Oliver to get his trip organised—'

'Why don't you go and see Dad?'

'Well . . .'

'Please, Jess. He'd appreciate it. It's been a rough few weeks.' Savannah pulled a face. 'And it's going to get rougher when the press find out about him and Mum splitting up. He needs someone to talk to, a real friend.'

Hmm, thought Jessie, or does he just need someone to sleep with?

'I thought he was off to the States. Oliver said something about a Spielberg film.'

'That's not until next week.'

'Oh. Well, maybe I'll give him a ring.'

Much as she hated fibbing, sometimes you just had to.

'Great. If anyone can cheer Dad up, it's you.' Savannah beamed at Jessie, oblivious to her reluctance. 'Now, any chance of another crumpet? Are you just going to let that one burn to a frazzle, or can I eat it?'

It was a miracle the press hadn't caught on to the story earlier.

'Just to warn you,' Deborah said on the phone from London, 'I got doorstepped by a couple of hacks from the *Mirror* yesterday. They knew something was up, so I told them we'd separated. All very amicable, nobody else involved, blah blah.'

'Right,' Toby spoke without emotion. 'I'll tell my agent to release a statement. How's Dizzy?'

'You mean Kenneth Branagh?' Deborah sounded amused. 'Up in his bedroom rehearsing a speech from *Hamlet*. Do you know, he hasn't switched on his computer once since we moved in?'

The phone didn't stop ringing the next day. Tantalised by the blandness of the press release, journalists and photographers descended on Upper Sisley in their droves.

Toby, in no mood to speak to them, disconnected the doorbell and drew the curtains. It was a damp, cold day, not great for hanging around. Maybe, with nothing to report back to their editors, they would get bored and drift away.

When Jessie pulled up outside Duck Cottage at six o'clock, covered in cobalt-blue paint and desperate for a bath, there were three journalists in her overgrown front garden and a photographer snapping away at the back of the house.

'I know it's an easy mistake to make,' said Jessie, 'but this isn't a stately home and these grounds aren't actually open to the public.'

'Jess, over here!' The photographer waved an arm to attract her attention. 'No, no, stay by the van! *Great* van—'

'Jessie, what do you have to say about the break-up of Toby and Deborah Gillespie's marriage?'

'Are you having an affair with Toby Gillespie?'

'How long have you two been seeing each other?' the third journalist piped up. 'Was Deborah devastated when she found out?'

'Jessie, are you expecting Toby Gillespie's baby?'

Another car roared up the lane. Two more photographers jumped out, flash units going off like fireworks.

Jessie clapped her hand to the front of her baggy dungarees. Honestly, the one day she didn't wear a belt . . .

'Jessie, is this the fairytale ending you always dreamed of?'

'Jess, Jess! When's the baby due?'

Hastily dragging two turps-soaked cloths and an unopened bag of marshmallows out of her front pockets, Jessie sucked herself in and patted her now much flatter stomach.

There again, a few sit-ups wouldn't go amiss . . .

God, journalists were cruel. But a snapped-out 'No Comment' would only convince them she had something to hide.

'I am not pregnant. Nor am I having an affair with Toby Gillespie.' Jessie spoke slowly and clearly, like a teacher addressing a bunch of unruly five-year-olds. 'The break-up of Toby and Deborah's marriage has nothing to do with me.'

The difference was, a bunch of five-year-olds might have taken a bit of notice.

'Jessie, how does Deborah feel about you being pregnant?'

'How do you and Toby see your future together?'

'So Jess, in your opinion, is Toby Gillespie a better lover now than when he was a lad?'

'You aren't listening,' Jessie said. 'I've just told you, there *is* no affair. I haven't seen Toby Gillespie for weeks . . . What are you *doing*?' One of the photographers was hauling cans of emulsion out of the back of the van and arranging them at her feet.

'Props, love. Don't worry, I won't spill 'em. Now, you just hold the paintbrush, rest one foot on this tin and give us a saucy smile. Confessions of a Painter and Decorator, that kind of thing . . .'

'You can't be serious!' Jessie was tempted to grab one of the cans and do a bit of spilling herself, but she needed the emulsion to finish a job. 'Look, see that For Sale sign? I'm moving to Cornwall. If I was having an affair with Toby Gillespie,' she pleaded, 'I'd hardly go and live one hundred and fifty miles away, would I?'

'Turn to the left a bit, Jess! That your craving, is it – marshmallows? Hold the bag up . . . Are you two hoping for a girl or a boy?'

Jessie lost her temper. She picked up the cans of paint and began slinging them into the back of the van. 'Look, I'm not interested in Toby Gillespie. He matters about as much to me as, as this . . .' she gestured with derision at a huge yellow slug, squirming in the wet grass at her feet, '. . . this *slug*!' She marched into the house, hideously aware that the dungarees were still bagging around her stomach. Before she could slam the front door shut behind her, one of the journalists called out, 'Jess, are you and Toby planning to marry before the birth?'

The next morning, like an answer to a prayer, a nice man in his early fifties came to take a look at Duck Cottage.

His name was Bob Keogh and he was a chemical engineer. Jessie, who didn't have a clue what that meant – something to do with designing chemical toilets? – also discovered that he was a widower with a nineteen-year-old daughter and enough money in the bank, thanks to his wife's life insurance policy, to buy the place outright. She wondered if he'd bumped his wife off in order to get his hands on the cash.

Bob Keogh seemed charming, but then those wife-murdering types generally did.

Anyway, Jessie didn't care. He liked Duck Cottage and that was far more important.

'You aren't wild about the colours, are you?' She watched

his gaze flicker doubtfully across the bottle-green hall ceiling and ruby-red walls.

Bob Keogh blinked, ashamed. 'I'm sorry. I know it looks good, but it just isn't my cup of tea. Plain white walls, that's what I go for.'

Jessie was busy, but she was also desperate. 'If you decide to buy this cottage, I'll paint every inch of it white. Whatever you want, I'll do.' Well, paint-wise, anyway.

Bob Keogh was looking thoughtful. 'Could I take another peep at the garden?'

'I'll paint that white too,' Jessie offered. 'Now, how about a cup of tea? Jaffa Cake? Chocolate Hob-Nob?'

Chapter 69

Twenty-four hours later, two things happened almost simultaneously: one good, one bad.

The knock at the door came first. When Jessie went to answer it, she found Toby on the doorstep, grim-faced and clutching a newspaper.

Well, hardly the surprise of the century.

'Look, I'm sorry. I told them and told them I wasn't pregnant but they just kept *on* about it, and I'm not trying to fob you off but I really am late for work—'

'Jessie, stop gabbling. Have you seen this?'

In the kitchen the phone began to ring. 'No, I've only just got out of— oh, hang on.'

Jessie listened in a daze to Harry Norton, the estate agent in Harleston, burble smoothly on about offers and asking prices, searches and surveyors' fees.

It was a while before she could get a word in. 'You mean Bob Keogh wants to buy the cottage?'

'If you decide to accept his offer of one two five.' Harry tapped his pen against the receiver as he spoke. 'We're talking twelve grand off the asking price, Jess. Bit of a drop. You could certainly hold out for more, but that's Bob Keogh's final offer.' Sounding intensely disapproving, Harry added, 'He seems to think you'll take it, too. Told me you sounded pretty desperate.'

Twelve thousand less than I was hoping for, thought Jessie – it's a hell of a drop. Then again, I *am* desperate.

She looked down at the newspaper Toby had opened and spread out on the kitchen table in front of her. Hmm, even more desperate than I thought.

'So I suggest you take a few days to think about it . . .'

A huge picture of a yellow slug occupied the top half of page five. Below was a smaller one of Toby. On the facing page, a headline proclaimed: I KNOW WHICH ONE I'D RATHER SLEEP WITH, SAYS PAINT-JOB JESS.

Beneath it they had used one of the dungaree-cum-barrage-balloon pictures in which she not only looked six months gone but was sporting a double chin.

Filled with indignation, Jessie thought, but I don't *have* a double chin.

Do I?

'You never know, play hard to get and he might up it a couple of grand . . .'

Next to her, still hatchet-faced and not showing the least sign of being sympathetic, Toby waited for the phone-call to end.

All of a sudden Jessie was tempted to stay chatting to Smooth Harry for the next hour at least – about his new car, his last holiday, his favourite music, maybe even his whole life.

'Then again, he could find somewhere else . . .'

Jessie could feel Toby's breath on the back of her neck and it wasn't a comfortable sensation.

Oh Lord, he really was livid with her.

'One two five, that's fine,' she blurted into the phone. 'Tell Bob Keogh I accept. How soon can we complete?'

When the receiver had gone down, Toby stood in silence – for all the world like an exam invigilator – while she read every word of the piece in the paper. When she had finished he said slowly, 'I've thought you were a lot of things, Jess, but I never thought of you as a coward.'

'A coward!' She jabbed at the newspaper, outraged. 'What's so cowardly about this? God, what did you *expect* me to tell them?'

'I'm talking about selling the cottage.'

'Selling the cottage? Good grief!' Jessie wailed. 'Can you blame me? I can't wait to get out of here!' She gave the newspaper another jab for emphasis. 'Do you know what this makes me look like? A sad substitute . . . second best . . . a devoted groupie rushing to fill Deborah's shoes – even if they are two sizes smaller than mine!' She was shaking now, with anger and humiliation. 'Because that's what everyone's expecting to happen, isn't it? You, the village, the newspapers—'

'I want it to happen,' said Toby, 'you know I do. And no, it doesn't make you look like a substitute—'

'Oh get real!' Jessie snapped back. 'It's like having your top-of-the-range Mercedes stolen. You might have to make do for a while with some rusty old banger – and at the time you're glad of it, because anything is better than no car at all – but sooner or later you know you'll dump it. Either your stolen car turns up again or the insurance company pays out and you buy yourself a brand new one. And that's it – bye-bye old banger, it was fun while it lasted. Well, I don't need that kind of fun. And I'm moving down to Cornwall BECAUSE I WANT TO!'

Heavens, where had all that come from? From some dark, guilty corner of her subconscious, obviously.

Never mind, it was good.

'But you don't want to,' said Toby. 'You *can't*—'

'Look, anything that gets me away from this kind of hassle sounds great to me.' Prodding was no longer enough; grabbing the paper, Jessie ripped it to shreds. 'Because I don't need it, Toby! I don't need people sniggering about me behind my back—'

'Jess, it's okay, calm down. It's just journalists, desperate to make something out of nothing.'

'Hah!'

Toby heaved a sigh. This wasn't why he'd come here. They were on the same side, for God's sake. It was the press he was furious with, not Jess. She'd done her best. She simply didn't have the experience to deal with them.

'You should have said "No Comment".'

How bloody patronising could you get?

'Oh yes! That would have done the world of good,' Jessie yelled, still shredding bits of newspaper and flinging them to the floor. 'They ask me if I'm pregnant with your child and I say No Comment!' Seething with indignation she cried,

'Even *I* know that people only say No Comment when the answer is yes. Jesus, I'm amazed *you* haven't asked me if I'm pregnant!'

Toby looked at her.

For a second he forgot to breathe.

'Are you?'

'NO!'

With an effort, Toby recovered himself. 'Look, it's a tabloid newspaper.' He gestured at the shreds of newsprint whirling around the kitchen like confetti. 'I know you didn't say any of this stuff.'

He was off to Los Angeles tomorrow and Jessie was glad. She could sell the cottage and be out of Upper Sisley before he got back.

'Ah well, that's where you're wrong,' she said bitterly, 'because the quote about the slug was true.'

Brrrrr-brrrrrugh-brrruggh.

Eleanor Ferguson exhaled slowly, removed her hand-knitted gloves and sat up a little straighter in the driver's seat of her highly polished Mini Metro. She turned the key in the ignition once more and willed the car to start.

Brrrrrrr-brrugh-bruuuugghh

For heaven's sake – today of all days! Why did cars always have to let you down when you had to be somewhere and couldn't afford to be late?

Grimly determined, Eleanor let off the handbrake and allowed the car to roll forwards down the sloping drive. The moment she reached the lane she would slam it into gear and hopefully it would bump-start.

Clu-unk.

Eleanor's mouth narrowed with annoyance. This was ridiculous – now she was stuck out in the middle of the road in pouring rain. Furthermore, it was only eight fifteen in the morning, which meant that there was no point even trying to phone the garage in Lower Sisley because it didn't open until nine o'clock.

Relief at hearing the sound of an approaching car turned to irritation when Eleanor saw who was driving it.

Drew Darcy, her daughter-in-law's fancy man. Well, that was just typical. Having made a particular point of not speaking to Drew since that sordid little liaison had come to light, she certainly wasn't about to ask him for help now.

The car slowed to a halt. Eleanor kept her gaze pointedly averted.

But moments later Drew was grinning at her through the driver's window, motioning her to open it.

'Problems?'

'Nothing I can't handle.' Eleanor spoke through stiff lips.

'Well, you're blocking the lane. Shall I give you a hand moving it?'

This was intolerable. Eleanor managed a curt nod and gripped the steering wheel.

Several seconds later Drew reappeared at the window. 'Actually, it helps if you free the hand-brake.'

Oh.

And it got worse, far worse.

'There you go,' Drew announced when the Metro had been manoeuvred to the side of the road, and it wasn't until Eleanor turned around that she realised he hadn't been the only one pushing the car.

'I heard you trying to start it.' Bernadette Thomas sounded almost apologetic. She was wearing a dark-blue kagoul and her face was wet with rain. 'If you put the bonnet up, I'll take a look. Could be the carburettor, or damp plugs.'

Eleanor, who had spent the last few weeks pointedly ignoring her next-door neighbour too, was tempted to say, 'No thank you, I would prefer to call the garage.' But this was her morning running the WRVS canteen at Harleston General and she had to be there by nine o'clock to open up. Nobody else could do it; she had the keys.

Unable to speak, she released the bonnet catch and climbed jerkily out of the car.

'I'm not great at this,' Drew was saying, his green Barbour already drenched and his unruly hair dripping into his eyes. But Bernadette was already busy checking leads with capable fingers.

'It's probably something straightforward. I spent a year on vehicle maintenance during my army days. Hmm, H-T lead seems okay. Right, let's have a look at these points . . .'

They were still trying to get the car started twenty minutes later. The rain was coming down in sheets now, whipped to an angle by the ferocious October wind.

Eleanor was in an agony of indecision. Every time she tried to say, 'Look, it doesn't matter, I'll phone the garage,' Bernadette and Drew dismissed her awkward protest and carried on working together, plunging their hands into the depths of the engine like surgeons in search of a lost swab.

'Can't get any wetter than this,' Drew told her cheerfully. 'May as well see the job through.'

The sense of obligation was crushing. Finally, unable to bear it a second longer, Eleanor blurted out, 'Let me ring for a taxi. I need to be at work by nine.'

Drew lifted his head above bonnet level.

'Why didn't you say? I'll give you a lift.'

'Really, there's no need—'

'Don't be daft. I'm not the chief mechanic here anyway.' He winked – ugh, actually winked – at Bernadette. 'I'm just the useless apprentice. Where d'you need to go?'

Only the thought of staff and patients waiting impatiently for the canteen to open forced Eleanor to reply. She couldn't, she just *couldn't* let them down. 'Harleston General. I run the WRVS shop two days a week.'

Drew nodded, wiping his oily hands on one of her pristine tea towels. 'The General. Where Doug used to work.'

'Where April works,' Bernadette added mildly.

'Who's April?' asked Drew.

'My ex-wife.'

Eleanor stiffened.

Glancing up at her, Bernadette said, 'She uses the WRVS shop from time to time.'

'I know.'

April was someone else Eleanor pointedly ignored.

'Right, it's a quarter to.' Shaking the rain out of his hair, Drew opened the passenger door of his own car and ushered Eleanor inside. 'Let's get you to work. Bernadette, okay if I leave you to it?'

'No problem.'

As Drew pulled away, Eleanor looked back at Bernadette, working diligently away beneath the bonnet of the Metro.

'Don't worry, she'll soon have your car fixed,' Drew told her with a grin. 'Bernadette's a good bloke.'

Four hours later, Eleanor was heaping doughnuts and flapjack on to plates when she saw April Thomas come into the canteen.

'Hello,' April said shyly, and because Eleanor was the only person behind the counter she was forced to mutter 'Hello' back.

Nervously, April pushed her short hair behind her ears. 'I'm April Thomas, Bernie's—'

'Yes yes, I know,' Eleanor blurted out before she could say the words aloud.

'Um . . . Bernie's just rung. He asked me to come over and let you know he's – sorry, *she's* – managed to fix the car.'

'Oh. Right.'

'It was something to do with the carburettor, apparently, but I couldn't tell you what.' April blushed and smiled. 'I'm useless with cars.'

Eleanor wondered guiltily if it had taken all this time – over four hours – to get her Metro going again. It was still bucketing down outside.

'Well, it was very good of . . . er, Bernadette. I'm most grateful.' Oh dear, she so hated to be the beholden one; she much preferred being the beholder. 'And . . . er, thank you for coming to let me know.'

'Actually, I'll have a doughnut now I'm here,' said April. 'You shut at four o'clock, don't you?'

'That's right.'

'I thought so. Bernie wanted to know.' April chose an apple doughnut and gave Eleanor thirty pence. 'She said she'll pick you up at five past four.'

★ ★ ★

'This is most kind of you. I could have caught the bus.'

'No problem,' Bernadette replied easily. 'Anyway, it's still raining.'

It was indeed, it was a filthy grey afternoon. As the temperature outside plummeted the rain intermittently turned to sleet.

A nice warming lamb casserole, thought Eleanor as they lapsed into silence. That's what I'll make when I get home. And steamed syrup pudding with custard.

'Would you mind stopping at the next rank of shops?' she asked Bernadette.

Emerging from the off-licence with a half-bottle of whisky – she didn't buy a whole one, it wouldn't do to encourage alcoholism – Eleanor said with a touch of asperity, 'It isn't for me, it's for Drew Darcy.'

Bernadette nodded. 'He seems charming.'

'Mm.'

'Your grandchildren adore him. I'm sorry,' Bernadette hesitated, 'I know your loyalties must lie with your son. It can't be easy for you.'

'It's hardly an ideal situation,' Eleanor admitted with reluctance. 'But at least the children are happy.' She sighed. 'I suppose it could be worse.'

They drove the rest of the way in silence. When Bernadette pulled up outside the cottages, Eleanor reached for her purse. 'I must give you something too. For the lift, and for mending my car.'

'Absolutely not.' Bernadette was firm. 'That's what neighbours are for.'

Even, it seemed, if your neighbour was a man in a dress and an ex-army boxer to boot.

Oh dear, how times have changed, thought Eleanor. Things like this simply didn't happen in my day. Although – irony of ironies – until she had made this bizarre discovery, she had actually liked Bernadette.

'In that case,' she spoke awkwardly, 'you must come over for supper tonight. I'm making a lamb casserole and steamed syrup pudding.'

Heavens, an olive branch. From Eleanor Ferguson.

In fact, never mind an olive branch, practically a whole tree.

Supper with Eleanor was hardly her idea of a relaxing evening. But under the circumstances, thought Bernadette, how can I refuse?

She hesitated. 'Really? Are you sure?'

Relief flooded through Eleanor. No longer beholden, she was back in charge.

So people in the village thought she was narrow-minded, did they? Well she'd soon show them.

Grandly she announced, 'I insist.'

Chapter 70

Jessie stood in the middle of the empty living room and gazed around her ex-home.

The papers were completed and Duck Cottage was no longer hers. It belonged to Bob Keogh and he had the newly painted walls and ceilings to prove it.

Which helped, in a way, because three coats of white vinyl silk emulsion throughout meant it no longer even faintly resembled Duck Cottage.

Instead of a bright purple cotton sweater, ripped orange jeans and a can of lukewarm Tizer, Jessie felt she should be wearing something white and elegant and sipping a glass of milk.

A resounding crash upstairs made her jump. The next moment Oliver clattered downstairs with a tea chest in his arms.

'Are you going to just stand there all day?' he panted, lugging the heavy chest into the hall. 'Or do you think you might be able to give me a hand?'

Jessie mustered a smile. 'Me? Your poor frail old mother?'

'I just dropped a bookcase on my foot up there,' Oliver grumbled.

'Have some Tizer. It's okay, the removals van won't be here for another hour. Actually, I thought I'd pop over to Lili's, say my goodbyes.'

'You've already been over to Lili's.' Oliver checked his watch. 'You said goodbye to her at ten o'clock.'

'I know, but Will was asleep then. He'll be awake now.'

But when she closed the front door behind her, Jessie didn't head across the village green towards The Old

Vicarage. Instead she found herself turning right along Compass Lane. As she passed Keeper's Cottage she heard a squeal of laughter coming from one of the open bedroom windows. Recognising the squeal as one of Savannah's – so she and Stevie were still at it like rabbits – Jessie walked on. With Toby still away filming in the States, that meant Sisley House was currently unoccupied.

When she reached the stone pillared entrance to the house she turned into it without even knowing why.

Walked slowly up to the leaf-strewn driveway without knowing why.

Stood at the top of the drive and gazed at the front of the house without kn—

Oh come on, who am I trying to kid? thought Jessie despairingly. Talk about pathetic delusions.

Dammit, *of course I know why*!

Anyway, what did it matter how pathetic she was being? There was no one to see her, the house was empty.

No more Deborah.

No more Dizzy.

No Savannah, who was far too busy next door having rip-roaring sex with gorgeous Stevie Harper.

And no Toby.

Who was also gorgeous . . .

And in America.

Her body ached with misery.

The house was empty.

Oh dear, thought Jessie as she blinked back tears, like my heart.

It was naff, but she couldn't help it. Knowing that you couldn't have someone – or that you could have them but it would be a relationship doomed to end in failure – didn't stop you loving them so much it hurt.

Nobody else had ever come close. No other man had meant a millionth as much to her as Toby Gillespie. She'd tried her hardest to find one, but it simply hadn't happened.

And I was tempted, Jessie finally admitted to herself, her scalp prickling with yearning and shame. I was so tempted to make a complete fool of myself and just go for it.

Knowing it wouldn't last.

Knowing that after a few months Toby would say, 'Look, it's been great, *but* . . .'

Knowing that he would move onwards and upwards, and find himself someone more famous and glamorous, someone infinitely more fitting for a film star of his stature.

Knowing that she would be left feeling a hundred times worse than she did now, and that behind her back people would be smirking and sniggering to each other, 'Well what did she expect?'

Oh shit, this was no good. The tears were coming thick and fast now and the last thing she needed was to be spotted emerging from Toby's driveway with blotchy cheeks and piggy eyes.

A sycamore seed, helicoptering down from an overhanging tree, landed on Jessie's head. Trying to disentangle it, she managed to pull out the old green pop sock she had used as a makeshift ribbon to tie back her unbrushed hair.

A bloody pop sock, for heavens sake!

If I were Deborah Gillespie, Jessie thought as she wiped her eyes with it, it would be a seven denier, Christian Dior, sheer black stocking.

'The solicitor just phoned,' Oliver announced when she arrived back at the cottage. 'He wants you to get over there as soon as you can to sign the completion papers.'

'He said three o'clock.'

'Change of plan. He's got a will reading in Cheltenham at two.'

Jessie sighed. Oh well, get it over and done with.

'Can you manage here on your own?'

His look told her that he had spent most of the morning managing on his own. 'I'll do my best.'

'Don't forget to label the crates.'

Oliver frowned. 'Have you been crying?'

'Me? Don't be daft.' Jessie reached hurriedly past him for the keys to the van. 'One of those sycamore things flew into my eye.'

★ ★ ★

434

Since she had to follow the removals lorry down to Cornwall, Jessie stopped at the garage on the outskirts of Harleston to give the van a once-over. It was boring, but not as boring as breaking down on the M5.

She filled up with petrol, squished air into the tyres, topped up the water and checked the oil. An uncharacteristic fit of conscience prompted her to put the van through the car wash. Well, it was indescribably filthy, and someone – probably Oliver – had written something rude to that effect across the back.

Anyway, that was why she was going, wasn't it? To make a clean start.

Sitting inside the van with soapy water streaming over it and the massive rollers thundering down the windscreen, Jessie didn't see Oliver's car race past the garage on its way into Harleston.

The removals lorry had arrived. Orders had been placed for tea. Oliver was heaping sugar into mugs when there was a knock on the kitchen door behind him. Expecting an overweight removals man with builder's bum and a swallow tattooed on his neck, he said, 'Coming up,' and was taken aback when he realised he was talking instead to a fragile girl with short black hair and slanting green eyes.

'Sorry,' she grinned at Oliver, 'the front door was open and a chap with a tattoo told me to come on through. I'm Sammy Keogh, by the way. Bob's daughter.' The unrepentant grin broadened. 'And I drink mine black with no sugar.'

She was gorgeous. A mischievous, emerald-eyed vision.

Oliver was instantly smitten.

'Right. I'm Oliver Roscoe. And you're . . . um, early.'

The green eyes sparkled. 'I drove down from Manchester, it didn't take as long as I expected. This is the first chance I've had to see my new home.'

'Hang on.' Hastily Oliver grabbed the mugs of tea. 'Back in a sec.'

When he returned, Sammy Keogh had refilled the kettle and was tapping her fingers restlessly on the worktop, waiting for it to boil. She was wearing a pale grey granddad vest and red Levi's, with a Manchester University sweatshirt tied around her narrow hips.

She studied him in turn, her head tilted appraisingly to one side. 'So, don't tell me, you're the only decent-looking guy in the village.'

'What?'

Oliver tried not to laugh.

'Story of my life.' Sammy heaved a sigh of resignation. 'Just as I move down here, you're moving away. We'll never see each other again.'

'You probably will, actually. My Dad still lives here, so I'll be coming back.'

'Great!' Her smile lit up her heart-shaped face. 'When, for Christmas?'

Oliver explained about his year off, back-packing around Europe. Happily the fridge hadn't yet been loaded into the van and there were still a couple of bottles of beer languishing at the back, waiting to be drunk. He talked about the countries he'd be visiting and showed Sammy over the cottage, determinedly ignoring the winks and nudges and leering grins of the removals men as they carted wardrobes noisily down the stairs.

'You're so lucky, it sounds brilliant.'

Sammy pushed her fingers through her dark hair, ruffling it into spikes as they wandered out into the front garden. The look of restlessness had returned to her eyes; something was clearly bothering her.

She smelled wonderful, like a bowl of freesias. Oliver, fighting the urge to kiss her neck, said, 'What's wrong?'

'Oh God, I'm just not used to being somewhere so *quiet*. I've never lived in a village before.' Her outstretched arm swept in an arc, encompassing the green and the collection of Cotswold stone houses surrounding it. She turned and gazed frustratedly at Oliver. 'I mean, how have you managed not to die of boredom? Does anything interesting ever *happen* around here?'

Chapter 71

There were never any spaces in the solicitor's minuscule car park, so Jessie left the van around the corner.

Well, this was it. Yesterday she had signed one set of completion papers, for Duck Cottage. Now she was here to sign the second lot. Once that was done, the house in Cornwall would be hers.

Wishing she could feel a bit more enthusiastic about the move, Jessie rounded the corner.

The first thing she saw was Oliver's battered black VW Beetle crammed into the already full car park, blocking in a couple of sleek BMWs with personalised plates.

God, what was Oliver doing here? Something awful must have happened—

The second thing she saw was Toby in the driver's seat.

Jessie froze. This couldn't be happening, it definitely couldn't be happening.

Toby was in America.

Except he wasn't. He was here. Looking at her and stepping out of Oliver's ancient car.

'You're late.'

Jessie's legs were shaking. She didn't have knees any more, she had castanets.

'What?'

'You left home forty minutes ago.' He checked his watch. 'Oliver said you were coming straight here. I left fifteen minutes after you and I still got here first.'

Is this an hallucination? Jessie wondered. Am I finally cracking up?

But hallucination or otherwise, Toby clearly expected an answer.

'Um . . . car wash.'

As they gazed at each other somebody inside the solicitor's offices tapped on a window, furiously indicating to Toby that he couldn't leave that heap of rust there.

Toby calmly ignored them.

'Car wash. Of course.'

Jessie's mouth was as dry as a sand pit. She tried to lick her lips. 'You're supposed to be in Los Angeles.'

'Flew back this morning.'

'Why? Did you get sacked?'

He almost – *almost* – smiled.

'O ye of little faith . . . Actually, I told them it was an emergency and I had to get back.'

'You told Steven Spielberg it was an emergency? How did he take it?'

Jessie was joking. Toby wasn't.

He shrugged. 'Pretty well. He said they could shoot around me for a couple of days. That's all he could give me, forty-eight hours. Still, long enough for me to find out one way or another what I need to know.'

The sash window behind him thudded open. A cross-looking secretary stuck her head out.

'Excuse me, you *have* to move that vehicle.'

'In a minute,' said Toby, 'I'm busy.'

The woman bristled. 'I'm warning you, if you don't move your car, our security guard will do it for you.'

Toby turned and smiled at her. 'He will? That's really kind. Thanks.'

The secretary's jaw dropped open. Jessie heard her whisper frantically, 'My God, it's Toby *Gillespie*.'

The next moment the window slammed shut.

'Look, I still don't know what you're doing here.'

Jessie's legs felt really peculiar, but if she tried to lean against one of the gleaming cars she was bound to set off some kind of screeching alarm.

'I've changed my mind about you. I don't think running off to Cornwall is a cowardly thing to do,' said Toby. 'I think it's brave. Misguided,' he added, 'but still brave.'

'It's n-neither,' Jessie stammered, 'I just want to, that's all.'

Toby ignored this. 'You love me, but you don't trust me. You see, that's the difference between us, Jess. I love you *and* I trust you. I've always loved you, more than you'll ever know. If anyone was the substitute, if anyone was ever second best,' he went on slowly, 'it was Deborah.'

Oh, this was too much. This wasn't fair. It was too *late* . . .

'The solicitor's waiting for me.' Jessie, her feet like jelly, tried to move towards the building's glass-fronted entrance. 'I've got to sign the completion papers.'

'Don't do it.'

'I have to! Duck Cottage is already sold. The removals men will be there by now!'

'I flew into Heathrow this morning.' Toby shook his head. 'I caught a cab home. I didn't know how I was going to persuade you to change your mind about leaving but I knew I had to try. And then I saw you standing outside my house and I didn't know what that meant either—'

'You were *there*?' Jessie gasped, dumbstruck. 'You mean you were there all the time, *watching* me?'

'Not all the time. I glanced out of the window and saw you, and I thought you might be crying but I wasn't sure.'

'I wasn't crying!' Jessie blurted out defensively. 'And if you saw me, why didn't you do anything? Why didn't you come out?'

'I had no idea why you were there.' Again, Toby nearly smiled. 'I half expected you to hurl eggs at the windows. But I didn't have a chance to react; the next thing I knew, you'd disappeared. And by the time I reached the cottage you were on your way here.'

Jessie couldn't take it in. Wearily she shook her head. 'It's still too late. I have to sign the papers.'

A muscle was twitching in Toby's jaw. 'This house in Cornwall. Does it overlook the sea?'

Wondering how this could be relevant, Jessie nodded.

'Okay. In that case we'll sign. I've always fancied a holiday home in Cornwall anyway.'

'*You've* always fancied a holiday home?' Jessie was struggling to keep up. What was he saying now – that he wanted to buy the house off her? Thoroughly confused, she stammered, 'B-but then where would *I* live?'

Dimly aware that they were being watched – a sea of faces had by this time appeared at the window behind them – Jessie stayed where she was and let Toby come to her.

He took her hands and looked into her stricken eyes.

'With me, of course. Sod the press. Sod what you think everyone else is thinking. I love you, Jess, and I'm pretty sure you love me too. What's more, when you've felt this way about someone for over twenty years, it's no flash in the pan. I want to spend the rest of my life with you. And if it helps at all,' he added drily, 'Steven Spielberg wants me to spend the rest of my life with you too.'

Jessie broke into something half-way between laughter and a sob. 'Truly?'

'Truly. I had to tell him all about you.'

'Name-dropper.'

'I'll stop at nothing.' Toby's hands were in her hair. 'Now, is that a yes?'

How could it not be?

Jessie nodded and breathed out slowly and at last, at long last, her knees relaxed and stopped doing their castanet impression. It felt blissfully, idyllically, like coming home. Not to Cornwall, but to Upper Sisley.

Well, sometimes to Cornwall. For long weekends . . . and whenever they could get away . . .

Reading her mind, Toby said, 'We'd better go inside, sign those papers.'

Jessie nodded, loving the idea already. A holiday home would be great.

'And give Oliver a ring. Tell him to send the removals van round to my place,' Toby went on. 'Until we sort ourselves out.'

Oh to be a fly on the wall in Myrtle Armitage's shop, thought Jessie, when word got out that she had moved into Sisley House.

'I can't believe this is happening.'

She clung to him, pressing herself against him, wanting to feel every inch of his body touching hers. Hmm . . . she wiggled her hips – was that a gun in his pocket or was he just pleased to see her?

Although, if it was a gun, wasn't it a bit . . . um, small?

Once again, miraculously, Toby appeared to guess what she was thinking.

'Ah yes,' he murmured, putting his hand in his pocket and taking out the rolled-up green pop sock he had found lying in his driveway earlier. 'I believe this belongs to you.'

Perfect Timing

To Lydia and Cory, with my love.
Special thanks as well to Postman Pat and Sooty,
without whose videos this book would have
taken twice as long to write.
Thanks also to Abby, my favourite step-daughter,
for all her help.

Chapter 1

The thing about going out on your hen night, Poppy Dunbar couldn't help noticing, was that nobody – but nobody – bothered to chat you up.

It possibly had something to do with the three inflated condoms tethered to the top of her hat and the L-plate hung around her neck, sending out the signal: 'Don't bother, boys.' She was about as off-limits as it was possible to get. All of a sudden – as far as men were concerned – she had become invisible. It felt weird, after years of nightclubbing and being chatted up. She'd never actually been unfaithful to Rob, of course, but it was still nice to be noticed.

'Tell me about it.' Dina, when Poppy had passed this observation on earlier, was able to sympathise. 'I'm in the same boat, aren't I?' She pulled a gloomy face. 'Nobody makes a pass at you when you're nine months pregnant. It's like being a nun.'

Not that Dina was in too much danger of being mistaken for a nun right now, not while she was smack in the middle of the dance floor giving it all she'd got. At her request the club DJ was playing the old Madonna song, 'Like a Virgin'. Dina's white Lycra skirt was edging its way up to mid-thigh and her black patent high heels reflected the fluorescent lights zapping and crisscrossing overhead.

For a pregnant nun she was doing pretty well, thought Poppy. If her husband Ben could see her now he'd have a fit. Dina's dance style bordered on the frenzied; much more of it and she would go into labour. If that happened she would miss both the wedding and her chance to wear her new pink straw hat. Oh dear, Poppy thought with amusement, what a wicked waste of twenty-two pounds ninety-nine that would be. Ben would be furious.

Poppy left her three fellow hens to it and made her way to the loo. Determined not to be hungover at her own wedding she had spent the night on 7-Up, which was going through her like Niagara Falls.

'Don't do it, pet,' said one girl, eyeing the hat and L-plate and rolling her eyes in mock-horror as she squeezed past Poppy.

'Getting married and not even pregnant,' teased another, 'there's posh.'

Studying her reflection in the mirror as she washed her hands, Poppy thought: Damn, I look a prat in this hat.

It would be more than her life was worth, though, to take it off. This was the ritual, the way things were done. Out on your hen night you were supposed to look daft and anyone who didn't was a complete killjoy. The girls would never forgive her.

Silly hat intact, Poppy emerged from the loos and began making her way back through the heaving masses. The dance floor, over to the left, was by this time as jam-packed as those Japanese commuter trains where everyone got levered in by merciless guards.

The air was stifling, smoky and multi-perfumed. Poppy turned right instead and threaded her way between tables. Double doors at the back of the club led down a flight of stone steps and out into a walled garden.

It was a heavenly summer evening. The sky was bright with stars. What she needed, Poppy decided, was five minutes outside before Dina and the girls realised she was missing out on all the fun.

Halfway down the broad stone staircase she passed a couple, arm in arm, heading back inside. With his free hand the boy was lighting a Silk Cut. Just for fun, once the cigarette was lit, he brushed it against Poppy's hat. One after

2

the other, like gunfire, two of the condoms exploded. Poppy, taken by surprise, promptly lost her balance and tumbled down the last few steps. With a squeal she landed in a heap on the grass at the bottom.

It was all highly undignified. Her skirt flew up and her L-plate ricocheted off her chin. The big toe on her left foot hurt like anything. Only her stupid hat remained intact.

People were staring. At the top of the steps the boy with the cigarette looked aggrieved. 'That's not my fault,' he told his girlfriend. 'I mean, it's not as if I *pushed* her.'

'Silly sod,' his girlfriend replied in loving tones. 'Come on, your round. I'll have a double rum-and-black.'

'It's okay, I've got you,' said a male voice. Poppy, who was busy cursing under her breath and tugging her skirt down, felt a supporting arm go around her waist. The voice went on, 'I don't think anything's broken. Can you make it over to that bench?'

She found herself being helped to her feet and led across the lawn by someone whose rumpled dark curls gave him the look of a wayward cherub. A cherub with cheekbones. His eyes, so dark they seemed black, were in marked contrast with his white shirt. He was tall, Poppy registered, and thin, and extremely brown. As he lowered her onto the wooden bench she also noticed very white teeth, two of them endearingly crooked, and a quirky infectious smile.

'Thanks.' Grateful to have her dignity at least semi-restored, Poppy straightened her L-plate. 'As if I wasn't already feeling daft enough.'

'I'm afraid your accessories have had it.' He indicated the burst condoms now dangling limply from the brim of her hat. 'I hope you weren't saving them for a special occasion.' He paused for a second, his dark eyes searching Poppy's face. 'When is it? The wedding?'

It was the weirdest sensation ever. Quite suddenly Poppy felt as if she'd known him all her life. Her breath caught in her throat.

'Tomorrow.' This was ridiculous; her heart was doing some kind of frantic can-can in her chest. In an effort to distract herself from the strangeness of what seemed to be going on, she bent down and pulled off one shoe. 'Looks like I'll be hopping down the aisle. I must have landed on my big toe. If it swells up I'm sunk.'

'My name's Tom, by the way.'

'Right. Tom. I'm—'

'Poppy. I know. I heard your pregnant friend say it earlier.'

Poppy, seldom at a loss for words, could only sit and watch as he reached for her foot, held it in the palm of his hand and carefully inspected her poor bruised toe.

'You'll live,' he finally pronounced.

'Ah, but will I limp?'

He smiled and Poppy's stomach turned over. Ye gods, she thought helplessly, what's *happening* here?

'It isn't swollen enough to be broken. We could put a cold compress on it if you like. Either that or cancel the wedding.'

'And give my future mother-in-law a nervous breakdown,' Poppy joked feebly, wondering when she was going to start feeling normal again. 'Please. Five hundred sausage rolls are baking as we speak.'

Several feet from where they sat was a lily pond with a small fountain. Tom took a dark blue handkerchief from his pocket and held it in the stream of water splashing down from the stone statue of a frog. Returning to the bench he rested Poppy's bare foot across his knee and wrapped the handkerchief around the injured toe. Without even thinking Poppy took off her hat and L-plate.

He glanced sideways at her. 'Won't your friends be wondering where you are?'

'Probably.' Poppy no longer cared. 'Won't yours?'

'Mine have left. I came down from London for the weekend,' Tom explained, 'to stay with my brother and his girlfriend. About an hour ago they launched into the most tremendous argument. The thing is with their fights, they're great ones for throwing plates at each other. So when they rushed off home,' he concluded with amusement, 'I thought I'd better stay put for a while. Leave them to it.'

He's from London and I've definitely never seen him before, thought Poppy in a daze. How, when I know absolutely nothing about this man, can I feel as if I've known him for years?

Tom slowly massaged her instep as he spoke. 'Of course, now I'm glad I stayed.'

'You are? You mean you have a thing about feet?'

He laughed. 'Maybe that too. Damn. Is this seriously bad timing or what?'

Poppy's heart did another ungainly flip-flop. If he meant what she thought he meant it was exactly what had been going through her mind too. Except that this whole thing was ridiculously far-fetched. A spot of instant mutual attraction was one thing, but actually falling in love – really in love – with a total stranger couldn't possibly exist. Could it?

It's a nervous reaction, she told herself, a subconscious last-minute panic. I'm just grateful someone's paying me a bit of attention at last, even if I did have to mangle my toe to get it.

'I wish you weren't getting married tomorrow,' said Tom.

'Coo-eee! There you are.'

Yelling over the heads of the dozen or so people separating them, Dina clattered down the flight of steps in her ludicrous high heels. Poppy whipped her foot off Tom's lap.

'Hiding away,' Dina chided, inspecting Tom with interest. 'Whatever are you doing out here? And who are you?'

'Your friend fell down the steps. She thought she might have broken her ankle,' said Tom. 'I'm a doctor.'

Poppy stared at him. 'You are?'

He grinned.

'Poppy, you're hopeless.' Dina turned once more to Tom. 'Well, *is* it broken?'

'No.'

'Good. So I can drag her back onto the dance floor.'

Dismayed, Poppy said, 'Oh but—'

'Come on now, no excuses.' Dina had her by the arm. She smirked. 'You don't have a leg to stand on.'

'But my toe,' wailed Poppy, who more than anything else in the world wanted to stay outside. 'It *hurts*.'

Dina rolled her eyes. 'If you think that hurts, try having a baby.'

'Maybe you should,' Tom said quietly. He was no longer smiling. 'Go back inside, I mean. I'm sorry about . . . you know, just now. I shouldn't have said it.'

'Said what?' Dina demanded.

'He told me I looked a prat in a hat,' lied Poppy, standing up at last and realising he was right. She had to go inside and pretend this encounter had never taken place. She had to look as if she was having heaps of fun. And tomorrow she had to marry Rob McBride.

'Go on.' Tom's coal-black eyes hadn't left her face. His smile was bleak. 'Happy wedding and all that.'

''Bye.' Poppy bit her lip.

'Quick!' screeched Dina, almost yanking her arm out of its socket as a change of music filtered out through the double doors. 'Gary Glitter, my *favourite*.'

Her big toe still hurt like crazy but Poppy no longer cared. She had danced non-stop for the past hour, forcing herself not to think of Tom. He had gone, anyway. She had seen him leave. It had just been one of those mad moments and now it was over. She was going to concentrate on real life instead.

By ten to two the DJ was winding up for the night. The last three or four records were always slow ones. Susie and Jen were dancing with two brothers who claimed, somewhat dodgily, to be airline pilots. Dina was massaging her aching ankles under cover of their table. She gave Poppy a hefty nudge. Poppy, who was hunting in the bottom of her bag for money for the taxi, didn't look up.

6

'Oh doctor I'm in trouble,' sang Dina. She didn't sound a bit like Sophia Loren.

'What?'

'That chap who couldn't keep his hands off your foot.' Triumphantly, she watched Poppy's head jerk up. 'Hmm. Looks like he can't keep away either.'

'You're having me on.'

'If you want to dance, dance.' Dina looked smug. 'Don't mind me.'

The last record of the night was 'Lady in Red'.

'Thank God you aren't wearing something red,' said Tom. 'That really would have been too kitsch for words.'

Poppy, whose heart was going nineteen to the dozen, didn't tell him she had red knickers on.

She said, 'I thought you'd left.'

'I did. Then I came back. I had to.' Tilting his head he murmured into her ear, 'I want you to know I don't make a habit of this. It isn't some kind of bizarre hobby of mine, in case you were wondering.'

Over his shoulder Poppy saw Jen and one of the airline pilots cruising at low altitude towards them. Jen winked.

'Watch what you're doing with my future cousin-in-law,' she instructed Tom. 'By this time tomorrow she'll be an old married woman. We're under instruction to keep our eye on her tonight.'

This is awful, thought Poppy, beginning to panic as the song moved into its final chorus. Any minute now the night will be over, it'll be time to leave. How can this be happening to me? I need more *time*—

In a low voice Tom said, 'Will your friends miss you if we sneak out now?'

'Of *course* they will.' Close to despair Poppy felt her fingers dig helplessly into his arms. 'Dina's already phoned for a cab to take us home.'

'Okay, I'll leave it up to you.' He shook back a lock of curling dark hair, studying her face intently for a second.

7

'Delgado's, that all-night café on Milton Street. You know the one, directly opposite the university?'

Poppy nodded, unable to speak.

'I'll wait there. Until three o'clock. If you want to see me, that's where I'll be. If you don't . . . well, you won't turn up.'

'This isn't funny.' Poppy realised she was trembling. 'I'm not enjoying this. I'm hating it.'

'You mean you wish you hadn't met me?' Just for a second Tom traced a finger lightly down the side of her quivering face. 'Fine, if that's how you feel. If it's how you *really* feel. Go home. Get a good night's sleep. Carry on as if tonight never happened. Get married——'

'Our taxi,' Susie declared with a melodramatic flourish, 'is waiting.' She passed Poppy her handbag and began to steer her in the direction of the door. Glancing from Poppy to Tom and back again she chanted, 'Ladies and gentlemen, your time is up. No more flirting, no more smoochy dances with handsome strangers, no more scribbling your phone number in Biro on the back of his hand and praying it doesn't rain on the way home. The girl is no longer available. Tomorrow, she gets hitched.'

Chapter 2

The journey from the centre of Bristol back to Henbury at two in the morning normally took ten minutes. This time the trip was punctuated with a whole series of stops and starts.

It's worse than musical bloody chairs, thought Poppy, willing herself not to scream as Jen, spotting a still-open burger bar, begged the driver to pull up outside. Susie had already sent him on a convoluted tour of local cash dispensers in search of one that worked. If Dina announced that she needed to find yet another public loo, Poppy knew she would have a complete nervous breakdown. At this rate it would be four o'clock before they even arrived home.

But they made it, finally. Dina, with her stressed bladder, was dropped off first. Then Susie, then Jen. Kissing each of them goodbye in turn, Poppy wondered how they would react if they knew what was racing through her mind. Jen was Rob's cousin, Dina his sister-in-law. Only an hour or so ago Susie had confided tipsily, 'If I could meet and marry someone even half as nice as your Rob I'd be *so happy*.'

'Edgerton Close is it, love?' asked the taxi driver over his shoulder when only Poppy was left in the car.

Poppy looked at her watch for the fiftieth time. Quarter to three. She took a deep breath.

'Delgado's, Milton Street. Opposite the university. Hurry, please.'

Delgado's was a trendy post-nightclub hangout popular with students and diehard clubbers alike. Poppy, who had visited it a few times in the past, knew its atmosphere to be far more of a draw than the food.

But with its white painted exterior and glossy dark blue shutters it certainly looked the part. On a night like tonight Poppy knew it would be even busier than usual, packed with people showing off their tans, making the most of the perfect weather while it lasted and pretending they weren't in Bristol but in the south of France.

As her taxi drew up outside Poppy wondered just how stupid she would feel if she went inside and he wasn't there. She looked again at her watch. One minute to three.

Then she saw him, sitting alone at one of the sought-after tables in the window. He was lounging back on his chair idly stirring sugar into an espresso and smoking a cigarette.

Poppy's pulse began to race. Twelve hours from now she was due to walk down the aisle of St Mary's church on her father's arm. Twelve and a bit hours from now she would become Poppy McBride, wife of Robert and mother – in due course – to three, maybe four little McBrides. It was all planned, right down to the middle names and the colour of the wallpaper in the nursery. Rob was a great one for thinking ahead.

'Here, love?' The taxi driver was showing signs of restlessness. When Poppy still didn't move he lit up a cigar and exhaled heavily, making smoke ricochet off the windscreen and into the back of the cab. This usually did the trick.

Poppy didn't even notice. She saw Tom look at his own watch then gaze out of the window. She knew, without a shadow of a doubt, that if she stepped out of the taxi now her life would be changed drastically and forever.

The taxi driver shifted round in his seat to look at her. 'Don't tell me you're dozing off back there.'

Hardly. Poppy, awash with adrenalin, wondered if she would ever sleep again. Her fingers crept towards the door handle.

'Look, love,' began the driver, 'we can't—'

'Edgerton Close.' Poppy blurted the words out, clenching her fists at her side and willing herself not to leap out of the cab. 'Please.'

'You mean back to Henbury?' The driver stared at her in disbelief. 'Are you sure about this?'

'No, but do it anyway.' She turned her face away from Delgado's and held her breath until the taxi reached the far end of Milton Street. It was no good, she couldn't go through with it.

The bad news was, she didn't think she could go through with the wedding either.

Since sleep was out of the question Poppy didn't even bother climbing into bed. Instead, making herself cup after cup of tea and pacing the moonlit back garden as she drank them, she went over in her mind what had happened so far. And, nerve-rackingly, what had to be done next.

By six o'clock the sun was blazing down out of a flawless duck-egg blue sky and upstairs Poppy heard her father begin to stir. She showered, pulled a comb ruthlessly through her tangled hair, cleaned her teeth and threw on a white tee-shirt and jeans. Then she tapped on his bedroom door.

'Dad? I've made you a cup of tea.'

Since the death of Laura Dunbar ten years ago there had been no other woman in her father's life. Poppy had missed her mother desperately following the nightmarish accident when an out-of-control lorry had careered down Henbury Hill smashing into Laura and killing her outright. Her mother had been fun-loving, vivacious and openly affectionate. She had also doted on Poppy, her much-loved only child.

In the first unbearable months following the accident Poppy had secretly wondered why the lorry couldn't have suffered brake failure in front of her father instead. It was shameful to even think it, but at twelve years old you couldn't always control your thoughts. And it would have been so much easier to lose the withdrawn, humourless, silent parent

11

who didn't even seem to like her that much anyway.

But it hadn't happened that way. Laura had been the one to die and Mervyn Dunbar had never made any attempts to replace her. Gradually Poppy had grown used to the fact that from now on there would be just the two of them. Poppy had made heroic attempts to learn to cook. A cleaning woman came in twice a week to keep the place hygienic.

Despite Poppy's best efforts her father had continued to treat her as more of a stranger in the house than a daughter. In turn she had taken to going out a great deal. He was her father but Poppy wasn't sure she loved him. It was hard to love someone who so plainly didn't love you back.

Now, having knocked on his bedroom door, she waited downstairs in the kitchen. Ten minutes later he appeared, fully dressed, in the doorway.

'Dad, I can't do it. I'm going to have to call the wedding off.'

Poppy watched him heave a sigh before reaching slowly for his cup of tea. When he had taken the first sip he would pull a face. She knew this because it was what he always did when she had made the tea.

'Why?' her father said at last when he had swallowed and grimaced. 'What's he done wrong?'

'Nothing. Rob hasn't done anything wrong.' Poppy pushed her fingers through her wet hair, wincing as a strand of it caught up in her engagement ring. The small diamond twinkled in the sunlight. She would have to give it back. 'It's me. I just can't go through with it.'

'And it's taken you until now to realise this?'

'I know, I know.'

'Do you enjoy it?' her father said bitterly. 'Causing trouble?'

She stared at him, appalled. 'Of course I don't!'

'You've always caused trouble.'

'I have *not*,' Poppy almost shouted, outraged by the lie. If there was one thing she'd never been, it was a troublemaker.

'You're like your mother.' Mervyn Dunbar's voice dropped

to a hoarse undertone. With her red-gold hair pushed away from her forehead like that, Poppy so resembled her mother it was unnerving. And she was twenty-two now; the same age Laura had been when he had first met her.

How he had loved Laura, he thought wearily. And how she had hurt him in return.

'What do you mean?' Poppy began to feel sick. She had never heard him say anything like this before. Her mother wasn't a subject he had ever seemed to want to discuss.

Mervyn Dunbar finished drinking his tea. 'Nothing. I'm just saying you like a bit of drama, that's all. So what happens after you've called the wedding off? Have you thought about that?'

'Not really—'

'And where will you live? Or,' said Mervyn heavily, 'does this mean you'll be staying on here?'

It was ironic, thought Poppy, that she should ever have worried about having to leave her father to fend for himself. Not normally slow, it had taken her until now to realise he would actually prefer her out of his way.

'It's all right, I'll move out.' She spoke jerkily, not having had time yet to think things through. 'I don't know where. Maybe out of Bristol. At least that way I won't keep bumping into Rob and his family. And all his friends—'

Poppy jumped as out in the hall the newspaper clattered through the letter box. She looked up at the clock on the kitchen wall. Ten to seven. Oh dear, she'd better get a move on. Poor Rob. He wasn't going to be very pleased.

Chapter 3

This was pretty much the understatement of the year. Having walked the half-mile or so to the semi-detached house where Rob lived with his parents and younger brothers, Poppy and her aching toe arrived at seven o'clock to find the McBrides already up and rushing about. Margaret McBride, who had insisted on doing all the food for the reception, was cling-filming everything in sight and ferrying trays of hors d'oeuvres out to the cars standing in the driveway. The younger boys were stuffing themselves with Scotch eggs while their mother's back was turned. Their father, sitting straight-backed on the kitchen doorstep like the army man he had once been, was vigorously spit-and-polishing a long line of shoes.

'You what?' said Rob, when Poppy told him in the privacy of the ultra-tidy sitting room.

'I'm sorry, I'm so sorry. I can't marry you.' She winced inwardly at the sound of her own voice saying the words. Poor Rob, he really didn't deserve this.

Poppy wished she didn't have to be here doing it, inflicting all this pain. The temptation to forget the whole thing – to just go ahead, what the hell, and marry the man – was huge. She could understand why not many people called off their wedding on the day it was due to take place.

What was really awful, she realised when she looked up moments later, was that Rob was smiling.

'Poppy. Come on now, love, calm down. It's *normal* to have last-minute jitters, you know it is. Don't you remember, there was a piece about it in that magazine of Mum's last week? She read it out to you.'

Poppy went rigid as, still smiling, he pulled her into his arms for a reassuring hug. Horrors, he didn't believe her . . .

'This isn't a last-minute jitter.' She lifted her chin, realising she had to make certain this time she was getting through. 'I mean it, Rob. I'm sorry, I know you're going to hate me for doing this but we have to cancel the wedding. We really *have* to.'

As Susie had observed last night, it would be hard to find a better husband than Rob McBride. He was charming, he was honest, he was generous to a fault. With his solid physique, his unflashy good looks, his heroic job as a fireman and his kindness to old dears and small children alike, he was everything a girl could want. He didn't drink, gamble or womanise. He knew how to put up shelves. He didn't even mind that Poppy couldn't cook.

Staring at her now, Rob said, 'Is this a joke?'

'No.'

'Poppy, you can't just cancel a *wedding*—'

'Yes we can.'

'But why would you want to?' Rob was no longer smiling. His complexion had turned three shades paler. His dark eyebrows drew together as he tried to make sense of what was going on. 'This isn't very bloody funny, you know. Come on, tell me what's happened. Why don't you want to get married?'

His body was well-muscled, honed to perfection with regular sport and weight-training exercises. Poppy could see that every one of those muscles was in a state of rigidly controlled tension. At least she didn't have to worry that he might hit her. Wife-battering wasn't something Rob would ever go in for. Except, Poppy realised belatedly, she wasn't going to be his wife. She was the bitch jilting him practically at the altar. He might not be able to resist giving her a quick slap across the face.

15

'I said,' Rob repeated stonily, 'why don't you want to get married?'

'Look, it's not you, it's me,' Poppy rushed to explain. 'You haven't done anything wrong. This is all my own fault. The thing is, it wouldn't be fair to marry you. Not fair to you or me. Oh Rob, I know I keep saying I'm sorry, but I *am*. You see, I don't love you enough—'

'Someone else.' The words came out through gritted teeth. Rob's light grey eyes were like ice-chips. 'Is this what you're trying to tell me? You've met someone else?'

It was no good. Poppy realised she might as well be honest. He deserved that much.

'In a way, I suppose. But—'

'In a way?' shouted Rob. 'In a *way*? And just what the fuck is *that* supposed to mean?'

Poppy tried to imagine what was going on at this moment on the other side of the sitting-room door. Rob's family must by this time be listening to every word. Their ears would be suction-cupped to the freshly glossed wood.

'I'm not leaving you for another man, Rob.'

The look of absolute horror on his face said it all.

'Not another woman either,' Poppy went on hastily. 'Please, try and understand. I'm not leaving you *for* another man but it is because of another man. He's someone I met, briefly. Very briefly. And I'm never going to see him again. But he made me realise I couldn't marry you,' she said with a helpless shrug. 'He made me realise I don't love you as much as I should. All I ever really wanted, you see, was an excuse to leave home and become part of a . . . a *happy* family.'

'So all the time I've been putting in extra hours, getting a bit more money together for the house,' said Rob slowly, 'you've been screwing some other bloke behind my back.'

'No. I wasn't. I didn't sleep with him,' Poppy explained. 'I didn't even kiss him. I know it sounds bizarre—'

'Bizarre's hardly the word I'd have called it. Will you look at the time?' He thrust his watch under her nose. 'Half past fucking seven. We're supposed to be getting married in six hours. What are you, some kind of sadist? If you had to call the thing off, couldn't you at least have done it before now?'

'No—'

'Who is this lover boy anyway?' Rob demanded furiously. 'For his sake it had better not be anyone I know. *And* you can tell me how long it's been going on.'

'It's no one you know,' said Poppy. 'It's no one *I* know, come to that. And it hasn't been going on any time at all,' she added wearily. 'I only met him last night.'

The next hour was so horrible it seemed to drag on for weeks. Poppy, effectively cornered by Rob's unhappy family, began to wonder if she would ever be allowed to leave. Most alarming of all was their absolute refusal to accept her decision. Margaret McBride carried on grimly clingfilming sausage rolls and plates of cheese-and-asparagus quiche.

'You don't mean it,' Rob's father said for the tenth time. He gestured towards the kitchen table, heaped with prawn vol-au-vents and tubs of Twiglets. 'You can't let good food like this go to waste.'

'I'll pay for the food,' Poppy said in desperation. 'I'll pay for everything. *Please* can't we phone the vicar—?'

'Never mind the cost,' shouted Margaret McBride. 'What about the humiliation? How's our son supposed to live this down? You're not even being logical, Poppy! If you were running off with another man I could understand it, but this . . . this is just a whim, a stupid idea you've got into your head. And it's selfish. *Selfish*,' she raged on, tears welling in her eyes, 'because you will destroy my son if you go through with this. How will he ever live down the shame?'

'What shame?' Rob demanded hotly. He had had enough of this. It was plain to him that Poppy had no intention of changing her mind. Sod it, why should he have to stand here listening to his own mother fighting his battles for him? She was making him sound a complete wimp.

17

He turned to face Poppy. 'You're the one who should be ashamed of yourself.'

'I *know*,' Poppy pleaded. She didn't care how angry he got – it would almost be a relief if he did punch her on the nose – she just wanted the showdown over with. 'I know and it's *all* my fault—'

'Damn right it is.' Rob's muscles were still bunched up, but he didn't hit girls. Never had, never would. That didn't matter though; there were other ways of getting back at Poppy Dunbar, better ways of hitting her where it hurt. Silkily he said, 'So what does your dear old Dad make of all this? You have mentioned it to him, I suppose?'

'He's not thrilled.' Poppy began to relax slightly. Rob sounded as if he were starting to accept the situation at last. 'He said I was causing trouble again—'

'You did enough of that, didn't you, when you were born?'

'Rob.' His mother spoke in warning tones.

Puzzled, Poppy echoed, 'When I was born?'

'Why should he give a toss, anyway, whether you get married or not? Mervyn Dunbar isn't your father.' Rob revelled in the moment. His mouth curled with pleasure. 'Dear me, so surprised,' he drawled triumphantly. 'I thought everyone around here knew that.'

Chapter 4

At twenty-two Claudia Slade-Welch had a great deal going for her. She knew this because people were always telling her so. She was lucky to have thick blonde hair, lucky to have splendid breasts – no need for a Wonderbra there – and lucky to have legs long enough to counterbalance what might otherwise have seemed a rather large bottom.

The luck didn't end there. As if all this wasn't enough for one girl, Claudia had also been blessed with an endlessly glamorous mother, and a father who wasn't only charming but famous to boot. Only when she was asked where she lived were people able – for a few fleeting seconds – to feel sympathetic towards her rather than envious. Renting a room in a friend's house didn't have much of a glamorous ring to it, they thought. It sounded mundane, if not downright dull. Until someone else happened to mention in passing that the friend in question was Caspar French. Then everyone, especially the women, changed their minds in an instant and gasped, 'My God, how fantastic! You lucky, *lucky* thing . . .'

The trouble was, as Claudia had come to realise over the years, she never actually felt as lucky as everyone else thought she should feel. As a child, reading endless Enid Blyton books, she had first suspected that her mother wasn't a normal Enid Blyton-type mother. Normal Enid Blyton-type mothers were never called Angie for a start. Nor did they wriggle into glitzy mini dresses and flirt with almost everyone in trousers, from her husband's celebrated circle of fellow actors to Claudia's own beloved form teacher at school, Mr Elliott.

Time hadn't improved matters. Normal mothers were supposed to be looked up to. Claudia, growing and growing like an over-watered sunflower, had overtaken tiny five-foot-tall Angie by the time she was eleven. Being ten inches taller than your own mother, she discovered, wasn't a comfortable sensation. Nor was it helped by Angie's habit of pointing it out at every opportunity, of faxing diet sheets to the matron at her daughter's school and of wailing loudly at parties: '. . . and I thought the whole *point* of having girls was so one could borrow their clothes! I mean, tell me, where did I go wrong?'

It wasn't the kind of remark an Enid Blyton mother would make. For a time Claudia's father had remonstrated with his wife, in that famously sexy, laid-back manner of his. But Angie, who had never taken any notice of anyone, least of all her husband, had carried on regardless. Then the divorce had happened and Claudia had seen little of her father for the next few years. On his infrequent trips back from Hollywood she hadn't dared to whinge. Instead she had stoically endured her mother's careless insults, pretending instead to be as happy as anything. As she grew older, she took care never to introduce Angie to any boyfriends she particularly liked.

One week after her eighteenth birthday Claudia had moved out of the family home and into the first of several chaotically shared flats.

But there was never any real getting away from Angie, short of upping sticks and emigrating to Siberia. For the past two years she had been passionately involved with an already married hotel owner on the Costa Smeralda and Claudia had enjoyed the break. Now that affair was over. The hotel owner, possibly fearing for his health, had decided to stay with his rich wife. And Angie Slade-Welch – together with her sickening twenty-one-inch waist and size-three satin stilettos – was back.

She hadn't been invited to tonight's party but had, predictably, turned up anyway. Watching from a safe distance as her mother approached a well-built sculptor friend of Caspar's and swung into action, Claudia absently helped herself to three prawn and cucumber canapés from the tray of a passing waitress.

'If you want to do something useful,' said a voice at her shoulder, 'you could always introduce me to that hunky chap talking to your mother. When she's finished with him of course.'

Claudia turned to Josie, an ex-flatmate from last year.

'By the time my mother's finished with him there might not be much left to introduce.'

Josie giggled. 'Well, if there is.'

'And I don't know who he is anyway.' Claudia tried not to sound annoyed, but it was a bit much. It was her birthday, supposed to be *her* party and she had forked out a fortune on caterers, yet Caspar had done his usual trick and casually suggested he might invite a few of his friends along too. 'Just to make up the numbers,' he'd said with a grin before she'd had a chance to object. 'No need to look so alarmed, Claudie, only half a dozen or so. No undesirables, I promise.'

It was her own fault, Claudia decided with a sigh, for having been stupid enough to believe him. But it was still irritating, having her own party invaded by so many of Caspar's friends that there were more strangers in the house than people she actually knew. They ate like gannets too. The expensive caterer, thin-lipped because she had only been asked to supply food for forty guests, had just warned her they were about to run out.

What annoyed Claudia most of all was the fact that – having successfully hijacked her birthday party – Caspar hadn't even had the common courtesy to show up. And everyone thinks I'm so lucky to be living in this house, thought Claudia, her expression mutinous. Huh.

'Where is Caspar anyway?' asked Josie, her appreciative eye still lingering on the broad shoulders of the sculptor.

Claudia pulled a face. 'Congratulations. You're the fiftieth person to ask me that question tonight.'

'Come on, cheer up.'

Claudia tried. 'Okay. Sorry. He's just impossible, that's all.' Flipping back her heavy blonde hair she shook her head in exasperation. 'D'you know, it's not as if he's even gone out anywhere. He's upstairs in his studio, bloody *painting*. I went up and banged on the door at nine o'clock. He wouldn't come out. He said he was on a roll and didn't dare stop.' Claudia, whose knowledge of art was pretty much limited to the water-lily print on her duvet cover, glanced up in disgust at one of Caspar's paintings hung above the mantelpiece. 'I mean, it isn't as if there's any hurry. His stuff sells really well now. He's hardly short of cash.'

Josie was slightly more knowledgeable. 'Money means nothing to these artistic types.'

'Evidently not.' Claudia spoke with feeling. 'Particularly when it comes to offering to go halves on the food.'

'Stop moaning. You don't know how lucky you are.' The waitress was back with her tray. Josie chose the canapé with the biggest prawn on top. Through a mouthful of puff pastry she said, 'I'd love to live here.'

'That could be arranged. Oliver's moving out at the end of the week. He's going back to New York.' Claudia's mind was on other things. This was the third time the red-haired waitress had circulated with the same tray. She touched the girl's arm. 'Excuse me. We'd like to try the blinis.'

'Sorry, they've gone,' said the girl with the red-gold hair. 'These cucumber thingies are all that's left.'

The mini blinis stuffed with Sevruga caviar, a speciality of Kenda's Kitchen, were what Claudia had been looking forward to all evening. Instead they'd been guzzled by a bunch of gastronomic philistines who would no doubt have been just as happy with sardines on toast. This really was the living end.

Bloody *bloody* hell, Claudia seethed inwardly, not trusting herself to speak.

'Um, if there's a room going free in this house,' said the waitress, 'I'd be interested.'

Claudia couldn't have looked more startled if one of the prawns had opened its mouth and asked the time.

Josie burst out laughing. 'Talk about seizing the moment.'

'Sorry,' said the waitress, registering the expression on Claudia's face, 'but if you don't ask you don't get. And I am desperate.'

Poppy wasn't exaggerating. Cancelling her wedding three months earlier had been the easy bit. Becoming known – practically throughout north Bristol – as The Girl Who Jilted Rob McBride, had been much more of an ordeal. An old lady whose ginger cat Rob had once rescued from a tree had shouted abuse through the letter box of Poppy's home. She had received horrible phone calls. One of Rob's ex-girlfriends from years ago, passing her in the street, had called her a bitch. And Poppy's father – except he was no longer her father – had said coldly, 'I think you'd better go.'

Which was why, just four days after her non-existent wedding, she had found herself on a coach bound for London. Poppy had chosen this city for three and a half simple reasons. Firstly, more coaches travelled more often to London than to anywhere else. She had also, on a school day trip years ago, fallen in love with the Portobello Road and Petticoat Lane antiques markets.

The third reason, so flimsy it only just qualified as one, had to do with her real father. Poppy needed time to make up her mind about this. Even if she wanted to try and find him, she realised her chances of doing so weren't great. All she did know was the name of the man who had had a brief but passionate affair with her mother, and that he had once – twenty-two years ago, for heaven's sake – lived in London.

But if this was flimsy it was nothing compared with the fact that London was also home to Tom, which was why she had only allowed it to count as half a reason. Poppy knew, with the benefit of hindsight, that she had been spectacularly stupid, but at the time she had made a conscious decision not to ask. And now it was too late, she thought ruefully. When you weren't even in possession of something as basic as a person's surname . . . well, then you *really* didn't have a hope in hell of finding them again.

Still, she had at least had one thing going for her on arriving in London. She hadn't expected too much of the place, hadn't imagined the streets to be paved with gold.

And she had been right, they weren't, but Poppy had taken the grim reality in her stride, refusing to be appalled by the low standard of rented accommodation available within her price range. She also refused to be offended by the amount of unfriendliness she encountered, which some people appeared to have elevated to an art form.

Mentioning no names, thought Poppy now. Manfully keeping her opinions on the subject to herself, she directed a guileless smile at the tall, blonde, stroppy-looking girl whose party – and home – this evidently was.

'The room,' Claudia said at last, 'isn't going . . . free. This isn't the Salvation Army.'

No, thought Poppy, they're far more welcoming.

'I didn't mean free-free,' she explained patiently. 'I meant available. Look,' she went on, 'this chap Caspar I keep hearing about, maybe I could have a word with him, see if he'd be willing to let me take the room.'

'Why are you desperate?' said Josie, who was incurably nosy.

'You should see the place I'm in at the moment.' Goodness, a friendly voice. Poppy turned to her with relief. 'Purple wallpaper with yellow lupins all over it. Holes in the carpet, missing floorboards, groping old landlord, incontinent cat – you name it. There's a heavy metal freak upstairs and a Glaswegian bloke with a beard who steams his own haggises. Or haggi. Anyway, the smell is terrible. The flat's a dump. But this,' Poppy concluded with an appreciative sweep of her arm, '*this* is a fabulous house. I mean it, I would be so happy to move in here! This place is a palace—'

'The trouble with palaces,' Claudia cut in, 'is they cost more to live in than dumps. I don't want to sound funny—'

Of course you do, Poppy thought.

'– but I doubt very much if you could afford the rent.'

'I might be able to,' Poppy said mildly. 'I only do this in the evenings. I do have a proper job.'

'Oh.'

'What is it?' Josie asked, warming to the girl who was standing up so well to Claudia at her huffiest.

'I'm a stripper,' said Poppy simply. 'It's great, and it pays well. I recommend it. If you ever want to earn good money, just become a stripper in a pub.'

Chapter 5

Poppy paused for breath at the top of the third flight of stairs then knocked on the dark green door as Claudia had instructed. Several seconds passed before an abstracted male voice said, 'Yes?'

'Um, hi. My name's Poppy Dunbar. I wondered if I could see you.'

'Let me guess,' said the voice through the door, 'you're a friend of Claudia's and she's sent you up here to act as bait. Your job is to lure me down to her party.'

'Not exactly.'

'Bullshit.' He sounded amused. 'I know the way her mind works. Don't tell me, you're a ravishingly beautiful blonde.'

'Nope.' Poppy smiled. 'A ravishingly beautiful redhead.'

'Hmm, shock tactics.'

'I'm not one of Claudia's friends either. She only sent me up here because she couldn't think how else to get rid of me.' Poppy thought for a moment then added, 'And maybe to punish you for not putting in an appearance downstairs.'

'Punish me? What are you, a tax inspector? A ravishingly beautiful redheaded tax inspector,' Caspar mused. 'Surely there's no such thing.'

'Open the door,' said Poppy, 'and find out.'

The attic studio was large, taking up the entire top floor of the house. There were canvases everywhere, propped against the white painted walls, stacked untidily on chairs and littering the polished wooden floor. Also occupying space were three sofas – one dark blue, one black velvet, one tartan. There was also, Poppy couldn't help noticing, an unmade king-sized bed.

'Good heavens, a choice of casting couches.'

Caspar French, who was tall and tanned and very blond, broke into a broad grin.

'We aim to please. I'm puzzled though.'

'Oh?'

'Well, I'm fairly sure we haven't met before. And you say you aren't a friend of Claudia's.' He paused, picked up an already opened Beaujolais bottle, held it up to the light and discovered it was empty. Reaching for a Kit-Kat instead, he dropped the wrapper on the floor, broke the bar in two and offered half to Poppy. 'So what I don't understand is how you came to be at the party. Unless we've been gate-crashed. Are you sure you aren't an undercover tax inspector?'

'I work for Kenda's Kitchen,' said Poppy, 'the caterers.'

'Ah.' Caspar nodded. 'And how's it going? Is Claudia happy with the food?'

'She might have been if your friends hadn't eaten it all. I'm afraid Claudia isn't very pleased with you.'

'I'll survive. I'm used to it.'

The area over by the window appeared to do duty as Caspar's idea of a kitchen. As well as chocolate to sustain him there were cans of Coke, a few half-full coffee cups littering the floor, an empty pizza box and several more wine bottles. Picking his way barefoot through the chaos Caspar discovered one that hadn't been opened. 'Hooray. White all right with you? Looks like something Australian.'

'Thanks but I can't. Much longer up here and I'll get the sack.' Poppy, suddenly nervous, wiped her damp palms on the back of her skirt. 'The thing is, I overheard your friend Claudia saying you had a room to rent. So, I'd like to volunteer myself for it.'

Unable to find a corkscrew Caspar had given up on the wine. Instead he began cleaning brushes, carefully soaking

27

each one in turn in a jug of white spirit before going to work on them with a rag which had evidently once been an evening shirt. He was wearing a pale yellow cotton sweater with the sleeves pushed up, and extremely paint-spattered white denims. The smell of the oils he had been using still permeated the air. On the easel in the centre of the room stood the current work-in-progress, two almost completed figures sprawling comfortably together on a sun-drenched lawn, their heads bent as though they were sharing a secret.

'Gosh, you're good,' exclaimed Poppy. Realising she sounded surprised she added hastily, 'I mean, I'm no expert—'

'That's okay. You're right anyway. I am good.' Caspar turned and winked at her. 'I'm up-and-coming. According to the dealers, at least.'

'You're certainly good at changing the subject.' Poppy was bursting with impatience. 'Go on, give it a whirl,' she begged. 'Say I can move in. I am house-trained. I pay my rent on the dot. I even Hoover occasionally.'

'You haven't seen the room yet. Are you an undercover journalist?'

'I'm not an undercover anything.' Poppy glanced at her watch. 'But I'll definitely get the sack if I don't shoot back downstairs. Look, will you at least think about it and let me know?' Seizing a nearby pencil – a sooty 6B with meltingly soft lead – she scribbled her address and phone number across the back page of an old *Daily Mail* and underlined it twice for good measure. Never again was she going to make *that* mistake.

'I'm trying to decide what it is you have,' said Caspar. 'Nerve or style.'

Poppy handed him the newspaper. 'Can't I have both?'

Back downstairs she found herself cornered almost at once by Claudia.

'Well, what did he say?'

'That I had a nerve,' Poppy dutifully replied.

28

'Just what I thought he'd say.' Looking immensely pleased with herself, Claudia smoothed back her blonde hair and waved hello to someone behind Poppy. When she chose to use it, Poppy thought, she actually had a nice smile. 'You see,' Claudia went on, 'maybe it's different where you come from but around here introducing yourself to total strangers and asking if you can come and live with them isn't really done.'

'No. Sorry.' Poppy hung her head. 'Sorry.'

'Well then, that's that sorted out.' Having won, Claudia was prepared to be magnanimous. 'I'm sure you'll find somewhere else to live soon enough,' she said kindly. 'By the way, did Caspar mention anything about coming down to the party?'

The words Caspar had affectionately employed were; 'Silly old bag, let her sweat.' But Claudia wasn't the only one who could be gracious in victory.

Poppy said, 'I'm sure he'll be here soon.'

'I say,' purred Angie Slade-Welch twenty minutes later. 'You have to admit there's something awfully attractive about a man who just doesn't give a damn.'

'Mother, Clark Gable's dead.'

'Never mind Clark Gable.' Angie was beaming away like a lighthouse. 'Your landlord's turned up at last. Does he cultivate that just-got-out-of-bed look or is it natural?'

'It's accurate,' said Claudia in pointed tones. 'He spends his life just getting out of bed. Beds, rather. Oh for heaven's sake,' she sighed, catching a glimpse of the paint-spattered white jeans. 'He could have changed into something decent before he came down. He's not even wearing *shoes*.'

'Nice feet,' Angie observed with a nod of approval. 'Anyway, why should he wear shoes? This is his house. He can walk round stark naked if he likes.'

Claudia cringed. 'Don't tell him that. You'll only put ideas into his head.'

'Or yours.' Angie loved to embarrass her daughter. 'Come on, you can tell me. What really goes on in this house when there are just the two of you here? Is anything likely to develop, do you think—?'

'Mother!'

Angie shrugged. 'Only asking, my darling. You never tell me anything so how else can I find out? And he *is* irresistible, isn't he? Go on, whisper it.' She lifted herself playfully on tiptoe, tilting her head. 'You can't tell me you don't fancy him rotten. And living together like this . . . well, he must have made a pass at you at some stage.'

A glass bowl of cornflowers stood on the marble mantelpiece. Claudia, in front of it, realised she had been abstractedly de-petalling the blue flowers. This was the effect her mother always managed to have on her. What Angie actually meant was that Caspar must have made a pass, *even* at her, at some stage.

He hadn't though. In all the time she'd known him, thought Claudia, there hadn't been the least bit of a pass made. Not even the teeniest hint of one.

As for the other less than delicately worded enquiry . . . of *course* she fancied Caspar rotten. She did feel, however, that she was hiding it well. To look at her nobody would ever guess. And, Claudia thought with feeling, just because she did fancy him didn't mean he wasn't also wildly infuriating to live with. Caspar might be irresistible but he was irresponsible too.

'No,' she told her mother, quelling the urge to seize the front of Angie's bronze satin bustier and haul it upwards. Over the past hour it had slithered lower and lower, revealing a perilous amount of pert bosom. Her mother had no doubt arranged for this to happen. She was proud of her small but perfectly formed breasts.

'No pass? Oh bad luck.' Angie's blue eyes gleamed like sapphires. 'Never mind, you can always live in hope.' The toe of her tiny shoe nudged a pile of shredded petals into the fireplace. 'Poor flowers, whatever did they do to deserve this?'

'Claudie, you look gorgeous. Happy birthday,' said Caspar, coming over at last and kissing her warmly on both cheeks.

It was the type of gesture that could never be mistaken for a pass. It was also, thought Claudia, the first time she had seen him all day. Having crawled home at dawn and slept until mid-afternoon Caspar had been closeted ever since in his studio, supposedly working.

He smelled of toothpaste and turpentine. He had also been using her Nicky Clarke shampoo again. As she breathed it in Claudia wondered how someone could be so incapable of remembering to buy his own shampoo, yet never *ever* run out of oil paints.

'You're late. Your friends have eaten all the food.' She turned and pointed to the guilty-looking lurcher brought along by Caspar's sculptor friend. 'And that hideous mongrel has slobbered his way through a whole basket of chocolates. Charbonnel et Walker champagne truffles,' Claudia added, though why she bothered she didn't know since Caspar was a stranger to remorse. 'They were a present from the girls in the office.'

'Dear old Hoover, such a connoisseur,' Caspar said fondly. 'He's always appreciated a decent class of chocolate.'

'And thanks for the birthday card.'

'Oh dear, you are cross with me.' He grinned. 'I know, why don't I paint you one?'

Claudia wasn't going to be won over that easily. 'Most people grow out of giving home-made cards by the time they're ten.'

'You'll have to excuse my daughter,' sighed Angie, 'it's so long since she last got laid.'

'Mother—'

'Only teasing, sweetheart.'

Realising she wasn't having the best of evenings, Caspar put one arm around Claudia's brown shoulders. 'I'm sorry I

31

didn't buy you a card. I thought maybe we could go somewhere nice for lunch tomorrow . . . as a kind of belated present.' His mouth twitched. 'Or do you hate me too much?'

'That depends.' Claudia's resolve began to weaken, as Caspar had no doubt known it would. 'Somewhere how nice?'

'The Marigold.' He knew it was one of her favourite places to go. Luckily it was one of his too. 'Come on, cheer up. We can go berserk on oysters and champagne. You know you want to.'

'I know *I'd* want to.' Angie's smile was catlike. 'Sounds heavenly. Is there room for one more?'

Caspar looked at Claudia.

Angie pouted. 'Just a little one. Oh please, couldn't I come too?'

'Um . . .' said Caspar.

The last person on earth Claudia wanted muscling in on their cosy lunch à deux was her man-eating mother.

'No,' she said before Caspar was obliged to be polite. 'You could not.'

Chapter 6

Becoming successful and earning serious money for the first time in his life hadn't changed Caspar one bit; he was as careless with it now as he'd ever been, only these days he had more to be careless with. Five years ago, as a poverty-stricken student, he would have spent his last tenner in the world on fish and chips and a bottle of Bardolino to cheer up a miserable flatmate. Now it was lunch at The Marigold and a bill that would run into hundreds of pounds. Caspar wasn't bothered; as long as everyone had a good time he was more than happy to sign the cheque.

When he looked back over the past decade Caspar marvelled at the way his life had changed. A much-loved only child, he had astonished his un-artistic parents from an early age with his passion for painting. Once over their surprise, they had supported him wholeheartedly. Money they might not have, but belief in their son's talent and their endless encouragement meant more to Caspar than all the financial help in the world. He would get by; he was used to being poor. Besides, poor was what art students were supposed to be. Leaving home, moving to London and struggling to survive on a grant the size of a peanut was what being a student was all about.

Henrietta Malone had lived at 15, Cornwallis Crescent for forty-eight years. A genteel, four-storey Georgian terraced house in East Kensington, it was the home to which her husband Edmund had brought her as a young bride almost

33

half a century earlier, a house large enough to accommodate any number of offspring and with a well-tended garden to match.

Sadly, Henrietta had been unable to bear children but by the time she and Edmund discovered this they had grown to love the house anyway. Only when her beloved Edmund died in his sleep – at the age of seventy-four and after forty-four years of quietly happy marriage – did the house seem too big to carry on living in alone.

Henrietta yearned for company, and not the kind you were apt to find in some depressing old folks' home. Instead, much to the horror of her more strait-laced friends, she pinned an advertisement to the notice board in the entrance hall of St Martin's School of Art.

Within a fortnight she had what she had always wanted, a house that shook with music, clattering footsteps and laughter, a house full of surrogate children who teased her unmercifully, shocked the neighbours and called her Hen. Broke but cheerful, they kept the most extraordinary hours and wore even more extraordinary clothes.

Henrietta adored them all but she especially adored Caspar, who had fallen instantly in love with the airy, skylighted studio on the top floor and who had moved in within hours of setting eyes on it. Over the course of the next two years other students came and went but Caspar stayed firmly put.

Henrietta never failed to be entertained by Caspar – her golden boy, as she secretly thought of him. Not only good-looking but charming too, he was a joy to have around. And he was talented. She was particularly touched, with Christmas approaching, when she discovered by chance that in order to pay his rent on time he was going without food.

In an effort to help out, Henrietta had visited Caspar in his studio, admired a recently completed painting and offered to accept it in lieu of money. But Caspar, politely refusing her offer, had by the skin of his teeth managed to scrape together just enough cash.

Two weeks later on Christmas Eve he had given Henrietta the painting she had liked so much.

Henrietta knew how much of a struggle it was for Caspar to find the rent each month, yet not once did he let her down. He was also unfailingly cheerful and willing to help out around the house if jobs needed doing which were beyond Henrietta's capabilities. She didn't care how untidy he was, how many girlfriends he brought back to his rooms or how many she had to fib to on the phone when Caspar absent-mindedly double-booked himself. He might be feckless but he made her laugh and she loved him to bits. He truly was the son Henrietta had never had.

Shortly after her seventy-fifth birthday Henrietta suffered a mild heart attack. 'Oh Hen,' Caspar chided when he had arrived at the hospital that evening armed with masses of yellow tulips, half a dozen Agatha Christies and a big bottle of her favourite scent, 'are we going to spoil you rotten when you come home.'

But Henrietta hadn't come home. A second heart attack three days later proved fatal. Caspar and the other tenants attended the funeral and simply assumed they would have to start searching for somewhere else to live.

Nobody was more astounded than Caspar when Henrietta Malone's lawyer informed him that 15, Cornwallis Crescent was now his. Henrietta, it transpired, had had no living relatives. With characteristic panache she had bequeathed hefty sums of money to Dr Barnardos, a donkey sanctuary in Sussex and the Chelsea Pensioners. Nobody who had known Henrietta had had any idea she was worth so much.

As far as Caspar was concerned this was the turning point of his life. Within the space of a few months he had acquired – thanks to Henrietta's amazing generosity – a house that was covetable by any standards. He had also graduated with honours from St Martin's and been showcased and favourably received in several prestigious Cork Street galleries. There was now a growing waiting list of customers eager to sit for

Caspar French, the rising young star of the art world. They wanted their portraits painted while they could still afford him.

The Marigold, in Covent Garden, was all oranges and greens with a tropical air to it and exotic waitresses in Carmen Miranda hats. It was popular with celebrity types, which meant everyone was always looking at everyone else.

This was why Claudia so loved the idea of coming here and being seen with Caspar French. It did her ego the world of good to see people clocking them together, assuming they were a couple. Besides, for all his faults Caspar was great fun to have lunch with. When he turned on the charm he could make a sack of potatoes feel chic.

As they walked in together and heads began to swivel, Claudia experienced that familiar surge of pride. Caspar, in a pale pink jacket and baggy cream trousers, was looking so effortlessly elegant and Brideshead-ish it quite hid the fact that in reality he couldn't give a monkey's what he wore. When he was this blond and tanned – and in such a good mood – he was just about irresistible.

Glad she had worn her most slimming black linen dress, Claudia held in her stomach and slithered gracefully between tables which at other times might have seemed too close together. She felt terrific. Caspar was treating her to a belated birthday lunch, she had successfully fobbed off her attention-seeking mother and grilled oysters were the dish of the day. What more could any girl want?

'You've got blue on the sleeve of your jacket.' Reaching across the table to touch the smudge of oil paint she found it was still wet.

'I was working before we came out.'

'Hiding, you mean,' said Claudia, 'in case I dragooned you into helping clear up the mess.'

'I'm no good at that kind of thing,' Caspar protested. 'Anyway, it was your party.'

36

'It was your friends who played skittles with beer cans in the drawing room. You should have seen the state of the place this morning. *And* all the flower vases were full of beer—'

'I thought we were here to celebrate. You aren't allowed to nag me to death,' Caspar argued good-naturedly. 'Not at these prices.' Turning to the wine waiter he pointed to one of the bottles on the list. 'A couple of these, I think, to start with.'

'And this can be cleared.' Claudia pointed to the third place-setting, taking up unnecessary space on the table. 'We're just two.'

The wine waiter, who knew better, hesitated.

'Oh, didn't I mention it?' Caspar looked amused. 'We're three.'

'Not my mother.' Claudia felt the hairs rise at the back of her neck. She was so outraged she could barely speak. 'Please, *not* my mother.' She did a double-take as a figure behind the wine waiter stepped to one side. Recognising with mounting horror that distinctive riot of red-gold hair and unable to help herself, Claudia wailed, 'Oh no, not *you*.'

'Oh dear, better break it to me gently.' Glancing at Caspar, Poppy started to laugh. 'Which am I then? The devil or the deep blue sea?'

'Come on now, you're over-reacting,' said Caspar when Poppy had beaten a diplomatic retreat to the loo. 'Oliver's moving out. We'll have an empty room. I don't see why you're so against her moving in.'

Claudia wasn't entirely sure herself, she just knew that if Oliver had to be replaced by a female she would much prefer a plain one.

'That girl eavesdropped on a private conversation,' she said crossly. 'Then she butted in. How pushy can you get?'

'She saw an opportunity and grabbed it.' Caspar shrugged. 'Makes sense to me.'

'You don't need to replace Oliver anyway,' Claudia

pleaded. 'You don't need the money any more.'

This was true, but tenants weren't only about money. Just as Henrietta had rented out her rooms for the company, so Caspar chose to do it for the simple reason that it made life so much easier for him. If he lived alone he knew full well he would never be able to fathom out the central heating system. He would leave gas rings burning and there would be no one else around to turn them off. He would be forever locking himself out of the house and there would be nobody else there to let him in, just as there would be no one else to wash up, maintain a modicum of order, remind him to pay bills and remember to buy all those boring but necessary items such as toothpaste, chocolate Hob Nobs and fresh milk.

'That's a selfish attitude,' said Caspar. 'Think of the housing shortage. All the homeless on the streets.'

'Bull.' Claudia wasn't falling for that. 'And she isn't homeless. She's a stripper in a pub.'

Caspar raised his eyebrows. Poppy, back from the loo, slid into her seat and wondered if Claudia would ever forgive her.

'I strip furniture.' She tried to sound apologetic. 'I work for a chap who runs a stall in Markham Antiques Market. He loaned me out to a friend of his who needed help renovating fixtures in a pub off the Portobello Road. I'm sorry,' she said to Claudia as the waiter refilled their glasses. 'I don't know why I made it sound the way I did. Sometimes I speak without thinking.'

'And sometimes you just lie,' Claudia replied stiffly. 'I asked you what Caspar said when you went up to see him. You told me he said you had a nerve.'

'Actually that's true.' Caspar was grinning. 'I did. But I also said she could move in.'

She had been made fun of, Claudia realised. For their own amusement. The fact that she hadn't approved of Poppy Dunbar was more than likely what had prompted Caspar to say yes. And now here they were, ganging up on her already . . .

'I'm really not as awful as you think I am.' Poppy was trying to be helpful. 'We just got off to a dodgy start.'

You're telling me, thought Claudia as Poppy offered up her glass for a clink. So much for her happy birthday lunch.

'Are you after Caspar?' she asked later, when he had disappeared up to the bar in search of cigarettes.

'Is that what you thought?' The look Poppy gave her was sympathetic. 'Not at all, and that's the honest truth. I'm a bit immune to men at the moment, if you must know. Had a traumatic time, not long ago, so I'm steering clear for the time being.'

From the way Poppy spoke Claudia knew she meant it. Reassured, she said, 'Oh.'

'Why, are you?'

'After Caspar, you mean?' Claudia blinked rapidly. 'Of course not.'

'Lucky old us then.' Smiling, Poppy acknowledged Caspar's imminent return to the table. 'From what I gather he has more than his share of a reputation.'

'Claudia once told me I was lucky to be male,' said Caspar, sitting back down, 'because if I were a girl I'd be a tart.'

'I like the word strumpet,' Poppy said dreamily.

Claudia was addicted to problem pages. Bursting to know, she leaned forward. 'So what was this trauma?' she said, her imagination working overtime. 'Was it something awful? What *happened* to make you immune to men?'

Chapter 7

Poppy couldn't wait to pack her bags and escape the gloomy confines of her Balham bedsitter. Moving into Caspar French's million-times nicer house was a dream come true, even if it did have Claudia in it.

Jake Landers, Poppy's boss at the antiques market, offered her the loan of one of his vans.

'Thanks – ' Poppy was touched by his kindness – 'but there's no need. All my stuff fits into suitcases.' At the expression on Jake's face she added lightly, 'I went minimalist when I left home.'

So minimalist that she no longer possessed so much as a living relative. Not one who would speak to her anyway. The truly ironic thing was, the shock discovery that her father wasn't actually her father hadn't come as that much of a shock at all. Not an awful one at least.

Surprise had swiftly given way to relief. Not being liked by your own father was unnatural and Poppy had always wondered what she'd done to deserve it. Now she knew the truth she could stop worrying. Not being liked by a man whose wife had made you the laughing stock of Henbury twenty-two years earlier was far more understandable. Only Mervyn Dunbar's determination to maintain outward appearances had kept the marriage going. The affair, once over, was evidently never mentioned again and Poppy, born nine months later and fooling no one, had been formally passed off as his own.

Dozens of people, including the McBrides, had known

about it. Poppy continued to be amazed by the fact that she had never learned the truth before now. All in all, she felt it was a shame it had remained a secret for so long.

'Well, if you need any help,' said Jake, 'you know you only have to ask.'

Poppy knew. She also knew how lucky she was to have landed a boss as brilliant as Jake. He was quiet, maybe even a bit on the shy side, but he had a dry sense of humour and the patience he exercised with Poppy – who was forever bombarding him with questions about antiques – was phenomenal. At twenty-eight he lived alone but Poppy knew nothing beyond that. Unlike her, Jake kept his private life pretty much to himself.

Another endearing quality about Jake was the way he genuinely didn't realise how good-looking he was. His own appearance clearly wasn't something with which he ever concerned himself. His dark hair was cut for him in a little shop three doors up from the antiques market, by a barber who might be unfashionable but who was at least fast. Jake's long-lashed dark brown eyes were hidden behind spectacles that looked like something his grandfather might have passed down to him. His body seemed all right – as far as Poppy was able to tell – but his dress sense was frightful. All she could say about Jake's clothes was that they were clean.

Poppy had fantasised once or twice that beneath the Clark Kent exterior was a Superman waiting to burst out, but she knew deep down there wasn't. From time to time Jake would find himself being chatted up on the stall, usually by women a few years older than himself in search of someone to mother. It was so sweet watching him because he obviously didn't have the least idea what to do with them. Eventually Poppy would take pity on him and intervene, allowing Jake to melt gratefully into the background.

He had never said as much but Poppy assumed he was gay.

'Thanks.' Poppy reached up to take the steaming mug of

tea Jake had brought down from the café on the top floor of the antiques market. She had enjoyed her week stripping in the pub in Portobello but it was nice being back here on the stall.

For a Friday afternoon the market was quiet. In between customers, most of them browsers who preferred to be left alone, Poppy had been reading up on Georgian teapots. Jake, just back from the monthly sale at Lassiter's Auction Rooms in Bermondsey, began unpacking a box of assorted silver photograph frames.

'Look at that.' Balancing her tea on the flat, glass-fronted jewellery cabinet, Poppy picked out one of the larger frames with its photograph still in place. The sepia-tinted print, dated 1925, was of a stiffly posed family. Mother, father and assorted children stared unsmilingly up at her. 'They all look like their father. Minus the moustache.'

'You could polish up these frames if you like,' offered Jake. He pointed to the hallmark on another frame. 'Date?'

'George the something.' Poppy wasn't in the mood for hallmarks. She looked again at the sepia print. A small knot began to tighten in the pit of her stomach.

'Fifth,' said Jake. 'George V.' He frowned. 'You seem a bit . . . are you all right?'

'Hmmm?'

'You don't look quite with it.'

Poppy broke into a grin. In his dark green cardigan full of holes, his blue and white striped shirt and brown houndstooth check trousers, if anyone was looking not quite with it, it was Jake.

'Sorry, I was thinking.'

Jake, who had heard about little else for the past week, said, 'About the move I suppose.'

'Actually no. I was wondering if I look anything like my father.'

'Ah.' He had heard about this too, over the course of the last three months. 'Well, I can't help you there.'

42

'I want to find him,' said Poppy, the words coming out in a rush. Quite suddenly it mattered more than anything else in the world. She felt like an alcoholic begging for a drink. 'I know I probably won't be able to but I have to at least give it a try. I *have* to—'

'Are you sure?'

Poppy had been um-ing and ah-ing about this for weeks. Jake's only experience in the matter was of an adopted schoolfriend who had managed to trace his natural mother then been traumatised by her refusal to meet him. Some things, Jake felt, were best left unmeddled with.

But Poppy had made up her mind. 'I must. It might be impossible. But it might not. He could be living just round the corner from me. Imagine if he was and I didn't *know* . . .'

'How are you going to do it?'

She nodded in the direction of the phone books stacked up beneath his cluttered desk.

'There are seventeen A. Fitzpatricks listed in the London area. I'll start by phoning them.'

'Try and be a bit discreet,' said Jake. He wouldn't put anything past Poppy. She was liable to turn up on their doorsteps armed with a do-it-yourself DNA testing kit.

The few details Poppy had been able to glean about her father had come from Dina, who had in turn learned them from her mother-in-law Margaret McBride. According to this third-hand information her mother had met Alex Fitzpatrick at a country club on the outskirts of Bristol. She was working there behind the bar and he had played the trumpet in the resident jazz band.

Alex had moved down from London to take the job, because even if the pay was peanuts it was better than nothing at all. He might have been poor but jazz was his great love; it was what he lived for.

Laura Dunbar, so legend had it, was finding married life less enthralling than she had been led to expect. Meeting

Alex Fitzpatrick, who kept nightclub hours, drank Jack Daniels on the rocks and laughed at the deeply suburban lifestyles of the members of Ash Hill Country Club, had knocked her for six.

Alex had a gravelly Cockney drawl, a quick wit and a career in what could just about be called show business. He also made Laura laugh, which mattered more than anything. She fell in love with Alex Fitzpatrick, ignored the fact that he had a wife waiting for him back in London and threw herself headlong into a recklessly indiscreet affair. It became the talk of the country club. It wasn't long before everyone knew, including Mervyn Dunbar.

But Mervyn, who loved his wife, sensed that if he kicked up a fuss he would only lose her. Electing to sit it out and pray that nature would run its course, he grimly feigned ignorance instead.

Six weeks later, as the summer season was drawing to a close, Alex Fitzpatrick's wife was watering a hanging basket when she fell off a stepladder and broke her leg in three places.

Alex explained to a devastated Laura that he had to go back to London. His contract at Ash Hill was pretty much up anyway, and now his old lady needed him. They'd had a laugh, hadn't they? They'd had a great summer together but now it was time to move on. She had a husband, he had a wife. Of course he'd loved Laura, but this was how things were. No need to get all dramatic over a bit of harmless fun.

Laura was devastated but she had her pride. To be fair to Alex, he had never talked about leaving his wife; she had just hoped he might.

Hiding her true feelings, refusing to cry in front of him, Laura kissed Alex goodbye. When she discovered three weeks later that she was pregnant she knew at once who was the father. She had been far too busy making love with Alex to have any energy left for Mervyn.

Mervyn, who wasn't stupid, was equally aware of whose

baby it was. When he'd wanted nature to take its course he hadn't meant in this fashion.

But at least he had his wife back, which was what Mervyn wanted most of all. He also privately suspected that he might not be able to father children of his own as a result of a nasty attack of teenage mumps. Maybe in time, he decided, he would be able to forget who the biological father of this child really was. Maybe he would learn to love it as if it were his own.

Poppy knew all this because her mother had confided as much in her small circle of friends, one of whom had been Margaret McBride. Pride had prevented Laura from ever contacting Alex Fitzpatrick to let him know she was carrying his baby. Instead she had immersed herself in the business of becoming a born-again good wife.

When Poppy had been born Mervyn had, in turn, tried his hardest to experience true fatherly feelings. The trouble was, they hadn't been there. And he had been unable to summon up any.

But the secret of Poppy's parentage had been kept, from herself if from no one else, and her mother's tragic death had only compounded people's determination to preserve it. To lose one parent was terrible enough, they whispered to each other. Imagine the effect it could have on a vulnerable twelve-year-old to discover that the one you had left wasn't a real parent at all.

If only they'd known, Poppy thought ruefully, how glad I would have been to find out.

But it was time now to go into action. She had waited long enough. Since she'd moved to London, wondering who her real father might be had knocked everything else out of her mind – even Tom. The sooner the noisy Australian from the basement flat stopped yakking to every friend he'd ever had and got off the communal payphone, the sooner she could make a start.

When he had at last finished Poppy ran downstairs and bagged the phone, kneeling on the dusty floor with her list of A. Fitzpatricks in one hand and a pile of twenty-pence coins in the other. Her heart pounded against her ribs as she began to dial. Imagine, within seconds she could actually be speaking to her father . . .

Each time the phone was picked up at the other end, Poppy asked in a businesslike voice to speak to Alex Fitzpatrick. Ten minutes later she was three-quarters of the way through her list, having got through to an assortment of Alans, Alistairs, Alisons and Andrews . . . even an Ahmed.

Then she struck lucky.

'Alex?' said a middle-aged sounding woman. 'I'm sorry, you've just missed him. May I take a message?'

Poppy gulped. This really could be it.

'Um . . . maybe I'll try again later. What time do you expect him home?'

'Well, nine-ish. He's gone to cubs.' The woman began to sound nervous. 'Is this about Ben's birthday party last week? Oh dear, you aren't Lucy-Anne's mother are you?'

Another ten minutes and she was finished. Not only a crushing disappointment, Poppy thought mournfully, but a waste of an awful lot of twenty pences.

How stupid to think finding her father would be that simple.

The next morning, bright and early, Poppy arrived on the doorstep of 15, Cornwallis Crescent.

'Please, it's only ten o'clock,' groaned Claudia, opening the door in her blue and white towelling dressing gown.

Poppy looked hurt. 'Caspar said any time I liked.'

'Caspar would.' Claudia was gazing askance at the two modest suitcases on the top step. 'He doesn't even hear door bells before noon. That can't really be all you've got.'

'I do what the glossy magazines say to do,' said Poppy. 'I may not have many clothes but I always buy the best.'

They both knew this was a big lie. For lunch at The Marigold, Poppy had turned up in cut-off black jeans and a Rocky Horror tee-shirt.

Claudia said gloomily, 'God, I hope Caspar knows what he's doing.'

'Oh look, I'm here now.' Poppy picked up her suitcases. 'And whether you like it or not I'm moving in. We may as well be friends.'

'Real friends,' Claudia pointed out, 'don't wake you up at ten o'clock on a Saturday morning.'

'I'm sorry, I won't do it again.' Carrying her cases through to the kitchen, Poppy heaved the smaller of the two up onto the fridge and began unzipping it.

Next moment a multi-coloured explosion of tights and tee-shirts hurtled out. It was like one of those trick cans full of snakes.

'What—' began Claudia.

'Come on, cheer up and grab a couple of bowls.' Having at last found what she was searching for, Poppy held them up. 'This one's to celebrate me moving in and this one's your belated birthday present.'

Claudia gazed at the two tubs of rapidly melting Ben and Jerry's. Other people celebrated with champagne, she thought. Poppy Dunbar had to do it with Chunky Monkey ice cream.

Chapter 8

Three weeks later, on a wet Wednesday afternoon, the weather was so depressing that Caspar decided he couldn't possibly work. This was the trouble with skylights and broad attic windows. When the rain came down, you knew about it.

To cheer himself up – and take his mind off the fact that the painting he was supposed to be working on should have been finished a week ago – Caspar watched a bit of lunchtime *Coronation Street* and polished off the bowl of cherry tomatoes he'd spotted earlier in the fridge. Then he helped himself to a cappuccino mousse with whipped cream on top.

By now *Coronation Street* had finished and been replaced by one of those audience participation talk shows. This one was about shoplifting. A skinny woman in an orange wig stood up to announce that she was a professional shoplifter. Another boasted about having once shoplifted a three-piece suite. The talk show host said this almost deserved a round of applause and the audience, unsure whether or not they were supposed to clap, looked nervous and fidgeted in their seats. The host then introduced this week's expert, a woman psychiatrist with a face like a bulldog, and Caspar fell asleep.

He was woken up an hour or so later by the door bell. Opening the front door he found Claudia's mother shivering on the top step. It was still pouring with rain.

'Come in, you're drenched.' Caspar pulled her inside and ushered her into the sitting room. 'Sorry, I was asleep.' He switched off the television and made a token effort to plump up the squashed sofa cushions. 'Claudia isn't home from work yet. She'll be back around five. Can I get you a drink?'

Angie Slade-Welch smiled at the sight of Caspar, so streaky-blond and deliciously tanned, in his turquoise tee-shirt and white shorts. He looked like a beach bum, and not a day over twenty-two.

'I knew Claudia wouldn't be here.'

She also knew that so long as you were prepared for it, a bit of rain didn't go amiss. The damp, dishevelled look suited her down to the ground. It was why, having been dropped off by her driver right outside the house, she had waited half a minute before ringing the bell. Plenty of Audrey Hepburn eye make-up and a fragile smile, and Angie could take on the world.

As long as the mascara was run-proof.

'You knew Claudia wouldn't be home yet? Oh dear,' said Caspar. 'In that case I hope you haven't come here to ask embarrassing questions behind her back. My mother did that once when I was in the fourth form. She cornered the French mistress, convinced that I was being led astray—'

'And were you?'

'Of course.' He grinned. 'But it improved my French no end. So, is that really why you're here? You want me to dish the dirt on your daughter's love life?'

'Not at all.' The only love life Angie was interested in was her own.

'You want to find out if she's happy here?'

Angie shrugged and shook her head. 'No, but you can tell me if you like. She's had a couple of moans about the new girl . . . what's her name? Poppy.'

Never one to boil a kettle when he could open a bottle instead, Caspar was relieved to discover an unopened bottle of Pouilly Fumée hidden behind the mineral water at the back of the fridge.

'Ah yes, Poppy and Claudia.' He filled two glasses and passed one to Angie. 'The harem, as some of my not very witty friends have taken to calling them.'

'And are they?' Angie raised an interested eyebrow. 'Your harem?'

Caspar pulled a face. 'They bear a passing resemblance. Claudia doesn't trust Poppy an inch. Now I know what it would be like, keeping a wife and mistress together under one roof. Except,' he added with a grin, 'I'm not sleeping with either of them.'

'How quaint.' Angie could imagine how desperately Claudia would have liked to. She would leap at the chance. Caspar evidently wasn't interested. Good.

'In fact neither of them are to my knowledge sleeping with anyone,' he went on, 'which means there isn't really any dirt to dish.'

'Some harem.'

'So if it isn't a rude question,' said Caspar, 'why are you here?'

'I'd like you to paint me.'

Angie crossed one slender charcoal-stockinged leg over the other. She was wearing an efficient-looking grey pin-striped suit today, tightly belted to show off her tiny waist. Unfastening her bag she took out a calfskin-bound diary.

'Um . . . no offence, but I'm pretty expensive,' said Caspar. It was always better to come out and say it straight away, particularly when the potential client was someone you knew. Even friends-of-friends had an embarrassing habit of expecting you to do it for free.

'That's all right, so am I.' Leaning closer, Angie gave him a conspiratorial look. 'The thing is, I want the painting for Hugo. It's his fiftieth birthday in December—'

'If you want it finished by December I'm going to have to charge more,' Caspar interrupted. 'Look, it's going to be six grand. I'm sorry, but my manager would shoot me if I said anything less.'

Privately he was marvelling at the choice of gift. How many men would want to so much as glance at a portrait of their ex-wife, let alone be given one for their birthday? What if he threw darts at it?

'Six grand, no problem.' Angie Slade-Welch was unperturbed. 'He'll be paying for it anyway.' She smiled. 'One thing I will say for Hugo, he's a perfect gentleman when it comes to alimony.'

Poor Hugo, thought Caspar. With four ex-wives to support no wonder he kept having to fly over to Hollywood to star in the kind of mega-budget movies he despised so much. Small wonder too that none of the ex-wives had ever bothered to remarry. When the payoffs were that generous, where was the incentive?

Caspar, who didn't have anything as efficient as a diary, led Angie Slade-Welch upstairs to his studio. The back of the door was covered with pinned-up business cards and scraps of paper with names and phone numbers scrawled across them. Some had dates and times added in brackets. This was Caspar's filing system. It was a miracle he ever got anything done.

'Mondays are good for me.' Angie was flipping through pages with beige, French-manicured nails. 'Wednesdays . . . no, that's aromatherapy. Um, Thursday afternoons could be arranged. Or maybe Friday mornings . . .'

They haggled amicably for a few minutes. Caspar never felt like doing much at all on Mondays. Finally they settled on three preliminary sittings to be going on with.

'This Friday then.' Caspar prepared to show her out. 'No need to worry about getting your hair done, not at this stage. But bring a couple of outfits so we can decide what'll look best. Nothing too fussy—'

'Nothing fussy at all,' Angie promised, her mouth registering amusement. 'Did I not mention it earlier? I want this to be a nude portrait.' She paused, waiting for his reaction. 'That's not a problem for you, is it?'

'Not exactly a problem for *me* . . .' Caspar was looking doubtful.

'Well then, that's fine. If you're worried about my daughter,' said Angie with a careless shrug, 'don't tell her. This is a private business transaction between consenting adults. Claudia doesn't need to know.'

After a rotten day at work and a rain-drenched dash from the tube Claudia wasn't thrilled to come home and find Caspar and Poppy gossiping together in the sitting room, cosily sharing a packet of Jaffa Cakes and showing no sign whatsoever of doing anything about the mountain of washing-up in the sink.

She was even less enchanted when she spotted the empty bottle of Pouilly Fumée up on the mantelpiece. Two glasses stood side by side on the low coffee table next to the carton that had earlier contained her favourite cappuccino mousse.

Next moment her attention was distracted by something more awful still –

'Ugh – UGH!' screamed Claudia, shuddering with fear and revulsion. She pointed at the carpet beneath the table. 'SPIDERS!'

Caspar craned his neck to see. He grinned, leaned over the edge of the sofa, scooped them up and lobbed them at Claudia.

'Don't get in a flap, they're only tomato stalks.'

'*Oh*.' Claudia was still trembling. 'You really are the living end . . .'

'Sweetheart, I wouldn't have thrown them at you if they'd been spiders.'

'Not that,' Claudia wailed, glaring at him. 'They were *my* tomatoes. This,' she jabbed a finger at the empty carton, 'was my cappuccino mousse. And I was saving that wine for a special occasion!'

'This afternoon was a special occasion.' Caspar thought of the six thousand pounds. 'That's why I opened it.' Then, since Claudia was looking very cross indeed, he added, 'I'll buy you another one.'

'That's not the point.' Claudia hadn't inherited her mother's gift for looking good when wet. Her hair was a mess and her navy mascara had run dramatically down her face. Turning to include Poppy in the diatribe she went on, 'You didn't even leave enough for me to have a glass. You had to jolly well drink it all.'

Poppy had only arrived home from work ten minutes earlier herself. She looked indignant. 'It wasn't me, it was—'

'Anton. From the gallery.' Caspar indulged in a bit of improv, sensing that now was not the time to tell Claudia her mother had been round. 'He dropped by to show me the brochure for next month's exhibition.' Ad-libbing shamelessly he went on, 'It looks completely brilliant. Anton says it's already attracting interest from dealers in Japan—'

The phone rang. Claudia picked it up.

'For you.' Tight-lipped, she handed the phone to Caspar. 'It's Anton. Calling from New York.'

Caspar, well and truly caught out, grinned. 'Told you Concorde was fast.'

'I'm not one of your girlfriends,' Claudia said bitterly. 'You don't have to lie to me.'

Chapter 9

'Didn't I tell you Angie Slade-Welch was trouble?' said Caspar when Claudia had disappeared upstairs to have a long hot sulk in the bath.

'You could have turned her down,' Poppy protested. 'You could have said no.'

He pulled a face. 'I'm not famed for my ability to say no.'

'Well, I just hope she's worth it. You haven't even seen her with her kit off yet.'

'I don't think there's any danger she'll fail the audition.' Caspar was doodling in the margins of the *Radio Times*. Glancing up, catching the expression on Poppy's face, he began to laugh. 'Well I'm sorry. I'm just being honest. You were the one who asked how my day had been. If you're going to disapprove, I won't tell you anything in future.'

'I'm not disapproving. I'm interested. It's the big difference between men and women, isn't it? You don't have to love someone, or even like them very much, but if you're a man you'll still sleep with them.' Poppy tore open a packet of crisps with her teeth. 'It's a bit of entertainment, a nice way of passing the time. Like doing card tricks or playing Trivial Pursuit.'

'I'm not completely indiscriminate,' Caspar protested. 'And okay, I might not be in love with these women but I do like them. Claudia's mother knows the score. She doesn't expect anything more than a fling. She certainly doesn't *love* me.'

'I suppose.' Poppy shrugged. 'It just seems weird.'

'You've had a sheltered upbringing.' Caspar drew a caricature of one of the ITN reporters, naked at his newsdesk.

'I have not!'

'What I'm saying is, you met this boyfriend of yours when you were seventeen. You went steady for a few years, got engaged, planned to get married . . . he's probably the only bloke you've ever slept with.'

'So?' Poppy demanded hotly.

'I just think you should get out and about a bit more,' Caspar explained. 'Live a little. Go to parties, meet new people.'

'Sleep with new men.'

'Yes.'

'Why?'

'Because,' Caspar sounded exasperated, 'you're twenty-two years old and you're single. It's what twenty-two-year-old single girls *do*.'

Poppy sighed. She only wished she could. It was over six months now since she had left Bristol and she was still unable to summon up so much as a flicker of interest in a member – any member – of the opposite sex.

She didn't even know if it had happened as a result of meeting Tom or as a side effect of calling off the wedding to Rob, but happen it had. The way things were going Poppy was beginning to wonder if, libido-wise, she would ever feel normal again. It wasn't as if she was unhappy or depressed either, because she wasn't. She just felt as if her heart had been snipped out and swapped for a block of ice.

And like the Cointreau lady, it was taking a hell of a time for the ice to melt.

Caspar was still watching her.

'Well I'm sorry,' said Poppy, 'but I don't want to run round London waving my knickers in the air. I told you before, I'm not interested in sex. I'm immune.'

'I just hope it isn't catching.' He grinned and held up the magazine so she could see his latest effort. A caricature of her with manic ringlets, a halo and a Just Say No tee-shirt stood alongside a wicked one of Claudia, looking hopeful, with Just Say Yes Please emblazoned across her vast bosom.

'Poor Claudia. Be nice to her.' Poppy, who had to be at work by seven, forced herself to her feet.

'What are you doing?'

'You told me I should go to parties and meet more people.'

'I'm talking about places where you aren't the one passing round the vol-au-vents,' said Caspar.

'Yes, well. I have an exorbitant rent to pay. And a pig of a landlord.' Hearing footsteps on the stairs, Poppy grabbed the *Radio Times* and tore out the page he'd doodled on. Claudia wasn't likely to appreciate the joke. She crumpled the un-flattering caricature into a ball and threw it just in time into the bin.

'Right,' Claudia announced, smiling at them both. 'I feel better now. Sorry I lost my temper before. Who'd like a cup of tea?'

Amazed, Caspar and Poppy both put their hands up.

'I'll make a big pot.' Claudia beamed again, to prove they were forgiven. 'And I bought some Hob Nobs on the way home. Oh great, my *Radio Times*. Let's have a look at what's on tonight . . .'

'Well?' Returning at midnight Poppy poked her head round the sitting-room door. 'At least you're still alive. But will she ever speak to either of us again?'

'I'm exhausted. I've spent the whole evening being nice,' said Caspar. 'Not that kind of nice,' he added as Poppy's eyebrows rose.

'All that fuss over one lousy missing page.' Working in the evenings meant Poppy barely got to watch any TV nowa-days. She glanced across at it as the film Caspar had been watching drew to an end. The credits began to roll. The name Fitzpatrick made her heart leap for a moment but it was only someone called Shona Fitzpatrick, one of the supporting actresses in the cast.

Sensing something was up, Caspar followed her gaze. He caught the name just before it slid off the screen.

Then he had a brainwave.

'Why don't you advertise on television for your father?'

Poppy looked at him. 'Now that is a terrific idea. Why didn't I think of it months ago? Hang on a sec,' she patted her jeans pockets, 'where's my purse? I know I've got sixty or seventy grand here somewhere.'

'Okay, okay. There is such a thing as free advertising,' Caspar reminded her. 'You could wait until the next big rugby international at Twickenham, make up a banner with Desperately Seeking Alex Fitzpatrick plastered across it, and streak across the pitch at half-time.'

'Desperately Seeking Attention, more like. Not to mention a chilly night in the cells.' Poppy conjured up a mental image of herself without any clothes on, being chased around the rugby field by a lot of smirking policemen. 'Anyway, I don't have the chest for it.'

'I'm trying to help,' said Caspar, 'and all you're doing is making feeble excuses. How about advertising in the newspapers then? That needn't cost much.'

'I know, but it's not very subtle either.' Poppy had already considered this idea. 'The thing is, I'm not looking for a missing person. I'm looking for someone who had – and probably still does have – a wife. The chances are that he has kids of his own. How are they likely to feel, discovering that he had an affair with my mother all those years ago? I don't want to hurt anyone,' said Poppy, 'or be the cause of some awful showdown. Any way of tracking him down would have to be discreet.'

'But you still want to try.'

Poppy was leaning against the sitting-room door restlessly turning the handle this way and that. She nodded.

'More than anything. I want to meet him, even if he

doesn't know who I am. I just need to know what he's like.' She took a deep breath, frustrated by her own helplessness. 'I might love him to bits, he might be perfect. On the other hand he could be awful.'

'Then again,' said Caspar, 'why should you be the only one around here with a parent who's awful?'

Poppy looked shocked. 'Your parents aren't, they're brilliant.'

'I didn't mean me. I'm talking about Angie Slade-Welch.'

'Goodness,' Poppy mocked. 'So does that mean you won't be sleeping with her after all?'

'I said she was an awful parent.' Caspar grinned. 'I daresay she's better in bed.'

Poppy went upstairs to catch a few hours' sleep. She was running the stall single-handed tomorrow while Jake toured the auction rooms. Ever since she had shooed away a wasp with her rolled-up programme and found herself the new owner of a twenty-foot refectory table riddled with wood-worm Jake hadn't let her within screaming distance of a gavel.

Caspar, who wasn't tired, spent the night working in his studio. He made great progress with the painting Angie Slade-Welch had admired earlier.

He wondered as he worked how long it would be before Angie made her move. That she would make a play for him wasn't in doubt; it was more a question of when. Caspar squeezed the dregs of a tube of cobalt blue onto his palette, chucked the empty tube in the direction of the bin and began blending the blue with viridian. Some women, enjoying the sense of anticipation, confined themselves to gentle flirting for the first three or four sittings. Others, eager not to waste a moment, made their intentions obvious straight away. Caspar had a bet with himself that Angie Slade-Welch would make her move at the end of the first sitting. She didn't seem the type to hang around.

He then surprised himself by wondering whether or not he should go along with it. This was startling because it had never before occurred to him not to.

Caspar put down his brush. Reaching absently for a can of Coke he drank from it, his gaze fixed on the ink-black sky through the uncurtained windows, his thoughts elsewhere.

This was all Poppy's fault. It was thanks to her that he was actually thinking of not sleeping with someone. Not because he had been lectured to, either, by some born-again do-gooder droning on about the evils of promiscuity. That was always guaranteed to backfire. It was, thought Caspar, enough to send anyone hurtling into the nearest bed.

But Poppy hadn't done that. Nor was she a droning do-gooder. She had simply wondered what the purpose of it was, when there was no love involved.

And now, for the first time in his life, Caspar found himself wondering if maybe she didn't have a point.

The rain had by this time stopped. There still wasn't a star in sight. Caspar wiped his paint-stained hands on his trousers and resumed painting, his brush moving more or less automatically over the canvas as he thought some more about Poppy Dunbar and the things she had said to him tonight.

The perfect solution, of course, would be to sleep with her.

Caspar grinned to himself and loaded a clean sable brush with cadmium yellow. He liked Poppy, had liked her from the first moment he'd met her. She had spirit and energy and she made him laugh.

She also had amazing hair and a flawless creamy complexion which was certainly undeserved considering the rubbish she ate. These plus points, combined with yellow-green eyes and a curvy mouth that always seemed on the verge of a smile, meant she looked every bit as good as the models who were forever throwing themselves at him.

But Poppy wasn't throwing herself at anyone. She had erected an invisible barrier around herself, a kind of aura

59

that sent out the signal: Definitely Not Interested. This was a natural enough reaction, considering what she'd gone through earlier in the year. Caspar had never experienced it himself because he'd never had to endure any form of emotional trauma, but he was perfectly prepared to believe it existed. He'd heard about all that stuff on Richard and Judy.

The thing was, it was beginning to intrigue him now. He couldn't help wondering if he could *make* Poppy be interested in him.

What a brilliant challenge that would be. He needn't bother with a pushover like Angie Slade-Welch, he could concentrate all his attentions instead on Poppy, who would be so much more fun to sleep with.

Caspar was painting faster and faster. The more he thought about it the more the idea appealed. He would be helping Poppy over her ice-block, as she called it. Mentally they were well matched. Physically – he just knew – they would be perfect. Damn, they'd be great together . . .

Watery sunlight streamed through the windows of the studio as Caspar put the finishing touches to the painting on the easel before him. He stretched, glanced at his watch – eight thirty – and wandered downstairs.

There was a plate of toast, thickly buttered just the way he liked it, on the kitchen table. Exerting tremendous self-control Caspar left it there and began breaking eggs into a frying pan instead. Moments later Poppy shot into the kitchen half-dressed to fill up the kettle and wrench the lid off the biscuit tin.

She looked stunned when she saw him.

'What are you doing?'

Caspar, who would have thought it was obvious, said, 'Cooking.' Proudly, he added, 'Eggs.'

'I mean what are you doing up? It isn't even nine o'clock.'

'I haven't been to bed. Damn—' Showing off with the fish slice he managed to break two yolks.

Poppy looked puzzled. 'Why on earth not?'

'I've been working.' He paused, meaningfully. 'And thinking . . .'

But Poppy was late for work. The kettle hadn't boiled because Claudia had unplugged it to make way for the iron. The iron was still there. With a mouth full of chocolate biscuit and her back to Caspar so he wouldn't see her knickers, Poppy seized the opportunity to get the worst of the creases out of her skirt.

'Most people take their clothes off before they iron them.' She turned and grinned at him.

'Most people take their clothes off the minute they walk into your studio, but it doesn't mean I have to. It isn't compulsory.'

The skirt, being only small, didn't take long. When Poppy had dragged a pair of tangled black tights out of the tumble drier, helped herself to another handful of Bourbons and located her black suede shoes under the kitchen table she blew a kiss in Caspar's direction and made a dash for the front door.

'Hell,' Caspar sighed, staring down at the eggs in the pan. Poppy had distracted him. They were hopelessly overdone.

'Yuk,' said Claudia, coming into the kitchen with her coat on.

She wrinkled her nose. 'How on earth did you manage to *burn* them?'

Caspar was starving and there weren't any eggs left. Nor, he discovered as Claudia finished her mug of tea, were there any more teabags.

'You haven't eaten your toast,' he said before she left.

'Oh . . . I wasn't hungry . . .'

When the front door had banged shut behind her, Caspar snatched up the toast he had so heroically resisted earlier. But it was too late, the butter had begun to congeal. The toast was soggy and stone cold. So much, thought Caspar, for being considerate and exerting self-control.

It didn't take much longer for his second good resolution

61

to bite the dust. What had seemed such a great idea last night was – in the cold light of day – becoming an altogether dicier prospect. As he went through the plan again and realised just how fraught with pitfalls it was, Caspar felt his resolve begin to drain away. By the time he'd finished the last piece of horrid toast he knew for certain he couldn't go through with it. There were heaps of reasons why not.

Poppy was a friend, for a start, a cheerful tenant he'd be sorry to lose should the plan backfire. Also, any kind of goings-on between the two of them would be bound to upset Claudia. She would *hate* it.

The major stumbling block, though, was Poppy herself. *She* might not be interested. She might not want to be won over, either. She might say no and mean it, and he would *really* hate that.

He would hate it even more if she laughed.

Damn, thought Caspar, why take the risk? Knowing Poppy she'd laugh her socks off. And even if she didn't, what could ever come of it anyway? He didn't exactly have the greatest track record in the world.

No, Caspar decided, the smart thing to do was to forget all about seducing Poppy, to put the idea completely out of his mind and simply think of her as one of the lads instead.

Far better to stick with the devil you knew.

Caspar sighed. It was seriously unlike him to change his mind like this; in fact, it had to be a first. But some weird inner instinct told him he was right to do so.

Bugger it, he might as well sleep with Angie Slade-Welch after all.

Chapter 10

Poppy couldn't help feeling sorry for the women in Caspar's life.

Not Angie, who was quite old enough to take care of herself. But Poppy certainly felt for the girlfriends who so patently adored him and whom he treated so casually in return. Fibbing over the phone to them on Caspar's behalf was one thing; Poppy had had plenty of practice doing that.

But when the girls were nice and you had to deal with them in person – actually face to face, with that awful trusting look in their eyes – it was hard, sometimes, not to interfere.

If you had an ounce of compassion in your soul, it could be downright impossible.

Jake was out on a buying expedition when Kate Mitchell came into the antiques market. She waited patiently for Poppy to finish selling a Staffordshire stirrup cup to a middle-aged Swedish woman in a purple mac.

Poppy liked Kate, who was sweet-natured, friendly and fragile-looking. When she discovered the purpose of Kate's visit she knew the time had come to start interfering like mad.

'I know it's only October but I always buy my Christmas presents early,' Kate explained with an apologetic smile. 'The thing is, I'm a bit scared of antique shops but I knew if I came here you wouldn't let me be ripped off.'

' 'Course I wouldn't.' Poppy thought what a shame it was that Jake couldn't be here to eavesdrop on such a compliment. 'And we've got some terrific presenty-type things. Who are you buying for, family?'

'Caspar actually.' Kate's cheeks went a fetching shade of pink. 'I don't have much money but I really want to get him something nice. In fact I spotted something a moment ago while you were with the lady in the mac . . .'

Poppy's heart sank. Kate was leaning over the glass-topped jewellery cabinet pointing an almost translucent index finger in the direction of a diamond tiepin. The ticket price was four hundred pounds, which she knew perfectly well Kate couldn't afford.

Poppy also knew it didn't matter how nice a person *she* thought Kate was; Caspar was beginning to tire of her puppy-like devotion. A turkey had more chance than this relationship did of lasting until Christmas.

'A . . . tiepin?' Poppy hesitated, stalling for time. 'Um, does Caspar *own* any ties?'

'It's all right,' Kate blushed again. 'I know he doesn't. It's kind of a private joke between us. You see, I was teasing Caspar, telling him he'd have to wear a tie one day when he got married.' Throwing caution to the wind she added in a rush, 'So I thought what a brilliant present it would be . . . and who knows, it might even prompt him to . . . well, think weddingy thoughts . . .'

Poppy felt numb. How embarrassing, and she wasn't even the one saying it.

'Couldn't you just buy him a tie?'

'Come on, unlock the cabinet,' pleaded Kate. 'It's okay, I know how much it costs. That doesn't matter.' Shyly she added, 'Caspar's worth it.'

He's NOT, Poppy wanted to shout, but all she could do was unlock the cabinet and hand over the tiepin. She could hardly cram it into her mouth secret-agent style and swallow it.

'Four hundred pounds,' Kate murmured, gazing at the centre diamond and turning it this way and that to catch the light. 'Four hundred pounds . . .'

This was what people did when they were too nervous to

haggle. Normally, to put them out of their misery, Poppy would have said, 'Well, for you, three fifty.'

'I know, and I'm afraid I can't drop the price.' She rolled her eyes. 'Jake can be so *mean* sometimes. If you ask me he's gone way over the top with this one. I doubt if it's worth two hundred, let alone four.'

'Oh, but it's so beautiful—'

'In fact,' Poppy had an inspired thought, 'I'm not even sure Caspar likes diamonds. I've got a feeling he thinks they're naff. What I know he *really* likes is topaz.'

Kate looked startled. 'Topaz?'

'Topaz and silver. He was talking about it just the other night. According to Caspar it's a classic combination, like Laurel and Hardy . . . caviar and vodka . . . Pearl and Dean . . .' Poppy waved frantically across to Marlene, whose stock of jewellery was more extensive than Jake's. 'Hey, Marlene! D'you still have that tiepin, the topaz and silver one I saw yesterday?'

Marlene nodded. Poppy turned triumphantly back to Kate.

'Take my advice, get him that one. It's a dream, Caspar will love it.'

'But—'

'And don't be afraid of Marlene. The ticket says eighty,' Poppy beamed. 'Be firm. Tell her you won't go a penny over forty-five.'

'G-goodness,' stammered Kate, backing away in the direction of Marlene's stall. 'Thanks, Poppy.'

'Thanks Poppy,' said another quiet voice behind her.

Brimming with guilt she spun round. Jake was back from trawling the auction rooms and had – quite unfairly, she thought – sneaked in the back way rather than through the glass double doors of the main entrance where she could have spotted him at once.

Poppy squirmed and wondered how long he'd been listening.

'Long enough,' said Jake, since the unspoken question was

fairly obvious. He took off his glasses and rubbed them on the elbow of his threadbare black cardigan. It was a habit he resorted to when his patience was tried, usually by Poppy. That and the sorrowful look he gave her – minus the terrible glasses – always made Poppy feel ashamed. It would be so much easier to bear if he'd only yell at her, call her an imbecile, give her a Chinese burn . . .

'Jake, I'm sorry, but I *couldn't* sell her the tiepin.' In the nick of time Poppy remembered to lower her voice. 'The poor thing's crazy about Caspar . . . she doesn't know he's about to dump her! And she's only an apprentice textile designer so she earns peanuts. Think about it, Jake, you *can't* stand by and let someone spend that much money when you know they're about to be ditched.'

Slowly Jake shook his head. He knew Poppy's intentions were good. He just wished they didn't have to cost him so much.

'Okay, I see your point. But Poppy, please. I have rent to pay, bills to settle –' he paused for added gravitas – 'your wages to find each week.'

Poppy looked miserable. 'I really am sorry.'

'Just remember, we're here to try and make a living. Caspar French's love life isn't my concern—'

He broke off as Kate returned. She was clutching the tiepin, now gift-wrapped.

'You were right,' she told Poppy happily, 'this one's perfect, much more Caspar's style.'

Poppy still thought it was like buying a CD for someone who didn't have a CD player, but that was up to Kate.

'Right, well, I'll see you on Thursday,' Kate went on, 'for Caspar's preview night. You're going, aren't you?'

Poppy nodded. The Denver Parrish Gallery on Cork Street was showcasing the work of three artists, one of whom was Caspar. The exhibition was attracting a huge amount of interest and the preview night promised to be a glitzy affair.

'And you too?' Kate turned and smiled at Jake, who looked uncomfortable.

'Oh no, I haven't been—'

'Yes!' exclaimed Poppy, seizing the opportunity to make things up to him. 'Of course you must come! You can be my partner. It'll be great, free champagne and all the pistachios you can peel—'

'I can't.' Jake cut across her frenzied babbling. 'I'm meeting someone on Thursday night.'

'He wasn't happy with me,' Poppy confided later on that afternoon. Jake had popped out to the bank and Marlene had wandered over for a gossip. They were sharing a bag of sherbet lemons. 'Poor old Kate, she doesn't have much luck with men. I even caught her discreetly giving Jake the once-over. Didn't have the heart to tell her he was gay.'

'Probably gay,' Marlene corrected. 'We don't know for sure.'

'Bet you fifty pence he is. Damn –' Poppy looked dismayed – 'is that the last one? We'll have to break it in half.'

The phone rang while Marlene was sawing energetically at the last sherbet lemon with an Edwardian letter opener.

'Hello?' said Poppy, picking it up.

'Oh, hi,' a male voice sounded surprised. 'Um . . . Jake not there?'

'I'm afraid he's popped out. Can I help you?'

'Okey-doke. If you could just pass a message on to him.' It was, Poppy realised, an extremely camp male voice. Like Julian Clary on helium. 'Tell him Ellis called and I'm ever so sorry but I can't make it on Thursday night after all. Something's come up –' he tittered – 'so we're going to have to get together some other time.'

'Gosh, this is a terrible line,' said Poppy, before pressing the phone triumphantly against Marlene's ear, 'could you say that last bit again?'

'Okay, okay,' Marlene grumbled two minutes later, 'you

were right and I was wrong, Jake's gay and I owe you fifty pence.'

'Not to mention half a lemon sherbet.'

'Consolation prize.' Marlene popped both halves into her own mouth.

'Poor Jake, stood up by Ellis. Never mind,' Poppy brightened. 'Now he can come along to Caspar's opening night after all.'

Chapter 11

Thursday evening hadn't got off to the greatest of starts as far as Claudia was concerned. Her period was due, which always made her puff up like an adder. This meant the dazzling new black dress she'd bought three days earlier – before PMT had struck – was showing the strain.

She began to feel better once she'd organised the narrow crisscross strapping across the back and trained herself not to breathe. Maybe she looked pretty good after all. The dress, from one of the new young designers at Hyper Hyper, had cost a bomb. Claudia gave herself an extra morale-boosting squirt of Arpège, checked her hair and make-up for the fifth time and sashayed downstairs to the sitting room where Caspar, Poppy and Kate were having a celebratory first drink.

'Oh,' said Claudia, coming to an abrupt halt in the doorway.

'Oops,' said Poppy, looking up.

'Snap,' said Caspar with a grin.

Claudia didn't know whether to stamp her foot or burst into tears. There was only one thing more galling than someone else wearing a dress almost exactly the same as yours, and that was discovering how much better they looked in it than you did. Damn, *damn* . . .

'When did you buy that?' Claudia blurted out, her tone accusing. More to the point, how could Poppy-the-pauper possibly have been able to afford it?

'Oh dear.' Kate was looking worried. 'I'm sorry, I lent it to her.'

Kate was even harder up than Poppy. Unable to help herself, Claudia declared, 'My dress cost three hundred and seventy-five pounds from Cher Balakiel at Hyper Hyper.'

'Blimey,' said Poppy. She looked at Kate in amazement.

'Mine was twenty-four ninety-nine,' Kate confessed nervously. 'From George at Asda.'

Claudia was unable to join in the cheerful banter in the taxi taking them from Kensington to Cork Street. She wished she hadn't been so stubborn now. All she would have had to do was run back upstairs and change into something else. It would have taken two minutes and then she could have put the incident out of her mind.

Instead here she was, looking like half a book-end – the *big* half – at the beginning of an evening that was bound to end in tears.

'Come on, cheer up,' said Caspar as he helped her out of the cab. 'It doesn't matter, really it doesn't.' He gave her a squeeze. 'Imagine what it's like for men. Is their day ruined if someone else turns up at the office in a grey suit?'

It was Caspar's big night. Claudia didn't want to be a party pooper. She watched Poppy and Kate walk into the lit-up gallery ahead of them.

'I'm sorry, I just . . .' She pointed helplessly at Poppy, with her red-gold hair swept up in a dashing topknot. Who needed a tan when you had skin like double cream? Poppy's colouring was the perfect foil for the intricately crisscrossed back and shoulder straps. Her figure was perfect. She was even wearing sheer stockings and black high heels.

'Don't be daft, you both look great,' said Caspar.

Claudia had spent years feeling inferior to her mother. Now it was happening all over again. She felt her lower lip begin to tremble.

'Poppy looks better.'

'Only because we've never seen her tarted up before.' Caspar had been pretty startled himself by the transformation. 'Whereas you always look smart. Let's face it, the way Poppy normally goes around she's hardly likely to be mistaken for Ivana Trump. I really thought she'd turn up tonight in jeans and Doc Martens.'

Claudia pulled herself together. She forced a watery smile. 'I wish she had.'

By nine o'clock the gallery was heaving. Among the guests were buyers, dealers, journalists and a sprinkling of rent-a-celebs, the kind who would jet in from Surbiton for the opening of a jam jar.

Claudia was putting a brave face on things but the fact that she didn't actually know anyone else there meant she was forced to stick with Poppy and Kate. Extra annoying was the way flashbulbs kept going off but every time she turned to see if she was included in the picture, the photographer seemed to have been aiming at Poppy instead.

Caspar had been commandeered by the owner of the gallery who was busily introducing him to all the most influential journalists and buyers. Kate, happy to watch from a distance as her future husband was fêted by a Greek billionaire, was dreamily imagining the blissful life she and Caspar would lead when they were married.

Poppy was determined to enjoy herself. Taking an evening off from Kenda's Kitchen made it doubly important that she should – if you were losing a night's wages you *had* to have a good time. She just wished Claudia would lighten up, start smiling a bit. And where was Jake anyway? He'd promised to be here by nine.

Claudia saw Jake first, threading his way quietly towards them through the squashed-together crowds.

'Good grief, train-spotter alert,' she crowed. 'How on earth did *he* get in?'

Then she cringed, realising who this must be, as the train-spotter touched Poppy's bare arm.

It was at moments like these that Poppy felt most

71

protective towards Jake. This must be what it was like for mothers when their child was pushed off the swing by a bully. Dying to punch Claudia on the nose she said brightly, 'Hooray, you're here at last. Jake, you've met Kate already. This is Claudia, who's in a stinking mood, so don't bother speaking to her.' She beamed up at him. 'And I'm Poppy, remember me?'

'Just about.' Jake smiled slightly. 'You've got make-up on. And you've grown a few inches since five o'clock.'

'Caspar said I had to look smart. These heels are murder. You don't know how lucky you are . . .'

Poppy's voice trailed off. She was somewhat hazy on the subject of gay men. Were they more likely to dress up in women's clothes than straight men? Was Jake a bit of a closet Lily Savage? Poppy's mind boggled at the thought. You never knew, maybe he had a suitcase hidden under his bed crammed with suspender belts and stilettos. It would certainly explain his absolute lack of interest in boring old men's clothes.

'Yes, I'm glad I'm not wearing high heels,' Jake said drily. Kate was peering at her. 'Poppy, are you all right?'

Poppy was envisaging Jake in a figure-skimming Shirley Bassey number. She pulled herself together. So what if he was a transvestite in his spare time? He could wear whatever he jolly well liked.

Jake had in fact done that anyway, turning up in threadbare beige cords, his favourite green sweater with the holes in the elbows and an equally ancient dark blue shirt.

Claudia, clocking each sorry item in turn, marvelled at Jake's nerve. He certainly stood out among the expensive designer suits and arty-farty, natty-cravatty outfits favoured by the other men in the gallery.

Nobody else was wearing an anorak.

Chapter 12

But as the evening wore on Claudia began to regret calling Jake a train-spotter. Granted, at first glance he looked terrible – and he especially didn't fit in with her mental image of how someone called Jake *should* look – but in a weird way he was beginning to grow on her. Claudia was used to noisy, flashy wine-bar types who drove fast cars and always did their chatting up with one eye on the door in case someone better walked in. Their interests in life were making money, getting legless and getting laid and they liked to do all these things as quickly as possible because – as they were so fond of saying – time was money.

Jake was unlike anyone Claudia had ever met before and she was confused. So confused that she couldn't even make out whether or not he was chatting her up.

Having excused herself earlier to visit the loo, Claudia now made her way back to the section of the gallery where the others were. There hadn't been any recognisable chat-up lines, that was for sure, but once or twice the look in Jake's eyes and the tone of his voice had made her think yes, he *was* flirting with her. It was subtle stuff, all very low-key, but she was almost certain it was there. And the more she thought it might be, the more attractive Jake became – in a subtle, bubbling-beneath-the-surface kind of way.

Something else that drew Claudia to him was the easy way he dealt with Poppy. When Poppy did something annoying at home, Claudia went ballistic. Jake's laid-back attitude was a revelation. It was also a bond, something they shared in common.

'It must be dreadful,' Jake had said earlier in his gentle, not-quite-serious fashion. 'She's bad enough to work with. Actually living in the same house must be hell.'

Now, returning from the loo, she saw that one of Caspar's friends had joined their party.

'. . . and don't expect any sympathy from Claudia,' Jake was saying, 'she's on my side.'

This time the look he gave her was almost proprietorial. Claudia experienced a warm glow in her stomach. She liked being on the same side as Jake.

'This is terrible,' complained Poppy, 'I'm being ganged up on. Thanks, Jake, I wish I'd never invited you now.'

Claudia was glad she had. In her excitement she downed her drink in one go. Goodness, it was warm in here. If she pretended to sway a bit in the heat she could brush her bare arm against Jake's woolly-jumpered one. Juvenile but exciting. Thank heavens he'd taken off his anorak.

'More drinks?' Jake said hurriedly. 'Same again all round? And, er, maybe we should take a look at the pictures. It's why we're here, after all.'

Kate was hailed by someone she knew. Poppy and Claudia trooped obediently across to the nearest wall to inspect a garish yellow and pink abstract by one of the other showcased artists. It was eight feet square and eye-bogglingly intricate. The title was 'Knitting; the dropped stitch'.

'Good job my granny's dead,' said Poppy, 'she'd have had something to say about that.' She peered over the shoulder of the Japanese man in front of her, studying the price list on his brochure. 'Fourteen thousand pounds, good grief.'

'Don't,' Claudia hissed. 'It's embarrassing.'

'Damn right it's embarrassing. Fourteen grand for that! I'd far rather have a Caspar French,' Poppy went on, 'in fact I'm going to ask Harry to buy me two. I overheard one of the

New York dealers just now saying they're the hottest investment since De Kooning.'

The Japanese buyer's ears twitched. Seconds later he moved off.

'You don't for one moment think he believed you,' sneered Claudia. 'Honestly, that is *so* juvenile.'

Poppy was stung. She'd thought it was a a brilliant ploy.

'It might work. If I heard someone saying something like that, I'd believe them.'

'Yes, well. You're gullible. Most people have more sense.'

'Thanks.'

Poppy gritted her teeth. If Claudia was going to start harping on about being gullible she might be forced to remind her who had just forked out three hundred and something pounds for a copy of a chainstore dress.

But this time, for once, Claudia backed down.

'Okay, I'm sorry.' She shook her head to show Poppy she meant it. This was Caspar's exhibition and it mustn't be spoiled. Besides, she was bursting to bombard Poppy with a million questions about Jake.

The apology had made Poppy instantly suspicious. She moved along and began studying another of the bizarre abstracts. This one, turquoise and grey, bore the title 'A Kiss in a Tree'.

'Anyway, you were right,' Claudia ventured, eager to clear the air. 'Caspar's stuff is tons better than this rubbish.'

A very tall, bearded man with hooded grey eyes gave her an angry stare.

'That's the artist,' murmured Poppy.

'Shit.'

'Only joking.'

Poppy grinned. Claudia suppressed the urge to throttle her. Instead, in casual tones she said, 'Jake's quite nice, isn't he?'

'Who, you mean Jake my boss? *Train-spotter* Jake?'

Claudia look flustered. 'It was only the anorak. Well, and the trousers. What I mean is, he's better than you expect

'. . . once you actually get to know him.'

Poppy looked amused.

'I'm sure he'll be flattered to hear it.'

'I can't remember,' Claudia blurted out in desperation, 'if you said he was married or living with someone.'

'Now this,' said Poppy, 'is what I call interesting. Don't tell me you're keen on Jake.'

Why did she have to look so . . . so *gleeful*? Affronted, Claudia lifted her chin.

'I'm only asking. Why shouldn't I? He's obviously keen on me.'

Poppy grinned. 'No he isn't.'

'Yes he is.'

'Claudia, I promise you. He isn't.'

'You don't know that.' God, Poppy could be a cow sometimes. 'What are you, some kind of world authority on The Kind of Girls Men Go For?'

'Calm down, calm down.' Poppy made soothing gestures with her hands. 'You've got hold of the wrong end of the stick.'

If I could get hold of the right end, Claudia thought vengefully, I'd hit you with it.

'Look,' Poppy continued, 'what I meant was, Jake doesn't go for *any* kind of girl. He's gay.'

Claudia was stunned. 'Gay? Are you sure?'

'Sure I'm sure. He keeps pretty quiet about it, but he definitely is,' Poppy explained in businesslike fashion. 'That's why there's no point trying to chat him up. So you see, I wasn't being bitchy when I said he wouldn't be interested in you, I was just being honest.' Unaware that Jake was back from the bar and standing right behind her, she went on: 'I know it's sad but what can you do? Jake's as bent as a nine bob note. Actually I think he may be a transvestite too—'

'RIGHT,' Jake hissed into her ear, 'that is ENOUGH. What in heaven's name do you think you are PLAYING AT?'

Poppy jumped a mile. The voice was so filled with fury

she barely recognised it. When she turned and saw the look in Jake's eyes she felt herself go white. She had never seen him so mad before. She wouldn't have believed him capable of such blood-curdling fury.

'Oh Jake, I'm sorry . . . I know it isn't something you make a song and dance about –' help, more visions of Shirley Bassey – 'but I just thought it would be easier to explain to Claudia why she shouldn't . . . um, why you . . . er, wouldn't . . .'

Jake looked ready to explode. Poppy gave up trying to explain. Cringing, she edged a few inches backwards. What a good job they were surrounded by people so Jake couldn't bellow at her.

'I-do-not-believe-this.' He wasn't bellowing. The words were spat out through gritted teeth, which was bad enough. 'Let's get one thing settled right now. I am not gay. I never have been gay and I never will be gay.' His dark eyes, like twin coals, bored through his spectacles and directly into Poppy's brain. 'And I'm sorry to disappoint you but I don't wear women's clothes either.'

'Oh,' said Poppy in a small voice. 'Jake, I'm sorry. My mistake.'

'You see, this is *exactly* what she's like,' Claudia told Jake with an air of triumph. 'She says things without thinking, just comes out with these ridiculous statements—'

'I didn't say it without thinking – ' Poppy was indignant – 'I just thought the wrong thing in the first place.'

Jake had begun to calm down. At least, steam was no longer billowing out of his ears. He frowned. 'But why, what made you think it? I never gave you any reason to believe I was gay.'

Poppy squirmed. Why *had* she thought it?

'I suppose because you don't have a girlfriend.' Oh dear, that sounded pitiful. 'And you never say much about your social life. Um . . .' Yes, that was it! '. . . and then there was that phone call from Ellis!' She seized gratefully upon it, like a lifebelt. 'You were supposed to be meeting him tonight, remember? But he had to cancel—'

'Ellis Featherstone,' said Jake with a sigh, 'lives three doors away from me. He's the local co-ordinator for Neighbourhood Watch. Yes, Ellis is gay,' he concluded evenly, 'but I'm fairly sure it's not catching.'

'Okay, so I made a mistake.' Poppy still couldn't get over the change in Jake. Talk about the worm turning, she marvelled. Jake had turned into a full-grown leopard.

Poppy wasn't the only one impressed by the transformation. Claudia couldn't stop gazing at Jake. The news that he wasn't gay after all had cheered her right up. Emboldened by all the adrenalin whooshing through her veins she seized one of the drinks Jake had carried back from the bar and glugged down another glass of slightly warm champagne.

'What made you say it tonight, anyway?' Jake persisted. In his other hand was Poppy's drink. Before he could pass it to her, Claudia whisked it from his grasp.

Poppy opened her mouth to explain.

'Well—'

'The truth is, she couldn't believe you were chatting me up,' Claudia blithely cut in, her tongue by this time thoroughly loosened. 'I told her you were, she said you weren't.' Breathing in, so her chest swelled out like a pouter pigeon, Claudia gave Jake the benefit of her perfect cleavage. 'Poppy can't believe any man would want to chat me up.'

It was like a mating dance, thought Poppy, struggling to keep a straight face as Jake's eyes inadvertently dipped into the cleavage then slid nervously away. It was like one of those displays of plumage you saw birds doing on David Attenborough programmes. Claudia was silently commanding Jake to respond and chat her up some more. Poor Jake, over his passionate outburst now, was looking downright scared.

Several minutes of awkward small talk later, Jake made his excuses and left.

'Well, thanks,' snapped Claudia when he had gone.

'Oh come on,' Poppy sighed. She had had more than enough of Claudia for one night.

'He would have asked me out, you know. You frightened him off.' Claudia glared at her. 'And don't tell me you didn't do it on purpose.'

By midnight the last guests were drifting away into the night. Only when Caspar had flagged down a cab and piled his own small party inside did he realise why Poppy and Claudia had spent the last couple of hours at different ends of the room.

'Come on, no need for this.' Buoyed up by the success of the exhibition, Caspar attempted a reconciliation.

'I'm all right,' sniffed Claudia. 'It's her. Jake would have asked me out if she hadn't stuck her oar in. If you ask me, she's jealous.'

'Jealous?' shrieked Poppy. 'You were the one who called him a train-spotter! Then you started flaunting your chest at him. He only left early because he was too embarrassed to look at you.'

'Girls, girls,' said Caspar. By the sound of her, Claudia had been drinking for England. He watched her struggling to light the tipped end of her cigarette. Luckily the lighter was upside-down too.

'*And* you're jealous because my dress cost more than yours did,' Claudia declared, giving up on the cigarette and chucking it out of the cab window.

'Oh yes, of course I am.' Poppy lifted her eyebrows in a what-can-you-do-with-a-mad-woman? kind of way.

'Don't do that with your eyebrows,' howled Claudia.

'I'll do whatever I like with my eyebrows. I paid three hundred and seventy-five pounds for them at Hyper Hyper.'

Claudia wondered if she'd ever wanted to strangle anyone this much before in her life. There was that hateful, barely-visible grin again, the one Poppy used when she was making fun of her.

'You're going to regret this.' Realising she didn't have the

79

strength for anything more physical, Claudia waggled an index finger at Poppy instead. 'I was going to tell you something. Something important. You should, you know . . . you should be *nice* to me . . .'

Poppy thought she'd been an awful lot nicer than Claudia deserved. Exerting superhuman control, she said, 'Go on then, what is this oh-so-important thing I need to know?'

'I'm not sure I want to tell you.' The pointed finger jabbed like a conductor's baton. 'I don't think you deserve to know. You shouldn't—'

'Oh for God's sake,' yelped Poppy, throwing herself back in her seat, 'will someone please shut this girl up? What have I done to deserve *her*?'

'Claudia,' said Caspar not unkindly, 'shut up.'

'But—'

'No, I mean it. You've drunk enough to float the QE2.'

'Oh well,' Claudia looked affronted, 'in that case I won't breathe another word.' She shook back her heavy blonde hair. 'Not one single word about the pianist at the Cavendish jazz club . . . the pianist whose name happens to be Alex Fitzpatrick . . .'

Chapter 13

Claudia woke up next morning with a cracking headache. When she rolled over and realised her alarm clock hadn't gone off, and that it was now nine thirty, she groaned aloud.

'It's okay,' said Poppy, nudging open the bedroom door with her elbow and plonking a tray on the end of Claudia's bed. 'I turned off the alarm. And I've phoned your office. I said there'd been a car crash outside the house and you'd rescued a little old lady from the wreckage. You had to wrap her severed finger in frozen peas and take it along to the hospital but you'd be back at work this afternoon.'

Claudia nodded, winced and clutched the side of her head. Getting into a sitting position was worse than climbing Everest. One thing about Poppy, she certainly came up with some inventive reasons for being late for work.

'Here, drink this.' Poppy passed her a cup of tea. She dropped three paracetamols into Claudia's trembling out-stretched hand. 'And I've made you some toast if you think you can keep it down.' She hesitated, then went on, 'And I'm sorry if I was horrible last night.'

'I'm sorry too.' Claudia looked shamefaced. It had all come hurtling back to her. 'I didn't behave very well either. I can't believe I threatened not to tell you about the Alex Fitzpatrick thing.' She gulped down the last few mouthfuls of too-hot tea. It singed her tonsils but quenched her raging thirst. 'I would have told you, of course I would.'

'I know.'

Poppy had barely slept. She still hadn't been able to get

81

over the hand fate had played in Claudia's revelation. To think, if Ellis Featherstone hadn't phoned up last week she would never have come to the inescapable conclusion that Jake was gay. She wouldn't have told Claudia, Jake wouldn't have overheard and the ensuing furious row would never have taken place. And if it hadn't, Claudia wouldn't have stropped off to the far end of the gallery and happened to overhear a couple of jazz-buff art dealers chatting amicably about the blues style of the resident pianist at a tucked-away little place called the Cavendish Club.

It was mind-boggling. As far as Poppy was able to work out, she owed it all to Neighbourhood Watch. Either that or to the entire criminal fraternity, because if it weren't for them the Neighbourhood Watch scheme would never have been invented.

'So d'you think he's the one?' ventured Claudia. 'Could he really be your dad?'

Poppy was sitting on the bed hugging her knees to her chest. No longer tarted up, as Caspar so romantically called it, she looked about sixteen with her red-gold hair flopping into her eyes and the remains of last night's hard-to-get-off mascara clinging to her lashes. She was wearing a yellow sweatshirt and polka-dot leggings, and her feet were bare.

'I think he really could be.' She nodded, resting her chin on one knee. 'But there's only one way to find out. I'm going along to the Cavendish Club tonight.'

Hopefully, Claudia thought, she would be over her hangover by then. 'Would you like me to come with you?'

'Would you?' The look Poppy gave her was one of amazement mixed with relief. 'I'd love you to. That'd be such a help.'

Heavens, thought Claudia, startled that she had even suggested it. Looks like we might be going to get along after all.

She glanced at her watch. It was now quarter to ten.

'Shouldn't you be at work too?'

82

'I phoned Jake.' Poppy helped herself to the toast Claudia was too hungover to eat. 'Said I'd be late.'

'Did you use the severed finger?'

'No. He never believes my excuses.' Poppy looked gloomy. 'It's a waste of time thinking them up.'

'But he's speaking to you, that's something.' Claudia felt her heart do a small practise flutter. 'Did he . . . um, mention me at all?'

'Actually he did,' said Poppy with a grin. Good old Jake, at least he hadn't borne a grudge. 'He said he had a hot date for tomorrow night and please could he borrow your little black dress.'

The Cavendish Club, in Covent Garden, was reached by teetering down a flight of steep, ankle-ricking steps. Converted from an old wine cellar with arched brick ceilings and uneven flagstone floors, it had a smell all its own – a sweet, pervasive mixture of damp, drink and nicotine. The regulars were the genuine jazz buffs, but the Cavendish was well-known enough to attract a wide mix of visitors ranging from students to tourists.

Luckily there were no dress rules.

'We look like The Odd Couple,' Claudia complained as they made their way there. She was wearing a charcoal grey polo-neck cashmere jersey, expensive black trousers and a discreet amount of gold, very chic if she did say so herself. Poppy had turned out in a miles-too-big white tee-shirt that kept slipping off her shoulders, and ancient jeans.

'You didn't like it when we wore the same thing.'

'I know. I just thought you might want to look smart . . . to meet your father . . .' Claudia began to wish she hadn't raised the issue '. . . that is, if it *is* him.'

Poppy wasn't going to admit she'd tried on practically every outfit in her meagre wardrobe before coming out. She glanced across at Claudia as they approached the Cavendish, already belting out music at only eight o'clock.

'What's he going to say, "Oh no, sorry, you aren't wearing top-to-toe Armani, I can't possibly acknowledge you as my daughter"? Please,' said Poppy defiantly. 'If he *is* my father, whatever he's wearing isn't going to make an ounce of difference to me. I daresay he'll forgive me if my tee-shirt isn't haute couture.'

The stage upon which the band played was situated at the far end of the largest of three interconnecting cellars. Their instruments were there, and a lanky youth was setting up mikes, but the music they had heard outside came from a tape deck at the back of the stage. The members of the band were, by the look of it, over at the bar getting a few quick drinks down them in order to sustain them through their set.

'Is that them?' whispered Claudia as they approached the bar.

Poppy was staring at the backs of their heads. Since the posters outside the club advertised Alex Fitzpatrick and the Cavendish Four, and there were five men talking music at the other end of the bar, it seemed more than likely.

'Well?' Claudia hissed excitedly, 'is one of them your dad? Can you tell just by looking? Is it the bald one, d'you think?'

Poppy's heart was flapping like a mad parrot in a cage. Which one of these middle-aged men was Alex Fitzpatrick?

This is crazy, she thought, sinking onto a high stool for support. How *can* I tell if one of these total strangers is my father? How can I possibly know?

Seconds later, she knew.

It happened so fast Poppy was glad she was sitting down. One of the men, the one on the far right with the dark red waistcoat and the hair just below collar-length, turned to speak to the barman. As she caught that first glimpse of his face Poppy felt as if all the air was being vacuumed from her lungs. The thud of recognition was so powerful it could have knocked her off her feet.

This is him, she thought dazedly. It *is* him. I know it, I

don't know how I know it, I just do . . .

'That one?' squeaked Claudia, intercepting the look on her face. She did a quick double-take, her own eyes registering doubt. 'You think so? He doesn't look a bit like you. I can't see any resemblance.'

The man they were both studying so intently wasn't particularly tall. He was solidly built with a well-developed paunch. His wavy hair, dark flecked with grey, was swept up at the sides and long at the back – this was clearly no bank manager they were looking at. His eyes were dark brown, his face generously lined. The nose was big, the chin a double. When he laughed a gold tooth glinted, matching the glittering chains around his neck and wrists, and the matchbox-sized rings on several fingers.

Poppy smiled to herself. Oh dear, Claudia must be horrified. She had been and gone and got herself a father with No Taste.

'Are you absolutely sure?' Claudia murmured at her side. Poppy nodded.

'But I don't . . . you aren't anything like him.' Claudia was floundering. 'Maybe it's one of the others . . .'

He was wearing a white shirt with diamanté buttons and a red velvet waistcoat. His dark green trousers were on the tight side. One of the other members of the band was telling a joke. When he reached the punchline Poppy saw her father throw back his head and roar with laughter. He had a loud, uninhibited gravelly laugh that made her tingle all over. She loved it. She had always adored men who laughed like that.

'It could be the one on the left,' Claudia suggested hopefully. 'His hair's kind of reddish. What about him, Poppy? He looks quite nice, don't you think?'

A woman had emerged from the cloakroom. Poppy and Claudia watched her clatter across the flagstones in her high heels and join the group at the bar. She kissed each of them in turn, saving the one in the red waistcoat for last. He got a noisy, enthusiastic, lipstick-loaded kiss on the mouth.

'Come on then, help me up!' The woman grinned broadly, holding out her arms so he could lift her onto the high stool at his side. When she was in position she leaned forward and kissed him again. 'Thanks love, and I'll have a gin and orange.' She turned and beamed at the rest of the band. 'Come on lads, time for one more before you go on. These are on Alex.'

Unable to handle anything stronger, Claudia ordered a bottle of Beck's for Poppy and a Perrier for herself. The band were up on the stage now, playing some clumpy-sounding jazz. The club was packed and everyone else seemed to think it was terrific. As far as Claudia was concerned, it sounded a lot like tuning up.

As for poor Poppy, how on earth was she feeling? She wasn't saying much, that was for sure. And no wonder, thought Claudia, who had every sympathy. As if Alex Fitzpatrick wasn't bad enough, there was that dreadful woman with him ... wife, lady friend, whatever she was. Either way, Claudia decided, she made Bet Lynch look demure. She sounded like something out of *EastEnders*. And she was downing gin and orange like it was going out of fashion.

Claudia flushed, remembering why she was on Perrier tonight. The difference was, this woman looked as if she drank gin for breakfast.

'So what happens next?' she said, because the appalling music was showing no sign of grinding to a halt. The band looked as if they could happily play on all night. How was Poppy planning to introduce herself to her father anyway? By leaping up onto the stage, grabbing a mike and doing an impromptu *This Is Your Life*?

Chapter 14

'Excuse me,' said Poppy, 'but is Alex Fitzpatrick the one at the piano?'

The woman, who was wearing Day-Glo pink nail polish, drew on her Rothman's and nodded.

'Yes love, that's him.'

'Um . . . right. He's good, isn't he?'

Brilliant, just brilliant, thought Poppy, realising that her wits had inconveniently upped sticks and deserted her. Oh, but trying to strike up a conversation with a complete stranger *was* hard when your heart was doing a triathlon in your chest.

'One of the best,' said the woman, blowing a flawless smoke ring.

Her hair was very blonde and fastened into a plait coiled like a snake on top of her head. Long twiddly bits curled in front of her ears, lacquered into place so they couldn't get tangled up with pink earrings the size of Jaffa Cakes. At a guess, she was in her mid-forties. The heavy make-up was very sixties, very Carnaby Street. She was wearing a tight turquoise blouse, a pink skirt and a pair of turquoise stilettos with stupendous heels. She also wore an amazing amount of jewellery, among it an ornate gold wedding ring, an eternity band and an engagement ring so colossal it couldn't be real.

'Um, could I borrow your lighter?' said Poppy, realising too late that she didn't have a cigarette. Didn't even know how to smoke, come to that.

The blonde woman passed across a heavy enamelled lighter. Claudia stared at Poppy. Poppy tugged at a loose thread on the side seam of her Levi's and burned it off.

'There, thank goodness that's done. It's been annoying me all evening.'

The woman smiled slightly. 'So long as you don't set light to yourself.'

Encouraged by the smile Poppy said, 'Look, sorry if I'm being rude, but are you Alex Fitzpatrick's wife?'

'I am, love, for my sins.' The woman began to take notice. Bright blue eyes studied Poppy's face. 'What's this then, twenty questions? Don't tell me you're his new bit on the side.'

'Oh no, *no*—'

'Joke, love. My Alex don't have bits on the side.' She laughed huskily then coughed and lit another cigarette. 'He wouldn't dare, he knows I'd kill him.'

'I'm not one, anyway,' said Poppy. 'I'm just a terrific fan of your husband's. You must be so proud of him . . . to have a talent like that.'

' 'Course I'm proud of the old bugger. What I don't understand – ' his wife gestured in the direction of the stage – 'is how you can be such a fan of his when you didn't even know which one he was.'

Poppy's mind raced.

'Well, you see, I'd never liked jazzy stuff before. But my boyfriend – ex-boyfriend – had a tape of this completely brilliant music, and I fell in love with it. He told me it was Alex Fitzpatrick,' she said brightly, praying that Alex had brought out a tape at some stage in his career, 'and I just thought he was the best jazz . . . um . . . player I'd ever heard. So that's why I had to come here. I'm sorry, this must be a complete pain for you, I'm sure you must be forever getting hassled by fans.'

'Not so you'd notice,' the woman said good-naturedly. 'Well well, so your ex bought a copy of Alex's tape. We always wondered where the other one went.'

'Mrs Fitzpatrick, could I buy you a drink?'

'Rita, love. Call me Rita.'

'And my name's Poppy Dun—' Poppy's mouth screeched to a halt; saying Dunbar could be risky. 'Er . . . Dunn. Poppy Dunn.' She swivelled round and tapped Claudia on the arm. 'This is my friend, Claudia Slade-Welch.'

Claudia had been trying to melt into the background. She managed a faint smile and a nod.

'Not enjoying yourself, love?' Rita evidently thought it was funny. 'This place not your cup of tea?'

Claudia sounded pained. 'Oh no, it's fine. Really—'

'I dragged her along,' said Poppy. 'That's the trouble with being a girl. Going out to clubs and things isn't something you can do on your own. I mean, I'd love to come here every week but I'd be dead embarrassed, sitting by myself—'

'No need for that.' Rita Fitzpatrick wiggled an over-here finger at one of the girls behind the bar. 'I'm always around, you can sit with me. I'm not wild about the music myself, mind, but we can keep each other company.'

'That's so nice of you,' Poppy said happily.

'I know.' Rita winked at the barmaid. 'I'm just an all-round terrific broad. Stand by, Effie. This young lady's about to buy me a drink.'

'Alex, you've got yourself a fan at last,' crowed Rita. She waved away the pea-soup fog of cigarette smoke swirling around her head and pulled Poppy forward. 'Meet Poppy Dunn.' Stifling yet another burst of husky laughter she added, "The other one's Claudia, but she ain't a fan. She reckons your music's the pits.'

'Oh but—'

'Never mind, at least one of them's got taste.' Alex Fitzpatrick grinned, mopping his forehead with a black silk handkerchief and glugging thirstily at the pint of lager Rita had just ordered for him. 'Poppy. Good to meet you.' He put his drink down and shook her hand, because Poppy had hers determinedly outstretched. 'So, not seen you before. First time, is it, here at the club?'

Poppy's shock of recognition earlier had been so vivid she hadn't been able to help wondering if he would feel it too. Of course, he hadn't. Trying not to feel let down, Poppy concentrated instead on his hand which was actually quite difficult to shake, what with all those thumping great rings in the way.

'First time.' She nodded in agreement, hoping she didn't look like one of those dogs in the back window of a car. Alex Fitzpatrick's hand was warm, squarish, capable-looking. The handshake was firm and perfectly ordinary. There were no special effects, no thunderbolts or lightning flashes, to startle him into realising who she really was.

'Effie, before I forget,' said Rita. She began rummaging through her handbag, a vast pink leather affair with gold elephants appliquéd around the base. 'Friday the fourth, make sure you get the night off.' She found a wad of invitations, flipped through them and handed Effie hers. 'Our silver wedding, we're having a bit of a bash,' Rita explained for Poppy's benefit. Gazing proudly across at Alex she went on, 'Twenty-five years, can you believe it? And we're as happy now as we ever was. I tell you, I wouldn't be without this gorgeous man, not for the world . . .'

'She adores him,' Poppy said gloomily.

It was midnight, they had caught a taxi home and met up with Caspar on the doorstep. Caspar had been out to dinner with a leathery Australian heiress called Darlene; since she had bought five of his paintings last night he had felt duty-bound to accept her invitation. The one for dinner, anyway.

'Darlene the Dingo?' Realising he'd come out without his key, Caspar waited for Claudia to unlock the front door. 'I know she adores me. I just don't want to sleep with someone who looks as if she might howl—'

'Not Darlene,' said Claudia. 'This woman we met tonight. Her name's Rita.' She paused for effect. 'She's Alex Fitzpatrick's wife.'

'Oh dear,' said Caspar when Poppy had run briefly through the events of the evening. 'I see why you didn't blurt it out. How to wreck twenty-five years of happy marriage in one minute flat.'

'Can you imagine?' Poppy sighed. 'The stupid thing is, they're such a . . . a *couple*, I don't think I could tell just him. They don't seem the type to keep secrets from each other. It wouldn't be fair.'

'If he's your father,' Caspar pointed out, 'he kept quiet enough about what he got up to with your mother.'

'I know, I know. But that was over twenty years ago.' Poppy realised she was instinctively defending Alex Fitzpatrick. 'Maybe he and Rita were going through a rocky patch. The thing is, they're happy now.'

'So what are they like?' asked Caspar as the living-room door opened and Claudia came in with a tray of coffee.

Poppy looked at Claudia.

'Go on. You tell him what they're like.'

'Oh . . . nice.'

Claudia did her best to sound as if she meant it. Personally she would have run a mile, if not several thousand, had Alex and Rita Fitzpatrick turned out to be related to her. But she was damned if she was going to give Poppy the chance to call her a snob.

'Is that it?' Caspar was waiting for more. 'Just . . . nice?'

'Well, charming,' Claudia floundered. 'And friendly . . . yes, friendly. Um . . .'

'Common as muck,' Poppy added, to be helpful. 'It's okay, you can say it. Dripping with the kind of jewellery you buy on market stalls. Loud. Liberace meets *EastEnders*, you know the kind of thing. And they know how to drink. He doesn't look like me but he definitely is the one. When he laughs – no, just *before* he laughs, he reminds me of me.' She swallowed, looking away as her eyes welled with unexpected tears. 'It feels so strange. He's my dad. I really have found him at last.'

'The thing is,' said Caspar, 'is he going to find you?'

'Bleeding caterers,' Rita grumbled the following Monday. 'Been and had a bust-up, haven't we? I told 'em last week I wanted one of them hollow cakes with a girl jumping out the top and they said no problem, they was all "Yes modom, no modom". Then this afternoon this poncy woman phones up and tells me they can't do it after all.' She lit a cigarette and heaved a sigh. 'So I told them to stuff their vol-au-vents, we'd get another firm to do the job. Boy, was Alex mad with me. He says serve me right if I end up having to do the bleeding lot meself.'

'It's short notice.' Poppy's brain was working overtime. This knees-up of Alex and Rita's was being held at their home in the East End of London. Poppy had a vivid mental image of the house, a modest two-up, two-down bulging with sixties' memorabilia to match Rita's clothes. Nothing exotic, that was for sure. Rita didn't go out to work and Alex played at the Cavendish because he loved it, not for the money it brought him. It was a standing joke in the club that the bar staff earned more than the band.

Poppy didn't care about that but she was burning with curiosity to see her father's home for herself. This could be my big chance, she thought. So long as Kenda's Kitchen didn't turn its delicate nose up at the idea of bridge rolls and bits-on-sticks for fifty in not-very-glamorous Bethnal Green.

'I work for a firm of caterers.' Poppy searched her jacket pockets and by some miracle came across one of Kenda's elegant dark blue and gold business cards. They were forever being urged to press them upon likely customers. Well, now she was. 'I know it sounds a bit posh but they're all right really. And there's a chance they may be able to fit you in. Shall I give them a quick ring and ask?'

Kenda answered the phone herself. She had a fluty, up-market voice that sounded like panpipes. Poppy asked if they could take on a booking for this Friday, raising her own voice to make herself heard above the music in the club.

'You'll have to speak up,' twittered Kenda, 'goodness, what a racket. But yes, we can manage Friday . . . there's been a cancellation. What would the client's requirements be?'

'She can do it.' Poppy turned with relief to Rita. 'She wants to know the kind of food you need.'

'Here, let me have a word.' Rita took over the phone and began to bellow down it. Poppy imagined Kenda cringing genteelly at the other end. 'Okay love? Top of the range we're after. Best you've got. Forty quid a head? Yeah, sounds about right. And numbers . . . ooh, to be on the safe side, make it two hundred and fifty.'

Caspar arrived at the club at eleven o'clock to give Poppy a lift home. He found her still shell-shocked.

'Two hundred and fifty times forty,' Poppy said numbly before Rita teetered back from the loo in her fake leopardskin high heels. 'I keep getting my noughts crossed. Is it . . .?'

'Ten grand.'

'Ten grand,' echoed Poppy. 'Hell's bells.'

'Why?' He looked amused. 'Have you been betting on the horses? Is this money you've lost or won? Careful how you answer that – I may have to ask you to marry me.'

'Sshh, can't tell you now.' Poppy elbowed him in the ribs. Rita was heading towards them. 'Here she is. And Alex is over there . . . up on the stage, purple waistcoat . . .'

'Honestly, Poppy,' Caspar chided as he drove her home, 'you are hopeless. You *and* Claudia. Couldn't you tell those diamonds were real?'

'Just don't tell Jake.' Poppy pulled a face. Jake had spent countless hours patiently teaching her the difference between clever imitations and the real McCoy. How stupid of her to assume that such vast chunks of gold and such super-sparkly stones had to be fakes.

Caspar grinned. 'You know what this means, don't you? All the evidence points to it.'

As far as Claudia was concerned it was the greatest sin of all. Her lip invariably curled in disdain whenever she uttered the dreaded words.

'Aaargh,' gasped Poppy, clutching her mouth in horror, '*nouveau riche*.'

Chapter 15

Caspar wondered idly if it had ever occurred to Claudia that she might be the product of *nouveau riche*-ness herself. After all, Hugo Slade-Welch had struggled as an actor for years before hitting the serious big-time. Thanks to intensive voice training and rather distinguished good looks he had cornered the market in David Niven-ish roles but he made no secret of having worked during those tough early years as a coal miner, a debt collector and a bricklayer's mate. Even Angie, before Claudia had been born, was rumoured to have been pressed briefly into service as a waitress in a transport café in order to make ends meet.

The difference, Caspar supposed, was that Hugo and Angie both looked and sounded as if they had been born into privileged lifestyles. They had good taste, they always knew which knife and fork to use and they wore exquisite clothes.

Well, most of the time.

Angie was draped across the bed, her golden body bathed in sunlight. She lay in a semi-reclining position with one arm flung above her head and the other resting on the pile of tasselled pillows beside her. One foot dangled lazily over the side of the bed. As middle-aged bodies went, hers was pretty much flawless. And Angie knew it.

'What are you thinking?' she purred.

'I hate that question.'

This was an understatement; it was one of Caspar's least favourite questions in the world. It was what girlfriends always seemed to start saying when they sensed they were on the way out. It was a bad sign and Kate had been asking it for the past fortnight. She had begun complaining wistfully that his mind always seemed to be elsewhere then looking terrified in case she was right. The trouble was, the more she said it, the more Caspar knew she would have to go.

Angie, who didn't fall into the category of about-to-be-discarded girlfriend, simply grinned.

'In that case,' she said unperturbed, 'why don't I tell you what I'm thinking instead?'

'Go on.' Caspar tried to look as if he didn't know what was coming next.

'I think we've waited long enough.' Mindful of the fact that he was putting the finishing touches to her upper half, Angie didn't move a muscle. All she did was smile. 'I think it's about time we got to know each other better. I think,' she added with a delicately raised eyebrow, 'it's time you joined me on this bed.'

To be fair, she had exceeded his expectations. Caspar had expected her to make her move much earlier than this, but here they were, five sittings down and only one to go. He was impressed.

'Look, thanks, but I can't.'

It was a toss-up which of them looked more surprised. Caspar even had the grace to blush. The dreaded N-word wasn't something that featured too strongly in his vocabulary.

As if realising that he might have a bit of trouble with it, Angie said, 'You mean you're turning me down? You're saying *no*?'

'Mmm.' Caspar frowned and pretended to concentrate on the canvas. Good grief, no wonder he'd never tried it before. Saying no was awful. It was embarrassing.

It was the last time he listened to Poppy too. This was what happened when you listened to a girl whose favourite film was *The Sound of Music*.

'Why don't you want to?' Angie sounded annoyed. 'What's wrong, am I the problem? Or is it you?' Her eyes narrowed, her tone grew scathing. 'What exactly do you mean by can't?'

Caspar gritted his teeth. Having aspersions cast on one's ability to perform was something else new to him.

'I'm not impotent if that's what you're getting at.'

Angie was really offended now. Rejection was bad enough on its own. To be buck-naked *and* rejected was the complete pits.

'So it's me,' she said flatly, although she still didn't see how it could be. Not with a body this perfect.

'Of course it's not you.' Caspar glanced at his paint-splattered watch. 'It's somebody else.'

'Not that clingy girlfriend of yours, the one who always looks as if she's just seen a ghost.'

'Not Kate.' He was damned if he was going to tell her it was Poppy.

'Who then?'

Thank goodness time was up. Caspar stepped away from the easel and began cleaning his brushes even more thoroughly than usual.

'Who?' persisted Angie, climbing irritably off the bed and into her discarded clothes. '*Who*?'

It was funny how fast you could go off people. In the space of a few minutes any lingering desire he might have felt for her had simply evaporated.

'What a coincidence,' said Caspar, wishing she would hurry up and leave, 'I hate that question too.'

Poppy hadn't spoken to anyone from Bristol for months. Finally, testing the water, she posted a birthday card off to Dina with her new phone number written inside. If she didn't hear anything back she would know she was still persona non grata and about as popular as bubonic plague.

The moment the card dropped through the letter box Dina was on the phone.

'You didn't even tell me you were leaving!' she screeched. 'I thought we were friends and all you did was bugger off

97

without a word. Poppy, how *could* you? Did you seriously think I wouldn't be on your side?'

In a word, yes. Poppy looked out of the window at a young girl pushing a pram across the road. She and Dina had got on well enough together but this was largely because of the McBride connection. It wasn't as if they'd been best friends since school or anything dramatic like that.

'Sorry,' said Poppy. 'I suppose I didn't imagine anyone would be on my side.'

'Thanks a lot!' Dina raised her voice to be heard above an infant wail. 'Shows how much you know. If I hadn't been stuck in that sodding hospital with me legs up in stirrups I'd have been round like a shot.'

Since Margaret McBride was an intimidating mother-in-law, this sounded a lot like bravado to Poppy.

'You'd have *been* shot, that's for sure.' She didn't bear any grudges. If she'd been Dina she'd have taken the easy option and gone into labour too. 'So, catch me up on all the gossip. How is everyone? How's that noisy baby of yours?'

'Oh, *he's* all right. I'm the one tearing my hair out.'

Poppy was sympathetic. 'Is he terribly hard work?'

'No. I just think I'm going to have to kill Margaret. Margaret-I-know-best-McBride.' Dina heaved a sigh that sounded as if it had been held in for weeks. 'Poppy, I mean it. You have no idea how lucky you are. You got out in the nick of time. She is the mother-in-law from hell, and if she tells me one more time how I *should* be burping, feeding, changing, washing and kissing my own child –' Dina's voice rose to a frenzied wail – 'I swear I'll boil the interfering old battle-axe in baby oil.'

Phew. Poppy, sitting in the window seat, hugged her legs and decided she had indeed had a lucky escape.

'Anyway,' Dina went on, apparently recovered, 'everyone else is fine. Rob's going steady with a nurse. Her name's Alison. Fat ankles, but she's okay. Ben's all right but he's working all the time so I hardly see him. Susie and Jen are the same as ever. I'm a bit bored with them, actually. Um, that's about it, there isn't really much else to tell you.'

Poor Dina. Not having a thrilling time, all in all. Poppy wondered idly what Alison looked like apart from the ankles and whether she and Rob would get married. She wondered if he would risk a second attempt and hoped he would.

'Oh, Mum said she saw your father in Debenhams the other day, arm in arm with Beryl Bridges. They were looking at duvet covers,' Dina related with glee, 'and they looked dead embarrassed when Mum said hello.'

Beryl had been widowed two years ago. She did tons of voluntary work and was an enthusiastic churchgoer. Maybe, thought Poppy, her father would marry again too, now he had the house to himself.

Except he wasn't her father.

Poppy debated telling Dina that she had tracked down the real one and decided against it. Dina was such a blabber-mouth. Besides, it hardly seemed fair when Alex Fitzgerald wasn't even aware of it himself.

'You know what I need?' Dina declared with an air of recklessness. 'I need to get away from here. I need a break, even if it's just a few days.'

Poppy realised where this was leading. Subtlety had never been Dina's strong point.

'How about that cousin of yours, the one in Blackpool?' she suggested. 'You and Ben and the baby could have a long weekend up there.'

'Oh, thanks a bunch,' Dina groaned, 'why don't I invite Margaret and all the rest of the sodding McBrides along while I'm at it? Poppy, they're the ones I need a break *from*. Ben included! All this happy families stuff is suffocating me. I've got to get out of Bristol . . .' This was it; this was what she'd been building up to. '. . . pleeease, Poppy, I'm desperate! And we're friends, aren't we? Be a doll. Say I can come and stay with you.'

'Dina, I would if I could. But I can't,' said Poppy. 'This

isn't my house. I can hardly ask Caspar to put up a friend and a baby—'

'No baby,' Dina responded like a shot, 'just me. Margaret'll be in seventh heaven,' she added caustically, 'having Daniel all to herself for a few days. Bloody old witch.'

She really was hell-bent on escape.

'The thing is,' Poppy prevaricated, 'my room's only tiny.'

'And who am I, two-ton Tess? All I'm asking for is a bit of floor space.' Dina was wheedling now. 'I'll sleep under the bed if it makes you happier. In the bath, even.'

'Well . . . I'll have to ask Caspar first.'

'Ask Caspar what?' said Caspar, pushing open the sitting-room door with his knee. His arms were full of canvases as yet unprimed. 'If it's "I'll have to ask Caspar if he'd like a cup of tea and a Marmite sandwich", the answer's yes.'

'Who's that?' Dina was all ears at the other end of the phone. 'Your landlord? Ask him now. Go on.'

Poppy was torn. Sorry though she felt for Dina, she didn't really want to be the one held responsible for whatever she might get up to. Dina's wild streak, tempered recently by marriage and motherhood, was clearly wrestling its way back to the surface. Poppy dreaded to think what the McBride mafia would have to say if they knew who was putting Dina up.

'Ask me what?' repeated Caspar, dumping the blank canvases on the sofa.

Dither, dither . . .

'I know what I forgot to tell you,' Dina cried, playing her triumphant ace. 'Guess who I bumped into at the club the other week? That chap of yours, the one with the dark curly hair.'

Saliva turned to sawdust in Poppy's mouth. She stared at her bare toes, pressed against the sash window frame. She wished Caspar wasn't there, shamelessly eavesdropping. She couldn't believe Dina had waited until now to mention it.

'Which chap?'

'You know, the dishy doctor who couldn't keep his hands off you.' Dina gurgled raucously down the phone. 'Well, your foot anyway. Come on, you remember! Couple of dances, couple of snogs and the next day you cancelled your wedding. *That* chap with the dark curly hair—'

'I did *not* snog him,' Poppy blurted the words out without thinking.

Caspar looked up in amazement.

Dina sounded gleeful. 'So you do know who I mean.'

'Did you . . . um, did you speak to him?'

'Hang on a sec, how completely weird, I can't remember.'

Dina was smirking, Poppy just knew it.

'Of course you remember.'

'Nope, it's gone.' Brightly, Dina said, 'Mind's a blank, a complete blank . . .'

Blackmail, how outrageous. Poppy sighed and turned to Caspar.

'Is it okay if a friend comes to stay for a couple of days?'

'A few days,' Dina corrected. 'Make it a few.' She giggled. 'I'll need time to get over the jet lag.'

'Of course.' Caspar was still stunned by the earlier mention of snogging. 'Of course it's okay.'

'So what's she like?' he asked when Poppy had hung up the phone. 'My type?'

Poppy wished Dina could have said something a bit more informative than a cheery 'I'll tell you when I see you.' She wanted to know *now* what Tom had said.

'Well,' demanded Caspar, '*is* she my type?'

Men. Poppy gave him a look. 'She's got a husband and a baby.'

Privately she thought that in her present mood Dina would be anybody's type.

'Talking of babies, I'll tell you what's really amazing,' said Caspar. 'Angie Slade-Welch. That woman actually gave birth to Claudia . . . and I swear she has no stretch marks at all.'

'Well, you'd know.'

Honestly, Poppy thought, how come everyone else seems to be so much more brazen than me? Am I abnormally repressed?

'It's my job to know.'

'And is she as great in bed as you expected her to be?' The words slipped out. She hadn't meant to ask. She didn't even *want* to know, for heaven's sake.

'No idea.' Caspar looked innocent. Then he grinned. 'Our relationship is purely professional.'

'And if you believe that,' said Poppy, 'you'll believe anything.'

Chapter 16

Poppy had braced herself beforehand but Alex and Rita's home still came as a shock when she saw it for the first time. In the dank back streets of Bethnal Green it stood out like a wolfhound among terriers, a wolfhound with a diamond-studded collar at that.

This was Southfork with sequins, Poppy realised. The house was immense. There was a chandelier the size of a hot-air balloon in the downstairs loo.

She couldn't help wondering where the money for all this had come from. Was her father a member of the infamous East End underworld? Was he a drugs baron? A porn king? Oh help, Poppy thought nervously, I hope it isn't anything too sordid—

'Chop-chop,' said Kenda, in her element as she bustled past. 'No daydreaming. Poppy, back onto this planet please. Stop wishing your rich friends could adopt you and get on with folding those napkins. Janet, straighten your apron. And Claire, get those ice buckets filled. I said stop daydreaming, Poppy—'

'Sorry.' Poppy bent her head and set to work but there were so many thoughts whizzing around her brain it was hard to concentrate on napkins. Apart from anything else, Kenda had just hit a particularly pointed nail on the head.

Poppy began to wish she hadn't come here. Seeing for herself just how rich Alex Fitzpatrick really was only made matters more complicated than they were already.

Until today her reason for not telling him who she really was had been Rita.

103

Now, Poppy knew she definitely couldn't say anything. If she did she would look like a fortune-hunter, desperate to cash in on the fact that the father she had never known had somehow managed to end up rolling in it. Alex would think she had only turned up to demand her rightful share.

If it was rightful. But . . . how *had* he made so much?

Behind her, Janet and Claire were discussing British Rail sandwiches. Poppy hoped her father wasn't one of the Great Train Robbers.

'There's a swimming pool outside you wouldn't believe,' said one of the other waitresses on her way back from unloading the second van. 'It's big enough to float a yacht on.'

Poppy hoped her father wasn't anything to do with Robert Maxwell. She hoped he wasn't Robert Maxwell reincarnated.

'Right now everyone, let's start carrying the food through to the dining room,' instructed Kenda. 'Smoothly and efficiently please, before the guests begin to arrive. And I know I don't need to remind you of this,' she added with a steely glimmer in her eyes, 'but I trust everyone will behave in a professional manner.'

Poppy flushed on Alex's behalf. What Kenda meant was no behind-the-back smirking at either the decor, the guests or Alex and Rita themselves. They might not live in Belgravia but they were paying an arm and a leg for the services of Kenda's Kitchen tonight. Kenda, who had been battling the recession along with everyone else, could do with a few more like them on her client list. She wasn't going to risk offending the Fitzpatricks or any one of their less than salubrious guests.

'Got you slaving, has she?'

Poppy grinned as Rita whispered the words not very subtly into her ear. 'What's she like then, this Kenda with the posh voice? Bit of a bossyboots, am I right?'

'Well, strict,' said Poppy, 'but fair.' Struggling to be loyal, she added, 'These things need a lot of organising. Someone has to be in control.'

'In control.' Rita rolled her eyes. 'Yeah, I can just see her in a leather basque and high heels, going, "You do as I say, you naughty boy", and beating her hubby with a bloody great whip.'

So much for everyone being on their best behaviour and not smirking at the Fitzpatricks, thought Poppy. Poor Kenda, if she knew she was being made fun of by Rita she would be appalled.

For tonight's party Rita was wearing a violet lamé dress with a seriously plunging neckline and high-heeled gold sandals. A couple of extra blasts on the high-velocity sunbed had deepened her tan and yesterday's trip to the hairdresser had resulted in a baby-pink tint on top of the blondeness. Her eye make-up, a symphony of pinks and mauves, matched her nail polish. Around her brown neck hung a new necklace studded with sapphires.

'Like it?' Rita saw Poppy's gaze linger on the necklace. Proudly she ran her fingers over the raised stones. 'Twenty-five sapphires, one for each year we been married. Alex designed it himself, got a jeweller mate of his to make the necklace up.'

Maybe Alex was a diamond smuggler. This possibility rather appealed to Poppy; it had a romantic ring to it. She knew she should be circulating with trays of food but her curiosity was threatening to get the better of her. She had spent the last two hours eavesdropping as frantically as she could, to no avail. The guests, a wide mix of down-to-earth Cockneys and members of the Cavendish jazz crowd, weren't telling her what she wanted to know.

Poppy had only the haziest of ideas when it came to property valuation but the house alone must have cost a million. Then there was the bright red Rolls Royce with the personalised plates out on the drive . . . goodness, you'd have to smuggle an awful lot of diamonds to support a lifestyle like this.

It was no good, she had to ask.

'Rita . . . I hope this isn't an incredibly rude question . . .'

'Mmm?' Rita's attention was being drawn elsewhere. At the other end of the room Alex and his band had launched into a rousing, jazzed-up version of 'Knees Up Mother Brown'. Suddenly everyone was dancing. Rita was clearly dying to rush over and join in.

'It's just, this house.' Having started, Poppy felt compelled to finish. 'Um . . . I couldn't help wondering where the money . . . I mean, it must have cost a fortune . . .'

Alex was belting out the chorus on his Bechstein. Everyone sang along. Rita, gazing in adoration at him, said, 'Sorry, what?'

'You and Alex,' Poppy shouted above the noise of the music. 'How did you GET SO RICH?'

'Mrs Fitzpatrick, I'm so sorry,' murmured Kenda, gripping Poppy's elbow with such force she felt her funny bone start to go. Smiling fixedly at Rita, Kenda wheeled Poppy round and propelled her in the direction of the kitchen.

'What in heaven's name do you think you're playing at?' She hissed the words, bullet-like, into Poppy's ear, as shocked as if Poppy had been asking how they'd caught syphilis. 'What did I say earlier about professional behaviour? I warn you, Poppy, you're treading a very fine line. Any more of this nonsense and you are *out*.'

Poppy did as she was told. She returned to the kitchen, armed herself with two fresh trays of devils on horseback and spent the next twenty minutes dutifully offering them around.

Then she watched one of the other musicians take over at the piano. Alex, kissing Rita's hand, led her into the centre of the room. Cheered on by the noisier guests he made a short speech thanking everyone for being with them tonight and Rita in particular for marrying him in the first place. Then they danced together to 'If You Were The Only Girl In The World'. Everyone whistled and applauded before piling back onto the dance floor themselves.

'What did you *do*?' whispered Janet as she passed Poppy going in the other direction. 'Kenda's blowing a gasket. She asked me if you were on drugs.'

'Honestly.' Poppy sighed. 'From the way she's going on, you'd think I'd been spitting in the soup.'

Janet said, 'If you had, you wouldn't be the first.'

Poppy carried on serving. Physically she was doing her job but mentally she was checking out every detail of the house. As much as she dared, anyway; she was going to get some pretty funny looks if she started rummaging through the cupboards under the stairs.

Still, she was seeing enough to get the idea. At a guess, a team of top-class interior designers had been called in. They had organised, amongst other things, the elegant pleated curtains, the concealed lighting, the dado rails and the white Italian marble kitchen. Rita and Alex had said how lovely, so as not to hurt the design team's fragile feelings. Then the moment they'd left, they had set to work putting their own personal stamp on the place.

Brightly patterned rugs were strewn around, probably to cheer up the tasteful taupe carpet. Even brighter lampshades, frilled and fringed to distraction, were perched on imitation Oscar lampstands. Ornaments thronged every available surface. There was enough Capo di Monte to stock a factory. Huge gilt-framed photographs of Alex and Rita hung on every wall.

One of the doors off the wood-panelled hall led into a library with no books but plenty of videos in imitation leather covers. There was also a cinema-sized television screen. The black leather sofa in front of it was piled high with fluffy toys. An oil painting of a liquid-eyed spaniel hung over the fireplace. Another, of Elvis, adorned the opposite wall.

Goodness, Claudia would sneer if she could see this. Poppy glanced down at the shag pile carpet, deep enough to need mowing. It wasn't her own taste but she felt oddly comfortable in the room. Alex and Rita had furnished it to suit no one but themselves. Which was, really, how homes should be furnished.

The door swung open behind her and Poppy jumped, guiltily aware that she had no business being in here.

'Aha,' purred a male voice, 'caught you.'

A stray remote control had been buried in the depths of the shag pile at Poppy's feet. When she jumped, she unwittingly turned the video recorder on. A naked couple romping together in bed appeared up on the giant television screen. Poppy went scarlet, dumped her tray of canapés on the gilt-embossed coffee table and grabbed the remote control. A million buttons later she managed to find Off.

'No need to look so shocked.' Her male intruder was grinning from ear to ear. 'Nothing wrong with a bit of nookie between consenting adults. All in favour of it, myself.'

Poppy remembered serving him earlier when she had been passing round the smoked salmon parcels. He was in his thirties, she guessed, with gelled-back hair, a reddish complexion and confident, wide-boy smile. He was wearing a well-cut grey suit, the jacket lined with bright blue silk. A mobile phone stuck out of his pocket. He was well-built but not particularly tall and spoke rapidly, like a stock market trader, with a slight London accent.

'Hey, hey, not so fast,' he said as Poppy seized her tray and attempted to breeze past him. He put out an arm to stop her. 'We can carry on watching together. Come on, sit down, take the weight off your feet. Let me have that remote control . . . hey, *relax*, I said . . .'

Poppy gave up on breezing. Breezing wasn't going to do the trick. This chap was one of those take-what-you-want types and his arm was tightening around her waist like a boa constrictor. Now she remembered he was the one who'd been drinking champagne out of a half-pint glass. He was drunker than he looked. Grinning triumphantly he flipped Poppy's silver tray over, catapulting two dozen angels on horseback in all directions. She felt his hot breath on her face as he yanked her towards him. There were bits of spit at the corners of his mouth. At such close quarters the smell of hair gel was overpowering.

'Let go of me,' said Poppy. Feeling wimpish, she added, 'Please.'

'Whoa, no need to panic! Nobody else is coming in here. I noticed you earlier, y'know. I like redheads. Sweetheart, sweetheart, stop fighting it! I fancy you, you fancy me. How about a little kiss to get us warmed up?'

'No.' Poppy hesitated. What would Kenda want her to say? 'No . . . thank you very much.'

He grew more insistent. The grip around her waist tightened another couple of notches. 'Just a little kiss. Don't be a spoilsport. This is what parties are all about, a bit of fun—'

Breezing was by this time out of the question. Poppy was hemmed in, pinned firmly against a black and gold lacquered sideboard with a heavy crystal whisky decanter on it, together with six matching tumblers. She felt behind her, located the neck of the decanter and picked it up. Heavens, it was even heavier than she'd thought.

'Please let me go.'

'Are you kidding?' He laughed, his mouth approaching hers, his left hand zooming in on her right breast. 'Just as we're getting to know each other at last? Baby, don't you know how to *have* fun—?'

It seemed an awful waste of whisky. It was bound to be a blended malt. Still, Poppy decided, better this way than a whack over the head with several hundred quid's worth of lead crystal. Less brain-damaging at least.

She tipped the contents of the decanter over his ultra-gelled hair. Glug, glug, glug . . . within seconds he was drenched from head to foot.

'Sorry,' said Poppy as he let out a bellow of rage. Next moment the library door was pushed open and Alex appeared.

He stared at Poppy with the empty decanter still in her hand. He looked at his whisky-soaked guest. Then he examined the sole of his left shoe and discovered one of the scattered angels on horseback clinging to his heel.

'Hmm.' Alex glanced with regret at the puddle of whisky sinking into the carpet around the other man's feet.

'Sorry.' This time Poppy meant it.

'No need. I can guess what happened. Derek been up to his usual tricks, has he?'

'She was begging for it,' Derek said irritably. 'I'm telling you, begging for it.'

'You always say that. You always *think* that.' Alex sounded resigned. He turned to Poppy. 'He's just a lech. Predictable too. As soon as I heard the racket I guessed he'd done it again. Are you all right, pet?'

Poppy nodded. Moments later she stopped being all right. Like a traffic warden turning up just when you'd parked somewhere clampable, Kenda loomed in the doorway.

'Right,' she said, taking in the scene far more swiftly than Alex had done and drawing her own tight-lipped conclusions, 'that is IT, Poppy. You have brought disgrace upon Kenda's Kitchen. I warned you earlier. I gave you every chance.' She paused. The performance was as much for Alex's sake as Poppy's. Clients who spent, spent, spent like the Fitzpatricks deserved nothing but the best. 'Your behaviour tonight has been abysmal,' she concluded rigidly. 'You are fired.'

Bugger, thought Poppy.

'Don't look at me,' said Derek, even though nobody was. 'It ain't my fault. She asked for it. Look at the state of my flamin' suit.'

'Please,' Alex said reasonably, turning to Kenda, 'there's no need to sack anyone. Derek's pretty tanked. He got carried away, that's all. Polly had to defend herself. She couldn't let herself be slobbered over, could she, without putting up a bit of a fight?'

'Poppy,' said Poppy, feeling hurt that he hadn't even

remembered her name. 'Not Polly. It's Poppy.'

'Sorry love.' Alex winked, then returned his attention to Kenda. 'Come on, give the girl a break. You don't really want to kick her out into the snow.'

'I'm afraid I have no other choice,' Kenda replied with an air of finality. She looked at Poppy. 'And before you leave you can clear up this appalling mess.'

There were angels on horseback everywhere. Bits of oysters and strips of smoked bacon were strewn across the shag pile. One oyster had landed on top of the framed painting of Elvis.

It *was* an appalling mess. Poppy prayed the carpet wasn't ruined beyond repair. She picked up the silver tray, bent down and began picking the oysters out of the carpet.

'Stop it.' Alex reached down, seizing her by the elbow. He pulled Poppy to her feet and gave her arm a reassuring squeeze. 'You don't have to do that. If you ask me, this woman here's been bloody rude to you. Well out of order.'

'I . . . I . . .' stammered Poppy.

'And if she's giving you the boot anyway, I reckon you ought to let her pick up her own sodding oysters. Why should you do it,' Alex demanded, 'if she's already sacked you? Tell the old cow to get stuffed.'

Poppy hadn't cried when she'd cancelled her wedding. She hadn't cried when she'd made the discovery that her father wasn't her father. She hadn't even cried the other night when Caspar had raided the freezer and pinched her last Magnum.

'There. *Now* see what you've done.' Alex pointed an accusing finger at Kenda. His identity bracelet glittered in the light. 'And you wouldn't even listen to her side of the story.'

Poppy wasn't crying because she'd lost her job. She was crying because her father had his arm around her. He was comforting her, defending her, just as a real father should. It was a feeling Poppy had never experienced before and she'd never realised until now how much she had been missing out on.

Since she didn't have a cold, Poppy didn't have a hanky. Alex whisked a red and white spotted one out of his waistcoat pocket and shoved it into her hand.

Derek, still dripping whisky, grunted something about a change of clothes and disappeared.

'Good riddance to him,' said Alex. 'Silly sod. His old lady'll give him what for when she sees the state of him.'

'I'll send one of the other girls in,' Kenda announced coldly. 'To clear up.'

'It's all right.' Poppy sniffed loudly and wiped her eyes with the spotted hanky. 'I'll do it.'

'Are you going to give this girl her job back?' demanded Alex.

'No, I am not.'

'Right then,' Alex said as he turned Poppy in the direction of the door, 'you're coming with me. What you need is a drink.'

Chapter 17

'I was going to ask if you're feeling better now, but I don't think there's much point,' said Alex.

Poppy was panting for breath, having danced non-stop for the past twenty minutes with a beaming barrel of a clarinet player called Buzz.

'Now I know how to jive,' she gasped. Buzz had to be in his early fifties. Who would have thought someone so old would be so amazingly mobile? Even now he hadn't stopped but had deposited Poppy on the arm of a chair and begun twirling Rita around the floor instead.

'Look at my girl,' said Alex, watching the pair of them with pride.

For someone who must get through forty fags a day Rita was doing pretty well herself. Her cocktail dress flared alarmingly out at the waist as Buzz launched her into a spin.

'Come on, have another drink.' Alex waved a bottle over Poppy's nearly-empty glass.

She let him pour.

'Thanks for sticking up for me earlier,' said Poppy. 'And for letting me stay on.' It was almost midnight. Kenda and the others had done their duty and left in the vans. Relations between Kenda and Alex had been frosty to say the least.

'Hang on, before I forget.' Alex dug in his pocket and pulled out a handful of crumpled notes. He passed Poppy a couple of tenners. 'For your cab home, seeing as you've missed your lift. We're carrying on for a few hours yet, mind. Not planning on having an early night, were you?

Not about to go and do a Cinderella on us?'

'What, and risk losing one of these elegant glass slippers?' Poppy waggled her black shoes, which were flat and sensible to match the plain white shirt and black skirt worn by all Kenda's employees. The female ones, anyway.

Alex looked appalled. 'You poor kid, I didn't think! How can you relax and enjoy yourself like that, stuck in that stupid uniform when everyone else is dinked up? Here –' he grabbed her arm and pulled her towards the door – 'come on, the least we can do is lend you something decent. Rita won't mind. Just have a rummage and pick out whatever you want.'

They were up the winding staircase, along the endless landing and into the master bedroom before Poppy could even think of a tactful reply. The bedroom, which had to be forty feet square, was lined with mirror-fronted walk-in wardrobes. The carpet was fluffier, thicker and whiter than Pekinese fur. Arranged along every window sill were yet more soft toys.

'Go on, help yourself,' Alex urged, plonking himself down on the rippling water bed as Poppy gazed helplessly at row upon row of Rita's clothes. 'Anything you like. Don't worry, it's good stuff. And it's all clean.'

Poppy pulled out the plainest dress she could see, of royal blue taffeta with long sleeves, an over-sized Peter Pan collar and a scalloped hem. It was a couple of sizes too big but the style of the dress meant it wouldn't matter too much. And unlike all the pinks, oranges and reds Rita favoured, it wasn't going to clash alarmingly with her hair.

'Good choice,' Alex nodded his approval. 'Know what colour that is, Poppy? Bristol Blue. Like the glass. I've got a few pieces in one of the cabinets downstairs. Beautiful stuff, it is, Bristol Blue glass.'

'I know it,' said Poppy. 'I'm from Bristol. I was born there.'

'Yeah? Great place.' Alex was still lounging on the bed, propped comfortably on one elbow. His dark eyes lit up at

114

the memory. 'I worked there once, years ago. In some poncy country club, playing in the resident band. I had a terrific time there.'

I know you did, thought Poppy. Her heart was hammering. It was now or never. She hadn't planned to say it, but how could she pass up an opportunity like this?

'What a summer that was.' Alex was half-smiling to himself. 'I'll never forget it.'

What do I say? Poppy's brain went into frantic overdrive. How do I say it? What if the shock's too much for him and he has a heart attack on the spot?

'Um . . . was that the Ash Hill Country Club?' Poppy ventured. She was trembling, she realised. Even her voice sounded shaky. At this rate she was the one heading for the heart attack.

'Ash Hill, that's the one!' Alex beamed. 'You know it?'

How about: No, but my mother was once on intimate terms with their pianist.

Or: Yes, Dad, actually I do.

Poppy practised the words in her head and chickened out. Her cowardly tongue had superglued itself to her teeth. How about if she could think of a less corny way of doing it? What if she just went for total simplicity and said, 'Look, Laura Dunbar was my mother.'

'L-look,' Poppy stammered, struggling frantically to free her tongue from her teeth. 'L-L-L—'

'There you are!' cried Rita, materialising in the doorway. Still barefoot, neither of them had heard her approach. 'Buzz said he saw the two of you disappearing upstairs.'

'It was Alex's idea. To stop me looking like a waitress.' Awash with guilt and praying Rita wouldn't leap to the wrong conclusions, Poppy held up the blue dress.

'I said you wouldn't mind,' Alex put in equably.

' 'Course I don't mind.' Rita sounded outraged by the suggestion. 'But that dull old thing? Are you sure?'

The dull old thing had the kind of designer label Poppy

had only read about in magazines. Her fingers curled around the padded silk hanger. 'Oh, it's great.'

'Well, I'll leave you girls to it.' Alex ambled out, patting Rita's generous backside as he went.

Poppy slithered gratefully out of her uniform. Rita sat at her Hollywood-style dressing table and primped. She glanced at Poppy's reflection in the mirror.

'I'm worried about you.'

'Me? Why?' Poppy was wearing a pale blue cotton bra and orange pants. She put the expensive dress on quickly, before Rita could change her mind about lending it to someone with such deeply unworthy underwear.

'Losing your job. I feel responsible.'

'Don't be! I'll be fine, really—'

'Bloody Derek, he's such a prat.' Rita whisked an extra layer of blusher onto her cheeks with a huge brush. Indulgently she said, 'I don't know, suppose it runs in the family.'

Eek! Poppy's blood ran cold. She hoped she hadn't just been snogged by her uncle.

'You mean he's related to Alex?'

Rita had begun vigorously Ultraglowing her neck and cleavage. She let out a bellow of laughter.

'Good job he didn't hear you say that! I meant *my* family, love. Derek's a cousin of mine. Been a prat all his life, too. Ow, I knew I should've given that jiving a miss.'

Poppy watched Rita flex her left knee as if it hurt.

'You were dancing like a pro. I was impressed.'

'Yeah, and it'll give me gyp tomorrow.' Rita carried on massaging the area below her knee. 'I broke my leg a long time ago. In three places. Nasty business it was.'

Of course, the fateful break. Poppy wondered what would have happened if Rita hadn't had her accident. Alex wouldn't have needed to rush back to London, her mother would have told him she was pregnant . . . who knows? He might have decided to stay with Laura after all. He might have divorced

Rita and married her mother instead. And I, thought Poppy, would have had a whole different life, an unimaginably different life . . .

'You're miles away, love.'

'I was. Sorry.' Poppy shook her head and grinned. What had Rita been talking about? Oh yes, the leg. 'I bet it put you off hanging baskets for life.'

Rita looked at her strangely.

'How on earth did you know that?'

Hell's bells, this was what happened when you didn't pay attention.

'You told me,' said Poppy.

'I don't remember.'

'A couple of weeks ago, at the Cavendish Club.' She improvised wildly, banking on Rita's fondness for a drink to get her out of this mess. 'I told you about Claudia setting her heart on a couple of hanging flower baskets and Caspar offering to kidnap next door's, and you said, "Bloody hanging baskets, I was nearly killed once, by a hanging basket". And then you told me about falling off the ladder and breaking your leg.'

'Blimey,' said Rita.

'It was the night you were drinking tequila slammers with Harry Osborne. You must remember that!'

'I remember the headache the next morning.' Rita pulled a face, gave her hair a one-for-the-road burst of hairspray, and stood up. 'Oh well, I'll blame Harry for that. Ready to go back down, love? The dress looks terrific.'

'This house is terrific.' Poppy seized her chance as they headed for the stairs. 'Have you lived here long?'

'Couple of years.'

It was no good, she had to ask.

'So does Alex have . . . um . . . another job?'

Rita glanced at her. 'You mean how come we're living in a place like this, Bethnal Green's answer to Buck House?'

'I know I'm being rude.' Poppy tried to look ashamed.

'I'm sorry, I'm the nosiest person I know.'

'That's all right, petal. Only natural to be curious. No mystery to it anyway,' Rita continued smoothly. 'Alex was just in the right place at the right time during the property boom.'

'Property? Buying and selling houses?'

'Yeah, that's it. Then he invested in a high-risk land deal in Spain. Three years ago the deal came off. And we woke up one morning a few million quid richer than we'd been the night before.'

The words sounded well-rehearsed, as if they'd been trotted out a few million times themselves. One thing was for sure, thought Poppy: Rita wasn't telling her the truth.

'Here we are.' Proudly, Alex steered Poppy into the drawing room where an illuminated cabinet contained his small collection of Bristol Blue glass. One shelf was occupied by a set of four goblets, three lozenge-stoppered decanters and a single spirit bottle.

Poppy recognised the spirit bottle at once. There was another one, just like it, in the house where she had grown up.

'Two hundred years old,' said Alex, 'can you credit it?'

'Cheeky bugger,' Rita retorted over his shoulder. 'I am not.' She winked at Poppy and said to Alex, 'Have you told her yet?'

'Told me what?'

'Me and Rita, we've had an idea.' He grinned. 'To make up for you losing your job.'

Poppy's heart began to race. She struggled to contain her excitement. This is it, she thought, hardly able to believe her luck, they're going to offer me work! They want to employ me as a . . . as a . . .

Poppy wasn't quite sure what, but she didn't care. She would clean, do odd jobs, mow the lawn, anything. Dammit, she'd even cook.

'Go on love, you tell her.' Rita gave Alex a nudge.

'The dress,' said Alex kindly. 'It suits you, love. We want you to have it. And no arguments; it's yours.'

Chapter 18

The last time Dina had visited London had been on a school trip to the Science Museum which had bored her stupid. The highlight of that outing had involved eyeing up another coachload of schoolboys from Birmingham, one of whom had thrown a doughnut at her in the Museum coffee shop. The lowlight had been getting a love bite on her neck from spotty Stuart Anderson on the journey home.

But that had been yonks ago, when she was just a kid. This is far more like it, Dina thought gleefully. No more stupid school uniform. No bossy Miss Wildbore, head of physics, barking at her to pay attention. No Mr Killjoy-Carter telling her to wipe off that lipstick or else.

Best of all, no baby.

'You jammy thing, have you fallen on your feet here or what?' Dina crowed with delight. She threw herself down on the sofa and gazed rapturously around the room.

Poppy knew she had to find herself another job fast if she wanted to stay here. At this rate she was going to end up a pub stripper after all.

'Never mind my feet.' She'd turn her attention to the job dilemma later. 'What did Tom say to you when you saw him?'

'Talk about uncool,' mocked Dina. 'Anyway, who said he said anything?'

'But he did.' Poppy knew Dina too well. She wouldn't have been able to resist talking to him.

'We-ell maybe. Good-looking, isn't he? All that curly hair. And those *brilliant* eyes . . .'

'I could always pull out your toenails one by one.'

Poppy was too shattered to play games. She had only managed three hours' sleep. She'd been hokey-cokeying and singing bawdy songs until five in the morning, in an haute couture dress.

Dina gave in. 'Okay. Well, I was there with Maggie and I spotted him right away. He was wearing a red and white striped shirt and white jeans. Brilliant bum, too. Well, I said "Hi" when we went past him to get to the bar and he didn't twig at first, what with me being a bit of a different shape.' Smugly, Dina patted her flat-as-a-pancake stomach. 'So I reminded him who I was and he kind of lit up and got interested. Asked me what I'd had and how the baby was getting on. Then he kind of took a deep breath and asked how you were.'

'*And*?'

'I told him nobody had heard from you for yonks. I said you'd called off the wedding and done a bunk. I'm telling you, you should have seen the look on his face . . .'

'What kind of look?' Poppy tried not to shriek. Dina was spinning this out on purpose.

'Oh, kind of . . .' Dina mimed it. 'No, hang on, maybe a bit more like . . .' She tried again, then shrugged. 'Well, pretty much gobsmacked. So I told him, then, all about you turning up at Rob's house the next morning, and how Rob wouldn't believe you when you said it was all off, and how Margaret was doing her nut and trying everything to make you change your mind because she'd never be able to live down the shame.'

'What did he say when you'd finished telling him all that? Or,' said Poppy evenly, 'was it kicking-out time by then?'

Dina looked offended. 'He said if I ever heard from you, to give you his phone number and address.'

'He *gave* them to you?'

Yes, yes! This was better than Poppy had even dared to expect. She had to control herself, sit on her hands. The temptation to frisk Dina, to rifle through her pockets for the precious information, was strong.

'He gave them to me.' Dina blinked. Nobody, thought Poppy, wore quite as much navy-blue eyeshadow as Dina.

'Well? You're here now, you can give them to *me*.'

'Except I kind of lost the piece of paper. Well, the beer mat,' gabbled Dina. 'You see, he wrote it down on the back of a beer mat and I put it in the side bit of my white handbag, the one with the chain strap. So it wasn't my fault,' she went on defensively. 'It's not as if I chucked it in a bin or something, like on purpose. It just . . . fell out of its own accord.'

'You've lost it,' Poppy echoed. Trust Dina to raise her hopes and then dash them. Anyone with a grain of compassion would never have done it like that. Anyone with an ounce of common sense, for heaven's sake, would have left out the whole bit about the beer mat.

Poppy wasn't yelling at her but Dina could tell she was upset.

'I'm sorry,' she said, looking perplexed. 'I didn't think it was that important. I mean, it wasn't as if you called off the wedding so you could run away with this chap instead, was it? You said you were never going to see him again. I didn't realise getting his number was such a big deal. You should have said.'

I hadn't realised it either, Poppy thought glumly. Until now.

When she had said goodbye to Tom that night she had still been intending to marry Rob the next day. The subject of phone numbers had deliberately not been raised because that would definitely have been tempting fate. When you felt that strongly about someone and you were marrying someone else, their phone number was a dangerous thing to know.

But she hadn't married Rob. She hadn't been able to stop thinking about Tom either.

'It's okay,' said Poppy wearily. 'You're right, it wasn't your fault. I should have said.' She heaved a sigh. 'Just, if you

122

ever bump into him again, could you take his number and not lose it?'

'Oh, I won't,' Dina shook her head vigorously. 'Bump into him again, I mean. He told me the brother he was staying with in Bristol was on the verge of emigrating to Australia.'

'Terrific.'

'I did kind of glance at the beer mat,' Dina was trying to be helpful, 'before I put it in my bag.'

'And?' Poppy hardly dared to hope.

'It said Notty something. Maybe Nottingham. Or Notting Hill.'

'In other words,' said Poppy, 'not a clue.'

A hyperactive six-year-old would have been easier to handle than Dina. By Sunday afternoon Poppy was on her last legs and down to her last fiver in the world. On Saturday they had shopped. On Saturday night they had visited more bars and clubs than she had known existed. On Sunday morning Dina had dragged her out again, to Camden Lock market. From there they had moved on to Covent Garden. At four o'clock they arrived back at Cornwallis Crescent. Dina had to leave at six to catch the coach home.

The trouble with Dina, Poppy decided, was she looked as if she were giving every man she met a lascivious once-over. She *was* giving every man she met a lascivious once-over. The drawback was letting them know it.

But Dina was unstoppable. She had been let off her leash for the weekend and was making the most of it. London was terrific, London was glamorous. It was also teeming with men.

And she hadn't had to change a nappy once.

'That girl is so brazen,' Claudia said scornfully when Poppy had dragged Dina downstairs to pack.

'I know, isn't it great?'

Caspar loved it, of course.

'It is not. She hasn't stopped flirting with you since she got here. And all you're doing is encouraging her.'

He grinned. 'Is that against the law?'

'She's married,' Claudia reminded him. 'And she's got a baby.' Acidly she added, 'Somewhere.'

'So, okay, chances are she isn't a virgin.' Caspar loved teasing Claudia. It was the perfect pastime for a Sunday afternoon. Well, maybe the second most perfect.

'All this promiscuity. Don't you get tired of it?'

'I'm getting tired of being lectured to about it.' First Poppy, now Claudia. Caspar was tempted to boast about turning Angie down, but sensed her daughter might not appreciate it, seeing as she didn't know about Angie's clandestine visits to the house in the first place.

Claudia was jealous. She knew this was because she'd been going through a bit of an arid patch recently, man-wise, but it only made Caspar's lack of interest in her more hurtful. Not to mention the shaming débâcle with Jake . . .

Things just weren't going her way right now. Claudia wished she knew what she was doing wrong. She flipped shut the copy of *Cosmopolitan* on her lap and gazed moodily at the model on the cover.

'So who's your ideal woman?'

'Someone who doesn't lecture me, who doesn't go on and on and on about boring morals—'

'Seriously.'

'Someone who doesn't take me seriously.' Caspar stretched. 'Oh, I don't know. Maybe I haven't met her yet.'

'But what's your ideal *type*?' Claudia was frustrated; she wasn't going to give in. 'I mean, short or tall, blonde or dark?'

No mention, Caspar couldn't help noticing, of medium-sized redheads.

'I like all kinds,' he said with unaccustomed tact. 'Anyway, personality's more important than looks.'

'Oh sure, as if you'd ever go out with some old boiler just because she told great jokes.'

124

Claudia abandoned *Cosmo* and started giving her nails their second coat of plum polish. Caspar couldn't figure out for the life of him why women wore the stuff.

'Depends how great the jokes are,' he said, 'and whether she laughs. Laughter's sexy. Men like girls who laugh.'

Right on cue, the sound of Dina gurgling like a drain drifted up the stairs.

'Okay,' Caspar amended, 'men like most girls who laugh.'

'Are you trying to tell me I've been a miserable old cow lately?'

'Well, the odd smile now and again might help.'

Claudia looked doubtful. She tried one.

'You mean like this?'

'Ravishing.'

She broke into a grin, blew on her wet nails and chucked over a pen.

'Go on then, get some paper. Write down all your best jokes.'

Chapter 19

Poppy gazed at the emerald earrings, pear-shaped and lavishly set in twenty-two carat gold. Jake was out at an auction and she wasn't – strictly speaking – allowed to do any buying herself. But even she could see these earrings were special; if she turned them down she could be missing out on a terrific deal. And where would be the sense in that?

The woman selling the earrings was middle-aged and frail, with a genteel manner and a high-pitched quavery voice.

'They were my grandmother's,' she explained to Poppy, 'but the time has come to sell. I don't want to, of course. Grandmother would be *so* disappointed ... oh dear, but Christmas is coming and since my husband died it's become harder and harder to manage.'

'The thing is,' said Poppy, 'my boss isn't here at the moment. If you could come back tomorrow—'

'I'm sorry, my dear. I really wanted to get it over and done with today. I'm afraid I find this whole business rather distressing.'

'How much were you hoping to get for them?'

The woman, close to tears, dabbed at her eyes with a pink hanky and shook her head. 'I don't know – whatever you think is fair. Maybe ... two hundred?'

Poppy reached beneath the counter and took out the cash box. The earrings were easily worth that. She smiled conspiratorially at the poor grief-stricken woman.

'I tell you what. Let's make it two hundred and fifty.'

Jake was right beside Poppy the next day when the policeman approached the stall. He didn't say anything, just held up a photograph.

'Nope,' said Poppy, having studied intently the face of a buxom girl in a dark green ballgown. 'Sorry, never seen her before in my life.'

Next to her, Jake groaned.

'Not the face, madam,' said the policeman with the merest hint of a sneer. 'The earrings.'

'Oh bugger,' wailed Poppy.

'We caught her this morning, trying to off-load more stolen goods.'

Poppy didn't dare look at Jake.

The policeman bent over to study the contents of the jewellery cabinet. Within seconds he spotted the earrings, marked at four hundred and fifty pounds.

'I'm afraid we'll need to take these from you, sir.'

Poppy stared at the policeman. Anyone could hire an outfit like that from a fancy-dress shop . . .

'Wait!' she yelled. 'You can't expect to waltz off, just like that, with a pair of valuable earrings! We'll see some identification,' she demanded hotly, 'if you don't mind.'

'Oh Poppy,' Jake sighed.

The policeman flashed his card at her. He smirked.

'What a shame you didn't think about that before.'

Jake was still speaking to her, but only just. The policeman, quite unfairly Poppy felt, had delivered a depressing lecture, warning her of the dangers of handling stolen goods. To listen to him, you'd have thought she was the mastermind behind Brink's-Mat.

The sight of Claudia colliding in the doorway with an impressively endowed woman in a fedora brought much-needed light relief to the afternoon. Their bosoms clashed. They ricocheted off each other like Sumo wrestlers. The woman in the hat glared at Claudia. Claudia, who felt she had right of way, glared back.

Poppy collapsed in giggles, which didn't help. Claudia had spent the last two hours planning her entrance and it hadn't included this. Trust it to happen when she was seeing Jake again for the first time in weeks. Just when she wanted to look cool.

Not to mention cheerful.

'Shame you weren't wearing a double-breasted jacket,' said Poppy, who was being a damn sight too cheerful. 'Then you might have won.'

Claudia tried to appear unconcerned. She smiled, as Caspar had advised her to do. It was a weird sensation, thinking about your smile while you were actually doing it. Claudia hoped it looked more natural than it felt.

She swung the smile from Poppy to Jake and quickly back again. Jake was wearing a beige and brown checked shirt and crumpled black trousers, and his dark hair was sticking up at odd angles at the back. Really, thought Claudia, if it weren't for those dark eyes of his, nobody would look at him twice. And even they were hidden behind Sellotaped-together spectacles . . .

Not that she was even interested, anyway, Claudia hastily reminded herself. An impoverished antique dealer in an anorak wasn't her idea of happy-ever-after. Jake was only someone she had decided she could practise on in the meantime. She could use him to try out her new smile.

'Well, this is an honour,' Poppy prattled on, since Claudia's collision appeared to have robbed her of the power of speech. 'Your first visit to our humble stall. You haven't come all this way, have you, to tell me off for leaving the butter out of the fridge?'

'Actually, I came to pass on a message. You had a phone call earlier, from some chap called Matthew Ferguson.' It was hard going, smiling and talking at the same time. Claudia's cheek muscles were starting to ache. 'He said to let you know the job was yours and he'd see you tomorrow night.'

'I've got the job,' squealed Poppy. 'Brilliant!'

'I didn't know you'd applied for one.' Claudia was curious.

'It was Caspar's idea. He had a word with a friend of his. I went to see him last night.'

Caspar's idea. Claudia experienced a spasm of jealousy. It sometimes seemed that all Poppy needed to do when she wanted something was ask Caspar. Place to live? No problem. New job? Here you are, take your pick! Like some fairy godmother he would wave his magic wand and effortlessly grant yet another wish.

'What is it, more waitressing?'

Several of Caspar's friends owned restaurants.

Poppy looked smug. 'Modelling.'

Oh, now this was too much.

'You can't be a model,' Claudia replied crushingly. 'You're too short.'

'Not a model-model. Not catwalks and *Vogue* covers,' explained Poppy. Her mouth twitched. 'What I'll be doing involves fewer clothes.'

'You mean topless? Oh my God!' Claudia gasped, no longer envious. How disgusting. How *degrading*. Furthermore, it wasn't even as if Poppy had an impressive pair of boobs.

Filled with indignation – not that she would do it for the world – Claudia thought: *I'm* the one with the boobs.

'Actually,' said Poppy, 'fewer clothes than that.'

'Nude?' Claudia gasped. 'You're going to be *nude*? What, like in . . . *Playboy*?'

By this time even Jake was beginning to look alarmed.

'It's for life drawing classes at St Clare's College of Art.' Poppy broke into a grin. 'There, you see? Nothing disreputable after all! I'll be doing four nights a week, for the students taking evening classes. All I have to do is lie back and think of . . . well, whatever I want to think of, and let everyone else do the work.' She beamed. 'Good, eh?'

'You're serious?' Claudia couldn't believe it. How could Poppy possibly think that what she'd be doing was respectable? 'You'd really parade around naked for a bunch of dirty leering old men?'

'I won't be parading around. And they aren't dirty old men. It's an art college,' said Poppy patiently, 'not a strip club in Soho.'

'Ugh. It's repugnant.' Claudia had forgotten she was supposed to be smiling. She shuddered in disgust. 'They'll see . . . *all* of you.'

'So? I'll be able to pay *all* my rent.'

'Well, you wouldn't catch me doing anything like that. I *couldn't*.' Claudia looked across at Jake for support. 'Could you?'

'Um . . . well, no, I suppose not.' Jake tried to bury himself in a brochure for Lassiter's next furniture auction.

'Look, it pays as much as Kenda's Kitchen and it's a damn sight easier on the feet. I'm doing it and that's that,' said Poppy. 'Now, is there anything else anyone would like to lecture me about or can I take my tea break?'

Claudia remembered her other reason for coming here and seized her chance. She turned to Jake.

'Well now, seeing as I've found you, I may as well spend some money. Perhaps you could help me choose a present for my mother. Something classy, elegant . . .'

I might not be classy and elegant like Angie Slade-Welch, thought Poppy resentfully, but at least I'm getting paid for being painted in the nude. I'm not the muggins who had to pay Caspar six thousand pounds.

'Actually,' said Jake, 'Poppy could be the one to help you there.' Claudia was smiling – no, baring her teeth – at him as if her life depended on it and it was making him nervous. 'I need to talk to Terry about picking up that set of rattan chairs,' he went on hurriedly, turning to Poppy for help. 'Is that okay? Can you take your tea break later? I really must speak to him now.'

'What's the matter with him?' asked Claudia, disappointed, when Jake had rushed off.

'I don't know. What's the matter with your face?'

Claudia looked alarmed. Her hands flew up. Was her foundation streaky, her mascara smudged?

'No, your mouth.' Poppy was genuinely trying to help. She did a fair imitation of the smile Claudia had practised for so long in front of the mirror. 'It's your wisdom teeth, isn't it? They're playing up again. You really should see the dentist and have them out.'

Upstairs in the coffee shop Jake sat alone. He was pretending to read the paper and thinking about Claudia. More to the point, he was telling himself what a hopeless coward he was when it came to socialising with the opposite sex.

The fact that he was even thinking about it was all Poppy's fault. For years he had led the kind of life that suited him most. Basically this involved steering clear of the opposite sex.

He had been comfortable doing this because the odd bit of loneliness was so much easier to cope with than the traumatic process of meeting girls, deciding which ones you liked, figuring out if they liked you back, plucking up the courage to ask them out . . .

As far as Jake could see, the whole tortuous dating business was a nightmare, an endless procession of trial and error that seemed far, far more trouble than it was worth. How many relationships lasted the course these days anyway? Look at the way his parents had fought before splitting up. No, those kind of complications he was better off doing without.

It was only since Poppy had come to work for him that Jake had begun to wonder if maybe there was something missing from his life. Not that he was secretly lusting after Poppy, because he knew he wasn't. It was more to do with the way she had taken control of her own future. She had seized it, given it a damn good shake and forced new things to happen. Poppy was fearless, impulsive and determined to make the most of every moment. She seldom bothered to worry about what might happen if she got something wrong.

This wasn't necessarily a plus, Jake thought with a wry smile. Especially when you were her employer. But at least Poppy had a go at whatever she set out to do.

He knew she must think his lack of a social life downright weird.

And now here I am, thought Jake, beginning to wonder if maybe she wasn't right.

He looked at his watch. Half an hour had passed. It should be safe by now to venture back downstairs.

It wasn't as if Claudia wasn't nice, because she was. It wasn't as if he didn't find her attractive, either, because he did. Perhaps if I take it slowly, one step at a time, Jake told himself, I could mentally gear myself up towards asking her out. In a couple of years time.

When he hit the bottom step he saw that half an hour hadn't been long enough. Claudia was still there, evidently torn between a pair of rococo candlesticks and a blue and white Florianware pottery vase.

'. . . are you serious? You've really never been to a car boot sale?' Poppy was saying as Jake approached. 'You don't know what you're missing – they're brilliant fun! If you want to give them a whirl, Jake can tell you the best ones to visit. He goes every Sunday, don't you, Jake?'

This was it, this was his big chance. Taking a leaf out of Poppy's book, Jake plunged in.

'There's a good one out at Henley this Sunday. I could pick you up if you like, we can go together . . . it's best to be there early, I'd have to be at your house by eight . . . and there's a pub overlooking the river, which does terrific food. We could have some lunch there afterwards . . .'

Jake ran out of words. Luckily he'd said all he needed to say. There, he'd done it. The last time he'd asked a girl out he'd been nine years old.

Golly, thought Poppy, astonished and impressed. She

132

turned expectantly. All Claudia had to do now was say yes.

'Oh, I would have loved to.' Claudia was stricken by the bad timing. If it had been anything else she would have cancelled like a shot. 'But I have to go to a christening on Sunday. My cousin's little girl. They're doing it in Brighton. What a *shame* . . .'

Poppy looked at Jake. It was like prodding a snail and watching the head shrink back beneath the shell.

'No problem. Just a thought. It really doesn't matter. Is this what you've chosen for your mother?' Jake held up the blue and white vase, his hands trembling slightly. 'Did Poppy tell you it's Florianware? Eighteen-nineties, and signed by Moorcroft—'

'How about the following Sunday?' Poppy couldn't bear it. She couldn't let him change the subject. 'You could go then instead. How about it, Jake? The Sunday after next?'

'I'm away that weekend,' said Claudia unhappily. 'Staying with Harriet and Tim in Wales.' Even to her own ears it sounded feeble, and she knew it was the truth. Heaven knows how it must sound to Jake.

'I'm busy as well.' Jake wished the ground would swallow him up. He wished he'd stayed put in the coffee shop for another thirty minutes. He definitely wished he hadn't made a complete dick of himself. How *could* he have been stupid enough to think Claudia would want to go to a car boot sale with him? I mean for God's sake, thought Jake despairingly; of all the glamour spots of the world, a *car boot* sale.

133

Chapter 20

Caspar was on his way out to a party in Belsize Park the following evening. He offered to drop Poppy off at St Clare's en route.

'Nervous?'

'What, of your driving?' Poppy grinned and shoved a jelly baby into his mouth. 'I'm used to it by now.'

'Nervous about the class. Getting your kit off.'

'Yes.' She could admit as much to Caspar. 'But that won't last, will it? The first five minutes will be the worst.'

'Sure you don't want me to come in for a bit, keep an eye on you?' He winked. 'Make sure they don't laugh? *Ouch*—'

Poppy whacked him on the arm.

'Thanks, but no thanks. I'll be okay. I just hope the heating's on.'

Caspar's petrol light flashed with renewed urgency. Spotting an Esso garage up ahead, he pulled onto the forecourt.

'Won't be a minute. Give me one more jelly baby . . . not another green one,' he protested, because Poppy always fobbed him off with those. His eyes lit up as he glimpsed a coveted red jelly baby in the bottom of the bag.

Poppy had seen it too.

'Here, have a lovely yellow one – no, no!' She let out a yelp as Caspar made a grab for the bag. They wrestled over it for several seconds. Then the bag split. Jelly babies catapulted in all directions.

Grinning, Caspar picked the red one off the dashboard and popped it into his mouth.

'You should know better than to fight with me. Don't I always win?'

'Petrol,' Poppy reminded him, because if he didn't get a move on she was going to be late.

While Caspar was filling up she slid off the passenger seat and began collecting the scattered jelly babies. By the time she scrambled upright he had disappeared into the shop to pay.

If she hadn't been so busy chasing jelly babies, Poppy realised afterwards, she would have seen Tom sooner.

If she'd stayed down on the floor a few seconds longer she would have missed him altogether.

But there he was, clearly visible under the bright fluorescent garage lighting, making his way back from the shop with a packet of Benson & Hedges and a can of Coke in one hand, a copy of the *Evening Standard* in the other. The tangled curls and glittering dark eyes were just as Poppy remembered them. He was wearing jeans – maybe the same pair he had worn last time she'd seen him – and a dark grey polo-necked sweater beneath a black leather jacket. The way he walked was the same. Nothing about him had changed. If she touched him, Poppy realised, she knew exactly how he would feel.

She sat frozen in the passenger seat, too shocked at first to react. It felt like hours but was probably no more than a couple of seconds. I've got to move, thought Poppy, dazed. I've got to attract his attention.

Tom's car was obscured from view by an RAC van. All she could see was the bumper. But he was heading for it, and if she didn't do something sharpish he was going to climb in, start the engine and disappear.

Galvanised into action, Poppy launched herself at the door handle. As she did so, the car Tom was about to get into started up. Someone else was driving. Poppy panicked and tugged again, frantically, at the handle. Slippery with sweat, her hand slid off. The car with Tom inside began to move and thanks to the angle of the RAC van and the petrol pumps she still couldn't get a good look at it.

'Stop ... help ... WAIT ... STOP!!' screamed Poppy, realising too late that she was the helpless victim of a child lock. Any second now the car would pull out into the road. This had been her chance in a million and she'd almost blown it. Her heart racing, Poppy threw herself across to the driver's side and leaned as hard as she knew how on the horn.

'Here. Don't say I never buy you anything.'

An unopened bag of jelly babies landed with a crackly thud in Poppy's lap. Caspar climbed back into the car.

'What's the matter with you?'

'Nothing.' Poppy was too shell-shocked to explain. She felt sick. She couldn't eat a jelly baby now to save her life.

'Last-minute panic?'

'No.'

'Well, something's happened.'

'Your car horn doesn't work.'

Caspar waved his keys at her. 'Not without these in the ignition.'

Hell.

'And there's a child lock on this door. You don't *have* children,' said Poppy.

'The chap I bought the car from had them fitted. Kate was showing me yesterday how to work them. Sorry, couldn't you open the door?' said Caspar. 'I didn't realise they were still switched on.'

Around Poppy, at varying distances, sixteen pupils stood before their easels observing, drawing, re-drawing and shading the contours of her body. Every detail mattered. Their concentration was total. When they spoke they did it in whispers.

The group comprised seven women and nine men, ranging in age from eighteen to eighty. The only disparaging remark about their new model had come from a tall older woman in a hand-crocheted tunic, complaining about Poppy's lack of saggy bits and wrinkles. Nobody had ogled her, either. They were too busy drawing to leer.

Poppy gazed at a peeling patch of wall. Her mind was elsewhere – back on a chilly garage forecourt on the Marylebone Road – but her body was right here doing its job.

At least seeing Tom again had given her something else to think about other than the fact that she was sitting here minus her clothes.

Money had been tight for the last few weeks and Poppy had been forced to give the Cavendish Club a miss. When she visited it the Friday before Christmas she heard the jaunty, bluesy sound of Alex on the piano as she reached the stone steps leading down to the entrance of the club.

Inside, half the office parties in London appeared to have crammed themselves willy-nilly into the three interlinked cellars. The place was heaving with tipsy secretaries and excitable clerical types with their shirtsleeves rolled up and their ties skew-whiff. Everyone was celebrating their last day at work. Ugly men waving scrawny bits of mistletoe were looking hopeful. There was a lot of smudged lipstick about. Poppy found herself fending off the enthusiastic attentions of a burly lad in a reindeer suit.

'If you don't give me a Christmas kiss, you'll hurt my feelings,' he pleaded.

'If you don't take your hands off my bottom,' said Poppy with a grin, 'I'll rip your antlers off.'

She found Rita in her usual corner of the bar, looking festive in a bright red dress and snowman earrings. The first thing she did was buy Poppy a drink.

'Still speaking to us then? I thought you might have decided you'd had enough of these jazz types.' She watched Poppy take a thrifty sip of her lager and downed her own drink in one. 'Come on love, get it down your neck. Don't worry, I'm buying.'

Was Rita looking older? Were there shadows under her eyes, carefully but not totally masked by concealer? Poppy watched her stub out one cigarette and straight away light up another. There was an air of recklessness about her tonight, a definite I-could-do-with-a-Valium look in her eyes. The smile was put on. And she kept glancing across in the direction of the stage, as if compulsively checking that Alex was still there.

Maybe they've had a fight, thought Poppy. Maybe Rita had been a bit free and easy with her own Christmas kisses and Alex had got jealous. Or vice versa.

Or there was more to it than that and she had discovered he was having an affair—

Poppy stopped herself before she got carried away. This was her trouble, she was always imagining things and leaping to conclusions. There were, after all, any number of reasons why Rita might be on edge.

Poppy glanced over her shoulder and saw a pregnant girl standing over by the fire exit. Rita had mentioned ages ago that she hadn't been able to have children. Briefly, almost casually, she had said, 'No, no kids. It just didn't happen. Still, never mind.' But behind the brave, don't-care façade Poppy had glimpsed the pain, and the number of soft toys in Rita's house had been another giveaway. The sight of a pregnant woman must remind her every time of what she had missed.

As for her and Alex having an argument . . . so what? It was what married couples did, and for the most mundane reasons. Alex had probably left his socks on the bathroom floor . . . squeezed the toothpaste in the middle . . . spent too long with his mates in the pub.

'Let's hear what you've been up to then.' Rita finished the second cigarette in a series of fast, jerky drags. 'Managed to get yourself another job?'

Poppy told her about St Clare's, which had now broken up for Christmas. Then she went on to tell her about the end-of-term party in a pub around the corner from the college, where during the course of the evening each student in turn had come up to her and said, side-splittingly, 'Gosh, I didn't recognise you with your clothes on.'

'They're a nice enough crowd,' Poppy sighed, 'but their idea of humour is to say, "What's this, cellulite?" And you should see some of the finished drawings. One old dear had me looking like Joyce Grenfell on speed. She's seventy-three and thinks she's Picasso, except she wears a black wig. Rita, are you okay?'

'Hmm? Sorry, I missed the last bit. Something about cellulite.'

'What's wrong?' asked Poppy.

She watched in horror as Rita's heavily mascaraed eyes brimmed with tears.

'Damn, this is doing my image no good at all.' Rita's voice cracked. She fumbled uselessly in her bag for tissues.

People were beginning to notice and Rita's make-up was woefully un-waterproof. Poppy led her through the crowded cellar to the exit.

'I hate these sodding steps,' mumbled Rita. 'Oh God, we're going to freeze to death. What do I look like? I *swore* I wouldn't let this happen . . .'

Poppy had brought her outside because she knew the ladies' loo would be packed. Now they'd reached the top of the steps she wondered what to do next.

'Where's your car?'

'Parked round the back.' Rita sniffed. 'I haven't got the keys. They're with Alex.'

A black cab turned the corner. Poppy flagged it down.

'Where to, love?'

'I don't know.' Poppy looked at Rita. 'Home?'

'Not without Alex. Oh, I get it.' Rita shook her head. 'You think we've fallen out. It's not that.' Wearily she added, 'I only wish it was.'

The streets were icy. Poppy's feet were numb. She started

to shiver. The cab driver was beginning to look fed up.

'We don't want to go anywhere,' she told him, pulling open the door and jumping inside. 'Just keep the engine ticking over. And the heater on.'

Rita sobbed noisily. The cab driver provided a box of Kleenex. Poppy had to wait several minutes before she heard what had happened.

'. . . you know what men are like, all this macho "I'm okay" stuff, when really all they are is scared out of their wits.' Rita sighed and blinked back more tears. 'Well anyway, Alex wasn't feeling so clever so in the end I made the appointment for him. We went together and the woman checked him out. Dead nice, she was. Kept saying she was sure it wasn't anything to worry about, but to be on the safe side he'd better go and have a few tests. So we went along for those this morning. We've got to see the specialist tomorrow for the results. Oh Poppy, I know what they're going to tell us.'

Rita's voice began to break again. The floor of the cab was covered with bits of damp shredded tissue. With practically no make-up left she looked quite different. Poppy held her hand.

Reassurance wasn't what Rita wanted. Cheer-up-it-might-never-happen speeches would do no good because as far as Rita was concerned, it already had.

'He's being so brave,' she told Poppy. 'Just carrying on as if nothing's changed. I'm the one showing myself up, bawling like a baby. It's just, I feel so helpless . . . and so bloody *angry* . . . Christ, I'm the one who drinks too much and smokes too much. If something like this has to happen, why can't it flaming well happen to me?'

All Poppy could do was sit there and listen while Rita ranted on. By the time the meter had clocked up eight pounds fifty, the tears had pretty much dried up. By ten pounds fifty Rita had renewed most of her make-up. Poppy paid the cab driver while Rita did her lipstick, and realised that she would have to go home now. All she had left was enough money for the bus.

'You're a good girl.' Rita gave her an awkward hug. 'And thanks for putting up with me. What a way to spend an evening, eh? You must've been bored stupid, having to listen to me droning on and on. God, I'm a selfish cow.'

'You aren't.' Poppy hugged her back. 'Look, I have to go now. Give my love to Alex.'

At home in bed, Poppy couldn't sleep. She lay staring up at the ceiling thinking about Alex and going over in her mind everything Rita had said.

I've only just found him, Poppy thought with trepidation. This can't happen. I can't lose him again. Not yet.

Chapter 21

Poppy caught the coach to Bristol on Christmas Eve. She hadn't told Dina she was coming down; she wasn't staying long. This was purely a duty visit.

When she arrived she felt even more of a stranger than she had imagined. Beryl Bridges was there, in a pale blue hand-knitted twinset, putting the finishing touches to plates of sandwiches and home-made cakes. There were doilies on the plates. The tea service was one Poppy hadn't seen before. When Beryl reached for the teapot and said coyly, 'Shall I be mother?' Poppy felt a twinge of alarm. Beryl was nudging sixty; surely she hadn't gone and got herself knocked up?

'We're getting married,' Mervyn Dunbar announced when the tea had been poured. He no longer took sugar, Poppy noticed. Beryl was probably behind that too.

'Oh . . . well, that's good news.' Poppy smiled at them both. 'Congratulations.'

'Next week,' said Mervyn. 'Down at the Register Office. Nothing fancy. No big party or anything.'

Of course not, Poppy thought. Wouldn't want to break the habit of a lifetime.

'Just a couple of my friends as witnesses,' Beryl put in hurriedly. 'And a spot of lunch afterwards.'

'So don't worry about having to trek down here from London all over again.' Mervyn blinked. Poppy turning up like this out of the blue had unsettled him. He had his own life now, and Beryl to share it with him. Knowing that Beryl would never sneak off behind his back with another man gave him indescribable peace of mind, whereas seeing Poppy again only served to remind him of all the misery and humiliation his first wife had put him through. 'There's no need,' he went on brusquely. 'We understand. It's a long way.'

It certainly was, Poppy mused. Even longer when you weren't wanted at the wedding.

'Still, you've got your own life to lead, haven't you?' Beryl said brightly. 'Up in the big city! Must be lots going on there, eh love?'

'Oh, lots.' Poppy nodded in agreement. She had no intention of telling them she had met her real father. She finished her tea and reached down to the raffia bag at her feet, pulling out Mervyn's wrapped Christmas present. Luckily, gardening books were his passion so he was easy to buy for.

Lucky too, thought Poppy, that I'm pretty passionate about washing. She thanked Mervyn for her own present, which she knew was Yardley soap. It was wrapped in last year's paper, which had been kept and recycled.

'Actually,' said Poppy, 'I was going to ask a favour.'

Mervyn looked wary. 'Oh yes?'

'You know that blue spirit bottle, the one on the shelf out in the hall. Was it my mother's?'

Bits of old glass were of no interest to Mervyn Dunbar. He nodded.

'She came home with it one day, before you were born. Bought it in Clifton. Waste of money, I told her.' His eyes flickered. 'Why? Valuable, is it?'

'Not really,' Poppy fibbed, because Bristol Blue glass of that age could fetch hundreds of pounds at auction. 'It's the same colour as the curtains in my bedroom, that's all. I wondered if I could have it.'

Claudia always enjoyed the *idea* of going along to her mother's drinks parties. Angie invited so many men you never knew who you might meet. It was only when she was there

143

she started wishing she hadn't come.

The trouble was, having spent ages looking forward to it, the event itself was bound to be a let-down. As in childbirth, Claudia conveniently forgot the bad bits – like the fact that her mother spent the whole time shamelessly hogging the limelight and always bagged the best men for herself.

'You look gorgeous, like an ice cream,' one of them told Claudia now. He was spectacularly drunk but so good-looking he could get away with it. 'Can I lick your shoulder? Do you taste as good as you look?'

Claudia began to perk up. How lucky she'd chosen to wear the ivory satin dress and not the blue wool one, and how right she'd been to keep up those sessions on the sunbed. She preened a bit, then squirmed with pleasure as the man began to drop nibbling little kisses along her collarbone.

With a whoosh of Chanel Number 5, Angie materialised beside them like an unwanted genie out of a lamp.

Her smile was provocative.

'Why bother with Walls economy-sized vanilla,' she purred, 'when you could be enjoying Häagen-Dazs?'

She slipped out of her jacket and offered the man her own bare shoulder. 'Go on, try me. And be honest, which would you prefer? A dollop of plain old vanilla or a little taste of heavenly Caramel Cone Explosion?'

'Honestly darling, I don't know why you have to be so touchy.' Mindful of the perils of dehydration, Angie poured herself another glass of mineral water and yawned. 'It was just a bit of fun. You're lucky Carlo only nibbled your shoulder.'

Claudia had managed to contain herself until the party was over. By the time the last of the guests had drifted off into the frosty night she'd had a good three hours in which to seethe.

'I'm not talking about my shoulder being nibbled,' Claudia howled. 'Having my shoulder nibbled doesn't *shock* me . . . what I can't bear is the way you always have to barge your way in and start showing off.'

Angie began to laugh.

'Oh dear, you mean the bit about economy blocks of ice cream? Sweetheart, you are so sensitive about your size! It was a joke, that's all.'

'You couldn't bear to think that someone like Carlo might have been more interested in me than in you.' Claudia glared at her accusingly. 'You had to shimmy up and start diverting his attention.'

'Fairly easily accomplished,' Angie retaliated. 'I mean, he hardly had to be prised off you, did he?'

'Now you're being spiteful.'

All the pent-up resentment of the past months was on the brink of spilling out. Having Angie back on the scene must have been more of a strain than she'd realised. Claudia gave her mother a measured look. 'And you're showing yourself up,' she said coldly. 'Has it ever occurred to you that some people might be watching the way you carry on and laughing at you behind your back? Not everyone thinks you're completely irresistible, you know. You aren't that perfect.'

Angie was no longer looking amused. If there was one thing she really couldn't bear it was the thought that she was being laughed at. It was only a cheap jibe of course – nobody *was* laughing – but the fact that Claudia could even make such a snide remark . . . well, it really pissed her off.

'I didn't say I was perfect,' she bristled. 'Or irresistible. Not that I can recall any complaints—'

'For God's sake, *there* you go again.'

'Oh please, can I help it if men find me attractive?'

'Not all men,' Claudia repeated through gritted teeth. This evening's episode had really bugged her. This time her mother wasn't going to get away with it. 'Not all men. Not Carlo, And,' she added for good measure, 'not Caspar either.'

Right. That was it. Mockingly Angie said, 'Caspar? Oh, you mean the Caspar *you've* had such spectacular success with? Dear me, so what you're saying is, if I were to make myself available to Caspar French, he wouldn't be the teeniest bit interested. Is that it?'

'That's it.' Claudia looked triumphant. Inwardly she thought: If I have to bribe him with every last penny I own, Caspar is never going to sleep with you.

Angie uncurled herself and rose from the sofa. She crossed the room to where the Christmas tree stood. It was an impressive ten-footer smothered in Victorian lace and beeswax candles. A mountain of exquisitely wrapped gifts was piled around the base. Angie reached for a large flat rectangular package done up in tartan paper. She handed it to Claudia with a tight little smile.

'Go on, open it.'

'Why? It's not mine.' Claudia looked at the label, which bore her father's name. Hugo was flying over from Los Angeles on Boxing Day.

'Just open it.'

The crimson ribbons unravelled, the paper fell open and the layers of tissue paper seemed to peel back of their own accord. Claudia sat gazing down at the picture on her lap. Her mother, naked and golden, sleepy-eyed and smiling, gazed back up at her. As if the carved wooden headboard of the rumpled bed on which she lay wasn't enough, there was the signature in the bottom right-hand corner to dispel any last lingering doubts.

'What a talented boy he is.' Smiling at the look on Claudia's face, Angie heaved a pleasurable sigh. 'And what fun we had! No wonder you're so keen to get to know him better,' she added in a taunting whisper. 'He even exceeded my expectations! Darling, you simply must give Caspar a try. I do recommend him. You're missing out on a treat.'

Chapter 22

With the proceeds of the Angie Slade-Welch portrait Caspar had sent his parents on a Mediterranean cruise. On Christmas night his mother, overwhelmed by the sheer opulence of the ship and two unaccustomed glasses of Amontillado, phoned to tell him there had been a choice of seventeen different vegetables served with lunch. There was also a waterfall – yes, an actual *waterfall* – inside – yes, actually inside – the boat.

'I've never seen anything like it before in my life,' she gasped happily. 'Talk about grand! Caspar, you should see it . . . this whole trip's like a dream come true. Oh, I do wish you could've come with us. You'd have had such fun—'

'I'm just glad you and Dad are enjoying yourselves.' Much as he loved his parents, the prospect of going away on holiday with them filled Caspar with alarm. 'And we're having fun here. We cooked a pretty mean lunch between us.'

'Not with seventeen different kinds of vegetables.'

'Maybe not.'

'And I'm not doing the washing-up,' his mother boasted.

'Neither am I.'

'Oh Caspar! You haven't left the girls to do it all.'

'Would I?' He grinned.

'You are naughty.'

'I am not. We used paper plates.'

People had been dropping in and out all day. Friends not caught up in the family-visiting routine had called by, staying for lunch or for a few drinks, enjoying the relaxed atmosphere and informal hospitality. At six o'clock Kate left to spend the evening with her parents. Claudia disappeared into the kitchen to deal with the washing-up.

'What washing-up?' Caspar protested.

'We didn't cook with paper saucepans, stupid.'

'Come on, leave all that. We'll do it tomorrow.'

'You mean I'll do it tomorrow.'

Caspar leaned against the kitchen door. He watched Claudia push up her sleeves in businesslike fashion and run a torrent of hot water into the bowl. He wondered if she'd had some kind of upset with her mother. She hadn't been in a bad mood today, but there had been a definite edge about her. He sensed something wasn't right.

Caspar wondered if it was him.

'Claudie, have I done something wrong?'

'Wrong? You?' Claudia was whipping up a mountain of bubbles. She shook her head. 'No. I don't suppose you have.'

'What's that supposed to mean?'

'It means you're the same now as you've always been. And I don't suppose you'll ever change.' She plunged her hands into the soapy water and began trawling for cutlery. 'After all, why should you?'

Claudia knew she shouldn't snipe, but she *was* fed up. It just seemed so unfair, Caspar and his endless capacity for sex, her with no sex life at all . . .

Caspar looked closely at her, but Claudia was busy looking closely at the washing-up. He assumed this was some veiled reference to the fact that he never did any.

It was Christmas. He experienced a pang of guilt.

'Okay, point taken. We'll go shopping next week. Get a machine to do the dirty work for us.' He gave her an encouraging nod. 'How about it, would that cheer you up?'

Claudia turned and stared. Surely he wasn't offering to buy her a vibrator! She went bright pink.

'Caspar, are you drunk?'

'No.' Well, not plastered.

'So what in heaven's name are you talking about?'

He looked perplexed. 'A dishwasher.'

Despite herself, Claudia began to giggle. This was why she could never stay angry with Caspar for long. Okay, so he had slept with her mother. But Angie was the one she was unable to forgive.

'Are you okay?' asked Caspar.

Claudia had no intention of bringing up the subject of his fling with Angie.

'I'm okay,' she said.

She was damned if she'd let Caspar think she cared.

The door bell rang. They heard the clatter of footsteps as Poppy raced across the hall.

'Who's that?' said Claudia.

'Could be Jake. She mentioned he might drop by.'

Claudia flushed again. Maybe she should nip upstairs quickly and re-do her make-up. She was sure her T-zone was shiny; a dab of powder wouldn't go amiss.

Poppy yelled to Caspar that *The Sound of Music* was on and Julie Andrews was going mad with a machete. Caspar took another bottle of wine from the fridge and made his way back to the sitting room. Claudia scrubbed away at a roasting tin and told herself that all she had to do when she joined the rest of them was act naturally, treat Jake as if he were any other casual dropper-in . . . and not make a prat of herself.

'Hello,' said Jake.

Claudia jumped, the sponge in her hand skidded up the roasting tin and a wave of greasy water shot over her white shirt.

'Sorry, I didn't mean to scare you.' Jake passed her a tea towel and watched as she mopped her wet front. 'Caspar forgot the corkscrew.' He paused. 'Merry Christmas, by the way.'

Act normal, act casual, thought Claudia frenziedly. She

wondered if a festive kiss on the cheek might be on the cards then realised at once she didn't have the nerve to try.

'Um . . . Merry Christmas. The corkscrew's over there. On the . . . um . . . fridge.'

And why do I get myself into this ridiculous state anyway, she thought crossly. I mean, look at him, look at that grey sweater . . . and those terrible trousers . . . how *can* I be nervous around someone who wears what looks like a school uniform left over from the last war?

He really really isn't my type, Claudia reminded herself. Apart from anything else he isn't even rich.

Moments later it struck her that she didn't need to be nervous anyway. Jake had invited her to visit those car boot sales the other week, hadn't he? And she hadn't been able to go. Maybe, thought Claudia, I could make up for it now. In, of course, a casual and natural manner.

'Will you be finished soon,' said Jake, 'or shall I bring a glass of wine through for you?'

'Don't worry.' Claudia smiled over her shoulder at him in Lauren Bacall-ish fashion . . . well, apart from the shiny nose. 'Almost done. Actually, I've been invited to a small party at a friend's house over in Baltic Wharf. If you'd like to come along you'd be welcome . . . I mean, we could go together. They're . . . um . . . nice people,' she added hurriedly, 'and very casual. Not a bit smart.'

Claudia winced; she hadn't meant to put it quite that baldly.

'Thanks, but I promised I'd call in on a friend of mine.'

For a second Jake looked amused. As well he might, thought Claudia. Here he was, getting his own back, turning *her* down for a change.

'Truly, or is that a bit of a flimsy excuse?' She tried to sound playful – like Lauren Bacall huskily asking Bogart if he knew how to whistle.

Jake reached for the corkscrew and moved towards the door.

'Truly. I'm expected for drinks at nine. At a friend's house.' Again that glimmer of a smile. 'You may remember me mentioning him once before. Ellis Featherstone. He runs our Neighbourhood Watch.'

By eight o'clock Poppy and Caspar were alone, sprawled in front of the television with a whole evening's uninterrupted supply of chocolate. *The Sound of Music* was over, Poppy had already eaten eleven feet of orange Matchmakers and neither of them could understand the rules of What's Your Fetish?, a board game given to Caspar by the hopeful blonde receptionist at the Denver Parrish Gallery.

'Maybe it's just as well.' Caspar abandoned the box of cards that went with it. The top card had begun, somewhat dubiously, 'Take two cans of whipping cream and a tin of pineapple rings . . .'

'We could watch my Gary Glitter video.' Poppy looked hopeful.

Caspar pulled a face. 'I bought the thing for you. Wasn't that enough?'

'You'd love it.'

'I wouldn't, I promise.'

'You are such a disappointment to me,' Poppy said sorrowfully. 'We like nearly all the same things. I don't understand how you can not love Gary Glitter.'

It was true, Caspar realised. They did like a lot of the same things. Well, as far as films and food and jokes were concerned anyway. Caspar smiled to himself. Morally, of course, they had their small differences.

'Now that we're on our own,' said Poppy, 'I have a bit of a confession to make.'

'Brilliant. Something sordid, I hope.'

'It's about that tiepin Kate gave you.'

When she had finished, Caspar grinned.

'Makes no difference to me. Diamonds or no diamonds. When am I ever going to wear a tie?'

151

'On your wedding day, according to Kate.'

'But I'm not going to be marrying Kate.'

'You see, that's why I made her buy the cheaper tiepin,' Poppy explained. 'I didn't even think you'd last this long. I was sure you'd have dumped her by now.'

'I tried, believe me.' Caspar shuddered at the memory. 'She got herself . . . well, into a bit of a state. She kept crying "Not before Christmas, not before Christmas", so in the end I gave up.' He shrugged and leaned over the edge of the sofa, delving into the box of Liquorice Allsorts Poppy had just opened. 'I'll do it properly next week.'

'Poor Kate.'

'Poor me.' Caspar looked indignant. 'It isn't fun, you know. Finishing with people who don't want to be finished with.'

'My heart bleeds.'

They watched a bit of the Bond film in companionable silence, Caspar stretched out across the sofa and Poppy sitting on the floor propped up against it.

She was right in front of him, hugging her knees and idly twiddling a purple sweet wrapper between her fingers, oblivious to the fact that Caspar's gaze had shifted from the television to the back of her neck.

He looked at Poppy, jolted to realise how much he still wanted her. She had tied her hair up with a black ribbon and loose red-gold tendrils curled around her ears. She was wearing the white stretchy top thing that Claudia had given her for Christmas and which, confusingly, appeared to be called a body. Caspar didn't care what it was called, he just liked the way the wide neckline curved, ballerina-style, around Poppy's slender shoulders, leaving the back of her neck bare.

Caspar realised he was fed up with trying to think of Poppy as just one of the lads. It wasn't working and it was as frustrating as hell.

It wasn't a sudden decision. He'd been exerting heroic self-control for weeks. Well, now it was Christmas night and what better time could there be to make his long-awaited move?

Reaching out, Caspar briefly touched the nape of Poppy's neck. His fingers rested against the sensitive ridge of bone where her spine began.

'Ooh, lovely,' Poppy squirmed with delight. 'Scratch my back.'

It wasn't quite the promising start he'd hoped to make. Every time Caspar tried to slow down to sensual-massage speed, Poppy shouted unromantically, 'Up a bit, left a bit – no, no, *much* harder than that!'

'Isn't it amazing,' she puffed minutes later, 'how just when you think you've got one itch sorted out, another three pop up out of nowhere. They must breed like rabbits.'

Lucky old itches. Caspar, unused to having to plan his next move – or, worse still, wondering if it would actually work – shifted a few inches further along the sofa. Now he was in line with Poppy's head. Surely, if he kissed the back of her neck, she'd begin to get the message?

Or would he be better turning her slowly round to face him? Then he could lean forward and kiss her on the mouth?

Damn, some things simply weren't meant to be plotted in advance . . . and seduction strategy was one of them.

'Poppy.'

'No I won't.'

Talk about flat-out rejection. Startled, Caspar said, 'Won't what?'

'Make the tea. It isn't my turn.'

'Oh.' He took a deep breath. As well as the white stretchy top thing, she was wearing the perfume Dina had given her for Christmas, an amazingly restrained scent considering who had chosen it.

'Yes, thanks, great,' prompted Poppy when he didn't move. 'I'd love a cup.'

Caspar breathed in again, inhaling the delicate peppery-flowery scent.

'I don't want any tea.'

Poppy, enjoying herself, twisted round and grinned up at him.

'I didn't ask you if you wanted any. I said I did.'

Right, thought Caspar, as nervous as any adolescent. *Now.* Go go go—

The phone rang, out in the hall.

'Three to one it's Claudia reminding me to switch her electric blanket on,' said Poppy, leaping to her feet. 'Evens it's one of your devoted girlies. Are you in or out?'

Caspar rolled onto his back and closed his eyes.

'Definitely out.'

Chapter 23

She came back looking sombre.

'It was Rita. I left a message on their machine yesterday. She's just got back from the hospital.'

'Bad news?'

'They don't know yet. Not for sure, anyway.' Poppy sighed and sank down onto the sofa, absently pushing Caspar's legs out of the way. 'They get the results of the exploratory op tomorrow. But the surgeon's already warned them not to get their hopes up.'

'Poor you.' Caspar gave her knee a comforting pat. It was surprisingly easy, now seduction was off the agenda.

Poppy sighed. There was no point feeling sorry for herself.

'Poor Rita.'

'At least you found him. That's why you came to London, isn't it?'

'Oh yes.' She nodded, then hesitated. 'Well, that was the main reason . . .'

'There was something else?' To cheer her up, Caspar gave her a nudge. 'What, you really came here because you'd read that piece about me in the *Sunday Times* and you thought here was a man you had to get to know?'

A flicker of a smile. 'Um . . .'

'Go on, you can admit it. You saw the photos of me and went "Cor!". You knew you had to leave Bristol and come in search of Caspar Fr—'

'I had to leave Bristol to escape the McBride lynch mob.' Poppy started to laugh. Since there was nothing she could do about Alex she was grateful for the distraction. Especially today.

Maybe making her laugh was the answer.

Caspar said, 'No, no, that wasn't it. You realised life would have no meaning until you met me. Don't you see?' He looked triumphant. 'This explains why you've never been able to summon up any interest in anyone else. It explains your ice-block. You've been crazy about me all along.'

Poppy blew him a kiss.

'I'd be even crazier about you if you made me that cup of tea.'

'There.' Back from the kitchen several minutes later, Caspar handed Poppy her mug. 'Talk about a one-track mind. There is more to life, you know, than tea tea tea.'

'Okay, if it'll stop you making fun of me, I'll tell you the whole story,' said Poppy. 'The real reason why I have such an abnormal lack of interest in men.' She gave him a warning look. 'And don't you dare laugh.'

'Me? Laugh? Why would I laugh?'

'Because it sounds too dopey for words,' said Poppy. She clutched her mug of tea in both hands and began to explain about Tom.

'Good grief,' said Caspar when she had finished. 'I thought it was just a case of cold feet. Why did you never tell us before?'

'Like I said, it sounds stupid.' Poppy bit one of her fingernails. 'And I thought it would have worn off by now. The thing is, it hasn't. I only have to accidentally *think* about Tom and my stomach goes all squirmy. I can't help it, I've never felt like this about anyone before. It's starting to make me nervous. I mean, what if this feeling never goes away?'

'Would it help,' said Caspar, 'if I told you he was probably married with three kids and a Volvo?'

'He isn't. I just know he isn't.'

They were employing different tenses, Caspar noticed.

156

'Was he good-looking?'

'Of course.'

Caspar experienced a stab of jealousy. 'What, better than me?'

Poppy smiled. He sounded so shocked.

'Oh, heaps better,' she teased.

'In that case he's bound to be a shit.'

'Oh well, you'd know.'

'The thing is,' Caspar said vigorously, 'you have to be practical about this. How long *can* you go on pining for this Mr Wonderful? I mean, let's face it. This is London. You're not going to bump into him walking down the street.'

Caspar stayed up long after Poppy had gone to bed. One way and another it had been an eventful evening. He understood a lot more now. The bad news was, it had made him want Poppy more than ever. Finding himself in competition with the absent Tom had only increased his interest. And to think that Poppy should have seen him in the petrol station only the other week . . .

I must have been standing right next to him, thought Caspar, trying to imagine what might have happened if Poppy had been able to get out of the car. No wonder she hadn't said much afterwards, as he had driven her to St Clare's.

But if she *had* told him then, he might have been able to help. Poppy had forgotten that all garages employ surveillance cameras. Caspar couldn't help thinking that a small bribe might have secured them a re-run of the video tape. Then all he would have needed to do was persuade a policeman friend of his to check out the car's registration number.

It was too late now. The video tape would be wiped over.

Caspar tried to decide if this was good news as far as he was concerned, or bad.

Poppy called round to see Alex when he had been out of hospital for a week. She was alarmed by how much older he

157

looked – and he wasn't the only one. It was the first time she had seen Rita in daylight and without make-up.

Now the initial shock was over they were being determinedly cheerful.

'Look at the state of us,' Alex mocked, squeezing Rita's hand as she bent over him to straighten his pillows. 'Couple of leftovers from Halloween. Can't see anyone wanting to paint us in the altogether, eh love?'

'You'd be surprised.' With a start of recognition, Poppy realised for the first time that one side of his mouth curled differently from the other. Hers did that sometimes, too. 'They like old models, they're partial to a few lines and wrinkles.'

Rita groaned. 'Blimey, you know how to cheer a girl up.'

'I do my best,' said Poppy. She looked at Alex. 'So what's happening? How do you really feel?'

'Like I've been kicked down the Mile End Road and back.' He managed a dry smile. 'But this is nothing, apparently. Once I get started on the chemo I'll really know the meaning of hell on wheels.'

'We're bracing ourselves for the worst,' Rita put in. 'That way, anything half bearable's a bonus. So people keep telling us, anyway.'

I'm not going to cry, Poppy told herself. She turned and stared very hard out of the bedroom window. The sun was shining, the sky was an optimistic shade of blue. Frost gleamed on the broad stretch of lawn below. She still didn't know how Alex and Rita had come by such a home, but what did that matter now? What good was all their dubiously-acquired money when all Alex wanted was a body not riddled with cancer?

She didn't stay long. Alex was clearly worn out.

'Thanks, love, for coming.' He nodded to show he meant it. 'A lot of people have steered well clear. It's all right turning up for the parties drinking my drink and having a knees-up, but when it comes to something like this you don't see 'em

158

for dust.' He coughed and laughed. 'Too scared we might start talking funerals.'

'They're afraid of saying the wrong thing,' said Poppy.

'Like mentioning the d-word. In case it hasn't occurred to us that I might kick the bucket.' Alex patted her hand. 'Anyway, you came. Bless you for that. And it's nice for Rita . . . does her good to see someone she can have a bit of a chat with.'

Not wanting to tire him too much, Poppy rose to leave. She pulled a newspaper-wrapped parcel out of the Sainsbury's carrier bag at her feet.

'I brought you something. I spotted it in an auction the other day. Thought you might like it to keep the other one company.'

Alex unwrapped the spirit bottle and gazed at it in silence for several seconds. Wintry sunlight reflected off the royal blue glass as he turned it slowly in his hands.

'Blimey, talk about coincidence,' Rita exclaimed. 'You always said it was one of a pair, didn't you, love?'

'Which auction room?' asked Alex.

'Oh . . . um . . . Lassiter's.' Poppy began to feel frightened. Had she gone too far this time? 'They do look like a pair, I know, but I expect there were hundreds made. Thousands, even. I mean,' she added hastily, 'it'd be a bit daft, wouldn't it, to only make two?'

'Oh well, never mind.' Alex shrugged; he was no expert. He smoothed the curved side of the bottle with an unsteady forefinger. 'I reckon they belong together now. If you ask me they make a pretty good pair.'

159

Chapter 24

The cold snap ended in the second week of January. Poppy, who'd complained bitterly about never being able to feel her toes, decided that rain was worse. One of her shoes had a hole in it. Her hair went completely mental in the wet. Her Shetland wool sweater smelled of damp sheep.

'And this is supposed to be a treat,' Poppy sighed as they trudged through a churned-up field. Her top half was splattered with rain, her bottom half with mud. She had, brainily, chosen today of all days to wear white jeans and a dry-clean only shirt. The shirt, a market stall bargain, was shrinking faster than you could say cheap import.

'It is a treat.' Jake was brisk. 'Honestly, all this fuss over a bit of rain.'

'A bit! A few dozen reservoirs-full.'

'Your first country house auction,' he protested, gesturing to the imposing building looming out of the semi-darkness ahead, 'and all you can do is whinge.'

Poppy wondered why the field-cum-car park had to be so damn far away from the house. She thought dark thoughts about the people who had organised today's shindig. She wished her shoes didn't squelch.

Jake grinned at the look on her face. 'Okay, okay. You can do some bidding.'

'Really?' Poppy perked up at once. She hadn't been allowed to bid for months, not since the wasp-swatting incident last summer. Still, no danger of any wasps today.

'We'll call it a trial run,' said Jake. 'I have to disappear at lunchtime to see a buyer in Windsor. You can take over while I'm away.'

Chartwell-Lacey Manor heaved with potential buyers. Dealers mingled with members of the public. An awful lot of mud was being trailed through the house.

Poppy envied the sensible people in warm coats and wellies. She queued up for plastic cups of coffee in the east-facing scullery, blowing on her icy fingers and eavesdropping on the gossip of two local women behind her. Jake had briefly outlined the story of Dorothea de Lacey, the recently deceased owner of Chartwell, but he was a typical man, hopeless in the gossip stakes. What these women had to say was far more revealing.

'. . . and what about them daughters of hers?' tutted the one in the purple tea-cosy hat, 'all but tearin' each other's hair out to get their hands on the best bits of jewellery. It's a disgrace, that's what it is. Shame on them, after the way they treated the poor old duck.'

'Except she was 'ardly what you'd call poor,' cackled the other one, pointing to the rolled-up catalogue she hadn't been able to resist buying, even though she had only come along for a nose. 'What about them chandeliers in the ballroom, eh? Imagine 'avin' to get up a ladder and dust all them bits o' glass every week! And did you spot that portrait of Mrs de Lacey when she was young? Up for sale, along with the bleedin' furniture.' She shook her head in vigorous disapproval. 'Those two money-grubbing bitches didn't even have the decency to keep a painting of their own mother. All they care about is gettin' their greedy 'ands on the cash. I tell you, Mabel, if I thought for one minute our Teresa'd play that kind of dirty trick on me, I'd turf 'er out o' the 'ouse so fast 'er 'eels wouldn't touch the ground.'

'Poor Mrs de Lacey, God rest her soul. Nice old duck, she was,' muttered purple hat. 'What she ever did to deserve daughters like that is beyond me.'

'What the daughters did to deserve all *this* is beyond me,'

161

the other one snorted. 'Eh? Millions, that's what they'll get when this lot's been sold off.'

'Should've left it to a cats' home,' growled purple hat.

The other one chuckled. 'Should've left it to me.'

By the time Poppy found Jake again his coffee was half-drunk and half-cold. He was studying dinner services, making careful notes in the margins of his sale catalogue and keeping a discreet eye on the other potential buyers swarming through the crowded rooms.

'Sorry, I kept getting my elbows bashed.' Poppy handed him his plastic cup with a grimace. 'I had to drink some to stop it being spilt.'

'What's the time?' asked Jake. Viewing went on until eleven thirty when the auction began.

'Only ten. How's it going? Any hot-lots?'

Hot-lots were those attracting a noticeable amount of interest from the dealers. Poppy loved to sound like a pro. When she'd first heard the expression she'd thought it meant stolen goods.

'We aren't interested in hot-lots,' Jake said mildly. He showed her the notes he'd been making, and the prices he'd scribbled next to the items he was interested in. 'Now, I'll be here for the first fifty or so lots. I'll watch you bid, and see how you get on, then head over to Windsor.' He paused and flipped over to the next page of the catalogue. 'Here, you'll be on your own. Carry on bidding and whatever you do, don't exceed the prices I've put down.' He gave Poppy a measured look. 'No getting carried away.'

'What, not even by a knight on a white charger?' Poppy grinned and gave him a nudge. 'You don't trust me an inch, do you? It's okay boss, no need to panic. I'm on my best behaviour. Even better now my feet have begun to dry out. I won't let you down.'

Jake said, 'Hmm,' and drew another Biro from the inside pocket of his ancient Harris tweed jacket. 'Here, you'll want to copy the prices down.'

'No need.' Having swung into super-efficient executive mode, Poppy tapped the catalogue with a forefinger. 'I'll use this.'

By twelve o'clock Poppy had cheered up no end. Chartwell-Lacey Manor was just like something off a film set, the auctioneer was unexpectedly handsome with an almost roguish twinkle in his eye – usually they looked like bank managers about to confiscate your credit card – and the atmosphere was building nicely. It was, Poppy felt, wonderfully dramatic and glamorous. Very Lady Jane and Lovejoy.

She could hardly wait for Jake to leave. She had already bid three times and been successful twice. The adrenalin was swishing through her like nobody's business; and if it was this good bidding with Jake beside her, how much more thrilling was it going to be when she was on her own? It would be like flying solo for the first time, she thought dreamily, without an instructor to stamp on the dual controls . . .

'Okay,' Jake murmured. 'I'm off. I'll be back before three.' He passed the catalogue across to Poppy and pointed to the lot numbers the auctioneer was currently dealing with. 'If you want to grab a sandwich, do it now. You've got twenty minutes before he reaches the Venetian glass.'

Poppy was seriously hard up this week. She batted her eyelashes at Jake.

'Be an angel. Lend us fifty pence for a sandwich.'

'Oh shit, oh help,' Poppy wailed a quarter of an hour later, her blood running cold as she realised what she had done. This was the other kind of adrenalin rush, the nasty kind that seized you when you realised you'd made a balls-up and it wasn't going to go down at all well.

It was the cheap shirt's fault for having shrunk in the rain. As the morning had worn on it had become tighter and tighter. It was like wearing a pantie-girdle over your shoulders.

Worried that at some crucial moment she might not be able to lift her arm to bid, Poppy had nipped into one of the downstairs loos, wriggled out of her sweater and blouse and dumped the blouse in a wastepaper basket. The Shetland wool itched like mad against her bare skin but at least she could breathe again. The sensation of actually being able to inflate her lungs had been positively exhilarating.

So exhilarating, thought Poppy with a sick feeling in her stomach, that she'd danced off to the makeshift canteen for cheese and pickle sandwiches and a Mars bar, quite forgetting to take Jake's copy of the catalogue with her when she went.

Poppy stared wretchedly at the sink where she'd dumped it while she was doing her quick change. That had been twenty minutes ago and the sodding thing had gone, been swiped no doubt by some rotten thieving opportunist too stingy to buy their own.

Stay calm, stay calm, don't panic, Poppy willed herself, before sweat could begin to prickle down her back. She couldn't cope with that *and* the Shetland wool.

Well, it's simple, she decided moments later. I have two choices here. Either I twiddle my thumbs until Jake gets back and tell him I haven't bought anything because I didn't bid for anything because I lost the catalogue with his price list on because I'm a complete wazzock . . . or I have a bash at doing it myself.

With no money left she had to relate her tale of woe to the man selling the catalogues and beg him to let her have one for nothing. Then, curling up on lot hundred and twenty-eight, a Victorian carved walnut balloon back armchair on cabriole legs, Poppy pored over the pages, willing herself to remember which of the items Jake had wanted her to go for. Lots seventy-three and seventy-five, the Venetian glass, she was sure about. And the satin-finished Lalique glass clock, hadn't he scribbled two thou by that? Then there were lot numbers eighty-three and eighty-four, the Ferdinand Preiss figures whose prices she couldn't be certain about. They would probably each fetch around five hundred pounds.

Poppy scribbled her own prices down, keeping her ears pricked to make sure the auctioneer didn't start on the Venetian glass without her. Lot eighty-nine . . . her pencil hovered over the page . . . was a box of assorted paintings. She knew Jake wanted them because when she'd glanced at his list earlier the number had rung a bell; eighty-nine was what she always ordered from their local Chinese takeaway: king prawns with mushrooms and egg fried rice.

'Lot number seventy-three,' announced the auctioneer, making Poppy jump. 'A fine example of Venetian glass, a handmade sweetmeat dish . . .'

Poppy scrawled four hundred next to lot eighty-nine and scrambled to her feet. She wriggled her way into the auctioneer's view and began bidding away. Oh, the giddy adrenalin rush now that she was actually doing it herself . . . no chaperone, no stabilisers!

She didn't get the dish, it went in a frenzy of dealing to a woman in a pink straw hat at the front of the room, but the auctioneer gave Poppy an encouraging wink afterwards. She wondered if it meant 'never mind, better luck next time' or 'hello darling, fancy a drink?' He really was good-looking. Pumped up with adrenalin, Poppy grinned back. Perhaps it meant both.

She didn't get lot seventy-five either, or eighty-three, but she hit paydirt with the second of the Ferdinand Preiss figures, beating off nervous competition from a housewifely-looking woman to clinch the deal for four seven five.

'Sold.' The auctioneer tapped his gavel and nodded at Poppy as if to say 'There, I knew you could do it!' He gave her an encouraging smile. 'Name?'

'Poppy Dunbar.' She had to say it; he looked as if he really wanted to know. Then she remembered who'd be writing out the cheque. 'Um . . . Landers.'

Did he seem disappointed? Did it make her sound married? Poppy ran the fingers of her left hand slowly, front-to-back, through her hair so he would see her ringless state. The exhilaration of bidding – and winning – was still with her. Was this surge of lust real or was she suffering an acute attack of auction-fever?

Poppy didn't know and didn't care. She just wanted to do it again.

And I can, I can, she thought joyfully, studying her catalogue and running her finger down the list. Four more lots, then it was the box of paintings, assorted. She hadn't seen them herself but Jake was always on the lookout for good picture frames.

She'd hazarded a guess and scribbled four hundred in the margin. Poppy bit her lower lip. Maybe, to be on the safe side, she should limit herself to three hundred . . .

' . . . three hundred and fifty, am I bid three hundred and fifty?'

The auctioneer's eyes flickered in Poppy's direction. The corners of his mouth twitched as if he were silently urging her on. She felt hypnotised by the look he was giving her, and by the breathless silence that seemed to have descended on the rest of the room. At this moment she had everyone's rapt attention. So this was how it felt to be the Queen.

Poppy wished she could do one of those slow Lovejoy winks but she knew she'd only look as if a contact lens had popped out. Instead, she nodded, twice, like a chicken.

'Three fifty to the lady on my left. Am I bid four hundred?'

The attention swung to the other side of the room. A male voice – she couldn't see who – said 'Yes.'

Outraged – and not wanting to appear cheap – Poppy shouted 'Four fifty.'

'Five hundred.'

Something weird was happening. Her fingers and toes had gone numb. And she was breathing much too fast. Heavens, never mind looking like a chicken . . . now she sounded like a dog.

Poppy tried to concentrate on the bidding. Even more weirdly, she realised, she no longer knew how much money five hundred and fifty pounds actually was.

'Five fifty? Do I have five hundred and fifty?' The auctioneer was gazing at her once more, lulling her with his voice, coaxing her into saying yes.

'Yes,' Poppy whispered. Then again, more loudly: 'Yes.'

There were no more bids. The gavel went 'tap' on the auctioneer's desk. 'Thank you,' he told Poppy, reaching for his pen. 'Landers. Right, ladies and gentlemen, we now come to lot number ninety...'

Chapter 25

'Lot what?' said Jake, his dark eyebrows drawing ominously close together. 'Eighty-nine? I didn't want lot eighty-nine.'

'Yes you did.' Poppy felt the first stirrings of panic. She nodded, to prove herself right. 'King prawns and mushrooms with egg fried rice.'

'*What*?'

'Jake, you definitely marked eighty-nine. I *know* you marked eighty-nine . . .' Her voice began to falter. Numbers were funny things; they played tricks on your brain. She could visualise the menu as plain as day now. King prawns and mushrooms were ninety-eight. Eighty-nine was beef chow mein.

'Poppy, you wrote four hundred pounds next to it.' Jake was sounding less amused by the second. He pointed to her hastily scribbled figures. 'Then you crossed it out and put three hundred pounds for a box of the tattiest and possibly the most terrible paintings I've ever seen in my life.'

'I – I didn't.' Poppy began to stammer. Oh help, now she was feeling really sick. 'Look, I'll p-pay you back . . .'

'You mean you went *over* three hundred? How much,' Jake thundered, 'did you bid?'

It was no good, he was going to find out in a matter of minutes anyway. Poppy braced herself.

'Five fifty.'

The explosion didn't happen. Cautiously she opened her eyes. Maybe he wasn't going to lose his temper with her after all.

'Right, that's it,' hissed Jake. He was white with rage. 'That *is* it. I've had enough. I can't afford you any more, Poppy. You'll have to go.'

Poppy waded through the churned-up field blinking rain out of her eyes. She no longer even cared that she was plastered with mud up to her knees. She was trying to do as Jake had instructed and dump the box of paintings in the back of the van but Jake hadn't told her where he'd parked the van and she couldn't find it.

She barely noticed as a loaded-up lorry trundled past, missing her by inches. All Poppy could think about was Jake, in front of an audience of fifty or so auction-goers, picking through the contents of the box, flaunting her stupidity for all to see. He couldn't have looked more disgusted if they'd been crawling with maggots. Each painting he picked up was worse than the last.

'All I can say about these,' he'd declared icily 'is the best thing about them is the frames.'

The rickety frames were mainly ex-Woolworth, circa thirty years ago. They were made of grimy off-white plastic.

A couple of dealers sniggered.

'I mean, for Christ's sake,' Jake raged, 'how could you even *think* I'd be interested in garbage like this?'

'I didn't see them.' Poppy's voice was small. She felt terrible and Jake wasn't even letting her apologise.

'Then you're even more stupid than I thought.'

'I'll pay for them.'

'Don't make me laugh. Only this morning you had to borrow fifty pence for a sandwich.' He glared at one of the larger pictures, a chocolate-boxy painting of two spaniel puppies peeping out of a flowerpot. Then he dropped it disdainfully back into the box. 'What I don't understand is how you managed to get *up* to five fifty. Was someone else really interested in this rubbish or was the auctioneer bidding off the wall?'

169

To suggest that she had been bidding against a non-existent buyer was the ultimate insult.

Poppy whispered, 'There *was* someone else.' She saw the auctioneer walking past. No, mincing past. He glanced at Poppy and glanced away again. Up close she saw his eyes were mean and his hair dyed. Bidding-fever had a lot to answer for. She wondered how she could possibly have found him attractive.

Now, out in the rainswept field, Poppy realised she was going round in circles.

The van was nowhere to be seen. She didn't have the nerve to go back inside and tell Jake she couldn't find it. He would only go even more berserk.

She had reached the main gate leading out onto the road. Without stopping to wonder if it was sensible, Poppy hoisted the box of paintings onto her hip and turned left. Left for London. He didn't want to see her again, let alone employ her. Well, Poppy decided, she couldn't face seeing Jake either. She'd been on the receiving end of quite enough fury for one day. All she wanted to do was go home.

'Eeyuch, look at you!'

Claudia, fresh from her bath, looked suitably horrified when she opened the front door.

'Sorry. My key's in my pocket.'

'You're all wet.'

'I'm not, am I?'

Wearily Poppy hauled the box of paintings into the house. What she really longed for was a hot bath but knowing Claudia she'd just emptied the tank.

Claudia, rosy-cheeked and bundled up in a fluffy white robe, padded after her into the sitting room.

'I say, is something wrong?'

'Jake sacked me. I owe him five hundred and fifty pounds.' Poppy collapsed on the floor, pulling off her sodden shoes and socks. 'And I've probably got trench foot. Otherwise everything's fine.'

Poppy was looking sad and bedraggled. To make up for pinching all the hot water Claudia made her a coffee with brandy in it. She listened to Poppy's sorry story while she was doing her make-up. She gave her nails an unnecessary manicure and a final coat of pink polish. She ran upstairs and came down again wearing a new sage green shift dress with expensive looking shoes to match. She squirted herself with heaps of Dior's Eau Svelte.

'Oh,' said Poppy at last. She had been enjoying having someone to moan to. 'Are you going out?'

'Wait until you see him,' Claudia confided gleefully, 'you won't believe it! He's heavenly, completely gorgeous. His name's Will.'

Poppy was astonished. She'd had no idea Claudia could be so enthusiastic.

'When did all this happen?'

'At lunchtime. A few of us from the office went to Rossini's for lunch.' Claudia was practically hugging herself at the blissful memory. 'And he was there with a crowd of friends. The girls kept saying he was looking over but I didn't believe them. Then, just as we were about to leave, he waited until I glanced across . . . and pretended to take one of his eyes out!' Poppy's face was a picture. To show her how he'd done it, Claudia mimed the action. 'He held it in his hand, bent down on one knee and rolled the pretend eyeball across the floor towards me.'

'What did you do?'

Claudia giggled. 'I rolled it back to him.'

'And then he came over,' prompted Poppy.

'And then he came over—'

'And said: "I was hoping you'd catch my eye."'

'Oh bum,' wailed Claudia. 'You've heard it before! I thought it was really original.'

'Sorry.' Poppy felt mean. She began pulling the paintings out of their box. Since she didn't have anything else to do she might as well polish up the few frames that weren't plastic.

'Anyway, his name's Will and he's a broker,' Claudia went on compulsively. 'He lives in Fulham and drives a red Lotus.'

Won't go with your nail polish, thought Poppy.

Claudia smiled a blissful smile. 'And he's taking me to Tatsuso.'

Poppy assumed this was good news. To make up for just now, she said, 'That's terrific.'

The door bell rang. Claudia let out a squeal of excitement. 'That'll be for me! You get it!'

Before Poppy could lever herself to her feet they heard Caspar making his way downstairs and the sound of the front door being opened.

Poppy said, 'It's been got.'

Chapter 26

Caspar had been working up in his studio for ten hours without a break. Coming downstairs in search of banana doughnuts and cadgable cigarettes, he answered the door en route.

'Who is he?' he whispered to Poppy, because Claudia was clearly far too excited to make proper introductions.

'The King of Smooth,' Poppy whispered back. She was marvelling at the sight of Claudia fluttering not just her eyelashes but her whole body at him. She looked at Will Smyth – not Smith – and wondered if he had really been born with that glamorous 'y' or if it was a recent addition, sneaked in there when no one was looking.

Poppy couldn't help comparing him with Caspar. Will's hair was dark and immaculately cut, Caspar's was blond and flopped all over the place. Will was wearing an expensive-looking suede jacket over an expensive-looking golfing sweater over a superbly ironed shirt, superbly pressed trousers and expensive-looking pigskin shoes. Caspar wore no shoes, ancient jeans and a tee-shirt that had been left behind years ago by one of his ex-girlfriends, with 'I love Jason Donovan' on the front.

'What's so funny?' Caspar had intercepted Poppy's side-long glance.

'I'm comparing the two of you. He smells of Givenchy for Gentlemen. You smell of turps.'

'I like the smell of turps.'

'His nails are manicured. Yours are covered in blue paint.'

'Damn, no wonder Claudia prefers him to me.'

'And he drives a Lotus.'

'Oh well, no contest.'

As long as Caspar's battered BMW got him from A to B, he was happy. He couldn't care less about status-symbol cars.

'It's Claudia's lucky day.'

Caspar lifted Poppy's chin, 'Doesn't look like yours.'

'It's been my unlucky day.' Poppy heaved a sigh. 'Claudia got pulled, I got fired.'

'So what else is new?' Caspar grinned. 'Okay, Claudia getting pulled is a bit of a novelty, I'll admit. But you're always getting fired. I thought you'd be used to it by now.'

'Don't make fun.' She prised a hideous old print of Westminster Bridge out of a frame that was at least made of wood, not plastic. If she polished it up it might fetch a fiver. 'I've been a prize prat. This time Jake isn't going to forgive me.'

After much high-pitched laughter and muffled shrieking in the kitchen, Claudia and Will came back. Claudia was holding a bottle of Krug and – precariously – four glasses. Will was holding Claudia around the waist, murmuring something into her ear that was making her blush.

'I thought we could have a drink before we leave.' This was Claudia's way of getting everyone to know each other. She wanted Poppy and Caspar to like Will as much as she did.

'You kept this well hidden,' said Caspar, meaning the Krug. He certainly hadn't spotted it in the fridge.

Claudia looked bashful. 'We only met six and a half hours ago.'

'She's the girl of my dreams,' said Will. He gave her a squeeze and winked at Caspar. 'I like a cosy armful, don't you?'

Claudia mouthed What Do You Think? at Poppy while Will unravelled the wire around the cork. Brightly, Poppy nodded, because if Claudia didn't mind being called a cosy armful who was she to object?

Seconds later the cork flew out of the bottle and bounced off the ceiling. As Poppy held her glass up to be filled, Will deliberately tipped some of the Krug down her front.

'Oops,' he leered, 'now I expect you'll need a hand getting out of those wet clothes.'

'It's a *joke*,' Claudia explained with a girlish giggle. 'He did it at lunchtime, to Daisy from accounts. Everyone thought it was a scream!'

'It's certainly a waste of champagne,' said Caspar.

Will winked again. 'I'd volunteer to lick it off.'

Poppy didn't dare look at Caspar. She took a great swig of her drink instead, so quickly the bubbles went up her nose.

'Well, cheers everyone,' said Claudia happily. Then, as the door bell rang again, 'Whoever's that?'

Will said, 'If it's the wife and kids, don't let 'em in.'

He winked so often, thought Poppy, it was practically a nervous twitch.

Caspar answered the door.

'It's your ex-employer,' he announced, coming back with Jake.

'Oh help,' mumbled Poppy, her gaze flickering nervously to the heap of paintings strewn over the carpet. She couldn't face another shouting match. If Jake accused her of absconding with lot eighty-nine she might have to burst into tears.

'Jake, what a surprise,' exclaimed Claudia. Eager to show off the dazzling new love of her life – ha! this would show Jake the calibre of man she was capable of attracting – she dragged Will towards him. 'You must meet Will . . . we're just off out to dinner . . . Will, this is Jake Landers. Jake, Will Smyth.'

Jake barely glanced at Will as he shook his hand. He muttered, 'Hi,' then turned to Poppy. 'Look, I'm sorry about earlier. I lost my temper and I shouldn't have. You aren't fired.'

'I'm not?'

Poppy's eyes swam. She'd been so certain he'd come here to give her another bawling-out.

'I overreacted. I was worried sick when I couldn't find you. How on earth did you get home?'

'A dealer with a van load of Victoriana took pity on me.'

'You accepted a lift from a complete stranger? For heaven's *sake*, Poppy—'

'It was a female dealer. I'm not a complete halfwit.'

'Is that the same as not half a complete-wit?' Caspar wondered aloud.

'Anyway,' Poppy felt honour-bound to tell him, 'she had a quick look at the paintings and said if you wanted to cut your losses she'd take them off your hands for fifty quid.'

'Oh well, I can do a bit better than that,' said Jake. 'After you'd done your vanishing trick I was approached by the chap who'd been bidding against you. His wife had her heart set on the painting of the puppies in the flowerpot – apparently they looked like a pair of spaniels they'd once owned – and he was desperate to get it for her. It's her birthday next week. He's not interested in the other pictures but he offered me three hundred for that one.'

Poppy bit her lip. 'The puppies in the flowerpot?'

'Oh shit.' Jake's face fell. 'Don't tell me. You've already sold it. You threw it in the Thames. You drew moustaches on the dogs.'

'No, it's right here.' Poppy grinned. 'I've even polished the frame.'

'Thank God for that. You had me worried.'

'How do you suppose I've been feeling since lunchtime? So, do I really have my job back?'

Jake nodded. He looked up in surprise as Claudia thrust a full glass into his hand.

'There we are, now we have something else to celebrate,' she said gaily.

'Is it somebody's birthday?' asked Jake.

Will slid his arm around Claudia's hip with a proprietorial air, pulling her against him.

'We're celebrating the fact that I've just walked into this gorgeous girl's life.'

Poppy wasn't the only one who'd been making comparisons. Claudia, revelling in Will's lavish compliments and scarcely able to believe her luck – to think, they'd so *nearly* lunched at Brown's instead – couldn't help comparing Will's suave glamour with Jake's painfully untrendy appearance. He looked dishevelled too, in a Bob Geldof-y kind of way, but you needed to actually *be* Bob Geldof to carry it off.

The thing about Jake, Claudia decided, was he didn't have the first idea about style and grooming and he didn't even have the grace to care. A make-over would do wonders. If he only bothered to smarten himself up he could probably look quite passable, maybe even handsome.

But that was the trouble; he never *would* ...

'What's the matter,' Poppy teased Caspar, 'jealous?'

He was looking through the untidy pile of paintings, running a finger through the layer of dust covering one of those she hadn't yet blasted with her trusty can of Mr Sheen.

'Mmm?'

He was miles away.

'Bet you wish you were that talented.' Poppy grabbed it from him, held it in front of her, pulled a face and turned it the other way up. 'Now this is what I call a masterpiece. What d'you suppose it is, an aerial view of Dorothea's crazy paving? And this brown splodge at the bottom; that could be a dead hamster . . .'

Caspar ignored Poppy's wittering. He took back the painting and gave it his undivided attention. It was smallish, fourteen inches by ten, and executed in oils. The frame was cheap, obscuring most of the signature. The aggressively abstract nature of the work and the unprepossessing colour scheme – greys and browns with the odd streak of black thrown in for light relief – ensured that neither the auctioneers nor the dealers had paid it more than a moment's attention.

To the casual eye it was a deeply unattractive example of the genre commonly referred to by the public at large as a load of old cobblers.

It had to be a fake, thought Caspar. A copy, an imitation, an 'in-the-style-of' . . .

'What did you say just now?' he demanded suddenly, making Poppy jump. 'Whose crazy paving?'

'Dorothea. Dorothea de Lacey. The woman whose stuff was being auctioned.' There was an odd expression on Caspar's face; Poppy wondered if he had known her. Damn, she hated having to break bad news. 'I'm sorry, she, um, died a few weeks ago. But I'm sure she didn't suffer. It was very peaceful . . . and she'd had a jolly good innings.'

This ludicrous expression always conjured up in Poppy's mind a vision of some tottering old dear in cricket pads and head gear, valiantly defending her wicket. She envisaged Dorothea hitting a nifty six.

Caspar was still studying the painting.

'How old was she?'

'No idea.' Poppy shrugged. So he hadn't known her after all. 'Pretty ancient.'

'Mid-eighties,' volunteered Jake, who had spotted a portrait of Dorothea as a young girl at the sale. It had been painted in 1925. 'Why?'

'Let me take it along to the gallery tomorrow. Show it to someone who knows a bit more about this kind of thing than I do.' Abstract art wasn't his forte. He wasn't going to raise their hopes on such a long shot. But Wilhelm von Kantz had once had a brief affair with an English girl known only as Dorrie. And if this was an undiscovered von Kantz, well . . .

'You mean it could be worth something?' Poppy gazed at the ugly little painting in disbelief.

'Maybe. A couple of hundred or so, anyway.' No one had had more practice at lying to the opposite sex than Caspar.

'Who knows? You could even end up in profit.' He gave her a nudge. 'You'll be asking Jake for a pay rise.'

Poppy's eyes lit up. 'Now there's an idea!'

'Thanks a lot,' said Jake.

Will touched Claudia's arm. 'We'd better be making a move.'

Claudia looked around for her jacket, which was draped over the back of the sofa. Spotting it, Caspar passed it across. He said, 'Home by midnight, okay? Don't do anything I wouldn't do.'

Claudia was glad she had at last been cured of her crush on Caspar. There was nothing, after all, more depressing than the prospect of fancying someone rotten for years on end and never being fancied in return.

Thank you, Mother, she thought drily, because the miracle cure was down to Angie. Before, Caspar's astounding success rate with women hadn't bothered Claudia. If anything it had only added to his allure.

Discovering that he had slept with her mother, on the other hand, had had much the same effect as a bucket of bromide. Yuck. Just the thought of them together made Claudia feel sick.

Anyway, she thought smugly, who needs that kind of hassle? I don't *need* to have a stupid crush on Caspar any more.

Nor did she need to worry about those other unfamiliar and even more embarrassing feelings, the ones she'd found herself quietly developing for Jake. Now they *had* been a worry. When you could overlook such diabolical fashion sense, you knew you were in big trouble. Heavens, thought Claudia in alarm, what with his shyness and that haircut and the general lack of interest in the opposite sex, Jake was even more of a no-hoper than Caspar.

But now, thanks to Will, she could put the pair of them out of her mind. He took her hand and gave it a loving squeeze.

179

I've got someone who thinks I'm the business, thought Claudia, and who isn't afraid to show it. What more could any girl want?

By midnight she knew what Will wanted.

'Oh come on, you know you do too,' he protested, trying to slide his hand for the third time up her leg. 'You invited me in for coffee, didn't you? You can't turn all heartless on me now.'

'I can, I can.' Frantically, Claudia wriggled out of reach. He was right, of course – she *wanted* him to stay the night – but she was even more determined not to be a pushover. She'd read enough women's magazines in her time to know how men operated. They'd take whatever they could get, simply because they were men. But when it came to settling down they wanted a nice girl, one whose bedposts were more or less intact.

Too many notches were a definite no-no, Claudia reminded herself. Okay, it wasn't fair and it wasn't liberated, but that was the way things were. Men respected girls who said no – for a while, at least. If she slept with me on the first date, they'd ask themselves, how many other men has she been with? Oh dear, tut tut, that will never do. Not for the mother of *my* children . . .

'What's the matter? We had a terrific evening, didn't we?' Will was looking hurt. 'I thought you liked me as much as I like you.'

'I do, I do.'

'Hang on, there's an echo in here.'

Claudia began to panic. What if he lost patience with her? What if he took offence at being turned down? What if he decided she'd had her chance and she'd blown it? She might never see him again.

'I just don't want you to think I'm easy, that's all,' she said nervously. 'Because I'm not, but if I let you stay tonight you might think I am.'

'I don't think that.' He gave her a lazy grin. 'I *wouldn't* think it.'

Claudia looked worried. 'The thing is, you *think* you wouldn't think it, but deep down you would. You see, you're only saying this now because—'

'Whoa,' said Will. 'Okay, enough. I give up.'

Claudia bit her lip. Was this the smartest move of her life, or the stupidest?

'I'm going now.' He yawned and rose with reluctance to his feet, avoiding her panicky gaze as he patted his pockets in search of his keys.

Oh God, I *have* blown it, Claudia thought miserably. Before she could stop herself she blurted out, 'Does this mean you don't want to see me again?'

'What? Oh . . . of course not.' He still wasn't looking at her. His manner was vague; he sounded as if he were making polite conversation to a stranger on the train.

'So you *do* want to see me again?'

'Yes, yes.'

'When?' said Claudia.

'What?' He was still hunting for his keys. He shrugged. 'Well, soonish. I'll give you a ring sometime.'

How quickly the best evening of your life could turn into one of the worst. Claudia felt her pride melt away.

'Okay,' she said in a shaky voice, 'you can stop looking for your keys.'

Will glanced at her.

'Why?'

'You can stay.'

He began to smile. The next minute he pulled her into his arms. 'You little beauty! Well, maybe not so little . . .'

Claudia clung to him.

'Just so long as you don't think I'm cheap,' she emphasised. 'I'm not a tart, all right? I don't make a habit of this. In fact, I've never done it before.'

'You mean the poor sods gave in,' Will drawled. He was

grinning broadly. 'When you said no, they thought you meant it. Damn, some men show no initiative.'

He had lifted her into his arms by this time. Claudia felt like a bride being carried over the threshold. As he headed for the staircase she prayed his back wouldn't give out.

She was so happy it took a while for his words to sink in.

'Hang on, you mean you were putting on an act just now? Deliberately making me think I'd never see you again?' She took a playful swipe at his shoulder. 'Oh . . . you!'

'Had to, didn't I?' He paused on the landing to kiss her. 'You were saying no. I had to make you change your mind.' He huffed on his nails and rubbed them with pride against his shirt front. 'Needs must, darling. Where there's a Will there's a way.'

Chapter 27

Poppy had never seen a transformation like it. The effect Will Smyth had had on Claudia was mesmerising. She looked prettier, she was happier, she couldn't stop singing. It went to show, thought Poppy, mystified. There really was no accounting for taste.

'You're home,' Claudia cried when she arrived back from work on Wednesday afternoon. 'Perfect, we can eat right away. I've made a chilli.'

'Made?' Poppy was startled. 'You mean poked holes in the cellophane and put in the microwave?'

'No, *made* made.' Claudia tried to look Delia Smith-ish, as if preparing meals from scratch was something that came perfectly naturally to her. 'Really made. And there's no need to stare at me like that,' she went on defensively. 'It's only chilli.'

'Oh, I get it. Will's coming round to dinner and you want him to see what a perfect wife you'll make.'

'Wrong –' Claudia looked smug – 'so there. I'm meeting him at Johnnie's Bar for a drink.' She beamed. She couldn't *stop* beaming. 'He's going to introduce me to his friends.'

And later, when he brought her home, she would casually ask if he was hungry and they would open the fridge in search of something to eat. Then she would say, even more casually, 'There's some leftover chilli here, we could heat that up. Or I could do cheese and biscuits.'

It was Claudia's subtle approach and she was proud of it. Anyone, after all, could knock themselves out producing a ravishingly formal dinner. Well, she was going to go one better. She was going to really impress Will by being the girl with the ravishing leftovers.

'You keep looking at your watch,' said Poppy, mopping up the last smear of sauce from her plate. She popped the bread into her mouth. 'That was brilliant. Should he have phoned by now?'

'No, no,' Claudia lied brightly.

'Only you seem nervous.'

'Me, nervous? Why would I be nervous? Oh—!'

The phone rang. Claudia leapt on it, her skin prickling all over with relief.

Seconds later she passed it across to Poppy.

'For you.'

Poppy winced. If Will made Claudia happy, she wanted him to phone. If Will made Claudia make stupendous chilli she wanted him to phone almost as much as Claudia did.

'Hi-ya!'

Five minutes later Poppy replaced the receiver.

'That was Dina.'

'I know it was Dina.' Twitchy with nerves, Claudia couldn't help sounding irate. 'I spoke to her first, didn't I?'

'She asked if she could come and stay with us again this weekend.'

'And you said yes. Again.'

'I couldn't really say no.' Poppy shrugged. 'She's hellbent on coming up here. I think she's going through a bad patch at home. Anyway, Caspar doesn't mind.'

Claudia was still fretful. She didn't even dare glance at the phone now. Maybe it was like a watched kettle never boiling . . . if she looked at it, it wouldn't ring.

'Well if you ask me, it's taking advantage. Why can't she book into an hotel?'

Poppy couldn't resist the dig.

'Maybe for the same reason Will didn't book into one the other night. Because it was more convenient to stay here.'

Poppy was lying semi-submerged in the bath an hour later when she heard the phone trill again downstairs. Before long Claudia was hammering joyfully on the bathroom door.

'That was Will, ringing to say he's finished work. Just to let you know I'm off out now to meet him.'

Phew, that was a relief. Poppy turned the hot tap on again in celebration, and added another dollop of Body Shop grapefruit shampoo because she'd run out of bubble bath.

'Okay, have a good time.'

'I will, I will!'

'Oh, and I've been thinking about what you said earlier,' Poppy added just for fun. 'The Dina thing. Maybe you're right. I'll tell her to find a B and B somewhere instead.'

Claudia hesitated for less than a second. Will had phoned and all was right with the world.

'Don't be daft, I was only joking,' she cried through the closed door. 'Of course Dina can stay.'

To while away a slow morning, Poppy and Marlene had been giving men marks out of ten for their bums.

'This is sexist,' Jake complained. No matter how hard he concentrated on his accounts he couldn't help but overhear their outrageous remarks.

'You're jealous because Marlene only gave you a seven,' Poppy told him.

'Marlene doesn't recognise quality when she sees it,' said Jake. 'And it's still sexist.'

'It's downright depressing if you ask me.' Marlene pulled a face like Les Dawson. 'I mean it's hardly Bondi Beach around here, is it? Hardly *Baywatch*.' She helped herself to another lemon sherbet, sucking noisily and twiddling the cellophane wrapper around her fat fingers. 'I mean, most of the blokes in here today have *been* bloody antiques.'

Glancing up, Jake spotted Caspar coming in through the double doors.

'How about this one? Is he more your type?'

'Average-looking,' said Poppy, sounding bored. She grinned as Marlene's jaw dropped open. 'A five, maybe a six. Not bad.'

'Not bad? Are you *kidding*?' squealed Marlene. 'Look at him, he's gorgeous! Talk about . . . Oh wow, he's winking at me.'

'Actually,' said Poppy, 'he's winking at me.'

It was very quiet on the ground floor. Caspar, whose hearing was excellent, said, 'If you must know, I was winking at Jake.'

'My lucky day,' Jake observed mildly. He gave up on the accounts, which were in a hideous state, and closed the book with a thud. Then he began cleaning the dusty lenses of his spectacles with the sleeve of his plaid shirt.

'It is,' said Caspar. He had come straight from Gillingham's, the prestigious firm of auctioneers in South Kensington whose name was right up there along with Sotheby's and Christie's.

Poppy looked confused. 'Is what?'

Jake, who wasn't so slow, said, 'Really? You mean that little picture's worth a few bob after all? That's great.'

'As a matter of interest,' said Caspar, 'hands up anyone here who knows the name Wilhelm von Kantz.'

Poppy looked blank. Jake looked blank. Marlene, hoping to impress the most heavenly body she'd seen in a long long time, screwed up her eyes and nodded slowly as if the name did mean something to her, she just wasn't sure what.

'Well?' Caspar turned his attention to her.

'Um . . . was he the Red Baron?'

He looked appalled by their stupidity.

'Hopeless, the lot of you. Okay, let me run through this. Von Kantz died two years ago at the age of ninety-three. He was a second-generation American of German-Dutch descent. He was a painter, a womaniser, a serious drinker, and he made a bit of a prat of himself publicly rubbishing the traditionalists and maintaining that his was the only form of art worth the canvas it was painted on.'

'Blimey.' Poppy shook her head in wonder. 'You mean the chap who did "Dead Hamster on a Patio" said that? Some people have a nerve.'

'What?' said Marlene, mystified.

'Go on,' said Jake.

'He came over to England just before the Second World War. He was married – well, married-ish – but he wrote in his diaries about an affair he had here with a woman called Dorrie.'

'Dorothea,' Poppy exclaimed. 'Oh, I love it when things match up! He had an affair with Dorothea de Lacey and he gave her a painting of a dead hamster to remember him by. How romantic can you get?'

'Who did you show it to?' Jake frowned. 'How much does he think it's actually worth?'

'I took it to Gillingham's on Monday. We had to wait until this morning for a couple of their experts to fly back from Boston. I've been with them all morning. They've verified the painting's authenticity. They asked if they could handle the sale.'

Poppy's eyes were by this time like saucers.

'You mean it's worth more than a couple of hundred?'

'Put it this way,' said Caspar. 'When he died, Wilhelm von Kantz was regarded as one of the greatest painters in the world.'

People were staring. The entire antiques market had gone silent. Poppy began to giggle. She punched Caspar on the arm.

'Okay, it's a wind-up,' she told Jake. 'We've been Beadled. Any minute now, the ghost of this loopy artist is going to burst in here and demand his picture back. Wilhelm von Kantz is probably an anagram of gullible nit wits. Watch out for hidden cameras everyone, and stroppy council officials with beards—'

'You really are a bunch of peasants,' said Caspar. 'How

187

can you *not* have heard of von Kantz? You'll be telling me next you've never heard of de Kooning.'

More blank faces. Edward de Kooning, for decades one of Wilhelm's friends and rivals, was possibly the greatest living exponent of this form of art, and nobody here even recognised the name.

'Picasso?' said Caspar. 'Ring any bells?'

'How much is this painting likely to fetch? Jake asked quietly.

Caspar rapped Poppy across the knuckles to regain her attention.

'Will you *stop* looking for hidden cameras? This isn't a joke.' Then he turned to look at Jake. 'Three quarters of a million pounds.'

Chapter 28

'You know what you are, don't you?' Dina said flatly. 'Weird, that's what. Mental. You bid for that picture. That means it's yours. Jake didn't even want the flaming thing. He *sacked* you, for God's sake! I'd tell the stingy bugger to stick his lousy job.'

It was seven thirty on Friday evening and Poppy was ploughing through a bowl of muesli. If she was going to keep pace with Dina in the Malibu and orange department it was best to give her stomach a rock-solid lining before they set out. She looked up at Dina, who was layering bright blue mascara onto her eyelashes.

'Jake isn't a stingy bugger. He's lovely. And I like my job.'

'Yes, but if you had three quarters of a million pounds you'd never need to work again! It'd be permanent holiday time. If I had that kind of dosh,' said Dina vehemently, 'you wouldn't see me for dust.'

Muesli took forever to chew. Gamely Poppy swallowed another mouthful.

'Anyway, it wouldn't be my dosh. It's Jake's picture. He paid for it.'

'He wouldn't *have* it if it wasn't for you.' Dina finished with the mascara and untwirled a bright pink lipstick. 'If you ask me, you should get yourself a bloody good lawyer. You're entitled to at least half.'

'But I didn't ask you.' Poppy wished she had never mentioned the painting now. All she wanted was for Dina to stop going on about it.

'Suit yourself.' Dina shrugged, mildly offended by the lack of gratitude. 'I'm on your side, aren't I? I'm your best friend.'

All of a sudden, Poppy thought drily. Money did that to people; it could have the weirdest effects. Like turning casual friends into best ones, as if by magic.

'I can't stay out too late,' she said. 'I've got to be at work by nine tomorrow morning. I'm not going on to any clubs.'

'If I had three quarters of a million pounds,' Dina said dreamily, 'I'd go clubbing it every single night. You wouldn't catch me sloping off early on account of some poxy job.'

Poppy must be going down with something, Dina decided as she let herself into the house much, much later. She hadn't seemed herself at all tonight. She'd been quiet. She'd even snapped once or twice when Dina had brought up the subject of the painting. And when she'd told Poppy about nosy Edna Frost who lived next door to the McBrides and who had last week been diagnosed with lung cancer, the oddest thing had happened.

'Snooping old cow, all she's ever done is make everyone else's lives a misery,' she had told Poppy. 'If you ask me it couldn't happen to a better person. She got what she deserved.'

Okay, Dina acknowledged now with a twinge of guilt, so it wasn't a very nice thing to say, but she had been on her sixth Malibu by then, and Edna Frost had been the neighbour from hell. But what she couldn't get over was the way Poppy's eyes had filled with tears – actual *tears* – as if the news really was upsetting. She hadn't said a word, just sat there with her eyes brimming and her fingers clenching and unclenching in her lap.

Still, never mind. Dina dismissed the bizarre episode with a shrug. Poppy was probably getting her period. And it hadn't mattered a jot that she'd gone home early, as it happened, because by the time the wine bar had called last orders Dina had found herself being chatted up by a couple of guys on a works night out. Once she'd been drawn into conversation with the rest of their party it had seemed only natural that she should go along with them to the Jack of Clubs.

And where's the harm in that, Dina asked herself as she headed through to the kitchen dumping her coat, hat and gloves along the way. What was wrong with a spot of harmless flirting, a bit of smooching to the slow numbers, a quick cuddle in the corner of the club with the less acne-ridden of the two lads who had chatted her up?

Dina wandered around the kitchen. Downstairs in Poppy's tiny room, on the floor beside Poppy's single bed, her sleeping bag beckoned. Except she wasn't in the mood for sleep.

London was for having fun in. Dina's veins were still pulsing with adrenalin. It was only three o'clock; she wasn't even ready to stop dancing yet. And she was so hungry she could eat a – oh wow! a massive helping of home-made lasagne.

How completely brilliant, thought Dina, grabbing the earthenware dish with both hands and knocking the fridge door shut with her hip. Normally when you arrived home starving from a club and looked in the fridge the best you could hope for was half a tin of dried-up baked beans and a bit of green bread.

She zapped the lasagne in the microwave, tuned the transistor radio on the windowsill to an all-night music station and began to sing and dance along to an old Adam Ant hit. She'd had quite a crush on Adam Ant yonks ago, Dina remembered fondly. God, she'd gone to a party once with a white stripe painted across her nose.

'Ant music yo yo yo yo yo,' she warbled, bouncing round the kitchen while the lasagne heated up. 'Ant music yo yo yo yo yo.' Funny lyrics really, when you came to think about it. Still . . . 'Ant music yo yo—'

Dina spun to a halt against the washing machine, clinging on for support. She thought for a moment about climbing inside. She wondered how long he had been standing there watching her. She really wished she hadn't been singing into an imaginary mike.

'Sorry.' He grinned, unrepentant. 'I heard a noise. I thought maybe we had a burglar. Is that what you are, an all-singing, all-dancing burglar?'

'I'm Dina. Poppy's friend.' Behind her, signalling that the lasagne was ready, the microwave went BEE-EEP. Dina jumped again. Heavens, her nerves were shot to pieces. 'Who are you?'

'My name's Will.' His mouth tweaked up at the corners. 'I'm Claudia's friend.'

He was wearing tartan boxer shorts and nothing else. Dina was impressed by his body – he looked as she imagined Will Carling would look in the locker room. He had sleek dark hair like a seal, small dark eyes and just the right amount of designer stubble. He also had excitingly hairy legs – a great weakness of Dina's. Her husband had a good physique but his legs weren't as hairy as these. Besides, when you knew a body as well as she knew Ben's, you were bound to lose interest in the end. As she'd tried explaining to Poppy, you could buy the most brilliant pair of shoes in the world but after a while, they just weren't as brilliant any more. You got bored with them, slung them to the back of the cupboard and bought yourself a thrilling new pair instead.

'Anyway, don't mind me,' Will gestured to the radio, where Adam Ant was still yo-yo-ing away. 'If you want to carry on, feel free.' He winked. 'I like a girl who knows how to have a good time.'

The cheeky bugger was eyeing her up, Dina realised with an involuntary shiver of excitement. She turned to deal with the microwave, standing sideways on so he could see how flat her stomach was. She was immensely proud of her figure and liked to show it off. Not many people could wear cropped tops and skirts this short and get away with it, even if her mother-in-law was forever making snide remarks about catching a chill.

Still, to look at her, Dina thought proudly, you wouldn't think she'd dropped a sprog. This guy Will, for example, would never guess.

'So you're the pushy tart from Bristol who's bored with motherhood and marriage,' Will announced.

Bang went that fantasy. So much for ticking the box if you wanted to remain anonymous. Dina bristled at the slur.

'That's what Claudia said, is it? She's an uptight bitch.'

'Unlike you.' Will looked entertained. 'You're the un-inhibited type. I can tell.'

'I like to have fun,' said Dina, 'if that's what you mean.' Her stomach emitted a terrific rumble. 'Sorry. I'm starving.'

'That smells good.' Will watched as she removed the lasagne from the microwave. Claudia had mentioned something about food earlier but he hadn't been interested then. Now he was quite peckish. He strolled across to the glass-fronted china cabinet and took out two plates.

'Mind if I join you?'

'Get some glasses. There's a bottle of wine in the fridge.' Dina batted her blue eyelashes at him. This was more like it. This was the kind of fun she liked to have. 'We'll have a midnight feast.'

They ate greedily. Dina giggled a great deal at the outrageous remarks Will came out with. He spilled some white wine down her top and told her she should get out of those wet things. He also told her some brilliant jokes. She told him he looked like Will Carling. By the time their plates were empty there were some serious undercurrents going on.

Will pounced as she was carrying the plates to the sink.

'Oooh!' Dina shrieked with laughter and almost dropped the dishes. She pressed her forefinger against her lips. 'Sshh.'

'You're the one making the racket,' Will grinned, 'not me.'

Now she was pinned up against the fridge. Dina could feel the hard ridges of his abdominal muscles pressing into her own bare stomach. She shivered with pleasure. He had a perfect six-pack. When you were married to someone with no visible muscles at all, you appreciated these things.

'What if Claudia wakes up?'

'She won't. She was snoring when I came down.'

'She'll know you've been up to something. You reek of garlic.'

'So do you.' Will's eyes didn't leave hers. His hands roved around her naked midriff. He sighed and his breath warmed her neck. 'You know, you are one hell of a sexy lady . . .'

Claudia had been dreaming about weddings when she was woken by the sound of a shriek followed by a burst of muffled laughter. Caspar and one of his girlfriends, she thought sleepily, or Poppy and Dina arriving back from their night out.

Moments later she woke up properly, her heart racing. Will had gone. And his side of the bed – she patted it frantically – was stone cold. He hadn't just popped to the loo, he had *gone* gone. Home.

Claudia sat up. She felt sick. He'd crept out, making sure not to wake her. She must have said or done something terrible.

Oh God, what if she was hopeless in bed?

She almost wept with relief when she switched on the bedroom light and saw his clothes were still there. No matter how much of a disaster you might be in bed, Claudia reassured herself, people didn't bolt in horror in the middle of the night without stopping to throw their trousers on first.

When she reached the kitchen doorway Claudia wished he had.

What was happening instead was far worse.

'What the fuck is going *on*?' yelled Claudia, and they sprang guiltily apart. Dina, the trollop, pulled down her practically non-existent skirt and combed her fingers hastily through her dishevelled hair. Since it was moussed to the limit, her hand got stuck halfway. Dina wrenched it free, reached for a cigarette instead and with an air of defiance lit it up.

'How could you?' Claudia hissed at her. 'What's the *matter* with you? Don't you care how many people you hurt?'

'Oh I get it,' said Dina, 'this is all *my* fault. I crept upstairs, knocked on your bedroom door and whispered, "Psst, any decent blokes in there? Fancy coming downstairs for a bit of a chat and a snog?" Well, I didn't, so there.' She looked half insolent, half amused. 'For the record, I was minding my own business when Will came down and joined me. We had a laugh, we had something to eat. We got a bit carried away, that's all.' Dina examined her cigarette, took a drag and breathed out a great plume of smoke. 'So don't make out I was the one who made all the running, because I wasn't.'

The little tart didn't even have the grace to apologise. Claudia longed to give her a slap.

'You could have tried saying no.'

'Jesus, will you calm down?' Dina raised her eyebrows in despair. 'It's not as if we were actually at it on the kitchen table. It was only a kiss, okay?'

Will had so far said nothing. Claudia realised she didn't dare look at him. How *could* he, she thought miserably, how could he do this to me? Is getting his end away really all he cares about?

But betrayals weren't only to do with sex. Something else Dina had said clicked into place. Claudia sniffed the air, belatedly recognising the significance of what she could smell.

Garlic, garlic . . .

'You had something to eat,' she said slowly. 'It'd better not have been my lasagne.'

Will spoke up at last.

'Sweetheart, you told me it was left over from lunch. You said it needed to be eaten.' He shrugged good-naturedly.

'Not by her!' howled Claudia.

'Well, how were we to know that? Come on now, no need to get yourself into a silly old state.'

'A silly old state? A silly old state! You were all over her!'

As he turned, Claudia glimpsed his left shoulder. 'You've got scratch marks all over your back! I thought you *loved* me—'

'Excuse me,' said Will stiffly, 'but did I ever say that?'

Dina decided to be helpful.

'Look, if you're one of these hyper-jealous types, maybe it's just as well you found out early on what he's like. You can get treatment for it, you know.'

'For what?' Claudia stared at her.

'Jealousy. They can sort it out these days, you know. On the NHS.'

Claudia spent the rest of the weekend in bed. Alone.

Will had lost patience with her on Saturday morning. He had told her, wearily, to give it a rest, to grow up, to say hello to the real world. Then he had dressed himself, bent over Claudia in bed and given her a perfunctory goodbye kiss.

The garlic fumes had almost knocked her sideways.

'Ciao, sweetheart,' said Will. 'It was fun while it lasted. And don't worry, I'll say hi if we ever bump into each other again.'

Claudia hadn't the heart to argue. She'd been so sure Will Smyth would turn out to be The One. Bloody men, she thought as she huddled miserably under her duvet. First Caspar had to go and sleep with her mother. Now Will had shown his true colours too. Why did they have to be so unfussy, so . . . indiscriminate? Weren't there any men out there for whom one woman was enough?

Poppy, who had slept through the night and missed the whole thing, was amazed by Dina's lack of shame.

'Come on,' Dina shrugged, 'I did the silly bitch a favour. He wasn't her type anyway. She's well shot of him.'

This was undoubtedly true, but there were ways and *ways* of finding these things out.

'You still shouldn't have done it. She was crazy about him.'

196

'All the more reason.'

Exasperated, Poppy said, 'I don't know what you thought you were playing at.'

'Oh, this is good.' Dina grinned, unrepentant. 'Coming from the girl who danced with a stranger on her hen night and ended up cancelling her wedding.'

'Hardly the same thing.'

'Isn't it?' demanded Dina. Her eyes narrowed. 'You *really* want to know what I was playing at? I was playing at having a bit of fun, just like you. I was playing at doing something out of the ordinary. Getting myself a life.'

'You're lucky you didn't get a wallop round the head. Anyway,' said Poppy, 'you've already got a life.'

'I'm bored with that one. I don't want it any more.' Dina had spent ages practising her Paula Yates pout in front of the mirror. She did it now. 'I want one like yours.'

'You've got a baby.'

'I've got a whole family,' Dina wailed, 'not to mention enough in-laws to fill Wembley sodding stadium. That's what's *wrong* with my life!'

'But—'

'Poppy, you don't know how lucky you are, not having any relatives.' She shook her head to show Poppy she couldn't possibly understand. 'I'm telling you, they wear you down.'

Chapter 29

It had only been a fortnight since Poppy's last visit but the change in Alex was shocking. His mind was still clear – he even managed to crack a couple of feeble jokes at Rita's expense – but his body was shrivelling away.

It was a heartbreaking sight.

One of the round-the-clock nurses hired to look after him chivvied Rita and Poppy out of the room after just a few minutes. Alex needed morphine and rest.

'I need a stiff gin,' Rita sighed when they reached the kitchen. She sat down heavily and rubbed her eyes with the heels of her hands. Then she looked up at Poppy. 'The cancer's everywhere. They've given up on the chemo. There's no point. All they can do now is control the pain.'

They drank massive gin and tonics. Rather unsteadily, but feeling that she should, Poppy made a plateful of cheese and tomato rolls.

Rita managed a couple of mouthfuls then gave up and smoked five cigarettes, one after the other, instead.

'Anyway, enough about us,' she said half an hour later. 'Time to change the subject. Come on, Poppy, cheer me up for Gawd's sake. Tell me what you've been getting up to in the last couple of weeks.'

Poppy told her all about the Wilhelm von Kantz painting, which was due to be auctioned at Gillingham's next week. The *Daily Mail* was running a feature on how the lost work of art had been discovered. Dorothea de Lacey's grasping daughters were wild with fury, foaming at the mouth and threatening to sue the auctioneers who had handled the sale at Chartwell-Lacey Manor. Thanks to their incompetence, the sisters had raged at the journalist who had gone to hear their side of the story, they had missed out on a fortune.

'It's quite good, saves us having to feel guilty,' Poppy explained. 'If they'd been nice we would have done. But they sound like complete witches. The journalist told me he'd spoken to practically the whole village. Not one person had a decent word to say about them.'

'So this chap of yours,' said Rita, 'this Jake. Pretty eligible now, is he?'

She was looking more cheerful, Poppy noted with relief.

'Don't start matchmaking. There's nothing like that between me and Jake.'

'All right, what about Caspar?' Rita thought Caspar was wonderful. Stupid name, but that wasn't his fault. Poppy rolled her eyes. 'There's definitely nothing like that between me and Caspar.'

'That's your trouble, there's nothing like that between you and anyone,' Rita pointed out with characteristic bluntness. 'You want to get yourself sorted, girl. Get yourself a decent bloke and settle down. Find one and grab him before someone else does.' She gave Poppy a sly look. 'Are you sure this guy Jake wouldn't fit the bill?'

The auction of the von Kantz at Gillingham's was over in no time flat. Four telephone bidders battled it out and in less than ninety seconds it was all over.

If Poppy had nipped to the loo she would have missed it. She clutched Jake's arm as the auctioneer's gavel fell. Dead Hamster on a Patio had just been bought by a New York collector for seven hundred and seventy thousand pounds.

'How do you feel?' asked Ross Wilder, the journalist from the *Mail* who was sitting next to Poppy.

'I need a pee.'

'Congratulations.' He shook Jake's hand.

'How do you really feel?' Ross murmured in Poppy's ear as they made their way out of the auction rooms.

'Look,' said Poppy, 'since I started working for Jake, all I've ever done is muck things up and lose him money. Now, for once in my life, I've done something right. I couldn't be happier,' she told him firmly. 'Nobody deserves it more than Jake.'

She meant it, she really did. And Ross was almost sure he knew why.

'You and Jake,' he said, nodding encouragement, 'tell me, are you two an item?'

Jake was walking ahead of them. Poppy caught up and tapped him on the shoulder. His green shirt had a nylony slither to it.

'Ross wants to know if you're going to make an honest woman of me.'

'Honest?' Jake looked incredulous. 'Remember a certain cheese and pickle sandwich? You still owe me fifty pence.'

The nurse gave Alex his midday morphine injection. He eased back against the pillows and felt the pain blessedly melt away. With it came the irresistible urge to sleep but he wouldn't. Rita was sending the nurse down for her lunch break, shooing her away so they could have some time alone together. It was like having a bleeding minder, he thought frustratedly. These days they never seemed to get a moment to themselves.

He had to stay awake a while at least . . .

When he woke up, Rita was sitting in the armchair next to the bed reading a newspaper. The play he'd been half-listening to on the radio earlier had finished; a boring lecture about economics burbled on instead.

For several minutes Alex lay there, just watching her. His woman. He loved her so much. They had been such a good team.

God, he hoped she wouldn't drink herself to death when

he'd gone. He hoped she'd meet someone else, in time. He wanted her to be happy again.

Rita looked up. Her face softened.

'You're awake. What are you thinking?'

'That you could do with a visit to the hairdresser. Your roots need doing, girl.'

'You always were a smooth-talking bugger.'

'I mean it. You could give that Nicky Clarke fellow a try. You fancy him, don't you?'

'Not so much as I fancy you.' Rita smoothed his hair away from his forehead. 'How are you feeling? Anything you need?'

Another wave of exhaustion swept over him. Alex squeezed her hand and felt his eyes close.

'You're here, aren't you? You'll do.'

Rita bent over to kiss him. The paper on her lap slithered off her knees and onto the floor.

'Why the *Daily Mail*?' he said as she gathered it up. 'You don't usually read that one.'

'It's got the piece in it about Poppy and that painting she found.' Rita held up the relevant page. 'I was going to show it to you. The reporter reckons there's a bit of a thing going on between her and Jake. Did I tell you how much that painting went for in the end?'

Alex didn't have the energy to study the article himself. His eyelids were closing again.

'Read it out to me.'

He kept his eyes closed while Rita began to read.

' "... and Jake's young assistant, twenty-three-year-old Poppy Dunbar." Talk about not believing what you read in the papers,' crowed Rita, 'they haven't even got her name right. It's Dunn, for Chrissake, not Dunbar. And look, they've done it again – ' she pointed to a section further down the page – 'what's the matter with these people? Why'd they keep putting Dunbar? What a stupid mistake to make.'

Some names you never forgot. Alex was glad his eyes were

closed. His mind flew automatically back to almost a quarter of a century ago. To a country club on the leafy outskirts of Bristol and a beautiful girl called Laura Dunbar.

And then it all clicked into place.

Of course.

It explained everything.

Poppy was Laura's daughter.

Alex frowned slightly. He wondered why Poppy had never told him. Then he remembered something else Rita had just said.

'How old did they say she was?'

Rita double-checked.

'Twenty-three. At least they managed to get that right. It's her birthday in May. Anyway, pay attention. Let me read you the rest.'

She carried on but Alex didn't hear another word.

Poppy Dunbar wasn't only Laura's daughter.

She was his too.

When Rita had finished she looked up. Alex was smiling to himself.

'What?' she demanded.

'Nothing,' said Alex.

Chapter 30

Caspar had spent the afternoon at the Serpentine Gallery supporting an exhibition organised by a friend of his. He had been plied with wine and invited to a party that night by a tall, spikily elegant PR girl called Babs.

He caught the tube back to Kensington. As he made his way out of the station he was spotted by one of the tramps he regularly gave money to.

'Fifty pence for a cup of tea, sir?' The tramp looked hopeful. Caspar normally bunged him a pound.

Caspar hunted in his pockets. Bugger, no coins. Lucky he was in a good mood.

He winked, gave the tramp a fiver and began to move away.

'Hang on a sec,' said the tramp.

When Caspar turned back, four pound coins were pressed into his hand.

The tramp, who had once been a bank teller, said, 'Your change, sir.'

The phone was ringing as Caspar let himself into the house. It was four thirty; Poppy and Claudia were both still at work. Miraculously the ringing didn't stop before he could reach it.

'Hello?' said Caspar.

'Is Poppy there?' said a quiet voice he didn't instantly recognise. 'I'd like to speak to her please. It's Rita.'

Poppy arrived home an hour later. She burst into the untidy

sitting room, hair flying, green eyes alight with happiness.

'Let me tell you, I have had *the* most brilliant day,' she declared with pride. 'Jake let me bid at Lassiter's and I got a Goldscheider face mask for seventy pounds! *And* a Barthelemy bronze for thirteen hundred – is that a bargain or what? Then we went to—'

She stopped abruptly. Caspar's face was sombre. He wasn't interested in her terrific bargains.

'What?' said Poppy, suddenly afraid. Her knees began to tremble of their own accord. 'What?'

'Rita phoned.' Caspar hesitated, then moved towards her. 'I'm sorry, sweetheart. Alex died this afternoon.'

He cradled her in his arms and let her sob.

Poppy got through half a box of tissues. Every time she thought the tears had stopped, they started again.

She was crying, she realised, for all those years she hadn't known her father. All the time she had missed.

Caspar stroked her red-gold hair. He kept his arms around her and couldn't help thinking back to Christmas night when he had so badly wanted to hold her like this.

That feeling hadn't gone away, but now was hardly the moment. All he could do now was comfort Poppy and pray she couldn't read his mind.

He made her a mug of tea, heaping in extra sugar.

'I feel stupid.' Poppy hiccupped, taking the mug and wiping her eyes with another tissue. 'Getting this upset over someone I didn't even know that well.'

'It isn't stupid. He was your father.'

'I got to know Rita better than I got to know him.' Poppy disconsolately blew her nose. 'That's another thing. When I see her at the funeral I can't be this upset. She'll think I'm downright weird.'

'You'll be fine,' said Caspar. 'People do cry at funerals.'

'Yes, but not buckets. Not this many buckets.'

The phone rang. Poppy flinched.

'Oh help, is that her? Did she want me to call her back?'

'No. She just said she'd let you know when the funeral was.'

'Look at me. Listen to me.' Poppy was pale and red-eyed. Her voice was clogged with tears. 'You answer it.'

It was Babs the elegant PR girl. Not thrilled.

'I thought you were going to meet me outside Langan's at seven.'

'Something else came up. Sorry, I won't be able to make it.' Caspar tried not to sound too insincere. He had forgotten all about Babs.

'Go,' sighed Poppy, nudging him. 'Don't stay in just because of me.'

'Oh come on, you said you'd come to the party,' Babs entreated. 'You promised.'

'Sorry, I can't.'

Caspar put the phone down. He turned to Poppy.

'Now you are being stupid. I'm not leaving you on your own.'

'But what about whatsername?' Poppy gestured helplessly at the phone.

'She had legs like Barry Manilow,' said Caspar. 'I'd rather be here with you.'

The phone shrilled again, shortly after Claudia got home.

'It's someone from St Clare's.' She came into the sitting room looking helpless. 'I told him you were ill but he isn't happy. He says he's got a classful of students waiting for a model and if you were ill you should bloody well have let him know.'

'Oh hell,' Poppy mumbled miserably, still on the sofa knee-deep in tissues. 'Look at the state of me. I can't do it.'

'He's not taking no for an answer. He won't get off the phone.'

Caspar looked at Claudia.

'You'll have to do it.'

'What? Are you *mad*?'

'Someone has to.' He shrugged. 'Like you said, they won't take no for an answer. I mean, come on. It's not such a big deal—'

'You bloody go then.' Claudia was staring at him in horror. 'I can't do that! If it's no big deal, you can strip off your clothes for a classful of students.'

Poppy, whose eyes were by this time so puffy she could hardly see, swivelled her head between the two of them. This was like Wimbledon.

'I would. But the class is Study of the Female Form.' Caspar played his trump card. 'And I'm a man.'

'You're a complete bastard,' wailed Claudia. 'No, I'm sorry, Poppy, but you cannot ask me to do this.'

'Please,' Poppy whispered.

'No, absolutely not.'

'Okay. Don't worry. Tell them I'm on my way.'

Claudia watched Poppy sweep a mountain of soggy tissues off her lap. White-faced, frog-eyed and fragile she hauled herself to her feet.

Claudia tried to imagine how she would feel if her father had just died.

Then she tried to imagine how it would feel to be naked in front of a classful of art students, all ogling those bits of her she had spent her entire life trying to keep hidden.

Her most hideous recurring nightmare involved walking into a party and suddenly realising she wasn't wearing any clothes.

'Oh sit down, dammit,' Claudia blurted out. 'You can't go anywhere looking like that. I'll do it,' she announced defiantly and with more than a trace of hysteria. 'Okay? I'll go.'

'Poor Claudia, I feel terrible,' said Poppy when she had left. 'It takes the students six sittings to finish each picture. She's going to be bamboozled into doing it now for the next fortnight.'

'She might enjoy it.'

Caspar had picked up a pencil and notepad. He did a lightning sketch of Claudia, spare tyres atremble, cowering behind a screen in her overcoat, refusing to come out until every student had his blindfold in place.

'She won't enjoy it. She'll hate every second.'

'It'll be character-forming. Anyway,' Caspar spoke with a casual air, 'you mustn't feel terrible. I don't.'

Poppy was instantly suspicious.

'Why should you? What have you done?'

'Nothing much.' Caspar put the finishing touches to his sketch. This time he was unable to hide his amusement. 'Just changed the title of the course from Study of the Human Form.'

'You mean you could have done it? You could have volunteered?' said Poppy accusingly.

'What, get my kit off for a bunch of strangers?' Caspar looked appalled. 'No fear.'

Chapter 31

'You haven't said a word about the money from the painting,' said Jake. Marlene was keeping an eye on the stall while they sat upstairs in a quiet corner of the café. He watched Poppy dunk doughnut number two into her cup of hot chocolate and wondered why she wasn't the size of a sofa.

'What is there to say?' Poppy licked the sugar off her fingers. 'That chap from the paper asked me what I thought you should spend it on and I said a decent haircut.'

'I want you to have half the money.'

Poppy looked shocked.

'I don't want it! It's nothing to do with me. Even if it was, what would I do with it? Seriously, Jake,' she shook her head so hard her spiral earrings almost flew off, 'what on earth would I spend that kind of money on?'

'Buy a house, somewhere of your own.'

The thought of living alone now filled Poppy with horror. As if the Balham bedsitter hadn't been awful enough.

'I don't want a house. I like it where I am.'

'A car, then.'

'I had a car once. All it ever did was break down and run out of petrol. Anyway, the tube's quicker.'

'Jewellery,' hazarded Jake.

'Real jewellery? God, I'd lose it.'

'I don't know.' He looked flummoxed. 'Maybe you could treat yourself to a few things.'

'If you can afford things,' said Poppy flatly, 'they aren't treats.'

'You are weird. Isn't there anything you want? Anything at all?'

I want Tom, thought Poppy. Sadly, he wasn't available in Harrods.

'I know what I'd really like,' she said.

'What?'

'To take you shopping.'

Nervously, Jake said, 'What for?'

'Among other things,' she replied, dunking the last of her doughnut, 'a decent haircut.'

Knowing Jake as well as she did, Poppy realised the key word was speed. No time could afford to be wasted. At the first sign of faffing around, Jake would lose patience and disappear.

They were going to shop SAS-style.

In.

Do the deed.

Out.

'If you make me look stupid,' Jake warned, 'I'll never speak to you again.'

'Don't nag.'

Minutes later he was gazing up in horror at the blue and gold frontage of the hair salon she had brought him to. In Knightsbridge.

'I'm not going in there. That's for girls.'

'It's bi-sexual.'

Poppy pushed him inside.

The male stylist she had booked for the job wore blue leather trousers. His hair was tied back in a blond ponytail.

But he was brilliant at his job.

And he was fast.

'What are we aiming for?' he asked Poppy.

Jake was beyond words. He sat in front of the mirror doing his impression of the incredible shrinking man.

'Think Pierce Brosnan,' said Poppy.

'Mmm, gorgeous.' The stylist ran his fingers experimentally through Jake's wayward hair.

'Is that it?' Jake demanded fifteen minutes later. 'Can I go home now?'

'Contact lenses,' she announced, just to see the expression on his face.

'No way.'

Poppy hadn't expected him to say yes. She took him to an optician and at lightning speed selected a pair of gold-framed, seriously flattering spectacles with amber tinted lenses.

'Don't do that—' Jake tried to stop her snapping his old taped-together horn-rims in half and tossing them into the bin under the optician's desk. 'They can be my spare pair.'

'They can't now.'

Since there was no point choosing clothes Jake would only flatly refuse to wear, Poppy kept it simple. She chose cotton shirts and faded jeans from The Gap, lambswool sweaters in plain colours, brilliantly tailored black trousers, a black leather jacket and three pairs of brogues.

Not a shred of Crimplene, not a pattern in sight.

Poppy surveyed her purchases with satisfaction. If he stuck to these, and only these, not even Jake could make them clash.

Unless . . .

'Socks,' she announced, but Jake had had it up to here with shopping.

'Enough. You can get them another time.' He grabbed the carrier bags from Poppy. 'When am I supposed to wear this stuff, anyway?'

'Every day. All the time.' Kindly, she added, 'You can take them off at night.'

'What about my real clothes?' Jake looked as if he was suffering withdrawal pangs already.

'They aren't real, they're unreal. And if you ever wear any of them again,' she told him, 'I will burn down your house.'

Poppy sat alone at the back of the church and watched her father's coffin slide silently from view. The curtains swished shut. That was it; he was gone.

He never even knew who I was, thought Poppy, biting her lip and willing herself not to cry. If she started again, she might not be able to stop.

The service at the crematorium didn't take long. Stragglers from the last funeral had been there when they arrived and when they emerged afterwards the next lot were already waiting to go in.

It made you think, Poppy reminded herself. All day long, six days a week, people were being brought here to be cremated. And it was happening all over the country . . . all over the world . . .

There was a lot of death about. She wasn't the only person mourning the loss of a parent.

Poppy told herself this, hoping it would help, hoping it might make her feel better.

It didn't.

'You all right, love?' Rita hugged her outside the crematorium while everyone milled around looking at the wreaths on display. 'You're coming back to the house, aren't you? D'you need a lift?'

'I'm okay, Caspar's lent me his car,' said Poppy.

'Sure you wouldn't prefer a lift? We'll be sinking a few.'

Poppy had guessed as much. Knowing she had to drive was her excuse for not getting plastered. Otherwise who knew what indiscretions she might helplessly blurt out.

She squeezed Rita's hands.

'I'll be fine. You're doing brilliantly.'

'Yeah, well. Got to give Alex a decent send-off, haven't we.' Beneath the broad-brimmed black hat and extra make-up Rita was baggy-eyed but determined. 'Flippin' heck, I'd never hear the last of it if I let him down now.'

Alex had his decent send-off. Back at the house it didn't take long for sober commiserations and much eye-dabbing to develop into a rip-roaring wake. Everyone from the Cavendish Club was there. Alex's band played all his old favourites. The dancing was uninhibited. At one stage Poppy found herself jitter-bugging with Rita's drunken cousin, who had no memory at all of the last time they had met.

'Come with me a sec,' said Rita, taking Poppy's hand and leading her into the deserted drawing room. 'I've got something for you.'

'What?' Poppy hoped it wasn't another dress.

'A present from Alex.'

Rita took the lid off a Bally shoe box. Poppy half-expected a pair of Day-Glo pink stilettos to wink up at her. She wondered if Alex had really wanted to give her a pair of shoes.

But when Rita peeled away the layers of black tissue, Poppy saw not the dazzle of pink patent leather but the rich gleam of cobalt blue glass.

Rita unwrapped the second spirit bottle, which nestled beside the first. She held them, side by side, up to the light.

'They are alike. I can't tell 'em apart. Anyway, they're yours. Alex wanted you to have them.'

'He did?' Mustn't cry, mustn't cry.

'Said they deserved to stay together.' She clinked the two bottles together and mimed a kiss. 'Reckoned they might miss each other if you split 'em up now.' Fondly, Rita said, 'Silly sod.'

Poppy's stomach did a slow somersault. She wondered if she was reading too much into Rita's recollection of Alex's words.

But could he – *could* he – have realised who she was? Was it possible that he actually could have made that connection, that he might have put one and one together and made three?

Surely not.

But then; maybe . . .

She would never know.

'Did he say anything else?'

Rita thought for a second, shrugged and shook her head. 'No.'

'Oh.'

'Although you can settle a silly argument.' Belatedly Rita remembered. 'Your middle name. It is Teresa, isn't it?'

Poppy looked blank. The subject had come up in conversation the other week. Rita knew it was Teresa.

She nodded.

'See! I told him!' Rita looked triumphant. 'I was right and Alex was wrong. Silly bugger, he was so sure it was Laura.'

It was serious hangover time. Poppy shuddered and gasped as an alarm went off inches from her ear. Now she knew how it felt to be trapped in the bell tower next to Big Ben.

She crawled out of bed, fumbled her way into the shower and clung to the sides while power-assisted needles of boiling water pummelled her brain.

God, that felt awful, worse than when she'd started. Whoever had dared her to down a pint of Malibu and milk deserved to be shot.

When she had finally managed to dry and dress herself, Poppy tottered downstairs.

Rita, in a canary satin robe and matching high-heeled mules, handed her a tumbler of frenziedly fizzing water.

'I know, looks like a volcano about to erupt. I thought four Alka Seltzers,' she said as Poppy peered nervously into the glass. 'Think that'll be enough?'

'I can't even remember setting the alarm clock,' mumbled Poppy. It was unlike her to think of something so sensible.

'You didn't. You just said Jake would swing you round by your earrings if you weren't on the stall by nine. I set it,' said Rita. 'Come along, drink that down. Now, d'you think you could manage a bit of toast?'

Poppy spread the marmalade with a trembling hand. This was kill or cure.

213

'At least it's shredless,' she said. 'I can't stand marmalade with bits in.'

'Neither can Alex; that's why I buy it.' Rita stopped. She shook her head and corrected herself. 'Neither could Alex.'

There was silence for a fraction of a second.

'Oh buggeration,' sighed Rita, reaching for her Rothmans. She lit one and inhaled down to her toes. 'You'll never guess what else the silly sod wanted me to do. Only give up smoking. Can you imagine?'

'Someone told me once that hangovers are worse when you smoke.' Poppy struggled to keep her toast down as a great waft of eau de fag drifted across the kitchen table. She clutched her head, which was still pounding. 'I can't imagine that.'

'You don't look great,' said Rita, who had probably shipped twice as much but had had far more practice.

'I feel diabolical. I especially borrowed Caspar's car,' Poppy groaned, 'to stop me drinking.'

'Then I went and spoiled it all and begged you to stay. Well, I'm glad you did, even if you aren't.' Rita pushed her fingers through her unbrushed hair. She winced as one of her rings caught in a backcombed bit. 'I didn't want to wake up on my own this morning.'

Poppy couldn't think of anything to say.

Rita twirled the end of her cigarette in an ashtray shaped like an elephant.

'No kids, that's my problem,' she mused. 'Other people have their children to rally round when this happens. Three different people yesterday said wasn't it a shame me and Alex never had any and why didn't I get down to the pet shop?' She said wryly, 'It's a great comfort apparently, when your old man's kicked the bucket. If you don't have kids, get a bleeding dog.'

'Would you?' Poppy looked doubtful.

'Would I heck. Doesn't seem like much of a deal to me. Does a dog argue with you about which channel to watch?

Does he moan about Crystal Palace playing like a wagonload of one-legged monkeys? Can he tell you which shoes look best with your new dress?'

Poppy had finished her toast, which mercifully appeared to be staying down. She knew she wasn't doing a great job conversation-wise but guessed that all Rita needed was someone to talk to.

'There, told you it'd help.' Rita nodded at her empty plate. 'How about a coffee now? I could do you a nice bacon sandwich.'

To Poppy's amazement her stomach gave a greedy rumble of approval. A bacon sandwich would be completely brilliant. She broke into a smile.

Rita jumped up from the table.

'Smoked or unsmoked? And d'you like your rashers crispy or soft? My God, listen to me. Is this what it's like to be a mother?'

'Not at all,' said Poppy. 'If you were my mother you'd be nagging me to tidy my room and telling me to cook my own sodding breakfast.'

'I wouldn't.'

'Oh yes you would. It's what mothers do. And they tell you your fringe needs cutting. Either that or do it themselves,' said Poppy with feeling, 'and never get it straight. In every photograph of me when I was young, my fringe is up to here and crooked.'

Rita laughed. She threw the bacon rashers in the frying pan and leapt back as the too-hot oil began spitting furiously.

'You turned out okay. Your mum would've been proud of you.'

'She wouldn't have thought much of my fringe.'

When the sandwich was made, Rita sat down to watch Poppy eat it.

'If I'd had a daughter I'd have wanted her to be like you.'

'Sure about that? I cheat at Monopoly.'

'Me too.' Rita stirred her lukewarm coffee and fiddled

with an unlit cigarette. 'We wanted children so much, you know. I'd always thought I'd have at least six. As it turned out, we couldn't even manage one.'

'That must have been awful.'

Poppy felt hopelessly inadequate. What else could she say?

'When we found out we couldn't have kids . . .' Rita paused, then shrugged and lit her cigarette '. . . I wondered if Alex would leave me.'

'But he didn't! Of course he wouldn't have,' exclaimed Poppy. 'You two were rock-solid.'

'We weren't always.' With a rueful half-smile Rita glanced up at her. 'We had our share of rough patches, believe me. In those early years.'

'I can't imagine that.'

'Oh yes. He had a bit of a fling once, you know. With some woman in Bristol. Your neck of the woods.'

Poppy's stomach squirmed. Her heart began to race. Thank goodness Rita was now gazing out of the window.

'I never told him I knew,' Rita said absently.

'How . . . how did you?' With difficulty, Poppy swallowed a mouthful of bacon. 'I mean, how did you find out?'

'I got a letter. Anonymous. Telling me my husband was getting up to no good with some married woman.'

'H . . . heavens.'

'I was all set to go down to Bristol and have it out with Alex. Confront her too, if need be. I was . . . *wild*,' declared Rita, her nostrils flaring at the memory. 'A thing possessed.'

Faintly, Poppy said, 'So what happened?'

Rita pulled a face.

'Fell off me bleedin' perch, didn't I? Of all the stupid things to do. There I was, in a right two and eight, about to drive down to Bristol, and I got it into my head that I had to water the hanging baskets before I went. Otherwise they'd have died.'

'Oh—' Poppy realised what was coming next.

216

'Yeah.' Rita nodded and grinned. 'I came off that step-ladder with a wallop and heard the bones snap in my leg. Crack, crack, crack,' she imitated the sound with relish. 'And that was it. That was me, buggered.'

'So . . . ?'

'So in its own way it did the trick.' Rita shrugged. 'Call it my lucky break. Alex came racing home. He didn't say anything, of course, about whatever he'd been getting up to in Bristol. I didn't mention it either. He was back and that was all I cared about. And from then on I made damn sure he didn't get the chance to do it again. Wherever he went, I went. Wherever he played, I watched. I didn't leave him any spare time for women. Simple as that.'

Poppy was struck by another thought.

'This letter. You never found out who sent it?'

'I had my ideas. Someone took the trouble to find out my address. My guess is the husband of the woman Alex was fooling around with.' Rita shook her head, unconcerned. 'That's something we'll never know.'

Poppy imagined Mervyn Dunbar writing his anonymous letter.

One thing's for sure, she thought: I'm not going to ask.

Chapter 32

Claudia nearly fell over backwards when she walked into the living room and found Jake deep in discussion with Caspar.

He looked so different, not nerdy at all. The haircut, no longer manic Worzel Gummidge, was sleekly dishevelled in a French film-starry way. Gone, too, were the disastrous Jack Duckworth specs. Even the clothes were . . . un-nerdy. Normal.

Jake looked great. Claudia, who hadn't for a moment believed the *Mail* journalist's hints that romance could be brewing between Jake and Poppy, felt jealousy slicing through her like a hot knife. It isn't fair, she thought helplessly, Poppy can't do him up and then decide to fancy him. Not when I've fancied him rotten practically from the word go.

The bad news about the disappearance of the heavy-rimmed Jack Duckworth's was being able to see Jake's long-lashed dark brown eyes that much more clearly. Since they were fantastically sexy eyes this should have been good news but Claudia, trying to smile 'Hi' at Jake without actually meeting his gaze, found it terribly disconcerting. Damn, she wished she'd known he was here. Especially looking like Alain Delon. Now she'd gone all tongue-tied and stupid.

And was it her imagination or had Jake's confidence grown along with the length of his trousers?

'Maybe Claudia can help,' he said, turning to her. 'We were just talking about this chap from Poppy's murky past. Tom. The one she met the night before her wedding.'

'And on that garage forecourt the week before Christmas,' said Caspar. 'Well, not met. Saw.'

'What about him?'

'Jake wants to have a go at tracking him down.' Caspar wasn't wild about the plan. 'He's been watching too much *Columbo* if you ask me. The thing is, even if we could find the bloke, is it a good idea?'

Jake looked at Claudia, willing her to be on his side. He tried not to picture her naked, modelling her glorious body for those lucky, *lucky* art students at St Clare's.

He tried so hard not to picture her naked he forgot why he had been willing her onto his side in the first place.

'Er . . .'

'Um . . .' said Claudia.

For crying out loud, thought Caspar, what is the matter with the pair of them?

'I think if she met him again she'd be disappointed.' Caspar wasn't examining his own motives too closely. All he knew was if Poppy were to fall in love with someone, he wouldn't like it one bit.

'But what if she isn't?' argued Jake. 'It's been almost a year now, and she hasn't been able to get him out of her system. This could be her one chance of happiness.'

'You're beginning to sound like one of Claudia's Mills and Boons,' mocked Caspar.

Claudia flushed angrily. She kept her Mills and Boons well hidden under her bed.

'And you're beginning to sound like a killjoy,' she snapped at Caspar. If it stopped Poppy becoming interested in Jake, she was all in favour. 'I think it's a great idea.'

'She needs cheering up,' Jake said firmly. 'She's been pretty low since the funeral. And since money's no longer a problem, it seems the least I can do.'

'How will you?' Claudia looked interested. Once she got into a conversation with Jake she was okay; the paralysing shyness abated. Those first couple of minutes were the worst.

219

'We'll take out newspaper ads,' said Jake. With heroic self-control he kept all Claudia's clothes mentally in place. 'The local press as well as the nationals. If that doesn't work we can try radio, maybe even TV. I've made out a couple of drafts, if you'd like to see them.'

'I'd love to see them.' Claudia leaned so far forwards her boobs teetered in their D-cups, on the brink of tumbling out.

Poor Jake's eyes nearly followed suit.

Grinning, Caspar said, 'I'd love to see them too.'

'Will you tell Poppy what you're doing?' Hurriedly Claudia changed the subject.

'Not until we get a result. If we get a result. No point raising her hopes,' said Jake.

Caspar had always run a complicated love-life but now, as spring approached, even he was beginning to get confused.

Kate was still around, chiefly because he hadn't had the heart to get rid of her. Caspar knew he was wasting both his time and hers but what could he do? Every time he tried to ease himself out of the relationship Kate gave him one of those puppy-eyed, please-don't-drown-me-in-a-bucket looks. If he persevered, she dissolved into tears and whispered, 'I don't mind you seeing other women. Really, I don't mind. Just don't finish with me, please . . . I couldn't bear it.'

Feeling trapped and uncomfortable but wondering what else he was supposed to do, Caspar had taken Kate at her word.

He had also got himself slightly more involved than he'd planned with an energetic aerobics instructor. Julia – 'call me Jules' – had a super-honed body, rippling white-blonde hair down to her twenty-two inch waist, and a sunbed tan the colour of Caramac. She also had an insatiable appetite for salad and sex.

Caspar was in favour of the latter but lettuce wasn't his thing at all. Jules had recently begun to take a distressing interest in his diet. 'We only have one body, darling. Think

220

of it as an investment for the future.'

Caspar's idea of investments for the future was buying a scratch card. Twice last week Jules had turned up at Cornwallis Crescent with cellophane-wrapped bowls of lollo rosso, frisée and rocket leaves in a special oil-free dressing, because 'No one can say they don't like salad until they've tried my dressing. I defy anyone to say it isn't out of this world.'

Jules made these pronouncements with missionary zeal. Caspar thought her lovingly prepared salads tasted like grass. He was more interested in her talent for undressing. Jules was wonderfully acrobatic in bed. And he enjoyed driving her to distraction with huge untidy honey and peanut butter sandwiches, currently his favourite après-sex snack.

Then there was Babette – Babs – the elegant PR consultant he had met at the Serpentine Gallery the other week.

Being stood up by Caspar that first night hadn't put Babs off. She had simply phoned him again the next day and asked him when he would be free for dinner. When Babette Lawrenson wanted something, she got it. She had sharpened her skills over the years, starting out as a double glazing doorstepper before moving into PR. Three years ago she had set up her own company. Now she represented a carefully chosen selection of actors, musicians and artists.

She had already offered to add Caspar to her list.

Babette had very short, glossy dark hair, cool blue eyes and a taste for expensive, sharply tailored business suits. She never went anywhere without twin mobile phones – sometimes one at each ear – and her Psion. She was the most organised person Caspar had ever met.

She didn't have time for aerobics classes and she wasn't wild about salad. She was neither thin nor fat, just average. But she knew how to dress to make the most of herself. She always looked, and smelled, stylish. She also had excellent legs.

'We'd make a terrific team,' Babette calmly informed

Caspar on their third date. They were eating roast pigeon with wild mushrooms at Neil's Bistro in Covent Garden. Jules would have shuddered at the sauce and said, 'Not for me, thanks. A minute on the lips and all that.'

'Team?' Caspar watched her neatly spear a mushroom. 'Sounds like a couple of carthorses pulling a plough.'

'That's a typical male ploy,' said Babette.

Caspar grinned. 'I said plough.'

'See, you're doing it again. As soon as a woman mentions emotional commitment, the man panics. He tries to turn it into a joke.'

'What d'you mean, emotional commitment? I thought you were talking about business. Me becoming one of your clients.'

'Oh well,' said Babette, 'that too.'

'Are you serious?' Caspar was enchanted by her upfront attitude. This was the kind of stuff girls kept to themselves. They might think it, but they would die rather than come out and say it.

'Of course I'm serious.' Babette stopped eating. She put down her knife and fork and rested her chin on her hand. Her fingers were strong and capable-looking, French-manicured and ringless. 'I know these things. It's my job to know these things, and I'm good at my job. I'm almost thirty, ready to settle down. So are you.'

'I'm not sure I—'

'Come on,' she chided humorously. 'You've sown enough wild oats to feed Russia. Be honest, aren't you bored with all that? It's time to move on, darling. I'm not saying decide right away, just give it some thought. I'd be perfect for you.' Her cool eyes appraised him for a second. Then she smiled. 'You're certainly perfect for me.'

She had guts, that was for sure. He had to admire her for that.

'Okay, I'll think about it,' Caspar nodded, to humour her. He wasn't entirely certain he knew what he was meant to be thinking about. Had she simply been recommending they carry on seeing each other or was she talking marriage, kids, two point two dogs and a pension plan?

Talk about efficient. Caspar was surprised she hadn't whipped out her Psion and keyed in: Neil's Bistro, 20:25 hrs, proposed to CF. Await decision.

It was an entertaining idea. She was talking about the future and he hadn't even slept with her yet.

Caspar wondered if she would time him in bed with a stopwatch.

'Do you like peanut butter and honey sandwiches?' he asked.

Babette looked amused.

'As a matter of fact, I do.'

Chapter 33

'I've double-booked myself,' Caspar told Poppy when she took a mug of tea up to him in his studio.

He had been on another painting bender, working through the night to finish a huge canvas in oils commissioned by a wealthy Italian banker. Cold sunlight streamed through the skylights, highlighting the thin layer of dust on the room's surfaces. The smell of oil paints, linseed and turps hovered in the air. Caspar took the Batman mug from Poppy, promptly covering it with cadmium yellow paint. His white sweatshirt was streaked with Venetian red.

'You look as if you've been shot.' Poppy unwrapped a Mars bar for him so he wouldn't get paint on that too.

'Probably will be.' He nodded at the door, which served as his diary. The haphazard assortment of scribbled notes pinned to it was escalating out of control. 'I'm supposed to be meeting Babette for lunch. She's introducing me to some journalist who might be interested in doing a piece on me for *GQ*. I'd forgotten I was meant to go with Jules to her best friend's wedding. She's expecting me to pick her up at one o'clock. She'll go ape.'

'Make that triple-booked,' said Poppy. 'Kate rang five minutes ago. She said to remind you about meeting her at one thirty.' Caspar looked blank. 'The preview at the Merrydew Gallery. You promised to take her.'

'Damn.'

'At least she won't go ape,' Poppy reassured him.

'No, just cry.'

'So who'll it be? Who's the lucky winner?'

'I'll think about it.'

Caspar began cleaning the worst of the paint off his hands. Poppy wandered over to the door to take a closer look at the pinned-up notes.

'B. McCloud,' she read, peering at the dreadful writing in green felt tip. 'Is that Bella McCloud the opera singer?'

He pulled a face. 'Ugly old trout wants her portrait done. At least she's keeping her clothes on. First sitting's next week.'

'Not next week. Two o'clock this afternoon.'

'You're having me on.' Caspar looked up. Poppy showed him the note. He winced. 'Bloody hell.'

'What it is to be popular,' she mocked. There was a smudge of blue paint below Caspar's left ear, nestling in the groove between his jawbone and neck. She took the spirit-soaked cloth from him and carefully rubbed it off. Those were the kind of tucked-away smudges Caspar was likely to miss.

He looked down at her, watching the expression of intense concentration on her face. When she had disposed of the smear she spotted another, this time hidden just beneath the hairline behind his ear.

Caspar said, 'It's midday. You aren't supposed to be here either. What happened, did Jake sack you again?'

There. Poppy had finished. Now, whichever of Caspar's girlfriends saw him this afternoon, they could safely nuzzle his neck without risking a mouthful of cobalt blue paint.

'For once, no. I've got a dentist's appointment.'

Poppy tried to sound grown-up and unconcerned. Only wimps were frightened of the dentist.

She just wished she hadn't had that toffee-chewing contest with Marlene last week.

And she wished dental surgeries didn't have to smell so . . . dentisty.

'Scared?'

'Scared? Me? Nooo.'

225

The trouble with Caspar, Poppy thought with frustration, was nothing got past him. He was brilliant at reading faces.

'So if you aren't scared,' he persisted with evident amusement, 'what are you?'

She may as well admit it.

'Um . . . more like pant-wettingly petrified.'

Downstairs the phone began to ring.

'That'll be for you,' said Poppy. 'One of your dates.'

'In that case, better not answer it.'

'You must. What if it's Bella McCloud?'

'All the more reason.' Just to be on the safe side, Caspar hung onto Poppy's wrist until the ringing had stopped. 'What time's this appointment of yours?'

'One o'clock. Why?'

'Okay. Come on, let's get out of here.'

'Where?' Poppy was confused.

'Don't say I never take you anywhere.' His grey eyes regarded her solemnly. 'We're going to the dentist.'

The surgery was off the Bayswater Road, across the park. Since Caspar's car had been clamped and the sun was shining, they decided to walk.

'You can't come in with me,' Poppy protested. 'I'd really look like a hopeless case.'

'I'm not staying out here,' said Caspar. The waiting room was heaving with kids flinging Liquorice Allsorts at each other. He pointed to a group photograph up on the wall, of the staff at the practice. 'Besides, I wouldn't mind meeting your dentist.'

Poppy's dentist didn't look like a dentist, she looked more like Joanna Lumley. Her tawny-blonde hair was swept back in a severely elegant chignon. Her white coat fell open to reveal a dark blue Lycra dress as tight as a bandage, and the best pair of pale-stockinged knees Caspar had seen in years. She reminded him, he decided happily, of one of those beautiful Russian scientists in *The Man from Uncle*, ice-cool on the outside but when you whipped off their glasses and let down their hair . . .

Poppy's wisdom tooth wasn't only badly cracked, she soon learned, it was growing diagonally and pushing her other teeth out of line. Her heart sinking, she heard the ominous pronouncement: 'You'll be far better off with it out.'

Poppy lay back in the chair, palms sweating, and marvelled at Caspar's idea of keeping her company.

The dentist – 'Please, call me Lisa' – was spending so much time flashing her flawless smile in his direction it was a miracle she hadn't taken out the wrong tooth. Unable to speak, what with the numbness and the mouthful of metal clamps and suction pumps, all Poppy could do was listen to the pair of them chatting each other up. When the thirty minutes of torture were over, the dumpy dental nurse gave Poppy a beaker of pink water and a funnel to spit into. Lisa gave Caspar her business card and scribbled her home number – in case of emergencies – on the back.

Poppy's frozen mouth had turned to rubber. She could no longer spit, only dribble pathetically into the gurgling silver funnel. Ribbons of blood-stained saliva dangled from her chin.

That's it, no toffees ever again, she thought exhaustedly.

It was also definitely the last time she let Caspar come along to give her so-called moral support.

'Don't forget, I'll be expecting to hear from you,' Lisa told Caspar with a dazzling white grin. 'Oh, 'bye,' she added to Poppy as an afterthought.

'Thankth a lot,' mumbled Poppy when they were out of the building.

'No problem.' Caspar was blithely unaware of his crime. 'How d'you feel, still a bit shaky? You've got blood on your shirt,' he pointed out, to be helpful. 'Come on, we'll get a cab home.'

'No, I want to walk,' Poppy said, to punish him. Caspar never walked anywhere if he could help it.

'Are you sure?' A fresh stream of dribble was sliding out of the corner of Poppy's mouth. One side of her jaw had already puffed up. She was beginning to look like a gerbil.

Stubbornly Poppy nodded. They set off up the road.

'Tho? Are you going to thee her?'

Slow to translate, Caspar frowned. 'Who?'

'My dentitht!'

'Oh . . . well, could do. Seems a shame not to.' He shrugged good-naturedly. 'It'd have its advantages, you'd never run short of dental floss.'

'Huh.'

'And she's a dab hand with a drill,' Caspar mused. 'I bet she's brilliant at putting up shelves.'

If not at putting up much of a fight, Poppy thought sourly. Somehow she had expected better of a dentist. It was almost undignified, like witnessing the Queen bopping along to the Spice Girls.

'Come on, cheer up.' Caspar took her arm as they crossed the road, heading for the park. 'It's over now. Look on the bright side; you'll never have to have that tooth out again.'

'Don't you have enough women to worry about already?' Poppy refused to join in. She wasn't in the mood. To punish him some more, she quickened her step. 'I mean, do you *need* to add another one to your litht?'

'Who says I worry about them?' Caspar grinned. 'I'm not worried. The more the merrier.'

'That ith *tho* immature,' snapped Poppy. She dragged another handful of tissues out of her jacket pocket and mopped irritably at her chin. The tissues came away crimson; all this stomping like a squaddie on a route march had brought the bleeding on again. And she might not be able to feel it, but she knew her left cheek was swollen. She must look completely mad.

'I don't know why you're in such a stinking mood,' said Caspar.

Poppy didn't know either. She didn't reply, striding on

across the grass instead. When she tried chewing her lip it felt disgusting, like a car tyre. Behind her she heard Caspar's far more leisurely footsteps, and the brief crackle of a sweet wrapper.

Go on, I hope both your front teeth fall out, thought Poppy vengefully. That would put the frighteners on his precious harem. That should do the trick.

The sun had disappeared behind a bank of ominous grey cloud. A cold wind whistled across the park. As Poppy tugged the flimsy bloodstained collar of her denim shirt up around her ears, fat raindrops began to fall.

To her even greater annoyance, she'd been so set on striding stroppily ahead at a rate of knots that she hadn't thought where she was going. Now, having veered left instead of right, they were closer to the boat houses on the bank of the Serpentine than to the bridge leading across it.

'Where are we going?' protested Caspar. 'This is miles out of our way.'

Poppy hoped he was freezing. She hoped he was hating every minute. It was a comforting thought.

'My feet are starting to ache,' Caspar complained behind her.

Without bothering to look round, Poppy murmured, 'Good.'

Chapter 34

They cleared the trees and approached the water's edge. Poppy, blinking rain out of her eyes, wondered why a dishevelled-looking pensioner would want to wade around in the muddy shallows on such a cold day.

Then she spotted the bottle – whisky-shaped – in the pensioner's hand. Poppy turned and waited for Caspar to catch up.

'He mutht be plathtered. Should we try and do thomething?'

'What did that dentist take out, your eyes as well?' said Caspar. 'It's not a he, it's a she.'

Poppy squinted across at the pensioner. In that battered trilby and long flapping raincoat it was hard to tell.

The next moment the pensioner was wading round in a semi-circle, shaking her whisky bottle at them.

'Bugger off!' The throaty, clearly articulated voice that floated across the water towards them was deep-pitched but definitely female. 'Sod off, the pair of you. Nosy bastards, come to gawk. What am I, some kind of peepshow? The latest tourist attraction?' She glared at Caspar and Poppy in disdain, then bellowed 'By God, it comes to something when a soul in torment can't even bloody top herself in peace.'

The voice wasn't only female, it was instantly recognisable.

'Crikey.' Poppy gazed transfixed. 'It'th Eleanor Brent.'

'Whatever you do,' said Caspar, 'don't ask for her autograph.'

Eleanor Brent was one of the darlings of British theatre.

She was practically a national treasure. Never what you could call a stunner, she had made up in talent and character for what she might have lacked in the looks department.

Eleanor's first fifty years had been spent ricocheting from one hopeless marriage to the next. She endeared herself to her public by proving you could be endlessly talented and still spectacularly unlucky in love. She was famous for smiling through her tears and insisting the show must go on.

Now she was in her mid-seventies, still much-loved, still working in the theatre, but no longer a slave to men.

'I've grown up,' she was fond of informing interviewers when they broached the subject. 'Put all that lovey-dovey stuff behind me, thank God. My days of romance are over. Such a relief.'

In which case, thought Poppy, what was Eleanor Brent doing, drunk as a skunk in the Serpentine, hurling insults at strangers and threatening to do herself in?

'I mean it.' The actress stumbled and waved her bottle wildly over her head to balance herself. Her trilby slipped over one eye. 'Get out of here,' she roared, sounding like Margaret Thatcher in need of Strepsils. 'Go on, bloody clear orf.'

To make sure they got the message she stuck two fingers up at them.

'No,' said Caspar.

The deadly glare narrowed.

'Look,' Poppy began to say nervously, 'how can we leave you here? You thouldn't be—'

'Jesus Christ, what are you, a pair of sodding Samaritans? Just turn round and start walking, can't you? I don't *want* to be lectured to about the joys of living by a couple of do-gooders. Apart from anything else, this water is fucking freezing—'

As she bawled out these lines, Eleanor Brent began wading clumsily backwards. Within seconds she was up to her waist.

The rain, pelting down even harder now, pitted the surface of the water like machine-gun fire.

The next moment she lost her balance and toppled over, losing her trilby in the process.

'For heaven's sake,' sighed Caspar, kicking off his shoes. He peeled off his jacket and handed it to Poppy.

'Quick,' Poppy squealed, shoving him forwards and promptly dropping his jacket in a mud slick. 'She'th going to drown!'

The torrential rain had emptied the park as efficiently as Domestos kills germs. There wasn't another soul in sight.

'Damn.' Caspar spoke through gritted teeth. 'She was right about something. It is bloody freezing.'

The trilby was sailing out into the centre of the lake. Eleanor Brent appeared to have sunk. Not without trace, though; a stream of bubbles broke the water's surface ahead of Caspar who was now struggling to keep his own balance.

The bottom of the lake was disgustingly slimy. The thought of what he could be treading in made Caspar wish he hadn't kicked off his shoes. Taking a deep breath he launched himself into a crawl in the direction of Eleanor's bubbles.

This was nothing like *Baywatch*. It didn't bear much relation, either, to the lifesaving techniques he had practised years ago at school, when all you'd had to save was a plastic dummy in a pair of striped pyjamas. Plastic dummies co-operated beautifully. They rolled over onto their backs, let you put one hand under their chins and allowed you to guide them effortlessly back to the side of the pool.

They definitely didn't kick, punch, bite and swear at the top of their voice. Nor did they bash you on the head with a bottle of Scotch.

'Drop it,' Caspar spluttered as Eleanor Brent simultaneously kicked him in the kidneys and lashed out at his face. God, for an old dear she had a grip like superglue. 'Drop that bottle and stop *fighting*—'

'Bog off,' howled Eleanor, her teeth bared with rage. 'Think I want to be rescued by some bloody blond nancy boy who dyes his hair?'

'My hair-is-not-dyed.'

She let out a turkey screech as he managed to prise the bottle from her gnarled fingers. Her nails clawed at his neck, drawing blood. Caspar began to wonder if he was going to have to knock her out cold; at this rate he didn't stand a hope in hell of getting her onto dry land.

The next moment, eel-like, Eleanor slithered from his grasp. She sank again. Caspar dived and dragged her back to the surface. This time she didn't fight back. All her strength had gone, he realised. She had also swallowed a couple of lungfuls of lake.

By the time Caspar managed to tow Eleanor Brent to safety, two cars had stopped. Poppy, who had flagged them down and dialled 999 on the second driver's mobile phone, waded in up to her knees to help Caspar haul the semi-conscious Eleanor out of the water and up onto the grass.

Eleanor promptly threw up. When she had finished she rolled over and aimed a wild punch at Caspar's knees.

'Raving bloody poofter. My second husband was one of 'em. And what the buggering hell have you done with my Scotch?'

'I'm not a poofter.' Caspar rubbed his eyes wearily, then blinked as a flashbulb went off six feet to his left. The driver of the first car was crouching on a muddy patch of grass to get the best camera angle.

'What the bloody hell was that in aid of?' Caspar demanded. Listen to me, he thought. Eleanor Brent's profanity must be catching.

'Come on,' reasoned the man, 'I've got a mate who works in a picture agency. You're Caspar French, aren't you? And that's Eleanor Brent.' As he spoke, he took another shot. 'I can sell these. You'll be a hero.'

'I can hear the ambulanthe,' said Poppy, whose mouth was

hurting horribly. She took off her shoes and emptied them of water.

'Come here.' Caspar patted the ground next to him, thinking that this could give Jake the break he'd been looking for. 'Come and sit down next to me.'

Chapter 35

Poppy spent the next day in bed nursing monumental tooth-ache – or, more accurately, gapache – and gazing morosely at the photographs of Caspar and herself in the papers.

Claudia, who had dumped the whole pile into her lap before rushing off to work, hadn't helped.

'I've heard of bad hair days,' she told Poppy with ill-concealed smugness, 'but this has to be a bad face day. You must be so embarrassed.'

Tactless but true. With her hair plastered down, her white face grotesquely swollen on one side and a dribble of blood smearing her chin Poppy was almost – but sadly not quite – unrecognisable. She looked like a cross between Quasimodo and a vampire left out in the rain.

Caspar, needless to say, looked terrific.

The day worsened as one by one, the women Caspar had stood up yesterday discovered the pictures in their own newspapers.

Caspar made his escape shortly after breakfast, murmuring something vague about having to meet a visiting Hong Kong collector. This meant Poppy was left in the house with only a packet of Nurofen for company.

And a phone that rang every five minutes.

Babette Lawrenson was the first, madder than a wasp because not only had Caspar stood up the journalist from *GQ*, he had made her look a fool into the bargain. It was unforgivable, she raged, not to mention bloody unprofessional. What the hell did Caspar think he was playing at?

Poppy, who hadn't so far met Babette, quailed beneath the onslaught. She wasn't up to this; her jaw felt as if it were being prised apart with the kind of equipment blacksmiths used on horses' hooves. She certainly didn't have the energy to defend Caspar, who might have let Babette down but who had saved someone's life.

As if sensing as much, Babette swapped targets.

'And I'm surprised you haven't seen fit to apologise,' she remarked acidly, 'seeing as you were the one who persuaded him to slope off yesterday afternoon.'

'But I didn't—'

'Funny, Caspar's talked so often about you, I'd imagined someone more attractive. When I saw the photo in the paper I couldn't have been more surprised. I had no idea you were so . . . plain.'

The calculated hesitation indicated that plain was Babette's way of saying she looked a complete fright. Poppy was rendered speechless by the jibe, all the more cruel because it was true.

'Anyway, make sure Caspar rings me the moment he gets in,' Babette concluded briskly. 'Oh, and tell him I spoke to my travel agent last night. If we want to go ahead and book, he needs confirmation by noon tomorrow.'

Wearily Poppy put the phone down. She wished she was one of those people who could leave it off the hook but she wasn't.

Minutes later as she was mournfully examining her reflection in a hand mirror, the phone rang again.

'I've just seen your picture in the paper,' Dina screeched joyfully. 'Not that I recognised you! God, Poppy – what have you been doing to yourself? You look like that chap in *Alien* just before the monster explodes out of his chest. Whatever's happened to your *face*?'

With friends like this, Poppy thought, who needs enemies?

She certainly didn't need Julia's barbed comments. They might not have been as deliberately cruel as Babette

Lawrenson's, but the implication was there; Caspar had failed to turn up for Jules' best friend's wedding and it was all Poppy's fault. Somehow she had forced Caspar to go for a walk with her in Hyde Park. He hadn't wanted to, of course; she had dragged him along, subjected him to some insidious emotional blackmail.

Whatever, she was the baddy. She was entirely to blame.

It was almost a relief to field the terse calls from Bella McCloud's manager. At least he didn't sling vile accusations directly at her or tell her she had a face like a monkey's bum.

The next call was from Kate, in tears as usual. She didn't have the nerve to point the finger at Poppy but she undoubtedly thought it. Listening to her being sweet and understanding and asking how she felt made Poppy feel worst of all.

'I'm sorry,' she told Kate hopelessly, 'I didn't ask him to come along with me to the dentist. He just . . . insisted. You know what Caspar's like when he makes up his mind.'

'Of course I know,' Kate sniffed. 'It's not your fault, Poppy. He just decided he'd rather be with you than with me. Oh bugger – ' she blew her nose noisily – 'how can s-someone you love so much make you so mis-mis-miserable?'

The last call came from her dentist, the lovely Lisa, who was too busy inflicting pain of her own to read newspapers. She hadn't heard about the rescue in the park, she was simply phoning to invite Caspar round to her house for dinner that night.

'He's busy,' snapped Poppy.

'Oh, shame. Well, do tell him I called. Maybe another night.'

'Maybe.'

'Is this Poppy?' As if remembering her for the first time, Lisa asked with professional politeness, 'How are you feeling today?'

'Like shit,' said Poppy, and hung up. She had had enough.

When Caspar finally rolled in at six o'clock, she had had time to build up to a simmering state of rage. Misery had given way to irritation. All the blame that had been so unfairly heaped on Poppy by the various women in Caspar's life, she was now ready to off-load onto him.

Her jaw had never hurt more. And the swelling was expanding to unimaginable proportions. The anger inside her grew.

First *Alien*, now *The Elephant Man*, thought Poppy as she caught sight of her reflection in the sitting-room mirror. At this rate I'm going to do John Hurt out of a job.

'You poor thing,' said Caspar, who was in great spirits. 'How about a brandy, would that sort you out?'

'I don't need sorting out,' Poppy snapped, itching to get started. 'You're the one who needs to get yourself sorted out. I'm sick of it, Caspar. Bloody sick of this.' She tried to hurl a piece of paper at him, which didn't really work. She should have written his messages on a brick.

'Ouch.' Caspar pretended to stagger backwards.

'It's not funny. This is the list of everyone who phoned you today. Sorry I didn't have time to type it up – ' Poppy attempted withering sarcasm – 'but I was in bed *trying* to get some sleep.'

'Sweetheart—'

'No! Shut up and let me say this. And don't call me sweetheart,' she yelled, 'because I've had it up to here with your sweethearts. That bitch Babette . . . Kate . . . Julia . . . they all blame me for you standing them up yesterday. It was all my fault, wasn't it, that you let them down! You should have heard the things they said—'

'I'll tell them,' Caspar shrugged. 'No worries. I'm sorry if they gave you a hard time, swee—Poppy, but I'll put them straight. You know I will.'

'That's not the point,' she howled. 'What you need to do is get your act together, stop mucking everyone around and . . . and . . . *grow up*.'

She shivered suddenly, hating the way Caspar was looking at her, half amused and half taken aback. In his eyes she was good old Poppy, someone he could have a bit of a laugh with, someone who would always listen to his mild grumblings when the endless stream of girlfriends made too many demands on his time. Oh, every now and then she might have put up token resistance, Poppy thought with fresh bitterness, but basically, as far as Caspar was concerned, she was on his side.

She was okay. A good sort. A pal.

Every time she had studied the photographs in today's papers Poppy had been struck, painfully, by the differences between the two of them. There was Caspar, blond and godlike, and herself, bedraggled and hoglike. And even though she knew she didn't normally look like that, it still hurt. Like hell.

No wonder Caspar had never made a pass at her.

Shocked that she could even think it – good grief, what was the matter with her today? – Poppy launched into the next wave of attack.

'You know what you are, don't you?' she demanded. 'You are just so damn *selfish*. You don't give a shit about anyone else. As long as you're all right, nothing else matters. What do you care about other people's feelings? Sod all, that's what.'

'You're beginning to sound like Eleanor Brent,' said Caspar. 'Good job we don't have a swear box.'

'Oh ha-bloody-ha.'

The door bell rang. Since Poppy was too busy seething and thinking up fresh home truths, Caspar answered it.

He came back into the sitting room with a cellophane-wrapped bouquet of orange roses and a bottle of Stolychnaya. They weren't for her.

Caspar tore open the envelope and read the accompanying letter aloud.

'Dear boy. Having sobered up, I now have to thank you for coming to my aid yesterday. I did a

foolish thing. Mercifully I have lived to regret it.
I can assure you I was – headache apart –
extremely glad this morning not to wake up dead.

Once more, my heartfelt thanks. Please enjoy
the vodka on my behalf, as my doctor informs
me I am now on the wagon. He's a bloody old
fool – still, this time I can see his point. There
shall certainly be no repeat of yesterday's performance. How depressing to think a bellyful of
putrid pond water might have been the last drink
of my life.

Thank you again. Eleanor.'

'How moving,' Poppy sneered because saying anything nice
was by this time completely beyond her. 'What a total hero
you are.'

'What a total strop you're in,' countered Caspar. 'Jesus,
next time I see some raddled old actress drowning I'll leave
her to it.' He frowned. 'Anyway, I still don't understand. Why
are you like this?'

'I'm like this because Eleanor Brent thinks you're the bee's
knees, and you aren't. You're a complete shit. What's more, I
bet you deliberately sloped off this morning,' Poppy accused
him, 'just to avoid all the phone calls you knew you'd be
getting. You left me to take the flak instead. And some bloody
flak it was too. Come on, admit it,' she snarled, 'you weren't
really seeing a collector from Hong Kong.'

'Okay, I wasn't. It was someone else. But it was still a
meeting I couldn't break.' Caspar looked uncomfortable. He
had actually been invited to Kensington Palace to discuss
the possibility of a royal commission, but he had been warned
not to broadcast this news.

'What kind of meeting? Horizontal, I suppose.'

'Now you're being childish.' He began to lose patience.
Poppy was standing with her hands on her hips like a
fishwife. 'Look at you—'

'Yes, look at me!' Poppy had spent most of the day peering into a mirror. Every time she did, it seemed she had slid up the ugly-scale another notch. 'Just look at me, fright-night on legs. One more example – as if we bloody needed it – of how self-centred you are.'

'*What*?'

She grabbed one of the newspapers and shoved it at him. Her grotesque, swollen face gazed up from the page.

'How could you have done it? Whatever possessed you?' Poppy demanded furiously. 'You knew how awful I looked, but you had to drag me into the picture anyway – never mind the blood on my chin and my hair being a mess and the fact that I looked as if I'd been chewing a brick. Do you have any idea how humiliating that is? Can you even begin to understand how ashamed I am? No, obviously you can't.' Since all Caspar was doing was looking bemused, she jabbed at the photograph again, so hard her finger went through his face. 'As long as you're looking great, nothing else matters. It doesn't matter how much of a fool you make *me* look. That's why you're selfish.'

So much, thought Caspar, for his spur-of-the-moment plan. If the ploy had worked, if Tom had spotted Poppy's picture in the paper and managed to track her down as a result, presumably Poppy would have been thrilled. As it was, she was all but unrecognisable and even if Tom did recognise her, she looked such a sight he would be more likely to emigrate.

But this was something else he couldn't tell her because as Jake had pointed out, it would be unfair to raise Poppy's hopes until they had a result.

Not that she was being exactly fair, thought Caspar. Talk about ungrateful. It was positively the last time he tried to play Cupid.

In all honesty, he hadn't thought twice about how Poppy was looking when the guy had shown up with the camera.

Poppy was Poppy, with her big eyes and her mad hair and the irresistible broad smile that lit up her face.

Not that her face was in much danger of lighting up just now.

'Have you finished?' Beginning to feel hard done by, he wondered briefly if Poppy expected him to apologise. Sod it, why should he? What, after all, had he done that was so wrong?

Poppy glimpsed the flicker of boredom in his eyes. There was resentment there too, resentment no doubt that she had dared to speak her mind. Caspar clearly had no intention of saying sorry.

'Yes,' she snapped. Then, as he turned towards the door, 'No! No I bloody haven't.'

Caspar suppressed a yawn. 'Okay, but try and fit it into the next two hours. I'm supposed to be going out tonight.'

'Don't worry, I won't keep you,' Poppy shot back. 'I'm just saying it's about time you grew up. Sorted yourself out. Why don't you do the decent thing for once, and put your fan club out of their misery? It's not fair on any of them, buggering them around like this. What you need to do is choose one. Go eeny meeny miney mo. Then get married.'

Caspar stared at her. He could still hardly believe they were having this row. He'd had no idea Poppy felt this way about him. She was positively oozing disdain from every pore.

'Right.' His tone was level. 'So. Is that it?'

'That's it,' Poppy's smile was saccharin-sweet. 'There, never mind two hours, I managed to fit it into two minutes. Rather like your sex life.'

Bewilderingly, Poppy realised she was on the verge of tears. She had no idea why, just as she couldn't imagine where all this pent-up fury had come from. God, she thought, appalled, I sound like some screeching fishwife.

But whatever happened, Poppy knew she mustn't let Caspar see her cry.

Chapter 36

Claudia wasn't nearly as sympathetic as Poppy would have liked her to be. Arriving home shortly after Caspar had left the house – without a word to Poppy – she was far more interested in rummaging through her wardrobe and swivelling in front of mirrors to see if last summer's bikinis made her bottom look big. Marilyn, one of the girls from the office, had split up with her boyfriend forty-eight hours before they were due to fly out to the Canaries. Marilyn wasn't heartbroken – 'Ah, he wasn't up to much; what can you say about a man who wears socks in bed?' – and Claudia, desperate for some sun, had offered to take his place.

'By this time tomorrow I'll be stretched out on a beach.' She heaved a blissful sigh and held up a parrot-green swimsuit. 'Does this look as if it's shrunk?'

'You're no help,' Poppy grumbled. 'I've had the biggest fall-out since Chernobyl, Caspar's never going to speak to me again, and you aren't even listening.'

'I am, I am.' There was a hole in the side seam of the green swimsuit. Claudia kicked it under the bed, rummaged in the wardrobe some more and unearthed a burnt orange bikini. 'Now this one's good for sunbathing. But if you try and swim your boobs fall out—'

'We may as well say goodbye now,' said Poppy. 'He's bound to have kicked me out by the time you get back.'

'D'you really think he will?' Claudia let out a shriek of delight as she spotted her favourite white espadrilles. 'You little darlings . . . I've been looking for you everywhere!'

'Not that you care.' Poppy was beginning to feel distinctly unloved. Claudia was hugging her espadrilles like puppies. Any minute now, Poppy thought, she'd give them a couple of biscuits.

'Look,' said Claudia, because Poppy's thunderous expression was putting her off her packing, 'I hate to say I told you so. But be honest, the reason you're upset is because you've only just realised what a shit Caspar is. I mean, isn't it what I've been saying all along?'

Claudia was lying; she *loved* being able to say I told you so. Poppy gritted her teeth and nodded. Under the circumstances she didn't have much choice.

'You always used to think it was funny,' Claudia went on, 'the way he got so muddled up about who he was supposed to be seeing. I felt sorry for them but you just thought it was hysterical.'

'I felt sorry for them too.' Poppy was stung. 'Well, Kate anyway.' She decided she might as well confess. 'I thought you were jealous because you fancied Caspar yourself.'

Claudia didn't howl with laughter; that would have been overdoing it. She just looked suitably amused, as if a small child had told a knock-knock joke.

'I've never fancied Caspar. Oh, I know he has the looks and the charm, but don't forget I've lived here longer than you. I've always known what he's like. Anyway,' she added with a genuine shudder, 'he had an affair with my mother. If that isn't enough to put you off someone, I don't know what is.'

Poppy had forgotten about that. Caspar and Angie Slade-Welch. He had laughingly denied it at the time but of course he had slept with her. As Claudia pointed out, it was pretty yukky. Angie might be glamorous but she was old enough to be Caspar's mother too.

Belatedly Poppy remembered that Claudia wasn't supposed to know about Angie's visits to the house.

'Your mum?' She raised a tentative eyebrow. 'And Caspar?'

245

Surely Caspar hadn't been indiscreet enough to spill the beans.

Claudia carried on packing. Her expression was matter-of-fact.

'My mother told me. She's on some kind of mission, if you ask me, to prove how attractive she still is to the opposite sex. I think she expected me to be impressed,' Claudia went on drily. 'The trouble is, having your portrait painted and getting slept with by Caspar isn't an achievement. It's par for the course.'

Arriving home from work the next day, Poppy found a note with her name on the front propped up against the biscuit tin.

The house was empty. Poppy's fingers shook as she unfolded the sheet of paper. She hadn't meant all those terrible things she'd said – well, maybe meant them a bit, but that didn't mean she wanted to be banished from Cornwallis Crescent for good.

But all the note said was: Poppy. Have gone away for the week, with Babette. As Claudia is away too, this leaves you in charge of the house (i.e. don't leave front door wide open when you go off to work.) I have bought an answering machine and set it up, so no need for you to take messages. C.

Having vented her spleen yesterday, Poppy had pretty much got her exasperation with Caspar out of her system. Now, re-reading the terse little note, she felt a lump expand in her throat. No Dear Poppy, no jokes, no lighthearted warnings about wild all-night parties. He hadn't even been able to bring himself to sign off with his full name; all she now merited was a chilly initial.

He was still angry with her.

She might not be out on her ear – yet, anyway – but they definitely weren't friends.

TOM: Are you the Tom who visited a Bristol

246

nightclub last June and met a girl, out on her hen
night, called Poppy?

If you are Tom or you think you may know him,
please phone this number, any evening . . .

Studying the advert in the personal column of the *Evening
Standard*, Jake experienced a rush of something that was a
mixture of excitement and pride. He felt quite private
detectivish, maybe even a bit James Bondy. It had taken him
hours to perfect the wording of the advertisement. He had
been tempted, at first, to put Desperately Seeking Tom. Then
he had toyed – quite daringly for him – with Did You Ever
Meet A Girl Who Wore Durex On Her Head?

In the end he kept it simple. He had bought a mobile phone
– okay, so the world and his dog carried mobiles around these
days, but it still secretly gave Jake a thrill – and arranged for
the ad to run every night for a week. He'd had two calls
already, from a girl offering exotic personal services and from
a man called James who would be more than happy to change
his name to Tom. So long as the money was good, he
explained matter-of-factly, he'd answer to any name Jake
liked.

'Fancy a trip to the cinema?' asked Poppy, who was
missing Caspar and Claudia dreadfully. The big house felt
strange without them and the weekend loomed emptily
ahead. She sat on a George III giltwood armchair with her
feet tucked under her and prodded Jake's copy of the
Standard. 'Whenever you like, tonight or tomorrow night.
Go on, have a look and see what's on. You can choose.'

'Can't make it,' said Jake, imagining his mobile phone
ringing in the middle of the film. He had already decided he
had to stay at home in order to take the calls that were bound
to flood in. 'Sorry, I'm . . . er . . . pretty busy just now.'

Jake never went anywhere in the evenings. Poppy
wondered if he was cinemaphobic.

'Okay, never mind seeing a film. How about coming round

247

to my place and letting me cook dinner? Nothing too glamorous, just chilli or something, but we could play Boggle, open a bottle of wine . . .'

Jake had compiled a series of questions to ask the potential Toms who phoned up, in order to weed out the cranks. The questionnaire was his version of Cinderella's glass slipper and he could hardly put it to each caller with Poppy there, her ears out on stalks.

'Sorry. I really am busy. Maybe another time.'

Poppy nodded without speaking. She tried not to feel hurt. Jake's manner had become almost abrupt; he clearly had better things to do these days than socialise with her.

I smartened him up, she thought with a twinge of resentment, and now I'm paying the price. Jake isn't busy, he's just seeing someone else.

As if on cue, two women who were regulars at the market approached Jake's stall. Hunched low in her chair pretending to read next week's Bonham's catalogue, Poppy watched them flirt gently with Jake. In the old days he would have blushed, stammered out some lame excuse and disappeared before you could say white rabbit.

To look at him now you wouldn't believe it. He was coping beautifully, taking their attentions in his stride and well on his way to making a sale. He wasn't flirting back at them, Poppy noticed, but he was certainly letting them think he might.

And all thanks to a new image.

Jake had discovered self-confidence and it suited him.

Poppy, whose weekend was looking emptier and more gloomy by the minute, thought: Fat lot of good it's done me.

Feeling faintly guilty, even though all she was doing was phoning a friend for a chat, Poppy rang Dina in Bristol.

'. . . it's so weird, I'm never usually like this. Six o'clock on a Friday evening and I'm already bored out of my skull.

You wouldn't believe how quiet the house is. Every room is so *empty*.'

'What do you look like?' Dina, ever practical, thought it best to check.

'Eh?'

'Your face. D'you still look like a gargoyle?'

'Oh! No, that's all gone down.'

'So you can be seen out in public?' In Bristol, Dina fluffed her hair up in front of the mirror and gave her reflection a knowing grin.

Poppy pretended not to understand. 'What are you getting at?'

'Come on! I can be there by nine. And if Claudia's not there I can't upset her, can I? While the cat's away and all that. We'll have a ball!'

Poppy felt guilty again.

'What about Ben? And the baby?'

'They'll manage,' Dina breezily dismissed that problem. 'You know Ben. If I'm happy, he's happy. He won't mind. And as for Daniel, he won't even notice! Tell you what, hang on a sec and I'll just square it . . .'

She was back on the line moments later.

'Get your kit on, girl. And do yourself up. This weekend is going to be wild!'

Chapter 37

Deciding to go for it was easy enough; actually going through with going for it was another thing altogether.

Hopelessly out of practice, Poppy took a leaf out of Dina's book and tripled her usual amount of make-up. Heaps of black around the eyes, more blusher and *gallons* more mascara. Rifling Claudia's dressing-table drawers in search of big earrings she came across a nice bronzy-looking lipstick and put it on. Bronze was good, it went with her hair and wouldn't make her look a complete tart.

Poppy stared at herself in Claudia's mirror as within seconds bronze turned to crimson. She looked at the label on the base of the lipstick. Damn, it was one of those Ultraglow indelibles.

Now she looked a complete tart.

'Hey, Morticia!' gurgled Dina when Poppy pulled open the front door at three minutes past nine.

By midnight Poppy's mouth was magenta. The lipstick, which couldn't be scrubbed off, not even with a Brillo pad, got darker the hotter you got. And Poppy was hot.

Matching Dina drink for drink had seemed the only way to banish the demons. By eleven o'clock they had jostled and scrummed their way through half a dozen packed-to-the-rafters South Ken wine bars. Poppy found herself drinking tequila and exchanging banter with a crowd of city types ready to celebrate the start of the weekend. Dina, whose skirt barely covered her bottom, kept rounding on innocent men shrieking, 'You pinched my bum! Right, you can buy me a drink for that. *And* one for my friend.'

When they eventually moved on to a club it was with half a dozen or so stockbrokers still in tow. Poppy, purple-lipped and light-headed, wondered if the tall one called Neil was really as good-looking as she was beginning to think, or just the best of an extremely average bunch.

Dina was dancing with B.J., the one who had started all the bottom-pinching in the first place. Poppy danced first with Tyler, then with Ken, then with an Austrian called Hans who galloped around the crowded dance floor like a camel. Feeling sorry for him, because everyone else was laughing and pointing him out to their friends, Poppy galloped like a camel too. By the time Neil managed to battle his way back from the bar she had worked up a raging thirst.

'Steady,' said Neil. 'Don't want you passing out cold.'

Poppy eyed him over the rim of her lager glass – well, maybe not *her* lager glass exactly, but the one she was drinking out of.

'I'm all right. I've got hollow legs.'

Weird, but true. Tonight, she decided, they were definitely hollow.

'You've got gorgeous legs.' Neil had an engaging lopsided grin and endearingly curly earlobes.

'You've got gorgeous ears,' Poppy heard herself say.

The grin broadened. 'You have . . . um, stupendous eyes.'

She wagged a finger at him. 'Are you making fun of me?'

'Absolutely not. Your eyes are stupendous. So's the rest of you.' His appreciative gaze flickered over the little white Lycra dress which clung lovingly to Poppy's every curve. 'I just wish you weren't so plastered. I'd really like to see you again.'

About time I got myself a boyfriend, Poppy thought. She nodded approvingly. Yep, that was what she needed. To sort herself out and settle down with someone nice. Normal and nice. She gave Neil an encouraging look and wondered if he squeezed the toothpaste in the middle. She hated people who didn't do that.

'The thing is, you're going to wake up tomorrow not even able to remember tonight.' He looked wistful. 'When I phone, you won't know who I am. You'll be too embarrassed to meet me ... we'll never see each other again ... bang goes our great love affair. We're *doomed*.'

Poppy thought at once of Tom, of the great love affair that had never happened. Thanks to her. Damn, how could she have been so stupid?

'Oh God, don't cry!' Neil was filled with dismay. 'Come on, cheer up. Have another drink.'

Poppy couldn't remember afterwards whose bright idea it was that the impromptu party should be carried on at Cornwallis Crescent. She vaguely recalled everyone piling out of three cabs, loaded down with bottles from an all-night off-licence, and staggering noisily up the front steps to the house.

Boisterous games were the order of the night. Dina, a Club 18–30 devotee, appointed herself games mistress and bullied everyone into teams. In her element, she demonstrated with B.J. how to play pass-the-banana. B.J., who was like someone out of *Baywatch*, kept whispering, 'Wait till this lot have gone. I know better games than this.' Dina shivered with pleasure; she could hardly wait.

Poppy knew if she sat down for a second she'd crash out, so she didn't sit down. If she was going to have a monumental hangover tomorrow – and really, there was no 'if' about it – she was jolly well going to get maximum enjoyment out of tonight. And if playing wheelbarrows around the sitting room – picking up matchboxes in your teeth along the way – wasn't sophisticated, so what? Who cares, thought Poppy as she was hoisted onto Ken's shoulders for the start of the next game. I'm having fun.

'Stop wobbling,' Dina shouted across the room. 'Don't hit the lights. And smile.'

A flash went off. Then another. Dina grinned and threw the camera to Hans. She grabbed B.J. 'Come on, now take one of us. *Ouch* –' she yelped with laughter as B.J's hand slid downwards – 'you sod, I told you not to pinch my bum again! I'll be black and blue tomorrow. What's my old man going to say when I get home?'

Waking up the following morning was awful. As soon as Poppy realised how bad she felt, she tried to go back to sleep.

But how could you possibly sleep when you felt this ill?

'Here,' said a male voice over her shoulder. Poppy jumped as a mug of hot tea was pushed into her hand. When she turned her head – ouch, *ouch* – she realised she wasn't in her own bed.

'I live here,' she groaned up at Neil, who had made her the tea. 'How did I get landed with the sofa?'

'It was more a case of you landing on the sofa,' Neil explained. 'Once you did, you were out cold. To be honest, none of us wanted to risk carrying you down the stairs to your room.'

'Oh.' Poppy thought for a moment. 'So who slept in my bed?'

Neil looked nervous. 'I did.' Hurriedly he added, 'I kept my clothes on.'

'What about everyone else?'

'Um . . . B.J. and your friend Dina disappeared upstairs. Tyler fell asleep on the bathroom floor – he always does that – and Ken's behind the sofa.'

'Ken,' said Poppy, 'are you behind the sofa?'

No reply.

'I can see his feet sticking out,' Neil explained. 'I didn't say he was conscious.'

'Hans,' mumbled Poppy.

'No, his feet.'

'*Hans*.' She tried to remember who else had been at the party. A couple of blonde girls, but they had caught a cab around four. Her last memory of Hans was of him dancing that astonishing dance again, round and round the sitting room like a wasp in a bottle . . .

Neil shrugged. 'Maybe he left.' His earlobes turned red. He cleared his throat and sat down on the far end of the sofa. Poppy shifted her feet over to make room. How embarrassing, had she really been irresistibly drawn to those glowing ears? Had she actually told him they were gorgeous?

In the harsh light of the morning after, it was immediately obvious that Neil wasn't the boyfriend she'd been looking for. Last night he had been good fun, really quite handsome, and flatteringly attentive. Today he was looking thin and gangly. He had adopted one of those eager-to-please, you-do-still-like-me-don't-you expressions that were always, as far as Poppy was concerned, an instant turn-off.

As for the ears: frankly, they were weird.

Guiltily, Poppy dropped her gaze. Since she wasn't looking so hot herself, there was every chance Neil was thinking the same about her.

But it was still embarrassing, having him perched at her feet like a puppy. She had had too much to drink and led him on. Shamelessly. She wondered if she could off-load the blame onto Dina.

'Well,' Neil joked feebly, 'at least you remember me. I was worried you wouldn't.'

'Oh, I remember.'

Sensing her discomfort, his shoulders sagged a good couple of inches.

'But now you're sober and you're having second thoughts.'

Defeated wasn't the word for it, Poppy decided. The boy looked positively trounced.

'Sorry and all that.' She felt rotten, but what else could she say? 'We had a great time last night. But really, to be honest—'

'You don't fancy me, you don't want to see me again, it isn't going to be the romance of the century after all.' Neil shrugged and managed a self-deprecating smile. 'It's okay,

I've heard it before. Story of my life.'

'Oh come on, it can't be that bad.'

'It can.' He was making light of the situation, but clearly meant what he said. 'That's my trouble, you see. If I meet a girl I like, I start fantasising. Oh, not that,' he added hastily as Poppy's eyebrows went up. 'I start fantasising about us getting married. I actually picture the church service, the whole bit. Then I imagine us with kids. Sometimes I even get as far as grandchildren. I know it's hardly macho.' He glanced, shamefaced, at Poppy. 'It's not what men do. But I can't help it. I want to live happily ever after. That was why I couldn't let you disappear last night. You might have been the one I'm looking for. I can't wait for it to happen,' he said sadly. Then, with a rueful smile, 'Of course it never does, because I scare girls off.'

Poppy said nothing. She was thinking about Tom again. And wondering if the magic of their all-too-brief encounter would really have survived.

It was a horrible feeling, like being six again and having to listen to the school bully jubilantly telling you Father Christmas didn't exist.

Poppy had believed unswervingly in Father Christmas, just as she had always believed in love at first sight.

Now, thanks to Neil, she was beginning to wonder if even that existed.

God, this was depressing. She pulled herself together and looked across at the lanky figure perched on the end of the sofa.

'You'll meet someone. One day it'll happen.'

'Yeah.'

'Truly. Loads of girls would kill for a man like you.'

'Yeah.' His tone was unconvinced.

'I mean, look at all the bastards out there who run a mile from any kind of commitment.' As she said it, Poppy thought of Caspar.

'Like B.J.' Neil nodded in agreement. 'He thinks I'm mad.

255

He says women are only good for two things and one of them's ironing shirts.'

'I'd iron B.J.'s shirt on one condition,' said Poppy.

'What?'

'That he stays in it.'

Chapter 38

Upstairs, Dina slowly regained consciousness. She listened for several seconds, bemused by the fact that the breathing she could hear appeared to be in stereo.

She turned her head to the left. B.J. lay with his smooth brown back to her. His dark hair stuck up at angles. Each breath he took was deep and regular, almost but not quite a snore.

Dina turned to the right. Another back, paler than the first and bonier around the shoulders. This time the hair was sandy-blond, finely textured and floppy like a child's.

Just to make sure, Dina levered herself up on one elbow. She peered over at the sleeping profile of Hans.

Blimey, thought Dina, don't remember that happening. She lay back down again and tried to rack her aching brains, in case it had. But the bedroom door was wide open, and Hans – another quick check revealed – was wearing trousers. He had most likely stumbled into the room in the small hours in search of something more comfortable to sleep on than a floor.

Dina wouldn't have minded a three-in-a-bed situation, but it would have been a shame not being able to remember it.

Reassured that she hadn't missed anything, and dealing with her hangover in the only sensible way, she closed her eyes and went back to sleep.

Tyler was something of a connoisseur when it came to bathrooms. He didn't know why, he certainly didn't do it on purpose, but every time he went to a party he woke up the next morning on the bathroom floor. Carpet if you were lucky, lino if you weren't.

Student flats were the worst.

No, correction: all-male student flats were the worst.

But waking up in a bathroom had its advantages. You could relieve your bursting bladder, splash cold water over your face and clean your teeth before anyone saw you and took fright. Tyler, who never went out on a Friday evening without a folding toothbrush in his back pocket, did all these things now. There, he felt better already, and the bathroom had been a positive pleasure to spend the night in. Thick carpet, he noted approvingly, a good quality bath towel that had rolled up to make a comfortable pillow, and plenty of expensive, girlie-smelling soap to wash with.

Tyler screwed the top carefully back on the toothpaste, replaced his folding toothbrush into its plastic case and slid it into his back pocket.

Halfway along the landing on his way to the stairs he passed an open bedroom door. Inside, in a row like the three bears – except these were all in the same bed – lay B.J., Dina and Hans.

They were all fast asleep. Hans had his arm around Dina, who in turn had her arm flung across B.J. B.J., stubbly-chinned and handsome, was snoring into his pillow like a train.

Tyler experienced a stab of envy. How did that lucky sod B.J. do it? How did chaps like him always manage to pull? Why did some blokes go through life effortlessly getting the girls while others spent their nights alone on the bathroom floor?

Still, that was B.J. for you. The man knew how to operate. Spotting a camera on the carpet beside the bed where it was likely to get trodden on, Tyler picked it up.

It was a good camera, an Olympus. Only one picture left before the film was used up. For Tyler, who was tidy by nature, it was as irresistible as the last window on an advent calendar.

He stepped back, took the photograph and rewound the film. He liked finishing things, rounding them off.

When the camera had stopped whirring he placed it on a chest of drawers where it couldn't get stepped on and went downstairs.

In the sitting room he found Neil talking to Poppy. From behind the sofa, Ken's feet stuck out.

'There was me thinking I was the first one up,' Tyler grinned at Poppy. 'And look at you, with your face done already.'

Poppy flew to the mirror over the fireplace. She clapped her hands in despair over her aubergine lips.

'I don't believe this stuff,' she wailed. 'It's still *on*.'

By Sunday night Jake had taken fifteen calls on his mobile phone and was no longer feeling like a secret agent with a walkie-talkie. The novelty had soon worn off. He was an old hand at this now. A pro.

The phone calls had been a let-down though. Mostly they had come from men claiming to be Tom.

'Yeah, mate, that's me. Met this bird down the disco, like your advert said. What's her name? Poppy, yeah . . . right, so I'm phoning you up, like you said. What do I get, like, a reward or something?'

Some made a better job of it than others, but all Jake needed to do was ask what colour Poppy's hair had been to prove they weren't the Tom he was looking for. 'Blonde,' most replied. 'Brown,' said two. 'She was so beautiful I didn't notice,' claimed one gallant soul.

'Okay,' Jake gave him another chance, chiefly to relieve the boredom. 'How did the two of you meet?'

'We were standing next to each other at the bar. I tipped out a handful of ice cubes and crushed them with my bare fist. I turned to her and said, "Now that we've broken the ice . . ." '

None of them had been the right Tom. Jake was far more disappointed than he had imagined and impatient to try again. He began to compile a new list. Plan B. The same ad, but this time all the papers.

He wasn't going to give up now.

Dina was smitten with B.J.

'Should you be doing this?' asked Poppy, as Dina punched out his number for the umpteenth time on Sunday afternoon.

'Of course I should.'

Poppy was beginning to feel like an old record.

'But what about Ben and Daniel?'

Dina heaved an impatient sigh. 'That's different. They're in Bristol, I'm here. Look,' she struggled to explain, 'B.J. and I just clicked. Really, we clicked. What happened on Friday wasn't a one night stand. There was more to it than that— Oh hi! Is B.J. there?'

He wasn't. Dina left yet another message for him to call her as soon as he got in, even though she had to leave in less than two hours.

'That was his flatmate again,' she said casually when the message had been relayed.

'Has it crossed your mind,' Poppy was exasperated, 'that he might be avoiding you?'

'I've already said, haven't I? It wasn't like that with us.'

Back in Bristol on Monday afternoon Dina was unbelievably restless. She was twitchy, too hyped up to relax. Poppy, who had promised to phone as soon as B.J. got in touch, wouldn't even be home from work before six.

But it was only three o'clock now and Dina was beginning to wonder how she was going to last. Margaret McBride had already popped-round-for-coffee and proceeded to deliver a pointed lecture on young women who don't know when they're well off. Dina, bored rigid by her mother-in-law's barbed comments about duties and responsibilities and the importance of the family – very *EastEnders* – hadn't been able to get rid of her fast enough.

Daniel, who was teething, had hardly stopped screaming all day, getting right on her nerves.

Ben had too. Placid, easy-going Ben. All he had said to Dina about her weekend away was, 'So long as you had a good time, love. That's all that matters.'

Dina wondered what she had to do to get a reaction out of Ben these days. If she told him what had actually happened to her in London on Friday night, would he even care?

By five o'clock, like a junkie no longer able to hold out for a fix, she fell on the phone and dialled B.J.'s number.

As it rang, Dina felt the fix begin to take effect. Even if he wasn't there it didn't matter; she felt better already, just knowing she had made the phone ring in his flat.

On the fifth ring, magically, the call was answered. Thrilled, Dina felt her heart leap into her throat. Adrenalin hurtled through her body. Her hands were all slippery with sweat.

She opened her mouth to say, 'Hi, it's me!'

But the voice at the other end continued. The laid-back drawl belonged to B.J. but his message was being relayed via an answering machine. Swallowing disappointment, Dina listened.

'. . . afraid neither B.J. nor Adam are able to take your call right now, but if you'd like to leave a message, feel free after the tone . . .'

Right, thought Dina, her eyes bright and her pulse racing, that's what I'll do. Just leave a friendly message reminding him he hasn't called me back—

'. . . unless, that is, you're the slag from Friday night,' B.J.'s voice went on, evidently amused. 'Nina or Dina or whatever your name is. The little tart, anyway, who keeps pestering me to phone her. If that's you, we'd much prefer you to hang up now. And please don't bother calling this number again.'

Ben, home early from work, came in through the kitchen

door and found Daniel alone, strapped into his pushchair. He unbuckled him and lifted him out, throwing his son up into the air to make him giggle and swooping him from side to side like an aeroplane. Then, with his elbow, he nudged open the door separating the kitchen from the hallway and aeroplaned Ben all the way through to the living room.

He found Dina sitting bolt upright on the sofa with tears streaming down her face. She was clutching the phone.

'What is it, is someone ill? Is someone dead? Oh my God, not Mum—'

'Nobody's dead.'

Dina wiped her wet face on her sleeve. She hadn't heard Ben arrive home. Damn and blast . . . that *bastard* B.J.

'So why are you crying?'

I don't know, I can't think of a good reason, Dina thought wearily. She didn't know if she could even be bothered to come up with one.

Ben, still holding Daniel, stared down at her. 'Tell me why.'

'Bloody double-glazing people.' She found a tissue up her sleeve, the one she'd used earlier to wipe puréed rusk off Daniel's face. 'Five calls in the last hour, from different firms, all trying to sell me bloody windows.' Dina mopped at her eyes with the Farley's-encrusted tissue. 'I'm sorry, it just gets me down.'

'Oh, love.'

Ben put Daniel down on the floor and placed an awkward arm around his wife. 'You can't let double-glazing salesmen reduce you to this. Maybe you should see the doctor. You could be depressed.'

I am, I'm *bloody* depressed, thought Dina, beginning to howl again.

Chapter 39

The house wasn't as much of a tip as Claudia had been expecting. When she arrived home, bronzed and glowing after six heavenly days in the Canaries, the place was actually clean. It was also empty. Poppy and Caspar must both be out. This was a big shame, because she was bursting to show off her glorious tan, but at least it meant she could lie in the bath, give her sun-bleached hair a hot oil treatment and unpack in peace.

After her bath, feeling extremely efficient, Claudia emptied her suitcases and sorted her washing into whites and coloureds. She loaded the washing machine, chucked her espadrilles into the sink to soak and lugged the empty cases upstairs. Since getting them back on top of the wardrobe was always a hazardous occupation – so much harder than getting them down – she left that task to Caspar. It was a job for a man.

Spotting Caspar's camera on her dressing table reminded Claudia that she had a film to be developed. What Caspar's Olympus was doing in her room was anyone's guess but that was Caspar for you; the other week she had found his sunglasses in the fridge. Caspar's film was used up too, Claudia noticed. He was so hopeless it would be months before he got round to doing anything about it. May as well take both rolls down to the chemist together, she thought a trifle smugly. Goodness, doing favours, I *must* be in a good mood . . .

* * *

She picked up both sets of prints two days later. Just to make sure they were Caspar's, Claudia flipped through the first few – taken at a friend's exhibition at some new gallery in Soho – and was soon bored. Modern art wasn't her scene. Shovelling the photos back into their envelope, she ran upstairs and drawing-pinned it to Caspar's attic door along with the rest of his mail, ready for when he arrived home. Claudia was far more interested in her own photos, the ones of her basking on the terrace by the hotel pool. She had been browner, blonder and bosomier than Marilyn and it hadn't escaped the hotel waiters' notice. She'd been whistled at nonstop.

Wait until Jake sees me looking like this, Claudia thought happily as she pored over the various pictures of herself, bikini-clad and positively oozing sex appeal. She was going to knock the unappreciative bugger's socks off.

Caspar had spent the first half of his holiday doing so much thinking it made his head ache.

Poppy was right; he knew that now. Keeping three girls on the go at one time was ridiculous. Disastrous. He might not be hurting himself but he was certainly hurting them.

And why? Caspar hadn't a clue. It wasn't as if he even enjoyed the subterfuge.

It was all so pointless too. None of them was exactly the romance of the decade. He wasn't madly in love with any of them.

He thought he was probably in love with Poppy.

He wasn't sure about this, not completely. It was a pretty bizarre situation, Caspar felt. Could you actually *be* in love with someone you'd never even kissed?

Anyway, that hardly mattered; it was beside the point. Because Poppy had made it abundantly clear to him that he was just about the least fanciable man on the planet. In her view, any girls interested in him needed their empty heads examined. Or, as Poppy had rather cruelly put it, if their IQs were any lower, they'd need watering.

The situation Caspar found himself in wasn't an easy one. The time had come, he decided, to put some distance between himself and Poppy.

Over dinner on the fourth night of the holiday he spoke to Babette.

'I've been thinking about what you said the other week.'

'Oh yes?' Babette knew at once what he meant.

'Have you ever wondered how it would feel, being married?'

They had parted on the chilliest of terms. Poppy, arriving home from work several days later, saw Caspar's car parked outside the house and felt a twinge of apprehension. She had never been one for holding a grudge or keeping a feud simmering. It wasn't in her nature. She hoped it wasn't in Caspar's either.

So how do I do this, she thought, loitering nervously at the foot of the steps. Burst into the house, give Caspar a big kiss and say sorry?

Act as if nothing's happened?

Or wait and see how Caspar handles it and take it from there?

At that moment Claudia pulled up. As usual she parked extremely badly and took an age doing it. Much squeaking of tyre against pavement ensued.

'Caspar's back,' Claudia exclaimed, having also spotted his car. Climbing out, she flashed a great deal of tanned leg. 'Come on, let's see what he's been up to. I'll kill him if his tan's better than mine.'

Poppy felt very much the poor relation. Claudia was brown but Caspar was browner still. And – something she hadn't been expecting – Babette was with him, all dark-haired and glossy and expensive-looking like something out of a Galaxy ad. She was wearing a long silk jersey dress the colour of peanut butter, and a modest smile. Caspar, in a dark blue tee-shirt and battered jeans, poured Bollinger into four un-matched glasses.

He handed one to Claudia.

'What are we celebrating,' she giggled, 'how glad you are to be back?'

Caspar passed the second glass across to Poppy, who was perched nervously on the arm of the sofa.

'Not exactly.' He was speaking to Claudia but his gaze was fixed on Poppy. 'I was given some advice a little while ago. You'll be amazed to hear I took it.'

Poppy glanced across at Babette, who was sitting there looking charming. This was the girl who had told her in no uncertain terms how plain she was. Presumably this meant Caspar had finished with Kate and Jules.

Caspar handed the third glass to Babette.

'And there we were, thinking you'd missed us like mad,' Claudia chirruped. 'We thought you couldn't wait to get home.'

'Actually,' said Caspar. 'I'm moving out.'

Claudia did a double-take.

'What do you mean?' she said finally. 'How can you move out? This is your home. You live here.'

'Like I said, I was given some advice and I took it.' Caspar couldn't help turning to look at Poppy again. 'And no,' he said coolly, 'I didn't go eeny meeny miney mo.'

Poppy felt sick.

'What are you *talking* about?' protested Claudia.

'I can't stand the suspense a moment longer.' Babette smiled and held up her left hand. 'We got married.'

Poppy drank her drink without noticing. She couldn't believe Caspar had done something so stupid. She couldn't believe he was putting the blame for his whim on *her*.

'. . . honestly, Antigua's just so beautiful, such a romantic place,' Babette chattered on, addressing Claudia rather than Poppy because Claudia was so obviously agog. 'The scenery is out of this world. Of course, that's why so many people are getting married out there nowadays. I mean, be honest, where would you rather exchange your vows? On a glorious beach with the sea lapping at your toes and tropical flowers in your hair, or in some musty old register office?'

'Oh well, goes without saying,' agreed Claudia, who would happily have exchanged her vows in a snake pit up to her neck in anacondas. Anywhere, so long as she got married.

'This wasn't planned in advance, you see. We were simply strolling along the beach one morning and we happened to pass a wedding ceremony in progress.' Babette dimpled and glanced across at Caspar, sharing the moment. 'Well, I'd love to be able to say he dropped down on one knee and proposed, but—'

'But I didn't.'

Confidingly, Babette told Claudia, 'He's not really the dropping down on one knee type. But he asked me to marry him and I said yes. So we made our way back to the hotel and spoke to the manager. He's an old hand at this kind of thing . . . he arranged everything.' Babette shrugged and spread her hands, the narrow gold ring on her third finger catching the light. 'Three days later it was our turn! What can I say? It was utterly magical. The most perfect day of my life.'

'It sounds amazing,' sighed Claudia. 'What did you wear?'

'A Liza Bruce swimsuit and an island sarong.' Babette reached for her bag and drew out an envelope. 'I'm sure the only reason Caspar went through with it was because he could wear his cut-off jeans. Here, have a look at the photos. See that confetti? Fresh flower petals. And this is the minister who performed the service.'

'Congratulations,' said Poppy, when Caspar had finished refilling her glass. It wasn't true; she simply couldn't think of anything else to say. Apart from bugger.

'All thanks to you.' He gave her a measured look. 'It was your idea.'

There was definitely no answer to that. Poppy bit the

corner of her mouth. She tried to imagine stamping her foot and yelling, 'Okay, I know it was my idea but I didn't *mean* it.'

Caspar said drily, 'And there was me thinking you'd approve.'

Poppy, all of a sudden dangerously close to tears, changed the subject.

'You still haven't explained why you're moving out. Isn't that a bit stupid? Claudia and I are the ones who should be doing that.'

'Doesn't seem fair, turfing you out.' Caspar shrugged, unconcerned. 'And Babs doesn't want to move. Her flat's her business base. It's easier for me to move in with her.'

Babette's flat, Poppy dimly recalled, was in Soho.

'What about your painting?'

'We'll be living together at the flat. I'll still have to come here to paint. If that's okay with you,' he added with a cool smile.

Poppy didn't smile back. She wanted to hit him. She still couldn't believe he had actually gone and got married.

'Poppy, you aren't looking.' Claudia passed the first handful of photographs across. Numbly, Poppy took them. Caspar and Babette, on the beach, grinned up at her. Their arms were around each other. The minister who had performed the ceremony beamed for the camera. In the second photograph, two small girls in white dresses and flower garland headdresses stood proudly on either side of them.

'Our bridesmaids,' said Babette, leaning across to see which one she was looking at. 'They're the hotel manager's daughters . . . aren't they simply angelic?'

Poppy turned to the next picture, taken in the hotel's beachfront bar. Caspar was kissing Babette on the mouth. Around them, a crowd of fellow holidaymakers clapped and cheered them on.

Jealousy, like bile, rose in Poppy's throat.

'Our wedding reception,' Babette explained smugly.

'Goodness, that was a party and a half. We sank some booze, I can tell you. Isn't it amazing, how a happy event brings people together? At breakfast we didn't know this crowd from Adam, and by nightfall we were practically best friends.'

'Talking of parties,' said Caspar, 'have we missed any good ones? What have you been getting up to while we've been away?'

Patronising bastard. Poppy handed the photographs back to Babette.

'Nothing. No parties.' She stood up. 'Actually, I think I'll have a bath.'

Claudia and Babette were wittering happily away to each other like new best friends. Caspar left them to it. As he went upstairs he passed the bathroom. The door was shut. Inside, hot water was running, and Bruce Springsteen was belting out 'Born to Run'. For once, Poppy wasn't singing along to the tape.

He wondered if what he had done was the right thing. Poppy had looked quite shaken when he and Babette had broken their news.

For the first time Caspar experienced a twinge of doubt.

When he reached the studio the door was festooned with messages and post. Caspar unpinned a dozen or so envelopes and a folder of photographs, and opened the door. The brown bills he didn't bother to look at. He skimmed through the more interesting envelopes – invitations to exhibitions and parties – then opened the folder. The first fifteen or so photographs had been taken at the Edison gallery. Not exactly riveting stuff.

Then he came to one of Poppy, though for a couple of seconds he wondered if it was really her.

Feeling odd, Caspar flipped through the rest of the photographs.

Looking as he had never seen her look before, Poppy was hoisted Gladiator-style onto the shoulders of some bloke. Her hair was wild, her eyes heavily made up. Her mouth was plastered with dark red lipstick. She looked like something out of the *Rocky Horror Show* and she was laughing uproariously, clearly having the time of her life.

In *my house*, thought Caspar, realising that the picture had been taken in the sitting room.

The rest of the photographs revealed more. Poppy and Dina, dancing with two men he didn't know. A couple of blonde girls kissing a dark-haired chap with a tea towel on his head and a bottle of vodka in each hand. Poppy again, in a wheelbarrow race around the sofa, flashing her knickers into the bargain. Dina, caught unawares, snogging in the kitchen with some muscle-bound hulk. And another one of Poppy lying on the floor shrieking with laughter as a blond guy in a torn tee-shirt tickled the soles of her bare feet.

The last photograph, taken in Claudia's bedroom, was of Dina fast asleep in Claudia's bed, flanked on one side by Mr Muscle and on the other by the blond guy. At the foot of the bed lay a tangled heap of clothes and an empty bottle of Jack Daniels.

So this was Poppy's idea of a quiet time. Caspar flipped through the relevant photographs again. By a process of elimination he worked out who must have shared Poppy's bed; either *him* or *him*. Or maybe they both had. Her bed was only a single, but would that have stopped them? Bitterly he thought, they could have taken it in turns.

Caspar realised he couldn't look at the photographs any more. He shovelled them back into the envelope, wondering if Poppy had used his camera on purpose to make her point. He also wondered if Claudia knew what Dina had been getting up to in her bed.

So much for wondering if he had done the right thing.

There was no going back now, Caspar thought grimly. He would move out tonight.

Chapter 40

Jake didn't care that the adverts he had placed in all the papers had cost him a fortune, but it annoyed him intensely that he wasn't getting a result.

Not the kind of result he wanted, anyway. Just more weirdos and practical jokers and hopeful lonely hearts offering themselves in Tom's place.

On his way into work the next morning he stopped off at his local newsagent for Polos and a ballpoint pen and the latest edition of *Antiques Monthly*. He waited to be served behind an old lady with a shopping basket on wheels, who was counting out change for a *Daily Mirror*.

'And you can take my card out of the window,' she told the newsagent, whom she evidently knew. 'Deirdre's back, safe and sound. Some kind soul rang me last night to say he thought he'd spotted her in Lavender Gardens. I rushed straight over, and there she was! Heaven knows what possessed her, but never mind, she's home with Mummy again now. Aren't you, my precious?'

The old woman lifted the lid of her shopping basket and devotedly stroked the pink nose of an ugly tortoiseshell cat.

'That's good news, Maud,' said the newsagent. 'Mission accomplished, eh?'

Jake looked at the cat. He had noticed the card in the window himself. Privately he had assumed Deirdre must have been run over by a bus.

But luck had been on Deirdre's side. The forlorn little message in the newsagent's window had done the trick.

Jake paid for his magazine and Biro and forgot all about the Polos. He had seen Maud's card; so had the person who had spotted Deirdre in Lavender Gardens; so must practically everyone who came into the little corner shop.

That was it, he thought with rising excitement. People bought newspapers but they didn't necessarily read the personal columns.

Just about everyone, on the other hand, had a newsagent they visited on a regular basis.

'How much does it cost to put a card in the window?' Jake asked.

The man behind the counter said, 'For a week, thirty-five pence.'

'Oh you poor darling,' cried Maud, clutching his arm, 'have you lost your cat too?'

Whoever said there was no point sitting around moping, Rita decided, didn't know what they were talking about. Sometimes a bloody good mope was what you needed more than anything else in the world.

It was what Rita had been doing for weeks, and she was buggered if she was going to feel guilty. She had drunk too much whisky, smoked far too many cigarettes, listened to hour upon hour of Alex's beloved jazz CDs and shed gallons of hot, aching, therapeutic tears.

Weirdly, having always thought she couldn't stand jazz, she now found herself beginning to quite like it after all. She was even getting to grips with Miles Davis. Since not having to listen to all that crappy music any more had been the only thing she had been able to look forward to after Alex's death, Rita thought this typical, and probably his idea of a huge joke.

But moping – or grieving – was something you had to go through and there wasn't a lot you could do to avoid it. Having realised this, Rita had kept visitors to a minimum, preferring to mourn alone. She had her beautiful house and her memories; it was all she needed right now. She was also, thank God, lucky enough never to have to worry about money again.

Unlike the old days, Rita reminded herself, thinking back fondly to the first years of their marriage and the grotty flat in Hackney, with the bucket on permanent drip-duty in the hallway and the rat-infested back yard. Bit different from what they had become used to here . . .

That's another stupid thing people say, thought Rita: Money doesn't buy you happiness. Okay, I might not be feeling that great at the moment, but I'd be a damn sight more miserable if on top of everything else I had to worry about paying bills.

What a load of tosh some people talked.

Today though, she wasn't in the mood for whisky and a mope. Spring had arrived, the sun was out and the temperature outside was on the verge of turning warm. Gazing down from the bedroom window at the daffodils bobbing in the garden below, Rita experienced an urge to embark on a bit of spring-cleaning.

The trouble was, there wasn't any to do. Her super-efficient cleaning women worked tirelessly all year round. Every window sparkled. There was no dust. If she were to drag her dressing-table chair over to the window, climb up on it and run her finger along the top of the curtain track, Rita knew it would come away clean. You could eat your dinner off the curtain tracks in this house.

But the urge to do something wasn't going to go away. If I can't clean up, Rita decided with a new sense of purpose, I'll clear out.

She flung open the fitted wardrobe doors and surveyed her clothes. Rail upon rail of gorgeous dresses. Bright oranges, violets, pinks and greens. Silver lamé. Blue and gold Lurex. Multi-coloured sequins and shimmering fringes. And all with shoes to match.

It was no good. Rita knew she couldn't do it. Alex had

helped her choose these outfits. He had loved to see her in them. How could she even think of throwing any of them away?

She slid the doors shut and opened Alex's wardrobe instead. After several minutes of deliberation she chose, for old times' sake, the crimson waistcoat he had worn for their silver wedding anniversary party and a pair of outrageous purple silk pyjamas she had bought for him on last year's happy trip to Lloret de Mar. Weakening briefly, Rita grabbed a favourite blue and yellow striped shirt of Alex's, and a hefty silver-buckled belt with the initials R. and A. intertwined.

Then, because she knew it had to be done, she swept the remaining contents of the wardrobe, hangers and all, into five black binliners. Boots and shoes filled another, sweaters two more.

Rita lugged the bags downstairs to be sent to Oxfam. Still bursting with energy she ran back up to the bedroom and dragged a motley collection of suitcases from the back of the wardrobe. Packed inside was everything they had brought with them when they had moved but hadn't known what to do with.

Now this, Rita thought with satisfaction, was stuff worth throwing out. A bag of tangled braces, years old, from when Alex had gone through a phase of wearing the things. A whole suitcase full of back copies of *Jazz Journal International*. Another case had been crammed with bits of a rusted old drum kit. The last one, with FRAGILE scrawled across it in green felt-tip pen, was stuffed with records in battered paper sleeves, old seventy-eights by ancient wrinkled Mississippians with names like Smokin' Joe Swampfoot.

Kneeling down, Rita sifted through them, deciding that rather than Oxfam she would drop these round to the Cavendish Club. Anyone who wanted the crappy things could have them. And the magazines.

At the bottom of the case, beneath the seventy-eights, were half a dozen hardback books, also to do with jazz. They looked deadly boring and as old as the records. Rita flipped though a few of the yellowed pages, wondering idly if Poppy would be interested in selling them on the stall. The date at the front of this one was 1954. Blimey, practically an antique.

When Rita picked the book up, a photograph fluttered out onto her lap. A small black and white snap, it was as discoloured with age as the pages it had been sandwiched between. With only mild curiosity -- she was by this time heartily sick of all things jazzy -- Rita turned the photograph over and took a closer look.

She knew at once when it must have been taken. She had bought Alex that patterned shirt the week before he'd left for Bristol, to spend the summer working at the Ash Hill Country Club. When she had broken her leg and Alex had come rushing back to London, he had turned up at the hospital wearing it. It had been bright green, with black Scottie dogs printed all over it. Each dog had been wearing a white collar. Rita, about as handy with a needle as a hippo, but so in love it hurt, had devotedly embroidered each dog's collar a different colour. It had taken hours but she'd done it anyway, and when she'd given him the customised shirt Alex had been thrilled.

So thrilled, thought Rita, that he'd worn it on an awayday to Weston-Super-Mare.

Or wherever it was. It might have been Weston, it might not. All Rita knew was that it was the seaside, somewhere with a pier. Alex was sitting on the beach, grinning broadly.

And he wasn't alone.

It had to be her. This time Rita didn't have any doubts. The way they sat together, her left knee brushing his right one, was a dead giveaway. Those knees said it all.

So this was what her rival had looked like. After years of wondering, it was a relief to find out -- like finally managing the last clue in a crossword puzzle that's been niggling away in your brain. Rita, still on her knees in front of the wardrobe, held the photograph up to the light.

The woman was nothing special. Okay, she was pretty, but nothing amazing. Having envisaged everything from Liz Taylor in her heyday to Brigitte Bardot, this came as a relief. The woman Alex had had an affair with had long curly hair, a heart-shaped face and a captivating smile. She was wearing a calf-length pleated skirt and a short-sleeved white blouse. Her feet were bare. There was a ring on her wedding finger.

Rita was surprised how calm she felt. What did it matter now anyway? Her curiosity had been satisfied, that was all. Alex's fling had ended twenty-three years ago and their marriage had been happy to the end. In a funny way, knowing about it – realising that she *could* have lost him to another woman – might even have helped the marriage.

Maybe I appreciated him all the more, thought Rita, gazing at his dear face in the photograph. There, that's female logic for you.

About to crumple the photo up and lob it into the waste-paper basket, she stopped and looked at it again. It was odd, but somehow she didn't have the heart to throw it away.

Instead, she slid it back inside the pages of the book and put the book on a high shelf right at the back of the wardrobe.

Then, suddenly fancying a gin and tonic and a nice fag, she went downstairs.

Chapter 41

'Do you have any idea how many newsagents there are in London?' demanded Claudia, when Jake arrived on Saturday morning at the house. She was dressed and ready to go but it didn't mean she was happy about the idea. In her opinion it sounded like the flimsiest of long shots. It was also a dismal way to spend a Saturday. She normally stayed in bed until lunchtime at least.

'That's why we're going to concentrate on Notting Hill,' said Jake. 'Here, I've got a map. We'll start at the centre and spiral out. With two of us, one can sit in the car and the other can zip into each shop. It'll save having to find parking spaces. Come on,' he added persuasively – heavens, thought Claudia, Jake's being *persuasive* – 'it'll be fun.'

'Sounds like *The Getaway*.' Having always longed to look like Ali McGraw, she began to weaken.

'Only with fewer bullets.'

'I hope you don't drive like Steve McQueen.'

'No, but I don't get chased by so many police cars either.'

Claudia began to forgive him for bullying her out of bed on a Saturday.

'You hope,' she said.

By one o'clock they had visited twenty-three newsagents, some smart, some unbelievably seedy. The cards Jake had had printed – on an eye-catching purple background – were pinned up alongside Megan-the-magnificent-masseuse type ads, rooms to let, sofas for sale, guitar lessons for aspiring rock stars and enough lost pets to fill a zoo.

277

Jake took Claudia to a wine bar for lunch. Okay from the outside but with an air of shabbiness inside, it served meals-in-a-basket at wonky tables. On each table stood a vase of plastic flowers. Claudia tried to control her upper lip, which wanted to curl in disdain. Jake, who had been doing so well all morning, spotted the lip. His confidence promptly ebbed away.

The bar manager had already handed them the menu (Today's Special, Spahgetti Bollonaise with mushroom's and chip's). Should he hand it back, say sorry they'd changed their minds and leave? If he did that, he would have to find somewhere else to eat, and knowing his luck it would be somewhere even worse. He wanted to appear assertive but he didn't know the area. Staring blindly at the menu, wondering what to do for the best, Jake reached nervously for the bowl of free peanuts on the bar. The moment the first one was in his mouth his panic intensified. Oh God, he'd eaten a free peanut. They couldn't leave now, they were trapped.

'Um, I'll have the lasagne,' he mumbled. Hopefully, the chef cooked better than he spelled.

By the time their food arrived, fresh from the microwave and cardboardy at the edges, the wine bar had begun to fill up. Jake, who was starving, chewed manfully and tried to pretend it was fine.

The spaghetti was the consistency of shoe laces and there was a dried lump of something hideous welded to the underside of Claudia's spoon.

'This is awful.' She laid down her fork. 'I can't eat it.'

'I'm sorry.' Jake looked miserable. 'We shouldn't have stayed.'

'It doesn't matter.'

But it did, and tact had never been Claudia's strong point. Petulantly, she moved the fake freesias away.

'I'm just surprised you come to places like this, when you could afford to eat anywhere.'

Lunch at the Ritz was hardly Jake's style, but he realised she was miffed.

'I didn't know it was going to be like this.' Falteringly, he tried to explain.

'You mean you saw a few plastic hanging baskets outside and thought, Oh well, this'll do, it's good enough for Claudia. Thanks.' She pushed her plate to one side. 'Excuse me if I'm not flattered.'

Jake could feel his neck reddening.

'Look, it's not as if we're out on a . . . a date. If we were, of course I'd take you somewhere nice. But we aren't.' The awful flush was creeping up to his face. He ran his fingers distractedly around the collar of his shirt. 'This was only supposed to be a quick working lunch. If I'd been on my own I'd have had a packet of crisps in the car. Okay, I wish we hadn't come here and yes, it's awful, but I . . . I really didn't think it mattered.'

As Jake spoke, a middle-aged man in a holey grey sweater was approaching their table. The next moment Claudia almost jumped out of her chair as he tapped her on the shoulder.

'It is you,' said the man, evidently delighted. 'I thought it was but I couldn't be sure. As the saying goes, I hardly recognised you with your clothes on!'

Claudia gazed at him, dumbfounded. It was her turn to blush. Unlike Jake's stealthy creeping redness, her face turned crimson in a flash.

'Mike Cousins, from the life class at St Clare's,' the intruder prompted jovially when she didn't react. As if she needed prompting after a remark like that.

'Of course,' murmured Claudia, not jovially at all. She was seized with the urge to strangle Poppy and Caspar all over again. The only way she had been able to endure those nightmarish classes was by telling herself she would never set eyes on any of its pupils again as long as she lived.

'Well, well, what a coincidence.' The beastly man, who

279

had never uttered so much as two words to her before, was now beaming matily across at Jake. 'This is some girl you've got there, if you don't mind me saying so. Splendid body. Rubensesque. You're a lucky chap.'

Jake, traitorously, was biting his lip and trying not to laugh. Claudia stood up, chair legs scraping noisily against the black and white tiled floor.

'Actually, we were just about to leave—'

'Bit of luck, too, bumping into you like this! Only last week I finished that oil I was working on . . . you know, the one with you lying on your side reading a book?' He mimed the pose, propping one hand dreamily beneath his chin. 'That one, remember? Bit of a success, if I say so myself. Thing is, I wondered if you'd like it. As a kind of memento—'

'No thank you,' gasped Claudia, snatching up her jacket and making for the door. 'Jake, we must *go*.'

'To remind you of your happy time with us at St Clare's,' Mike Cousins persisted, bemused by her reaction to his well-meant offer.

'Jake,' she almost shrieked, 'come *on*. NOW.'

Back in the car, Jake wisely made no reference to the incident. For the next three hours he and Claudia drove around Notting Hill placing another twenty-eight cards in newsagents' windows.

He dropped her off at Cornwallis Crescent at five o'clock before Poppy, who had been left running the stall single-handed, could arrive home and demand to know what the pair of them had been getting up to.

'Sorry about the pervert,' Claudia muttered as she undid her seatbelt.

'Sorry about lunch.'

Her lips tightened. 'Pretty disastrous all round.'

Jake took his courage in both hands.

'Look, I meant what I said earlier. If we went out . . . you know, properly, on a *date* date, I would take you somewhere nice.'

She stopped fiddling with her front door key.

'How nice?'

'As nice as you want.' Encouraged by the question, Jake said, 'Tablecloths, the works.'

Claudia very nearly smiled.

'Heavens, how posh.'

'Anywhere. You could choose. Any restaurant you like.'

'The thing is . . . is this a hypothetical question or are you actually asking me?'

Jake looked at her. 'That depends on whether or not you'd say yes.'

'I'd say yes,' she murmured, 'if you took me to Chez Nico.'

'Sure it's expensive enough for you?' Even Jake had heard of Chez Nico.

Claudia had got what she wanted. This time her smile was triumphant.

'You can afford it.'

Chapter 42

Jake, back from a spectacularly unsuccessful car boot sale in Chigwell, sat peacefully in front of the TV eating a Birds Eye frozen dinner for one. Claudia would not have been impressed.

Jake didn't care. It was Sunday afternoon. The Birds Eye roast-dinner-on-a-plate was actually quite edible, especially when you were as hungry as he was after a long day sifting through boxes of Barbie dolls with matted nylon hair, bent cutlery, dodgy electrical items and chipped tea sets. And he was watching *The Antiques Roadshow*, one of his favourite programmes. What more could a man want?

One of the furniture experts was assessing a French provincial chestnut armoire carved with vines and acanthus scrolls. The owner was pretending to be interested in the age of the piece. Lying through her buck teeth, she said, 'Well no, we never have,' when the expert asked if she'd ever wondered about its value.

'Two thousand six hundred,' muttered Jake, chasing the last potato around his plastic plate. 'Maybe two eight.'

'Well,' said the expert, prolonging the agony, 'it is a particularly charming example of the period.'

'Come on, come on,' Jake urged.

'On the other hand, this split in the wood will obviously have an effect on the value.'

'Okay, two four,' amended Jake. He cursed as the phone rang. Didn't these crank callers have any sense of timing?

The owner of the armoire was looking mulish. 'Actually,

282

I'm sure that split wasn't there this morning. Are you sure your cameraman didn't do that when he bumped into it just now?'

Great, a fight.

'Hello,' said Jake, answering the phone. If it was yet another nutter he was hanging up.

'Oh . . . hi.' The male voice at the other end of the line sounded briefly taken aback. 'I was kind of expecting to speak to Poppy. Is she there?'

'No.' Jake's tone was brisk. He had dealt with enough of these dirty phone callers by now. 'And before you say anything else, your number can be traced.'

'Just as well.' This time the voice sounded amused. 'That's rather the point of the exercise, isn't it? To trace me. Besides, if I didn't want to be found, would I be ringing you now?'

He didn't sound like an obscene phone caller. Adrenalin began to fizz through Jake.

'Are you Tom?' He spoke cautiously, hardly daring to believe it could have happened at last. 'Are you really *that* Tom?'

'Of course I am,' said the voice. 'I fell in love with Poppy when she fell down that flight of steps. When she didn't turn up at Delgado's I thought that was it. I couldn't believe it when I heard she'd cancelled the wedding.' He paused then added drily, 'I suppose that dippy friend of hers didn't pass on my address.'

'My God, it is you.'

'If you like, I can tell you about the hat she was wearing.'

'It's okay.' Jake glanced at the television, where the credits were rolling up the screen. The jolly signature tune signalled the end of the show; now he would never know how much that armoire was worth.

'Anyway,' said Tom, 'if it isn't a rude question, who are you?'

'Jake, you just caught me.' Poppy sounded pleased to hear

from him. 'I was about to jump in the bath.'

'You still can. Claudia's the one I want to speak to.'

'Oh charming. What's she got that I haven't?'

Exhilarated by success, Jake grinned and said, 'Big boobs for a start.'

But Poppy had already chucked the phone over to Claudia, who was on the floor doing sit-ups. Mike Cousins' remark about her Rubensesque figure had hit a nerve.

'Thanks a lot,' said Claudia. Jake, who was managing to offend everyone, didn't even blush.

'Listen, we did it. He phoned. Just now. We've *found* him.'

'You mean—?'

'Don't say it! Yes, Tom of course – who else? But not a word to Poppy, okay? We want it to be a surprise.'

'So what was that about?' Poppy asked nosily when Claudia had hung up. 'Is something going on between you and Jake that I should know about?'

Claudia fished around for inspiration. 'He just rang to say he was looking forward to tomorrow night.' She looked vague. 'You know, at . . . um . . .'

'Chez Nico,' Poppy supplied, straight-faced. As if Claudia had forgotten. She still found it hard enough to believe Jake was taking Claudia somewhere so smart. And now . . . luurve messages, no less. He was actually phoning, in true teenage fashion, to say he couldn't wait.

Something was definitely up.

When she didn't move, Claudia said, 'I thought you were having a bath.'

'Just wondering what kind of hat to wear at your wedding.'

'Typical.' Claudia resumed her sit-ups. 'You always have to make fun of people. You're only jealous because nobody ever takes you out, let alone anywhere nice.'

She was pleased with this bit of jokey repartee. Knowing that Tom had been found – and that Poppy would at last have a love life of her own – made it extra amusing.

Poppy, who didn't get the joke, was less amused. Since

Caspar had moved out she hadn't been in the greatest of spirits. A twittery, about-to-sit-an-exam kind of feeling had taken up more or less permanent residence in her stomach, a sensation so weird that if she'd had sex any time in the last century she might have wondered if maybe she wasn't the tiniest bit pregnant.

But she hadn't, so she definitely wasn't that.

Cheers Claudia, Poppy thought, for reminding me what an empty, wizened-old-spinster life I lead. In case I'd forgotten, thanks for pointing it out.

'. . . forty-seven, forty-eight, forty-nine, fifty,' fibbed Claudia, collapsing on her back with a groan. 'God, why do sit-ups have to hurt so much?'

'All this,' Poppy mocked, 'for Jake's benefit.'

'No. Well . . .'

'Don't tell me. He's *so* much more attractive now he's got money to throw about.'

What was Poppy implying, that she was a fortune hunter?

Huffily, Claudia said, 'That's not true.'

'You mean you'd be just as happy eating fish and chips in a bus shelter?'

Even Claudia didn't have the nerve to lie her way out of this one. Instead, as if the question simply wasn't worth answering, she sighed and stretched her arms lazily above her head. 'Oh please. You're not happy so you can't bear anyone else to be, is that it? I don't know what's got into you tonight.'

Nothing, thought Poppy. Not for ages. Maybe that's the trouble.

'I'm just warning you. Jake's my friend.' She spoke through gritted teeth. 'And I don't want to see him get hurt.'

'. . . I'm not trying to be a killjoy, okay? I'm just saying bear it in mind.'

Hoping she hadn't upset him, Poppy offered Jake her last Juicy Fruit.

He shook his head. 'No thanks. Should you be eating that now?'

Jake was far too hyped-up to pay much attention to Poppy's lecture. Tom was due any minute now and he wanted Poppy to make a good second impression. Sartorial elegance might not be Jake's forte, but even he knew the sight of someone chewing chewing gum wasn't the ultimate turn-on.

'Why not?' Poppy stared at the unwrapped stick.

'Um . . . won't it ruin your appetite?'

She broke into a grin and folded the gum expertly into her mouth. 'Jake, five doughnuts and a chip sandwich don't ruin my appetite.'

'Oh well, suit yourself.'

Jake was definitely odd today. Poppy guessed he was on edge about dinner with Claudia. She waited until a pair of Americans had finished examining a pewter mug ('Look at that silver, Herman, you'd think they'd take the trouble to polish it') before trying again.

'Jake, were you listening to me? I know it's only a dinner date, but I'm just saying don't get too carried away.'

'Hmm?' Jake couldn't stop glancing across at the main doors. What if Tom didn't turn up?

'Tonight. Claudia. The thing is, I know you like her and you think she likes you because she's having dinner with you—'

'You're chewing and talking at the same time.'

'Sorry. Look, what I'm trying to get across is, Claudia's always gone on and on about how when she gets married it's going to be to someone seriously rich.'

Was Jake listening to her? Or was he only pretending to ignore her because she was telling him something he didn't want to hear? Dramatically, Poppy launched into the next phase, 'And when she *does* finally land some dopey rolling-in-it idiot, she's going to murder him the minute the honeymoon's over. I'm serious, Jake, she told me so herself. A quick splash of weedkiller in the casserole, that's how I reckon she'll do it. With Claudia's cooking, who'd notice?'

'Stop wittering, Poppy,' said Jake, 'and serve the customer.'

The customer said, 'I'd like three condoms, please, and a stupid hat.'

Chapter 43

She turned her head in what felt like slow motion and there he was. Those dark, dark eyes, thickly lashed and as bright as coal, were watching her reaction. The tangled black curls were damp from the rain. He was wearing a dark grey sweater and faded jeans and he smelled exactly the same as he always had in her dreams.

Poppy wondered if she *was* dreaming, but no, she was fairly sure this was real.

Oh damn, she thought vainly, why didn't I listen to Jake? What kind of a gormless Gertie do I look like with my mouth hanging open and my chewing gum on show?

But it was no good wishing she'd got make-up on, or that her hair could be looking a bit more glam, a bit less as if it had been given a brief going over with an egg whisk. This was the day the extraordinary coincidence she had waited for for so long had actually happened. She was wearing a battered sweatshirt and her least flattering leggings – the ones with the exhausted Lycra, that gave her wrinkled knees like an elephant's – but it was no good panicking because there wasn't a damn thing she could do about it.

By some miracle, at least Tom had still recognised her.

Hastily, before it fell out of her open mouth and put him off completely, Poppy swallowed her gum.

'My God, it's you! How amazing . . . Jake, this is someone I haven't seen for ages . . . his name's Tom . . . and this . . . this is Jake . . .'

Poppy's voice trailed away. Introductions always floored

her; she could never remember the proper way, which had something to do with age, but how were you supposed to go about it if you didn't know who was the eldest, ask to see their driving licences before you began?

'I think she's in shock,' said Jake. 'Poppy, are you okay? Do you want to sit down?'

'I really wish I'd thrown these leggings away now,' said Poppy. She gripped the sides of the cashbox until her fingers ached, and forced herself to concentrate. She needed to pull herself together, fast. What must Tom think?

'It's – it's great to see you again,' she heard herself stammer idiotically. 'Is there something you're in-in-interested in, or are you just having a browse?'

Tom said, 'Oh no, there's definitely something I'm in-in-interested in.'

He was teasing her. It struck Poppy that he didn't seem nearly as astounded to see her as she was seeing him. She tried to say something sensible, without stammering, but her chewing gum had got itself wedged at epiglottis level. This time all that came out was a mousy squeak.

'Lost for words,' observed Jake. 'Now there's a first.'

'And here we are, making fun of her.' Tom grinned and ran a finger lightly over her knuckles, white where they still clutched the cashbox. 'I suppose we aren't being very fair. Poppy, this isn't a coincidence. I didn't just happen to be passing. Jake found me.'

This was getting more bizarre by the minute. Behind Tom, an old dear in an ochre Pakamac was hissing crossly, 'If you'd move out of my way, young man, I'd quite like to have a look at that Staffordshire pig.'

Poppy swallowed again. This time the chewing gum went down and stayed down.

'Jake what? What d'you mean, *found* you?'

With some pride, Jake said, 'I advertised.'

Was this how it felt to be Tango'd? Poppy shook her head. 'Advertised how?'

'In all the papers. But that didn't work.' Jake was beaming like a new father. 'So we tried newsagents' windows. And bingo.'

She knew she was parroting everything they said, but it was all she was capable of just now.

'You put an advert in a newsagent's window,' Poppy said carefully. She turned to Tom. 'And you *saw* it?'

'Well, the girl who lives in the flat downstairs saw it, and remembered me telling her about the night we met.'

He'd told other people about her . . .

'And it wasn't actually me who put the ad in that window,' said Jake, not to be outdone. 'It was Claudia.'

Tom took Poppy to a tiny restaurant just off Kensington High Street. Like a sleepwalker Poppy allowed herself to be helped into her seat.

'Jake was right, by the way, about me being lost for words. I'm not usually like this.'

'Look,' said Tom, 'maybe there's something we should get straight before we go any further. Is my turning up out of the blue a nice surprise or a bloody awful shock? Are you happy about it, or not?'

'God yes, of *course* I'm happy.' Flustered, Poppy realised she sounded like some hopeless lovestruck groupie. 'I mean . . . I mean . . .'

'Good.' Beneath the table, Tom's foot touched hers. His smile reassured her. 'Seeing as Jake's been to all this trouble. Imagine how offended he'd be if we took one look at each other and went Ugh!'

'Dina told me she'd bumped into you. She lost your address. I wanted to kill her!'

'Don't worry, I'll do it when we next see her.' He lit a cigarette and exhaled with relief. 'It'll make up for all those weeks afterwards, twitching every time the phone rang and being disappointed when it wasn't you.'

'I saw you, just before Christmas.' The words began

tumbling out. 'At a petrol station. I tried to get your attention but you disappeared so fast—'

'What I don't understand,' said Tom, 'is why you didn't turn up at Delgado's that night. Did you think I wouldn't be there?'

'I knew you *would* be there. I did turn up. I saw you, at that table in the window.' There was so much to say, so many things to explain. A waitress was hovering behind them. Poppy glanced at the menu in her hand, knowing she wouldn't be able to eat.

'It's okay, you choose,' Tom told the waitress. 'Anything you like. And a bottle of something to go with it.'

'I panicked,' Poppy admitted when they were alone once more. 'I was meant to be getting married. Meeting you wasn't supposed to happen.'

Tom grinned. 'I think it was. Anyway, you didn't get married.'

'I couldn't.'

'Can't have been easy.'

'It was awful. Like the end bit of *The Graduate*, but without anyone to jump on the bus with. In the end I jumped on by myself,' Poppy said drily, 'and came to London. Before I could be burned at the stake.'

'What about your family?' Tom stubbed out his cigarette, half-smoked. 'Were they okay about it? Did you ever regret calling off the wedding?'

'Not for an instant.' He was running an index finger idly over the veins on the inside of her wrist. Distracted, Poppy trembled with pleasure. 'As for my family . . . I would never have found my real father if it hadn't been for you.'

Tom frowned. 'You've lost me.'

'It's a long story. And no, I haven't lost you,' said Poppy, realising that there was simply no point in being coy. 'I've found you. God, that sounds naff.' Laughing, she buried her face in her hands. 'I can't believe I just said it.'

'Here comes the food. We're going to have to pretend to eat.'

Their eyes locked. Over the worst of the shock now, Poppy had begun to relax. The last time they had met, it had been the middle of the night, pitch-black and tropically warm. Ever since, trying to conjure up a mental image of Tom, she had only been able to picture him in darkness.

Now, almost a year later, it was daylight. Unforgiving drizzly grey daylight at that. It was a huge relief to discover he was as breathtakingly handsome as she remembered. The sight of him still made her stomach disappear.

The magic was still there. Remembering her elephant-kneed leggings and out-of-control hair, Poppy amended that. It was still there, on her side at least.

'What's the matter?' said Tom.

'I wish I wasn't wearing these clothes.'

'You look fine.'

'I can look better.'

'I know.' That knee-trembling grin reappeared. Heavens, he was gorgeous.

'Everything all right?' enquired the waitress, who evidently thought so too. She was addressing Tom. Poppy, watching the way she looked at him, spotted the quick glance down at his left hand. The ring-check, every single girl's reflexive response to a good-looking man . . .

Poppy followed the waitress's gaze.

'Oh bloody hell, I don't believe it,' she wailed. 'You're married!'

Chapter 44

'No I'm not,' said Tom.

'Yes you are.' Poppy jabbed an accusing finger at his hand. How could she not have noticed it before? After all those things she'd said, too. How embarrassing.

'No he isn't,' said the waitress, looking at Poppy as if she were mad. 'That's his right hand.' Nodding at the other half of the pair she added kindly, 'That one's his left.'

'Sorry.' Poppy tried to shrink into her chair. 'I'm dyslexic.'

'The thing is,' said Tom when the waitress had sauntered back to the kitchen, 'I'm not married. But I am kind of . . . well, involved with someone.'

Buggeration. In an effort to appear laid-back, Poppy picked up her glass and swilled the wine before sipping it. Sadly it swilled out of the glass and onto the white table-cloth.

'I see.' So much for laid-back. 'How involved?'

'On a scale of one to ten? Five. Maybe six.' He watched her mop ineffectually at the wet tablecloth and smiled. 'But at least I won't have to get a divorce.'

'I'm single. Unattached, I mean.'

'I know. Jake told me.'

'What else has he said?' Poppy wondered if she wanted to hear this. If Jake had made her out to be some kind of sad charity case she would die. Her heart skipped a couple of uncomfortable beats as another thought struck her. 'My God, he didn't pay you to come and see me, did he?'

Tom burst out laughing.

'This is getting less romantic by the second. Do I look like a gigolo?'

The thing was, he was so gorgeous, he did rather.

'You could be.' Poppy felt herself going pink. 'I'm sorry, I'm a bit confused. I keep wondering if this is a huge joke. I don't know what's supposed to happen next.' She glugged down the remains of her wine. 'I feel like I've been given an instruction manual and it's in Japanese.'

'Not that bad.' He was teasing her again. 'At least I speak English.'

'I don't even know your surname.'

'That's an easy one. Kennedy.'

'Are you really a doctor?'

'Did you think I was?' Tom grinned. 'No, it was all I could come up with at the time, to explain away the fact that your foot was in my lap. Somehow chiropodist didn't have the same ring.'

'You're a chiropodist?' Poppy bit her lip. She didn't know if she could fall in love with someone whose life revolved around other people's feet.

'I'm an architect.' His smile broadened. 'Is that all right with you?'

Phew. 'Oh yes, much better.'

'Next question.'

The waitress returned with more wine, giving Poppy time to gather her scattered thoughts. Her lamb cutlets looked heavenly but she hadn't been able to eat a thing.

'Go on,' prompted Tom while she dithered with her napkin.

'That night. What would have happened if I'd met you in Delgado's?'

He grew serious. 'We wouldn't have wasted the past year.'

It hadn't been wasted. She had found Alex. Still, Poppy held her breath.

'We might not have got on.'

'You felt the same way as I did. How often does that kind of thing happen?'

Helplessly she said, 'So . . . what now?'

'We make up for lost time.' His dark eyes were intense. 'We aren't going to eat this, are we? I'll get the bill.'

'But . . . this girlfriend of yours.'

Tom shrugged. 'It's over.'

'Oh God, won't she be upset?'

Taking Poppy's hand, he drew her to her feet and kissed her full on the mouth. Almost instantly he pulled away.

'No, not here. I can't kiss you how I want to kiss you. Of course she'll be upset. I imagine your chap was upset when you called off the wedding. But you and me . . . when these things happen, they happen.'

Quivering, Poppy said, 'Yes, but—'

'Don't argue. It's destiny. I'm not going to lose you again.'

Tom settled the bill. Outside, he hailed a cab. It was still raining.

'You don't have to go back to work, by the way.' He brushed droplets of rain from her flushed cheeks. 'Jake's given you the rest of the day off.'

'That's even more of a miracle than you turning up,' Poppy joked feebly.

The cab had drawn to a halt in front of them.

'I know how I'd like to spend the afternoon,' said Tom as he helped her in, 'but say if it's too soon. I don't want to pressure you.'

'Are you kidding?' Poppy was practically melting with lust. 'I thought you'd never ask.'

'Right, it's make your mind up time,' said the world-weary driver. 'Your place or his?'

So the nosy cabbie couldn't hear, Poppy whispered, shamefaced, 'I've only got a single bed.'

Tom squeezed her hand. 'That's nothing. I've got a girl-friend with a key to my flat.'

The house was empty when they reached it. Claudia was at work and there had been no sign of Caspar for days. Poppy, who knew what a state the kitchen had been in when she'd raced out of the house that morning, took Tom straight downstairs.

'Welcome to my rabbit hutch.' She gestured around the tiny, messy room. 'If I'd known you were coming I'd have made the bed.'

Tom took her into his arms.

'Are you nervous?'

'Of course I'm nervous. Would I be making this many bad jokes if I wasn't?'

'Sshh.' He pulled her closer. 'No more jokes. Time for that kiss I couldn't give you earlier.'

The one good thing about horrible clothes, thought Poppy, was you couldn't wait to get them off. And they made your body look better by comparison.

'You are beautiful,' said Tom. 'I mean it.'

'Don't sound so surprised.'

'Well, you never know. Some girls look stunning until you see them naked. Then you realise it was all industrial-strength knickers and Wonderbra. One minute they're up here, the next . . . whoomph. Talk about a let-down.'

Poppy glanced at her own modest breasts. 'I don't have enough to let down.'

'I said no more jokes.' His dark eyes softened. 'You're perfect.'

'Well,' said Poppy an hour later, 'that was definitely perfect.'

'Not to mention long overdue.'

She lay in his arms and gazed around her room, seeing it as Tom must see it.

'Sorry. This place is such a tip.'

'Never mind, I'm here now.' He raised himself up on one elbow and planted a necklace of kisses around her throat. 'I'll take you away from all this.'

'That won't help.' Poppy closed her eyes, squirming with pleasure as he ran warm fingers across her bare stomach. 'I can be untidy anywhere. It's pro rata. The bigger the space, the more mess I make.'

'Sshh.' Tom kissed her again. Then he made love to Poppy a second time, slowly and thoroughly, until overcome by the events of the day she sobbed with joy.

A sheen of perspiration covered Poppy's body. The duvet cover was sticking to her hips.

'A bath.' She reached over Tom, peering at her wristwatch on the bedside table. 'That's okay, only four o'clock. Claudia won't be home for ages yet.' She double-checked the time. 'How amazing.'

Tom seized her arms and pulled her down on top of him.

'What?'

'It's only four o'clock,' Poppy sighed between kisses. 'I feel as if we've been in bed together for days.'

Shaking off rain like a dog, Caspar let himself into the house. Getting away from London for the weekend was all very well – he and Babette had driven down to the Cotswolds and stayed in an hotel teeming with golfers in loud sweaters – but his commissions were piling up. Back in the real world he had work to do.

Incredibly, Bella McCloud had decided to forgive him. Now back in the country following a triumphant appearance at La Scala, the diva had instructed her manager to re-schedule a series of sittings with the so-handsome young artist who had had the audacity to stand her up.

She was meeting him here in – Caspar checked his watch – twenty minutes. He lit a cigarette, since her manager had already warned him he wouldn't be able to smoke in La McCloud's presence. Wondering if this meant opera singers *never* went into pubs after a hard day's warbling, Caspar made his way slowly upstairs.

When he reached the first-floor landing he realised the house wasn't empty, as he had first thought. Something was going on in the bathroom. And whoever was in there clearly wasn't alone.

Claudia? Had she and Jake got it together at last? Or was she here with her new boss, having sloped out of the office for a naughty afternoon off? Amused by this idea – giving Claudia a lift into work the other week, he had seen her middle-aged boss ogle her across the car park – Caspar listened to the sounds of shrieks and splashing filtering through the bathroom door.

Then he heard Poppy, helpless with laughter, scream 'No, no, not the cold water – oh you sod!'

Not Claudia. Poppy.

Caspar's blood ran cold. What the bloody hell did she think she was playing at? Even more to the point, who was she *with*?

More giggles and shrieks. Caspar felt his hands curling into angry fists. Of course he knew who Poppy was with. It had to be that prat from the photographs, the lanky one with the inane grin Poppy had so boisterously entertained here while he and Claudia had both been away.

Without stopping to think what he was doing, Caspar marched up to the door and hammered on it. The door, which had been left unlocked, burst open.

Chapter 45

'Jesus!' exclaimed a dark-haired, dark-eyed Adonis he had never seen before in his life.

'Aaargh!' screamed Poppy, who had streaked along the landing earlier to grab a couple of dry towels from the airing cupboard and forgotten to re-lock the bathroom door. Like a scene from a Whitehall farce she made a lunge for the nearest towel, which was slung around the Adonis' hips. He hung onto it. Yelping, desperately trying to cover herself with her hands, Poppy scuttled sideways and snatched the other towel from the rail.

If he hadn't been so furious Caspar would have found it funny.

'What are you *doing* here?' Poppy shouted, her face burning with embarrassment. She clutched the yellow towel to her chest like a toddler's security blanket.

'It's my house.'

'How dare you come barging in! You must have heard us,' she seethed. 'Couldn't you have knocked?'

'I did. I thought you'd have locked the door.'

'I forgot!'

'And I heard you screaming.' Caspar looked pointedly at her companion. 'What was I supposed to do? How did I know you weren't being murdered?'

'Oh, please.' Poppy's eyes were like chips of ice. 'Now I've heard bloody everything.'

'Look—' began the bloke in the towel.

'No, *you* look.' Ignoring him, Caspar pointed an accusing

299

finger at Poppy. 'Listen to me for once in your life. I'm not talking morals here, just plain common sense. Picking up total strangers and bringing them back to an empty house is a dangerous hobby. You're not stupid, Poppy. You read the papers. Girls get attacked. They get raped, murdered—'

'You've got a nerve!' Poppy was so agitated she almost dropped her towel. 'How many girls have you brought back here? I bet you didn't lecture them about how stupid they were being! Anyway,' she yelled, 'I haven't picked up a total stranger. This is Tom. Tom Kennedy.'

'Oh well done, you know his name,' Caspar's voice dripped sarcasm. 'He actually bothered to introduce himself. That's okay then, he can't possibly be a psychopath.'

But as he spoke, the significance of the name sank in. Tom. This was *that* Tom. Jake's hare-brained scheme to find him must actually have worked. He was here with Poppy and things were obviously going with a swing.

Great.

'Okay?' demanded Poppy. 'Does it all make sense now?'

Caspar was buggered if he was going to apologise.

'So you met him once before. Big deal. You still don't *know* him.'

'I know enough,' Poppy countered hotly.

'Please,' said Tom, who was far too handsome for Caspar's liking, 'could we all calm down? I'm really not a psychopath.' He turned to Poppy. 'But you can see Caspar's point. He only has your best interests at heart.'

'Like hell he does.' Poppy glared at Caspar. 'He's just pissed off because he thinks he's the only one around here allowed to have any fun.'

'Now you're being stupid,' Caspar snapped back.

'If you had my best interests at heart, you'd be happy for me.' Poppy was startled to find herself thinking that if he'd had her best interests at heart he would never have married Babette Lawrenson. 'If you *really* had my best interests at heart,' she shouted, 'you'd get the hell out of this bathroom and leave us to get dressed in peace!'

Bella McCloud had a disappointing afternoon. Having looked forward to meeting and being gently flirted with by the famously attractive Caspar French, she was feeling deeply let down. Oh, he had been polite enough, and the preliminary drawings he had done of her couldn't be faulted – if you didn't count the fact that he had insisted her hint of a double chin stayed in – but that had been as far as it went. Where was the charisma, the easy charm Bella had heard so much about? Caspar French had been quiet, almost abstracted. He had simply got on with the job. Not a flirtatious grin in sight.

In the back of the cab as it took her back to her hotel, Bella McCloud dug in her bag and flipped through her diary. She tapped a long red fingernail thoughtfully against the number of the Harley Street surgeon all her friends had been raving about. Maybe it was time for that face lift after all.

Tom's flat was on the third floor of a huge Victorian house in the smarter section of Notting Hill.

'Well? Do you approve?' he asked when the guided tour was over. She had seen the kitchen, the living room, the bathroom and both bedrooms.

'Very smart.' Poppy ran her hand over the matte black wooden shelving. Recessed lights cunningly illuminated a selection of steel-framed black and white prints. The walls were pale grey, as was the almost futuristic sofa. 'Very . . . architecty.'

He looked amused. 'I don't like clutter, if that's what you mean.'

'I don't think you and Laura Ashley would have hit it off.'

'Judith, the girl who lives downstairs, calls it stark. She hates my kitchen, says it's like being on board a bloody spaceship.'

'It's not stark,' Poppy lovingly assured him, 'it's manly.'

Tom put his arms around her. 'I know. Maybe what it needs

is a woman's touch. I've just been waiting for the right woman to come along.'

He's probably envisaging fresh flowers, thought Poppy; five perfect irises faultlessly arranged in a conical vase. Since her version of a woman's touch was more likely to be cake crumbs all over the pristine kitchen worktops and blobs of mascara on the bathroom mirror she realised she was going to have to buck up her ideas pretty damn quick.

'Right, down to business.' Tom glanced at his watch as the oven timer in the kitchen went ping. 'Sit down, sweetheart. Make yourself at home. I have a phone call to make.'

Thinking he meant work-type business, Poppy happily made herself comfortable on the grey sofa and chose a magazine from the coffee table. Called *Architecture Today*, it made her feel jolly intelligent.

She was gazing at a picture of an office block when she realised to her horror that Tom wasn't phoning the office at all.

'. . . no, it's better if you don't come over. Jan, listen to me. I'm sorry, really I am, but we can't see each other any more. Hang on, let me explain . . . Jan, please . . . I've met someone else. It's serious. This is the real thing.'

He was standing with his back to Poppy, looking out of the window. Even from ten feet away she could hear the anguished wail on the other end of the phone.

Poppy squirmed. Tom listened in silence for several seconds. Then he said, 'Jan, calm down. I know it isn't fair but there's nothing I can do about it. Yes, yes, I know that too. I'm a bastard. And a shit. What else can I say? I *am* sorry. If we could be friends, that'd be great. Look, can I ask you to do something for me? Post your key back? No, just send it in the post . . .'

Cringing, Poppy watched him listen for a few moments more. When he had put the phone down he turned round.

'She doesn't want to be friends.'

'Oh, I feel terrible! That poor girl,' Poppy gasped. 'She sounded dreadfully upset.'

'She'll be fine.' Tom's smile was rueful but dismissive. 'It just came as a shock, that's all. She wasn't expecting it.'

'Neither was I.'

'Come on, it's over now.' He drew her to her feet and kissed her again. 'We can't have you feeling sorry for Jan. It's not as if it was the love affair of the century. We weren't even living together.'

'Why did she have a key?'

He led her through to the kitchen. Through the smoked glass door of the oven a casserole was in the process of being heated up.

'It made life easier,' said Tom. 'Jan finished work an hour before me. She used to let herself in and make a start on the evening meal. She made this this morning,' he went on, 'before she left. Actually, she's a bloody good cook.'

He was taking plates down from a steel-fronted cupboard. Then he slid open the cutlery drawer and began picking out knives and forks.

Poppy blurted out, 'I can't eat that casserole!'

'Oh God, you're not a vegetarian?'

'No! I mean I can't eat something your girlfriend made for the two of you to share tonight!'

Tom frowned. 'Ex-girlfriend.'

'Okay, ex-girlfriend.' Poppy started to laugh. Men, honestly. 'Don't you see? All the more reason why I can't eat it.'

'Oh.' He nodded. 'Right. Bugger, I'm starving.'

She decided to take the plunge. He was going to have to find out sooner or later. 'We'll make something else. Except . . . I have to warn you, I'm a pretty hopeless cook.'

'So am I.' Tom held her face between his warm hands. 'It doesn't matter. Nothing else matters, Poppy. I love you.'

'You're in a grumpy mood,' observed Babette. Since

303

emerging scented and revived from her bath an hour earlier, Caspar had hardly said more than two words. She rubbed the last vestiges of moisturiser into the backs of her fingers and glanced at her diary, lying open on the sofa. 'What was Bella McCloud like, a pain in the neck?'

Caspar stopped pretending to watch whatever was on TV. He gazed across the room at Babette, who had now finished efficiently rubbing in hand cream. She fished in the pocket of her white silk dressing gown, clipped her watch briskly onto her wrist and slid the narrow gold wedding ring back into place.

'Pain in the chin, if anything.' He shrugged. 'She was okay.'

'Well, something's bothering you.' Picking up her diary, Babette came over to his chair and draped her arms lovingly around his neck. 'Cheer up, darling. Look who I'm seeing tomorrow.' She pointed with pride to the name she had underlined in red, belonging to the owner of one of the smartest galleries in Knightsbridge. 'He wants me to promote his next exhibition. Is that a coup or what?'

Becoming known as Caspar's wife had done Babette's career no harm at all. There had been a flurry of interest in the media and Babette had handled it superbly, in interviews playing up the differences between the super-organised businesswoman and the laid-back artist. Their marriage certificate, Caspar joked, had been photocopied in triplicate and filed away in her office under M for marital status.

'Great.' He forced a smile. She was right, he was being grumpy and it wasn't her fault. 'Sorry. Headache.'

'You don't get headaches. Come on, something's up.' Babette slid onto his lap. 'Isn't this what wives are for? You can tell me.'

'Nothing to tell. Poppy's taken up with some old flame, that's all.' Caspar didn't want to elaborate; this was close enough. 'She thinks she's in luurve. I just hope she isn't making a horrible mistake.'

304

Babette checked her watch. It was early yet; if they made love now she would still have plenty of time to work on tomorrow's presentation.

'If it's love, you could soon be losing yourself a lodger,' she pointed out. 'That's good news.'

'Why is it good news?'

'No need to jump down my throat! I mean if Poppy moves out, maybe Claudia will go too. You'd get more money renting the house out to a family. Financially it makes far better sense.'

Caspar grinned. 'So organised. So efficient.'

Babette shifted position on his lap and began undoing his shirt.

'Not to mention,' she said happily, 'so great in bed.'

Chapter 46

Jake didn't know what he'd eaten, but something was doing its damnedest to wrench his stomach inside out.

'I'm sorry, this evening's off,' he told Claudia. He felt so dreadful it was a struggle even to hold onto the phone.

'Food poisoning?' Claudia had spent enough time working in offices to know this was the oldest and least original excuse in the book. Along with funerals. 'Sure it isn't a funeral?'

'What?'

She looked at her glamorous reflection in the mirror above the fireplace. All that make-up, all that careful hair tonging, all for bloody nothing.

'Are you really ill?'

Jake closed his eyes. His stomach was churning ominously.

'Of course I'm ill. Why would I invite you to dinner and then cancel?'

Claudia's self-confidence was deserting her. All she knew was that she was being stood up. Insecurity flooded through her like poison.

'Maybe you found out how much dinner was likely to cost.'

'Oh come *on* . . .'

'Okay, I know. I'll drive over. I can look after you.'

Jake hadn't been sick for almost fifteen minutes. Sweat prickled across his icy skin, reminding him it was time he headed for the bathroom again.

'Please don't,' he said urgently. The prospect of having

Claudia here to witness his condition was too awful to contemplate. 'I mean it. You mustn't.'

You mean I mustn't come over and find out you aren't really ill, thought Claudia. Mentally she was ten again, in an unflattering pinafore dress, and Angie was trilling to all and sundry, 'With hips like mine, I can't imagine how I managed to produce such a gawky great lump of a girl!'

'You won't, will you?' Jake had to double-check.

'Of course I won't,' Claudia snapped back.

A great wave of nausea swept through him. Jake lurched unsteadily to his feet. 'Sorry, got to go—'

It gave Claudia the tiniest amount of satisfaction to hang up first. She kicked off her high heels and stomped barefoot through to the kitchen. No Caspar, because he was too busy being happily married to Babette. No Poppy because she was busy being even happier with Tom.

No Chez Nico.

And no Jake.

Claudia, whose own stomach was growling with hunger, peered at the contents of the fridge. I'll have scrambled eggs on toast, she decided, trying hard to be brave. And lemon pudding.

Then she burst into tears.

Ben McBride took the message on Friday afternoon while Dina was out at the supermarket. Returning weighed down with nappies, she spotted the brief note propped against the phone.

'Poppy rang! What did she say? What's this bit?' Dina dropped the nappies and wandered into the kitchen, where Ben was mending the toaster. 'Your writing's in a world of its own. She's found what? *God*?'

'Tom.' Ben was poking and prodding amongst the wires with his screwdriver. 'She said to tell you she found Tom. Whoever he is.'

Dina didn't tell him. Tom was, after all, the reason why

307

Poppy hadn't married Ben's precious brother.

'He's an old friend. That's brilliant news.' It was like giving up smoking, then breathing in the seductive whiff of a cigarette; the urge to zip up to London came over her in an instant. Eyes shining, she turned to Ben. 'You aren't working this weekend, are you?'

He gave her a weary look.

'What does that mean? You, buggering off again, leaving me stuck here with the baby?'

'Poppy's my friend.' Dina's arms were crossed, which meant she wasn't going to give up without a fight. 'She's had some good news. Is there anything wrong with seeing a friend, helping her celebrate?'

The look of defiance on her face was what Ben couldn't bear. Dina always made him out to be some kind of ogre, the boring grown-up out to spoil her fun. And all he wanted was for them to have fun together . . .

'Go,' he said stiffly, 'if that's what you want.'

'Thanks.' It was so easy to twist him round her little finger. Dina dropped a triumphant kiss on top of his head. Now she could ring Poppy and fix things up.

She pulled a face when Claudia answered the phone.

'Poppy's not here,' said Claudia in a 'so-there' voice. 'She'll be at Tom's flat. And no, I don't have the number. Sorry.'

Bitch. But Dina's weekend was at stake, so she forced herself to sound friendly.

'Great news, isn't it, about Tom? Actually, Poppy suggested I came up this weekend—'

'She isn't here,' Claudia repeated.

'Yes, but I can still crash in her room, can't I?' Dina's manner was confident, all-girls-together. 'I mean, I don't want to play gooseberry at Tom's place.'

'Look, I'm just on my way out. Staying here isn't really on, I'm afraid. Maybe you should make other arrangements.'

Bitch, *bitch*. Claudia was giving her the kind of brush-off normally reserved for double-glazing salesmen. Except double-glazing salesmen weren't allowed to bite back.

'Okay, no problem,' said Dina breezily. 'I'll give Jake a ring.'

It was a shot in the dark, but Poppy had told her Claudia was keen on Jake.

'Jake? You can't do that! You've never even met Jake.'

Dina grinned. Bingo. The bitch was rattled.

'So?' she countered innocently. 'He's a friend of Poppy's, isn't he? I bet he'd put me up.'

'My God, you have a nerve.'

'Anyway, I've been looking forward to meeting him for ages. Poppy says he's lovely. And now he's got all that money stashed away—'

'He's not going to want you turning up on his doorstep,' Claudia interrupted furiously. 'I'll tell you that for nothing.'

Before putting the phone down Dina purred, 'Want to bet?'

Ben had finished mending the toaster. Testily he said, 'What was all that about?'

'Poppy shares a house with a complete cow.'

His face reddened with suppressed rage. 'And who the bloody hell's Jake? Dina, you're not going up to London and staying at some bloke's house. Not some bloke you've never met. I won't have it.'

'Don't get your knickers in a twist. Of course I'm not going.' She didn't even know where Jake lived. The weekend was off. Upstairs, Daniel began to wail. With bitter satisfaction Dina said, 'I was just geeing her up.'

Claudia, who had been lying about going out, was so angry she couldn't even manicure her nails straight. She gave up and ran a bath instead, tipping in half a bottle of hair conditioner by mistake.

It was four days since Jake had cancelled their date and there had been no word from him since.

If I phone to warn him about Dina, she thought miserably, he'll think it's just a pathetic excuse to speak to him.

It wasn't as if they'd parted on the sunniest of terms. Oh, but if that slut Dina really did have plans to get her claws into Jake, how could she *stand* it?

The bath water was weirdly slippery. Unable to relax, Claudia climbed out and ran downstairs. She found Jake's number in the phone book, picked up the receiver and dialled. Then, her courage failing her, she put the phone down after the first ring. Jake hadn't bothered to make contact all week. She would sound so obvious, so . . . desperate.

Claudia forced herself to sit through *Coronation Street* and *The Bill* in her dressing gown. By eight thirty her agitation was at fever pitch and most of the nails she had lopsidedly manicured earlier were bitten to the quick. If Dina had caught the coach straight up to London she'd have arrived by now. She would be wearing a skimpy top and an up-to-the-bum skirt, and carrying a change of clothes in that cheap leather-look bag of hers. With her cat-like smile and sickeningly tiny figure, Claudia realised, Dina was a low-rent version of her mother. Except even Angie didn't have quite that much barefaced cheek.

By nine o'clock she couldn't stand it any more. Not knowing what was happening was the worst torture of all. Leaping to her feet, Claudia raced back upstairs and pulled on a white sweater and pale green trousers. Moments later she tore them off and changed into a black sweater and black jeans. It made her look like something out of a Milk Tray ad, but maybe that was what she needed . . .

She was so nervous she could hardly drive. By the time she reached Jake's road she had taken four wrong turnings and her *A-Z* was practically in shreds.

Trembling like a leaf, Claudia parked four doors away and switched off the ignition. The lights in Jake's house were on and the living-room curtains had been drawn, but carelessly. One of the curtains had got hooked up against a pile of books on the windowsill, leaving a smallish triangular gap.

There could be no backing out now. She had come this far and she had to know. Fuelled by jealousy, Claudia slid out of the car and crept, Milk Tray-style, across the road. Thankfully, there was no one else in sight.

Not so good was the way the house had been designed. Five steps led up to the front door and the minuscule front garden, surrounded by railings and planted as a rockery, was eight feet below the window-ledge. If she clambered over the railings and onto the rockery, there was no way she could see into the window. If she mounted the steps and leaned across as far as she possibly could . . . well, she would fall over.

Claudia hovered agonisingly on the pavement wondering what to do next. She jumped as a front door opened and shut at the far end of the street, and watched a fair-haired man climb into a van and drive off. Moments later, realising what the van had been parked behind, she experienced a surge of adrenalin and raced up the road to investigate.

The skip was three quarters full, packed mainly with builders' rubble and planks of rotted wood. But thrown in on top, by some miracle, was a dining chair. Granted, a chair with the seat missing and only three legs, but enough to do the trick.

Joyfully, Claudia hauled herself into the skip, seized the chair and eased herself out onto the pavement. She ran with it back to Jake's front garden, climbed over the rusty railings and wedged the chair against the front of the house with the missing leg nearest the brickwork to keep it secure.

The street was silent. All she could hear was her own breathing. Balancing herself carefully, one foot at a time, on the frame of the chair to which the seat had once been attached, Claudia edged her bitten fingernails up the wall. She was safe, she wasn't going to topple over, all she had to do now was grab the window-ledge and pull herself from a crouch to a standing position—

311

'Oi, you!' yelled a voice from the other side of the road, 'Stay right where you are! Smash that window and I'll smash your head in.'

Claudia almost wet herself. Whimpering with fear she tried to climb down. Her fingers scraped against the wall, losing what feeble grip they might have had. One knee gave way. The chair wobbled in the opposite direction and cracked under the strain.

She landed in the rockery with a scream and a bone-crunching thud.

Chapter 47

'Don't move!' ordered the rough male voice, now close behind her. 'Thieving bastard, I hope you've broken both your bloody legs. Don't you move a muscle. Jake, GET OUT HERE!'

It was a nightmare. Everything hurt. Too appalled to cry, Claudia lay in the darkness amongst the rocks and splintered chair legs wishing she could at least have been knocked unconscious. Anything to be spared the humiliation of the next few minutes.

Above her Jake's door opened, spilling out light.

'What's going on?'

'Bloody cat burglar. Saw him from our bedroom window. It's okay,' the rough voice declared with satisfaction, 'I've already phoned the old Bill. They're on their way.'

Not okay. Not okay at all. Struggling to raise her head from the ground Claudia heard herself moan pathetically, 'Oh please, not the police.'

'Flaming Nora,' the rough voice exclaimed, 'it's a bird.'

'Jake, it's me. Make them go away. Not the police, *please*.'

'*Claudia*?' Jake leapt over the railings in amazement and appeared beside her. 'Are you hurt? Can you move?'

'Ouch, I think so. Oh no—'

The wail of a police siren shattered the night. Gritting her teeth – at least they were all still there – Claudia let Jake help her slowly into an upright position. Somehow, between them, he and the man from across the road managed to lift her back over the railings. She sat on the steps of the house

313

with her head buried in her hands and listened to Jake explaining to the police officers that she wasn't a burglar; it had all been a mistake.

You're telling me, thought Claudia, hot tears of self-pity seeping through her aching eyelids and dripping onto her wrists.

'Well, well, you're a dark horse and no mistake,' marvelled his neighbour when Jake had persuaded the police to leave. 'Never had you down as the type to have a fan club, Jake. What are you, some kind of rock star in your spare time?'

'His name's Dan. He's very into Neighbourhood Watch.'

One way and another, Claudia thought morosely, Jake's Neighbourhood Watch scheme was out to ruin her life.

'Now –' he put a mug of coffee into her hands – 'are you sure you're all right?'

'Is that meant to be a joke?'

'I mean if you want to see a doctor I could drive you to casualty.'

Claudia shook her head. The last thing she needed was a gaggle of medical students with smirks on their faces prodding her bottom. By tomorrow it would be one huge bruise. The least she could do was keep it to herself.

'Sorry about the chips,' said Jake, breaking the silence.

'What?'

He pointed to the mug she was holding, chipped around the rim.

'I'd have thought you could've treated yourself to new ones,' said Claudia. 'Now you can afford it.'

It wasn't the first time she had made that kind of remark. Jake really wished she wouldn't. He wished he didn't keep remembering Poppy telling him that Claudia was only interested in men with more money than sense.

Ironically, it was probably thanks to Claudia that he was still living here. The more digs she made, the less keen he became on the idea of moving to a smarter address. And it wasn't as if he was cutting off his nose to spite his face, Jake reassured himself. There was no rush, and he'd always been happy here. He loved this house.

He glanced briefly around his cluttered, comfortable-but-shabby living room, seeing it through her eyes.

'Would you like to criticise my home too, while you're about it?'

Claudia shook her head. The room was actually quite cosy, though clearly the domain of someone whose priority in life was not interior design. The carpet was threadbare in places, the furniture old and functional rather than elegant. Those striped blue and green curtains didn't match anything else in the room . . .

Bloody curtains, she thought crossly. If he'd only taken the trouble to draw them properly there wouldn't have been that enticing gap and she wouldn't be here now, nursing a bruise the size of a pizza and looking a complete prat into the bargain.

'So what *were* you doing outside my front window?' asked Jake at last.

Claudia couldn't look at him.

'I wanted to find out if Dina was here.'

'Who?'

'Poppy's friend. From Bristol.' Painfully, she forced herself to meet his astonished gaze.

'I've never even met Dina!'

'I know. But I wouldn't let her stay at the house tonight so she said she'd ask you instead. She told me you wouldn't turn her down and anyway, from what she'd heard, you sounded right up her street. She's a shameless uppity trollop.' Claudia was indignant. 'And a gold-digger to boot.'

Mildly, Jake said, 'Well, she isn't here. You came up my street instead. If you were so worried, why didn't you just phone?'

'After you'd stood me up on Monday and hadn't bothered to get in touch all week? You'd have thought I was chasing

315

you,' Claudia snapped. 'That would have looked great.'

'You lying splattered all over my front garden didn't look that great,' he pointed out. 'A phone call would have been easier. Anyway, why would I think you were chasing me?'

'Oh come on! It happened to Caspar all the time. He spent his life getting us to field phone calls from besotted girlies.' Her lip curled. 'They were a standing joke.'

As opposed to a flat-on-your-back-in-the-rockery joke, thought Jake. Diplomatically, he didn't say so.

'I'm not Caspar.'

'No.'

'I'm not anything like Caspar.' Drily he added, 'And I've never had a phone call from a besotted girlie in my life.'

Claudia thought it was just as well everyone wasn't like Caspar. Imagine a world full of them . . .

'What, never?'

Jake shook his head.

'Why not? You aren't that ugly.'

'Thanks.'

Flustered, Claudia said, 'I didn't mean it like that.'

He smiled slightly. 'You should have seen me as a teenager. When you're awkward and shy *and* you wear NHS specs, girls don't exactly swoon at your feet.'

'But you must have had a girlfriend at some stage.'

'I had a girlfriend for five years. Emily. She wore glasses too,' said Jake. 'The first time I kissed her, at the school Christmas disco, it was like antlers clashing. Everyone saw us go clunk.' He mimed the jarring action. 'We didn't live it down for months.'

'Yes, but you were together for five years, so it must have been serious. What happened?' Claudia was burning with curiosity.

'She had cystic fibrosis. She died.'

Claudia's hands went up to her mouth. 'No! How awful. God, I'm sorry . . . Poppy never told me.'

'Maybe because Poppy doesn't know.'

'But that's so sad—'

'It was a long time ago.' Jake shrugged off her sympathy. 'Do you want another coffee? If you want to use the bathroom to tidy yourself up, feel free.'

It was pretty galling, being told to tidy yourself up by Jake – rather like Harold Steptoe suggesting your teeth could do with a scrape and polish – but when she reached the bathroom Claudia saw what he meant. The rubble in the skip had left a layer of grey dust over her black sweater, and her hair was thick with it too. There were twigs in her fringe and a smudge of mud across one cheek.

What a fright.

'I'd better go,' she said when she had made her way back downstairs.

Jake, rather touchingly, was emptying a packet of peanuts into a dish. Next to it stood a bowl of Ritz crackers.

'Do you have to? I still don't know why you came.'

You blind bat, can't you see I was jealous? Why else would I leap about in a skip like a demented monkey? Why else would I try and climb up the outside of your house?

Claudia couldn't say it. She gazed hard at a frayed patch of carpet and wondered why getting it together with someone you fancied had to be so fraught. Why couldn't she make something approaching a first move? If Jake really did like her, why couldn't *he*?

For a mad moment she wondered what he would have done if she'd come back downstairs naked, if she'd just ripped off all her clothes and presented herself to him in all her wondrous glory.

But if she had, she would have looked a berk, what with all the crease marks on her stomach from wearing too-tight jeans, not to mention the whacking great bruise on her bottom.

Wondrous glory was hardly the phrase most likely to spring to Jake's mind.

'Here,' he offered her the dish, 'have a peanut.'

I'm such a failure, thought Claudia miserably.

The peanuts were stale. They tasted disgusting.

'Come on, sit down,' Jake urged. '*Raiders of the Lost Ark* starts in a minute. You know, with Indiana Jones.'

Indiana Jones. Wild, brave, reckless and passionate. Claudia, her imagination running riot, wondered if some of that recklessness and passion might rub off on Jake. She sat down cautiously – ouch – at one end of the sofa.

'You'll be more comfortable if you stretch out,' said Jake. 'Put your feet up. Here, have a cushion.'

She uncurled her legs a few inches, wondering if he was inviting her to rest her feet on his lap.

'Am I taking up too much room?'

'Don't worry about me. You're the invalid. I'll sit on the chair.'

'Eh up,' said Poppy at work the following week when Jake accidentally let slip that Claudia had spent Friday evening at his place. 'I saw Claudia yesterday and she didn't mention any of this! Come on, tell. Are we talking true romance here or what?'

'Actually, we're talking about watching *Raiders of the Lost Ark* and sending out for a Chinese. That's all.'

'What? Claudia hates takeaway Chinese! She calls it repulsive slop.'

Jake flushed. This explained why Claudia had left most of hers. Probably not expensive enough for her; he should have ordered a takeaway from the Savoy Grill.

'You aren't telling me everything,' Poppy persisted annoyingly. Her own current state of bliss had got to her like religion. She longed for the rest of the world to be as happy as she was with Tom.

If she'd been a Jehovah's Witness, thought Jake, he could have closed the door in her face. But she wasn't, she was here on the stall, with an awful gleam in her eye.

'Jake, I have to know! Did she stay the night?'

'No!'

'Oh well, maybe that's too much to hope for.' The gleam was still there. 'How about heavy petting?'

'Poppy, stop it.'

'Snogging, then. You must have kissed her.'

There might not be a door to slam in Poppy's face but there was a cash register he could bring down on her head. Taking off his glasses so at least he couldn't see her any more, Jake said wearily, 'No.'

'Not even a weeny one? On the doorstep? A goodbye peck on the cheek?'

Of course he had kissed her, a million times and a million different ways . . . in his dreams. All the time Harrison Ford had been swashing and buckling his way across the screen, sweeping his heroine masterfully into his arms, Jake had imagined doing the same to Claudia. The trouble was, the more he had wanted to, the more firmly he had remained welded into his chair. Crippled with uncertainty, he hadn't dared move so much as a muscle. What if he tried it and she screamed? Or laughed? Or slapped his face?

As for the dreaded saying-goodbye-at-the-front door scenario (surely the ultimate doorstep challenge) . . . well, he *had* been gearing himself up to it. A friendly kiss on the cheek, Jake had assured himself, wouldn't be out of order. Not a slapping offence, at least.

But as Claudia had hovered and he had wavered, a motley crew of lads from the Crown and Feathers had been making their way noisily up the street. Spotting Jake and Claudia in the lit-up doorway they had passed by chanting, 'Give her one, give her one, give her wo-on,' and that had been that. Chance blown.

Hugely embarrassed, realising he couldn't possibly kiss her now, he had taken a step back.

With an awkward little wave Claudia had scuttled across the road to her car and driven off.

Jake looked so sad, Poppy rushed to reassure him. 'Oh

well, never mind, she was only interested in your bank account anyway. And imagine, if you married Claudia, you'd have Angie as a mother-in-law.' She giggled. 'She'd have your Y-fronts off in a flash.'

'How's Tom?' said Jake, because Poppy was easily diverted these days and he didn't want to imagine marrying Claudia.

Poppy heaved a besotted sigh.

'What can I say? He's wonderful. I'm so happy I could burst. The more we get to know each other, the better it gets. I'm meeting all his friends, and he's so *proud* of me.' Dreamily she shook back her hair. 'I know it sounds sick-making, but I had no idea it was possible to feel so . . . so *special*.'

Poppy had got it bad and Jake was glad for her. He just wished it didn't make his own life feel so empty in comparison.

Chapter 48

Tom emerged from the shower drying his dark hair with a towel. He came up behind Poppy, who was sitting cross-legged on the bed doing her eyes with the help of a shaving mirror.

'You look gorgeous. Take that dress off.'

It was Poppy's favourite dress, one of her charity shop bargain buys from Help The Aged. When Caspar had first seen her in it he had whistled and said, 'Help the Aged on their way to a heart attack, more like.'

She grinned at Tom's reflection in the mirror.

'No time for that now. We're supposed to be meeting your friends at eight.'

'Dress,' murmured Tom, unzipping it in one smooth movement, 'off.'

'Oh God, we'll be horribly late.'

But instead of ravishing her body, Tom was pulling a carrier bag out of the wardrobe.

'Surprise.'

Poppy realised he wanted her undressed for quite a different reason. He wanted her out of her short white strapless number with the flirty hem and into a far more elegant affair in navy blue crêpe, with a high neckline and below-the-elbow sleeves. It was calf-length, clearly expensive and extremely grown-up.

'It's beautiful,' she said, touched by the trouble he had taken. If you didn't count the Motorhead tee-shirt Rob had once given her for Christmas, no man had ever bought her clothes before. 'Um . . . do you think it's quite me?'

'This one's nice,' Tom picked up the white dress, then pointed to the navy one Poppy was wriggling into, 'but that one's better.' His dark eyes softened as she zipped herself into it. 'There, see the difference.'

Poppy saw. She looked positively nun-like.

'Don't you like it?' He sounded concerned.

Hastily she looked ecstatic.

'Oh yes, yes! It's just the length. I'm not used to . . . well, so much material.' She kissed him. 'All my dresses are short. But this is . . . it's brilliant.'

He smiled, reassured.

'I prefer long. You're mine, Poppy. I don't want other men ogling your body.'

'Sure you wouldn't like me to sling on a yashmak?'

'No, that's okay. They can ogle your face.' Tom looked amused. 'I'd just rather keep the rest of you to myself.'

They were meeting his friends at a restaurant in Hampstead. Richard Mason worked with Tom and his wife Anna stayed at home to look after their two children.

'You'll like them,' Tom assured Poppy. 'Better still, they'll like you.'

As usual, he was right.

'We've heard so much about you,' Anna told Poppy when they were seated at their table. 'We couldn't believe it when we heard Tom had found you again. It's just so romantic, like something out of a film. Not like Richard and me.' She pulled an unromantic face. 'All we did was get pissed and crash into each other one night in a pub.'

'Ah, but we had a happy ending,' Richard put in. 'I made an honest woman of you, didn't I? And now here we are, two kids and a gerbil later.' He gave Anna's hand a squeeze. 'It might not be the stuff of film scripts but we're a good team.'

When they had ordered from the menu Richard went on, 'Anyway, talking of happy endings. How long before we can expect a bit of knot-tying from you two?'

322

'Oh yes,' Anna exclaimed with longing, 'I could buy a new hat!'

Poppy gulped a lungful of wine and spluttered into her hand.

'We've only known each other a month.'

'Listen, when Tom met you last year he told me he knew in an instant you were The One for him. The other week he said This Is It, Together Forever and other such tosh.' Richard, who played rugby and didn't much go in for soulful declarations of love, mimed sticking his fingers down his throat. A nearby waiter looked alarmed. 'I wouldn't ask, only it's going to be fun watching the secretaries in the office hold a communal wake.'

'Stop it, you're embarrassing Poppy,' said Anna. She leaned across the table, bright-eyed. 'He's such a nosy bugger. Don't tell him, okay? Tell me.'

'Of course we'll be getting married,' said Tom. In his right hand he held his glass. Beneath the table his left hand stroked the inside of Poppy's thigh. 'But big weddings take time to organise. Besides, this is the nineteen nineties. These days it's pretty much compulsory to live together first.'

Poppy turned to stare at him. They had talked about it, of course, but only in a desultory fashion. No definite decisions had been reached.

'You mean . . . ?'

'As Richard says,' Tom grinned, 'why wait? It's what we both want.'

'Fab!' Anna clapped her hands. 'Can we order champagne?'

'You really want me to move into your flat?' Poppy was thrilled but nervous. 'Are you sure? I'll turn it into a terrible heap.'

Tom started to laugh. 'No you won't. It's just a matter of getting you house-trained. Anyway, once you give up work you'll have more time to clear up after yourself.'

Richard was busy ordering two bottles of Bollinger. At the same time, their food arrived.

'Give up work?' echoed Poppy. This was definitely news to her. 'What, and be like a . . . a *housewife*?'

'Why not?' Tom's fingers were still caressing her leg. He looked pleased with himself. 'I can afford to support both of us. Darling, you don't *need* to work.'

'She's in shock,' said Anna. 'Poppy, don't look like that . . . you'll love it! Take it from me, not having to go out to work is the best thing ever.'

Stunned, Poppy glugged down more wine. This wasn't something she had ever considered. Surely, giving up work was what you did once you had children.

'I'm not pregnant,' she blurted out, in case Tom thought she was.

'Give me a chance.' His dark eyes regarded her with affection. 'It's only been a month.'

'Think about it,' Anna went on enthusiastically, 'you'll be a lady of leisure! No beastly early mornings battling through the rain, getting crushed to a pulp on the tube, never having enough time to do lovely things like shopping for clothes because you've got to work instead. I used to be a nurse.' She pulled a face. 'The sister in charge of our ward was a right cow. I tell you, jacking in my job was the best move I ever made.'

The conversation moved on to Bastard Bosses each of them had been forced to work for over the years. Since Jake wasn't a bastard, Poppy used the breathing space to turn Tom's suggestion over in her mind. Okay, she liked her job, but maybe Anna had a point. To be unemployed and forced to survive on some miserable dole cheque was depressing beyond belief, but giving up work knowing you were financially secure was surely the height of luxury. It was why people did the pools, wasn't it? Instead of slaving your life away in some smelly office you actually got to sit back and enjoy all those acres and acres of delicious free time.

I could go to the theatre, thought Poppy, who had never

been to a theatre in her life. I could take long walks, go to coffee mornings, meet friends for lunch, join a health club like Princess Di, have – what were they called? Oh yes, that was it – *pedicures* ...

'What are you thinking?' Tom whispered, his mouth brushing her ear.

It was Poppy's turn to squeeze his leg. He was so perfect for her; he knew her better than she knew herself.

'Just how clever you are,' she murmured back. 'I think I could enjoy giving up work.'

'I love you. I want to look after you.'

It was such a novelty. No one had ever said that to her before. Poppy felt dizzy with desire.

'I love you too.'

It wasn't exactly the surprise of the century but that didn't mean Caspar had to like it.

'I'm moving in with Tom,' Poppy announced, almost bashfully. Her eyes were bright and there were spots of colour high up on each cheekbone.

Tom, who was holding her hand, said easily, 'You've had her long enough. My turn now.'

Haven't had her at all, thought Caspar, hating the way Tom's fingers stroked the inside of Poppy's wrist almost as much as he hated the aura of blissful happiness surrounding them like ectoplasm.

'First you and Babette,' said Poppy, 'now us. It must be catching!'

'Yeah, well, that's great.' Caspar knew he didn't sound as thrilled as he was supposed to sound. 'When are you off? Straight away?'

'Well, Tom's having the bedroom redesigned. The decorators arrive tomorrow and they reckon it'll take a week. So if it's okay with you, I'll move out next Saturday.'

Tom said, 'It'll be chaos until then.'

'It'll be chaos when I move in.' Poppy grinned.

'No it won't. I told you, it's simply a matter of getting you trained.'

Caspar tried to imagine the new, improved, fully house-trained Poppy Dunbar, the perfect Stepford Wife.

'Are you okay? I know it's not much notice,' Poppy put in hurriedly, 'but I can still pay the rent up to the end of the month.'

She was beginning to look hurt. Caspar pulled himself together.

'Don't be daft. Sorry. I was miles away.' He broke into a smile. 'Trying to figure out who we can invite to your leaving party.'

She brightened. 'Oh, you don't have to—'

''Course we do. Next Saturday. It's about time we had another party anyway. It'll be a bloody good bash.'

Poppy looked excited. 'Can I invite everyone from the antiques market?'

'Actually,' said Tom, 'I was planning something for next Saturday. Dinner with the head of our firm. Perhaps you could hold your party on the Friday?'

'Afraid not,' Caspar lied smoothly, for the hell of it. 'I'm busy then. You'll just have to put your boss off.'

Chapter 49

'Daddy! I didn't know you were in London! When did you sneak back?'

It was Saturday afternoon and the phone had been ringing incessantly all day. As word spread that Caspar was holding another of his infamous parties, friends and friends-of-friends had been calling up out of the blue on the off-chance of being asked along.

'Last night.' Hugo Slade-Welch's deep hint-of-Edinburgh voice was as unmistakable as ever. He sounded amused. 'And I don't sneak anywhere. I'm staying at the Hyde Park Hotel for a few weeks, taking a break between films. I wondered what you were doing this evening. Thought I might take my little girl out on the town.'

Claudia melted when her father called her his little girl. He was such a hero in her eyes, not least for having put up with her mother for as long as he had. And it was such an age since she'd last seen him, not since Christmas in fact, when Angie had given him that nude portrait of herself and he had carted it back unwrapped through customs at Heathrow, telling the press he couldn't have hoped for a better Christmas present, his old dartboard was worn right out.

'Oh Daddy, I'd love to see you. But Poppy, who's been living here with us, is moving out tonight. Caspar's holding the most massive party.'

'Is he indeed? What, young people only or are old fogeys allowed in as well?'

'Of course you could come!' Claudia swivelled round as

Caspar, lugging two crates of wine, pushed the hall door open with his elbow. 'It's my father. He'd like to come tonight.'

'Just what we need, more bloody gate-crashers,' said Caspar loudly. 'And a struggling no-hope actor at that.' He dumped the crates and grabbed the receiver.

'Hello, you old bugger. When are you going to get yourself a proper job?'

'Daddy?' said Claudia, when she had wrestled the phone back. 'No, of course you don't have to bring a bottle. I just wondered, are you bringing anyone else?'

'You mean Alice, presumably?' Hugo's tone was dry. 'No, Alice and I have had a parting of the ways. When I left Bel Air she was throwing all her shoes into cases. Shouldn't take her more than a week. By the time I get back next month she'll be gone.' He didn't sound too upset. 'Ah well, at least we weren't married.'

Alice was a silicone-boobed aspiring actress who had once had a walk-on part in *Baywatch*. Or as Hugo had once been heard to remark, a bounce-on part.

'Well, she was too young for you, Daddy.'

'I know, I know. Women are like cigarettes, I guess. A hard habit to break.'

'She was quite fun,' Claudia admitted.

'Oh, Alice was okay. Drew a moustache on that expensive painting Caspar did of your mother.'

'Did she?'

'Mm.' Hugo chuckled. 'And it wasn't on her face.'

By nine o'clock the house was filling up fast. In the sitting room, now minus most of its furniture, music blared. As usual the kitchen was bursting at the seams.

Another crowd of guests piled in through the front door. Luckily it was a warm dry evening, which meant the garden – even if it wasn't the best tended in Cornwallis Crescent -- could be pressed into service to take the overspill.

Caspar was watching Poppy introduce Tom to her friends

from the Markham Antiques Market.

'No wonder she's so besotted,' said Babette, holding out her glass for a refill of Chablis. 'He's definitely gorgeous. Looks like Rufus Sewell.' She raised her brimming glass to smiling lips. 'In fact he's nearly as handsome as you, darling one.'

'What I don't get,' said Caspar with a touch of irritation, 'is the first time he saw Poppy she had her skirt up round her ears. He obviously liked what he saw. So what's with this new look?' He nodded in the direction of Poppy who was wearing yet another long dress bought for her by Tom, a high-necked black jersey affair with a bias cut skirt that swirled just above her ankles. It had clearly cost a great deal and would have suited any number of women to a tee, but it still wasn't Poppy.

'Maybe he wants to make sure it doesn't happen again,' Babette said calmly. 'Some men are like that. It's the whore-madonna thing. They don't mind seeing other girls with their bits on show, but their own wives and girlfriends are another matter.'

Crossly, Caspar said, 'I know that, but what the hell's Poppy doing, going along with it? She looks about forty.'

'She's flattered.' That was the thing about Babette; she had all the answers. 'He adores her and she loves it that he cares. It's why some women stay with their men, even when they're being battered senseless every Friday night. They think it shows they care.'

'Christ.' Caspar wondered wildly if that was why Poppy was keeping her legs hidden. Maybe beneath all those yards of exquisitely draped jersey her thighs were beaten black and blue. He experienced a sudden urge to rush up to Poppy and do a Bucks Fizz, rip her skirt clean off . . .

Thinking better of it, he poured himself another drink. It crossed his mind that Tom Kennedy was clearly the possessive type and that upstairs in his studio he still had, somewhere, the interesting selection of photographs taken

329

of Poppy getting up to all sorts while he and Claudia had both been away.

Caspar shook his head. Bloody hell, what was the matter with him tonight? As if he didn't know. He was more jealous than he'd ever been in his life and it wasn't a happy experience. Of course he wouldn't stoop so low, shatter Poppy's newfound happiness . . .

It would just be nice if someone else did.

'Look, there's Claudia,' said Babette excitedly. 'With her dad. Now that would be a catch. Imagine handling *his* PR.'

'Oh no, what's *she* doing here?' wailed Claudia as Angie, in a flesh-coloured chiffon dress and the highest of high heels, made her impressive entrance at nine thirty. She looked more burnished and golden than ever and her perfume was apparent even at twenty paces. Before she had time to do more than wave gaily across at her daughter and ex-husband she was accosted by Caspar's sculptor friend, all but foaming at the mouth with lust.

'Darling, I assumed you'd invited her. When she rang me this afternoon I mentioned I was coming along to your party tonight. All she said was fine, we'd bump into each other then.' Hugo's smile was rueful. 'Should've known better, I suppose, after all those years of practice. My dear ex-wife evidently hasn't lost her touch.'

'She'll tell me I've put on weight.' Claudia, who had, looked miserable. For weeks now she hadn't been able to stop thinking about Jake. Unfortunately she hadn't been able to think about him without reaching for the biscuit tin. She had put on a terrifying seven pounds and the bugger of it was, he still hadn't phoned.

When an extremely famous person puts in an appearance at a party, the non-celebrities generally pretend they haven't spotted him. Only when they know for sure he can't see them will their eyes swivel furtively in the VIP's direction.

Not Dina.

'Oh wow, you're Hugo Slade-Welch!' she squealed, charging up to him and all but ricocheting off his broad chest. 'Am I a big fan of yours! I've seen all your films. You were brill in *Black Thursday*. I'm Dina, a friend of Claudia's – hi, Claudia – God, I can't believe I'm standing here talking to you, I've never met a film star before! Here, have a fag.'

Claudia glared at Dina, who was thrusting a crumpled packet of Embassy Regal practically up her father's nose. This girl really did have an endless supply of nerve. And to say she was a *friend* of hers . . .

Hugo, looking amused, said, 'Actually, I don't smoke.'

'Oh well, never mind. You can still autograph the packet.'

'Daddy, why don't we—?'

'Hang on, not so fast. Who's got a pen around here? Hugo, how about you?'

Claudia was about to spontaneously combust at the chummy use of her father's Christian name when she realised Dina was actually pulling open his jacket. Locating a fountain pen in Hugo's inside pocket, she whisked it out.

'Ooh now, there's posh! I might have known a big star like you would have a real ink job. And feel how heavy it is! How much did that set you back?'

'Dina—'

Claudia's eyes were almost as narrowed as her mouth. Snotty bitch. Dina refused to be cowed.

'Okay, no need to get your knickers in a twist. I'm not going to nick it. Here –' she offered the uncapped pen back to Hugo – 'tell you what, real ink won't work on the fag packet. How about autographing me instead?'

Dina was wearing a sequinned boob tube and skin-tight blue satin trousers. She thrust her chest forward and pointed to the area midway between the top of the tube and her left collarbone.

Outraged, Claudia hissed, 'Do you have any idea how stupid you're making yourself look?'

'Come on, it's only a bit of fun! Everyone'll think it's a tattoo.'

'Leave my father alone.'

'It's okay, really,' Hugo placated his angry daughter. In an attempt to defuse the situation he smiled and winked at both of them. 'I've been asked to autograph stranger parts of the anatomy in my time. Claudia, would you be an angel and fetch me another drink?'

All Claudia wanted to do was slap Dina's ridiculous over-made-up face, but her father was clearly anxious to avoid a scene. She stomped off, cannoning into people on all sides, unaware that Dina's cigarette had burned a neat hole in the back of her dress.

'Please excuse my daughter,' said Hugo, his famously blue eyes twinkling. 'She is rather protective.'

'Jealous, more like. What with your last girlfriend being exactly the same age as me. And I'm very into older men,' Dina told him, cleverly blowing her cigarette smoke out sideways so it didn't go straight in his face. 'You can understand why she's worried. If we got married, I'd be her step-mother.'

'Now there's a thought.' Since Dina was still pointing to her chest, Hugo leaned forward and signed his name with care. 'You aren't married yourself then, I take it?'

'Well . . . kind of. But you know how it is. If a better offer came along it wouldn't be a problem.'

'That can't be easy for you.' Hugo was sympathetic. 'I mean, a lovely young girl such as yourself must receive offers all the time. I daresay they're hard to resist.'

He's chatting me up, thought Dina, so dizzy with excitement she could hardly breathe. Here I am, in London, at a party so glamorous you aren't even expected to chip in for the booze, being chatted up by an honest-to-goodness movie star.

In an instant her mind conjured up a whole series of thrilling fantasies: Dina and Hugo whizzing round the world

on their private jet . . . sunning themselves on the deck of a
yacht . . . arriving at the Oscars ceremony hand in hand . . .
being photographed for *Hello!* magazine . . .

'So Hugo, what kind of car do you drive?'

'Well—'

'D'you know what I'd have, if I was loaded? A bright green
Rolls Royce.'

'Well now, that sounds a wonderful choice.' He smiled
down at her. 'I did own a Silver Shadow many years ago—'

'Are they good? I'd still rather have a Rolls. Tell you what,'
said Dina, slipping her arm through his, 'why don't we go
out into the garden? Before that old crosspatch Claudia gets
back.'

Chapter 50

Claudia wasn't in any hurry to get back. If her father was so set on humouring Dina – and he was famous for his patience with members of the public when they took the liberty of introducing themselves – she didn't want to be around to witness it. Serve the silly old fool right.

She had just finished pouring Hugo a quadruple Scotch when Angie materialised at her side.

'Darling, you forgot to send me an invite! If Hugo hadn't mentioned it this afternoon I'd have missed the party altogether.' Ostentatiously reaching up on tiptoe she kissed her daughter's rigid jaw. 'And look at you in a pretty new dress. Such a shame about the cigarette burn.'

'Where? Oh *no*!'

'Never mind, make a few more holes and pretend it's the latest Vivienne Westwood. Where's Hugo?'

'Talking to some little tart.'

'Oh well, what's new?' Angie looked amused. 'You don't look terribly cheerful, my darling. If there's some kind of problem, tell Mummy.'

Well Mummy, you see the thing is, I'm completely besotted with someone and I don't know if he likes me and I'm way too embarrassed to ask and he's really shy so he might fancy the pants off me but he keeps his feelings so much to himself it's just about impossible to tell.

'I'd rather die,' Claudia said aloud. 'Since when were you interested in my problems anyway?'

'I love hearing about problems! I'd make a wonderful

agony aunt,' Angie protested, laughing. 'If only people would have the nerve to take my advice.'

Nerve was what Angie possessed in abundance. Claudia definitely didn't want to be Angie but she wished she could have inherited a bit more nerve. It was a handy thing to have around. Especially right now.

Jake was heading almost straight for them. He was wearing the plain dark blue sweater and a pair of the well-cut trousers Poppy had chosen for him. His dark hair, freshly washed, was flopping onto his forehead. Behind the tinted gold-rimmed spectacles his dark eyes searched the room. He looked so smart and so quietly handsome Claudia felt her heart leap into her throat like a fish. And he had come in search of *her*.

'Jake,' she said, because he was in danger of veering off to the left.

'Oh. Hi.' He stopped dead and the look on his face told Claudia he hadn't been searching for her at all. 'Um . . . I thought Marlene would be in here. How . . . how are you?'

'Oh, I'm fine. Yes, fine.'

Jake hesitated then said, 'Fallen off any good windowsills lately?'

It was meant to be a light-hearted quip, an ice-breaker, and it was clearly a line he had prepared earlier, like a Delia Smith soufflé.

Except Delia's soufflés never fell this flat.

Angie, her tinted eyebrows up in her hairline, said, 'Heavens, I *am* intrigued.'

Claudia took a gulp of her drink, clean forgetting it wasn't her drink. She had never been able to get to grips with Scotch.

'Aaargh.' Spluttering helplessly, unable to swallow the burning liquid, she was forced to spit it back into the tumbler. Her eyelids felt as if they were on fire.

'You must excuse my daughter,' Angie said smoothly, 'she has the manners of a wart-hog. I'm Angie, by the way. And of course I've heard all about you! Now Jake, what an enthralling remark. There must be a story behind this. Do tell.'

'Mother—'

'Claudia, throw that Scotch-and-saliva away before someone else drinks it. And go and clean yourself up, you've got dribble on your chin.'

In desperation Jake said, 'Actually—'

'No, no, I insist,' Angie lowered her voice a conspiratorial octave. 'I can't wait to hear what my daughter gets up to on windowsills when I'm not around.' Reaching up, she smoothed a section of hair behind Jake's left ear. 'There, that's better. It was sticking out. Goodness me, what glossy hair you have, you must take tremendous care of it. And I adore your aftershave.'

'I'm not wearing any.' Jake looked nervous. 'It must be deodorant.'

'Mum, please.'

'No, it's definitely not Mum. And Claudia, what did I just tell you to do? Chin, darling. Chin.'

'It's going to seem weird here without you,' said Caspar. Tom, who had barely left Poppy's side all evening, was deep in conversation across the room with one of Caspar's artist friends, who had once been an architect. 'We'll miss you.'

'Me too.' Poppy grinned. 'Listen to us. Anyone would think I was disappearing up the Amazon. We'll still see each other.'

'Yeah.'

'We will! Tom's already said we must have you and Babette over for dinner.'

'Well,' Caspar struggled for something to say, 'that sounds . . .'

'Like your idea of the dinner party from hell,' Poppy suggested drily. 'I know. Babette and I haven't exactly hit it off. And you and Tom didn't get off to the greatest of starts. But he did say he liked Babette.' She pulled a face. 'She's

336

got her act together, apparently. Tom approves of people whose acts are together.'

Now there was a thought. Caspar glanced across the room at Babette, chatting animatedly to a tall antiques dealer. Poppy followed the direction of his gaze.

'Can I ask?' she said suddenly. 'Why *did* you marry her?'

But Caspar's expression was unreadable. He raised his glass of Beaujolais to the light, apparently studying the colour.

'Because you told me to.'

'Really?'

'I thought it would simplify matters. And I wanted to know what being married would be like.'

'And has it? Simplified matters?'

'Of course.' Was Caspar mocking her? It was impossible to tell. 'Only one notch on my bedpost nowadays. I'm a respectable married man.'

'You must still get chatted up.' Poppy was disbelieving. 'That hasn't stopped, it can't have.'

Caspar broke into a grin. 'Oh, I get my share of offers. But being married is a great excuse for saying no. They don't get offended. Some of them are even impressed.'

'I'm definitely impressed.'

'So how about you?' Swiftly Caspar turned the tables on her. 'Are you happy? Sure you're doing the right thing?'

Poppy gave him a strange look.

'Of course I'm sure.'

'Because—'

'What a bloody stinking awful pig of a party,' howled Claudia, barging up to them. 'If there wasn't such a queue for the bathroom I'd slash my wrists.'

Caspar said, 'Don't tell me. Someone else has turned up wearing the same dress as you.'

Claudia commandeered his glass and downed the contents in one.

'My unspeakable mother is chatting up Jake. My father is

337

being chatted up by your even more unspeakable friend Dina. And some total bastard has burned a sodding hole in my dress.' Gathering up material from the back, Claudia showed them the evidence. 'If I find out who did it, I'll kill them.' Her eyes narrowed to slits. 'Does that look like the kind of hole an Embassy Regal would make?'

Poppy left them to it. She had spotted Rita in the doorway.

'I'm so glad you're here.' She hugged Rita, who was wearing an orange and white polka-dotted frock and matching shoes. 'I thought you weren't coming.'

'Said I would, didn't I?' Rita lit a cigarette. 'Never been one to miss out on a good party. How's it going?'

'If you don't want to be depressed, steer clear of Claudia.' Poppy took her arm. 'Come on, let me introduce you to some people.'

'Don't worry about me, love. I don't need looking after. Just point me in the direction of the drinks. When I see someone I like the look of, I'll introduce myself.'

It was dark outside in the garden, apart from the coloured lights Caspar and Poppy had strung up somewhat haphazardly in the trees.

'Aren't they pretty?' sighed Dina, gesturing dreamily with her cigarette at a ball of lights Caspar hadn't been able to untangle. 'It's like a fairytale. Like . . . Cinderella.'

'Mind your glass slippers don't get stuck in the mud.'

She looked down at her stiletto heels, ringed with earth and leaves.

'That's not very romantic. Fine Prince Charming you'd make.'

Hugo smiled. 'I'm rather afraid my Prince Charming days are over. Far too old.'

Dina's stomach did a cartwheel. She flicked her cigarette into the bushes and turned to face him.

'I don't think you're too old. I said, didn't I? I like older men. Especially you.'

She half-closed her eyes, waiting for him to kiss her. They were away from the house, unobserved. All he had to do was take a step forward and pull her into his arms.

But Hugo tilted his head to one side and gave her a look of affection mingled with genuine regret.

'Oh, my dear. It's delightful young things like you who get men like me into trouble.'

'I wouldn't.' Dina shook her head eagerly. 'Honest. I'm on the Pill.'

Hugo's mouth twitched.

'You're very sweet. Nevertheless, maybe we should be making our way back to the house. Before people start to wonder where we are.'

Claudia waited until Jake had taken her mother's empty glass and disappeared in search of a refill. She was over in a flash.

'Hello darling, fancy bumping into you again so soon,' said Angie. Claudia had been scowling at her from a distance for the past ten minutes. She unclipped her evening bag, took out a mirror and calmly re-did her lipstick. 'I must say, I can quite see why you're so keen on Jake. What a poppet.'

A *poppet* . . .

'You always have to ruin everything,' hissed Claudia, 'don't you?'

'Ruin everything?' Angie looked surprised. 'Baby girl, I had no idea there was anything to ruin. I assumed he was a free agent. I'm sorry, are you saying you and he are a couple?'

'You know I'm not!' Claudia spoke through gritted teeth. 'You just come out with the most embarrassing remarks, like, "I've heard all about you." Viciously she imitated her mother's words. 'That was a lie for a start. I've *never* told you about Jake.'

Angie's smile was pure Cheshire Cat.

'I didn't say you had. Caspar did, while I was sitting for my portrait. He told me all about your crush on Jake.'

Bloody Caspar.

'But that was months ago,' Angie shrugged. 'Let's face it, sweetheart, if he was interested he'd have made his move by now.'

Since there was no answer to that, Claudia scowled and said instead, 'So what were you talking about?'

'Oh, money mainly. Jake's little windfall . . .'

'How typical.'

'. . . how to spot gold-diggers . . .'

'Well, you'd know about that,' Claudia said bitterly.

Angie looked at her. 'You should try smiling occasionally, darling. It does wonders.'

'Don't—'

'Just a suggestion. Ah, there's your father. Speaking of gold-diggers, who *is* that frightful creature with him? He looks as if he needs rescuing.'

As Angie drifted away, Claudia wondered if the evening could possibly get worse.

Chapter 51

Bursting for the loo, Dina excused herself seconds before Angie reached them. She slipped into the downstairs cloak-room, relieved herself, then studied her flushed reflection in the small mirror above the basin.

Hugo Slade-Welch had called her delightful. And sweet. He fancied her like mad, she knew, but was holding himself back because he thought it was the gentlemanly thing to do.

Dina, whose maxim when it came to make-up was more-is-more, rummaged around in the bottom of her shoulder bag. She applied an extra layer of metallic Bahama Blue eye-shadow, another generous coat of blue mascara and re-did her lipstick. When someone tried the door handle she called out, 'Hang on a sec,' but as her mouth was in lipstick-receiving mode at the time, the words came out oddly. Hey, Dina marvelled, I sound dead posh.

But there were evidently two people on the other side of the door. A woman, in a low voice, was saying '. . . but darling, where on earth did you find her? Talk about Girl at C & A. I can't believe you brought her over with you from the States! I mean, she'd still be in quarantine . . .'

When Dina heard Hugo's unmistakable laugh, she froze.

'Angie, didn't anyone ever tell you? You're supposed to mellow with age.'

'I am being mellow. I could think of far worse things to say about her. Come on, Hugo, spill the beans. Who is she and where *did* you pick her up? King's Cross?'

Dina's hands were shaking so hard she almost dropped her lipstick in the basin.

'Do I look as if I found her anywhere?' she heard Hugo reply with amusement. 'She found me. I hadn't been here more than ten minutes when she latched herself onto me. Her name's Dina, she knows Poppy and Claudia and she's spent the last hour telling me how much she loves older men, especially ones who star in Hollywood movies. She made me autograph her chest, she told me I should try a splash of Pepsi in my Scotch. As for Girl at C & A,' he added drily, 'you couldn't be more wrong. She told me herself, her boob tube cost seventeen pounds ninety-nine at Top Shop.'

Dina didn't know why this should be so funny but it clearly was. Angie snorted with laughter and Hugo joined in. She clutched the sides of the basin as Hugo, recovering himself, went on, 'And when I said I was due to play Othello at the Royal Court next year, she said yeah, Charles Dickens is brill, she's seen all his films but *Oliver!* is her favourite.'

Dina didn't move. Eventually she heard Angie say, 'Darling, whoever's in that loo has obviously died. Could you be an angel and find me another drink? I'm going to have to run upstairs.'

When they had both gone, Dina looked up again at her face in the mirror. Bahama Blue tears ran down her cheeks and plopped steadily into the basin.

When the door bell rang at ten thirty, Caspar answered it.

'Bloody late as usual,' he grinned at Patrick Dennehy, who was lugging a huge canvas-shaped parcel tied up with brown paper and a lot of frayed string. 'What's this, homework?'

Patrick was the evening class tutor at St Clare's, which wasn't the kind of career he'd dreamed of during his art student days but was still better than the dole. Since his arms were aching, he thrust the parcel at Caspar with some relief.

'Kind of. Here, you can take these through. Presents for the girls.'

'Great,' lied Caspar. Patrick was an old friend but his paintings were crap, hopelessly modernist and quite without meaning. Still, it was a kind gesture. Caspar just hoped Claudia would be diplomatic when the paintings were unwrapped.

He had to clear a space in the sitting room for the opening ceremony. Neither Claudia nor – more surprisingly – Poppy seemed overjoyed to see Patrick there.

'Try and look thrilled,' Caspar murmured in Claudia's ear. 'It's probably three black splashes and a blue triangle. Patrick's only ever sold one painting in his life. And that was to his mother.'

It was like pass-the-parcel. Both paintings had been extremely thoroughly wrapped. By the time the last layers were ready to come off, the carpet was strewn with brown paper and a sizeable crowd had gathered to watch.

Claudia, who had thought the night couldn't get any worse, realised it could. She screamed and tried to cover the painting up with a crumpled sheet of paper which had unaccountably shrunk.

A howl of protest went up from the audience.

Next to her, Poppy froze. 'Oh shit.'

'You bastard,' wailed Claudia, swinging round to glare at Patrick.

'You didn't paint those,' said Caspar, starting to laugh.

'I didn't say I had.' Deeply offended by such a suggestion, Patrick failed to see what all the fuss was about. 'One of my students did them. Mike Cousins. When I mentioned I was coming here tonight, he asked me to bring them along.' He turned back to Claudia. 'Mike bumped into you the other week, right? He was worried you might have got the wrong idea and thought he'd wanted you to buy the picture. He didn't mean that at all, he just wanted you to have it.'

Claudia just wanted to die. One of Caspar's friends had whisked the brown paper from her grasp, leaving the painting exposed for everyone to see.

And, dreadfully, everyone had. Some people were laughing, others applauding. Next to her, pink to the hairline and similarly humiliated, stood Poppy.

'Mike wanted you to have yours too,' Patrick assured her. 'You don't have to buy it. It's a gift.'

To add insult to injury, Mike Cousins was an enthusiastic artist rather than an accomplished one. He had given Claudia a hint of a squint and a right breast larger than the left.

Poppy hadn't fared much better – one arm was longer than the other and her hair looked like a wig put on in a rush – but at least she was thin. Depressingly, one aspect of Claudia's figure Mike Cousins had got off to an absolute tee was her awful undulating stomach.

Caspar came up and stood between them. He put his arms around Poppy and Claudia and said, 'You both look great.'

Jake, over by the doorway, agreed. Seeing Claudia naked was something he had dreamed of. And he wasn't disappointed. She looked beautiful, even more beautiful than he had imagined. He adored every curve, every perfect voluptuous inch of her . . .

'Christ Almighty, who's the blob?'

The voice, loud and slurred, belonged to a late arrival. Jake didn't know him but he appeared to have tagged along with a group of Caspar's friends. He leaned in the doorway, his arm draped around the waist of an anorexic-looking brunette.

'Shut up,' said Jake.

The bloke grinned. 'Come on, look at it! What a whale! Imagine getting trapped under something like that.'

The room fell silent. Glancing across at Claudia, Jake saw the anguish in her eyes.

'Move,' he instructed the skinny girl.

She looked blank. 'What?'

Jake placed her to one side and punched the smirking heckler so hard he was catapulted through the doorway. Out in the hall, sprawled on his back on the floor, the man

344

groaned loudly and clutched his face.

'You've broken my nose . . .'

'Good,' said Jake. He wrenched open the front door, surprising two more late arrivals on the doorstep. 'Now get up and get out. You too,' he told the skinny brunette, who was kneeling beside her boyfriend, using the hem of her cheesecloth skirt to wipe the blood from his face. 'Come on, out you go.'

The open-mouthed couple on the doorstep stood aside to let them past. When they had gone Jake said, 'Sorry about that. You can come in now.' To be on the safe side he added, 'You're friends of . . . ?'

'We aren't really friends of anyone,' replied the girl, who was plump and sensibly dressed. 'We're just looking for someone. Maybe you can help us,' she went on, sounding like an efficient policewoman making enquiries. 'Her name is Dina McBride.'

Claudia had disappeared upstairs. Caspar gathered up the offending paintings and dumped them in the broom cupboard out in the hall.

'Well,' said Tom icily, 'that was fun. Anything you'd like to do as an encore? Rip your dress off, maybe, and dance on the table? After all, it's hardly going to make a difference now. Everyone here already knows what you look like.'

His eyes glittered, reflecting his disgust.

Since there wasn't much else she could do, Poppy attempted to brazen it out.

'It was just a bit of life-class modelling,' she said lightly, with a shrug. 'I don't do it any more. I needed to earn some money to pay the rent. I thought I'd *told* you about St Clare's.'

She hadn't, of course she hadn't. For this exact reason.

'No, you never did. I think I might have remembered.' Tom's jaw was set like concrete. 'Jesus. I wondered how you could afford to live in a house like this. How long ago did you stop doing it?'

'February. Three months ago. Before I met you.'

'And how have you been managing to pay the rent since then?' His gaze flickered dangerously in the direction of Caspar. 'In kind?'

After the von Kantz had sold at auction, Jake had doubled her salary. Tom knew that.

Poppy looked at him.

'What are you trying to say, you don't want me to move in with you? It's all over between us? You don't want to see me any more?'

Tom didn't speak for several seconds. Finally he shook his head.

'Don't be stupid, of course I still want you to move in. I love you, Poppy. More than words can say. You know that.'

The tiny hairs at the back of Poppy's neck were standing to attention. Abruptly a lump came into her throat.

'But—'

'Come here,' murmured Tom, drawing her to him and wrapping his arms tightly around her. 'You silly thing. If I didn't love you I wouldn't care, would I? But I do care. You're mine and I want to be the only man who sees you without clothes.' He kissed her, lingeringly, then stroked her pale cheek. 'I want to keep you all to myself.'

'Um . . . excuse me,' said Jake, embarrassed to be butting in. 'Poppy, some people are here looking for Dina. I can't find her. Any ideas?'

Extricating herself from Tom's embrace, Poppy turned and came face to face with the man she had once so nearly married, Rob McBride.

Chapter 52

'Rob!'

'Hello, Poppy.'

She felt her mouth drop open. This party was in danger of becoming seriously bizarre. Who was going to turn up next, Elvis?

Rob was suffering from something approaching shell-shock himself. The last time he'd seen Poppy had been on the morning of their supposed wedding. When she had scuttled off to London he had imagined her living in some godawful bedsit. He'd certainly hoped it was godawful anyway.

But he had been wrong. Instead she was here, in this palatial house where wild parties were held, huge parties where gate-crashers got their noses broken and good-looking men strolled through the hall, clutching paintings of the girl he had once almost married. Only the one glimpsed by Rob had been no ordinary painting . . . in this one Poppy had definitely been *naked*.

To add to the air of surreality, he was almost sure the middle-aged man standing less than three feet away from him was the film star Hugo Slade-Welch.

'Rob. It's nice to see you again.'

He pulled himself together.

'Yeah, you too.' A small lie. It was downright weird seeing Poppy again. And that bloke over there definitely *was* Hugo Slade-Welch. 'Sorry . . . uh, this is Alison.' Awkwardly he made the necessary introductions. 'My fiancée.'

Poppy smiled and nodded and said 'Hi.' Dina had told her all about Alison, the nurse with the unfortunate ankles. Unable to help herself, she glanced anklewards. Yep, there they were. Alison's legs, encased in woolly blue tights, went straight down. She was wearing sensible shoes with real laces.

'Sorry, I'm a bit confused,' said Poppy. 'Did Dina invite you along to the party?'

'I'd better explain.' Rob was still staring goggle-eyed at Hugo Slade-Welch so Alison put herself in charge. It was what she was good at. 'Ben didn't want Dina to come here tonight. They had a major row and she stormed out. The thing is, as far as Ben's concerned, this is the last straw. He's in a dreadful state, but absolutely determined. If Dina doesn't come home tonight, their marriage is over. He'll divorce her. He says he never wants to see her again and he'll fight for custody of little Daniel.' Alison paused for a second. Ever practical, she added, 'He probably won't win, of course. The courts almost always favour the mother. But he does mean it. If we can get Dina back tonight, they can try again. Otherwise that's it; Ben's had enough.'

'Oh Lord.' Poppy bit her lip. If the remarks Dina had been making recently were anything to go by, they might as well book the solicitors now. She had a sneaking suspicion Dina would declare this the best news she'd heard all year.

'So you see why we had to come. Sorry to have intruded on your party. We tried phoning a few times but it was always engaged. In the end we thought we'd better drive up.'

'Alison found the address in Dina's diary,' Rob put in. He didn't add what else they had found in the diary. 'Ben doesn't know we're here.'

Poor Ben. Poppy peered in desperation over the heads of the milling guests. She hoped Dina wasn't nearby doing something horribly indiscreet.

'She could be anywhere. Why don't you two help yourselves to a drink now you're here? Let me go and look.'

But she found Dina almost straight away, sitting on her

own on a wooden bench at the bottom of the garden.

'What happened to your make-up?' said Poppy, joining her. Dina was sitting very still, gazing blankly ahead.

'Washed it off.'

'Have you been crying?'

'No.'

Since it was obvious she had, Poppy proceeded with care. 'Rob and Alison are here. They want to take you back to Bristol. Look, I heard about your fight with Ben. If you don't go home tonight, he's going to divorce you.'

'Okay.'

'Okay what?' Poppy leaned closer. Dina didn't even sound like Dina. 'Okay you'll go back or okay he can have a divorce?'

Dina heaved a long sigh. 'I'll go back.'

This was so unlike her Poppy thought there must be a catch.

'Really?'

As Dina took out a cigarette her hands trembled. The brief flare of the match lit up her face. Fresh tears slid down her white cheeks.

'Oh Poppy, I thought I could do it. I thought I could change my life, like you changed yours . . . for the better. But I can't. It's no good, I just bloody can't. It worked out for you but it wouldn't work for me.'

'I don't get it.' Poppy frowned; an hour ago Dina had been in tearing spirits. She couldn't imagine what must have happened to knock her down like this. 'Has somebody said something to you?' Claudia, perhaps? Surely not Caspar . . .

'Not to my face.' Dina's voice wavered. 'But it's what they say behind your back that counts, isn't it?'

'Who?' For a wild moment Poppy wondered if Caspar had been leading Dina on.

'Doesn't matter who. Everyone probably. Anyway, sod them.' Dina ground her cigarette out with her heel and stood up. 'I don't care any more. I've got a husband who loves me. And a baby. I may as well go back home.'

349

Worried, Poppy said, 'Do you love them?'

'Of course I do.' Dina's answering smile was bleak. 'Oh, I know I said I was sick of it all, but that was when I thought I could find something better up here. Meet someone richer, more exciting. Like you did.' She shoved her cigarettes and matches into her bag and looked down at the angry red mark on her chest. Hugo Slade-Welch's scrawled signature had taken ages to scrub off. 'But now I know I can't, I'll be all right. Might even have another baby. Ben's been going on about a little brother for Daniel for months.'

'You might have a girl.'

'Yeah.' As they made their way back to the house, Dina gave Poppy's arm a squeeze. 'Poor kid, if we do. We'll just have to hope she doesn't take after me.'

'Now there's a blast from the past,' remarked Hugo, inhaling pleasurably as he found himself next to Rita. 'That takes me way back. All of a sudden I'm twenty-five again.'

'In your dreams,' replied Rita good-naturedly.

'Mitsouko. Guerlain. I'm right, aren't I?'

She nodded. 'My husband bought it for me.'

'I haven't smelled it for years. Reminds me of a beautiful woman I once knew, back in Edinburgh. I was madly in love with her.' Hugo's eyes crinkled. 'Sadly, her husband had bought her that scent too.'

'Did you have an affair with her?'

'Even more sadly, no. She wouldn't. I was a penniless drama student, not much of a catch. And she was a lady of expensive tastes.'

'I bet she was gutted when you became famous.' Rita looked entertained. 'Did you ever hear from her again?'

Hugo shook his head.

'But for years, every time I was interviewed on television, or one of my films was being shown, I imagined her sitting at home watching me. And hoped, of course, that she was . . . gutted.'

'If she'd really loved you she wouldn't have minded you being skint. When I met my husband he didn't have a bean.'

Unlike Poppy, Hugo was able to tell real diamonds from fakes.

'And what does he do now?' he enquired with genuine interest.

'Nothing much. He died in January.'

Hugo was appalled. 'I'm so sorry.'

'On the other hand,' Rita went on easily, 'he could be getting up to all sorts. We don't know, do we? He might be having a high old time, banging away on some piano, vamping it up with Louis Armstrong and Count Basie, playing up there in the clouds where the bar never closes, the beer's free and the audience always knows when to clap.'

'Your husband was a jazz pianist!' Hugo looked delighted. 'I'm a bit of a jazz buff myself. Would I have known him?'

'He wasn't famous. Alex Fitzpatrick. I shouldn't think you'd—'

'Alex Fitzpatrick? I have heard of him! I even saw him playing once, many years ago, at a club in Soho. He was excellent. I say, what a small world.'

'Bugger it!' exclaimed Rita as a blonde trailing a handbag squeezed past. Looking down, she saw that the clasp on the girl's handbag had caught against her tights. When she bent her knee to examine the hole, a ladder promptly slithered the length of her leg. She rolled her eyes at Hugo Slade-Welch. 'Shit, don't you just hate it when that happens?'

He started to laugh. 'Where are you going? Don't disappear . . . we've only just met. I don't even know your name.'

'Rita. And if you want to make yourself useful, find me another gin and tonic.' She moved away, trailing Mitsouko. 'That way you can guarantee I'll be back.'

'Sorry to interrupt, pet, but look at the state of my tights. Is there an all-night garage anywhere near here, or a late-opening corner shop?'

351

'I've got a spare pair.' Poppy, who had just waved off Dina, Alison and Rob, was talking to Jake. Luckily, Rita's torn tights were Barely Black. 'Same colour, one-size-fits-all, still in the packet.' Feeling madly efficient she said, 'You can have those. Hang on a sec, Jake . . .'

'Don't worry, I can get them. Just tell me where to look.'

Following Poppy's directions Rita made her way downstairs. The tiny bedroom Poppy had occupied for the past eight months was almost empty now, most of her belongings having already been packed into suitcases and moved into Tom's flat. The narrow bed was stripped, the wardrobe empty. Only an overnight case remained, crammed with toiletries and the contents of the bedside table. The tights, Poppy had explained, were somewhere in the case.

Rummaging carefully, Rita found them near the bottom. As she slid the oblong pack out, her rings clunked against glass. Silly girl, thought Rita, glimpsing the silver edge of a photograph frame squashed against a can of hairspray, that could get broken.

She pulled an ancient pink tee-shirt out of the bag, to wrap around the glass and keep it in one piece. Then she levered the photograph frame upwards.

The woman in the photo, smiling up at her, was instantly recognisable.

She stood in a small garden, holding a newborn baby in her arms.

She was wearing a white blouse and a full, flower-patterned skirt, and her curly hair was tied back from her face with a white scarf.

She was, Rita realised, Poppy's mother.

And although there was no date on the back of the photograph Rita also knew when it must have been taken.

Nine months, give or take a few weeks, after she had broken her leg.

Chapter 53

Jake knocked on Claudia's bedroom door.

'Go away.'

'No.' Standing his ground he said firmly, 'It's me. I want to come in.'

When Claudia opened the door, her eyes brimmed at the sight of him.

'What a fiasco. Has everyone stopped laughing yet?'

'No one's laughing. Nobody has laughed. Why would they?'

'Oh come on.' She rubbed her face with the sleeve of her dressing gown. '*I* would have, if it hadn't been me. As my mother once so thoughtfully pointed out, I've got more spare tyres than Kwik-Fit.' Almost as an afterthought Claudia added wearily, 'Thanks, by the way. For punching him.'

Exasperated, Jake said, 'Why do you suppose I did?'

'Because there are some things it's kinder not to say.'

'Dammit, what's the matter with you?' shouted Jake. 'I punched him because what he said wasn't *true*.' Reacting physically had unleashed something in him; the adrenalin was still pumping, making it easier to say what he had never before had the courage to put into words. His dark eyes were alight with almost missionary fervour. 'You looked beautiful . . . dammit, you *are* beautiful. If you don't want the painting, I'll have it. I could happily look at that portrait of you every day for the rest of my life.'

Masochistically, Claudia whispered, 'But he called me a blob.'

'And did you see that stick of celery with him? That scrawny girlfriend of his? Some men like shrimps,' Jake declared with reckless abandon. 'Others prefer... well, langoustines. Stop *looking* at me like that,' he went on, close to despair. 'I wouldn't say it if I didn't mean it. And I don't make a habit of punching people, either. I've never done it before ... oh, don't cry. He isn't worth it. He deserved to be punched.'

'I'm not crying because of him,' Claudia sniffed. Her dressing-gown sleeve was really quite soggy now. 'I'm crying because I'm h-h-happy.'

I will never, ever, understand women, thought Jake.

But Claudia, who had made up her own mind, moved towards him. If she was going to do anything, it had to be now. Jake had rushed to protect her earlier. He had called her beautiful. He had even – well, it was the thought that counted – told her he preferred langoustines to shrimps.

She kissed him. On the cheek. Just a peck.

Jake stopped being angry. Instead he looked nervous. Not very romantically he said, 'What was that in aid of?'

'I just wanted to do it.'

'Why?'

This was make or break time. Claudia heard the sound of her own blood drumming in her ears. She took a shuddery breath and threw herself into the breach.

'Why d'you think? Because I've wanted to do it for months but I never knew if you liked me, but now I think maybe you do after all. Because *you* never kiss *me*. Because ... because you're hopeless and it's about time one of us did something. Now, shall I try again or would you rather I didn't?'

There, she'd said it. God, thought Claudia, I feel sick.

Jake smiled.

'Try again. Definitely try again. I'd much rather you did.'

'You came back.' Evidently relieved, Hugo Slade-Welch

handed Rita the gin and tonic he had been holding onto. 'You've been ages. The ice has melted.' He glanced down at her shapely legs. 'All okay now?'

'What? Oh . . . yes. All okay.'

'You're looking more cheerful.'

'I've just made a discovery.' Rita nodded. 'You know that feeling you get when the last piece of the jigsaw slots into place?'

'I'm not a great one for jigsaws,' Hugo admitted. 'I like crosswords though.'

There was laughter in Rita's eyes.

'Either way. It's a great feeling, isn't it? Suddenly figuring everything out?'

Hugo nodded. He didn't have a clue what she was talking about, but he knew what he wanted to say next. He had spent the last ten minutes rehearsing his lines.

'Look, I'm staying in London for a while. Say if you don't feel up to it, but would you like to come out with me one evening? Have dinner, maybe, and visit a jazz club afterwards?' He glanced across, trying to gauge her reaction. 'We could go to Ronnie Scott's.'

'It's a funny thing,' Rita mused, 'all those years with Alex, I used to think I couldn't stand jazz. It wasn't until he died and I found myself going through his old LPs I realised I'd got to like the stuff after all.'

'Is that a yes?'

She looked tolerantly at Hugo. 'What is this, a set-up? Did Poppy tell you to be kind to me? There's no need, love. Really. I'm fine as I am.'

'I'm not being kind. I'd like to get to know you better, that's all.' Hugo was wounded. 'And I've never been turned down before. Please say yes, for the sake of my ego if nothing else.'

'Tights all right?' said Poppy, joining them.

'They're fine.'

Rita's smile was affectionate. There was no hurry; she

could tell Poppy about her discovery another time. And she could give her the other photograph too. It would mean a lot to her—

'Poppy, do something,' Hugo pleaded. 'I've invited this lady to have dinner with me and she's making excuses. I'm on the verge of rejection here. Help.'

'It's too soon, love. Nothing personal, I just wouldn't feel right. Ask me again in a year.' Rita patted his arm equably. 'That's if you aren't married again by then.'

'But—'

'Don't try and argue,' said Poppy. 'Not with Rita. She had the best husband in the world. You can't compete.'

The party finally broke up in the early hours. Caspar stood in the lit-up doorway seeing out the last of the guests. Earlier he had watched Tom carry Poppy's overnight case to the waiting taxi, and had thought how like an amicable divorce it felt as Poppy, hesitating on the doorstep, had slipped her still-warm front door key into his hand.

'Thanks for everything,' she had whispered almost shyly, brushing Caspar's cheek with her lips. 'And the party. See you soon.'

'Darling?' Babette appeared behind him, holding his leather jacket. She had to be up at six, for a breakfast meeting with a new client. 'Ready?'

'You go.' Caspar knew he wouldn't sleep. 'I've got some work to do. A painting to finish.'

Babette raised her eyebrows sympathetically. 'Sure?'

'Sure.'

'Okay darling. Make it a masterpiece.' She lifted her face up to his for a kiss. 'See you when I see you. 'Night.'

Caspar took a half-full bottle of warm Chablis up to the studio with him and began to paint. He wasn't in the mood but anything was better than sleeping. Or thinking.

He especially didn't want to think.

* * *

At four o'clock in the morning the phone rang. Caspar picked it up.

'Hello?'

'What are you doing still there?' whispered Poppy. 'I wanted to speak to Claudia.'

'Bit of an odd time for a girly gossip, isn't it? What's wrong, did nobody ever tell you the facts of life?'

Clearly put out, she hissed, 'I wasn't expecting you to answer the phone.'

'I'm working. And Claudia isn't here. She left with Jake and a terrifying smirk on her face.'

'Oh.'

'Won't I do?' asked Caspar.

Sounding nervous, Poppy whispered, 'This is embarrassing.'

'What's it about? Contraception? Come on, you were going to ask Claudia. Ask me instead.'

'Okay.' He heard her rapid breathing. 'I was going to ask Claudia to leave a key under the mat.'

'Who for?' Caspar was less than enthusiastic. 'Not Dina again.'

'No. Oh Caspar.' For the first time, Poppy's voice broke. 'Can I come home?'

Back on the front doorstep, Caspar watched as the taxi pulled up at the kerb and Poppy – this time carrying her own cases – jumped out. It was like déjà-vu on rewind.

At least the long black dress had gone. Poppy's hair swung loose around her shoulders and she was wearing a white shirt tucked into tightly belted Levi's.

'Get inside,' said Caspar, taking the two largest cases from her. 'What was that business with the bracelet?'

The silver bangle she always wore had disappeared with the taxi driver.

'Couldn't pay my fare.' Poppy avoided looking at him. 'Oh God, I'm sorry about this. Am I a prat or what?'

In the sitting room Caspar plonked her down on the sofa

357

amid the party debris and pushed an abandoned drink into her hand. Her face seemed okay, but you could never tell.

'What happened, did he hit you?'

'Hit me?' Poppy looked amazed. Then she sank wearily back into the sofa. 'He didn't hit me. I almost wish he had. It'd make all this a damn sight easier.'

'All what?'

Poppy pushed her fingers through her hair. Her sigh blasted a layer of ash from a nearby ashtray.

'It's no good, I can't do it. Tom . . . *worships* me. I know how stupid that sounds, but he does. And it's too much. He loves me too much. If I stayed with him I'd . . . well, I'd drown.'

'He doesn't love you too much,' said Caspar. 'He's just possessive. Jealous. Desperate to keep you to himself. If he loved you,' he added, unable to resist pointing it out, 'he'd have bought you a dress that suited you. Not a bloody marquee.'

'I was flattered,' Poppy said sadly. 'Nobody's ever cared that much before. I thought it was so great . . . so romantic.'

'So you've left him.'

'It's a good job I wasn't expecting you to be sympathetic.'

Poppy's look of indignation was adorable. Bottle it, thought Caspar, and you'd make a fortune.

'Is that what you want? Sympathy?'

She lifted her face to him. 'I know. I'm sorry. The party must have cost a bomb.'

'Sod the party. Your moving out was only an excuse to throw one,' said Caspar.

'And now I want to move back in.' She bit her lip. 'Can I?'

'Am I likely to say no?'

'Thanks.' Poppy drank her drink and pretended she hadn't really been nervous at all. After a while she said, 'I've been so stupid, kidding myself everything was all right.'

'Why?'

'Because I desperately wanted it to be, I suppose.'

'Should have listened to me,' Caspar said lightly. 'I knew he wasn't right for you.'

Poppy heaved a sigh.

'The trouble is, I knew it too, practically from the start. I just wouldn't admit it to myself.' She paused, lost in thought, then glanced up again at Caspar. 'He was jealous of you, you know.'

Caspar grinned. 'Surely not.'

'He said did I have to snog you in front of everyone, as we were leaving earlier.'

'Oh yes?'

'I said it wasn't a snog, and anyway I'd been living here since last September, if anything was going to happen between you and me it would have happened by now.'

Caspar felt his heart begin to race. He picked up an abandoned cigarette packet; annoyingly it was empty.

'Would it?'

'Well, before you got married, anyway.'

He spotted a crumpled Marlboro pack behind a cluster of glasses on the mantelpiece and went to investigate. Bingo, three left. His hand unsteady, Caspar lit one.

'Poppy, listen to me—'

But when he turned to face her, she was crying.

'Shit, what a mess. I've done it again, haven't I? Run away.'

'But it was the right thing to do.'

'All I ever wanted was to be happy.' Poppy grabbed a crumpled-up napkin and sobbed into it. 'God, I'm such a failure. There must be something horribly wrong with me. Why can't I meet someone like you did? Why can't it be for me like it is for you and Babette?'

'Poppy, stop crying and listen—'

But when she started, Poppy didn't stop easily. With a wail she held a cushion over her face.

'Mmf Tom mmmff mff furry mmf...'

'What? I can't hear you.' Leaning across, Caspar whisked the cushion away. '*What* did you say?'

Red-eyed and miserable, she gazed up at him.

'I said Tom's going to be furious when he finds out.'

Chapter 54

Furious wasn't the word. Caspar, enjoying every moment and making only a token effort not to show it, lay across the sofa with his feet up pretending to watch The Open University.

Poppy stood with her back to the bottle-strewn fireplace. Tom endlessly paced the room.

'Can't we at least have some privacy?' he demanded, glaring at Caspar's suntanned feet. The fact that they were propped up on the arm of the sofa seemed to annoy him more than anything else. 'This is ridiculous. Does he have to be here?'

'I want him to stay. I'm not going to change my mind,' said Poppy. 'You shouldn't have come. I told you not to.'

'Shouldn't have come?' Tom stared at her in disbelief. 'Are you mad? You left me a *note*, Poppy. I woke up this morning and found a fucking note, telling me it was all over. Did you seriously expect me to leave it at that?'

'Well, yes.' Poppy deliberately didn't look at Caspar, who was half-killing himself trying to keep a straight face. 'It was what you did, to Jan, after you met me. The only difference is you did it on the phone. I heard you, remember?'

'That was different,' he shouted. 'That was only Jan. We weren't even living together.'

Poppy stood her ground. 'Neither were we. Two and a half hours doesn't count.'

'But we were going to get *married*,' Tom raged, unable to understand why he wasn't getting through to her. 'This is ridiculous. Poppy, you can't *do* it.'

'I can. I have. It wouldn't work,' she told him simply. 'I'm staying here.'

Tom's black eyes blazed.

'Who put you up to this?' Furiously he jabbed a finger in Caspar's direction. 'Him? What happened when you were making that exhibition of yourself on the doorstep last night – did he make you a better offer?'

'Now you're just being stupid,' Poppy wailed. 'I told you before, there's nothing going on between Caspar and me. He's *married*.'

Caspar, gazing steadily at a sociologist in flares being witty on the TV screen, thought, So I am; I nearly forgot.

'Oh my God,' shouted Claudia, jerking awake and clapping her hands over her ears as an alarm clock three inches away from her head exploded into life. 'Turn that thing OFF!'

'Sorry.' Leaning across, Jake silenced the terrible jangling. He hadn't even been asleep. For the past hour he had been watching Claudia beside him, reminding himself that last night really had happened and wondering if it was humanly possible to be happier than this.

She groaned aloud and squinted at the clock.

'It's eight o'clock. On a *Sunday*.'

'There's a car boot sale in Hertfordshire.'

'A car boot sale . . .'

The look of undiluted horror on Claudia's face brought Jake out in goosebumps.

'I won't go. It's just what I normally do on Sundays. I set the alarm yesterday, before the party. Before . . . oh hell,' he shook his head in resignation, 'this is a good start.'

Claudia lay back against her tartan pillow, overcome with remorse. I'm so used to feeling miserable, she realised, I've forgotten I don't need to be any more.

'My fault. I'm a terrible grouch.' Her fingers brushed Jake's bare shoulder, cold to the touch because in her sleep she'd managed to hog most of the duvet. How typical of him, she thought with a rush of love, not to have grabbed it back.

By the time Jake had finished making the coffee and carried it upstairs, the bed was empty and the shower was going full pelt next door. When Claudia emerged ten minutes later she was fully dressed.

Having rather hoped for a repeat performance of last night, his face fell.

'You're going?'

'Not unless you want me to.'

'I don't want you to.'

Claudia took one of the mugs from him. Crossing the room, she drew back the faded blue curtains. Sunlight poured in. 'It's morning. Sure you still respect me?'

Jake said quietly, desperately, 'I *love* you.'

'Oh Jake.' Claudia bit her lower lip, willing herself this time to say the right thing. 'If you truly mean it, then I love you too. But you'll have to be patient. I'm not used to being happy and I'm not used to being nice. I'm especially not used to men being nice to *me*—'

Clumsily, since they were both still holding brimming mugs of coffee, Jake kissed her. He felt Claudia's mouth begin to tremble against his own.

'Come on. You aren't going anywhere.' With his free hand he began unbuttoning her navy cashmere cardigan. 'Let's go back to bed.'

Claudia wanted to, like anything, but the urge to start being nice – to show Jake she could be if she really tried – was overwhelming.

'No.' She pulled away, wincing as hot coffee slopped over the back of her hand. 'I want you to take me to a car boot sale.'

Jake, who would a million times rather have stayed in bed, said, 'But—'

'I mean it. Get dressed,' Claudia told him firmly. 'We're going to Hertfordshire.'

* * *

363

'Well well, it just goes to show the quiet ones are always the worst.' Angie, phoning up for a post-party gossip, sounded amused. 'We did wonder what had happened to you after that thrilling punch-up. And what a very Clint Eastwoody thing to do! Who'd have thought dear old Jake had it in him?'

'Mum—'

'And how wildly romantic, darling! What did he do, carry you off into the sunset on his white Vespa?'

'Don't you dare make fun of Jake,' said Claudia, her knuckles turning pale around the receiver. 'I mean it, don't start. I love him and he loves me. I'm happy. Just this once, don't try and ruin everything, okay?'

'Sweetheart, as if I would!' Angie sounded contrite. 'Baby girl, I *want* you to be happy. Daddy and I were discussing it at the party, in fact – saying wouldn't it be wonderful to see you off that lonely, dusty old shelf.'

Pride mingled with recklessness.

'Yes, well, maybe I'm off it now.'

Claudia had to hold the phone away from her ear. For a small woman, Angie had a loud laugh.

'What's so funny?'

'Oh sweetheart, have a bit of fun with Jake by all means. But you can't seriously want to spend the rest of your life with him!'

'Why not?' Claudia countered hotly. It was what she wanted more than anything.

'Darling, darling.' At the other end of the line Angie was still gurgling merrily away. 'Jake's a nice enough lad, bless him. But let's face it, he's hardly going to set the world alight. He's not exactly a thrill-a-minute merchant, is he?'

'For God's sake, I don't want—'

'Listen to me, Claudia, I'm your mother. I know you and I know the kind of man you need. A risk-taker! Someone to make your pulse race! Someone,' Angie declared passionately, 'who rides a Harley Davidson, not a Vespa.'

Claudia howled, 'Jake doesn't have a Vespa!'

'I know he doesn't. I talked to him on Saturday night, remember?' Her mother's tone was cutting. 'He drives a van.'

Claudia was still boiling with rage when Jake and Poppy arrived at the house an hour later. Jake, who had given Poppy a lift home from work, was looking forward to taking Claudia out to a popular new Italian restaurant in Fulham. Now, to his dismay, Claudia was insisting she was too wound up to eat.

'You can share my Welsh rarebit,' said Poppy, who knew Jake was ravenous. She offered him the least burnt slice, which he wolfed down in seconds. Generously – because she was hungry too – she gave him the rest.

'My mother is the bitch of bitches,' Claudia seethed.

Poppy tore open a packet of chocolate digestives and emptied them onto a plate.

'Yes, but what exactly did she say?'

'I can't tell you.'

'Why not? Was it something awful about me?'

'No.'

Jake finished the last of the incinerated Welsh rarebit and reached for a biscuit.

'I expect it was about me.'

Claudia didn't deny it, so he knew he was right. He shrugged and helped himself to another biscuit.

'Don't let her get to you. It doesn't bother me.'

'She just doesn't want me to be happy. She always has to stick her oar in.'

If Jake wasn't bothered, Poppy didn't see why they couldn't all know what Angie had said to upset Claudia so much.

'Go on, you may as well tell us,' she wheedled. 'What *did* she say?'

It was a relief to blurt it out.

'That Jake isn't very exciting.'

Jake looked amused. 'I'm not very exciting. I already know that.'

'She said what I needed was a man to make my pulse race. Someone who takes risks. A red-hot chilli pepper,' Claudia recited bitterly, 'not a wet lettuce.'

Jake rather wished he hadn't asked now. He pretended not to mind.

Across the table Poppy sensed his discomfort. Rushing to his defence she declared, 'Chilli peppers make my eyes water and my nose run. And some lettuces are great. You could be a cool iceberg, Jake. Or a drop-dead trendy lollo rosso.'

But Poppy was trying too hard to help. Jake wondered if maybe Claudia was upset because there was an element of truth in what Angie had said.

'*Is* that what you want?' he said quietly. 'A risk-taker? Someone who'd make your pulse race?'

'No thanks. My mother has spent her life making my pulse race.'

Claudia stared hard out of the window. She loved Jake, she really did, but Angie's cutting remarks had unsettled her. Outside, it was raining. A sleek, dark green Lotus shot up the street, the driver tooting his horn in appreciation as he passed a pretty girl in a miniskirt. Across the road, parked beneath dripping plane trees, stood Jake's rusty old van with Landers' Antiques stencilled across the side.

'How about some ice cream?' suggested Poppy brightly. 'I've got Chunky Monkey or New York Fudge Crunch.'

'Vanilla?' asked Jake.

'That's so boring! Come on, live a little.'

Abruptly Claudia turned away from the window.

'We'd better get a move on. Our table's booked for seven thirty.'

'You said you didn't want to eat.' Jake looked startled.

'I changed my mind. I do now.'

'But I've just . . .' he gestured towards the empty plates littering the table. Between them, he and Poppy had finished the whole plate of biscuits. 'I'm not hungry any more.'

'Oh I don't believe this!' shouted Claudia. 'You are so

selfish. All that money of yours and you won't even take me out for a lousy pizza.'

Poppy stared at her.

'Claudia, you said you couldn't eat a thing. You can't blame—'

'It's okay,' Jake cut in, 'we'll go.' He knew why Claudia was so on edge. He just wished she wouldn't drag his money into every argument they ever had.

'Mind your tights, by the way, on the passenger seat,' Poppy called out as they left the house. 'There's a hole in the plastic with a spring sticking out.'

Claudia, who was wearing a cream linen dress and Donna Karan ten-denier stockings, said, 'Your van is the pits. Why don't you buy something decent?'

'I am. I've ordered a brand-new one.' Jake looked pleased with himself.

'I didn't mean another *van*. Why can't you get a Mercedes? Or . . . or a Lotus?' she demanded fretfully. 'You can afford it.'

Chapter 55

'Oh flaming Nora, what are you doing here?' groaned Rita, opening the front door with a headful of fluorescent pink curlers and no make-up. .

'I came to apologise.' Hugo modestly inclined his head and handed her a bunch of tiger lilies.

'Blimey, no need to bow. I'm not the Queen.' Grinning, she took them from him. 'Come in. Sorry about the hairdo. Serves me right for thinking you were the milkman. Anyway, what have you got to apologise for?'

'I didn't know if I'd offended you the other night, inviting you out to dinner.' Hugo followed her through the vast wood-panelled hall and into the swimming-pool-sized kitchen. He watched Rita fill a fluted vase with water and begin to arrange the flowers. 'Do you remember what Poppy said, that you had the best husband in the world and that I couldn't hope to compete? Well, I've been a pretty lousy husband in my time and I'm not even trying to compete. But I would very much like us to be friends.'

While not strictly true, it would do for a start. Hugo didn't know why he should have been so instinctively drawn to Rita. She was hardly his usual type. But there was something about her, maybe something that reminded him of the women he had knocked around with back in the old days in Edinburgh, those lusty, straight-talking, honest-to-goodness *real* women he had known – and frequently bedded – before acting had changed his life and the fiendish Hollywood bug had bit.

Rita regarded him shrewdly, her head on one side.

'Friends, eh?'

'Purely platonic,' Hugo assured her.

'All the rage, is it, in California this year?'

He liked the way she made fun of him, refusing to be impressed by his fame. Although with a house like this, he thought dryly, why on earth should she be impressed?

'Oh, absolutely. The latest thing. And so much less painful than body-piercing.'

Rita cackled with laughter, stifled a cough and patted the pocket of her cardigan. 'Bugger, I forgot.'

'Forgot what?'

'Gave up smoking yesterday. I keep thinking it's time for a fag. It's murder.' She pulled a face. 'Can't see me lasting.'

'In that case, what you need,' said Hugo, 'is the help and support of a friend. A non-smoking platonic friend,' he added in his most beguiling tone, 'to take your mind off the fact that you've given up.'

He took Rita, minus fluorescent rollers, to Little Venice. They ate lunch at The Glassboat, a floating restaurant moored on the Regent's Canal, and listened to the jazz being played by a quartet out on the deck. The sun shone and the sky matched Hugo's cobalt blue shirt. Rita's dress, which was peony pink shot through with lilac, clashed exuberantly with the restaurant's Rosie-and-Jim style decor.

Hugo, as deft a storyteller as David Niven, told Rita how utterly hellish each of his marriages had been, and showed her the photographs in his wallet, of his three glossy ex-wives. He carried them with him at all times, he explained with suitable gravity, as a salutary reminder never to do it again.

'Maybe I should carry a picture of a packet of Rothmans.'

To steer the subject away from cigarettes, Hugo said, 'Do you have a photo of your husband with you?'

She shook her head.

'Don't need one. I can remember what he looks like.'

'Tell me all about your happy marriage –' he refilled their

369

coffee cups – 'and your perfect husband. I want to hear about Alex.'

'He was a wicked old bugger and he made me laugh.' Rita heaped sugar into hers. 'But he wasn't perfect. He was no Jane Asher.'

Hugo raised a quizzical eyebrow. 'Would you have wanted to be married to Jane Asher?'

'She'd be a whizz with home-made Christmas decorations.'

'Ah, but sit her in front of a jazz piano and what would she do?'

Rita roared with laughter.

'Stencil it.'

After lunch they walked along the canal path.

'I want a cigarette.'

'Here, hold my hand instead.'

'Can I smoke it?'

Hugo took her hand anyway.

'Try patches. They worked for my agent and he was a twenty-a-day man.'

Only a lifelong non-smoker, Rita thought affectionately, could think twenty a day was a lot.

'I was a fifty-a-day woman.' She looked depressed. 'Anyway, why d'you suppose I'm wearing long sleeves? I've already got a week's supply slapped on all over me. Underneath this dress I look like Mr Blobby.'

It was five o'clock when they arrived back at Rita's house, almost five fifteen by the time she'd finished deactivating the elaborate security system.

'It's a bugger but you have to have it. D'you want a drink or is it time you were off?'

Hugo, following her into a sitting room so big you'd need binoculars to watch television, realised she wanted him to leave. Feeling distinctly put out, because he'd thought she was enjoying his company – and because nobody ever wanted him to leave anywhere – he made himself comfortable on an indigo velour upholstered sofa.

'I'll have a brandy, thanks.'

He watched Rita pour two incredibly small measures.

'There you go. Cheers.'

Before Hugo had finished saying cheers back, her drink had vanished. She was hovering in front of him, willing him to drink up and go.

'Well, thanks for today. It's been great, really. I've enjoyed it.'

'But,' drawled Hugo.

Rita looked evasive. 'But what?'

'But it's time I left? But it's time for your bath? I don't know,' said Hugo. 'You tell me.'

'I thought you'd have other plans. Places to go, VIPs to see.'

'No.'

'Oh.'

She was jittering; he could see it. If he reached across and touched her it would be like resting his hand on the bonnet of a Volkswagen Beetle.

Hugo said evenly, 'Why do you want me out of here?'

'I d-don't—'

'Unless you have a secret lover tucked away upstairs.'

'Ha ha.' Rita laughed nervously.

'Or, better still, a secret stash of cigarettes.'

'You sod!' She went bright red and covered her face with both hands. 'Oh God, and after all your hard work. I'm so ashamed . . . what must you think of me?'

'I think you're human. And being with you today hasn't been hard work. Go and get them.' Enormously relieved, he added, 'Now, can I stay?'

He insisted on peeling the nicotine patches off Rita's arms first.

'Otherwise you'll overdose.'

'Ouch!' She winced; he was being careful but it still hurt. 'This is worse than having your legs waxed.'

'Sorry. Tenacious little buggers. There, last one. You can light up now.'

'Bliss,' sighed Rita, taking her first toe-tingling drag. 'Right, we'll have a proper drink this time.' She grinned happily at Hugo. 'You pour, I'll forget to say when.'

The level in the brandy bottle went steadily down. Swathed in smoke, Rita relaxed visibly, regaling him with stories of growing up in the East End.

'So when did all this happen?' Hugo gestured around the sitting room, at the three chandeliers, the football-pitch sized carpet, all the gold-plated trappings of wealth. 'And how did it happen?'

'Property deals.' Rita stubbed out a cigarette and promptly lit another. 'Buying, doing up, selling on. That old routine. You know the kind of thing.'

'Yes, but—'

'And then two years ago,' she continued blandly, 'a high-risk deal came off. In Spain, it was. This massive company was so desperate to get their hands on our bit of land, we could pretty much name our price. Alex thought of a number, doubled it, and the daft buggers said yes. We made three million, overnight.'

'Whereabouts in Spain was this?'

'Barcelona.'

'I know Barcelona quite well,' said Hugo, who wasn't an actor for nothing. If Rita could lie through her teeth, so could he. He'd make a far better job of it too. 'Which company negotiated the deal?'

Rita's eyes flickered. She tried to light another cigarette, then realised she already had one on the go.

'God, I can't remember. Los something . . .'

'Loss of three million, I should think.' Hugo leaned towards her, his mouth twitching. 'Come on, you can tell me. What really happened?'

Rita looked even more agitated than when she hadn't been allowed to smoke.

'I can't . . .'

'If it helps at all, I asked Poppy when I rang her to get

your address. She seems to think Alex was something to do with the Great Train Robbery.'

'My Alex? He couldn't have robbed anyone to save his life! Anyway, he got travel-sick on trains.' Flustered, Rita tried to stub out her lighter. She sighed. 'It wasn't anything illegal, okay? Oh hell . . . the thing is, we made a pact never to tell anyone. It just seemed safer, easier . . . people can get so *funny* . . .'

She rubbed the ash off the gold Cartier lighter. Hugo was sitting there looking at her, not saying a word.

But he's come up from nothing, thought Rita; he's got money now, enough to appreciate the problems.

In fact if anyone could truly understand why she and Alex had done what they had, it was Hugo.

'People *do* get funny,' she said again, psyching herself up to confess. 'When you've got money and they haven't, they treat you differently. If you've earned it, at least they can respect you for that. It's when you haven't earned it they really give you a hard time.' She took a gulp of brandy; she'd started, now it was too late to stop. 'Two years ago, me and Alex watched one of those documentary thingies on TV, about people who'd won tons of money and how it had fucked up – sorry, *messed* up – their lives. They didn't know who their friends were any more. They got hate mail. Death threats. They argued about how much to give to their relatives. Their marriages broke up, they wished they'd never won it . . . I'm not kidding, it was real Hammer Horror stuff, the scariest thing I've ever seen.'

Still Hugo didn't speak.

'Well, you can guess the rest,' Rita went on. 'We said right, that was it, no more lottery for us. Except Alex had already bought our tickets for Saturday's draw.' She paused then said simply, 'Three days later, we won.'

Margaret McBride looked as if she'd won the lottery and lost her ticket. When Ben and Dina finally clattered into the sitting room that night, she greeted them with a disapproving glare and her arms tightly folded across her chest.

'It's one o'clock in the morning,' she announced grimly, 'and you promised to be back by eleven. It's downright inconsiderate, that's what it is.'

Dina, clinging to Ben's arm, did her best not to giggle. Ben nudged her in the ribs and tried to look suitably apologetic.

'Mum, we're sorry, we didn't mean to be late—'

'But you are,' his mother interjected, 'and being sorry just isn't good enough. Apart from anything else, the pubs shut at eleven. I can't imagine what you've been doing for the last two hours.'

Dina couldn't help it; a great snort of laughter escaped and she had to hide her face in Ben's shoulder. If Margaret McBride knew what they'd really been up to, she'd have a heart attack. Making riotous love in the bus shelter around the corner simply wasn't what respectable married couples did in their free time.

'Margaret, it won't happen again, I'm really, really sorry.' Dina made an effort and pulled herself together. 'There was a party at the pub, an after-hours thing, that's why we're late. How was Daniel, anyway? Did you manage to settle him all right?'

Her mother-in-law's expression softened. Daniel was the absolute light of her life.

'No trouble at all. Went out like a light.' She looked proud. 'He's always a good boy for his Nan.'

'I don't know what we'd do without you, Mum,' said Ben, because outrageous flattery always went down well.

'The best babysitter in the world,' echoed Dina, secretly sliding her fingers under Ben's shirt at the back and running them up his spine. She stifled a grin as he squirmed and made a dash for the kitchen.

'I'll put the kettle on, shall I? Mum, fancy a cup of tea before you go?'

Margaret McBride hesitated, then smiled and nodded.

'Just a quick one then.' Now why was Dina giggling like that? Still, at least the girl seemed more cheerful these days. 'So you enjoyed yourselves this evening,' she said to her daughter-in-law. They'd apologised for being late; she couldn't be cross with them for long. 'Had a good time, by the look of you.' Not to mention a few drinks.

'Oh yes, we definitely enjoyed ourselves. It was brilliant.' Dina realised as she said it that she meant every word. She nodded happily. Who would've thought you could have so much fun with your own husband? 'We had the best time in the world.'

Chapter 56

'Smile,' said Jake, 'you're frightening the customers.'

Poppy knew she was looking down in the dumps. It suited her mood. Down in the dumps was how she felt.

'I'll read this, then they won't be able to see my face.' She reached for her dog-eared copy of *Miller's Guide* and opened it at random.

Rifling through the pages didn't help. Poppy chewed her thumbnail and gazed morosely at the photographs: a pair of Tiffany peridot and diamond earrings, pairs of candelabra, *endless* pairs of wheelback, ladderback and splatback chairs . . .

With a mammoth sigh she slammed the book shut, making Jake jump.

'What is it?' He knew something was up. Poppy hadn't even been able to finish her mid-morning banana doughnut.

'Nothing. Just . . . oh, nothing.'

'Tom?' Jake looked worried. He wished he'd never tracked Tom Kennedy down now. The fairytale happy ending hadn't taken long to turn sour.

'No.' Sensing his discomfort, she managed an invalid's smile. 'I'm glad I got out when I did. And I'm glad you found him for me. If you hadn't, I would always have wondered. It's just such a let-down,' Poppy said sadly, 'spending your whole life believing in love at first sight then discovering it doesn't exist. It's worse than finding out about Father Christmas.'

The tatty *Miller's Guide* slid off her lap. When she leaned over and picked it up, it fell open at a page of Staffordshire figures, every one a perfectly matched pair.

'Ohhh,' Poppy wailed in frustration, convinced the book was doing it on purpose. 'Couples, couples everywhere I bloody look! It's not *fair*.'

Trying to help, Jake said, 'You'll find someone else.'

Wearily, Poppy turned and looked at him.

'Oh, I've found someone else.'

'You have? Who?' Bewildered, he wondered why, in that case, she was so miserable.

'Doesn't matter who.' Poppy looked evasive. 'He's already one of a pair.'

Jake was shocked. 'You mean he's married? Poppy, are you mad? How could you get yourself involved with a—'

'I'm not,' she intercepted, her cheeks reddening. 'Anyway, he wasn't married when I met him.'

'For God's sake, Poppy.'

'I didn't *want* it to happen.' Poppy rolled her eyes at his stupidity. 'You can't always help who you fall in love with. You of all people,' she added, unable to resist the dig, 'should know that.'

Jake ignored it.

'Look, having an affair with a married man isn't the answer.'

'I'm not having an affair with him. And don't preach at me,' Poppy said sulkily. 'Stop sounding like a Relate counsellor.'

Thank goodness there were no customers within earshot. Jake, determined to make her see sense, said, 'Listen to me, Poppy. Get out while you can. It's for your own good. They never leave their wives. Promise me,' he said urgently, 'please promise me you won't see him again.'

Poppy had finished chewing her thumbnail. She'd chewed so far down it hurt.

'Could be tricky.' She examined her thumb. 'Seeing as I live in his house.'

377

Up until now Jake had somehow assumed she'd fallen for a fellow trader, most probably the dark-haired, notoriously charming – and married – ceramics expert who was always timing his coffee breaks to coincide with hers.

But Caspar . . .

He opened his mouth to speak.

'Don't,' Poppy blurted out. 'Just don't, okay? I know it's totally pathetic of me. Dammit, I know better than anyone what Caspar's like!' She was twiddling her hair furiously, a sure sign of agitation. 'And you don't have to lecture me – I'm not planning to do anything drastic. It's like measles. I'll get over it.' She winced as a strand of hair got caught up in her earring. More entanglements. Irritably she said, 'Claudia did. I suppose I will too.'

Whoever said confession was good for the soul? Some berk. Poppy was already deeply regretting telling Jake.

He was still looking appalled.

'Does Caspar know?'

'Are you mad? Of course Caspar doesn't know! Nobody knows.' It occurred to Poppy that newly-in-love people had a sickening habit of telling each other everything. 'And you aren't going to tell anyone either. Especially not Claudia.' She gave Jake a deadly, I-mean-it look. 'If you breathe a word, I'll break your new glasses.'

Jake still missed his old, taped-together pair, the ones Poppy had so triumphantly snapped in half.

He looked rueful. 'What's new?'

Claudia was surprised how easy it had been to feel comfortable in Jake's house. Accustomed as she was to opulence, elegance and space, clutter and fraying curtains weren't her line of country at all. But somehow the fact that his style was less *Homes and Gardens*, more *Exchange and Mart*, didn't bother her nearly as much as she expected it to. The effect was cosy, undemanding, as relaxed as Jake himself.

More and more easily, Claudia realised, she could

envisage living here. Threadbare carpets weren't the end of the world. Besides, she thought, once I persuade Jake to part with a bit of money we can buy new ones. Together we could really do this place up.

That evening, having come straight from work to his house, she had made a lasagne and opened a bottle of Chianti. Another thing she loved about Jake was how appreciative he was of her cooking.

'This is terrific. Better than Findus,' he told her as he mopped up the last of the sauce with ciabatta.

This, coming from Jake, was the ultimate compliment. Glowing with pleasure, Claudia caught sight of her candlelit reflection in the big mirror behind him. She looked so bright-eyed and happy, for a split second she barely recognised herself.

'It's Poppy's favourite. She's always nagging me to make it.'

Jake poured more wine.

'Maybe we should have invited her over here tonight. There would have been enough for three.'

'I prefer it like this,' said Claudia. 'Just us. Anyway, Poppy's been such a grouch lately. She even had a go at me last night for leaving my clothes in the washing machine. I mean, honestly, the nerve of that girl! I told her she had a bloody cheek and the next thing I knew, she'd dragged all my stuff out of the machine and dumped it on the floor.'

'She's going through a bad patch,' said Jake, ever the peacemaker.

'Don't start feeling sorry for her! If you ask me,' Claudia pronounced bluntly, 'she's behaving like a spoiled brat. Everything Poppy wants, Poppy gets. Even Tom Kennedy, thanks to all *our* hard work. And then what does she do? Dumps him, for no sensible reason at all. I still can't figure out why. What was wrong with him, for heaven's sake? Nothing, that's what.' With an air of triumph, Claudia waved her fork at Jake. 'Which is why she's being so grumpy now,

I bet you anything. She regrets it. She probably went to see him and begged him to have her back, and Tom told her to take a hike. Well, good for him,' she declared roundly. 'Serves Poppy jolly well right.'

Having a go at Poppy was one thing but elevating Tom to hero status was quite another. Claudia made him sound like Rhett Butler telling Scarlett he didn't gave a damn.

This was so unfair Jake couldn't – simply couldn't – let it pass.

'Look, if I tell you something,' he lowered his voice, 'will you promise, absolutely *promise*, not to breathe a word to another soul?'

Claudia leaned towards him. She adored secrets.

'Jake, you can trust me! What is it? Of *course* I won't tell.'

Chapter 57

Having spent a long afternoon upstairs in the studio, working on a canvas commissioned by a wealthy factory owner – 'Summat blue and green, lad, to hang in t'boardroom' – Caspar was cleaning brushes over the sink.

As Claudia switched the kettle on, the phone rang.

'Oh hi,' said Babette's voice. 'Is Caspar with you?'

'Hang on, he's covered in paint. I'll have to put the phone to his ear.'

'Don't worry, I just called to remind him about tonight.' Babette sounded cheerful. 'We're off to a bash at the Wellington Gallery. Tell him I've got his jacket back from the cleaners, I've booked the cab for eight thirty and if he's hungry there's a dozen oysters sitting here waiting for him.'

'Heavens, you know what they say about oysters.'

'Yes, well, the cab can always wait.' Babette was laughing. 'Damn, there goes my other phone. Blow him a kiss from me, okay? Tell him to hurry home. Byeee.'

Caspar nodded when Claudia relayed the message, and carried on cleaning his brushes.

'She won't keep the cab waiting. Babette's never been late for anything in her life.'

Claudia, who liked Babette, said, 'She's exactly right for you. The perfect wife. I can't imagine what you've done to deserve her.'

He grinned. 'Maybe I'm a perfect husband.'

'Are you?' Daringly, overcome with curiosity, Claudia said, 'Are you faithful?'

'Don't look at me like that. Yes, I am.'

When Caspar had finished cleaning himself up with another spirit-soaked rag, she passed him his coffee. Across the hall, the clock struck six.

'Poppy should be home by now.'

'Been and gone,' said Caspar.

'Really? Where?'

He looked out of the kitchen window at next door's cat launching itself at a starling.

'For a walk, she said.'

'A what?' Claudia was incredulous. 'Poppy doesn't go for walks.'

Caspar shrugged. It had happened the last three or four times he had come to the house. Poppy had made some bizarre excuse or other and promptly disappeared.

'Looks like she does now.'

Claudia watched him drink his coffee. When she sipped hers, she almost gagged.

'This has got sugar in it! You've got mine. Here –' she swapped mugs, gazing at him in disbelief – 'didn't you even notice?'

But Caspar, clearly distracted, only shook his head. Something was on his mind.

Claudia wondered if Poppy had been making a nuisance of herself.

'She's been a bit odd lately,' she ventured. 'Had you noticed?'

Caspar was trailing his forefinger through a pile of sugar he had spilled earlier on the worktop. He drew an unsmiley face.

'Not really. Well . . . maybe a bit.'

He was being evasive. More than likely, Claudia decided, he was playing the situation down in order to protect Poppy. In the past they had always got on so well.

But Caspar was married now. There was Babette to think of.

Claudia had promised Jake she wouldn't tell anyone what he had told her, but what he'd really meant was don't embarrass Poppy by blabbing to all their friends. Surely, she thought, it was only fair to put Caspar in the picture, to give him some warning. Then if Poppy did do anything stupid – like fling herself at him – he'd be able to handle it. He wouldn't be caught off-guard. Better still, aware of the potential awkwardness of such a situation, he could make sure it didn't have a chance to happen in the first place.

'Actually, there's something I think you should know about Poppy.'

Caspar's jaw tightened. When Claudia put on her compassionate face, the news had to be bad.

All of a sudden he knew what she was going to say. In an odd way, he realised, he had been dreading this moment for weeks.

'Don't tell me. She's pregnant.'

Claudia almost dropped her coffee mug. The pain and guilt in Caspar's eyes was unmistakable. He wasn't asking, he was telling her.

'What? You mean she's having your baby?' She gasped and covered her mouth. 'Oh Caspar, how *could* you? Poor Babette . . .'

He frowned. 'Hang on a sec, it's not mine. I thought you meant she was having Tom's baby.'

Bewildered, Claudia said, 'But I didn't even know she was pregnant.'

'In that case,' Caspar heaved a sigh of relief, 'she probably isn't.' His eyes narrowing, he looked at Claudia. 'But why on earth did you think it was mine?'

'I d-didn't really.' Stammering, she tried to explain. 'It . . . it just kind of tied in with what I was about to tell you. The thing is, Jake told me and I thought you should know . . . but then I thought maybe you knew already . . .'

'If I wanted a cryptic crossword, I'd buy the *Telegraph*. Get to the point.'

383

Claudia took a deep breath.

'Poppy's got a thumping great crush on you. Actually, she told Jake she was in love with you, but you know how Poppy exaggerates. Anyway,' she chided, 'it's probably your own fault. You know what you're like – half the time you flirt without even realising you're doing it. And Poppy's vulnerable right now – she's single again and probably panicking that she'll never meet the right man. Look,' Claudia went on, because Caspar seemed too shell-shocked to say anything, 'I'm just saying watch yourself. The way Poppy's feeling at the moment, you could end up getting pounced on. Don't give her any encouragement, that's all,' she concluded kindly. 'It wouldn't be fair to Poppy or Babette.'

The private viewing at the Wellington Gallery hadn't gone well for the exhibiting artist, who only sold two paintings, but the evening had been a profitable one for Babette.

'Networking, that's what it's all about,' she told Caspar in the cab as they made their way home. She flipped through her Filofax, happily pointing out the names and numbers of influential contacts she had made during the course of the evening. 'Damn, I'm good! Play my cards right and I've got myself another fifty grand's worth of business here. Are you okay, darling? You've been quiet. Come on, cheer up. Play *your* cards right and you could make love tonight to a future Businesswoman of the Year.'

Caspar shook his head.

'Sorry, sweetheart. It's over.' Reluctantly he closed the bulging Filofax and took her hand in his. 'It's been fun, we've had a great time. But I'm moving out tomorrow.'

'Oh.' For a second Babette looked as if she was about to cry. 'Oh, right. Okay.'

'I know this is all rather sudden. I'm sorry, but I can't help it. I just have to go.'

She leaned her head against his shoulder.

'Where?'

'Home,' said Caspar.

'To . . . ?'

He nodded. 'Yes. Well, hopefully.' Gazing out through the window at the wet street, he realised the alternative was too horrible to contemplate.

'Oh well, here's to the good times.' Recovering herself, Babette reached up and planted a kiss on his cheek. She even managed a smile. 'After all, we had fourteen good weeks together.' Wryly she added, 'And you did say it wouldn't last.'

Chapter 58

Jake, arriving back from a house auction at four o'clock the following afternoon, found Poppy sitting with her bare feet tucked cosily under her on the bottle green velvet chaise longue he had sold that morning. She was curled over a folded-up copy of the *Evening Standard*, so absorbed in what she was reading she hadn't noticed the top fall off her felt-tip pen. Having clearly spent the last twenty minutes absent-mindedly flicking the pen against her thigh, the leg of her white jeans was now crisscrossed with red ink.

Jake dumped a box of copper jelly moulds on the floor.

'These need cleaning. Have you finished pricing the cutlery?'

Poppy nodded.

'Been busy?'

She shook her head.

Exasperated, Jake picked up a pile of glossy brochures. Poppy hadn't exactly been working her socks off in his absence, even if her feet were bare.

'What are these doing here?'

At last she looked up. 'Claudia came by earlier, dropped them off for you to have a look at.'

They were sales brochures for new cars. BMW. Mercedes. There was even – for heaven's sake – one from the Rolls Royce showroom in Mayfair.

Jake tipped the brochures into the bin.

'Feet off that chaise. The buyer's picking it up at five.'

It's one hundred and fifty years old, thought Poppy. If it

can survive that much action, I don't see what difference another hour of my feet can make.

But she swung her legs down, dumping the paper on top of the jewellery cabinet. Jake looked at the ads she had circled in red.

'What's this? Flats and bedsitters?' He raised his eyebrows at Poppy. 'I thought you didn't want to move.'

'That was then, this is now.' She shrugged and began listlessly unpacking the jelly moulds. 'I thought about what you said and decided you were right. I'd be better off living somewhere else.'

'What happened to getting over it, like measles?'

'It might not be measles,' said Poppy. 'It might be something that goes on for years, like TB.' She took the paper back from him, tore out the page she'd been studying and folded it, tucking it into her shirt pocket.

'You could stay at my house,' Jake offered.

'Claudia would love that. Fifty ways to irritate your lover.' Poppy's smile was dry. 'It's okay, I'll be fine. There's a bedsitter in Peckham that doesn't sound too bad. I'm going round to have a look at it after work.'

'Go now,' said Jake, 'if you want.'

'No hurry. They aren't expecting me until six.' She opened the cupboard, took out a couple of cloths and a tin of Brasso. 'I'll do these first.' Spotting the brochures sticking out of the bin she said, 'Aren't you interested? From the sound of it, Claudia has her heart set on a Merc.'

Not looking amused, Jake said, 'Claudia can take a running jump.'

Poppy was on her knees engrossed in an extra-vigorous bout of polishing when Caspar came through the glass doors.

Jake said, 'Caspar's here,' and the tin slipped out of Poppy's hand.

'Oh fuck.' She let out a wail as escaped Brasso soaked into her jeans. From her position on the floor she glared defensively up at Caspar, who was wearing a blue and white rugby shirt and dark blue chinos. 'What do *you* want?'

'I can see why you employ her,' Caspar told Jake. 'Cheerful, polite, eager to assist the customer—'

'You aren't a customer.' Poppy gazed down in dismay at her now totally wrecked white jeans.

'Yes I am.' Grinning, he waved his wallet. 'I want to buy a ring, a big glittery one. Come on, Poppy, wipe that gunk off your hands and sell me something expensive.'

Poppy guessed it must be Babette's birthday. If past experience was anything to go by, it was probably her birthday today and Caspar had forgotten. Now he had to buy something fast. Guilt always made men spend more.

Jake sat pretending to read the BMW brochure while Caspar studied the trays of rings. To impress Jake, Poppy reeled off dates, carats and settings. She described the way the stones had been cut, and the meaning of the different hallmarks. What she didn't know, she made up.

'This is completely riveting stuff,' drawled Caspar some time later, 'but I'd rather know which one you like best.'

Poppy didn't see why; about the only thing she and Babette had in common was they both had periods.

But, to humour him, she pointed to a diamond gypsy ring, heavy, totally unfussy and worn smooth with age.

'Okay. I like that one. But I really think Babette would prefer this.' Picking up a ravishing solitaire with rose diamond three-stone shoulders, she held it up to the light. 'Look at the cut of those stones. You could send morse code signals across Kensington. Of course it costs fifteen hundred more—'

'Try on the gypsy one,' said Caspar. 'I want to see how it looks. No,' he ordered, 'put it on the third finger.'

Poppy did as she was told. The ring was miles too big.

'Bloody typical,' said Caspar. If this was a film with Meg Ryan in it, it would have fitted.

'Doesn't matter.' Shifting from one bare foot to the other, wishing she didn't reek so overwhelmingly of Brasso, Poppy pointed towards the far end of the market. 'Dennis, over there by the fire exit, does alterations. He can take it down a few sizes. You mustn't just guess, though,' she went on, remembering that Caspar was probably desperate to get the thing home. 'Can you remember what size Babette's wedding ring was when you bought it?'

'No. What size are you?'

'Don't look at my hands,' Poppy said irritably. 'Babette's fingers are fatter than mine.'

Caspar burst out laughing. 'Oh, you bitch.'

'I'm not being bitchy, I'm just stating a fact. She isn't going to be thrilled if she can't get the bloody ring *on*.'

He was still shaking with laughter.

'Poppy, now listen. Do you love me?'

For a moment Poppy thought she must have misheard. How embarrassing, for a moment there, she thought he had said love.

Poppy's mind worked feverishly, struggling to figure out what he had actually said.

Try as she might, she was unable to come up with another word that sounded like love – glove? lug? nudge? – and still made sense.

Finally she said, 'What?'

'Do you?' Grinning, Caspar leaned across the counter towards her, his grey eyes searching her face. 'The thing is, you see, rumour has it you do. But I don't always trust rumours. I prefer to hear things from . . .'

'. . . the horse's mouth?' suggested Jake.

'Thank you.' Gravely Caspar nodded. 'I didn't quite have the nerve to say it myself. Anyway, where were we? Oh yes, the rumour. Is it true?'

'Ouch – no!' shouted Jake, clutching his naked face, but Poppy, fuelled by adrenalin, was too fast for him. She snapped his expensive spectacles in two, tore the arms off for good measure and hurled the bits into the bin.

'You snake! You complete lowlife,' she hissed at Jake. 'I can't believe you told him!'

He looked indignant. 'I didn't. I only told Claudia.'

'And Claudia told me,' Caspar said cheerfully. 'Come on, Poppy, I'm still waiting. Do you love me?'

Poppy's fists were bunched in anguish. She wanted to break a lot more than a pair of lousy glassess. And her face, her treacherous face, felt as if it was on *fire* . . .

'Dammit, what kind of a question is that?' she howled at Caspar. 'I'll tell you, it's the most stinking rotten bloody question I ever heard! You can't go around asking people things like that, for crying out loud! You're *married*.'

She was trying to make a bolt for it but Caspar had somehow managed to grab hold of both her hands.

Still smiling broadly he said, 'No I'm not.'

It seemed safest, as Caspar drove her back to Cornwallis Crescent, to say nothing. Poppy closed her eyes and didn't open them until they reached the house. The smell of Brasso in the car was overwhelming.

When they were inside she bent down automatically to pick up the morning's post. The folded-up piece of newspaper slid out of her shirt pocket. Caspar picked it up, glanced at it and crumpled it into a ball.

'You won't be needing that.'

'This is bizarre,' said Poppy finally. 'If you aren't married, why on earth did you say you were?'

He shrugged. 'Seemed like a good idea at the time. You said I needed to sort myself out, to stop pratting around and settle down. You told me I should get married,' Caspar reminded her. 'So I told you I had.'

'But *why*?'

'I realised I was crazy about you,' he said simply. 'I also knew that as far as you were concerned I was the worst news since Hiroshima. The last person you'd *ever* be interested in was someone like me, with my abysmal track record.'

'I still don't see—'

'So I thought I'd give it a whirl, see what being married

felt like. I wanted to find out if I could be happy with one person, turning down offers from other women instead of always thinking what the hell, go for it, why not?' Looking pleased with himself, Caspar added, 'And I discovered I could. I actually enjoyed it. I was pretty bloody amazed, I can tell you. But it was great.'

'If it's so great,' demanded Poppy, now experiencing a horrible mixture of confusion and jealousy, 'why don't you marry Babette for real?'

'I like her. A lot. But I don't love her.' Caspar half-smiled. 'And before you say anything else, she doesn't love me either. She went along with the idea, got herself and her beloved company a ton of publicity . . . where was the harm?'

Poppy shook her head in bemusement; her insides felt so scrunched up she could hardly breathe.

'So what happens now?'

'I told her last night. She wished me good luck.' His mouth began to twitch. 'Even though, personally, she'd far rather I got together with Claudia than you.'

Fat-fingered cow, thought Poppy. But what Caspar had been saying was beginning, finally, to sink in.

'Look, do you mean this?' She spoke with a touch of belligerence. 'Are you serious? Because I'm warning you, if this is some kind of joke—'

'What, you'll break my glasses too? Really, Poppy, violence isn't the answer.'

He certainly picks his moments to get witty, thought Poppy. Aloud she said, 'I'm not sure I even understand the question.'

'Sorry, I don't appear to be making a great job of this.' No longer grinning, Caspar pushed his sunbleached hair away from his face. 'I'm nervous too, okay? I've never told anyone I loved them before. This is scary stuff.'

'It's supposed to be nice stuff.' Poppy was beginning to feel decidedly weak-kneed.

'I know. But what if it doesn't work? We've been friends for almost a year.'

'Maybe you should try kissing me first. See what that's like.' As she said the words, Poppy began to tremble. 'Then, if it seems okay, we can carry on. If it's weird or awful . . . well, we'll just forget it.'

She was standing there waiting for him, but Caspar was making an unhappy discovery. He couldn't move. A lifetime of confidence had abruptly deserted him – now, when for the first time it really, truly mattered. It was ridiculous. Walking into the antiques market had been easy. Telling Poppy he wasn't married to Babette had been easy. But this . . . this . . .

This wasn't.

Watching Caspar, knowing him as well as she did, Poppy realised what was happening.

It's up to me, she thought, bracing herself against the fridge. If I don't do it we'll still be here at midnight.

The trouble was, her knees were feeling horribly unreliable.

'You'll have to come here,' she told Caspar. 'I can't walk.'

When he did, she slid her arms slowly around his waist. Holding her breath, feeling as if her lungs were about to burst, Poppy touched her mouth to his.

'Okay so far?' She murmured the words against his lips, amazed she could even speak, what with all the firework effects zapping through her body. 'If not, I can always stop—'

In reply, Caspar held her so tightly and kissed her for so long, neither of them heard the front door open and close.

'Well?' gasped Poppy, her heart hammering like a road drill when they finally paused for breath, 'how was it for you?'

She was grinning. Caspar, hopelessly aroused and wondering whether to carry her upstairs or just ravish her right here on the kitchen floor, bit her earlobe.

'I suppose you'll never let me forget this. For the next fifty years, at every party we go to, you won't be able to

392

resist telling people about the time I lost my bottle.'

'You lost your bottle?' Poppy kissed him again, pressing her hips against him. Starting to laugh, she glanced down at the front of his trousers. 'There, I've found it again. Gosh, it's a magnum.'

Caspar began undoing the buttons of her white cotton shirt.

'I love you, even if you are a mickey-taking bitch.'

'I love you,' Poppy retaliated, 'even if you did sleep with Angie Slade-Welch.'

'I didn't.'

'Yes you did.'

'Bloody hell, I did *not*—'

'We'll argue about that later. We can make a list of things to argue about. Right now I'd far rather be doing something else.' Overwhelmed with lust, Poppy leaned back against the fridge and watched him unfasten the last couple of buttons. 'Um . . . shouldn't we find somewhere a bit more private?'

Caspar smiled.

'We have some serious catching up to do. I'm going to make love to you in every room in this house.'

As he began to kiss her again, Poppy glanced up at the clock on the wall.

'Look, Claudia could be home at any minute. We don't want her to see us . . .'

Behind them in the kitchen doorway, a clear voice rang out.

'I've already seen you,' Claudia announced, her eyes glittering with anger, 'and the pair of you disgust me. You, especially, should be ashamed of yourself.' She turned her disdainful attention to Poppy's flushed cheeks and unbuttoned shirt. 'How could you do this to poor Babette?'

Chapter 59

'They're completely sick-making,' Claudia grumbled, struggling to scrape caked-on mud from the soles of her Hunter wellies while Jake loaded the morning's bargains into the back of the van. Though she would rather die than admit it, Claudia was beginning to enjoy these Sunday car boot sales. Last week at a particularly upmarket one in Virginia Water she had come away with three Jean Muir dresses and a Moschino jacket. If the woman – who owned a Range Rover – wasn't embarrassed to be seen selling them, Claudia decided she wasn't ashamed to buy them. And the Range Rover had been an N reg.

'What?' Straightening up, Jake slammed the rear doors shut. Rust showered off. Never mind, he thought contentedly, by this time next week he would have his brand-new van.

'Poppy and Caspar. You have no idea what they're like.' She pulled a face. 'They can't keep their *hands* off each other. I mean, how much sex can one couple have? It's indecent. Embarrassing.' Claudia climbed into the passenger seat and wound down the squeaky window. 'I feel so . . . in the way.'

'Do they make you feel in the way?' Jake started up the engine, which spluttered with damp.

'They go out of their way not to.' Darkly, Claudia added, 'Which makes it worse.'

Jake watched his fingers tighten around the steering wheel. It wasn't the most romantic of situations but it was the opportunity he had been waiting for. He had to ask her; had to know.

For the second time in a fortnight he said, 'You could move in with me.'

When he had made the offer to Poppy she had turned him down.

Claudia went pink with pleasure.

'Really? I'd love to.'

'Okay. We'll do that.'

Oh, what a momentous occasion! Jake had asked her to live with him and she had said yes. This, she thought excitedly, is the next best thing to getting married.

Claudia longed to fling her arms around Jake and cover him in kisses, but he was driving and the lane was narrow. She dug in her coat pocket instead and found half a packet of Fruit Gums, selflessly offering him the red one although it was her favourite.

'Well,' she said, chewing happily, 'that's solved that problem.'

It wasn't the most romantic of acceptances either. Jake braked as a sleek black top-of-the-range Audi pulled out ahead of them.

'That's a nice car,' said Claudia.

'If you like that kind of thing.'

She glanced across at him.

'I don't know how anyone could not like that kind of thing.'

But Jake wasn't going to get into an argument. Saying nothing, he concentrated on the road. As they rounded a bend, a glorious old house came into view, an ivy-clad rectory with a Victorian-style conservatory built onto the side. A For Sale notice swung above the driveway.

'Imagine living in a place like that,' Claudia sighed.

'I'm happy where I am.'

She gazed with longing at the house as they rattled past. Then she saw Jake's expression, which was grimly uncompromising.

'If you won't move, you could at least have a conservatory

built,' she pointed out, her tone fretful. 'You've got room. Go on, go mad.' It was almost – *almost* – a taunt. 'You could at least splash out on one of those.'

'Where are we going?' asked Claudia twenty minutes later. It was lunchtime, she was hungry and Jake had driven past endless promising-looking country pubs. She wished she hadn't given him that fruit gum now.

Jake carried on driving. Claudia wondered if he even knew where he was headed; this certainly wasn't the way home.

'Why are we *here*?' she demanded when they reached the outskirts of Purley. Spotting a sign for another car boot sale, her voice rose. 'Oh God, I don't want to traipse round any more bloody playing fields.'

But Jake, still looking as if all he wanted to do was waste petrol, swung the van right instead of left.

'Okay, this'll do.'

'For what?' Claudia stared incredulously at the dilapidated row of shops, nearly all of them closed. Spotting a frightful-looking transport café, she said, 'If you think for one minute I'm eating my Sunday lunch in that greasy spoon—'

'We aren't going in there,' said Jake, opening the passenger door and practically dragging her out. 'We're going to go mad, like you wanted.' He pointed to the seedy-looking betting shop next to the café. 'We're going to live a little. Have a bit of fun. In there.'

Claudia winced as Jake held the door open for her. A thick sea of cigarette smoke made her eyes water. The shop was full of men, the floor awash with discarded betting slips and stamped-out fag ends. There were sheets of newspaper detailing the day's racing pinned up along every wall, and half a dozen TV sets tuned to the afternoon's racing.

'So this is your idea of a bit of fun.' Claudia, who had never stepped inside a betting shop before, felt her upper lip curl with distaste. 'Go on then, hurry up. Have your stupid bet and let's get out of here.' Ostentatiously she shuddered. 'My jacket's going to reek.'

Jake studied the list of runners and riders flickering on one of the screens above their heads.

'Flirty Fay, evens. The Goodbye Girl, seven to one. Tango, nine to two.' He paused. 'Fortune Hunter, eight to one.'

'Bored and Hungry,' intoned Claudia without looking up. 'Dead cert.'

'Come on.' Jake took her hand, pulling her over to the cashier sitting behind her till. The woman – the only other female in the shop – smiled through the security glass at them. Claudia couldn't be bothered to smile back.

'Yes, love?' The cashier turned her attention to Jake.

'Fortune Hunter, running in the two thirty,' said Jake. 'Um . . . do you accept cheques?'

'Yes love, we do.'

'Half a million all right? It won't bounce.'

'Half a million pounds.' Echoing the words, the woman looked dazed. 'On the nose, sir?'

Jake nodded firmly. 'That's right. To win.'

'Hang on a sec, I'll have to check this with the manager.'

Fed up, Claudia had been leaning against the glass watching an old man smoke two cigarettes at once. No wonder, she thought disgustedly, the floor was inches deep in ash.

The next moment, Jake's words belatedly filtered through to her brain. She jerked upright and did a cartoon double-take.

'*How* much?'

'Sshh,' said Jake. 'She's asking her boss if it's okay.'

'For God's sake, have you gone completely mad?' Sounding like McEnroe, Claudia hissed, 'Jake, you can't be serious!'

'No problem at all, sir,' the woman announced, re-emerging from the office. 'Just so long as you can show us some form of identification. Oh yes, a driving licence, that's fine.'

'Jake, stop it,' howled Claudia as he filled out the betting slip. 'You can't *do* this—'

'You want to marry a millionaire, don't you?' He shrugged off her desperate pawing hands, wrote the cheque and signed it. Before Claudia could stop him he had pushed both the slip and the cheque beneath the glass. 'Well, right now, I'm only half a millionaire. Not really enough, is it? This way, ten minutes from now I could be four million pounds richer.'

Gibbering with rage, Claudia yelled, 'But what if the horse doesn't win? Then you won't have anything!'

'Of course I won't. That's what makes it exciting. I thought you *wanted* a bit of excitement,' protested Jake. 'You keep telling me to live a little, to splash out.'

Claudia wanted to cry. She even wanted a cigarette. The one thing she definitely didn't want was this kind of excitement.

When she finally looked up, the middle-aged cashier said, 'Cheer up, love. Fingers crossed, eh?'

'If I win,' said Jake, 'you can have that big house you liked.'

There was a new air of recklessness about him, a wild kind of glitter in his dark eyes. Demented with worry, Claudia snapped back, 'And if you lose, you can just fuck off.'

She couldn't bear to watch the race, and she didn't need to.

'. . . and Fortune Hunter has fallen at the second furlong,' relayed the commentator, 'Fortune Hunter's taken a tumble, both horse and jockey appear to be unhurt . . . and Tango and Flirty Fay are neck and neck going up to the third . . .'

Jake crumpled his betting slip into an ashtray.

'Looks like Fortune Hunter's having a bit of an off-day.'

Claudia snapped. 'She isn't the only one.'

'That's that, then. It's all over.'

'You bloody, *bloody* fool.' Feeling sick at the thought of half a million pounds wasted, she shrugged off Jake's tentative hand on her shoulder. All around them, other punters were urging on their horses. Only the woman behind the till was watching Claudia rather than the race.

'Well,' said Jake slowly, 'is it all over?'

She wanted to cry. 'Of course it is.'

'I meant us. Are we all over too?' He stood in front of Claudia, forcing her to look at him. 'The money's gone. I'm pretty much where I started. Do you still want to move in with me, or not?'

Cheers and groans erupted around the smoke-filled room as Flirty Fay won by a length. A volley of balled-up betting slips hit the floor.

'What is this, some kind of test?' said Claudia.

'If you like.'

'You sick bastard.' Her eyes filled with tears of dismay. 'You thought I was only interested in your money?'

'Call me a pessimist,' said Jake steadily, 'but it had crossed my mind. You certainly seemed interested in helping me spend it.'

Claudia couldn't speak. Didn't Jake understand how unfair he was being? Of course she was interested in helping him spend his money. Money was wonderful, it was there to *be* spent. And now it was gone.

'Well?' he demanded, 'what's the verdict? If you don't want to see me any more, I'll understand. I never thought I was much of a catch anyway.' His fingers were shaking as he pulled the van's keys out of his jacket pocket. 'Don't worry, I'll still give you a lift home. No hard feelings. We'll just say goodbye.' Jake's voice began to falter but his mind was clearly made up. Since it was the polite thing to say, he added stiffly, 'I daresay we can stay friends.'

A terrible sinking feeling swept like a tidal wave through Claudia's gut. Desolation mingled with panic. She could bear the loss of the money – just – but she couldn't lose Jake too.

'I don't care,' she whispered, because some of the old men nearest to them had begun to eavesdrop. 'I don't care how much money you haven't got. Of course I still want to move in with you.'

'What?' Jake had to raise his voice; another race was in progress.

'I love you.' The old men were nudging each other now, chuckling between themselves and ignoring the race being screened above their heads. 'Wasting that money was the stupidest thing you ever did, but I still love you. Anyway, my mother was the one who said I needed excitement,' said Claudia, 'not me.'

Overjoyed, Jake took her in his arms and kissed her and didn't let her go.

'Bugger me,' guffawed one of the men, 'better than a flamin' cabaret. Wait till I get home and tell my missus about this.'

'Mine gives me earache if I lose more'n a fiver,' marvelled another.

'I didn't think you'd still want me,' Jake murmured in Claudia's ear. 'Oh God, I was so afraid you wouldn't.'

'Maybe it'll be fun, being poor,' said Claudia bravely. As long as she had Jake, nothing else mattered. Feeling giddy with happiness she whispered, 'I'll learn to economise. No more Manolo Blahnik shoes, no more getting my hair done at Nicky Clarke's. No more eating out,' she went on, improvising wildly. *Coronation Street* was full of poor people, wasn't it? 'I'll . . . I'll learn to make Lancashire hot-pot . . .'

'My mother has a brilliant recipe for hot-pot.'

This was love, this was serious. No longer caring that they were the focus of attention, Claudia clung to him and kissed him again, extravagantly, on the mouth. 'I want to meet your mother.'

The next moment Jake was unwrapping her arms from around his neck and the cashier was no longer behind her till, but standing beside them.

'What's wrong?' said Claudia, wondering if they were about to be asked to leave, kicked out for indecent behaviour.

'You said you'd like to meet my mother,' Jake explained, 'so here you are. Wish granted.'

'Hello love, I've heard so much about you.' Jake's mother smiled. 'Not all of it good, I have to be honest, but never mind, you saw sense in the end.'

Claudia stared at them both.

'Are you serious?'

'Of course I'm serious.' Jake grinned. 'I just wanted to find out if you were.'

'Here, love.' Jake's mother produced the cheque from the pocket of her uniform. 'Tear it up quick and for God's sake don't tell the boss. He'll have my guts for garters if he ever gets to hear about this.'

'But . . . but . . .' Claudia spluttered helplessly. 'You can't do that, you'll get the sack.'

Entertained by the look on Claudia's face, Jake explained, 'She didn't place the bet. It didn't go through the machine.'

Chapter 60

'Come on, get up,' Caspar announced, throwing back the duvet. 'Things to do, places to go. You can't spend all morning in bed.'

Poppy winced and tried to curl herself into a ball. 'It's my day off.'

'And we're going out.'

'Somewhere nice?' Cautiously she opened an eye. Caspar had showered already, and left it running for her. She watched him throw on a crumpled white rugby shirt and jeans.

'Somewhere extremely nice.' Hauling Poppy out of bed, he pointed her in the direction of the bathroom. 'The electricity showrooms. We need a dishwasher.'

'Why?'

'Because Claudia doesn't live here any more.' He threw a pair of Poppy's leggings after her. 'Hurry up.'

Outside the sun blazed down from a cloudless sky. They made their way towards the shops on foot.

'I can't believe you're making me do this,' grumbled Poppy, glad of her sunglasses. 'Not on my day off. Talk about domesticated.'

They were passing a delicatessen. Caspar glanced at their reflections in the window. Poppy's still-damp hair was piled haphazardly on top of her head, tied with a red scarf that was already coming undone. She was wearing RayBans, a cropped red tee-shirt, white leggings and gold sandals.

'You don't look domesticated. Cheer up –' he gave her waist a squeeze – 'think of all the washing-up we won't have

402

to do. You'll be able to spend more time in bed.'

'Only if you're there too.' Reluctantly, because she was still supposed to be cross with him, Poppy broke into a grin. Sex with Caspar had been a total revelation; she couldn't imagine ever tiring of it. He had made her life idyllic.

How long did it take to choose a silly dishwasher anyway? Poppy brightened at the prospect of enticing Caspar back into bed. They could be home in less than an hour.

Recognising the glint in her eye, Caspar said, 'You are disgraceful. A shameless hussy.'

'I'm a happy hussy.' Reaching up, she kissed him. 'You're not bad, you know. Even if your idea of a romantic day out is a trip to the electricity showrooms.'

'Actually, I thought we might visit B & Q afterwards.' Caspar sounded amused. 'Take a look at kitchen units.'

'That would be too much excitement for one day.'

'I know how to give a girl a good time.'

'Come home with me,' said Poppy, 'and I'll show you a better one.'

As they began to cross the road she spotted a familiar figure, a vision in billowing violet chiffon, hurrying up a broad flight of steps leading into an official-looking building.

'Look, it's Rita! Wearing a hat,' Poppy exclaimed. 'Isn't that the Register Office? She must be going to someone's wedding.'

'Must be.'

'But that's weird. I asked her if she wanted to meet me for lunch today and she said she was visiting a friend in Kent.'

As she gazed over the tops of cars, Poppy's bewilderment grew. Rita re-emerged from the building, hanging onto her flower-strewn, Queen-of-Ascot hat with one hand and lighting a cigarette with the other. Behind her, clutching a suitcase, was . . . of all people . . . Claudia.

'Hang on, what's happening?' Astonished, Poppy pulled off her sunglasses. Now Jake had joined the small group at the top of the steps. And, looking intensely glamorous in a

403

dove-grey morning suit, Hugo Slade-Welch.

She turned to Caspar. 'Is something going on that I don't know about? Is . . . is Rita marrying Hugo?'

'No. You're marrying me.'

'I'm *what*?'

They were still halfway across the road. Caspar steered Poppy safely onto the pavement. Fishing in his shirt pocket, he pulled out the heavy, diamond-encrusted gypsy ring she had last seen on that eventful afternoon on Jake's stall. The one she had thought he was buying for Babette. The one Jake had later told her he'd sold to an Australian tourist.

'Well, I'd like you to.' Caspar waved the ring at her. 'It rather depends on you saying yes.'

Shakily Poppy said, 'Are you serious?'

'Never more so.'

'You mean, you – you *planned* all this?'

'It helps,' said Caspar, 'if you want the guests to turn up.'

'My God, I can't believe it. But – my hair!' she wailed, clutching her head. 'And my *clothes* . . . whatever made you do it like this? Why did it have to be a surprise?'

'Look.' Caspar turned her to face him. 'With your track record, I thought it was the only way. Every time someone wants to marry you, you do your party trick and run a mile. Sometimes a hundred miles,' he added drily. 'I didn't want you pulling that one on me.'

'But I wouldn't!' Poppy stared at him, amazed he could even think such a thing. 'It's different this time. I love you.'

'Yes, well. I wasn't prepared to risk it. This way, you don't have a chance to get cold feet. Everyone's here already, waiting for us. In half an hour it'll be done.' Caspar took her trembling hands in his. 'That is, if you want to.'

Poppy frowned. 'You haven't asked me yet.'

He half-smiled, inwardly far less confident than he appeared. He just wished she would put him out of his agony and say yes.

'Sorry. Will you marry me?'

'On one knee.'

'Come on, not here.'

'Yes here.'

Caspar looked appalled.

'In the street?'

'Not in the actual road,' Poppy said generously, 'in case you get run over by a bus. You can do it on the pavement.'

Passers-by were beginning to take notice. An ear-splitting, four-fingered whistle rang out from the top of the Register Office steps. Rita yelled, 'Blimey, you two, are you getting hitched or what?'

'Hurry *up*,' shouted Claudia, holding up the suitcase. 'I've got your clothes in here. You can change in the loo.'

Further up the road the traffic lights had turned red. Cars, cabs and a couple of double-deckers ground to a halt. Interested faces peered down at Caspar as he sank to one knee.

'Say you'll marry me,' he hissed. 'Quickly.'

Poppy thought her heart would explode with joy. She flung out her arms and kissed him. Between kisses she said breathlessly, 'Yes, yes, of course I'll marry you.' Car horns tooted all around them as Caspar stood up, hugely relieved that ordeal was out of the way. The passengers on the nearest bus applauded.

'You look great.'

Rita, crammed into the loo behind Poppy, was handing over eyeshadow, mascara and lipstick like an efficient nurse in an operating theatre. Except efficient nurses in operating theatres didn't pass sterile instruments with cigarettes dangling from the corners of their mouths.

Poppy finished her make-up with sixty seconds to spare. She fiddled with a few tendrils of hair and hastily checked her overall reflection in the mirror.

'I'm getting married. I'm actually getting married.' As she spoke, a horrible thought struck her. 'Oh help, where are we going after this? The house is a complete tip—'

'Don't panic, that's all sorted. Everyone back to my place.'

Poppy was touched. 'Oh Rita, you are brilliant. What would I do without you?'

'Silly girl. D'you think Alex would have wanted your wedding reception held anywhere else?' Rita hugged her. 'Oh Lord, don't you dare cry...'

'I wish he was here.' Poppy grabbed a handful of loo roll and dabbed her brimming eyes.

'I know, love. So do I. Now come on, we've got a wedding to go to. Anyway,' Rita announced, to distract her, 'there's another little surprise for you when we get home.'

Poppy didn't know if she could cope with any more surprises.

'What?'

'I've got Kenda's Kitchen doing the food.' Rita's grin was mischievous. 'For old times' sake.'

Nadia Knows Best

Jill Mansell

When Nadia Kinsella meets Jay Tiernan, she's tempted, of course she is. Stranded together in a remote Cotswold pub while a snowstorm rages outside . . . let's face it, who would ever know?

But Nadia's already met The One. She and Laurie have been together for years – they're practically childhood sweet-hearts and she still gets butterflies in her stomach at the sight of him. Okay, so maybe she doesn't see that much of him these days, but that's not Laurie's fault. She can't betray him.

Besides, when you belong to a family like the Kinsellas – bewitchingly glamorous grandmother Miriam, feckless mother Leonie, stop-at-nothing sister Clare – well, someone has to exercise a bit of self-control, don't they? I mean, you wouldn't want to do something that you might later regret . . .

Acclaim for Jill Mansell's novels:

'Fast, furious and fabulous fun. To read it is to devour it' *Company*

'Slick, sexy, funny stories' *Daily Telegraph*

'A sure-fire bestseller from the queen of chicklit' *Heat*

'An exciting read about love, friendship and sweet revenge – fabulously fun' *Home & Life*

'A jaunty summer read' *Daily Mail*

'Riotous' *New Woman*

'A romantic romp full of larger than life characters' *Express*

0 7472 6488 0

headline

Staying at Daisy's

Jill Mansell

Daisy MacLean runs the country house hotel owned by her flamboyant father, Hector. When she hears who's about to get married there, she isn't worried at all – her friend Tara absolutely promises there won't be any trouble between her and ex-boyfriend Dominic, whom she hasn't seen for years. But Daisy *should* have been worried. Dominic has other ideas. And seeing Tara again sets in motion a chaotic train of events with far-reaching consequences for all concerned.

While Daisy spends the ensuing months doing battle with Dev Tyzack (Dominic's so-called best man), Tara battles with her conscience. Meanwhile, Hector's getting up to all sorts with . . . well, that's the village's best kept secret. And then Barney turns up, with a little something belonging to the husband Daisy's been doing her best to forget.

That's the thing about hotels, you never know who you're going to meet. Or whether they're going to stay . . .

Acclaim for Jill Mansell's novels:

'A jaunty summer read' *Daily Mail*

'An exciting read about love, friendship and sweet revenge – fabulously fun' *Home & Life*

'Slick, sexy, funny stories' *Daily Telegraph*

0 7472 6487 2

headline

Head Over Heels

Jill Mansell

Jessie has kept the identity of her son Oliver's father a secret for years. She's stunned when she discovers that the man in question, actor Toby Gillespie, has just moved in next door. The truth's about to come out.

One glance at Oliver, and a little mental arithmetic, and Toby has the situation sussed. Meeting the son he never knew he had is the shock of a lifetime. It's a shock, too, for Toby's wife, the beautiful Deborah, though she seems to take it in her stride.

Would Deborah be so relaxed if she knew just how close Toby wants to get to the mother of his firstborn? As the attraction between them flares up again, Jessie just can't see her way to a happy ending. But no one is quite what they seem, and there are more surprises to come . . .

'A light-hearted and likeable tale' *Prima*

'Fast, furious and fabulous fun, to read it is to devour it' *Company*

'Slick, sexy, funny stories' *Telegraph*

'A riotous romp' *Prima*

0 7472 5736 1

headline

Now you can buy any of these other bestselling books by **Jill Mansell** from your bookshop or *direct from her publisher*.

FREE P&P AND UK DELIVERY
(Overseas and Ireland £3.50 per book)

Two's Company	£6.99
Nadia Knows Best	£5.99
Open House	£6.99
Staying at Daisy's	£5.99
Fast Friends	£6.99
Millie's Fling	£5.99
Sheer Mischief	£6.99
Good at Games	£6.99
Miranda's Big Mistake	£6.99
Head Over Heels	£6.99
Mixed Doubles	£6.99
Perfect Timing	£6.99
Kiss	£6.99
Solo	£5.99

TO ORDER SIMPLY CALL THIS NUMBER

01235 400 414

or visit our website: www.madaboutbooks.com

Prices and availability subject to change without notice.